"Dinna be afraid of me, lassie," the earl murmured softly. "I am said to be a skilled lover, and I will treat ye gently."

Still aggravated with herself, Arabella snapped, "Is your manroot as big as your pride, my lord?"

"Only sometimes, lovey," he shot back with a chuckle, and kissed her mouth.

With the touch of that firm mouth against hers, Arabella felt her body flooded with a delicious warmth. Thoughts not in her head minutes before were suddenly swirling about in her brain. She was in bed. *Naked*. With a handsome man. *Equally naked*. They were going to make love, a not wholly unpleasant prospect, even if she was more frightened than she chose to admit. Well-schooled in kissing by her husband over the autumn months, Arabella opened her mouth to him, and his tongue plunging between her lips began a leisurely exploration.

THE
SPITFIRE

Bertrice Small

BALLANTINE BOOKS • NEW YORK

Copyright © 1990 by Bertrice Small

All rights reserved under International and Pan-American Copyright Conventions. Published in the United States by Ballantine Books, a division of Random House, Inc., New York, and simultaneously in Canada by Random House of Canada Limited, Toronto.

Library of Congress Catalog Card Number: 89-92612

ISBN: 0-345-37565-3

Manufactured in the United States of America

First Trade Edition: September 1990
First Mass Market Edition: February 1992

OPM 16 15 14 13 12 11 10 9 8 7

FOR MY SON, TOM,
who grows more like my heroes with each passing
year. This one's for you, Bun, with much
love from your doting Mother. . . .

⚜ *Prologue*

*B*y the body of Christ crucified!'' swore Tavis Stewart, the black-browed Earl of Dunmor. *"By the body of Christ crucified, and by the tears his blessed mother Mary shed upon the hill of Calvary, I will be avenged!"* He stood amid the smoking ruins of Culcairn House, his nostrils burning with the acrid scent of death. A fine mist of rain had begun to fall, and the damp but sharpened the unpleasant stench.

"She brought it upon herself! Upon us all!" said Robert Hamilton, the young laird of Culcairn. The boy was close to tears. In the last three years he had lost his mother to a childbed fever, and his father to the never-ending border wars. His home had been all he had, and suddenly it was gone. How was he to shelter and to protect his younger sisters and brother now? How could he even seek out a wife without a decent home to which he might bring her? It was gone. And why? Because of his bitch-in-heat of an elder sister! Beautiful Eufemia with her dark red hair and bright blue eyes. Eufemia with her quick laughter and mocking smile. *Eufemia, the whore!* It was time that Tavis Stewart knew the truth. He need seek no vengeance over Eufemia Hamilton, whose honor was long gone, had the earl but known it.

"Robbie, please!" Eleven-year-old Margaret Hamilton put a gentle hand upon her brother's arm, sensing his dangerous thoughts, his dark, rising anger. These last few hours had made her older and wiser beyond her years. "Eufemia is dead, and to have died in such a way as she did is too horrible to contemplate any further." The young girl began to tremble, shaking so hard her teeth chattered. "I . . . I sh-shall hear her sc-screams until my d-dying d-d-day."

The laird put a comforting arm about his sister, but his voice was hard and bitter as he spoke. "Eufemia is to blame, Meg, and there is no use in denying it. She brought the English down upon us, and cost us all dearly in her jealous folly. She had no care for any of us. Neither you, nor me, nor Mary or Geordie. We might hae all been killed because of her! Damn her black soul to hell!''

The Earl of Dunmor glowered down at the laird from beneath his thick and bushy eyebrows. His dark green eyes were icy with his anger. He was twenty-seven years old to the boy laird's fifteen, and though Robert Hamilton stood six feet in height, the earl topped him by a good four inches. ''Yer quick, laddie, to make allegations, but slow to gie me the whole truth of this matter,'' Tavis Stewart said in a dangerously soft voice. ''Ye'll tell me now, or as God is my witness, I'll kill ye where ye stand!'' His hand went to his jeweled dagger as if for emphasis.

''Noooooo!'' Margaret Hamilton pulled away from her brother. White-faced, she put her slender child's form between the two, her little hands stretched out as if she might actually prevent them from assaulting one another, for her brother's hand had gone to his dagger as well. ''Has there not been enough killing here?'' she sobbed. ''Is that all men are good for, my lord? Killing, and looting, and ravishing?'' She wiped the hot tears from her cheeks, smudging the soot upon her pretty little face.

About her the kilt-clad borderers looked shamefaced for a brief moment, remembering other raids, other smoking ruins, other women who wept. There wasn't a man standing within the sound of Margaret Hamilton's voice who was not moved by the sweet-visaged girl and her poignant words. She looked so vulnerable, but then they always did. She was too young to have suffered so terribly, but then they always were. The Earl of Dunmor's face, however, was impervious, and he gave no sign of relenting.

''Come, Mistress Meg, come wi me, lassie.'' An old servant woman finally took the girl by the shoulder and gently led her away. Meg looked back to her brother and the earl. Then, torn, glanced toward her six-year-old sister, Mary, and their three-year-old baby brother, George, who huddled together whimpering in the lap of another servant. Her maternal instinct rose strong, and she immediately decided that Rob and the earl could solve their own problems. The bairns needed her more. She hurried toward them.

''The truth, Rob! I want the truth, and I want it now!'' the earl growled at the laird once more.

"Eufemia was a whore, my lord," began the laird, and then he staggered with the blow that the earl delivered to his jaw. Grim-faced, he continued. "A born whore though she hid it well, or so she thought. Most knew, though none would dare to say it aloud."

"I did not know," Tavis Stewart said gruffly.

"Ye cared nothing for my sister," Robert Hamilton said quietly. "Ye wanted a wife. Eufemia was convenient, for our lands abut, and she was beautiful. 'Twas all ye cared to know, my lord, and my sister was ambitious. She wanted a good marriage, and would have probably been a faithful wife to ye if ye serviced her with regularity, for her passions were great. She lay wi those men who could not for fear of retribution brag on it." The boy sighed sadly.

"Last year, however, my sister fell in love, God help her. He was English, Sir Jasper Keane, by name. They were well suited to one another, for the Englishman was as rash and as reckless as was Eufemia. They met while out riding the borders. 'Twas dangerous for my sister to ride alone, but she would have none wi her. Even our father could not control her. She was wild for her Englishman. Wild to the point of madness.

"Once she learned he was seeing another lass along the borders, she followed him upon the moor until she had located the wench's cottage. Eufemia burned that cottage to the ground, my lord. Sir Jasper, I am told, found her behavior most amusing, although he beat her black and blue for it. She showed me her bruises as if they were badges of honor instead of her dishonor. Eufemia believed he cared for her because he beat her.

"My sister thought to be the bastard's wife," Robert Hamilton said, shaking his head. "She truly loved Sir Jasper, and she refused to believe him when he told her he would have an heiress of good character to wife, not a red-haired Scots whore wi but a small dowry; but Eufemia laughed when she told me his words. She did not believe that the Englishman would wed another. She thought he but said what he said to taunt her and make her jealous.

"At first those words did not fret her, but eventually, I think she began to be afraid Sir Jasper meant them, though she would nae admit it even to me. She began to be jealous of every minute he was nae wi her; jealous of his other women, and there were several, I am told, for the Englishman is as randy a borderer as any I hae ever heard. Women are drawn to him even as flies to a honey pot.

"Then you came to us, Tavis," continued the laird, "and ye asked me for Eufemia's hand in marriage. God knows ye could hae made a better match than my sister, but I understood yer reasons. Ye wanted a wife and an heir, but ye were not of a mind to quibble over the matter, which ye should hae had to wi a greater name or fortune. I should hae refused ye, my lord. I knew what my sister was, for she had confided her passion to me from almost the beginning, although I dinna know why. Eufemia always held herself aloof from the rest of us." The boy's shoulders slumped with his exhaustion and dejection. For a long moment he was silent and there could only be heard the sound of the wind and the sobbing of the survivors of Culcairn House.

Briefly the earl felt pity for the young laird, but he both needed and wanted to know the entire story of this tragedy which certainly, to a great extent, concerned him as well. "The rest of it, laddie," he said quietly. "Tell me everything, Rob."

The laird sighed deeply and then continued. "Eufemia would nae let me refuse ye, my lord. She swore to me that if the match was struck she would be a good wife to ye; but the truth was that she could barely wait to tell her English lover of her *good fortune*. She wanted to make him envious of her *earl*, for he was but a simple knight. How she laughed at being able to repay him in kind. She told him he was welcome to his heiress if he could even find one who would hae him. She would be a *countess*; the wife of the king's half brother, despite her small dowry. Now that I think on it, I believe my sister gave me her confidences because she was fearful. 'Twas a dangerous game she played with a dangerous man.

"Sir Jasper told my sister that he would bring her to England and gie her her own house. Eufemia replied that she was tired of being his mistress and would not be publicly shamed. He would either wed wi her or she would wed wi ye. Several weeks ago she told him she would nae see him again; that she was finished wi him, and she would tell the world so. That she preferred being a wife, and if nae his, then yers. She was stubborn, my elder sister, but the break pained her, I know. Her temper was foul these past weeks, and she cried easily."

Robert Hamilton's eyes dimmed with his memories. He could

once again hear the stamping of hoofbeats outside of his home, the hard jangling of bridles, the menacing rumble of voices that forewarned him of trouble to come. He moved swiftly to the library windows, and saw outside in the light of the smoking torches a large party of men. The burning brands flamed eerily in the rising wind, sending an equal measure of light and shadow over the mounted troop, none of whom, the young laird noted, wore plaids. *English!*

"God in his heaven!" he whispered softly to himself, fearing the worst even while hoping for the best. Culcairn House had originally been a hunting lodge, and although added on to over the years until it had become a house, it had never been fortified; although it should have been, considering its precarious location so near the border.

Robert Hamilton heard a mighty hammering upon the door. He ran from the library downstairs to the main level of the house, directing his servants even as he came to seek safety for themselves and the other young Hamiltons. The hall was emptied as if by magic as he, himself, flung open the stout oak door of his home to face a deceptively handsome gentleman who stepped quickly over the threshold, saying as he came,

"I am Sir Jasper Keane. I wish to see Mistress Eufemia Hamilton."

"I am her brother, the laird," Robert Hamilton answered, "and the hour is late to come calling, my lord."

"Yet I am here, sir, and you will not, I think, send me away," came the arrogant reply. "Surely you will permit me to speak with Mistress Eufemia after the long hard ride my men and I have undertaken this night."

Robert Hamilton laughed bitterly. "I am nae in a position to refuse ye, my lord, am I? Still I am uncomfortable, for I dinna think much honest business is conducted in such a manner in the deep of night."

The Englishman flushed, but before he might reply to the laird's sharp words, Eufemia Hamilton herself appeared at the top of the stairs.

"How dare ye come here!" she hissed at Sir Jasper Keane. "Get ye gone, my lord!" Then turning, she disappeared into the upper reaches of the house.

Sir Jasper leapt up the stairs after her, but the laird's voice caused him to stop in his flight.

"*My lord!* I will nae hae this shameful matter between ye and my sister made any more public than ye hae both already made it. Let me escort ye to my library, and I will send for Eufemia to come and join us there. I would bid ye remember that this is *my* home."

The Englishman nodded, but said, "My men must be allowed entry to the house, sir."

"There is nae any danger to ye here, Sir Jasper," the laird replied stiffly. "I will open my door to show my good faith, but yer men will remain outside."

"Very well," came the agreement.

Robert Hamilton opened his front door and said to the assembled troop, "Yer master bids ye await him here." Then turning back to his unwanted guest, he led him upstairs to the second level of the house, into his library. "There is wine, my lord. I bid ye help yerself while I go and fetch my sister." He hurried from the room and up the staircase to the third story of the house, where the bedchambers were located.

In the upper hall he met with old Una, the children's nurse-maid.

" 'Tis a wicked man that comes courting wi a troop of armed rogues at his back," she noted matter-of-factly.

"Aye," he concurred. "Take the bairns to safety, and if there be those amongst the servants who have nae hidden themselves, bid them do so before it is too late. We may get out of this alive, old woman, and we may nae. It is too late to seek help from the earl, I fear."

He continued down the hallway to his eldest sister's room, entering the chamber without even knocking. There he found Eufemia, flushed, excited, and as anxious as a maid with her first love. He marveled that anyone as willful and selfish as she was could be so beautiful. Her sapphire-blue eyes were almost black with her mood, and he observed she was wearing her very best gown, a dark green silk with pearls embroidered on the bodice.

"He hae come for me, Rob!" she said excitedly. "I knew he would!"

"Dinna be a fool, Eufemia," the young laird said sharply. "If the Englishman had come to offer marriage to ye, he would hae asked me first, as 'tis proper. Certainly he knows yer willing, sister."

Eufemia Hamilton frowned. "Yer right," she said slowly, as if unwilling to admit to the truth of his words. Her eyes flashed angrily as her mood turned. "Damn him, Rob!" Now she was almost close to tears. "Damn his black soul! Send him away!"

" 'Tis easier said than done," Robert Hamilton replied quietly. "Only ye can send him away."

"I'll nae see him!" she said petulantly.

The laird gripped his sister's arm in a bruising grasp, and his voice was so uncharacteristically harsh that Eufemia's eyes widened in surprise. "I may be yer junior in years, sister mine," he told her, "but I am the head of this family, and as such, *I will be obeyed!* Ye've endangered us all wi yer shamelessness, and by God, ye'll put an end to it this night before the earl hears about it. Do ye understand me, Eufemia?"

"Aye," she whispered.

"Then come down to meet wi yer *lover*. He's awaiting ye in my library."

"Ye'll nae come wi me?"

"Nae unless ye want me to, sister."

She shook her head in the negative.

"Then bind up yer hair and go before his men start stealing the livestock."

"He likes my hair loose, Rob, and so if I would appeal to his softer side, 'tis best I leave it," she said. Then she hurried from the room.

The laird as quickly exited his sister's chamber, and hurrying to his own, shut the door firmly, bolting it behind him. Moving to the fireplace wall, he felt along the molding. A small door, well hidden in the paneling, sprang open. Stepping through, the laird closed the door behind him, and slipped down the interior staircase within the wall. He knew the way well and had no need of a torch. Reaching the bottom of the stairs, he stood quietly, peering through a small opening cleverly concealed in the wall from anyone on the other side of it. He saw the door to the library open and Eufemia enter the room.

Sir Jasper Keane strode masterfully across the room and, sweeping her into his arms, kissed her fiercely.

Eufemia pushed him away impatiently. "Dinna touch me," she said coldly. "Ye disgust me, Jasper."

"And you fascinate me, you border bitch!" he answered her.

"Why are ye here? My brother is most angry wi me, and ye've frightened the bairns wi all yer men," she told him.

"You know why I'm here, Eufemia. I've come to take you back to England. You have not yet formally celebrated your betrothal to this earl of yours. 'Twill be no shame to him if you cry off now. You know I love you. At least as much as I can love any woman," he amended.

"Are ye asking me to be yer wife, then, Jasper?" Eufemia Hamilton somehow managed to keep the eagerness out of her voice, although it trembled just slightly.

Sir Jasper Keane took the girl into his arms. His mouth traveled over her face as he left a trail of hot kisses upon her cool skin. A hand slid into Eufemia's bodice to fondle a plump breast, tweaking at the nipple until it was rigid and puckered with her unspoken desire for him. For a minute Eufemia Hamilton sagged against her lover, enjoying the moment, but she stiffened sharply when he said softly, his tongue licking at the shell of her ear as he spoke, "You know my position, my pretty pet. I shall have an English heiress to wife, and I shall have a Scots border bitch for my mistress."

"Nae this border bitch," she told him furiously. "Ye know *my* position in this matter, Jasper. I shall be yer wife, or I shall be the wife of the Earl of Dunmor, and quit of ye! Can some milk and water English virgin love ye like this?" she demanded, pulling his head down and kissing him passionately.

He returned her kisses with equal fervor, and then raising his head, he looked down into her eyes and told her, "I'm taking you back to England with me tonight, Eufemia, and if your puppy of a brother attempts to stop me, I shall kill him. You were never meant to be any man's wife, my pet, for there is too much fire and wickedness in you. You will be my mistress, my leman, for all of England to see, for I shall be proud to flaunt your beauty before the world itself. Why would you want to be my wife? My wife must be a brood mare. I will not love her. Her sole function will be to birth healthy children for me. No one will care about her, Eufemia, but you they will gaze after with envy, some even daring to imagine what it would be like to ride between your milky thighs. Nay, my pet, what I offer you is far better than to be a mere wife."

Eufemia's dark eyes smouldered dangerously at his words.

"And for how long will I be yer leman, my lord? Will our union last forever?"

He grinned back at her. "You are a practical woman, Eufemia," he said. "You will be my mistress as long as it pleases me you be."

"And afterward, Jasper?"

"If you still retain your beauty," he said bluntly, "I expect you can find another protector."

She pulled from his embrace, and raising clenched fists, began to beat him about the head and chest, all the while shrieking her outrage. "Yer a bastard, Jasper Keane! An English bastard! Am I some peasant wench that ye would dare to offer me such a life? I am a woman of a reputable family, a member of the lower nobility! I am meant to be wedded, not just bedded! I will nae go wi ye! Ye canna make me!" She slapped him as hard as she could.

Laughing, he caught her hand and placed a burning kiss upon the palm. "I do not doubt your family's repute, my pet, nor even your nobility, but you are a whore nonetheless, Eufemia. Some women are born to it, and you are one of them."

They continued to argue back and forth, and suspecting that they would be at it for a while longer, Robert Hamilton hurried back to his bedchamber. Undoing the bolt, he slipped into the upper hall and, moving swiftly, checked all the rooms to be certain that they were empty of their inhabitants. He was relieved to find that he, Eufemia, and Sir Jasper were undoubtedly the only ones left in the house. The servants and his younger siblings were safely away. Returning to his hiding place in the wall, he discovered that his sister's anger had not abated even in the slightest.

"For God's sake, Eufemia," he heard Sir Jasper say, "you are the only woman for whom I've ever felt such passion! Is that not enough for you?"

"Passion?" Eufemia Hamilton laughed almost hysterically. "Ye know nothing of passion, Jasper. Yer naught but a rutting boar compared to the Earl of Dunmor!" She laughed again at the look of surprise upon Sir Jasper Keane's face. "Aye," she said, confirming his suspicions. "He's already bedded me, and his stallion's rod makes yer own tool look like the puny worm it is!" she lied boldly, attempting to rouse his jealousy.

The Englishman's visage darkened and, his mouth drawing

back into a snarl of rage that overflowed with his rising anger, he slapped Eufemia so hard that her teeth rattled. "You claim you are meant to be a wife, you border bitch, but I tell you that you have the cold, black heart of a born whore!" he shouted.

"Yer a jealous fool, Jasper Keane," Eufemia mocked him. "Ye hae nae ever really pleased me. Ye hae the manhood of a feeble bairn, and so I'll tell the whole world if ye steal me away and dinna make me yer wife!"

"If I displease you so, my pet, why would you want to wed me instead of your fine earl?" he demanded cleverly.

"Because I love ye, God help me!" Eufemia admitted.

"Then you will come away with me this night!" he said, his anger softened by her declaration, and the belief that he had the upper hand over her. If she continued to resist him, she would regret it.

"Nay, I will not," she replied stubbornly.

"Aye, you will, my pet," he replied firmly, and if Eufemia Hamilton did not see the determination in her lover's eyes, her brother in his hiding place did. "You are mine, Eufemia, and I will allow no one, even King Jamie's bastard brother of Dunmor to have what is mine until I am finished with it." His eyes narrowed dangerously, and with a sudden viciousness, he knocked her to the floor, and falling upon her, pushed her skirts up to her waist with one hand while loosing his cock from his breeches with the other. " 'Tis past time, my pet, that you re-acquainted yourself with my puny worm!"

Eufemia screeched like a scalded cat with the unexpectedness of his attack. She pummeled him with her knotted fists even as he thrust into her, but then her protests began to fade, her passions blossoming as the Englishman rode her. She began to moan with her own pleasure in the union, her fingers tearing open his shirt, her sharp nails raking down his back. He pleasured her thrice as he indulged his own lusts, which did not seem to be easily sated.

Robert Hamilton saw fear begin to enter his sister's countenance, and silently he opened the hidden door to step into the library. She saw him, and her frantic eyes warned him away. The young laird hesitated. This was his sister for all her wickedness. The Englishman's buttocks tightened and contracted with his efforts, and he began to roar loudly as he approached his own peak. Eufemia thrust her own hips up firmly to meet his violent downward motions.

"*Save the bairns!*" she cried out but a single time, and waved him away, praying her lover lost in his lusts would not comprehend her words.

Robert Hamilton hesitated, once again torn with his love for his elder sister despite everything.

"*Quickly! Quickly!*" she urged him.

"Not yet, my border bitch," Sir Jasper Keane growled, thinking that she spoke to him. " 'Tis the last time I intend fucking you, and by God, I'll have my fill of you!" Redoubling his efforts, he began to shout once again, pumping her hard as he approached his crisis.

Hearing the Englishman's words, Robert Hamilton withdrew as silently as he had entered. It would appear that Sir Jasper had finally accepted Eufemia's decision, and when he had finished taking his pleasure of her, would withdraw with his men, leaving them in peace. Still, it would be better to remain hidden until the English had gone. He knew instinctively where his younger siblings would be concealed. The land about the house offered little cover to an escaping party of people, but there was a large, thick bramble of a hedge that encircled the building. They would be secluded in the ditch that paralleled that hedge, and sure enough, there he found them.

Old Una was clutching little Geordie to her shriveled bosom in an effort to keep him from crying and betraying their presence. Meg and Mary clung to each other for solace, their eyes wide with their fright.

"It will be all right, bairns," he told them as he joined them, crouching low in the hidey-hole. "The English will soon be gone, but ye must remain as quiet as wee mousies hiding from the cat."

"Will they kill us if they find us, Robbie?" little Mary quavered.

"Aye," he said honestly. It was best to be direct in a situation like this. Their very lives depended upon it.

At the sound of Eufemia's voice, he turned his gaze back to the front of the house, which he could see quite clearly from his vantage point just at one of its corners. Sir Jasper Keane was half dragging her from the house while she struggled and cursed him with all the pent-up violence in her soul. As they passed over the threshold, the laird saw flames leaping behind the two figures. He groaned softly with despair. The damned bastard had fired Culcairn House!

"Jasper! Jasper! Don't do this to me!" Eufemia was desperately endeavoring to escape her lover's grasp.

The Englishman laughed, and his hand wrapped itself even more tightly in her dark red hair, forcing her face to his. He kissed her hard, and then said loudly, "I told you, Eufemia, that you would be mine only as long as you pleased me. You no longer please me, my border bitch."

"Then let me go," she pleaded, and Robert Hamilton could see the terror in his sister's face. Her dark blue eyes were almost rolling in her head like some panicked animal.

"Let you go? To the Earl of Dunmor? Nay! If you will not be mine, then by God, you will not be his either! I don't want you as my whore any longer, Eufemia, but it is my right to decide your fate." He yanked her about so that she faced his troop of men, and using his other hand, he tore her clothes from her, rendering her naked.

"Dinna look," Robert Hamilton commanded his younger sisters, knowing what was about to transpire, and feeling a deep dread in the pit of his stomach.

" 'Tis poor pickings we'll have this night, my lads," Sir Jasper Keane told his followers, "but you may want this pretty piece of goods for your amusement. She's hot and juicy, and I've already primed her well, so that she's ready for the taking. *Have her!"* And he brutally shoved Eufemia forward.

She stumbled, but somehow managed to keep her balance. The ring of English borderers about her closed even as she looked wildly about for a chance to elude them. Belatedly her hands moved to cover her bosom and the triangle between her thighs. The flames from the burning house threw dappled shadows over her fair, white body, and but for the crackle of the fire, the night was suddenly, for a brief moment, deathly silent. Then a large borderer moved forward from the circle of men, loosening his engorged male organ free of his breeches as he came toward her. Eufemia shrieked and whirled wildly about, seeking an avenue of escape, but there was none.

"Come on, lassie," the man crooned, moving stealthily onward. "Johnny will fuck you nicely." He reached out his hand to her. Eufemia screamed again and made to bolt, but two other men jumped forward, wrestling her to the ground even as the one who called himself Johnny stepped to stand over Eufemia and then smilingly fell to his knees to straddle her.

Robert Hamilton shuddered with the violence of the memory. Now haunted and hollow-eyed he looked up at the Earl of Dunmor. "In a moment's time all discipline was gone, and they violently savaged her. Before my very eyes, and those of my sisters, they ravished her again, and again, and again. Like Meg, I shall hear Eufemia's screams until my dying day! I shall never forgive myself, my lord! I might have saved her earlier, but I did not. I crouched helplessly in a ditch while my elder sister was murdered before me. I could not help her. It was all I could do to soothe Meg and Mary, and to keep little Geordie from crying out, for he was terribly frightened.

"I was one. The English were many. The girls and old Una clung to me, begging me not to leave them. What was I to do? I could not sacrifice my younger sisters and brother to the brutality of those devils! *I could not!* And when they had finished with Eufemia, they threw her naked body into the flames of our home. She was long dead by then, I am certain, for she had made no sound for several minutes before.

"Then the English took my horses and my cattle, and drove them off across the border. Despite my love for Eufemia—and I did love her for all her wild ways, my lord—none of this would have happened had my sister not been the whore that she was. Now ye know the truth of this matter. *The whole truth!*" the young laird concluded defiantly, looking up at the earl.

A deep silence prevailed for a long minute between the older and the younger man. Then Tavis Stewart put a comforting hand upon the laird's shoulder. " 'Tis done then," he said quietly. "Yer family and servants will come back wi me to Dunmor Castle, and there ye will stay until yer home can be rebuilt." His voice was devoid of emotion. "Whatever else she was, Eufemia Hamilton was to have been my wife. I'll nae let her family suffer. The English, in murdering yer sister, have besmirched the honor of the Stewarts of Dunmor, as well as the Hamiltons of Culcairn. As the Earl of Dunmor it is my right to wreak my vengeance upon this little English lordling. We'll hae our revenge, laddie, that I promise ye!"

"What will we do, my lord?" Robert Hamilton asked.

"Och, Rob, we must first find where this English fox has his den, and then we'll burn it to the ground, even as he burned yer home. We'll take back yer horses and cattle, and of course we'll hae his horses and cattle as well in forfeit. That done, I expect the Englishman will think us finished wi him, but we will nae be, Rob. We will wait, and we will watch. Sir Jasper bragged to yer sister that King Richard would make him a fine match.''

"Perhaps 'twas all it was," the laird said, "idle boasting and nothing more. Why would the English king be bothered with a petty vassal? I dinna know a great deal about the man other than what Eufemia told me. I dinna even know if he has a house, but my sister never spoke of any important connections that this man might have.''

"Patience, lad," the earl counseled. "In time we will learn everything we need to learn about Sir Jasper Keane. If indeed King Richard makes an advantageous match for this man, we will know it, and it may be we will make this unknown heiress a widow before she is a bride. The English will pay a heavy forfeit for this night's work at Culcairn.''

"But how will we find Sir Jasper's home?" the laird persisted.

"Think, Rob! The man canna keep his cock to himself, and has lasses, ye've said, on both sides of the border. God only knows we Scots hae our share of randy borderers, but last night this Englishman murdered a Scotswoman of good family. He did it deliberately, cruelly, and wi malice. We will find him, lad, for someone is certain to know the location of his lair, and they will talk. Either from their own outrage over this crime or from their own greed. I intend offering a reward for information that can lead us to the treacherous bastard. Gold is often a more powerful weapon than even the sword.''

The young laird thought a moment and then nodded his agreement at the earl's words. An impatient tug upon his sleeve caught his sudden attention, and he looked down into the wizened features of a tiny woman who glowered balefully up at him. "What is it, Una?''

"What is it?" the old woman repeated irritably. "I'll tell ye what it is, Master Robert. Mistress Meg is near collapse, and Mistress Mary and wee Geordie chilled to the bone and hungry. I've already lost one of my precious bairns.'' Tears ran down her cheeks, though her voice remained strong. "Am I to lose another while ye two plot a vengeance that could just as easily be plotted before a warm fire and a plate of hot food?''

The barest hint of a smile touched the corners of Tavis Stewart's stern mouth as Una loudly scolded the laird. She was a tiny bit of a wiry woman, but it was pointedly obvious she feared little. "Can yer bairns sit a horse, old woman?" he demanded of her.

"Aye," she answered him. "I'll ride pillion wi Mistress Mary. Mistress Meg can ride wi Master Robert, but someone will have to take our Geordie. I would wish for a cart if I could, for I dinna like the four-legged beasties myself. And where are we to go, I should like to know?"

"Ye'll be coming to Dunmor, good dame, and I'll take yer littlest bairn wi me. My mother, Lady Fleming, will advise me in the matter of these little ones; and ye'll stay at Dunmor until Culcairn House is rebuilt," the earl told her.

Dame Una nodded. " 'Tis right ye gie us shelter," she said matter-of-factly. Then she moved off to where her charges waited, seated upon large stones that had once been a part of their home.

"She was one of our great-grandsire's bastards," the laird explained. "Her mam nursed his legitimate bairns."

"I understand," the earl replied. "She is kin, and that is a good thing, for kin are usually loyal."

The laird flushed as if the words had been meant as a rebuke. "I did nae know what to do about Eufemia," he explained helplessly, as if the explanation were required of him. "She was my elder by three years. After our mother died birthing Geordie, our father gave into her every whim. She was his eldest and always his favorite, though he never said it. Then father was killed last year, and I could nae more control her than he could. She had a way wi her, my lord," Robert Hamilton finished simply.

"Eufemia cast no spell over me, Rob, though I should have probably beaten her if she had been my sister and behaved so. I hardly knew her, though I did hope in time we would come to like and respect one another. Ye know why I asked for her. It is time for me to wed, as my mother is ever preaching at me. I like the idea of having kin whose lands abut mine. Then, too, Eufemia was a pretty creature, and a man likes a pretty woman in his bed, for it makes his bedsport pleasant."

"Aye," the laird agreed cheerfully, "and 'tis nice when they smell good too. Eufemia always smelt like wild roses." Then remembering himself, Robert Hamilton said, "I do thank ye for coming to our aid, my lord, and for the shelter ye offer my family and servants." The earl's reasons for marriage did not surprise Robert Hamilton, for they were sound and practical reasons. Love was generally something that came later in a marriage, if it came at all. Love, more often than not, had little to do with a good match. He was flattered that the Earl of Dunmor had asked for his elder sister's hand in marriage, for indeed, as King James's half brother, Tavis Stewart might have sought far higher. Until this possibility of an alliance between their families had arisen, he had not known the earl, for Dunmor was often at court in his brother's service. His reputation, however, was that of a fair, though hard man.

"There's serious rain threatening, Rob," the Earl said, breaking into his thoughts. "Spring is early this year. Yer sisters and little brother dinna look to me as if they'll last much longer. We hae best be going."

The laird cast a worried glance at his younger siblings. "Aye," he said, and suddenly he felt exhausted again.

The earl saw the look upon the young man's face, and he said, "The sooner we get to Dunmor, laddie, the sooner we may begin to plan a fine revenge upon Sir Jasper Keane and his ilk. Neither my honor nor yers will be satisfied until the Englishman has paid for Eufemia's life wi his own, but first we'll hae a bit of fun wi him." He waved his hand and the horses were brought. Mounting his stallion, he took little George Hamilton from old Una and placed the sniveling child on the saddle before him. "Dinna greet, Geordie," he warned the boy sternly, "else ye frighten the horses. Yer a Hamilton, and Hamiltons are nae afeared of anything save God himself, eh?"

The little lad turned large blue eyes upon the earl and nodded solemnly at the fierce-browed man who held him and whose words were strangely comforting. Then he looked about him for a brief moment and felt proud. No one else had so fine a horse as this one. Old Una and his sister Mary were pillion upon a small gelding, and Rob was forced to ride wi Meg. "I'll nae greet," he lisped up at the earl.

"Good lad!" came the reply as their party began to move off.

Robert Hamilton, his sister slumped half conscious behind him, glanced back for just a moment at his family's home as they rode away. Culcairn House stood bleak against the lowering skies. Its blackened stones and charred timbers, still smoking, seemed to cry out to him for vengeance. In the rising wind he would have sworn that he could yet hear Eufemia's screams. *Aye!* The earl was right, and he, too, wanted his revenge. Only when he had taken that revenge would Eufemia be put truly to rest. Whatever her behavior, she had been his sister. When he thought of her in the future he would remember the happy times. Remember her last words to him: *Save the bairns!*

In the end, the goodness that Robert Hamilton believed in all women had overcome everything else wicked that had festered in his elder sister's soul; and for the first and only time in her life, she had thought of the rest of them. She would be revenged. *Aye! She would be revenged!* The laird of Culcairn turned his face from the tragic ruins of his ancestral home and, digging his heels into his horse, rode off into the rising storm.

Part I

THE BORDER

BRIDE

M iddleham Castle sat firmly upon the southern hills, its great gray walls and towers looming over the village of Wensleydale. The king was in residence on this fine late September day, for his banner with its white boar flew from the topmost turret. His coronation was almost three months past, and his entry into his city of York several weeks ago had been an incredible triumph. How they loved him, his beloved northerners; and how warmly they had taken Anne and little Edward to their hearts as well. It had been such a triumph that he had stayed longer than he had anticipated, allowing the investiture of Edward as Prince of Wales to take place in York Minster. Now, when he should be on his way south, he had escorted his son and his queen here to Middleham, his favorite home, that he might have a few days respite before picking up his duties again. Neddie, as the little prince was fondly called by his intimates, would, of course, remain here when his father, the king, departed.

Richard, King of England, reached for his goblet and gazed with a beneficent look about the family solar. His wife's widowed cousin, Lady Rowena Grey, and her little daughter had come to stay these few precious days with them. Sweet Row, born into a lesser branch of the Neville family, had been orphaned young and raised by his father-in-law, the Earl of Warwick, with his own dear wife. She was, in fact, the best friend that Anne had, although the two women had been separated for many years.

Anne Neville's first husband had been a prince of Wales, the son of King Henry VI and his queen, Margaret of Anjou. Rowena, on the other hand, had been married on her thirteenth birthday to Henry Grey, Baron Greyfaire, an unimportant border lord who possessed a small but strategic keep. Sir Henry, as Richard remembered him, was a loyal and kindly man, some years his wife's senior. He had died the previous year, another victim to the incessant undeclared war between England and

Scotland that had raged for centuries along the border between the two kingdoms. Sir Henry had left but one living child, Arabella, who was a year older than the king's own son, her cousin.

The difference in age between the two children was not readily apparent, for although Neddie was ten to her eleven, and frail of body, Arabella Grey was still petite, not having attained her maturity yet. She had a quick mind, though, the king noted, for she not only held her own at the chessboard with Neddie, she had already beaten him once this afternoon. The girl, Richard mused with a small smile, had obviously inherited her father's intellect, for sweet Row had never been able to play chess or concentrate on anything more complicated than an embroidery pattern. The child had looks too, not that her mother was lacking there, but Rowena Neville Grey, with her light blue eyes and thick wheaten-colored hair, appeared almost plain next to her daughter; for Arabella, with that odd, pale gold, almost silver-gilt hair, and those light green eyes that slanted up slightly at the corners and which were overshadowed by dark brows and lashes, was a rare beauty. The king chuckled softly to himself. Why was it, he considered, that the heiresses from great families were more often than not horse-faced, while the daughters of the less distinguished were usually the beauties? It was obvious that God had a great sense of fair play.

"Is she promised?" he asked aloud, nodding his head toward Arabella, even as he directed the question to her mother.

"Henry and I had planned to match her with a cousin, but the boy died of a spotting sickness last autumn, my lord," Rowena Grey replied. "Ohh, Dickon!" Her pretty face grew hopeful. "Would you make a match for her? I am so helpless when it comes to things like this, and who else can I turn to? Oh, I know how busy you are now that you are king, but could you not take but a moment of your time to find Arabella a husband? We desperately need a man at Greyfaire. I live in terror lest the Scots come over the border. I would not even know how to defend the keep."

"Why do you not remarry, Row? Arabella is young yet, but it would be easy to find you a new husband," the king said.

"Nay! I have naught to offer a man but the little dowry my lord of Warwick gave me when I was wed to my Henry. I fear a suitor might cast covetous eyes upon Greyfaire, and find a way to do my daughter a harm in order that he might gain her inheritance. If once Arabella is married there is one who would have me, then so be it; but I shall not take another husband until my child's future is safe," Rowena Grey said firmly.

"I think you show surprising good sense, cousin," Queen Anne remarked. Then she turned a melting glance upon her husband. "Come, Dickon, find a husband from amongst your retainers for little Arabella. You would have Greyfaire in safe hands, would you not? Remember that Arabella's father was a cousin to Lord John Grey, he who was the first husband of your late brother's wife."

"Henry was ever loyal to your grace, however," Lady Rowena quickly interjected, for although King Richard had loved his elder brother, Edward IV, and had always been his most loyal liegeman, he detested his brother's queen.

Elizabeth Woodville, several years King Edward's senior, had, it was believed by many, entrapped her king into marriage. She had—in fairness, Richard thought—been a good wife to her husband, and given him a large family of children, including two sons; but she had used her position to enrich and ennoble her family excessively. Few called themselves her friends, and consequently, after his brother's death last April, there were few to take up her cause when the church declared her marriage to Edward IV invalid, and her children bastards unable to inherit their father's throne. Edward IV, the church declared, had had a previous marriage contract with Lady Eleanor Butler, who was yet living when Edward IV had eloped with the widowed Lady Elizabeth Grey and secretly married her. England's powerful had not wanted a minority rule, for even though Edward IV had made his brother his sons' protector, the queen's relations were immediately maneuvering to gain control of the government. Declaring little Edward V ineligible to rule and passing the crown to his uncle, Richard III, had solved the problem.

Richard had placed his two little nephews in protective custody so that they could not be used by others to foment rebellion. Already the rumors abounded that he had harmed them, but the king loved all children and was incapable of such violence. Besides, trueborn or not, they were his brother's sons, and Richard had loved Edward with all his being. But from her sanctuary at Westminster, the former queen screeched and howled her outrage over her double loss: that of her prestige, and the custody of her sons; even as she dealt, not so secretly, in an attempt to match her eldest daughter, Elizabeth, with the Lancaster heir, Henry Tudor, Richard's sworn enemy.

Queen Anne had made a small miscalculation in reminding her husband of Arabella Grey's distant connection with his sister-in-law's family. The north of England—York, Northumberland, and Cumbria—had always been loyal to her husband, yet even now Richard had begun to see enemies where none existed. He considered Greyfaire Keep. It was small, but it was strategic to the defense of the border, being so close to it. Greyfaire Keep was always the first to raise the alarm when the Scots came swarming over the Cheviot hills; and the Scots were always treating with the king of England's enemies. It could be danger-ous for little Greyfaire Keep to fall into unfriendly, unloyal, or opportunistic hands. He would not be ill-advised to find a hus-band for the little heiress. A man who was unquestioningly loyal to Richard of England and no other master.

"I think you are correct, sweeting," he said to his spouse. "We must find our little cousin Arabella a husband, *and* before we leave Middleham."

"She is far too young to wed," Rowena said with obvious emphasis.

"Yet the bridegroom can be chosen now," the king said. "Your fears for Greyfaire are realistic, Row. I need a strong man in charge there, that I may be reassured of the continued safety of my northern borders. I will think on it, Row. You may rest assured that I shall not allow you to remain unprotected any longer. Indeed, you should have come to me sooner about this."

"Dickon," she began out of habit, and then amended, "sire, my child and I are the least among your subjects. Had not my dearest Anne sent for us to come to Middleham, we would not be here at all and I should have never presumed upon your kindness in finding my daughter a husband."

The king took Lady Grey's hand in his and patted the plump flesh. "Rowena, you are family. My sweet Anne's most favorite companion from her childhood, and her cousin. Had you not been matched to Sir Henry and wed upon your thirteenth birth-day, you would have remained with her, and thus now been a part of our court. That your life took a different path makes you no less beloved of us." He lifted her hand to his lips and kissed it before releasing it.

"Sire . . ." Her blue eyes filled with tears.

"Dickon, Row. As ever, Dickon," the king replied.

"Dickon, you are so kind. You have always been kind to me. I remember when we were children and Anne's elder sister, Isabel, was always so cruel to me, except that you would not allow it when you saw it. You have always cared for those weaker than you. England is fortunate to have you as its king, but one favor I beg of you."

"Whatever you desire, Row."

Rowena Neville Grey was forced to smile. "You speak too quickly, and are too generous as always, Dickon, but I shall not take advantage of you, my lord. My request is simple. Though I loved my Henry, I was too young for marriage when my lord of Warwick sent me off to Greyfaire. I lost two sons before Arabella was born, and miscarried of another daughter afterward. Make the match that Greyfaire may have a master again, but let there be no formal ceremony until my daughter is old enough to be a wife in the fullest sense."

Richard looked to his wife, and the queen nodded her agreement with her cousin. "Pick the man," she told him, "but there should be no formal betrothal or marriage until little Arabella is older. Greyfaire will have its protector, its kingsman; but should my little cousin grow up to love another as I have always loved you, my lord, at least she will not be forced to the altar with other than her true love. If we formally betroth her, she will be formally bound. Should the day come that she desires a husband other than the one you have chosen, Greyfaire's protector can be offered a suitable compensation for his loss, can he not?"

"You have a tender heart, my love," the king replied, "but it will be even as you have suggested. Will that suit you as well, Row?"

"Aye, Dickon, it will!" Lady Grey said, smiling. She was very relieved that the king had taken a hand in this matter. It was unlikely that Arabella would marry any other but he whom the king chose, and there would once again be a master at Greyfaire. It had been so frightening these last months since her husband's death. He had died in the late summer a year ago, and she truly believed that it was only through the personal intervention of the blessed Mother herself that the Scots had not raided in the vicinity since Sir Henry's demise; but how much longer could she count upon divine protection? Greyfaire needed a new lord.

She had not been entirely helpless, however. There was her husband's faithful captain, FitzWalter, and he had remained in his position after Henry's death; but FitzWalter was not Greyfaire's lord. He had appeared at Greyfaire in Henry's youth, offering his fealty and service. No one knew from whence he had come, and FitzWalter never bothered to divulge that information to any, even the wife he took after several years in residence. He had begun as a simple man-at-arms upon the walls, working his way through the ranks until one day he became Greyfaire's captain. His wife served as the keep's laundress, even as she produced a bevy of healthy daughters and one fine son for her husband. The boy, Rowan FitzWalter, was a year older than Arabella, and along with a younger sister, Lona, was the little heiress's closest companion. FitzWalter would be as relieved as she was, Rowena thought, to have a master once more. He had done his duty, but she knew that the full responsibility had fretted him. He was not a man to overstep his position. The king had given her his word, and she would not discuss it with him again unless Dickon broached the subject first.

Prince Edward and Arabella, their game of chess completed, wandered over to their parents. The boy's color was high with his excitement, and the queen reached out to feel his forehead. Edward pulled away irritably, but Queen Anne drew him back into her embrace, saying, "Your father has promised to find a fine husband for your cousin Arabella, Neddie. Is that not nice?"

"I wish to marry my cousin," the boy said imperiously. "I like her. She makes me work to win at chess."

"You cannot marry me, Neddie," Arabella said. "It would not be right."

"Why not?" the lad demanded.

"Because, silly, you are a prince. Princes marry princesses. One day you will be king," Arabella said, sounding just a trifle annoyed that he should not have known this himself.

"If I am to be king," the boy replied with perfect logic, "then why can I not make you a princess so that we may marry? Kings are allowed to do anything they want."

"Not always," said his father, and though his tone was serious, his eyes bespoke his amusement. "What your cousin Arabella means is that boys who are to be kings must make very advantageous marriages in order to help their countries. Your bride will come from a country who can be of help to England against her enemies. Perhaps she will even be the daughter of an enemy, and your marriage will end a dispute. She will have a good dowry; not just gold, but lands as well.''

"Arabella has Greyfaire," the prince said.

"Greyfaire," Arabella told him, "is a little keep, Neddie. Your castle of Middleham is five times as big. Besides, my husband must come and live with me, for Greyfaire helps to protect the Middle Marches from the Scots. A king must travel all about his kingdom. I cannot be your wife, but can we not remain friends?''

"I suppose so," the prince said, sounding somewhat disappointed, and then he brightened. "Would you like to see the new puppies that my father's best bitch has just whelped? She's in the kennels here. They are mine to do with as I please, my father says. Would you like one, cousin Arabella?''

"Ohh, Neddie, yes!" the little girl replied excitedly, and then looked to her mother. "May I, Mama? May I?''

Rowena laughed. "I suppose that Greyfaire can house another hound, Arabella. Aye, if Neddie wishes to give you a puppy, and it is all right with the king, aye, you may have one.''

The two children scampered out of the family solar as their fond mothers looked after them.

The king chuckled. "She has a good head on her, Row, your wee lass. Her father's daughter, I must assume.''

The queen and Lady Grey laughed, for Rowena Neville had never been a scholar in their shared school days. She could barely read, and wrote her name but legibly, and her sums had always been more wrong than right. In the wifely arts, however, she had excelled. There was not a recipe, household or medicinal, that she could not concoct to perfection. Her soaps were like bathing with pure silk, her conserves and sugared comfits without equal, her embroidery an art form. Her home in the foothills of the Cheviot range had the most exquisite flower garden for miles, but she had no true intellect, and she admitted to it with a cheerful honesty.

"Aye, she is Henry's child in every respect, Dickon. She reads for pleasure," Lady Grey said wonderingly, "and when our bailiff took ill and could not keep the accounts, she kept them for her father, even discovering where poor old Rad had made several errors. She speaks French and Latin, for Henry enjoyed teaching her, and she was always quick to learn. If she has any fault, Dickon, it is that she is too outspoken for a girl. You saw how she was with Neddie. She seems to have no fear at all.''

"She will be an interesting woman one day, Row," the king said, and smiled comfortingly at his wife's cousin. Sweet Row, but how Henry Grey had stood being wed to her he never knew. You certainly could not speak with her for very long without being bored to death, but his dearest Anne loved her even as he had loved Anne since their childhood.

"Dickon will find Arabella just the right husband, Rowena," the queen said, and then the two women began to gossip quietly about a mutual acquaintance, leaving the king to his solitary thoughts.

Soon, the king considered, he would have to leave Middleham and attend to the business of his kingdom, which was not a stable kingdom at this moment in time. He had not sought to be king, whatever others might think, and the clergy's disclosure of his brother's previous contract of marriage with Lady Eleanor Butler had been as much a surprise to him as to anyone else. He had always intended supporting his nephew named Edward, even as his own son. His late brother had made him the children's protector in order that he defend the kingdom against Elizabeth Woodville Grey's greedy and overly ambitious relations, who had, upon his brother's demise, rushed to take custody of the boy king.

Lord Hastings had gotten word to him, and Richard had intercepted the queen's party and their royal prize upon the road to London, taking charge of the boy before any harm might be done. The queen's party, of course, wished to crown young Edward immediately, doing away with the protectorate and appointing themselves regents of the young king. Although he was willing to see his nephew crowned as soon as possible, Richard knew that he must be England's regent if he was to protect the boy, the nation, and his brother's dreams.

. In the beginning the queen's party had lost ground because of the very nature of Elizabeth herself. Then came the disclosure regarding Lady Eleanor Butler, and though none could be found to refute the charges, despite the lady in question being deceased

now, Richard still did not seek the throne. The throne was offered to him in order that there be no doubt cast upon England's
rulers. He had demurred at first, disliking the position in which
he found himself, knowing that there were those who would
protest this removal of his beautiful golden brother's eldest son.
In the end he had accepted, for there was no other choice. He
had stamped out the protest by immediately executing those who
could continue the strife, thereby weakening England, making
her vulnerable to France, to Spain, to Scotland. Lord Hastings,
who had earlier supported him, was one of his victims, and
Richard wept at this ruthless necessity.

Now he was an anointed and crowned king, and his beloved
Anne had been crowned queen. Little Neddie was invested as
the new prince of Wales; and Elizabeth Woodville Grey was
stirring up trouble in the south from the safety of her sanctuary.
His nephews were hidden safely, though not in the Tower, as
many supposed. They were far too vulnerable in the Tower. He
had arranged that their warders be given drugged wine, and then
he personally escorted young Edward and Richard, the younger
lad who was his namesake, from their quarters in the Tower and
sent them here to Middleham. They were bright children, and
they had understood the need for secrecy. They were safe within
their own wing of the castle; and carefully shepherded over the
next few years until his kingdom was secure, they would be kept
hidden from everyone, even his own son, their cousin, who
made his residence here.

Another day. He promised himself one more green and gold
September day here at Middleham before he would take up his
king's mantle again. And he must settle the matter of little Arabella Grey, for he had promised Row that he would. *Who?* Who
among his people was highborn enough, but not a great name,
for Arabella did not merit a great name. Who was without wife?
Who was a widower? Who could he trust with Greyfaire Keep?
Trust to warn the Middle Marches of the coming Scots. Who
would keep faith with him and not pledge his loyalty elsewhere?

Richard remembered a soldier who had fought with his brother
and with him in the past. He was a northerner, the king remembered, but he could not remember the man's name. Waving a
servant to his side, Richard sent for Lord Dacre, who wasted
no time in bowing himself into the private solar and accepted
an offered goblet of wine. The king explained his difficulty. "I

cannot," he said, "for the life of me remember the fellow's name. Wait! Jasper! 'Tis his Christian name. *Jasper!* But Jasper what?"

"Sir Jasper Keane, my liege," replied Lord Dacre.

"Aye, that's the fellow!" The king grinned, pleased, then a frown crossed his features. "Is he wed, Dacre?"

"He has been widowed several times, my liege, but has no wife at the present time, to my knowledge."

"Children?"

"Nay, sire."

"What's his age? I would not force an old man upon the girl," the king said.

"I am not certain, for we are not intimate, my liege, but I would say that Sir Jasper is nearing his thirtieth year."

"A good age," the king noted, "and he is a good fighter. What do you think, Dacre? Would he be a good choice to defend Greyfaire Keep, and would he make my wife's young cousin a good husband? Is he to be trusted?"

"His loyalty is unquestioned, my liege, and I believe he would, indeed, be a good man to place upon the border in England's interests," replied Lord Dacre. He did not mention to the king Sir Jasper's reputation with women, for Richard did not approve of such men. It was the one area in which he had disagreed with his late brother, who adored the ladies. Richard had always been loyal to his Anne, but he was unique in such behavior. England's interests came before any form of morality, and so Lord Dacre remained silent on this matter.

"Has he lands of his own?" demanded the king. "His birth must be at least equal to my cousin's."

"His family has connections, distant however, with my own, and closer ties with the Percys," Lord Dacre answered. "He has property of his own, but his home, Northby Hall, was recently burned to the ground in a savage, but isolated attack by the Scots. No one was killed, but his cattle, horses, and sheep were all driven off. He's a good man, my liege, and I imagine such a fine match would cheer him greatly and bind him even closer to your side."

"A king," observed Richard, "cannot have too many friends, eh Dacre?"

Lord Dacre laughed politely. "Sir Jasper is here at Middleham, my liege, should you decide to favor him."

"Is there anyone else, Dacre, to whom I might give this rich plum? The girl won't be marriageable for at least two years, and I will have no formal betrothal lest they do not suit. My queen is firm upon this point, having suffered from personal experience an unhappy marriage. She would have her cousin's child happy, and I am inclined to give her this small boon, for Anne asks for very little."

Lord Dacre thought for a time and then replied, "Nay, sire, I believe Sir Jasper is eminently suited for both Greyfaire Keep and as little Lady Grey's husband."

"Say nothing of this," the king warned him. "I must think on it further before I make my decision."

"As my liege commands," Lord Dacre said, and bowed himself from the king's presence. He had no sooner left the royal solar than he hurried to find Sir Jasper Keane to tell him of his possible good fortune. "Keep your cock under control," he warned Sir Jasper, "that the king does not hear of your loose behavior. He will not award you the girl and her lands should he learn of your extreme penchant for female flesh. King Richard III is a moral man."

"I know of Greyfaire Keep," Sir Jasper replied. "It is a cozy little castle. Is the heiress rich?"

"There is some small wealth, but were she rich, my friend, I should have had her for my own bastard son," came the answer. "You will not be uncomfortable, but the king will not have the wedding for a year or two. It pleases his queen that the girl like you. If she does not, there will be no wedding. Be warned."

In the Great Hall of Middleham Castle that night the king called Sir Jasper Keane to his side and told him that he would match him with his wife's young cousin, the heiress of Greyfaire Keep, Lady Arabella Grey. Expressing his delight at this honor, Sir Jasper pleased his liege lord, showing no displeasure at the terms to be imposed.

"Shall I be permitted to meet my bride, sire?" he asked politely.

"I see no reason why not," the king replied. "I will ask you to escort Lady Rowena and her daughter, Lady Arabella, back to Greyfaire that you may judge the condition of its defenses and make any changes you so desire. This keep is the first warning beacon upon my borders with Scotland, and the safety of Middle

Marches depends on Greyfaire Keep remaining in English hands.''

"I will not fail you there, my liege," Sir Jasper replied with complete sincerity. He was a soldier first, and the challenge presented him was a pleasing one. He did not fear that the little girl would not like him, for he had never met a woman who did not like him. Tall, with bright gold hair and light golden-brown eyes, few females looked past his pleasing features with his oval face, high cheekbones and forehead, straight nose, dimpled chin, and sensuous mouth, to see that those eyes were cold and fathomless. That the sensuous mouth could grow narrow with cruelty. He was as skilled a seducer as he was a soldier, although as a soldier he had never been known to take a foolish chance. A man did not live to enjoy the fruits of his labor by being reckless and foolish in war. Only in passion did a man dare to be reckless.

"Come to the queen's solar tomorrow morning after the mass, Sir Jasper," the king said, "and you will be introduced to your proposed bride and her widowed mother."

"Thank you, my liege," Sir Jasper Keane replied.

"And be prepared to leave immediately afterward for Greyfaire Keep," the king said. "It will take you a week or more traveling with the ladies to reach there. You are not used, I would imagine, to traveling at such a slow pace, but it will give you time to get to know Lady Rowena and her daughter. It is best you leave tomorrow before the autumn rains begin. The ladies will not like traveling in the rain."

"I shall endeavor to make the trip as easy and as pleasant for the ladies as possible, my liege," Sir Jasper replied, and he gave the king a warm smile.

In the morning Sir Jasper Keane made it a point to attend early mass that he might secretly observe his bride-to-be and her mother. They were obviously amongst the women attending the queen, but all he was able to see was the backs of heads and gowns. It was not until the queen departed the chapel with her ladies that Sir Jasper saw the petite girl with the pale hair, the only child, excepting the little prince, amongst the others. This then was his bride, but which of the ladies was his mother-in-law he could not tell. Waiting for a few discreet minutes, he finally made his way to the queen's solar and was admitted.

Sir Jasper bowed elegantly to Queen Anne and kissed her hand politely. "Madame."

"You have come that we may introduce you to our beloved cousin, Lady Rowena and her daughter, Arabella, whom the king has chosen as your prospective bride, my lord. Welcome," the queen said.

"I am honored that you would consider allowing me this connection with your own family, my gracious lady," Sir Jasper replied.

"What elegance of speech, my lord," the queen answered him. "Why, you might be a clever courtier instead of the soldier my lord, the king, says you are. I am glad to know that Arabella's husband will be a man who is able to use pretty words as well as a sharp sword, Sir Jasper, but I imagine you grow impatient to meet your bride. Come forward, dear child, that I may introduce you to Sir Jasper Keane. You, also, Rowena, for I know you will want to meet your son-in-law to be."

Mother and daughter stepped forward and curtsied politely to Sir Jasper Keane. His bride was quite lovely upon closer inspection, but hair that pale had never really been to his taste. The mother, however, was another matter. The wheaten-colored hair was lovely, and her bosom, rounded where the child's was flat, was delightfully enticing. He felt a familiar tightening, a stirring of interest in his nether regions, which his handsome face, of course, never betrayed. "I am honored, my lady Arabella, that you would consider me for a husband," he said smoothly, taking the child's hand in his and kissing it.

Her heart was pounding furiously, and she felt her cheeks grow pink and warm even as she met his gaze with her own cool green one. He was surely the most handsome man she had ever seen. She had absolutely no idea what she should say and felt extremely foolish as he released her hand.

"My lady Rowena." Lady Grey's hand was saluted.

I shall swoon dead away, Rowena Grey thought, both horrified and thrilled by her reaction to this man. These were feelings that she thought had died with Henry, and yet she could feel the wetness between her thighs already. "I am grateful, my lord, that you have come to our rescue," she said with far more calm than she was feeling. What kind of a woman was she to have such thoughts about the man who would be her daughter's husband? God forgive her!

No one else would have seen these thoughts which she labored so hard to mask, but Jasper Keane saw them deep within Rowena's light blue eyes. A young widow, he almost purred with his pleasure. A young widow hot and ripe for the plucking. Mother and daughter, his for the taking. He had never had both a mother and her daughter. The thought was almost unbearably exciting, and he thanked God that his clothing hid the state of his lust. He could imagine, but vividly, the entire scene.

Strangely, it was his bride-to-be who rescued him. "My cousin, Prince Edward, has given me a deer hound puppy," she said. "It will have to stay here at Middleham until it is weaned, however."

"Have you ever trained a dog, my lady Arabella?" he asked her.

"Nay, my lord, but I watched my father, and FitzWalter's son, Rowan, has a touch with the dogs, our kennel master says. FitzWalter says, however, that the kennel master, having no sons, would like to steal his from him. He says that Rowan will be a soldier like he has been, and if he is a very good soldier, he might one day be Greyfaire Keep's captain too."

The queen laughed. "As you can see, Sir Jasper," she said, her tone doting, "my little cousin is full of news. I think she loves her Greyfaire even as much as my lord, the king, loves Middleham. I hope you will be happy together. When Arabella reaches her fourteenth birthday in another two and a half years, you may plan to wed with her, provided that she is of a mind to wed with you; but I am certain that if you treat her with loving kindness, she will be content to have you for her husband. If, however, she is not, you will be compensated by the crown for the time and care you have given Greyfaire Keep."

"I shall do my best, my lady queen, to keep faith with your majesties," Sir Jasper said.

Queen Anne nodded, satisfied. "Then it is settled," she said, and turning to her cousins, kissed them both in farewell. Removing a small ring from her littlest finger, she gave it to Rowena. "Should you ever have need of my help, Rowena, send me back the ring," she told her favorite cousin, slipping the little signet upon the other woman's finger. "I will aid you as long as I shall live." Bending down, she spoke softly to Arabella so that only the young girl might hear her. "Wed him only, my child, if you truly love him. If you find that you do not, do not be afraid to tell him no. I would not have you unhappy. These few years before we will allow your marriage to be celebrated will give you time to know the man."

"He is most beautiful to look upon, madame," Arabella said shyly.

"Beauty does not always mean goodness, little cousin," the queen warned. "You must ever look beyond beauty for the truth." Then she hugged Arabella hard, sending her cousins and Sir Jasper upon their way.

They took their final leave of King Richard and rode out from Middleham Castle on a warm and sunny late September morning. There were a dozen men-at-arms from Greyfaire who had escorted the women from their home, and Sir Jasper had another dozen men which added to their little troop, making it quite formidable. Watching them go from his place upon the castle's ramparts, the king wished with all his heart that all his problems were as easy to solve as had been the matter of Lady Arabella Grey and Greyfaire Keep.

Chapter 2

S ir Jasper Keane could not remember when he had ever been so content in his entire life. A man could go soft living so comfortably, he thought, as he gazed with a pleased eye about the little hall at Greyfaire Keep. It was a pleasant place, with four windows that held real glass to keep out the winter winds which, even now, blew about the small castle. The stone floors were swept daily, their rushes and sweet herbs totally replaced, for Lady Rowena was an excellent housekeeper and could not abide evil odors. There were two fireplaces in the hall, and neither smoked. Consequently, the hall was relatively warm and cozy.

Before him upon the burnished oak table of the highboard was a polished pewter plate with a hollowed-out trencher of freshly baked bread. A silent servant ladled hot oat porridge into the trencher, while another set a second plate with bread, a wedge of cheese, and a slice of ham by his side, and a third filled his goblet with brown ale. Jasper Keane began to eat with good appetite, smiling as he discovered sweet chunks of dried apple in the cereal, for he had mentioned in passing to Lady Rowena that he did not care for the bland oat dish that was served daily each morning. It took but a word to Row, and she would immediately endeavor to correct the problem.

Sir Jasper Keane had been at Greyfaire Keep for five months now. He had been extremely pleased by what he had found upon his arrival. Everything was in good order, and FitzWalter, the keep's captain, had immediately deferred to him, readily accepting him as Greyfaire's new lord. Consequently, it would not be necessary to replace him or demote him, which relieved Sir Jasper. He did not intend to remain upon the border forever, and when he went off, he would have two needs: to know that his home was in capable hands, and to have Seger, his own captain, by his side, for Seger was invaluable to him.

His little bride-to-be was an amusing, if somewhat outspoken girl, but there was time enough to correct her behavior. If he

36

had one complaint, it was the fact that he had had to curb his behavior in order that these two females who held his future in their hands not take offense. He had refrained from using the keep's women servants to service his needs, instead roaming the border for his amusement while the weather had remained clement. For the last few weeks, however, the weather had been foul, and he had been forced to remain within his walls.

His loins ached for a woman. He wondered if he might, now that several months had passed, seduce Rowena. That she desired him he had absolutely no doubt, although she struggled mightily to conceal her longing. He had no doubt that he was responsible for the increasingly long hours she spent in the keep's chapel upon her knees; but he knew she had not confided her *sins* to Father Anselm, their resident priest, for the cleric's kindly manner toward Jasper Keane had not changed since their first meeting. *Sweet Row*, he had heard the king call her. Was she indeed sweet?

Jasper Keane's eyes narrowed in contemplation. He imagined Rowena, whom he now knew to be four years his junior, naked. She had fine, full breasts and a still slender waist, he could see. She was small of stature, which he liked in a woman, and he did not imagine her legs would be long. Were her thighs soft and rounded? Her Venus mont pink and silky-skinned? Would her bottom be plump? He hoped so, for nothing irritated him more than a woman with skinny shanks. A woman with a fat rump displayed well the marks of his palm upon her fair flesh.

Rowena Neville Grey had a pretty face. He liked her round and trusting light blue eyes. He particularly liked her full and pouting lips. It was a voluptuous mouth which he did not doubt would be skilled at kissing. Did she have other skills at which her lips were equally as deft? If she did not, he would soon teach her. The thought of that sensual mouth expertly mastering him was almost more than he could bear. He wanted her. He would have her. He had waited long enough. The question of how to persuade Rowena to overcome her scruples was something he must ponder, and then the answer became crystal clear.

Arabella! His little bride-to-be was the answer. He would threaten to debauch the girl, who was the apple of her mother's eye, if Lady Rowena did not yield herself to him. The lady, already struggling against her own lustful nature, could surrender herself to him with a clear conscience and the belief that she was protecting her daughter. He almost laughed aloud at his own cleverness. He would accost her this very day, and tonight he would enter her bed, wipe away her few guilty tears, and she would be his for as long as it amused him.

And suddenly, as if he had called her, she was at his side, smiling hesitantly. "Good morrow, my lord. Was the porridge more to your liking this morning?"

"Aye," he answered her. "Where is Arabella? I have not seen her yet today."

"She has taken a chill, and I have told her she must remain in her bed this day. It is rare she is ill."

"Come," he said, standing up. "Let us go and see her. I'm certain our company will cheer her up."

"My lord, she is in her shift. I do not think it proper that you see her in her shift," Rowena protested nervously.

He took her by the shoulders and looked down into her face. He could feel her quivering beneath his fingers, and he smiled a slow smile. "Arabella is to be my wife, sweet Row. Soon enough I will see her both in and out of her shift. There is no lack of propriety here. Will you not be with me?" Then taking her hand, he practically dragged her off to Arabella's chamber, which was located on the floor above the hall.

FitzWalter's young daughter, Lona, sat upon the bed, playing a game with pebbles with Arabella. Looking up at him, they both began to giggle, and Sir Jasper playfully threw himself on the bed between them. Lona shrieked a sound that was almost kittenish, and he reached out to tickle her ribs. Lona squirmed and wiggled, her laughter rising even as Arabella threw herself upon them.

"No! No! Lona is the most ticklish girl in the world, my lord. Have mercy!" Arabella cried.

For a moment he ceased his frolic, and then turning his gaze on her, he said, "And are you ticklish, Arabella, ma petite?"

"Nay!"

"Liar!" he retorted, and before she might escape him, his fingers reached out to find her.

"Ohhhhh!" Arabella gasped, laughing wildly, tears coming to her eyes. "Stop! Stop!" And she writhed desperately to escape, her shift riding up to display her naked legs and bottom.

"Arabella!" Rowena's voice was shocked, but her shock was more due to the fact that Sir Jasper's hands seemed to be every-

where upon her daughter's body. They skimmed lightly over her newly-forming breasts, brushed casually over the girl's belly and lower. "*Arabella! Sir Jasper!* Stop it this minute. Lona! Get off the bed this instant and pull down your skirts!" She dragged the little girl onto her feet and then reached out for Sir Jasper.

At the touch of her hand upon his shoulder, he immediately ceased his frolic with Arabella and, turning, looked full into her face as he said, "If our life together is to be so happy, I regret the necessity of our waiting to celebrate this marriage." He stood up, giving Arabella a pat upon her bottom even as he drew the negligent shift back down to a more respectable level.

"My lord!" Rowena said angrily. "Arabella is ill and must have quiet. I cannot allow this outrageous rollicking. Lona! Go to your mother and help her with the laundry."

With a sudden chastened look, Lona curtsied to her mistress and scampered from the room.

Rowena took her daughter's rosary beads from the girl's bedside table, saying as she did so, "Say your beads, Arabella. It will calm you and hopefully restore you to a more obedient spirit." She handed the rosary to her daughter. "Come, my lord. We will leave Arabella to her meditations."

"I wish we were wed now too," Arabella said defiantly to her mother. "Then I should be my own mistress here at Greyfaire!"

"Apologize to your mama, ma petite," Sir Jasper said quietly. "She thinks only of your good."

Arabella's lower lip quivered mutinously, but then she said, "Pardon, Mama."

Rowena flew across the room and, bending down, hugged her daughter. "You are forgiven, my darling, but now rest. I know how very much you dislike being ill." She kissed her child upon the forehead and then led Sir Jasper from the bedchamber.

Once again in the keep's hall, Sir Jasper turned to Rowena and said, "Arabella will be twelve at the end of March, will she not?"

"Aye, my lord," Rowena said, giving him a goblet of wine as he stood by the fire.

"Plenty of girls are married at twelve, lady. I will not truly be master here at Greyfaire until I am your daughter's husband."

"None here have denied you, my lord, and both the king and

the queen have said the wedding may not take place until Arabella is fourteen, or more.''

"But if you asked them to allow the marriage now, I doubt that they would gainsay you,'' he said. "I have needs, madame, if I may be blunt with you.''

"Needs?" For a moment she was puzzled, and then Rowena's cheeks flamed.

He shrugged his shoulders. "I am a man, madame. If I do not have a wife with whom to satisfy these needs, I must find another. Sooner or later word of my nocturnal roamings will reach your daughter's ears. She will be hurt, and she will be angry. Virgins like Arabella, raised gently, do not understand the darker nature of a man. I regret my weakness, sweet Row, but what can I do?''

"Could you not take a mistress, my lord? Many men do,'' she said.

"Whether I visit one woman or a dozen, my comings and my goings would still be commented upon,'' he said. "I can see but one solution. I must wed your daughter in the spring.''

"No!"

He saw the agony in her eyes, and suddenly he decided that the idea must come from her own lips and hers alone. "What other choice have I, sweet Row? For months I have kept my desires in check and at bay, but even as winter draws to a close and the sap begins to rise in the trees, so my passions begin to rise once more.''

Rowena swallowed hard. "My daughter is still a child, my lord, and not yet ready for childbearing.''

"She can still be a wife in the fullest sense,'' he said with meaning.

"She is not ready for such things, my lord. I fear that you could injure her, though certainly you would not hurt her deliberately, I know. What can I say to you that will convince you not to force this marriage?'' Rowena's pretty face was a mask of motherly concern and fear. She could not help wringing her hands with her worry.

He took one of those hands, and turning it palm up, planted a kiss upon the fragrant flesh. Then their eyes met, even as he said softly, "What other choice have I, sweet Row?''

She knew. She knew what she must do to save her child from what would amount to virtual rape. This, then, was to be her punishment for her lustful and wicked thoughts. She would become Sir Jasper Keane's whore that Arabella might be spared his *needs* until she was old enough to serve them herself as his wife. So great was Rowena's shame and her guilt that she could bring herself to say nothing more but one word, *"Tonight,"* before she turned away from him, pulling her hand from his grasp and walking from the hall.

The log in the fireplace cracked and collapsed into a heap of orange coals.

"Masterfully done, my lord," came the soft hiss of congratulation.

"You move like a cat, Seger," Jasper Keane said, never turning. "I never know when you are there, but discretion, my friend, is called for in this matter. I do not want the heiress running to her royal cousins, lest I lose this plum."

"I would not harm your lordship," Seger replied. "Even I, ignorant wretch that I am, understand the delicacy of the situation. The keep folk love their ladies. It would never do for them to think you were hurting them."

"Cleverly said, Seger," Sir Jasper told his man, "but one day, I think, that clever tongue of yours will be your downfall."

"Until that time I but live to serve your lordship," Seger answered, and Sir Jasper Keane laughed at his boldness. "I have, in anticipation of your lordship's direction, already seduced the lady Rowena's personal serving maid, who lives in terror that her mistress discover her loose ways. You need not fear any indiscretion on her part, my lord," the captain finished with a toothy grin.

"There is no one like you, Seger," said his master admiringly.

"No, my lord," came the agreeable reply.

Blessed Mary! How her conscience assailed her, but what else could she do, Rowena thought as she went through the familiar routine of her day. She was only a woman. A helpless woman. Dickon and Anne were so far away, and outside the keep a blizzard was raging, and she simply didn't know what else she could do. It wasn't as if she were a virgin. She well knew what it was to have a man impale her on his lance. Henry might have been many years her senior, but he had always been a vigorous lover, and she had enjoyed his attentions. *Too much!* Did the church not teach that the sole reason for the coupling of a man and a woman was for the procreation of good Christian children? Nothing was said about pleasure, but it was pleasurable, and she had missed it.

Henry, of course, had been the only man she had ever known. Were men different in their lovemaking? She felt an anticipatory thrill of excitement race down her spine, and she bit her lip with her vexation. She was betraying her own child! What kind of a wretched creature was she that she could look forward to breaking faith with her own daughter? He was so handsome, yet as attracted as she was to him, she would have never allowed him her bed but for their conversation this morning. He had not said it aloud, but she had well understood his meaning. He had intended ravishing Arabella even before their marriage was celebrated, in order to satisfy his manly desires.

Pray God and his blessed Mother that she could please Sir Jasper Keane, that she could sate his lusts. How else could she protect her child? Surely God would forgive her? She would not, however, confess her indiscretion to dear Father Anselm until Arabella was happily wed. How could he understand the position in which she found herself? He would counsel her to seek grace in prayer, and he would lecture Sir Jasper sternly; but Sir Jasper would not listen, Rowena knew. He would force Arabella to his bed, and it could kill her child to have her innocence breached so soon. No. She would bear this burden silently and alone. Was it not, after all, a woman's lot to bend like the flowers of the field before a wind?

Lona had waited until Sir Jasper and Lady Rowena had departed, and then hurried back into Arabella's bedchamber. "Ahh, 'Bella," she sighed gustily, "you are so fortunate! He is the most handsome of men. I shall probably be matched with old Rad's sniveling grandson, the bag of bones with the long pointed nose that always drips."

"He is beautiful to look upon, I will grant you," Arabella said, pulling her friend down to sit once more upon the bed. "Yet there is something . . ."

"What, you goose? Sir Jasper is perfect, although I will allow that I do not like his captain, Seger," Lona said.

"You only say that because Sir Jasper might have given Seger your father's position," Arabella returned.

"Nay," Lona said, her dark brown braids shaking vigorously, her blue eyes serious. "Seger almost slithers like a snake, and

I have seen him with my aunt Elsbeth on several occasions. They were kissing, and once I saw his hand up her skirt; yet in the hall he ignores her. It is as if he does not even know her.''

"Perhaps I should speak to my mother," Arabella considered aloud. "After all, your aunt does serve her. Mayhap I will speak to Sir Jasper, for Seger is his man.''

"I do not think it would be wise, 'Bella. Perhaps it was nothing more than a quick kiss and a cuddle. Lads and lasses are apt to do such things. Then, too, Sir Jasper might think we feared Seger, which would not reflect well upon my father. My aunt is grown, and if she were having difficulties, she would go to your mother, I am certain, but she will thank neither of us if we interfere and tell tales on her. I should not have spoken to you at all.''

"Oh, Lona, we are friends, and have been since our infancy," Arabella reassured the other girl.

"But you will wed Sir Jasper in two years, 'Bella, and then you will be the lady of Greyfaire Keep. You will change, but I will not. I will always be Lona, one of FitzWalter's lasses.''

"You will be Lona, the lady Arabella's personal maidservant, you goose! You will have every bit as much stature as your mother and father, and you do not have to wed with old Rad's bony grandson if you do not wish it. As my personal servant and my friend, you will have your pick of the handsomest lads around. I promise you!" Arabella said generously.

"As long as I don't have to wed with spindleshanks," giggled Lona. Then she grew serious again. "Am I really to be your maid, 'Bella?''

"Aye, if I say it," Arabella said, "and I do.''

"And you really do like Sir Jasper, don't you?" Lona asked.

"My cousin, the queen, says that beauty does not always mean goodness in a person," Arabella said slowly. "I have heard whispers that Sir Jasper is a man for the ladies. They say he cuts quite a swath on both sides of the border.''

Lona's blue eyes grew round. "Who told you such a thing?" she demanded indignantly.

"Is it true?''

"I would not know, 'Bella.''

"But you have heard the rumors too, have you not, Lona?''

"The old women will gossip, 'Bella, and they best like to gossip about a handsome man or a pretty woman. Have not most of the men on both sides of the border poached in forbidden waters?''

''The man I marry must be true to me, Lona. Never did I know my father to stray from my mother's side, and I will have the same respect from my husband.''

''You are not wed yet, 'Bella,'' Lona reminded her friend. ''Sir Jasper is a grown man and may dally hither and yon before your marriage. You have not the right to chastise him for it, at least not until after you are wed!''

''If I ever find that he has betrayed me with another, Lona, I shall take a knife and cut his black heart from his chest!'' Arabella said fiercely.

''Has Sir Jasper seen your evil temper yet, 'Bella?'' Lona teased. ''Beware, lest you frighten him away!''

The day seemed to go quickly, and soon it was evening. In her bedchamber with its little corner fireplace, Lady Rowena stepped from her tub to be toweled dry by her maidservant, Elsbeth. In the pier glass, the wedding gift of her late husband, she stared self-consciously at herself with a critical eye. Child-bearing had not destroyed her body, for only two of her four children had come to term; a boy they had named Henry, who had not survived his first year; and Arabella, whom she had been carrying when he died. Guiltily she turned her eyes away from the mirror. She was wicked. *Wicked!*

''Which gown, m'lady?'' Elsbeth inquired.

''My head aches,'' Rowena complained. ''I do not think I shall go down to the hall this night. I will get into bed and sleep.''

''Shall I have Maida mix a potion, m'lady?''

''Nay. I shall not need it,'' Rowena replied. ''I have been fretted about Arabella all day, but a night's sleep should cure me.''

Elsbeth slipped a simple shift over her mistress's head, and opening the bed, helped her lady into it, tucking the coverlet about her. ''I will bid you a good night then, m'lady,'' she said. ''When I have had my meal, I shall return.''

''*Nay!*'' Rowena forced her voice to a more normal level. ''I shall not need you again tonight, Elsbeth. You may sleep at home if you like, or in the hall.''

''Thank you, m'lady!'' Elsbeth was delighted. An evening

off meant she might lure Seger into another tryst. She curtsied and hurried from the bedchamber.

She had a lad, Rowena thought, not fooled. I wonder who he is? It did not matter. She was FitzWalter's youngest sister-in-law, and he would see that any difficulties were smoothed over so that Elsbeth could have her happiness. But what of my happiness? Rowena thought. Oh, Henry, why did you go and leave me? Did I not beg you not to go off that summer's morning? I knew you would not come back that day. Somehow I knew. I am all alone, and I must whore in order to protect our child. It is not fair, and it would not have happened if you had but listened to me! A small tear of self-pity rolled down her face.

Rowena Neville Grey had only vague memories of her parents, Edmund Neville and Catherine Talbot. They had died of plague when she was four, and her paternal grandparents with whom they lived, being elderly, had brought her to the family's head, Richard Neville, the great Earl of Warwick, to foster. She had been raised by his countess along with his daughters, Isabel and Anne. She had been treated with loving kindness by all but Isabel Neville, who was overproud and given to meanness. Had Lady Isabel singled Rowena out, it might have been different, but her ill-temper was reserved for none in particular. It was generously spread amongst all her siblings.

That the great earl, called the Kingmaker by his contemporaries, bothered to find a husband for his unimportant relative, and to dower her was a kindness, Rowena knew. She might have spent her life an unpaid servant once she had left her childhood behind and her more important companions had been wed into other great houses. Instead, she had been informed upon her twelfth birthday that she would be married on her thirteenth birthday to Sir Henry Grey, Baron Greyfaire, the holder of a crucially placed keep along the English border with Scotland. Sir Henry needed a wife, and King Edward wished to make friends where he could. His predecessor was somehow managing to give him difficulty even from the Tower of London, where he was imprisoned. King Henry VI had, following his defeat to Edward IV, taken refuge in Scotland, and for over three years until his capture given his former subjects a great deal of trouble. Edward needed his borders secure, and so his sometime ally, the Kingmaker, who had aided him in gaining his throne, supplied the necessary bride in the person of his young relation and ward, for by this time Rowena's grandparents had died.

Their marriage was celebrated on the sixteenth day of May, 1469. Rowena was given a dowry by her powerful relative that consisted of ten pieces of silver and five pieces of gold; a white mare with its saddle and bridle; and two fine oak chests bound in iron. The first chest contained all the linens she had been embroidering over the past year in anticipation of her new status as a wife; a pound bag of salt; a set of six silver spoons; and a bag containing four sticks of cinnamon, two nutmegs, and a half pound of peppercorns. The second chest held her clothing, two bolts of fabric, and the little jewelry she had inherited from her late mother, as well as a small strand of freshwater pearls given her as a wedding gift by the earl and his wife. It was not the dowry of an earl's daughter, but neither was it a dowry of which she need be ashamed. She came to Henry a well-propertied woman able, despite her youth, to command his respect by not only her important connections, but by her possessions as well.

But now Henry was dead, and to protect her child from the lasciviousness of Sir Jasper Keane, she must yield her body to him. There was no one left to protect *her*, and so *she* must protect Arabella. She would have never imagined, long ago in the happy childhood she shared with her cousin Anne at Warwick and Middleham castles, that it would in the end all come to this. She sighed deeply, and then her ears, sharp with years of practice, heard his footsteps outside her door. Rowena half closed her eyes and feigned sleep.

Jasper Keane entered her bedchamber quietly, yet there was nothing stealthy in his coming. He came as a husband might come into his wife's rooms, with a certainty of the warm welcome awaiting him. From beneath her eyelids she watched as he removed his clothing, not even realizing her breathing had become shallow as his body, every bit as attractive as his face, was revealed to her. Long legs, a long slim torso, a well-furred chest, the hair strangely darker than that upon his head. Having lain his garments neatly where he might regain them quickly, Jasper Keane walked over to the edge of the bed, and drawing back the coverlet, pulled Rowena to her feet. Her blue eyes flew open with surprise as his hand hooked itself into the rounded neck of her shift and, with a quick motion, ripped it in twain, carelessly tossing the two halves aside.

"In future, my pet," he said in a pleasant, low voice, "you will sleep as God fashioned you. I prefer it." Then, without further preamble, he kissed her a long, hard kiss, finally releasing her to say, "You kiss like a girl, Rowena. Open your mouth so I may have your tongue." Obedient, she complied and he sucked her tongue into his mouth, even as his fingers cupped and kneaded her buttocks, drawing her tightly against him.

Her head swam as familiar sensations, newly awakened, surfaced, and her knees seemed to turn to jelly beneath her. It had never been quite so intense with Henry, she thought, moaning as he broke off the kiss and, lifting her up, began to lick her skin. She threw her head back, the veins in her throat straining in her effort to remain quiet, lest her cries of pleasure bring the entire keep awake. His broad tongue slid over the taut skin, moving on to the softer flesh of her breasts.

He laughed aloud as her whole body first stiffened and then shuddered as she attained her first crisis. Her pretty head fell forward upon her chest, even as he sat down upon the edge of the bed, cradling her within his arms. His fingers probed her, and finding evidence of her passion, he smiled broadly. "You are a passionate little piece, my pet," he approved. Then he turned her over so that she lay facedown across his knees, and stared with delight upon her pretty, rounded posteriors. Still bemused, Rowena came quickly to herself as his hard hand smacked down upon the tender flesh. "Ohhhh!" she cried, startled.

"Be discreet, my pet," he warned her. "We do not wish to share our interlude with anyone else. Put your hand in your mouth if you must." And he commenced to rain a series of stinging blows upon her helpless bottom while she whimpered and squirmed beneath his punishing hand, his other hand firmly upon her slender neck. When the globe of her skin had turned a deep burnished pink and he could feel a heat rising from it, he reached beneath her to ascertain her condition, and smiled at the sticky wetness his fingers encountered.

He placed her facedown upon the bed, and mounting her, entered her woman's passage from the rear; his hips finding the perfect rhythm. To his delight, she immediately pulled herself to her knees and her own hips thrust back at him. "Very good, my pet," he purred in her ear. "Very, *very* good!" he continued to approve as, lifting her carefully, he slowly turned her about onto her back, and holding her legs apart, probed her deeply.

She was dying, Rowena thought, and she deserved to die for this betrayal of Arabella that was so heavenly. She had no right to enjoy his lascivious attentions so greatly, but she was enjoying them. Enjoying them more than she had ever enjoyed making love with Henry, and she had always enjoyed making love with her late husband. Jasper Keane, however, was a master of passion; and if she must protect her dearest child from him, Rowena considered, what was wrong with enjoying this pleasure? She had not initiated this erotic bout. She was not to blame. Why should she be punished for it? Her nails dug into the muscles of his shoulders, and he thrust almost brutally.

"Aye, my little pet," he growled softly, "claw me, for I do not mind your marks upon me."

She barely heard his words, nor did she remember very clearly the rest of that night of fiery and tumultuous desire. In the early minutes before the dawn she awoke to find herself alone amid the tremendous tangle of bedclothes. Though replete with satisfaction, her body ached, particularly her woman's passage, which had been so long denied a mate. Jasper's manhood was larger than Henry's had been, but she had seemed to have no trouble accommodating him.

Rowena longed to remain abed, for she was drained of energy. He had used her vigorously throughout the night, his great lance never seeming to flag or grow tired, and now as she lay exhausted, he was already up and gone. Reluctantly she arose from her bed and straightened the bedclothes so that Elsbeth and the other maids would not be suspicious. Then she took the two shredded halves of her shift and laid them on the barely glowing coals of her fire, watching as the fire sprang to life, adding a log that any evidence of her shameful behavior be fully eradicated. She would indeed sleep naked from now on, for she could not afford to lose any more of her undergarments.

Taking an earthenware pitcher of water from a corner of the little fireplace, she poured the warmed liquid into her basin and scrubbed herself clean with a small cloth. Then taking a clean shift from her storage trunk, she quickly dressed herself and sat down to do her hair, brushing the floor-length wheaten-blond hair free of tangles, braiding it and winding the braids atop her head to be pinned securely. She had just finished when Elsbeth entered the room.

"M'lady! Forgive me for being tardy, but I fear I overslept," the woman said.

"Is it late?" Rowena asked.

"Nay, m'lady, not the hour," came the reply.

"I awoke early," Rowena said, "and so I decided not to await you. There is no harm done, Elsbeth. Is anyone else up and in the hall, girl?"

"Sir Jasper and his man, Seger," Elsbeth said, avoiding her mistress's gaze, but Rowena did not notice, for she was hoping her own guilt did not show upon her face.

"I must first go to see how my daughter does," she said almost to herself, and hurried from the chamber.

Arabella was, of course, fine, rarely being ill and having little toleration for the state. She was already up, and Lona was helping her to braid her own hair.

"I want Lona for my servant, Mama," she said by way of a greeting. Her light green eyes challenged her mother to refuse.

"I think that would be an excellent idea," Rowena agreed. "I am certain that Rosamund can spare one of her daughters from the laundry, and I must agree you will need someone other than old Nurse Ora to look after your needs. After all, you are to be married in two years, but Ora, I know, persists in treating you like a child. We shall retire her to her cottage until you have your own children for her to look after. Lona can learn from her aunt Elsbeth what she must know to care for a lady properly."

"Ohh, thank you, m'lady Rowena!" Lona cried, delighted, and even Arabella smiled, pleased with her victory.

In late April there came word that little Prince Edward had died at Middleham on the ninth day of the month. Rowena longed to go to her cousin Anne and comfort her, but Jasper Keane would not allow it. His sly innuendos regarding Arabella's fate should she leave him for even a short time frightened as well as angered her, for she knew he was once again prowling the borders like a tomcat.

"Then let Arabella go, my lord, for I cannot bear the thought of my cousin, the queen, believing we do not care."

He considered her request and then, to her surprise, acquiesced. "Aye, let the king see our sympathy and loyalties are with him in his time of sorrow. Besides," he grinned, pinching one of her nipples fondly, "you are far more entertaining these days than my little bride-to-be. While she is gone we shall ride the hills together and visit some of my pretty little friends. We shall have a ménage à trois, my pet. I enjoy being entertained by two women at a time. Once Arabella and I are wed and I have broken her to my bridle, you will join us in our bedsport, Rowena. Will you not enjoy that, or will it make you jealous to share my favors?"

"*My lord!* You forget yourself! I will never partake in such a vile debauchery," she cried, shocked.

He laughed. "Ah Row, sweet Row. You will do precisely as you are told, because if you do not, I have the means by which to make you suffer as you have never suffered before." He tipped her face to his and kissed her lightly. "You know that in your heart, my pet, do you not?"

And she did. She had known almost from the first night that this was a terrible and dangerous man. She knew, but she was also aware that the king was not knowledgeable of Sir Jasper Keane's dark soul. Richard was a noble and decent man with a good heart, but she could not go to him and expose Jasper Keane, for to reveal the true nature of Sir Jasper was to reveal her own shame.

"Arabella must start tomorrow," she said quietly, pretending not to have been frightened by his implied threats.

"I shall arrange a suitable escort, my pet," he replied, knowing she feared him now and would do whatever she had to in order to protect her child. For now it contented him to leave the child alone, although of late he had noticed her little breasts beginning to bud quite prettily beneath her bodice. A tasty dish was best savored over time, he thought.

Arabella was gone several weeks, most of her time spent traveling back and forth between Greyfaire and her royal cousins. The queen, she reported upon her return, was inconsolable at the loss of her only child.

"Ahh, Mama," she said. "It would break your heart. Poor cousin Anne weeps constantly. Neddie's death has fair destroyed her."

"But was she glad to see you, Arabella?" demanded Sir Jasper. "I hope your presence was not an additional pain to her, lest she think ill of us all."

"Nay, my lord," Arabella said a trifle stiffly. "My cousin,

the queen, was happy for the company. She said I reminded her of better times and took away some of her sadness."

"I am glad for that," Rowena said softly, "but what of the king? He must be as devastated by little Edward's death as is poor Anne."

"He is, Mama," Arabella replied. "Sometimes he does not even hear what is being said to him. His heart and the queen's have been broken, especially as the physicians say cousin Anne can have no more children. There are some who say the queen will die of her sorrow."

"Then the king can take a younger, more fertile wife," remarked Sir Jasper.

Arabella rounded on him. "*My lord!* Where is your heart, or is it true as I have heard, that you have none?"

Jasper Keane was momentarily stunned by her words, which were both sharp and knowing. He stared at the girl, seeing her as he had not seen her before. True, she was Row's daughter, but her outburst made it more than clear she was more her father's daughter. Henry Grey, a man who had doted upon his sweet and helpless wife, was also a man with a famous temper. Arabella had obviously inherited that temper.

"What, poppet?" he said in a bantering tone, for Sir Jasper had decided not to be angry with her. He rather liked this new and fiery disposition she was showing. Row's meekness was pleasant, but it was also dull. "Have you been listening to gossip, Arabella? I would have thought better of you," he mocked.

"In gossip there is always some grain of truth," she answered him tartly, "but we are not speaking of my behavior, sir. We speak of yours. My cousin, the queen, suffers greatly her loss. Neddie was her only surviving child, and she birthed him at great risk to herself. Perhaps you did not know that, for men are not interested in such things, I am told. She has striven over the years to make him strong and healthy, which is why he lived at Middleham, away from the court, the crush of crowds and possible contagion. If, my lord, you can have no sympathy for the pain she is feeling now, and the greater pain the king feels, at least have the decency to be silent, lest your words be repeated and heard by your enemies, who would use them against you. Since you are to be my husband and the lord of Greyfaire Keep, such indiscretion on your part endangers not only you, but me and mine as well," Arabella concluded furiously.

"You and yours?" he said softly, his irritation rising just slightly.

"Aye, my lord. Greyfaire is mine, and you become its true lord *only* when you become my husband," Arabella reminded him.

"Arabella! You must be more biddable," Lady Rowena wailed nervously. "Must she not be more biddable, Father Anselm?" The despairing mother turned to the keep's priest, who also sat with them at the highboard.

Father Anselm, who had come to Greyfaire in the year of Arabella Grey's birth, hid a smile. He knew the mistress of the keep far better than anyone else, even her own mother. His gray eyes twinkled as the hapless Rowena chattered on nervously.

"We need Sir Jasper, my darling! We need a man to hold Greyfaire for the king!"

Arabella snorted. "I am the Grey of Greyfaire, Mama. I am perfectly capable, with FitzWalter's help, of holding this keep for the king, though I doubt there will be a need for it soon. The Scots may swarm over the border at regular intervals, but the worst they do is drive off the livestock, take whatever of value that is not nailed down, and steal the pretty girls away. Then our English borderers reciprocate in kind. *This keep is impregnable.* Father said it, and he would know. Besides, we are not a tempting target on our little, lonely, out-of-the-way hill. We are hardly a great castle."

"Greyfaire is small, my lady, but hardly as unimportant as you try to convince yourself," the priest said quietly. "It has great strategic value to the land south of it, as it is usually the first to know of a Scots invasion. This little castle is built upon the walls of a Roman fort. If you would go to the cellars you would see the evidence for yourself of my words. This site has always been of value to someone."

"That is why the king arranged this marriage for you with Sir Jasper," Rowena said. "You must have a husband, Arabella!"

"My marriage is not to be celebrated for two years, Mama," Arabella replied irritably. "Until then I am sole mistress of *Greyfaire*, and women have held castles against invasion in the past. If I must, then I assure you I will."

"Women holding castles in siege more often than not had strong families behind them, and husbands as well," Father Anselm noted in a reasonable tone. He knew to annoy Arabella was to incur her undying enmity. Young girls her age were given to moods.

"I am but two months past my twelfth birthday," Arabella said in a quieter manner. "After my fourteenth birthday, Sir Jasper and I will wed. He is the husband chosen for me by my king, and I have sworn my fealty to King Richard. Like my father before me, I shall not break my oath."

"Nor would I expect it of you, poppet," Sir Jasper said softly, pleased. The little wench had definite possibilities. She became more interesting with each passing day, and perhaps he would learn to like pale gold hair after all.

The argument was over, but Rowena, unable to realize the subtleties of the situation, nattered on heedlessly. "You are a female, Arabella! A mere female, and women are weak of spirit. Is that not so, Father Anselm?"

At the moment her thoughtless words fell upon his ears, the priest found himself closer to murder than he had ever been in his life. How could the lady Rowena be so harebrained and rash as to arouse her daughter's ire just when he had managed to calm Arabella? What was worse the silly woman had unknowingly boxed him in, for he could not deny her words without coming into direct conflict with his religion. Forced to promulgate the teaching of the church, he nodded dourly, although he did not believe for one minute that Arabella Grey was a weak vessel. Most women, perhaps, but not all, and certainly not this young girl. "The church teaches us, my daughter, that the female of the species is indeed the weaker vessel in some respects, but she is strong in others, else God would not have given her the heavy burden of bearing children. St. Paul teaches that women should be obedient to their husbands, and I know that when Arabella weds with Sir Jasper, she will be a good wife to him, even as you were a good wife to Sir Henry. I think that you worry needlessly."

"Indeed you do, Mama," Arabella said. "I will do my duty, for I am, above all else, my father's daughter, and my father laid down his life for England in doing his duty. I am not my brother, but I am a Grey. I can do no less."

"Yes, yes, of course," Lady Rowena fluttered nervously.

Jasper Keane forced down a chuckle. Aye, Arabella was indeed becoming more interesting as each minute passed. "Why, sweet Row," he murmured, "it would seem you have birthed a spitfire in this child of yours. I do not know that I should not be taken aback by this turn.''

"Would you have me be weak as water, my lord?'' Arabella snapped. ''What kind of children should I give you then? I have ever been accustomed to speaking my mind, and I shall not change.''

He laughed aloud and nodded his handsome blond head. "Aye, a hot-tempered spitfire. I think I shall enjoy taming you, Arabella Grey.''

The priest was too innocent of matters between men and women to hear the implied threat in his voice, but Rowena heard it. Arabella, however, also innocent, looked at her future husband and said boldly, ''And just how shall you tame me, my lord?''

"Why, with sweet songs, and soft words, and pretty gifts,'' he said with a charming smile, for it amused him at the moment to play the gallant.

"Indeed, sir?'' Arabella's young heart fluttered at this sudden attention, for until this moment he had treated her as he might have treated a child.

Sir Jasper saw her confusion and the softening of her attitude. Reaching over, he took her hand in his and kissed it lingeringly. "I shall never be able to repay the king for the great kindness he has done me by bestowing upon me such an exquisite bride . . . even if she is a spitfire who shall undoubtedly give me a great deal of trouble.''

Unaware of how to respond to his wooing, Arabella giggled girlishly, and Rowena felt the worm of jealousy turn sharply in her heart.

"You are too extravagant with your compliments to my daughter, my lord,'' she said sharply. ''I would not have her overproud.''

"Pretty words do not fool me, Mama,'' Arabella said, aggravated that her mother had spoiled such a lovely moment, ''but those same words are still pleasant to hear.''

The girl was not stupid, Sir Jasper considered again, as he had in the past. Innocent, yes, but not stupid. He had seen her green eyes widen at his compliment, seen the blush that stained her pale cheeks pink. ''A man is bound to spoil a beautiful wife,'' he said simply.

Afterward, in her own chamber, Arabella considered Sir Jasper once again as she had considered him in the past. He was handsome, he was kind to both her and her mother, FitzWalter respected him, and he certainly knew how to speak prettily to a woman. What more was there to a man than that? In many ways he appeared to be like her own late father, and yet . . . there was something that she could not quite put her finger upon that niggled at her. Some unknown voice that seemed to shriek a warning, but what was it warning her of, or of whom was it warning her? Or was it merely her overstimulated imagination? In a sense she was resentful of Sir Jasper's coming, for once he became her husband and her lord, it would be he who became the possessor of Greyfaire, not she.

It was difficult to think of Greyfaire belonging to anyone else but her. She had grown up knowing that it would one day be hers, and she was certain that if her father had lived, he would have seen it remained hers no matter her husband. Greyfaire was all she had in the world. It was as much a part of her as she was of it. Without it she was valueless. In a way, she resented losing it to another. *To a man.*

Sometimes she wished she had been born a boy, and this was one of those times. Men certainly had all the fun, and if she had been her father's son rather than his daughter, then no one could have taken Greyfaire from her! Perhaps if she loved Sir Jasper, she would not have minded, but having observed her parents all her life, she thought it must have something to do with a deep sharing of not simply one's body and emotions, but one's possessions as well. For now she did not feel that way about Sir Jasper. Perhaps in time she would.

Chapter 3

*I*n the previous autumn of 1483 there had been three areas of anti-Richard activity. Kent and the southeast section of England; the south-central counties, and the West Country of Cornwall and Devon. The rebels in the Home Counties about the capital planned to secure London and to also free the dowager queen, Elizabeth Woodville, and her daughters from their sanctuary. The Duke of Buckingham—once Richard's staunch ally, but now suddenly his enemy—along with the Earl of Dorset, intended raising armies in Wales and the West Country to support a prearranged invasion by Henry Tudor from Brittany.

The rebels, however, had no central authority to coordinate this rebellion. The rising in Kent broke out too early and failed. Buckingham could not even raise his own tenantry, let alone a real army. Dorset found that he was unable to guarantee a safe landfall for the Tudor claimant, who, caught by the autumn gales mid-channel, was finally forced to return to the continent.

The rebellion was a total failure, but not simply because of the rebels' lack of organization. Richard had his support. At the first sign of trouble the Duke of Norfolk moved to defend London, and that done, destroyed the rebellion in the southeast. Humphrey Stafford of Grafton contained Buckingham by gaining control of all the bridges along the river Severn. As the king's army moved southwest, the rebels lost heart. Buckingham, who himself had a tenuous claim on the throne through his ancestor, Edward III, was captured, brought to Richard in chains, judged guilty, and executed on November second, All Souls Day. The king's army mopped up the last vestige of resistance and settled down for the winter.

The new year, however, brought disquieting news. While the men had fought each other upon the battlefields of England, Henry Tudor's mother, Margaret Beaufort, who was now Lady Stanley, had been in negotiation with Elizabeth Woodville for the hand of her daughter, Elizabeth of York. On Christmas Day 1483, Henry Tudor, from his exile in Brittany, solemnly prom-

ised before God and man in the cathedral at Rennes to marry
Elizabeth of York, thereby laying formal and unmistakable claim
to England's throne. It was a clever ploy, but at the time no one
in either England or Europe took this betrothal seriously.

In the summer of 1484 the Breton government, for so long
the Tudor refuge, agreed to allow extradition of Henry Tudor of
England. Warned by his friends, Henry escaped into France, to
be followed by his own adherents. He was warmly greeted by
the French king, Charles VIII, who was unable to resist the
opportunity to irritate France's age-old enemy, England. For
several months Tudor and his people followed the French court.
Word came that little Prince Edward had died and that the queen
would bear no other children.

There was further word. Richard had designated his nephew,
John de la Pole, the Earl of Lincoln, his heir-presumptive. Queen
Anne was ill. The dowager queen, Elizabeth Woodville, had
supposedly made her peace with Richard. And the nastiest of
all possible rumors—the king was casting incestuous eyes upon
his niece, Elizabeth of York, intending to replace his old and
fruitless queen with a young and fruitful one.

Richard was himself horrified by the rumor, particularly as
he could not find its source. Neither could he quench it. Each
time he believed the vile rumor had finally disappeared from
whence it came, it would spring to life anew. It was frustrating
and embarrassing to a king who was not only a strictly moral
man, but a deeply religious one as well. Worse, it hurt the woman
he so deeply loved and who could not seem to recover from her
little son's death. And it made impossible his future relationship
with his nieces, which had always been a good one. But for now
that seemed to be the worst of Richard's troubles, and for a time,
the threat of Henry Tudor banished, he attempted to rule his
kingdom.

At Greyfaire it was the happiest summer of Arabella Grey's
young life, for she believed herself to be in love for the very first
time. How could she have been so childishly blind, she asked
herself over and over again, growing up with her wonderful
parents and their deep love of each other as an example? But
then how could she have really known what love was until she
found it for herself? She sighed happily. Jasper was *so* very
handsome to the eye with his rich, wavy gold hair, and eyes that
seemed to be the color of Spanish wine. When he looked at her

with those marvelous eyes, the effect was just as intoxicating, she decided. He had good teeth too. Even and white, and his breath when he whispered to her was always sweet, always fresh.

She could not forget the queen's warning that beauty to the eyes was not always true beauty, yet Jasper was charming and very witty. He told her his amusing tales of court life in the days of the late King Edward IV, and those tales were just a trifle bawdy, for King Edward was a naughty man, Jasper said, where the ladies were concerned; Arabella could not help but giggle at the humor Jasper imparted in his stories. Sometimes when Rowena was near enough to hear, she would scold him for telling her daughter these stories.

"She does not understand half of what you say, my lord," Rowena would scold. "She is my innocent little country child."

And Arabella would more often than not explode with anger at these maternal sallies, furious that her mother continued to treat her like the baby she no longer was. Irately she would remind Rowena that she was twelve and a half. That it was she, and not her mother, who was Greyfaire's mistress. That in less than two years' time she would be Sir Jasper's wife, and hopefully, pray God, a mother herself soon after.

The day she had said that, her mother had gone white with her own distress, and Jasper had taken Arabella onto his lap, an arm about her slim waist. "Mignon," he said softly, kissing her cheek lingeringly, "no one can long for that day more than I do," and when she nestled her head against his shoulder, his other hand brushed with seeming carelessness across her young breasts, sending a shiver down her spine.

"My lord!" Rowena's voice was tight.

"What is it, sweet Row?" His tones were dulcet.

"I do not think you should treat Arabella in that fashion," she said.

Arabella slid her arms about Jasper Keane's neck and, turning her head, stared boldly at her mother. "We are to be married soon," she said coolly. "Is it not right that lovers court, Mama? Jasper is hardly a stranger to me, having been at Greyfaire this past year. Would you have me go to my marriage totally ignorant?"

"Arabella! You will not speak to me that way," her mother cried.

"I think you are jealous of me, Mama," the girl said heedlessly. "I think you are jealous that the king has given me such a fine man to be my husband. You are still young and pretty. Perhaps you should find yourself a new husband too."

"Ohhhhh!" Rowena gasped with outrage.

"Ah, mignon," Jasper Keane said quietly, "that is very wicked of you. I will not have you speaking to your mother like that." He gently tipped her from his lap and turned her about so she faced him. "You are to go out of the keep and onto the hillside, Arabella. You will bring me back a fine switch of this thickness." He held up a single finger.

"You would beat me?" Arabella's young voice was filled with disillusionment.

"Until we are wed, mignon, your mother is your governor. Afterward I will assume that position," Sir Jasper explained patiently. "If you are disobedient to your mother now, does it not follow that you will attempt that same disobedience with me?"

"I would never be disobedient to you, my lord," Arabella whispered.

"Good," he said with a broad smile. "Then you will seek the switch as I have ordered you, mignon, will you not?"

Her eyes filling with tears, Arabella nodded mutely, and curt-sying to him, ran from the hall. Jasper Keane chuckled softly.

"Do not beat her, I beg you, my lord," Rowena half moaned, kneeling before him and clutching his hand.

"I will not harm her, Row. Six strokes and that is all. I would just test her mettle. Now get up. You look positively tragic there at my feet."

They sat in silence for some time, until at last Arabella re-turned carrying a stout hazel switch which, with downcast eyes, she brought over to him. He took it and waved it several times as if testing it, and then with a smile of satisfaction he said to her, "You will lay yourself across my lap, Arabella."

She complied immediately, not even casting a look at Ro-wena, who sat weeping softly, wringing her hands; nor did she even wince when he lifted her skirts up and drew aside her undergarments so that her posteriors were bared to his gaze. She started slightly when she felt his hand smooth lingering over her skin, squeezing it slightly, and she distinctly heard a sound very much like a hum of approval. But before she might consider it, the first blow fell with a stinging pain and she shrieked, although she had not meant to and, helpless, tried to wiggle away from the hurt.

"That was one," he said dispassionately. "There will be five more strokes, mignon, and then having kissed the rod, you will kneel to your mother and beg her pardon. Is that understood, Arabella?"

"Yes, my lord," she said tightly, determined not to cry out again, if she died in the attempt. To her great satisfaction she did not, although she would have sworn the last two blows were the hardest of all, almost as if he were trying to make her scream. The last blow completed, Arabella squirmed off Sir Jasper's lap to quickly kiss the outstretched hazel switch. Then turning, she knelt before her mother.

"I ask your pardon for my wayward tongue, madame," she said coldly, and when Rowena murmured a loving reply, Arabella stood up, straightened her skirts and walked from the hall.

When she had gone, Rowena said softly, and there was a sound of pleasure in her voice, "You have made an error, my lord. Arabella will accept almost anything but an affront to her dignity. She will not forgive you easily, if she forgives you at all."

"We will see," he said, and then he thought it made little difference if Arabella forgave him or not. He had entrenched himself here at Greyfaire now, and he did not intend to give up possession of this keep to anyone, let alone a silly chit of a girl. His own home, Northby Hall, had been burned to ashes. Nothing remained of the two-hundred-year-old house his family had built in the reign of Edward I, who had been known as "Longshanks." His livestock had disappeared over the Cheviot hills with the Scots who had destroyed his house. Retaliation, he had no doubt, for his destruction of Eufemia Hamilton's home.

If the truth be known, all he possessed was the land, what small income he could wring out of his few tenant farmers, his horse, and his arms. He liked Greyfaire. It might be small, but it was well-built, and could, he was more than certain, withstand a serious siege should anyone ever decide to pen him within the keep. Greyfaire would not be easily demolished by an enemy. The land about it was good, for a little valley surrounded the castle's hill. There were several fine farmsteads, rich fields, and even an apple orchard. The king was paying him a small subsistence to husband the keep, which allowed him to retain his own men, but allowed for precious few luxuries. There was trouble coming, he knew, for he could smell it in the air as one could smell a city in a downwind. *King Richard. Henry Tudor.* He would have to make a choice eventually. Not too soon, but not too late, lest he lose out on all the favors the victor would grant those who had the good sense to support him. It was a good time for an ambitious man to be living, and he already had his toehold on the future.

Arabella Grey was a strong, healthy girl, for all her pale coloring. She should give him healthy children and live to raise them. He had had two previous wives. The first he had wed the year he was sixteen. She had been his orphaned cousin and only ten years of age. They had never cohabited, and his mother had hoped to raise Beth to be the kind of wife she thought her only son should have. Unfortunately, both his mother and his child-wife had died in the early spring of 1470 of some pestilence that was scourging the surrounding countryside. His father survived long enough to arrange a second marriage for him, which was celebrated that same December at his dying parent's bedside. His second wife, Anne Smale, had died less than three years later, having never conceived despite his unrelenting attentions to her.

Sir Jasper Keane had found himself at twenty-one answerable to no one, and so he had pledged his fealty not to the most powerful nobleman in the north, the Earl of Northumberland, but to King Edward himself. He was loyal and self-effacing and served the king in a number of discreet matters. Though he was a lascivious man by nature, he hid that part of himself from the licentious king lest his baser nature be considered a weakness to be used against him. It was this seeming morality in the face of immorality that brought him to the attention of the king's brother, Richard, the Duke of Gloucester. He was quick to pledge his service to Richard upon the king's death, for Sir Jasper Keane was no fool, and he could see more advantage in allying himself to a grown man than kneeling at the feet of a child monarch.

His instincts had proven sound, although he had never expected the turn of events that followed. Jasper Keane knew he was of very little import in the world of English politics. He could only hope that eventually his dedicated service would be taken note of and rewarded. He sought but two things: gold and

a healthy, hopefully well-connected wife. Some high lord's bastard by a daughter of the merchant class perhaps. A daughter
who was loved, or at least remembered with fondness. Greyfaire
and Arabella Grey were far more than even he had dared to
hope. Jasper Keane knew that his luck was riding high. He had
been in the right place at the right time, and to add a sugared
topping to it all, there were two pretty birds in the nest, not one.

He would have to take Rowena in hand, however. She was
showing distinct signs of jealousy with regard to his courtship
of her daughter. He had allowed Arabella several days to regain
her equilibrium and was concerned when she did not come
around, for women always did. A morning did not pass that he
hadn't had a small gift or trinket delivered to the girl who would
be his wife. He picked these small treasures carefully from the
loot of his border raids. Two gifts were of particular value: gar-
net ear bobs, and a beautiful pair of red Florentine leather riding
gloves with tiny pearls sewn upon the turned-back cuffs. Other
gifts were as simple as two cream-colored silk ribbons tied about
a posy from the garden. More experienced women had melted
before such wooing, so he was surprised when Arabella did not.

Then he had the good fortune to overhear Rowena encouraging Arabella to continue in her anger. Indeed, the mother
actually incited the daughter in her attitude. Sir Jasper had sent
his man, Seger, to waylay Lady Rowena and bring her in secret
to his private chamber. There, Seger had stifled Rowena's cries
of agony while his master, having stripped his victim naked,
proceeded to whip her fiercely with a leather tawse until her
back and bottom were raw and bleeding. Then, before the very
eyes of his captain, Sir Jasper Keane had satisfied his lusts in a
particularly cruel manner.

When he had finished, he yanked Rowena up by her wheaten-
colored hair and snarled, "You will soften your daughter's manner toward me, sweet Row, even as you have encouraged her in
her hard-heartedness. If you do not, I will not hesitate to kill
you."

"You would not," she whispered. "You could not! I love
you!"

"Let there be no mistake in our relationship, sweet Row. You
are my whore. Nothing more. You will obey me. Some months
back I had a highborn whore named Eufemia Hamilton of Culcairn. She defied me once too often, and I killed her even as I

burned her family's house to the ground. Do you understand me?''

Rowena shuddered. She did not want to believe him, but she could see in his eyes that he was telling her the truth. ''How could you do such a thing?'' she said, appalled. Appalled that she had allowed herself to love him. Appalled that the king had chosen this man for her daughter's husband.

''They were Scots,'' he answered simply, as if that was all the explanation necessary. ''Now will you obey me, sweet Row? Or do you need another taste of the tawse?''

Rowena Grey nodded her assent wordlessly, in shock as she gathered up her garments and began to dress herself. She was heedless of Seger, heedless of Sir Jasper, heedless even of her bleeding back and buttocks. She sought but one thing. Escape from him. She needed time to think. She finished fastening the last garment and smoothed her hair into a semblance of order.

''Tonight,'' he said. ''You will go to your daughter tonight and tell her that you were wrong; that she must forgive me and cease holding her childish grudge. You will suggest to her that I love her, else my desire for her perfection would not be so strong. If I did not love her, I should not have beaten her in an effort to gain that perfection. You will tell her that, won't you, sweet Row?''

''Yes, my lord,'' Rowena said. Anything so that he would let her go.

Jasper Keane smiled his beautiful smile. ''Then you may go, my pet,'' he said in a kindly tone, and Rowena fled him.

But when she knelt in the chapel to think and to pray, she found that she could excuse him, even though she could now feel the burning ache he had inflicted on her; feel her shift alternately sticking to her back, only to pull away and irritate her painful wounds. She had been wrong to stoke the fires of Arabella's great pride to deeper anger. She had been jealous of the attentions he was paying her daughter, she admitted to herself. It was only right he give his attention to Arabella. It was she who was to be his wife, not her. If Rowena had been foolish enough to fall in love with this man, then it was but God's judgment upon her for enjoying their shared passion. Not for her liaison with Jasper, for that was but to protect Arabella, but she should not have enjoyed him. She sighed with resignation, and rising from her knees, went off to speak to her daughter.

Arabella, however, was not as easily convinced as her mother was as to Sir Jasper Keane's motives. "I have heard unpleasant rumors these past few days," Arabella said darkly.

"What rumors?" Lady Rowena asked, knowing her daughter's firm moral stance on infidelity, and nervous as to what might have been said.

"It is said Sir Jasper is overfond of the ladies, Mama, and I can well believe it, for it is clear he thinks highly of himself. The king has said the choice is mine to make regarding this marriage. Would you have me wed to a lecher and a womanizer? The man I speak my vows with must be true to me." Arabella's jaw was firm with her determination.

"Father Anselm!" Rowena wailed. "You must help me explain."

"Men are weak where the flesh is concerned, my daughter, and the world offers many temptations," said Father Anselm, dutifully coming to Lady Rowena's aid. "I will not deny that I, too, have heard that Sir Jasper enjoys feminine company perhaps more than he ought to, but he is, after all, a bachelor. Marriage to a beautiful and virtuous wife will settle him. Of that I am certain."

"He beat me," Arabella said, outrage sparkling in her green eyes with memory.

"There is no sin in a man beating his wife," the priest said honestly. "It is man's duty to teach his wife acceptable behavior. I see many good qualities in Sir Jasper, my child. He is loyal to the king, and he is a good soldier, FitzWalter says."

"And you will forgive him, Arabella?" Lady Rowena said nervously.

"I do not know if I will forgive him, Mother. My father never beat you, nor did he beat me," Arabella remarked. "I will allow the incident to be forgotten, however."

"Ohh, Arabella, you *must* be more biddable!" Rowena counseled, looking to the priest for support. "Men do not like women who speak their minds as plainly as do you."

"I cannot be meek and silent as you have always been, Mama," Arabella said ominously. "I will make peace with Sir Jasper, but you must be satisfied with that, for I shall offer no more."

Seger, hidden in a corner of the hall, reported the conversation in careful detail to his master even before Rowena came fluttering in to him with her carefully laundered version of her discussion with her daughter. He had already decided what he would do. It was unthinkable that a headstrong girl like Arabella Grey should unseat him from his position here at Greyfaire, but nothing, he had learned in his lifetime, was impossible. He kissed Rowena tenderly and said, "My pet, you have done well, and I am grateful for your intercession." And she had simpered happily at him, her foolish love shining brightly in her pretty face.

Jasper Keane then set about to once again court the heiress of Greyfaire Keep. Confused by his sudden kindness, Arabella began to question her former judgment, yet still in the back of her mind a tiny dark doubt lingered and refused to be dispelled. In a flash of understanding she began to comprehend how his reputation with the ladies had grown so mightily. He was charm itself when he chose to be, which seemed to be most of the time these days. She tried to put the last year in true perspective. Only once had he been unkind.

Of course women would be attracted to this handsome lordling. It was easy to see how his legend might have grown as a ladies' man. Arabella was young, but she knew enough about gossip to know that most of it could be discounted, however savory. Other than his one cruelty, his behavior toward her had always been most circumspect. Not once had he attempted to steal a kiss from her lips, or approach her in any way but a most courteous manner—but for the one cruelty. Why did that keep weighing on her so?

It was quite obvious to everyone that Sir Jasper Keane was every bit as fine a gentleman as her own dear father, God assoil him, and her own mother appeared content with the match. In fact, Arabella had not seen Rowena so complacent since her father had died. Jasper had even, in her hearing, assured Rowena that he expected her to remain at Greyfaire after their marriage. She could, he said, have the Dower House, and there would be no need for her to remarry. He was happy to provide for her. That was most thoughtful, Arabella considered. They were all really quite fortunate in the king's choice, and it was time she stopped behaving like the child she claimed she no longer was. It was time, Arabella decided, to make peace with her future. If Jasper made no further slip in his behavior, then she would accept him for her husband. She would force that nagging little uncertainty from her mind. Wisely, however, she kept these thoughts to herself.

Throughout the autumn of 1484 and the winter of 1485, Sir Jasper Keane courted Arabella Grey with charm, and guarded both his tongue and his actions. Toward her mother he was publicly kind and polite. Privately, his passion for Rowena did not abate, and he kept her well satisfied. Their liaison would continue after his marriage, when she would take up residence in the Dower House. Arabella need never know, he soothed his mistress, and they would all be quite content. He no longer brought up the possibility of sharing the two women simultaneously, for he had forced Rowena into that situation the previous summer with great disappointment. Still, he thought with a smile upon his handsome face, there were other compensations.

Arabella's thirteenth birthday on March twenty-ninth was barely remembered, for word had come several days prior that Queen Anne had died at the palace of Westminster on the sixteenth day of the month and had been buried in the abbey of the same name. Rowena's sorrow was greater than anyone else's at Greyfaire, for she and the queen had been as close as sisters. For almost two weeks a mere word could send her into fits of weeping.

The queen's death galvanized Sir Jasper into action. Only once since he had come to Greyfaire Keep had he left it for any period of time; and within that time frame there had been no serious border disputes, only sporadic raiding back and forth on both sides. Now he knew if he was to learn precisely the true state of affairs in England, he must go south to visit friends and acquaintances, perhaps to the court itself. A mistake at this point in time could be fatal. He could not rely on gossip. FitzWalter could be trusted to defend the keep, and Jasper Keane considered himself fortunate to have inherited such a good captain.

"Why must you go?" Rowena wailed the night before his departure. "What if the Scots come?"

"Rowena," he explained patiently, "your *Dickon* is in serious danger of losing his throne to Henry Tudor. I may have to choose sides now, but before I do, I must learn which of these men has the better chance of winning. The king, or the pretender. Our very existence depends upon my choice. Can you understand that, my pet, or is it all too much for your foolish little brain to comprehend?''

"I am not so silly, Jasper," she answered him, "that I do not see you contemplate breaking your oath of loyalty to the king. Why would you betray Richard when he has lifted you up from the ashes of Northby and given you Greyfaire? Is this how a gentleman repays his good lord?''

He nodded slowly. Sometimes Rowena surprised even him with an astute observation. "There is a strong possibility that the king may not be able to retain his throne, sweet Row. Too much controversy swirls about him, and has since the death of his brother, King Edward, several years ago. Now his wife is dead, and he has no direct heir of his own body. The rumor about his lust for his niece is not pleasing to the commons, and his refusal to show the people his little nephews gives proof to the tale that they are dead.''

"They are not dead!" she cried. "They are at Middleham. Dickon took them there himself in the summer of his coronation. We spent a good part of our childhood there, and it is Dickon's favorite home. He wanted the boys to be raised there secretly in safety, where they could have good country air and not be a magnet for every malcontent.''

Here was an interesting piece of information, Sir Jasper thought. "How do you know this, sweet Row?" he queried her gently.

"Dickon told me so himself when we visited him after Neddie's investiture as prince of Wales," she answered.

"Perhaps he lied to you," Sir Jasper suggested.

"Dickon never lies!" she told him indignantly. "I cannot tell you how many beatings he got when we were children because he would not lie, even to protect himself from the littlest offense. No, if he told me Edward and Richard are at Middleham, then they are there.''

It was possible, Sir Jasper thought as he kissed her absently. It was worthy of Richard, who had a too kind heart. Having sat in the seat of power, however, even the king, who was an ethical man, would not be able to give it all up. He would not reveal his nephews' existence in order to protect his position, for Richard loved England above all else. Two contestants for the throne was bad enough, but Henry, like himself, was a grown man. Richard would believe he had a far better chance of retaining his throne against Henry Tudor than he would have against Elizabeth Woodville's sons. Besides, it was entirely possible that Henry Tudor, squeamish as his reputation claimed he was, might harm the boys. Richard would keep their whereabouts a secret no matter what, in order to protect his nephews.

"I must still go south," he told Rowena, "and learn the truth of this situation."

He rode forth from Greyfaire Keep in the first week of April. He visited York and went as far south as London. The situation was volatile at best. People changed sides daily, and no one could really be sure of what would happen. Only one thing was certain, Sir Jasper decided. There would be an invasion this summer. He began his return north, stopping at Nottingham, where the king was in residence, but for some reason he did not go to court. Nothing he had learned had aided him in deciding what to do. His fealty was to Richard, but he did not want to be placed in the position of having to reaffirm that fealty.

When war came, he would have to make his decision. He laughed ruefully to himself. Rowena and Arabella feared for Greyfaire, but whichever man won, Richard or Henry, they and Greyfaire would be safe, for the keep belonged to Arabella, and a woman could not fight. If he declared for Richard and Richard lost, Sir Jasper decided, he would lose Greyfaire. If he declared for Henry and Henry lost, he would lose Greyfaire. There was, Jasper Keane finally decided, only one way to protect himself without losing everything. He must return to Greyfaire, marry Arabella immediately in order to safeguard his claim to Greyfaire, and then avoid declaring for either combatant.

If Richard won and demanded an explanation, he would say that he but sought to protect England's back door in the event the Scots took the opportunity to invade while the king was busy defending his realm from the pretender. He could not be faulted for that. If Henry Tudor won, the same explanation would suffice, particularly if he stressed his loyalty to England first. Sir Jasper Keane knew he was not important enough for either combatant to spend a great deal of time bothering with; and the information he possessed about the whereabouts of Edward IV's two young sons should certainly ingratiate him with Henry Tudor and dispel any doubts a new king might have regarding his loyalty. *Yes!* That was the path he would take, and he would lose nothing by it. His decision made, Sir Jasper Keane and his captain, Seger, spurred their horses northward.

"She is too young yet," Rowena protested his determination when he told her of it. "She is only thirteen!"

"Girls have been wed younger, sweet Row. It is not unusual. Thirteen is an average age for marriage," Sir Jasper reasoned with his mistress.

"She is too young," Rowena insisted stubbornly.

"You were thirteen when you married Sir Henry," Jasper Keane said. "It was your thirteenth birthday, you told me."

"And I bore a stillborn before I was even fourteen, my lord, and another son eleven months later who lived but a short time," Rowena said. "I was too young, and so is Arabella!"

"Henry Tudor's mother bore him before she was fourteen," he told her. "Plenty of women Arabella's age marry and have children without ill effects. Are you trying to tell me that her monthly woman's flow is *not* upon her? That she cannot yet conceive and bear children?"

She considered lying to him. She needed time to think. There were things he had to know, things he must consider before he wed with her daughter. Then she saw the look in his eye and knew that he already knew the answer to his questions. Once he told her that he would kill her if she ever defied him again. She had believed him then, and she knew now that nothing had changed. "Arabella is fit to be a wife in every sense of the word, my lord," she told him truthfully, and Sir Jasper Keane smiled, well pleased.

"Good! Then have Father Anselm quickly cry the bans, sweet Row, for on the first day of June I shall take your daughter to wife," and he smiled at her again, "in every sense of the word, my lady," he concluded, laughing when she blanched at his none-too-subtle meaning.

"You are vile!" she whispered, near to weeping.

"You are jealous," he chuckled, enjoying her pain. "Will you tell Arabella or shall I?"

"She is so young and inexperienced," Rowena said. "She is still foolish enough to be romantic. Keep the illusion alive for her at least until after she marries you. How sad that it will be too late for her when she learns the truth of you, Jasper."

"Do not be bitter, sweet Row," he mocked her. "I shall not neglect you just because I am wed to Arabella."

"You bastard!" she flung at him.

"A show of spirit, sweet Row? No, no, my pet, that will not do. I can only handle one little spitfire, and Arabella is she. You are the biddable one, and so you must remain lest I become angered," and laughing, he went off to find Arabella.

"But this is the twenty-fifth of May, my lord," Arabella told him. "We were not to be wed until next summer."

Quietly he explained to her. He knew that unlike her mother, Arabella had an intellect, although that was unique in a woman. "We are safest not taking sides in this matter, mignon, although, of course, our loyalties lie with the king," he finished.

"But the question is *which* king," Arabella said astutely. "I know I am a woman and not supposed to understand such matters, but I do, Jasper." It was the first time she had ever called him by his given name without his title, and he was not displeased at her acceptance of their new relationship. "We must think of Greyfaire first, I know. I love my cousin, the king, and I pray that he will surmount this challenge to his lawful authority, but who are we in the face of the mighty? I shall never withdraw my loyalty, having sworn it before God, but it is God who will decide this matter, not you or I. His will be done, and while it is being done, we will protect England's back here in our little keep, free of all controversy, my lord."

"You surprise me, mignon," he admitted frankly. "I know that you are not your mother, but such wisdom from one so young is perhaps a bit frightening. I salute you, *wife*!" He bent and brushed her lips lightly with his.

Immediately Arabella flushed with confusion and not just a little pleasure. She was suddenly very aware of him in a way she had never been before. The very air about them was charged with an excitement she had never experienced until now. Suddenly she was very curious to know exactly what it was that Jasper did with other ladies that made his reputation as a great lover such a legend. She found herself longing for their wedding day, their wedding night, even though she knew little of what was involved. She had attempted to question Rowena, but her mother's answer, given with a strangely flushed face, had been brief and not particularly informative.

"It is too soon for you to ask me such questions, Arabella," Rowena had said sharply. "I shall explain everything that you need to know just before you go to your marriage bed. I am disturbed that you would ask me such things now, for it bespeaks a lack of chastity on your part.''

Arabella was not put off by her mother's harsh and unfair words. "Is it like the dogs in the hall, Mama? When the males mount the bitches?'' she persisted. "Come, Mama, what difference does it make when you tell me? I would digest your words at my leisure in the event that I must ask you further questions. You know how I dislike being at a disadvantage. I would not have Jasper think badly of me, or that I am an ignorant country girl.''

''A bride should most certainly be ignorant of what transpires between a man and a woman, Arabella! I am shocked by your attitude,'' Rowena said irritably. Then she arose from her place by the fire and left the hall, her skirts swishing with a strangely angry sound.

Arabella watched her go, wondering what on earth she had ever said to distress her mother so. Then she shrugged. Rowena was probably nervous about the wedding, but then so too was she. Rowena at least knew what being married was all about. She did not. Oh, she knew how to run her household, for Rowena had been certain her knowledge there was complete, but that wasn't all to it. She had spoken to Father Anselm on the matter, but the dear old priest was full of vague platitudes about a woman's duty toward her husband. But what of love? Where did that come into it? Her mother had learned to love her father. Would she learn to love Jasper? What exactly was love?

The next few days were filled with activity as Greyfaire Keep prepared for the nuptials of its heiress. Rowena spent most of her time in the kitchens overseeing the menu for the feast to follow the ceremony, though there would be few guests because of their isolation and the suddenness of the wedding. The wedding gown was quickly fashioned. Arabella was busily engaged seeing to the decorations in the Great Hall, as well as those in the church, which was situated in the little village that clustered at the foot of the castle hill.

Rowena was relieved that her activities prevented her from seeing much of her daughter. It meant she might avoid Arabella's probing questions about the relations between a man and a woman. Thinking of Jasper and her child together filled her with impotent and unhappy distress. It wasn't fair. *It just wasn't fair!* She was still young and beautiful. Why should she not be the bride? She had to talk to Jasper. There were other things he must consider before he was irrevocably bound by this marriage.

Jasper Keane contemplated his bride-to-be in the hall the night before their wedding. Over the last months he had become acutely aware of how very innocent Arabella really was, and he was not only astounded, but delighted by this knowledge. He certainly expected Arabella's maidenhead to be firmly lodged and totally intact; but the fact that she was so totally virginal in her person, particularly as she was so outspoken a girl, surprised him. He had broken a few maidenheads in his time, of course, but the girls involved were worldly wise, with lips used to kissing and breasts well fondled. It excited him to think of a female totally without carnal knowledge. When he lay with Row later he would instruct her to tell his bride nothing of a man and a woman. He would teach Arabella everything she needed to know. She would be without inhibitions, and she would please him as no woman ever had.

He looked down at the girl next to him, and taking her hand, smiled down into her face. "I have a small gift for you, mignon," he told her, and reaching into a pouch that hung from his side, he drew forth a delicate gold chain from which hung a thistle carved from a single piece of pale violet quartz crystal which was banded in gold.

Her eyes grew bright with her pleasure as she took it from him and slipped it over her head. "It is beautiful, Jasper! Thank you. I shall cherish it always."

"Wear it tomorrow, mignon. It would please me to see you in your wedding finery with this little jewel nestling between your pretty breasts." He bent so only she might hear his bold words. "I long to caress those sweet fruits, mignon." Then he dropped a kiss upon her shoulder. "How I hunger for the morrow when you will truly be mine!"

Arabella colored with his words. "My lord," she said, "you should not speak to me so."

"Why, mignon, you are to be my wife, and a husband may speak so to his spouse," he told her. "Once we are wed I shall not simply speak of love. Do you not long for my arms as much as I long to hold you in them, Arabella? Do you know how difficult it becomes with each passing day as you grow in beauty before my very eyes, not to kiss or caress you? Not to love you as I so very much want to do?"

"I know naught of love, my lord," she answered him. "It is not seemly, my mother says, for a girl to know such things before her marriage, although I think it foolish to be that ignorant." Arabella's heart was skipping beats within her chest. Jasper was being more attentive to her than he had ever been. Was it possible he was in love with her?

"Your mother is wise, mignon," he purred low, his warm breath soft in her ear. "A husband should indeed be the only font of knowledge a wife has. It is he who should tutor her in all that would please him."

For all her excitement over her marriage, Arabella slept well that night. The first day of June dawned unusually warm for the north. The mists cloaked the surrounding hillsides and draped themselves over the keep's towers. The sun, a blur of mother of pearl, struggled to assert itself through the thick fog, but so far had not been successful. The wedding ceremony was to be solemnized early so that the rest of the day might be spent in celebration of the event, Greyfaire's people having been excused from their labors today.

Rowena, overseeing her daughter's bath and other preparations, looked exhausted. There was a mark upon her bared left shoulder that resembled a bite, but of course that could not be. The tawny orange of her gown, usually a most flattering color for Rowena with her rich gold hair, somehow looked all wrong today against her pale skin with those purple-black circles beneath her blue eyes. Lady Grey, considered by all who knew her to be a pretty woman, was definitely not at her best this morning.

She had left *his* bed to come to her only child. Left after a night of incredible passion and savagery that should have turned her against this man who was to wed her daughter. She could not dissuade him from marrying Arabella, though God knows she had tried. As wicked as Jasper Keane was, she loved him. She knew that he did not love her, but perhaps, just perhaps, he would love Arabella, and then her sacrifice would not be for naught. It would be for Arabella, even as everything she had done had been for the girl. Aye, Jasper was a wicked and cruel man, but if he loved Arabella, then mayhap he would not be wicked and cruel to her.

"How beautiful you are," she said quietly to her daughter when at last the girl was dressed in all her nuptial finery. "You are so much like your father. If only he might be here today to see you.''

''Am I really beautiful, Mama? Do you think that Jasper will think it? He has, after all, been to court and seen so many really lovely women.''

''None as fair as you, my daughter,'' Rowena said sincerely, a great sadness overwhelming her as she spoke, though she knew not why.

''I think I love him, Mama, and I would be the most beautiful woman in the world for him!'' the bride enthused.

''Arabella, you know nothing of love,'' Rowena said. ''You are flattered by Jasper's attentions and delighted that he is so fair to look upon, but that is not love. In your secret heart you know it. But come to my pier glass and see for yourself.''

''I do love him, Mama! *I do!* '' Arabella cried earnestly, even half believing it herself.

''Perhaps,'' Rowena answered, ''or perhaps you but think you do. It does not matter which. He is to be your husband whether you love him or not. If believing you love him makes it easier for you, then believe it. But be warned, Arabella: never give yourself so wholly to a man that when you finally discover he is but a mere mortal and fallible as we all are, it breaks your heart and spirit. You must be strong to be a woman. Your strength must be beyond that of all others if you are to survive. Remember that, and remember that I love you!'' Then giving her child a kiss upon her cheek, Rowena left her for a few moments to her own thoughts.

Arabella Grey was surprised. In her entire lifetime she had never heard her mother speak so profoundly. Rowena had always reminded her of a pretty, fluffy kitten, or a bright, darting butterfly. Charming, beautiful, sweet, and sometimes even amusing; but with little of a serious nature to recommend her. It startled Arabella to think that perhaps she did not really know her mother at all; or else perhaps it was just the excitement of today that made her feel that way. Rowena, undoubtedly, was moved to bestow upon her daughter some words of wisdom before her marriage, and indeed, her mother's words had given Arabella pause for thought. How strange. She had never before thought Rowena wise.

Arabella turned her eyes to the pier glass to gaze upon her image once again. The glass was one of the castle's most precious possessions, having been brought back to England by a Grey ancestor who had fought in the Holy Land and passed through Venice on his way home to England. Her wedding gown was the most beautiful garment that she had ever possessed, or she believed she would ever possess. Both skirt and bodice were of cloth of silver, embroidered with gold threads and small pearls. It was rather tight-fitting, with a long waist, long, close-fitted sleeves banded in ermine, a wide shawl collar of rich, soft ermine, and a low vee-neck which offered a tempting view of her breasts. A delicate gold tussoire hung from the jeweled girdle holding up her long skirt. On her feet she wore a pair of round-toed sollerets, fashioned from soft, gilded kidskin.

Her hands were free of rings, as she would receive her wedding band, but she had worn Jasper's lovely chain, and a small jeweled rosary also hung from her girdle. Her elderly nurse had brushed her beautiful hair out so that it hung to her ankles, a gossamer cloud of pale-golden silver gilt. She looked very grown up, she thought, and yet at the same time she looked so very young. Suddenly she was afraid. What was she doing? She was about to marry a man she wasn't even certain she wanted to marry.

"Come, dearie," the old nurse said, breaking into her thoughts. " 'Tis time to go to the church. Yer fine laddie will be awaiting ye."

Arabella swallowed back her nerves. It was all right. Everything was perfectly all right. She was going to marry Sir Jasper Keane, a man she could certainly learn to love. They would live a happy life together. They would have many children. Oh, yes! She wanted children. Jasper was everything she had ever dreamed of in a man. It would be a good life.

The keep seemed empty as they passed out into the courtyard. It was only a short walk over the drawbridge, down the hill to the church. Arabella found herself relieved to see Jasper waiting to escort her. His eyes widened with approval as he saw her, and a small sigh of relief escaped her lips. The servants and all of her people were lining their path. They called out their good wishes as she passed with Jasper. They were not invited into the small church, for it would not have been able to contain them all; but having seen the bride in her wedding finery and the groom in his scarlet robes, they were content to return to their tasks until the feasting began, for Lady Rowena had promised there would be cakes and ale for all.

It was a strange sort of day, for the mists had still not lifted by the time they arrived at the church where the invited guests had assembled. Inside the stone structure the air was damp, but the flickering candles upon the altar threw a hazy golden light over all. The stone altar was laid with a fine embroidered linen cloth upon which sat a beautiful jeweled cross and a pair of golden candlesticks. As they neared the altar where Father Anselm stood arrayed in his finest gold and white robes, Arabella could suddenly smell the white roses that had been brought in to decorate the church. *The white roses of York.* In the oaken pews that flanked the church's single aisle were some Grey relations of her father's—elderly souls, for the most part—a few male friends of Sir Jasper's, and the castle servants who were the most privileged of Greyfaire folk. Arabella and her bridegroom knelt before the priest upon a velvet-cushioned double prie-dieu. Behind them Arabella could hear Rowena softly sobbing.

For a moment all was silence, and then raising his hand to bless all, Father Anselm intoned, *"In nomine Patris, et Filii, et Spiritus Sancti, Amen."*

"Amen," echoed the congregation, but some, sharper-eared than others, thought they heard the sound of horses' hooves beneath the sound of their own voices.

Father Anselm placed his hands upon the bowed heads of the kneeling couple, and suddenly there was no mistaking the tramp of uninvited booted feet upon the stone porch outside. As the male guests arose to their feet in alarm, the double doors to the church were burst asunder by armed and kilted clansmen who poured into the holy place, blocking all possible routes of escape, successfully imprisoning the wedding guests, none of whom were armed. To have come armed to a wedding would have been considered an offense to the laws of hospitality. The men in the wedding party remained silent, but there were small cries of alarm from the women. Then all was silent. This was, after all, the border, and they were used to such raids.

"My sons! My sons!" Father Anselm spoke up. "Why have you come armed into God's house, and on this particularly joyous occasion?" The priest was a small man, but he had a commanding voice when he chose to use it. He had spent his life on this border, and he recognized the plaid that most of these borderers were wearing as Ancient Stewart, although there were several men in the Murray tartan. It did not bode well, for the Stewarts were the royal family, and he could not possibly think what they wanted with unimportant little Greyfaire unless an invasion was imminent. The keep and its people were relatively safe from everyday raiding.

The clansmen filling the aisle parted as if in response to a silent command. A tall gentleman wearing the crest badge of a chieftain came forward to face the priest. "I am Tavis Stewart, the Earl of Dunmor," he said in a strong voice heard by all in the church. "I have come for only one thing, holy father. *That man!*" A long, elegant finger pointed at Sir Jasper Keane. "That cowardly dog who now stands before ye in his wedding finery is mine! I thank God that I have at least saved yon innocent maid from the terrible fate of being his wife. Gie me Jasper Keane, and I will leave Greyfaire in peace."

It was generously said, for everyone within the sound of Tavis Stewart's voice knew he might take Sir Jasper, slay all within the church, and pull Greyfaire to bits, stone by stone, if he so chose. The guests were frankly curious as to what Sir Jasper had done to bring down the wrath of the Royal Stewarts.

"My son," Father Anselm replied. "Ye seek to do murder, for I see it in your eyes. I cannot turn this man over to you under such circumstances. 'Twould make me every bit as guilty as you will be should I allow you to commit such a folly. Whatever ill will may be between you two gentlemen, can we not reason together?"

"This devil is guilty of murder himself, holy father," the earl replied. "Does not the bible say that they who live by the sword are fated to die by the sword? I would meet Sir Jasper in single combat."

"Tell me what he had done, my son, that has earned him such a fierce enmity on your part," the priest said quietly.

"He has wantonly murdered the Lady Eufemia Hamilton, my betrothed wife, holy father. For that act I will have his miserable life!" The earl looked hard-eyed at Jasper Keane, who now stood, dragging Arabella to her feet with him. "He came over the border fifteen months ago to Culcairn House, where he foully murdered Lady Hamilton. Then he fired Culcairn and drove off the young laird's livestock. The lad managed to escape and take his two younger sisters and little brother to safety.''

"Sanctuary!" The strangled cry rang throughout the small church. "I beg sanctuary of the church, Father Anselm!" cried Sir Jasper Keane.

Rowena pushed forward through the kilted men to put comforting arms about her daughter. Arabella, however, shook her mother off. Rowena paled with fear as her only child placed herself squarely before the Earl of Dunmor and, looking up at him, shouted angrily.

"How dare you, sir! How dare you break into *my* home, and interrupt *my* wedding?! You are naught but a filthy Scots liar! A low border bandit! Begone this instant! I am the king's cousin, and I will have royal justice from Richard if you trifle with me further!''

For a moment no one even dared to breathe, and then the Earl of Dunmor said in an icy voice, "Madame, I have killed men for fewer words than ye have just now uttered. Did ye not hear what I said, or are ye too daft to comprehend my tale?" He looked down on her and thought she was a pretty wench, even if she was stupid enough to be besotted by his enemy.

"I do not believe you," Arabella answered him rudely. "Sir Jasper is every bit the parfait and gentle knight. He would not murder a woman, my lord." Then her voice softened. "You are but grief-stricken for your lady, I can see."

"Grief has nothing to do with it, madame," the earl answered coldly. "Yon coward has besmirched the honor of the Stewarts of Dunmor by his cruel act. My betrothed, I have learned, was his most willing mistress. This *gentle* knight of yours refused to wed wi her, but he wanted her to come wi him to England. When she refused, yer *parfait* knight raided her home, and when he had finished amusing himself wi Eufemia, madame, he gave her to his men for their sport. When all had been taken from her that could be taken, Sir Jasper's men threw her battered and ravished body into the fire of Culcairn House, where she perished; if she was not already dead, which I pray she was.''

Several of the women in the church fainted with the recitation of the earl's tale, and Rowena herself felt bile pushing up into her throat. This, then, was the woman Jasper had bragged to her about killing. It had been no idle boast, as she had fervently prayed it was. Arabella, however, reached up and slapped the earl with all her strength.

As the stain made by her little palm print spread across Tavis Stewart's face, the earl looked away from Arabella and said scathingly to Jasper Keane, "Will ye let a wench do yer fighting for ye, then, coward?"

An air of expectation hovered over them all as everyone waited to see if Sir Jasper Keane would rise to the earl's blunt challenge and come out from behind the sanctuary of the church.

Father Anselm spoke once more. "I will not dispute the truth of your words, my son, but Sir Jasper has asked for sanctuary from the church. I cannot, as you well know, refuse him, despite the vileness of the charges you have made against him. I grant that sanctuary, and having granted it, you cannot touch him while he remains within this church, to the peril of your immortal soul."

Jasper Keane felt the blood flowing within his veins once again now that his safety had been insured. He almost laughed aloud as the earl's hand worked itself, frustrated, upon the hilt of his sword.

"Tavis!" A sandy-haired young man in the red Murray plaid spoke warningly. "Dinna do it, laddie!"

Arabella rounded fiercely on her bridegroom, unbridled rage pounding in her veins. Her wedding was ruined! *And Jasper!* The man she was about to give her heart to did nothing except cower behind the priest's robes. She glared furiously at him. "Surely you will not let this Scots savage insult and slander you, my lord? Accept his challenge, and let us have this matter over and done with, I beg you! I will not have Greyfaire and her people endangered by this man. We want no breach of peace with the Scots, especially on this, our wedding day."

A small light of admiration lit the earl's eyes for a brief moment. The girl was loyal, he'd give her that, though it was plain she knew little of the truth of Sir Jasper Keane. She knew her duty to her people, however, and put it above all else. Obviously she was a good chatelaine. He turned his gaze to Sir Jasper. "Well, coward?" he demanded mockingly. "Will ye do battle wi me or continue to hide behind yon cleric's skirts?"

"And when I destroyed you, my lord," Sir Jasper answered, bold in the security of the church's protection, "your men would tear me apart. I should be a fool to accept such an offer. Nay, I refuse ye.''

"*If* you can beat me fairly, sir, I gie ye my word that my clansmen will depart peacefully,'' the earl replied.

"I do not believe you, my lord. Who would trust the word of a thieving Scot?'' Sir Jasper said insultingly. Then he turned to Father Anselm. "Perform the marriage ceremony, Father. I have kept this lady waiting too long as it is, and would have her for my wife.''

The Earl of Dunmor stepped between the bride and groom with a suddenness that sent the color draining from Jasper Keane's face, for he thought the Scotsman, ignoring the church, was about to do him a harm. Brief amusement lit the earl's dark eyes, though his face was grim and his voice icy once more. "I think ye will nae wed wi this lass today, coward," he said quietly. "Ye hae taken my betrothed wife from me, and so I will now take yers from ye!" He put a hard arm about Arabella's waist and pulled the startled girl to his side. "The bride goes wi me, and when ye see fit to accept my challenge, coward, *and if ye overcome me in fair battle*, then, and only then, may ye hae her back!"

"*Nooo!*" Rowena cried in a gasping and terrified voice.

"Savage!'' Arabella shrieked, and twisting from the earl's grasp, she kicked him in the shins. "I will not go with you!" Whirling about, she grabbed up a sword from one of the startled clansmen and attacked Tavis Stewart with it.

Surprised, the earl nonetheless managed to defend himself long enough to disarm the girl, who kicked and screamed vigorously, all the while hurling pithy epithets at him. He tossed the short sword back at his embarrassed clansman and ordered the others, "Take this damned spitfire outside and put her on my horse.'' He was suddenly overwhelmed by a great desire to laugh, for there certainly was humor in the situation. "Methinks the bride is far more of a man than yon cowering groom," he mocked Jasper Keane. "Dinna fear, Englishman. I will keep yer hot-tempered little lass safe for ye—if yer brave enough to come after her. I will treat her wi far more kindness and respect than ye showed to poor Eufemia Hamilton.''

"My lord! My lord!'' Rowena Grey fell to her knees before the earl. "Do not, I beg ye, take my child away! She is all I have left since my husband fell in battle after Berwick.''

Tavis Stewart gently raised Rowena to her feet, thinking that she was a very pretty woman, even with the tears running down her cheeks. "I must take her, madame, and ye well know it. Yer brave husband, may God assoil his soul, would understand that; and so, I suspect, do ye deep in yer heart. I will nae harm yer little lass. She is but my hostage, and will be returned to ye unscathed when honor has been satisfied." The earl then kissed Lady Grey's hand and turned to depart the church.

"Do you not want the gold candlesticks or the jeweled cross upon the altar, my lord?" Jasper Keane said insultingly, but Tavis Stewart never even paused in his stride as he passed from the church followed by his men.

Within moments the sounds of horses' hooves rang out, but no one amongst the guests moved until all was finally silent. Then Rowena spoke.

"You will go after Arabella immediately, will you not, Jasper?"

"Why?" he demanded. "I do not need your daughter to have Greyfaire. The king wants it in a man's hands. Besides, do you think I want the Scotman's leavings, my pet? He will have your daughter in his bed and squirming on his lance before the sun sets this day. Tavis Stewart is the finest soldier in Scotland, and although I am good, I could not possibly beat him. To accept his challenge is to seek my own demise. Do you think I am mad? I will not go willingly to my death for the sake of a mere wench."

"But he promised not to harm her, Jasper! He said we might get her back unscathed," Rowena sobbed. "She is my child! My only living child!"

As Rowena's voice rose slightly in her distress, the assembled congregation behind her leaned forward almost to a man in an effort to hear what was going on between the weeping woman and Sir Jasper Keane. They were doomed to disappointment, for the distance was a little too far. Father Anselm, however, was privy to all, and his kindly visage darkened as Sir Jasper continued harshly on, unthinking of Rowena's anguish.

"I will give you other children, my pet. If I am not mistaken, though ye strove to hide it from me, you are already ripening with my seed. Will you deny it?" he asked the white-faced woman. "I will not have my son born illegitimate now that I have the choice."

"And what would you have done, Jasper, if Arabella had not been kidnapped by the Scots?" she demanded of him. "This child would have been born nameless, and you would have had no choice in the matter! Why should you suddenly care now that my daughter is gone?"

"If the babe was a male child, I would have legitimized it, though it could not have inherited Greyfaire if Arabella gave me sons. Now there is no question of that, Rowena, so you will marry me this day, that my claim to Greyfaire be even stronger."

"I will not!" she cried furiously, surprising even herself in this show of spirit.

"You will," he said ominously, and turned to the priest. "Father Anselm, you will marry me to this lady now. Waive the bans and perform the ceremony."

"My son!" The priest was shocked, and felt that most un-Christian of emotions—anger—beginning to rise within his soul. "You cannot do this. It is immoral."

Sir Jasper Keane smiled his most winning smile. "I must insist, Father Anselm, that you do your duty. The king would be certain that Greyfaire is in loyal hands and protected from the enemy. I can hardly wed with the lady Arabella now, can I? I cannot retrieve her without mortal peril to my own life, and for what? The long-lost honor of a Scots whore named Eufemia Hamilton? There is not a man on either side of this border that did not know of Mistress Hamilton's wildness, but the earl who was so puffed with pride in his own importance that he heard not the rumors. If I cannot wed Arabella Grey, then I must, of necessity, wed Rowena Grey in order that this keep remain safe and loyal to England's king."

"But what of the heiress of Greyfaire?" Father Anselm insisted, his love and loyalty to Arabella evident, to Jasper Keane's annoyance, particularly as there was a low murmur of disapproval from the pews containing the Grey relations.

"Arabella Grey is lost to us," Sir Jasper said in a firm, even voice, easily heard by all within the little church. "If, by chance, she should return, she will be a dishonored woman, and I will not accept her as my wife. We were not betrothed, Father, and you well know it. Our arrangement was made by the king for the safety of this keep, but never was it formalized. Now perform the ceremony between myself and Rowena Grey or I will send my captain, Seger, to find a priest who will. If you force me to such an act, I will banish you from Greyfaire forever! Think of the scandal, and think of the lady Rowena, who will bear my child before year's end, good father.''

"You leave me no choice, my lord," the priest said bitterly. "It is obvious to me that you are not the man I believed you to be."

Sir Jasper Keane laughed aloud, and it was an unpleasant sound. "I do not leave you a choice, do I?" he said, smirking. Then he turned to the assembled guests and told them, "You have come for a wedding, and by the rood, my friends, you shall have one! Begin the ceremony, Father," and taking Rowena's hand firmly in his, he half dragged her to the double prie-dieu and pushed her to her knees. "We are going to be very happy, my pet," he told the softly weeping woman, and then he chuckled, but Rowena did not hear him.

This, she thought bleakly, was the final punishment for her lust. When Arabella found out, she would never forgive her. Her daughter was as lost to her as if the Scots had slain the girl this day instead of carrying her off. And she, Rowena, was condemned to live in hell with the devil himself for the rest of her natural life. And what of the child who even now ripened and grew beneath her heart? Would he be like his father? Pray God, no! Better he be born dead!

Chapter 4

A rabella Grey sat stony-faced atop the Earl of Dunmor's big, gray stallion. Her captor, who was mounted behind her, kept one arm lightly about her while guiding his horse with his other hand, a feat at which he seemed quite adept. Arabella kept her head carefully turned so that she should not have to look at him. She was tired and not just a little frightened, although she showed none of these emotions, nor would she show them to the enemy, for the Scots were England's enemy. She would not quickly forget that they had killed her father.

Arabella was angry, but not so much at the earl, for though she was but a woman and therefore assumed to be ignorant, she knew enough of the code of honor to understand that Tavis Stewart had done the only thing that he might have done under the circumstances. Arabella found, not greatly to her surprise, for she was a practical girl, that her anger was directed more toward Jasper Keane for having caused this impossible situation.

It was with a harsh and dawning cognizance that Arabella realized she believed her captor's version of events past. Why she believed this stranger she could not fathom, but there was something so innately moral and honest about the earl of Dunmor, something that caused her to trust him, and distrust Sir Jasper about whom she had already had doubts. Doubts she had so resolutely tried to deny. She almost squirmed with annoyance remembering her girlish ravings of this morning, when she had declared to her mother that she loved Jasper Keane. How could she have loved a coward? A man who would not satisfy a debt of honor in single combat. Not that she would admit her error to this hawk-browed Scot.

What a fool she had been! Oh, she had heard the rumors about him, but for the sake of imagined love she had been willing to overlook the gossip that had swirled about him. Had not Father Anselm assured her that all Jasper needed was a virtuous wife? She wondered now if the old priest had known the truth of Jasper Keane, or if, innocent like her, he had merely hoped for the best. *Murder.* Sir Jasper Keane had murdered a helpless woman. No matter that the earl himself admitted that the lady was no better than she ought to be. Murder was a heinous crime, particularly the murder of a woman or a child.

And like a lamb to the slaughter she had tripped down the aisle of Greyfaire church less than an hour ago, eager to wed with Sir Jasper Keane. Would he have murdered her too, had she not pleased him? What of her poor mother, left to the mercy of the man? And would Sir Jasper come after her? Well, she certainly did not intend marrying him now! As soon as she returned to Greyfaire she intended going to cousin Richard herself and exposing Sir Jasper Keane for the blackguard that he was!

They rode relentlessly on, crossing over the Cheviot hills, which were clothed in the green of their summer mantle. The day, however, remained mist-filled despite the smoky sun which could not quite burn away the fog. The dampness seemed to eat through her beautiful gown, chilling her to the bone. They stopped once, and the earl told her most bluntly that if she needed to relieve herself she must do so now behind the nearest bush. Arabella blushed to the roots of her pale gold hair, for no man had ever spoken to her of such a private function; but she grimly followed his instructions, for she knew that this was no time for outraged modesty. If he said that she would not get another chance, then she believed him. She was both hungry and thirsty. Because of the early hour of the wedding with its mass, she had not yet broken her fast. She had seen some of the clansmen chewing on oat cakes they had drawn from their pouches, and drinking from flasks as they rode along, but no one had offered her either food or drink.

As if he were reading her mind, the earl said in a kindly tone, "We will soon be at Dunmor, lassie, and I'll wager there's a joint already on the spit roasting for supper. Are ye hungry?"

"I'd sooner starve than eat a morsel of your food!" Arabella lied hotly.

"I doubt ye'll eat much in any case, for that yer a wee bit of a wench," the earl noted, ignoring her obvious anger. "We'll have to see if we can fatten ye up, lassie."

"Are you so thick-headed, my lord, that you do not understand me? I will starve myself before I accept your hospitality!" Arabella hissed furiously at him.

"If ye starve yerself, lassie, ye'll not have the strength to fight wi me, *or* to revenge yerself on Sir Jasper," he said calmly.

"Why on earth would I want to revenge myself on Sir Jasper?" Arabella said sweetly, the lie almost choking her. "I love him, and he will kill you when he comes to rescue me. On reflection, perhaps you are right. I should accept your hospitality so I am alive and well to see the horrible death you will die at Sir Jasper's hands!"

Tavis Stewart found it impossible to restrain his laughter, and it burst forth, echoing across the hillsides, much to his captive's outrage. Turning, she glared up at him as he wheezed with mirth. "Lassie, yer Sir Jasper has nae the courage to come after ye, nor has he the skill to win in a fair fight wi me, for I am a better swordsman than most. Why do ye think he refused my challenge this day? I expect ye'll be my guest for some time."

"Then why did you kidnap me, my lord?" she demanded.

"Yer Sir Jasper gave me no other choice, lassie, but dinna fear. I expect yer pretty mother will appeal to yer king, who will appeal to my king, and all will be well in the end for ye. I will have to catch yer Sir Jasper another way, but if ye marry him ye'll be a widow sooner than ye'll be a mother, I promise ye."

"Sir Jasper will come for me," Arabella said with more conviction than she actually had. "He must, for he cannot have Greyfaire without me." She did not bother to tell the earl of her decision to unmask Jasper Keane and his perfidy to King Richard. Another husband would be found for her to help defend Greyfaire, but this time she would insist the king allow her to choose. She was tired of having her entire life ruled by men. It might suit her mother, but it did not suit her!

"So he canna have yer inheritance wi out ye, eh lassie?" the earl said thoughtfully. "Perhaps his greed will overcome his good sense and he will come after ye. Who made the match between ye? Yer mother?"

"No," Arabella said proudly. "The king himself. The late queen was my mother's cousin. Mama was fostered by the Earl of Warwick, and Queen Anne was like her sister."

"Yer king did well by Sir Jasper, lassie. He will want to keep yer Greyfaire, for he has no other home now."

"You are mistaken, my lord," Arabella said. "Sir Jasper is the master of Northby Hall, though it is currently in ruins."

"I know," the earl told her, "but it was a poor place scarcely worth the burning."

"*You burnt Sir Jasper's home?*" She was secretly glad.

"Aye," the earl replied. "In retribution for Culcairn House. 'Twas fair."

Arabella was silent, but she agreed with him. She had been as shocked as any by the earl's tale of rapine and violence. She realized that Tavis Stewart would not have come over the border after Jasper Keane had he not been certain. He had witnesses in the surviving Hamilton family. She had quickly ascertained by his manner, his horse, the handsome chieftain's ring upon his finger, and the deference with which his men treated him, that the Earl of Dunmor was a great nobleman. Why would a man of his stature want to pick a fight with Sir Jasper unless it was justified? He would not.

"Ahhh, lassie, look! There is Dunmor," the earl said, pointing ahead to where a small castle sprang from a distant hillside. "Ye'll be sore with the long, hard ride we've had this day."

"Savage," she snarled at him, "have you no delicacy at all?" She struggled about on her precarious perch to slap him, and he laughed again, skillfully managing his dancing stallion, all the while avoiding her blows.

"What a little spitfire ye are, lassie," he said, and chuckled, not in the least offended. "There must be some Scot in ye, I'm thinking. Grey is a Scot's name as well as an English one, and the border Greys are a sept of the Stewarts, ye know. Perhaps we are related, lassie."

"I'd sooner be related to a donkey than to you, my lord!" she replied spiritedly.

He chuckled again. "I wonder if Jasper Keane knew just what it was he was getting in you," Tavis Stewart remarked. "It will take more of a man than he is to handle ye, lassie. Yer more woman, I'm thinking, than he could have ever managed."

"*Handled? Managed?* My lord, you make a woman sound like a disobedient animal to be properly trained. A good wife is a man's helpmate, though she be but the weaker vessel. She is not a possession to be handled and managed!" Arabella retorted angrily.

"Indeed, madame?" he gently mocked her. "Where did a little English lass get such bold ideas? Certainly not from yer gentle mother, who looks as if she would fear her own shadow.

These ideas are more suited to a Scotswoman than a weak bit of a lassie from the other side of the border,'' he teased.

"You great buffoon of a Scot!'' she fumed. "What could you possibly know of the English that was truth?''

Before the earl might reply, however, the young man who had earlier cautioned the earl within the church rode up next to them. "Tavis, why not let us take the lass on to Mother at Glen Ailean?'' he said. "She'll hae companions in Ailis and the two Hamilton lasses to help her while away the hours until her release.''

"Nay, Colin,'' the earl said. "Dunmor is impregnable to attack, and I would have the lassie where I know she is safe. Arabella Grey, this is my half brother, Father Colin Fleming. If ye fear for the lass's virtue, Colin, I will put her in yer charge. No one can then say that I mistreated her, for ye will guard her vigilantly. The English will nae disbelieve a priest, for the church wipes away all nationalistic boundaries, does it not, little brother?''

"You are a priest?'' Arabella said, surprised, looking at the young man in his plaid. There was nothing to distinguish him from any of the other borderers.

"I am, my lady,'' was the quiet reply.

"And you are *his* brother?''

"Aye.'' Colin Fleming grinned lopsidedly at the tone of her voice.

"Then why do you wear different plaids?'' Arabella asked pointedly.

"Because I am a Fleming, my lady Arabella, while my eldest brother is a Stewart.''

"Eldest brother? There are more of you?''

The young priest chuckled, a warm sound filled with genuine humor. "I am the youngest. The others are Gavin and Donald Fleming, and we have a little sister near to your age as well.''

"You are the children of your mother's second marriage?'' If she was going to be forced to remain in Scotland for any length of time, and it appeared that she was, Arabella thought it would be best to sort out the family relationships at the start.

"We are the children of our mother's *only* marriage, my lady,'' Colin Fleming said, his eyes twinkling with mischief. "Tavis's father was King James II, our mother's distant cousin. The Stewarts are a close and loving family, as those of us who are not Stewarts well know.''

''You're a bastard?'' It was out before she could stop herself.

The earl, however, laughed. *''A royal bastard*, lass, which makes all the difference in the world here in Scotland. The Stewarts, a loving clan, as Colin points out, are gracious wi their favors. When my mother's only brother died wi out legitimate heirs of his own, my father made me my maternal grandfather's heir, which is how I came into my earldom.''

''Then you are King James III's half brother,'' Arabella said, astounded.

''Aye, though Jemmie be my elder by some six years; and in answer to that unspoken question I see quivering on yer lips, my half brother and I are on the most cordial of terms. I barely remember my father, however, as he managed to get himself killed before my third birthday,'' the earl told her, and again there was a hint of laughter in his voice. ''Jemmie's mother, Queen Mary, was a kind and devout lady who never held my birth against me, and who was always a friend to my own mother, who, though she loved the king, was somewhat embarrassed to find herself enceinte with his child. She had the good sense not to flaunt herself at court, but rather asked the queen's pardon, and thereby gained her undying friendship.''

Seeing her shock, Colin Fleming spoke up in an attempt to turn the subject away. Lady Arabella Grey had obviously lived a most sheltered life. ''Ye'll be quite safe and comfortable at Dunmor, my lady,'' he told her. '' 'Tis a fine castle, and our mother lives nearby.''

''She dinna need cosseting, little brother,'' the earl said, chuckling. ''She's a wee spitfire, our little English captive, are ye not, lassie?''

''Go to hell, my lord,'' Arabella snapped angrily. She was tired, sore, and hungry. ''I despise you for what you have done to me this day!''

''Lassie, I've done little to ye but save ye from a bad marriage,'' Tavis Stewart replied. ''Ye owe me yer thanks, nae yer anger.''

''You expect gratitude from me? You are daft, my lord!'' Arabella said angrily.

Tavis Stewart said nothing further on the matter. The girl was young and inexperienced. She obviously had no knowledge of the vicious beast Sir Jasper Keane really was. Some day she would realize that she had been fortunate to escape him, but for now the earl knew he was wise to place her in his priestly brother's charge. Arabella Grey would remain his honored captive until Sir Jasper either accepted his challenge or Jemmie Stewart ordered her returned to her family for an appropriate remuneration to be paid both to himself and to the Hamiltons in the matter of Mistress Eufemia Hamilton's death. There would be time enough to kill the Englishman, for he was unlikely to change his ways, and would eventually find himself another border mistress. When he did, the Earl of Dunmor would know, and he would trap the English fox that he might send him to eternal damnation.

Arabella had let her gaze wander to Dunmor Castle. It was not as big a castle as Middleham and other large fortresses she had seen when she and her mother had gone south almost two years ago. It was certainly larger than Greyfaire, and from the weathered darkening of its stone, which was covered with gray-green lichen, it was surely as old as Greyfaire. It was a squared building with four towers, one at each corner of the structure. Upon the crenellated tops of the walls she could see men-at-arms, alert to any danger, pacing. As they began their climb up the hill upon which Dunmor was perched, Arabella saw that there was also a water moat about the castle.

"Where does the water for the moat come from, Father Colin?" she asked the kilt-clad priest.

"There is an underground spring within the castle courtyard, which is why Dunmor has always been so impregnable to attack, my lady. Tavis's maternal ancestor cleverly diverted that spring into two streams. One provides freshwater for the castle's inhabitants, and the other keeps the moat well filled. Since the mouths of both channels are within the castle, neither can be dammed by an enemy."

The drawbridge to Dunmore lay open to the visitors, for the earl was recognized and expected. They clattered across it into the castle courtyard. There were many open-mouthed stares directed toward the girl with the beautiful, flowing mane of pale gold gossamer hair who sat so regally in her silver gown before the earl upon his saddle. Arabella held her head high and refused to lower her glance. Let them all see how a brave Englishwoman behaved before her captors.

Drawing his great stallion to a halt before a wide swath of stairs leading up into his home, the earl slid to the ground. He reached up to help Arabella dismount, but the girl pushed his hand away, protesting,

"I am quite capable of dismounting a horse myself, my lord," but then to her intense mortification as her feet hit the ground, her legs collapsed beneath her.

"Dinna be such a proud little fool, lassie," he admonished her as he scooped her up and carried her up the steps into the castle. "Yer legs are tired from the long ride." He carried the irate girl into the Great Hall of Dunmor and deposited her as gently as he might into a high-backed chair by the fire. Then, looking down at her, he took her chin in his hand and tipped it up so he might see her face. "This is my house, Arabella Grey, and I will nae be shamed wi in it by anyone, least of all a wee slip of a girl. Yer my captive, but I will treat ye wi kindness and honor as long as ye merit it. Try my patience, however, and I will lock ye in the north tower and toss the key down my well."

"Nicely done, Tavis," came an amused voice as it moved nearer to them. "If I were this young lady, I think I should be tempted to find something sharp and stick it in ye." The voice gained a face and form as an elegantly dressed woman moved gracefully across the hall and joined them. "Where have you been, my son? Did you forget that today is Ailis's birthday and the family has come to Dunmor to celebrate?"

"Mother!" Tavis Stewart kissed the lovely lady and then apologized. "I did forget. There was an opportunity to settle this matter with Sir Jasper Keane, the man who murdered Eufemia, and I simply took it." He went on to explain to his mother.

Arabella tried to be discreet in her examination of the earl's mother, but she was frankly curious about this woman who had loved, and been beloved of a king. Margery Stewart Fleming was almost six feet in height. She had dark red hair and her eyes were dark green, like her son's. Her features were strong for a woman, and Arabella would have called her more handsome than beautiful. Her voice was deep, but mellifluous. She had beautiful hands, which she used to punctuate her speech, and her fair white skin made even more dramatic her coloring.

Behind Lady Fleming clustered three young girls, one who looked so very much like her that it could only be her daughter.

As for the other two, the elder had lovely chestnut-brown hair
and large blue eyes, and the younger was a brown blond with
the same blue eyes. Sisters, perhaps, Arabella considered. She
blushed when she saw that she was under as intense scrutiny
from the girls as they were by her.

Lady Fleming turned her gaze to Arabella, and she immediately arose and curtsied to her elder.

The older woman smiled, well-pleased. "What pretty manners you have, my child," she said, then slapping her big son
on the arm, she demanded, "Introduce us properly, Tavis!"

"Mother," the earl replied, "may I introduce to you Lady
Arabella Grey." He directed his speech next to Arabella. "Lassie, this is my mother, Lady Margery Fleming."

"You poor child," Lady Fleming said almost immediately.
"You must be chilled to the bone coming across the hills on
such a damp and cold day wi out not even a cloak. Ye'll come
wi me, and I'll see ye hae a nice hot tub. Then we'll see if we
can find ye something more comfortable to wear, and we'll do
what we can to salvage yer beautiful gown. Are ye hungry,
child?"

"Aye, madame," Arabella said, "and thirsty too. The wedding was to be early, and I had not yet broken my fast because
there was to be a mass."

"Ye hae nae eaten or drunk this day?" Lady Fleming looked
astounded. "Tavis! Yer a brute to treat this poor little thing so
badly. Did I raise ye, then, to think so poorly of women and
their needs?"

"Peace, Mother!" the earl said. "When I went over the border this morning I did nae think I should be returning wi a
captive."

His mother continued to look somewhat askance at him.
"Continue wi yer introductions, then, my son," she replied.

"Lady Grey, my sister, Ailis Fleming."

Ailis Fleming curtsied to Arabella, who said, "Felicitations
on your birthday, Mistress Fleming."

"Lady Grey, Mistress Margaret Hamilton, and her sister,
Mary."

The Hamilton sisters curtsied to Arabella, who returned their
greeting in kind.

"I'm a wee bit taller than ye, Lady Grey," Meg Hamilton

said, "but I think we might alter some of my gowns to fit ye, though none would be as beautiful as the gown yer wearing."

Arabella smiled shyly. " 'Tis the finest dress I have ever owned," she admitted. " 'Tis my wedding gown."

"Aye, Meg," the earl said wickedly. "Lady Arabella was to have wed this day wi yer sister's murderer. She has had a most fortunate escape, although she canna seem to see it that way, can ye, lassie?"

"You really are a bastard, my lord," Arabella said furiously.

There was an awkward silence, and finally the earl said, "Will no one say anything?"

"What do you expect them to say?" snapped Arabella. "You have just introduced me to the Mistress Hamiltons as the bride-to-be of a man who must surely be their bitterest enemy. Do you assume that Mistress Margaret and Mistress Mary can so easily overlook that? Whatever she may have done, Mistress Eufemia was their elder sister and they loved her. Once again you display to me a lack of delicacy of feelings, my lord earl."

Lady Fleming almost laughed, but she restrained herself with much difficulty. This petite young girl's attack upon her son was most refreshing. Women were usually apt to make fools of themselves over Tavis. His title, his royal relations, and his handsome face seemed to be irresistible until now.

"Oh, please, Lady Grey," Meg Hamilton said earnestly, "do not think that we would hold you accountable for anything that Sir Jasper Keane did. I know I speak for my whole family when I tell ye that we dinna. Indeed we are most astounded by yer appearance in our midst, but ye must believe the earl when he tells ye that ye have had a most narrow escape. Sir Jasper is nae a kind or a good man."

"Where do ye intend housing this child, Tavis?" demanded his mother.

"In the west tower, mother. There is but one entrance and exit to the west tower apartments. Lady Grey is not, I suspect, above attempting to escape my custody, are ye lass?" He said with a grin.

"Are you asking for my parole, my lord?" Arabella said sweetly. "Well, I'll not give it you! Offered the opportunity, I will escape you!"

"I know," he replied quietly, "and so ye'll be guarded at all times, lassie. If ye behave yerself, however, ye may have the freedom of the hall, the chapel and my gardens. Misbehave, and ye'll find yerself confined most strictly."

She glowered at him. "I understand, my lord," was her icy answer.

"This child must have someone to look after her, Tavis," Lady Fleming said.

"I know, Mother." He turned and called to a motherly-looking woman across the hall. "Flora, to me!"

The woman, obviously an upper-servant, hurried over to the earl. "My lord?" she said, curtsying.

"This is Lady Grey, Flora. She is both my prisoner and my honored guest. She is to be lodged in the west tower, and I would hae ye look after her wi kindness. She is never to be left alone, and Father Colin is responsible for her. Ye will go to him, unless, of course, the matter is a serious one."

"Aye, m'lord," Flora said, "and I'll take good care of the little lassie for ye, dinna fear. I'll go now and see that her rooms are prepared and a fire lit, for the day has been cold for June and the night will be as well. The west tower can be damp in weather like this." She curtsied again and hurried off.

Arabella was well warmed now, and she allowed the earl to lead her to the highboard, as the dinner hour was upon them. He seated her on his left, his mother on his right. Sitting next to Margery Fleming was her husband Ian, a large, bluff man who kissed Arabella's hand as he introduced himself. They were joined by the earl's sister, Ailis, Meg and Mary Hamilton, the earl's three half brothers, and a handsome young man who was introduced as Robert Hamilton, the laird of Culcairn. Below the highboard, tables were brought, and placed along with benches, which were quickly filled with the earl's retainers and servants. Other servants began entering the hall with steaming platters, bowls, and plates filled with hot food.

Arabella was ravenous. Forgetting her threat to starve herself, she heaped her silver plate high with salmon, lamb, several slices of sweet pink ham, a wedge of rabbit pie, a spoonful of small onions and carrots covered with a sherried cream sauce, some braised lettuce, and a bit of raw cress. All of this she liberally washed down with a large goblet of rich red wine, mopping the juices from her plate with a small trencher of bread which she daintily broke into little pieces.

About her the talk swirled, and though she half listened, she did not join in while she ate, giving all her attention to her food. She was determined to dislike Tavis Stewart for using her as a pawn in his game with Jasper Keane; yet those about her, his family and servants alike, treated the earl with a mixture of respect and fondness. Perhaps he was not as bad as Jasper, but he had used her. Still, Jasper Keane had used her as well. Used her to gain a foothold at Greyfaire, which she realized now was his only interest in her. His own home—a poor place, the earl had said—was destroyed. He needed Arabella Grey for but one thing: Greyfaire Keep. And the king had used her as well. He had used her, and he had used her inheritance to bind Sir Jasper Keane to him in loyalty. Arabella considered that perhaps cousin Richard had not known Jasper Keane at all, for he was, Arabella now suspected, loyal only to himself. Arabella spooned up the last bit of a sweet tartlet with its blanket of heavy cream.

"I think we may be of an age, Lady Grey," said Meg Hamilton, leaning over to speak to her. "I am almost fourteen."

"As am I," Arabella replied. "Will you call me Arabella, and may I call you Meg?"

"Aye!" Meg replied, and when she smiled, Arabella could see tiny golden flecks in her eyes, which were more gray than blue and fringed in short, thick sandy-colored lashes. "I realize 'tis a difficult situation in which we both find ourselves, but can we nae be friends? After all, neither ye nor I are responsible for the difficulties that surround us."

Arabella nodded. "Men," she said irritably. "They cannot seem to live in peace. I would like to be friends with you, Meg. I have a friend at Greyfaire. Her name is Lona, and she is FitzWalter's daughter. FitzWalter," she explained, "is the keep's captain." Then, "Did Sir Jasper really burn your house to the ground? It was a beastly thing to do!"

Meg nodded. "Rob brought us all—Mary, the baby, Geordie, old Una, and me—to safety. We saw everything . . ." Her voice trailed off even as Arabella remembered what the earl had said about Eufemia Hamilton's death.

"Ohh, I am sorry, Meg! I have been thoughtless." Arabella's voice was genuinely regretful. "Forgive me. It is just that I am so surprised to have discovered that Sir Jasper is such a villain," and as she spoke, Arabella remembered the day that Jasper Keane had beaten her. Why had she not known then?

"You did not really know him," Meg said quietly.

"Nay, not really. The king chose Sir Jasper to be my husband because he knew Greyfaire must have a lord to defend it. He is very handsome, and I, to my shame, am very inexperienced in these matters."

"And I would certainly hope a lass of yer tender years would be inexperienced in the matters of men," Lady Fleming said. "Yer king, if he cared, should have known better, but I've heard nae good of King Richard."

"Oh no, madame!" Arabella cried. "King Richard is a good man, I vow it! I have known him my whole life, as has my mother, who was Queen Anne's cousin. I believe that Sir Jasper put on one face for the king and yet a different face for each person he met. 'Tis a most handsome face too," Arabella concluded.

" 'Tis always difficult to believe the worst of a handsome man," Lady Fleming noted sagely, and the gentlemen hearing her remark laughed.

"Are you betrothed?" Arabella asked Meg. She had decided that she liked this pretty Scots girl. They would pass the time most pleasantly until she could discover a means of escape. Who knew? Perhaps Meg Hamilton would help her.

"I am nae betrothed," and Meg lowered her voice, "but I am in love!"

"You are?" Arabella said. "How wonderful! Are you certain? I thought I was in love with Sir Jasper, but now that he has proven himself so cowardly, I realize I could have never really loved him. How do you know, Meg, if it is really love? Can you tell me who he is? Will your family approve? Will they make the match?"

Meg giggled. "So many questions!" she teased Arabella, smiling. *"He* is Gavin Fleming, the earl's half brother; and aye, my brother approves; and aye, Gavin loves me too. It is wonderful! Tell me, Arabella, did yer toes feel all curled up in yer shoes when Sir Jasper kissed ye? Mine do when Gavin kisses me. That's one way I know. I never felt that way before when the lads would steal a kiss. Wi Gavin I dream about my own home, and about the bairns we will have." She blushed. "I nae thought about having bairns before wi another lad. 'Tis love, I'm certain! Gavin will ask his father's permission to wed wi me when they return home to Glen Ailean in a few days. Lord Ian will agree, for there is nae impediment to our union. Rob has promised that he will add half of Eufemia's dowry to my dowry. The other half will go for Mary when she weds one day. I am a well-dowered lass and need nae be ashamed that I would be Gavin Fleming's wife. Gavin will one day inherit his father's house and lands, ye know."

"You are fortunate to be a laird's sister, Meg," Arabella said sadly. "No king is concerned with you or your property. You may follow your heart. I thought the king had sent me a fine man to be my husband, but now I realize he cared naught for my happiness. I am chattel to the king, and I am chattel to any man who will wed me." She made a small moue with her mouth. "I do not like being another person's possession."

"Nor should ye, child," said Lady Fleming. "I am going to gie ye a wee bit of advice given me when I was a girl. Depend on no one but yerself in this life and ye'll be happier. Trust only yer own instincts; that little voice we Celts call the 'voice within,' and ye'll nae go wrong. I have followed that advice for many years, and I have nae been disappointed."

Arabella considered Lady Fleming's words and then asked her, "Who gave you such good advice, madame?"

"Tavis's father," Lady Fleming replied. "He was called James of the Fiery Face, for he was born wi a great purplish splotch on his face. He was a good man, but he was a soldier wi little liking for his own court. His father was murdered when he was six, and he spent his childhood as a pawn between our constantly warring nobility. When he was ten his governor, the Earl of Douglas, died. Douglas's ambitious sons hoped to follow in their father's footsteps and have charge of the king. They were murdered before the boy king's eyes by other jealous nobles who wanted James's custody. It was not an easy childhood, and my James learned early that he could only depend on himself, for those who did not seek his custody for their own gain were repelled by his face, half of which was the color of an amethyst. He was as handsome as any Stewart but for that. His mother was an Englishwoman, Lady Joan Beaufort. The Scots and the English like to fight wi one another. Yet they have a history of being friends and lovers."

"I could never be your enemy, madame," Arabella said.

Margery Fleming smiled warmly at the girl and then turned back to her husband and eldest son, thinking that perhaps this young Englishwoman would be a good match for her Tavis.

There was no question of the girl marrying Sir Jasper Keane
now. Of course the girl had nothing but Greyfaire, and the English were not going to let the Scots have even a small keep on
their side of the border. Still, in the past Scots had held castles
on the English side of the Cheviot, and the English had held
Scots' strongholds. Why, Berwick had belonged to Scotland
until recently. Eufemia Hamilton was dead and gone, and Tavis
had shown no interest in finding another wife. It was unthinkable that Dunmor should be lost to the Stewarts just because her
stubborn eldest son could or would not settle down.

Arabella Grey was beautiful and obviously intelligent. She
was not overawed by either Tavis's face or rank. She was young
enough to learn and change. She was just the sort of girl that
the earl should have for a wife, Lady Fleming considered, for
she had not liked Eufemia Hamilton at all, and thought her son's
hasty choice a very poor one indeed. Fate had given him a way
out, and now once again fate was providing him with the perfect
solution to his problem of a wife, if he could but see it. Why
was it that men were so dense when it came to practical matters?

Arabella leaned over to once again talk with Meg Hamilton.
"The earl is the most arrogant man I have ever met!" she said
in an angry whisper.

"He's a Stewart on both sides," Meg said with a small smile.
"They're a proud family."

"How did it happen that the king became his father?" Arabella was frankly curious, in spite of her dislike of her captor,
and it was not a question she felt she should ask Lady Fleming.

Meg arose from her seat and beckoned to Arabella. "Let us
walk about the hall," she said, "and I will tell you."

Arabella also stood, and after the two girls had curtsied to
their host, they stepped down from the highboard and began
their stroll arm in arm.

"The previous Earl of Dunmor was Tavis's grandfather, Lady
Fleming's father," began Meg. "He was Kenneth Stewart,
called Kenneth Mor. Mor is the Celtic for large or big, and Lady
Margery's father was a big man who stood six feet, eight inches
tall. They say he was the tallest man in Scotland in his time.
Mor of Dunmor. He had a wife he loved dearly, and when she
died, he would take no other despite the fact he had but two
bairns; a son, Fergus, and a daughter, Margery. Fergus was
killed at the battle of Arkinholm. Old Kenneth Mor had been

very sick and could not answer the king's summons, and so his son had gone. He died defending King James II from an enemy's blow; a blow he took himself when he threw himself in front of the king, who had been momentarily disarmed, in order to protect him. By the time the king rearmed himself, Fergus Stewart was mortally wounded. King James II killed his slayer.

"After the battle had been finally won, the king himself came to Dunmor Castle, bringing with him the fallen hero's body that it might be buried among its own. He praised Fergus's bravery to the skies, but after that old Kenneth Mor was a broken man. It was here that the king saw Lady Margery for the first time. She was fifteen, and they fell in love. After that, whenever the king was in the borders, he visited Margery Stewart, and soon it was known that she was his mistress. When Tavis was born of their union, the king decreed that he would be his grandfather's heir, as there were no other near male relations.

"The king then permitted Kenneth Mor to arrange a match between Lady Margery and the laird of Glen Ailean, Lord Ian Fleming, who had been her childhood sweetheart. The old earl was dying, and the king knew he could not give his time to protecting the rights of his infant son. Ian Fleming, however, would. He was honored to be entrusted with the raising of the king's son. It had always been thought that Lord Fleming would one day wed Margery Stewart, and it is said that she swore to him of her own free will on the day she agreed to wed with him that she would never again enter the king's bed. She then affixed the date of their wedding vows for six months hence so that none could say that any child she bore her husband within the first year of the marriage was not Ian Fleming's get.

"Ten months after her wedding, Gavin was born, his parentage undisputed and blemish-free, for Lady Margery had kept to Dunmor Castle during her betrothal period, and King James II had not once come to visit her. He did come, however, to congratulate the proud parents upon my Gavin's birth. It was the last time they ever saw him, for he was killed at the siege of Roxburgh several months later when a cannon, whose firing he was supervising, exploded from an excess of gunpowder and killed him. In the next few years Lord and Lady Fleming added to their family. Donald came next, and then Colin, and finally Ailis, who is fifteen today."

"I like Lady Margery," Arabella said. "She is so kind."

"She can be fierce too, Arabella," Meg replied. "The men in her family all adore her and defer to her wisdom in most things. She can be most formidable."

"My lady?" Flora was at her side.

"Aye?" Arabella responded.

"The earl thinks perhaps ye might wish to seek yer bed now. He believes ye must be tired after all the excitement this day had held for ye."

Arabella's first instinct was to deny her exhaustion, but she quickly decided against such a childish action in the face of the reality that she was indeed very tired. Then Meg spoke up, saying that she too was ready for her bed, and yawned as if to punctuate the point. Arabella grinned at her new friend, knowing full well that Meg had only feigned sleepiness so that Arabella would not feel singled out. She walked back to the highboard, and reaching up, helped herself to a slightly wizened apple from the silver bowl upon the table. Then turning, she followed Flora and Meg.

"I'm glad to see the distress of losing a possible husband has nae spoilt yer appetite, lassie," the earl called mockingly after her.

Furious, Arabella whirled about and, with an unerring aim, threw the apple at the earl, hitting him mid-chest. The men in the hall burst into delighted guffaws of loud laughter, partly at her obvious outrage, partly at the earl's surprised expression.

"Ah, laddie, if that had been an arrow, we'd all be mourning ye now," his stepfather said with a chuckle.

"Sleep well, my lord," Arabella said in sugared tones, curt-sying, and then she turned on her heel and departed the hall.

"How did ye dare to do that?" Meg giggled. "Tavis can be so terrifying at times. I frankly admit to being a little afraid of him."

"He is an odious bully!" Arabella fumed. "If I had had a sword, I should have run him through!"

Ahead of them Flora smiled to herself. The little English lassie was strong-willed, and Flora did not believe for a moment that given the chance, the girl wouldn't do just what she threatened to do. They were not so unlike—the border Scots and the border English. Like Lady Fleming, she thought Arabella the earl's match. She wondered if he would see it. Flora was relieved to have Eufemia Hamilton in Dunmor's past, but she would not be unhappy if Arabella Grey was its future, even if she was English.

Outside the hall Meg left them for her own rooms, which were in another part of the castle. Arabella obediently followed the older woman as she hurried down a corridor and then began to climb a narrow flight of stone stairs at the end of the hallway. The steps twisted up and around. It was cold and dank within the tower. Flora moved so quickly that Arabella several times lost sight of the flickering torch she carried to light their way. Only by continuing to climb could she be certain of eventually reaching her own shelter atop the tower; and sure enough, as she moved around one more turn she saw Flora ahead of her, the torch already set in an iron holder attached to the wall, standing in the warm golden light of a doorway, beckoning to her.

" 'Tis a long climb the first time, m'lady," Flora said, ushering her charge into a small windowless room. A little fireplace blazed merrily, and next to it was a small wooden settle with a woven cushion. Beyond, through a second open door, was another room. Flora closed the door to the stairs firmly and said, "Ye'll be snug as a wee bug up here." She escorted Arabella into the next room. "I took the liberty of having a bath brought up for ye. I thought ye might feel the need of one. Let me help ye wi yer gown, m'lady," and without waiting for an answer, Flora began the task of assisting the girl.

Arabella looked about the little room, which was a bedchamber. Both the walls and the floor were of gray stone. A fireplace without a mantelpiece was set into a section of the outside wall, and upon the floor was a large, woolly sheepskin. There were only three pieces of furniture in the room. The bed with its heavy hangings was large and looked big enough for two. A small square table was set on one side of it, and at its foot was an iron-bound chest for storage. Without the small round oak tub before the blazing fireplace, which crowded it badly, the room would just be passable, but it was certainly not a spacious chamber.

There was but one narrow window, a casement, which to Arabella's relief was glassed. It was not an unpleasant place, but Arabella hoped she would not have to spend a great deal of time living in it. One thing she had already decided. There was no escape from this tower other than the door to the stairs. The single window was far too attenuated to allow passage of even her slender, small frame; and she suspected that the drop, now obscured by the night, was much too steep for safety's sake. Tavis Stewart had obviously meant it when he said that he would not allow her the chance to escape. Arabella smiled grimly. She might be but a woman, but she was clever nonetheless. Cleverer than any female he had ever met, she would wager.

"I will have to sleep in my chemise," Arabella said when she finally stood unclothed and ready for her bath.

"Nay, m'lady, I've a fresh one for ye," Flora told her. "I'll launder the other, and when I've brushed the dirt of the borders from yer beautiful gown, I'll store it all safely away. I've already raised the hem on one of Mistress Meg's chemises for ye, for she said I might. Using yer own gown for measure, we'll hae a new wardrobe for ye in a few days' time, one far more suitable than this delicate garment of fairy dust ye wore today."

Arabella was forced to laugh at the woman's words, for it was obvious that Flora was torn between admiration and disapproval of Arabella's wedding gown. "Thank you, Flora," she said. "You are most kind. Will you help me with my hair? I must pin it all up if I am to bathe, and it is difficult to manage by myself."

Flora was a plain, big-boned woman, perhaps six inches taller than her new mistress. Wisps of graying auburn hair were visible beneath her white linen wimple. Her eyes, however, were as lively and brown as a thrush's; they looked with frank admiration upon Arabella's long hair. "I've nae seen hair so beautiful, lassie," she said softly. Then wrapping the hair in two thick hanks about her hand, she carefully pinned it atop Arabella's head and helped the girl into her tub.

Arabella sat down in the warm water and a beatific smile lit her features. The soreness immediately began to ease in her posterior and her legs. She had not realized until this very minute how very much she ached, but now the warmth began to soothe her muscles. "Ohhh, Flora," she said with heart-felt gratitude in her voice, "thank you! I can but imagine the trouble you had to go to just to bring me this lovely water up to my little tower."

"Bosh, lassie, just a few stout lads wi buckets at me beck and call," Flora replied with a chuckle. "I've taken many a long ride along this border meself, and I know the toll a prancing horse can take. Now ye just rest in yer tub while I take yer gown downstairs to brush it. There's a towel warming on the stones by the fire, should ye want to get out afore I'm back. Yer clean chemise is upon the bed. I'll nae be long." Then she was gone.

Arabella closed her eyes and began to relax for the first time this day. The tub was pleasant and there was, she thought, just the faintest scent of heather in the air. Opening her eyes, she saw a tiny cake of hard soap on the stone floor next to the tub. Reaching out and picking it up, she sniffed at it. Aye! Heather. Her favorite fragrance. Dipping the soap in the water, she washed herself most thoroughly and rinsed the lather from her skin. Tiredness was beginning to seep into her bones again. Reaching out once more, she drew the towel to her, and standing up, she began to dry herself off, even as behind her she heard the door to the little apartment opening again.

"Flora, you run up and down those stairs like a young girl," Arabella said as she turned around, and then she shrieked loudly, clutching the scrap of towel to her as her light green eyes focused upon the earl. She was pink with embarrassment, the color made all the more vivid by her pale hair.

Tavis Stewart flushed himself and found himself momentarily at a loss for words. He had but come to see that his reluctant guest was as comfortable as she might be under the circumstances. It had never occurred to him that she might be bathing. His personal knowledge of women was limited to that of a son, a brother, and a lover. He had been practically grown when Ailis had been born, and living at Dunmor while his sister had been brought up in her own house at Glen Ailean. He had never kept a mistress at Dunmor, for this would be his wife's home one day, and he did not want it tainted by a lesser woman. He was, therefore, not particularly familiar with a woman's habits, and right now he was not quite certain where to look and where not to look.

The furious girl was simply lovely and appeared far more mature without her clothes than with them. Her legs were much longer than he might have thought for one so petite, for Arabella Grey certainly stood no higher than five feet three inches. Her breasts, however, were small; but they were also magnificent high cones of pale ivory flesh, each one topped with a bright berry of a nipple. Her narrow waist slid down into well-rounded hips and slender, but firm thighs. He couldn't stop looking.

"M-Madame, I beg your pardon," he finally managed to say,

trying desperately to tear his eyes away from this glorious sight, for the tiny towel did little to hide her splendor.

"Get out!" Arabella gasped, as surprised by his appearance as he was by hers.

"I but came to inquire if ye were comfortable," he attempted to explain his sudden arrival.

"Get out!" she shouted, and threw the cake of soap at him.

Ducking her accurate aim, the earl backed from the room, out through the antechamber, and closing the door behind him, retreated down the staircase. At its bottom he met Flora and began to berate her. "Did I nae tell ye the lass was nae to be left alone, and yet ye leave her in an unlocked room free to roam."

"The wee lassie was in her tub," Flora retorted spiritedly, "and wi out her clothes, my lord. Ye could hardly expect her to flee into the night wi out a stitch on her, and especially into unfamiliar territory. Dinna fuss at me now." She looked at him slyly. "She's a beautiful lass, or perhaps ye didna notice."

"I noticed," he said with a wry grin. "How could I nae notice? I got a cake of soap pitched at me for my troubles. 'Tis twice this night she's thrown something at me, and the wench's aim is unerring. She's got a temper on her bigger than she is, Flora. Ye had best beware."

"Ye should hae a wife like Lady Arabella, my lord," Flora said boldly. "A hot-spirited lass who will breed Dunmor up strong sons and daughters." Then she turned on her heel and hurried back up the stairs before the earl might scold her for her daring tongue.

Behind her Tavis Stewart laughed at her words. After Eufemia Hamilton, he wasn't certain he wanted a wife, at least not now. Women seemed to be more trouble than they were worth—his mother excluded, of course. Eventually he would wed for Dunmor, and no other reason. The earl returned to the Great Hall where his brothers and Rob Hamilton were drinking companionably about the fire. His mother, his stepfather, and the others had obviously gone off to bed. Taking up a newly filled goblet, he joined them and related his adventure, to their vast amusement.

"So she's a real beauty, is she, Tavis? What a pity she's a maid, or ye might take her for yerself, even as Sir Jasper took

Eufemia. Yer pardon, Rob," Gavin Fleming amended, nodding to the young laird of Culcairn. "Are ye certain she's a maid?"

"Aye, 'tis obvious no man's ever touched her, but having glimpsed what I just did of the lass's charms," the earl said, "I will admit to be tempted. She's lovely enough wi her clothes on, but wi out them, lads . . ." He sighed gustily, as one unjustly denied.

"Swallow yer lust, brother," Colin Fleming said sternly. "The lass is an honored hostage, and ye promised her poor mother that ye would return her daughter unscathed. Besides, she is nae to blame for the behavior of Sir Jasper Keane or Eufemia Hamilton. The poor little lassie hardly knows the bastard. I would remind ye, Tavis, that Arabella Grey is under the church's protection at yer own request. Ye'll nae touch her, at the peril of yer immortal soul."

"Gie over, Colin," Donald Fleming teased his youngest brother. "Tavis has simply decided he'd rather have the lass under him than under the church's protection. Who knows? She might be happier for it, eh?" And he made an obscene gesture with his finger, laughing.

"Why not?" Gavin Fleming joined the discussion, half drunk. "Did not the English coward besmirch our brother's good name and his honor? If Tavis wants the wench for his pleasure, I for one say let him have her, Colly! Who has a better right?"

"Nay," the young priest said firmly. "He does not! Arabella Grey is innocent of this matter. A pawn of her king and of Sir Jasper, and now of ye, Tavis. Eufemia hid her vices well, but had ye been of a mind to listen, my brother, ye would have heard the whispers, for they were there. Ye sought to avoid yer duty, Tavis, and because of that ye chose the simplest path, as ye always do when ye must do something ye dinna like to do. Ye looked about for the nearest, available, attractive woman of good family, and then wi out even getting to know her, ye made her an offer of marriage. Ye are living proof, my lord earl, that God looks after fools! Now ye will treat Lady Grey wi respect, and tomorrow ye will send a spy over the border to learn what nefarious plans Sir Jasper Keane may be planning in order to retrieve his intended, if indeed he intends retrieving her."

"Aye, Colin," the earl admitted, "yer right, but the little lass has certainly lit a fire in my loins that I will find hard to quench, but I'll do as ye say."

"And ye'll hae the comfort of knowing tonight as ye lay alone in yer bed, elder brother, that the church's blessing is upon ye," Gavin said drolly.

"Lust is nae love," the young priest said quietly.

"If yer cock had ever been as hard for a woman as yer pretty head is for God, little brother," teased Donald, "perhaps even I would pay some attention to ye, but a man who doesna eat oats can scarcely comment on the taste of the porridge."

"I was a man before I was a priest, Donald," came the amused reply. "Do ye nae remember all those lasses I managed to steal away from ye? I did nae gie up what ye hae lightly, and there are times, I freely admit to ye, when I still miss the lasses. Still, I could nae serve God wholly had I nae given up a wife and bairns. For me there is nae other way but the way I walk. Perhaps because I dinna use women as ye do, I see them in a different light. Mayhap ye should try to see them my way instead of simply creatures upon which ye slack yer carnal appetites."

Donald Fleming groaned dramatically. "I nae liked lessons when I was a wee lad, Colin, and I like them nae better now. I'll be yer spy, Tavis. I canna stay here watching ye thirst after that pretty piece of English flesh while this priest prays over ye both!"

" 'Tis past time, Donald," his younger brother admonished him, "that ye stopped thinking wi yer cock and used yer head instead."

The brothers laughed, and then the young laird said, "I hope that ye do not do all of this for Eufemia's sake, my lord. I loved my sister, but she was nae worthy of ye."

The earl grimaced. "Ye should hae told me that the day I came to sue for her hand, Rob, but I dinna blame ye. What I have done today is for my lost honor and not yer sister's, although I will, in the end, avenge her death. Eufemia had great charm when she chose to exhibit it, and I dinna doubt she wrapped ye about her little finger despite yer aching conscience. Ye were but a lad, alone and wi out an older head's guidance. Ye did yer best, and saving yer younger sisters and little brother was a feat worthy of any man."

By the time Arabella opened her eyes the following morning, Donald Fleming had long since departed Dunmor Castle and crossed the nearby border over into England. Reaching the vicinity of Greyfaire Keep he noticed that despite the fact the day was at least an hour past the sunrise, and that the morning was fair unlike the previous day, the people seemed slow to rise. His disguise as a peddler rendered him fairly safe, and finally spotting a farmwife drawing water from a well in her yard, he stopped.

"Good morrow to ye, madame," he said cheerfully. "Might I be troubling ye for a wee drink from yer well?"

"You're a Scot!" the woman accused, looking him up and down with a hostile air.

"Aye, but dinna hold it against me, m'dear," Donald said winningly. "Me da came from t'other side of the border, 'tis true, but me ma, God assoil her, was a good lass from York. I'm a peddler by trade, I am, and me mixed blood allows me the freedom to travel both sides of the border with impunity." Donald Fleming took a bundle off his horse, and opening it, spread the contents out upon the ground before the farmwife's eyes to show her an array of threads, laces, silk ribbons in all the colors of the rainbow, small metal cooking utensils, and carefully sealed packets of rare spices. "I'm carrying some fine cambric cotton and a few wee bolts of silk, very rare, if yer of a mind, m'dear, but perhaps while yer thinking about it, ye'll choose a packet of spice for yer kindness in allowing me and me poor beastie to water ourselves." He smiled broadly; a trustworthy smile that reached all the way to his blue eyes.

The farmwife looked him over again, but the suspicion was gone from her eyes, to be replaced by a frank admiration for Donald Fleming, who was, with his big frame and auburn hair, as handsome a man as she had ever seen. His good looks, coupled with his easy manner, which just bordered on flirting, immediately lulled the farmwife into a sense of security.

"Well," she said, offering the bucket to the horse and looking up at Donald coyly, "perhaps a little bit of saffron, if you have any to spare."

"Only for ye, madame," Donald replied, respectful, but willing to lead the good woman on in order to obtain the information he needed. " 'Tis late," he noted, handing her a paper packet of the chosen spice, "and yet yer the first person I've seen up and about this morning."

"Aye," she answered disapprovingly as she pocketed her gift, "the men are probably all still drunk after yesterday." She offered Donald a dipperful of cool water, which he accepted gratefully, for he was really thirsty. "We had a fierce mite of excitement yesterday, and 'tis for certain. The young mistress of Greyfaire Keep, a dear little lass, was to have been wed in the morning. She's related to our King Richard, you know, and 'twas he who chose her husband. There's been no man at the keep these last few years since Lord Henry was killed, and the king wanted a man there to defend it, though if you ask me, FitzWalter, the captain, was capable enough. Well! Didn't those thieving Scots take the very moment our Lady Arabella stepped into the church to be wed to come raiding! Ach! Such a sweet lassie, our little mistress! Tiny like a fairy's child, with long hair just like thistledown, the very color of a golden summer's moon and hanging to her little feet. Stole her away, they did, those Scots! Took her right from the church and rode away with her!" The farmwife wiped her eyes with her apron.

"To hold for ransom, no doubt," Donald said soothingly. "Her bridegroom will get her back when he pays. 'Tis an old trick, m'dear, stealing the bride. 'Tis nae the first time 'tis happened. When yer new lord opens his purse and pays, the lassie will be back quick as a wink, I'm thinking."

"*Our new lord!* Humph!" the farmwife sniffed. She obviously viewed the gentleman in question with great disfavor. "A proper villain he turned out to be, though my husband says I must hold my tongue now, for he's the new master of Greyfaire, and there's none who will deny him, even FitzWalter, but Father Anselm was shocked right enough, as were the rest of us!"

"Shocked? Over what, m'dear, and who is yer new master?" Donald asked gently.

"Sir Jasper Keane is his name, my lad, and the Scots had no sooner ridden off with our little mistress than this Sir Jasper turned about and forced poor Lady Rowena to the altar, claiming he could not now wed with Lady Arabella, for even if they got her back, she'd be thoroughly dishonored by the Scots! Ohhh, he's a wicked one!"

"Who is Lady Rowena?" Donald inquired softly, fascinated by this new turn of events.

"Why, she's Lady Arabella's mother. 'Tis a scandal, it is, whatever my husband says!" the farmwife cried indignantly, her two-and-a-half chins quivering with her outrage. " 'Tis said poor Lady Rowena wept all through the wedding ceremony, so distraught was she."

Donald pretended to be puzzled, and the truth was that he was puzzled. He needed further answers to unspoken questions he now voiced to the farmwife. "How could Sir Jasper wed with this other lady if he was betrothed to yer Lady Arabella? How could yer priest dare to marry to them? The marriage would be invalid under such circumstances as a prior commitment. Why, 'twas a similiar situation that brought King Richard to the throne instead of his nephews."

"Sir Jasper was not betrothed to Lady Arabella," the farmwife said knowledgeably. "The king sent him to be her husband, but the choice was to be hers, for our dead queen loved the girl and did not want her unhappy should she dislike Sir Jasper. He seemed such a fine gentleman," the farmwife sobbed, wiping her eyes with her apron, "but now I do not know what will happen to our little mistress."

"Ach," Donald sympathized, " 'tis a terrible tale. This Sir Jasper of yers would nae appear to be such a fine gentleman as he pretended. Poor lassie. Well, I must be on me way," and he began packing up his goods.

"I'll take a bit of black thread," the farmwife said, now that she had unburdened herself and had a good gossip, "and perhaps a scarlet ribbon for my youngest daughter, who is to be wed come Michaelmas, and I could use a knife for my kitchen, if you've one with a good strong handle."

Donald dutifully extracted the required items, haggling spiritedly with the farmwife over the price, finally accepting the copper coin, the small cheese, and a newly baked cottage loaf she offered in exchange. Replacing the pack upon his horse, he mounted the animal, and with a broad smile, thanked his hostess again for the water.

"Why don't you go up the hill to the keep," she suggested to him helpfully. "The new lord may be in a benevolent mood after his wedding night and might buy some of that silk of yours for Lady Rowena."

"Perhaps I will, and thank ye for the thought," Donald answered her, and set his horse in the proper direction. Once out of sight, however, he turned back and circled around, heading for the border. He had considered going to Greyfaire, but then he remembered that he had been in the forefront of his brother's attack on the church yesterday. He might be recognized by Sir Jasper or one of his retainers. His features were not disguised, and he had nothing with him with which to alter them suitably. Besides, he had more than enough information for his brother. The English fox had outflanked his Scots pursuer once again, and Tavis Stewart was not going to be pleased.

Chapter 5

Y e've been neatly checkmated, Tavis,'' said Donald Fleming to his eldest brother as he finished the story of his
morning's adventure. It was early evening, and in the Great Hall
of Dunmor Castle the sun sent bright rays of clear light across
the stone floor. "Sir Jasper Keane has got Greyfaire Keep in his
clutches, and the girl is useless to ye now."

Seated next to the earl, Arabella's pale skin grew even paler
with her shock. "It is not true!" she whispered hoarsely. "You
are lying to me! Jasper could not have wed my mother. 'Tis
absurd!"

"Donald would nae lie to ye, lassie," Colin Fleming said
gently. "He's a roughneck and bit of a braggart, but he's nae a
liar." The young priest wished with all his heart that his mother
had not returned to Glen Ailean this afternoon, but she had,
taking his sister Ailis and Mary Hamilton with her. Tavis would
not release Arabella Grey into her custody, for the house at Glen
Ailean could not be defended as easily as Dunmor. The earl
feared that Sir Jasper would learn of Arabella's whereabouts,
thereby endangering the Flemings. At least he had allowed Meg
to remain for Arabella's company, but still, Colin thought, he
would send to his mother for advice.

"I thought he loved me," Arabella said, puzzled, "at least a
little. I thought I loved him, until he proved to be a coward.
Greyfaire is mine, not my mother's. He cannot have Greyfaire
by simply marrying my mother. The king will not allow it! Ohh,
poor Mama!" Her eyes filled with tears, but whether they were
for her own loss or her mother's plight, Arabella knew not.

"Yer king wanted Greyfaire in a man's hands," the priest said
with calm logic. "He has many difficulties at this time. If Sir
Jasper tells him that ye were stolen by the Scots and killed, that
he wed yer mother to protect the king's border, yer king will
believe it. He has nae time right now to check the veracity of
Sir Jasper's words. Yer king will gie Greyfaire to Sir Jasper

111

Keane under the circumstances, and there is naught ye can do, lassie."

"What will become of me?" Arabella demanded, her voice rising in intensity. "Without Greyfaire I have nothing. *I am nothing!* 'Tis my dowry, and all the lands and goods that belong to it are a part of me as well. If Sir Jasper has stolen all that away from me, what will happen to me?" Then suddenly her green eyes flashed furiously and she rounded on the earl. "This is all your doing, you bastard Scot! You have ruined my life with your damned bravado and your prattle about honor! *What of my honor!* I am sick unto death of my fate being planned by others!" And grabbing up the earl's dirk which lay upon the table, for he had been cutting cheese with it, Arabella attacked him.

"Jesu! Mary!" the earl exploded as he felt the knife slamming into his shoulder, slipping easily through the silk of his shirt and into the thick muscle beneath the fabric. Instinct brought him to his feet, and grabbing her by her wrist, he cruelly twisted the blade from her hand. "Wench," he roared, "that is the second time in two days that ye hae attacked me meaning to do bodily harm! I'll nae have it, d'ye hear me?" His other hand staunched the flow of blood from his shoulder even as he released her wrist.

Arabella rubbed her injured wrist for a moment, certain the earl had broken it. Then stepping back a pace, she slapped Tavis Stewart with all her might. "If you did not wish my enmity, my lord, then you should not have stolen me away."

The earl rocked back on his heels with her blow, astounded that someone so little had such strength. "I should hae let ye wed wi yer coward, for ye surely would hae killed him a lot sooner than I'll hae the chance, lassie," he said wryly, closing his eyes a moment as the hall began to revolve.

"Sit down, Tavis," Colin advised, pushing his elder brother back into his chair. "The knife touched nothing vital, but yer going to be weak wi loss of yer fine, blue blood."

Grinning at his younger brother's words, Donald pressed a goblet of red wine into the earl's hand, while Gavin began to clean and bind the wound with cloths brought him by the frightened servants.

Meg Hamilton drew Arabella back into her seat and gave her hand a reassuring squeeze. She thought the English girl terribly brave.

"Well, now," the earl said insultingly, "what the hell am I

going to do with this spitfire, since she's no longer of value to me, or to anyone else for that matter?''

"Yer going to wed wi her, brother," Colin Fleming said quietly.

"Never!" Both the earl and Arabella spoke in unison.

The young priest ignored them. "Ye need a wife, Tavis, and once she's yers, ye can claim her inheritance, or at least remuneration from the English king for Greyfaire Keep. 'Twill gie Sir Jasper a bad turn, I've nae a doubt. No one yet knows of Sir Jasper and Lady Rowena's marriage outside of Greyfaire. There hasn't been time to get word to the king. 'Twill seem a great insult that ye stole the coward's bride from the very church itself where he demanded sanctuary, *and* then brought her back over the border to marry yerself. *And*, 'twill make it seem as if Sir Jasper wed wi the lassie's mother in a desperate attempt to steal the girl's wealth. He'll be a laughingstock, particularly if ye get our own king to back up yer demands for the girl's dowry wi the English king. Jemmie 'twould do it for ye.''

"Richard of England will nae gie the rights of an English border keep to a Scot," the earl said.

"But he might pay ye a forfeit for it. He canna disinherit the lass wi out cause, and none of this is her fault. He might hold Greyfaire in trust for yer eldest daughter, provided an English match were made for her while she was in the cradle. She could be sent to be fostered by her betrothed's family when she was six. There hae been many border matches made over the years. This solution has always been the one used to settle the disputes of ownership and guarantee fealty to the right king.''

"Are ye mad, Colin?" Donald Fleming demanded. "The lass will kill him! She's already tried twice!''

They all spoke as if she weren't even in the room, and Arabella could feel her anger seething.

"I'd thought to ask Rob for Mistress Margaret's hand in marriage since she's of an age now," the earl remarked casually. "She's a gentle and biddable lass.''

"Not so biddable that she'll wed wi ye, Tavis Stewart," Meg said boldly, surprising even herself with her words. "Besides, I love another, and I'll wed wi no one but him, my lord!''

"What, lassie?" He found himself amused by this situation. "Ye'd hae another to me? Who is this paragon that ye prefer to an earl?''

" 'Tis the earl's brother," Meg said boldly. "Gavin and I love each other, Tavis. Rob approves, and Gavin is to speak to his father as soon as he can."

The earl laughed, looking over to his red-faced brother, whose adoring look toward Meg Hamilton finished the tale. "I canna interfere wi the course of true love," he said, "and I would nae make an enemy of my brother. I wish ye both happy. 'Twill be a good match," he finished graciously.

"So would a match between ye and Arabella Grey," Colin persisted.

"I'll not wed him," Arabella said firmly. "I'd sooner take the veil!"

"The church will nae hae ye wi out a dowry, lassie," the earl replied dryly. "My priestly brother is correct, and as much as the prospect terrifies me, Arabella Grey, a marriage between us would seem the ideal solution. Only a noble husband can regain yer inheritance for ye."

"I can regain my own inheritance!" Arabella said angrily.

"I think not, lassie," the earl said quietly.

"There are others who would have me," she told him.

"Perhaps," Tavis Stewart agreed. "As long as they did not incur yer fierce temper, spitfire, they would be dazzled, for yer surely fair to look upon, Arabella Grey."

She flushed, confused. She did not know if he were giving her an honest compliment, remarking upon her general beauty, or if he was referring to his untimely entry into her little tower the previous evening.

"In order to find yerself a proper husband," he continued, "ye must return to England and plead yer case before yer king. Surely ye do not propose to travel alone? How will ye pay yer way along the road? Sir Jasper has wed wi yer mother to hae Greyfaire Keep. He believes he does hae it now. Yer return would threaten his position. I believe he would not hesitate to permanently remove such a threat. He's murdered one woman that we already know of, lassie. Do ye think the fact that ye are his wife's child would protect ye? He wants Greyfaire, and if he must, he'll kill ye to get it. Ye need a husband who is willing to defend not only yer person, but yer rights as well. What Englishman will defend ye against the king's chosen man, Arabella Grey?" he finished. He had seen her blush, and for a brief moment his heart had softened toward her, even as his shoulder

ached with the pain of her attack. Poor wee lass. She really had
no choice, and now neither had he.

"I'll not wed with ye, my lord, if I die for it, and there is no
way you can force me to your will," Arabella said icily. Then
she stood up and stalked from the hall.

Meg rose quickly to her feet, and with a curtsy to the gentlemen, hurried after her friend.

"She is angry, and rightly so," Colin Fleming said. "Let her
go, Tavis. Once she has slept on it, she will see the wisdom in
it. I'll waive the banns and marry you to her tomorrow."

"Yer mad, all of ye," Donald said. "The lass has twice tried
to kill ye, and yer going to force her to the altar? Yer stark raving
daft, Tavis Stewart!"

"I will try and reason wi her once again on the morrow," the
earl said. "She is a lass well-versed in her obligations, and she'll
wed me if for no other reason than to save her people from Sir
Jasper. I dislike admitting it, but none of this would hae happened had I not stolen her away in my anger against Sir Jasper
Keane; but when I saw that exquisite girl standing there in her
wedding finery, and realized that within hours that devil would
have her in his bed and at his mercy, I could nae leave her to
wed him. I owe Arabella Grey the protection of my name as
well as my sword."

"The whole fault lies wi my sister, Eufemia," Robert Hamilton said drunkenly. " 'Tis I who should wed Lady Grey. If
Eufemia had nae been the whore she was, none of this would
hae happened." He hiccuped twice, and then sliding slowly out
of his chair, he fell asleep beneath the table.

"Poor laddie," the earl said. "He still feels guilty over this
matter. Still, once he's back at Culcairn, he'll get his feet under
him again."

"When will the house be rebuilt?" Gavin Fleming said.

"The Hamiltons will return home by summer's end," the earl
told him.

"How old is Rob now?" Colin asked. "Culcairn is rich in
lands, and wi a fine new house he'll be a good catch. Has he
chosen a bride yet?"

The earl chuckled. Colin was more like their mother than any
of her other sons. "Rob is almost sixteen, and I believe Mother
is just waiting until he returns home to propose a match between
him and Ailis," he told Colin.

"Best we approach him sooner than that," the priest said wisely. "He's restless, I can see, and if we can make the match, they could be wed before year's end. There will be others who will appreciate Culcairn's fine acreage, Tavis, and if ye canna have a Hamilton to wife yerself, then 'tis best we gie Rob a Fleming to wed, and secure yer flank."

"And rid the laddie of his thoughts of Lady Arabella Grey," Gavin laughed.

"The lass would eat him alive," Donald Fleming said grimly.

"I'm tougher meat," the earl said quietly.

"Aye, and she's twice tried to carve ye up," was the quick reply. "The next time she could be successful."

"I think ye worry needlessly, Donald," the priest said.

"And I think yer solution is too pat, Colin. We hae no guarantee that Tavis will be able to regain Greyfaire or its worth in gold. The lass has no dowry."

"Nay, Donald, Colin is right," the earl told his middle brother. "I dinna need a dowry, should it come to that; but I do need a wife to replace the one Sir Jasper murdered. What better choice than the lass the Englishman was to have wed? If we put it out, the gossip will say I came raiding for the express purpose of stealing his bride to replace the one he stole from me. 'Twill seem a good revenge, and 'tis a good solution!"

"And what of the king?" Donald said. "Ye know ye need his permission to wed, as yer his half brother."

"James has already given me permission to wed," the earl replied.

"He gave ye permission to wed wi Mistress Hamilton, not some distant cousin of the English king," Donald said stubbornly.

"There is nae time for me to sue James for permission anew, Donald. When Sir Jasper learns, and he will, that Arabella is well and healthy, he may decide to solve his problem by sending an assassin after her. I can better protect her as my wife, and Jemmie will understand when I explain the situation to him. Jesu, Donald, do I need the lass's death on my conscience?"

"So it's settled? Ye'll wed the little English lass?" Donald said. "I canna change yer mind?"

"Nay, ye canna, and aye, I'll take the girl to wife in the morning." Tavis Stewart stood up. "And now, brothers, I'll bid ye a good night," he said, and departed his hall. Behind him the three remained at the highboard drinking and arguing the merits of the matter, unaware that the earl was at this very minute climbing the steps to the west tower.

"I would speak wi Arabella Grey," he told Flora, who answered his knock. "Wait below."

Flora curtsied, and closing the door behind her, hurried off down the stairs.

The earl walked into the little bedchamber and seated himself upon her bed. Wide-eyed, Arabella clutched the bedcovers to her chest.

"Get out!" she squeaked.

He took one of her hands in his, and smiling, said, " 'Tis a little bit of a hand, but it delivers a mighty blow, Arabella." Then he kissed her hand, and Arabella felt a tingle race up her spine. "Ye know ye must go willingly to the altar, lassie," Tavis Stewart said quietly. "Both yer honor and mine demand it. I dinna believe ye ever really loved Sir Jasper Keane, but he is lost to ye now. We find ourselves in a situation neither of us expected, lassie; but let us make the best of it. I will be a good husband to ye, and ye will lack for nothing, I promise ye."

"I have no other choice now, my lord," Arabella said, hating the weakness that caused a tear to slide down her cheek. It seemed to her that she was more tired now than she had been yesterday evening.

"Ahh, lassie," he said, feeling unaccountably moved by that single tear. "Dinna weep. Ye would break my heart, and I am nae a cruel man." Reaching out, the earl brushed the little tear away with his finger.

Arabella's green eyes widened at the gentle touch. She would not have thought this big man with his fierce dark brows, set in a face whose angles and planes made it seem harsh, had a soft side. Her lips parted with her surprise, for that simple touch was sending further ripples down her backbone.

Whatever happened, Tavis Stewart thought to himself, he had to have a kiss of her. He was astounded with himself, but she was totally delectable, and he could not resist. Leaning forward, his hand cupped her little pointed chin tenderly and his mouth touched hers.

He was going to kiss her! She knew it, and yet she could not resist him as his lips touched her. She had never been kissed. Not even by Jasper. With an instinct as old as woman herself,

Arabella's lips softened beneath his mouth. The kiss deepened, and she only realized it when she fell back upon her pillows, feeling the down give beneath her even as the passion suddenly ignited between them began to mount in its intensity.

What was happening to her? Arabella thought fuzzily. This man was her enemy, for all she must wed him, and yet she was wantonly accepting his advances. She had never thought about kissing Jasper Keane, but neither did she consider refusing Tavis Stewart. *What was the matter with her?* Marshaling every ounce of self-discipline she possessed, Arabella pushed the earl away, sputtering angrily, her hands slapping at him. "Villain! How dare you!"

The earl was not so bemused by the sweetness of the kiss that he had not realized it was her first kiss, no matter how agreeably she had accepted his lips, or now how volubly she protested the action. He caught her hands in his, and with maddening charm, kissed them. "I think, lassie, that I would dare far more were ye nae so sweetly innocent. Ye will wed me, won't ye?" and he smiled as she nodded, albeit reluctantly. "Then I will leave ye now, for if I stay longer there are those who will believe I have had yer maidenhead of ye. Yer old enough to wed, Arabella Grey, but I dinna think yer experienced enough to be a wife yet. Sleep well, lassie," and he arose from the bedside.

"I would have love!" Arabella cried to him. "I do not even know ye, my lord."

"Ye did nae know Sir Jasper either, lassie," Tavis Stewart said.

"Nay, I did not," Arabella agreed, "and see what kind of a villain he turned out to be!"

"Touché, lassie." The earl chuckled, grinning ruefully. He continued, "But I promise ye I hae no such skeletons in my cupboard." Then he was gone out the door.

Flora returned, smiling broadly. "They say in the hall that yer to wed wi the master on the morrow, m'lady."

"Aye," Arabella said thoughtfully.

"Thank God!" Flora exclaimed with a broad smile, and then she pulled her trundle from beneath Arabella's bed.

The serving woman was quickly asleep, but Arabella lay awake for a time. She had gone wandering about the castle with Meg this afternoon, and her friend, with a giggle, had pointed out a little-used postern gate nestled into the walls of the castle

courtyard which was used by the servants to sneak out and meet
their lovers. The gate was rarely locked.

Arabella had been given that day a light woolen skirt, a silk
shirt, and a plaid shawl to replace her own gown, which was far
too elegant for daily life at Dunmor. In a few days, she had been
told, she would have a more suitable wardrobe made for her.
Her simple clothing and her knowledge of the postern gate would
aid her in her escape. She had not intended attempting an escape
so soon, but the earl's determination to marry her in the morning
left her with no other alternative.

If she braided up her long hair and used her shawl to hide her
features, she just might be able to escape the notice of the guards
upon the wall. She would appear to be just another serving girl,
slipping out in the early morn for a quick assignation before she
took up her duties for the day. A servant taking advantage of the
excitement generated by the earl's wedding. All she had to do
was not allow herself to sleep too deeply despite her weariness.

Arabella dozed on and off throughout the long hours of the
night, forcing herself back to consciousness whenever her body
was tempted to relax into deep sleep. It would take her longer
to walk back across the border to Greyfaire than it had taken to
ride across the Cheviot hills, but if she could just have the benefit
of an early start before they discovered her gone, she might hide
from the Scots whenever she heard their horses. They would
seek to recapture her, she knew, but the advantage would be
hers!

She had a score to settle with Sir Jasper Keane. The man was
a damned fool if he thought she would allow him to take Greyfaire away from her by marrying her mother; and his talk of her
"dishonoring" was just that. Talk. And even if the earl and his
entire troop of borderers had raped her in sight of the keep's
walls, it still did not change the fact that it was she, Arabella
Grey, who was the heiress to Greyfaire. King Richard had sent
Jasper Keane to wed with her, not her mother. It was hardly her
fault, Arabella considered, that she had been carried off by the
Scots; but it was certainly Sir Jasper's problem that instead of
rallying the keep and following after the Scots to rescue her, he
had turned coward and attempted to steal her inheritance by
marrying Lady Rowena before the Scots were barely over the
hill with their captive. It had been Jasper Keane who had first
called her a spitfire, but he didn't know the half of it. She would

give him a dressing down the likes of which he had probably
never had in his entire life. Cousin Richard was going to learn
just how loyal his parfait knight actually was. It was obvious
that Sir Jasper had more an eye for his own good than for the
king's good. A man like that was no asset to a border keep as
strategic as Greyfaire, and Arabella intended telling the king so.
She was not frightened by the earl's thought that Jasper Keane
might do her harm should she return to Greyfaire now. He
wouldn't dare!

Anxious for the morning, Arabella slipped quietly from her
bed and across the room to peep out the narrow little casement.
Behind her Flora snored lustily, and Arabella thought that a
troop of horses could not awaken the sleeping servant before
her accustomed sunrise hour. Peering through the window, Arabella saw that though the top of the sky was yet black as pitch,
the edges of the horizon were beginning to grow gray with the
coming day. Arabella slowly crept across the chamber and lifted
the lid on the storage trunk, pulling her few garments out.

Silently she put on the silk shirt and drew the dark wool skirt
up over her chemise to fasten it at her narrow waist. Sitting down
upon the trunk, she pulled on a pair of knit stockings, but her
shoes she stuffed into her skirt pockets so she might move
through the castle proper more quietly. Carefully, Arabella
braided up her hair, using her tortoiseshell pins to fasten the
braids most tightly so that they should not come down and betray
her. Finished, she tiptoed back over to her bed and took one of
the fine down pillows, tucking it beneath the coverlet so that it
would appear to a quick glance that she still slept there. Satisfied
with her handiwork, Arabella moved back to the window to see
a wider band of pale gray inching up the horizon while the sky
above it was now ash-colored.

It was time! Quietly she slipped from the bedchamber, moving across the narrow space of floor separating her from the hall
door. She felt the handle beneath her clammy fingers, and turning it, Arabella drew the door open just wide enough to slip
through to the landing beyond. She drew the door shut as quietly
as she might and then stood for a long heart-pounding moment
listening, but Flora's snores never wavered in their rhythm. Convinced she had not awakened the servant, Arabella almost flew
down the steep staircase to the hallway below.

Cautiously she looked about, and then seeing no one, swiftly hurried through the castle until she at last reached the small, unobtrusive door that led into the castle's courtyard. Pulling up her shawl over her head, Arabella slipped out the door and across the courtyard in the half shadow, heading directly for the little postern gate. She could not believe her good fortune in having encountered no one so far. In a short while the entire castle would be stirring with preparations for the wedding.

Reaching the gate, she slipped the bolt, and the gate opened out with a faint creak that set her heart hammering wildly, for in the silence it sounded uncommonly loud and she was sure someone had heard it. Without a backward glance, however, Arabella boldly stepped through, and slipping on her shoes, hurried across the narrow little earthen dam that stretched across the watery moat. In times of war the dam was broken so that the castle's only access was its drawbridge.

Arabella never stopped her forward movement, for she knew that should she hesitate for even a moment, she could draw attention to herself and risk being recognized and recaptured. Above her she could hear the watch upon the walls, but no one cried out an alarm, and Arabella was torn between weeping with joy and shouting her relief.

Ahead of her she could see the faint beginnings of the sunrise, and so she turned onto the path leading south, which was to her right. If by nightfall the sun had moved to her right hand, then she would know she was still headed directly south. If not she would correct her direction. She did not think she could go too far wrong. Then she began to smile with delight over her success, and took a deep breath of the fresh morning air. It smelled sweet, but then freedom was always sweet!

In Dunmor's west tower Flora awakened with the sunrise, as was her custom. For a moment she lay upon her trundle bed as her consciousness restored itself. Then rising up, she drew on her garments, turning for a moment to look at her charge, but the little lassie was still sleeping, snuggled deeply beneath her coverlet. Flora nodded. The girl had looked exhausted last night. She would get a bucket of water to warm before she awoke her new mistress, that the girl might wash before her wedding.

Hurrying off, she returned a few minutes later, but her charge had not moved. Flora poured the bucket into the open iron kettle hanging over the hearth and encouraged the embers into a strong flame. Smiling, she walked over to the bed to shake the lass from her slumber, and quickly discovered Arabella's deception. With a shriek, Flora ran from the tower directly to the earl's apartments, startling the earl's body servant, Calum, as she came through the door gasping.

"The lassie is gone! She's gone, I tell ye! Get the earl, ye fool! Get the earl!"

Hearing the uproar in his dayroom, Tavis Stewart came from his bedchamber. He was as naked as the day he had been born, but Flora never noticed, so deep was her distress. "The little lassie, my lord! She's gone!" Flora cried.

"Gone? Precisely what do ye mean by gone, Flora? Did I nae instruct ye to stay wi her at all times?" the earl demanded.

"I was wi her, my lord! I put her to bed last night after ye had spoken wi her, but when I awoke at dawn, she was gone!"

"Ye may be upsetting yerself for naught, good dame," the earl said in a kinder tone. "It is our wedding day, and she may have been unable to sleep. Go to Mistress Hamilton and see if Arabella Grey is wi her. If she is nae there, then ask in the hall if any have seen her this morn."

Flora scurried off, to return several breathless minutes later. "Mistress Hamilton says she has nae seen Lady Arabella since last night, and no one else has seen her either, my lord," the serving woman reported. "Mistress Hamilton, however, says that the lassie showed an interest in the postern gate while they were walking about the courtyard yesterday."

"The postern gate?" the earl inquired.

"The servants use it to slip in and out unnoticed when they want to meet wi a lover," Calum said dryly with a knowing grin.

"Jesu!" The oath exploded from the earl's mouth, and then he turned to the cringing Flora. "Run to the stables, woman, and have them saddle the gray stallion! I'll be in the courtyard in five minutes! Calum help me dress, damnit!"

Flora flew from the earl's apartments as if she were being pursued by a pack of wolves. Once in the stables, she urged the groom to speed. By the time the earl came down the main staircase of his dwelling, Flora was waiting, holding his horse herself. "Watch says a servant girl left by the postern gate no more than a half an hour ago, my lord. No one else has left this morning."

"Which direction was she headed in?" he demanded, already knowing the answer.

"South, my lord," Flora answered with predictability.

The earl vaulted into his saddle and turned the horse about, pushing him into an instant canter as he headed out across his drawbridge. "Tell Father Colin to be ready to perform the marriage the moment we return," he called back to the woman.

"Dinna be harsh wi her, my lord," Flora cried after him. "She's but a little lass."

The earl grimaced at her words and muttered beneath his breath. "She may be wee, but she's given me more trouble than any six females, I'll vow. She'll nae be an easy wife, I'm thinking." His horse's hooves now hit the hard dirt road, turning south as his master urged him onward. The earl's plaid began to blow in the morning breeze.

It was Arabella's bad fortune that she was crossing a relatively flat stretch of ground when the earl finally caught her in his sight some long minutes later. Although she had heard him coming, there was simply nowhere for her to hide, and she sincerely wished she might be a bird so that she could fly away. For a brief moment she considered that it might not be him. Hesitantly she turned about to look at the horseman who was fast closing the distance between them. She had known him but three days, but she recognized him immediately, even imagining the grim expression upon the face that she could not yet see plainly. Heart pounding, Arabella began to run, but her legs suddenly felt leaden in her fear. He would surely kill her!

Tavis Stewart almost laughed aloud, seeing her pick up her skirts to flee him. Then he considered that she had made a fool of him, promising to marry him and all the while planning her escape. He kicked his stallion into a steady gallop, and when he was abreast of his quarry, he leaned from his horse and, lifting her up, threw her none too gently facedown over his saddle before him.

"Let me go!" Arabella shrieked furiously, kicking and squirming.

Angrily the earl brought his hand down upon her wriggling backside. "Madame!" he roared. "I have had all I will take of yer duplicity! Be silent now, or as God is my judge, I will strangle ye!"

The blow shocked Arabella more than it hurt her, for her

clothing took the brunt of the smack. Its effect, however, was
to startle her into silence, and she lay quietly, albeit uncomfortably, as he returned them the short distance to Dunmor Castle.
As they clattered over the drawbridge, the men-at-arms broke
into laughter at the sight of the English girl slung so rudely over
their master's saddle.

Stopping his mount in the courtyard, the earl slid easily from
the animal, turning to yank the girl off the horse. For a moment
she reeled giddily as the blood rushed to her head, but then as
the dizziness faded, Arabella swung on the earl with a furious
fist. Anticipating her action this time, he ducked, and fingers
fastening about the nape of her neck, he hustled her into the
Great Hall, where Meg Hamilton, her brother Robert, and the
earl's brothers awaited.

"Sweet Mary!" whispered Meg to her Gavin. "They look as
if they would kill each other."

" 'Tis a mistake, I tell ye, but he'll nae listen to anyone,"
muttered Donald Fleming darkly.

"Shut yer mouth!" hissed Gavin as the earl pushed Arabella
to the forefront of the little gathering.

"Perform the marriage ceremony, Colin," the earl ordered
his youngest brother.

"Nay, Tavis, I will not do it until ye and Arabella have both
cooled yer tempers," the priest said. "Yer to go to opposite
ends of the hall and calm yerselves. I will nae wed ye for at least
an hour. Meg, keep Arabella company, and I will come to ye
in a few minutes to hear yer confession, for marriage is a sacrament, and ye should enter into it honestly shriven."

"Colin," the earl growled warningly, but he stopped when
the priest held up his hand.

"Be warned, Tavis, I serve God first, and man second,"
Colin Fleming said quietly. "Now on yer knees, or I swear I
will order yer excommunication, brother mine."

Sudden laughter lit the earl's eyes. He was not so filled with
pride that he did not see the humor of the situation. He was *the
Stewart of Dunmor*, the head of his entire family. Even his stepfather deferred to his judgment; yet here he was, in the twinkling
of an eye, made painfully aware of his own mortality, and by
his little brother to boot. Tavis Stewart knelt meekly before the
priest.

At the other end of the hall Arabella grumbled to Meg about

the earl's high-handed treatment, and Meg, somewhat astounded by the English girl's ferocious anger, listened quietly. Colin came, and in his capacity as a priest spoke with Arabella, hearing her confession, but failing to cool her anger. Finally the hour was up, and the priest led the English girl back down the hall to where the earl awaited her.

"Perform the marriage ceremony now, Colin," the earl said, repeating his words of an hour before.

"Am I to be wed like *this*?" Arabella demanded, outraged. "In these rags?"

"I'll nae let ye out of my sight again until we're man and wife," Tavis Stewart said grimly, feeling his own anger beginning to rise once more. "If it would please ye, however, I'll hae Flora bring yer wedding gown, and ye can change here in the hall."

Her green eyes narrowed dangerously. "I will never wear that accurst garment again!" she said vehemently. "But neither will I wed ye dressed like this!"

"Then ye'll wed me in yer shift, madame, but wed me ye will, for I'll hae no more shilly-shallying about it!" he told her furiously.

"Wed ye in my shift?" Arabella's voice rose to a shriek. *"Never!"*

"Then, by God, ye'll wed me wi out, Arabella Grey!" the earl raged at her; and before any of them might stop him, Tavis Stewart had torn the clothing from Arabella's slender form, leaving her naked for all to see.

Meg's hand flew to her mouth in shock and she gasped.

"Holy Mother!" Gavin half whispered, though both Donald and Colin were struck dumb by their elder brother's actions.

For a moment Arabella was stunned, unable to believe what had happened. Her instinct was to run and hide, but then it occurred to her that to do so would indicate weakness on her part. She would not let Tavis Stewart defeat her. A slow, proud smile lit her features and she stood straight. Then lifting her arms up, she undid her pale golden hair from its braids, handing the tortoiseshell pins to Meg. Arabella's hair swirled about her like a silken veil as she said, "Since I am yet a virgin, my lord, it is my right to wear my hair unbound to my wedding." Her voice was clear and firm.

He nodded, her elegant actions having returned him to his

senses. He was more than surprised by his own behavior, but there was no help for it now. To apologize or back down would be to show a lack of strength on his part; and he would be master in his own house. "It is yer right, indeed, as ye are a virgin, Arabella Grey," he answered her gravely. Then he turned to the priest. "I believe we are ready to begin, Colin."

To his credit, Colin Fleming did not falter as he spoke the words of the marriage ceremony. He had never wed a couple before where the bride was naked, but he knew of no clerical impediment against it. His beautiful, well-modulated voice, intoning in perfect church Latin, never wavered in its recitation. It was not easy. He remembered the teasing Donald had given him only recently regarding women, and although he had done his share of coupling with the lasses before he had taken God's path, he had never before seen a woman totally naked. Arabella Grey was undeniably beautiful, and the priest suddenly understood for the very first time the true nature of Adam's temptation.

Gavin and Donald Fleming spent the ceremony looking everywhere in the hall but at the bridal couple. Gavin felt quite guilty that his glimpse of Arabella had set his own pulses raging, particularly as his own sweet Meg was even now by his side, holding his hand so trustingly. Donald considered that perhaps his elder brother's marriage was not quite the mistake he believed after all.

Most marriages were between strangers, and the best one could hope for was a pretty woman with a ripe body. Arabella Grey certainly qualified, and he could almost feel her firm, cone-shaped breasts nestling in the palms of his hands right now. The plump pink mont between her slender, rounded thighs was a most tempting sight. He could but imagine delving between those thighs, and thanked heaven that his kilt covered his rising lust, for he would not have offended Tavis for the world. He should never have coveted his new sister-in-law for even the briefest moment had not her lovely charms been so generously displayed.

Next to Donald stood Robert Hamilton, who was suffering the effects of too much wine last night. He had spent the early morning retching his guts out and now, his legs weak, his skin pale and clammy, he was in no mood to appreciate the sight before him. He wished for only one of three things. A clear head, a settled belly, or a quick and merciful death.

"Ye will both kneel for the blessing," Colin Fleming finally instructed the bridal couple, and they knelt. Colin made the sign of the cross over the pair, saying as he did, *"In nomine Patris, et Felii et Spiritus Sancti. Amen."* There was a pause and Colin said, "Yer wed now, Tavis."

"My lord earl!"

They all turned to see Margery Fleming striding into the hall. Her hair was disheveled from an obviously hasty ride, and none of her four sons could ever remember seeing her so angry. Reaching the wedding party, Lady Fleming removed her cloak and put it around Arabella's shoulders. Then she turned to Tavis Stewart.

"Good morrow, Mother," he said calmly, experience having taught him the folly of arguing with her.

"When," Lady Fleming demanded of her oldest son, "did I ever teach ye to abuse women, or perhaps ye think yer rank entitles ye to such behavior? I am appalled that ye would mistreat this poor child in such a fashion."

"This *poor* child, as ye mistakenly refer to her, Mother, has twice taken a knife to me. This morning, knowing full well that I intended marrying her, she attempted to escape Dunmor, and when I brought her back, she attempted to hit me. I would hardly call making this virago the Countess of Dunmor mistreating her. I hae given her a better name than her own king would have."

Lady Fleming was secretly delighted that her son had finally taken a wife, but there was much she did not understand about the situation. Before his mother might consider further, the earl enlightened her as to the events that had led up to his wedding. She listened quietly, but when he had finished, she looked between her son and Arabella and said, "Tavis, I dinna know if I can forgie ye yer behavior here today, and I wonder if yer wife can. I am taking Arabella home wi me to Glen Ailean, and I will hear no talk of any danger she might be in, for Sir Jasper Keane is too busy consolidating his own position at Greyfaire to be bothered wi this wee lassie. And if he were of a mind to come after her, who will tell him where she is? If I take her now before the rest of the castle is awake and stirring, few will even know where she has gone."

"Arabella is my wife, Mother, and I will nae hae her living anywhere but Dunmor," the earl replied.

"Indeed, my lord?" Margery Fleming drew herself up to her full height. She was a most formidable sight. "I would remind ye, my son, that I know all yer weaknesses as well as yer strengths. I gave ye life, and there are but two people upon the face of this earth whom ye must respect and obey wi out question. Yer brother, the king, and *me*! Yer countess comes wi me. You are welcome to visit us at Glen Ailean once Arabella's anger cools. Ye might consider courting yer wife, my son. If I am to hae grandchildren of ye, she should see that ye hae a softer, kinder side to ye than ye hae shown her. Now step aside, Tavis Stewart, or as God is my witness, I'll knock ye down!" Lady Fleming put a protective arm about her daughter-in-law.

"Mother!" The earl was chagrined.

"Stand aside, Tavis!" she repeated.

"Arabella!"

"She'll nae speak wi ye, my lord," his mother said. "Come, Margaret Hamilton, ye canna remain here wi these rough men. If ye've clothing ye might share wi poor Arabella, we can be on our way. I'm taking Flora too, Tavis." And she walked regally from the hall with her two charges.

Chapter 6

*R*ichard, king of England, fell in battle on August 22, 1485, hacked to death by Welsh pikemen who butchered him in a muddy mire after his horse became stuck. Within two hours the battle that had been fought between the Yorkists and the Lancastarians for England's throne was over, and Henry Tudor, to be called Henry VII, was acclaimed king of England by his jubilant troops. It was the last serious battle in the long and tortuous conflict that had been called the War of the Roses. The white rose of York and the red rose of Lancaster would unite to become the Tudor rose. The new king entered London on September third, welcomed and feted by all.

At Glen Ailean, Arabella wept for the cousin whom she would always remember with fondness. The news had been delivered to her by Tavis Stewart, who brought a copy of the parchment sent Scotland's king.

> *"Henry by the grace of God, king of England and of France, prince of Wales and lord of Ireland . . ."*

announced to all who would listen that:

> *"Richard, duke of Gloucester, lately called King Richard, was slain at a place called Sandeford."*

"They say," the earl said, "that King Richard might have fled but he would not. He fought with incredible bravery, cutting down the Tudor standard bearer, William Brandon, and sending the Red Dragon pendant into the dust before he himself was killed." Tavis Stewart did not relate to his young wife of how Richard's body had been stripped of its armor and dishonored by his enemies. It was an act unworthy of telling.

"It is most kind of you to bring me this news, my lord," Arabella told him. She had not seen him since their wedding day in June, for Lady Fleming, true to her word, had whisked her new daughter-in-law away from Dunmor Castle. She had spent a long and pleasant summer at Glen Ailean, but until now Tavis Stewart had not been able to find an excuse to visit his bride, and was too proud to simply come, hat in hand, to settle their differences.

"I fear for my mother and for Greyfaire, my lord," she told him. "What if the new king should hold my mother's blood against her?"

"I thought perhaps that ye might worry about her, Arabella, and so I sent a man across the border to learn how Lady Rowena is getting on," the earl told his wife. "Sir Jasper quickly consolidated his own position in regard to Greyfaire by sending his pledge of fealty to King Henry before King Richard's defeat. There were others more powerful—neighbors of yours, I am told—who also did the same. Sir Jasper excused himself from battle by claiming he was keeping the border safe for England. As to yer mother, she is great wi a bairn; due, they say, before year's end." Tavis Stewart had considered lying to Arabella, but he knew that such lies were eventually found out.

"But they were only wed in June," Arabella exclaimed, and then she paled. "Ohhhh!" she whispered as the realization of his words dawned upon her. Then looking up at him, she burst into tears, the knowledge of how great a betrayal had been perpetrated upon her totally complete.

The earl took his wife into his arms and comforted her, saying, "Dinna weep, lassie, for I canna bear a woman's tears. Ye know it."

"I'm not a woman," Arabella sobbed, her tears soaking through his silk shirt.

Tavis Stewart closed his eyes for a moment, his big hand smoothing Arabella's beautiful hair. Nay, he thought, she wasn't a woman yet, nor likely to be soon unless he could make his peace wi her. He hadn't had a woman since the day of their marriage, for he somehow knew that Arabella Grey—Arabella *Stewart*, he corrected himself mentally with a small grin—would not tolerate infidelity on his part, even if their marriage hadn't been consummated as of yet. "There, lassie," he said, "I know it hurts ye, but yer mother was probably lonely, and Sir Jasper has some fame as a seducer of hapless women. At least the bairn will hae a name now, which it should not have, had ye wed wi that wicked devil. Think of yer poor mother's shame, and if she hae any kind of a conscience, she feels guilty even so.''

"I am not angry at my mother," Arabella told him. "I fear for her, my lord, for it is obvious to me now that Sir Jasper is both cruel and evil.''

"Yer mother will be safe wi him, lassie," the earl told her, although he himself was not certain of his words. "He did nae hae to wed wi her to steal Greyfaire from ye, but he did. She is to bear his child, and I am told Sir Jasper does nae have any children of his own. All men want children, lass, and so I believe he will treat the mother of his child wi great care." He liked the feel of her against his chest, Tavis thought, as he held Arabella in an easy embrace.

Arabella found herself loath to pull away from the comfort of his arms. "Do you have children, my lord?" she asked him.

"Aye," he said honestly, and her head shot up, the green eyes half curious, half shocked. "I am a grown man, lassie, and I enjoy women," he admitted honestly. "There are several bairns attributed to me, and I hae seen no reason to deny them, since Stewarts tend to hae a certain look about them. I hae had no woman to my bed, however, since the day we were wed, Arabella *Stewart*, though my needs hae not lessened over these past few months."

"I do not know you, my lord," she said low. "I . . . I . . . cannot.''

"I am a patient man, Arabella *Stewart*, but ye will nae learn to know me if ye remain here at Glen Ailean wi my mother," he said, his dark eyes twinkling. "What's done is done. Can we nae make a new beginning, my wee English spitfire?''

Arabella sighed deeply. She was beginning to really like this big man who was her husband. She realized now that she had never liked Sir Jasper Keane. She had never felt anything for Sir Jasper. He was the king's choice for her husband, and she had simply accepted it blindly with the certainty of youth that she would live happily ever after. Still, the thought of riding off back to Dunmor with the earl was a little frightening. She drew a deep breath and said, "I would welcome a new beginning, my lord, but I would also prefer remaining here with your mother until we know each other a bit better. Would you really mind that, sir? Dunmor is not far, though one might think it so, this being the first time I have seen you since our marriage," she finished with a little twinkle in her own eyes.

He chuckled, delighted by her small scold. "Can it be that ye hae missed me, lassie?"

"Oh, aye, my lord, I have indeed missed you, and I have missed being hauled all over the borders upside down on your fine horse, and having my clothing destroyed, and living in a cramped and chilly tower as well," Arabella told him mischievously.

The earl burst into good-natured laughter. "Lassie, ye'll nae be easy on me, will ye?"

Arabella considered, and then said more seriously, "I shall always speak the truth to ye, my lord."

"My name is Tavis, lassie, and it would please me to hae ye call me my name."

"Tavis James Michael," she answered him. "James for your father, your mother says, and Michael because she liked the name and could not decide between the two. Your grandfather settled the matter by having you baptized Tavis James Michael, Lady Margery says," Arabella told him. She pulled away from him now, suddenly shy.

He caught her hand and pulled her back. They had been standing in his stepfather's library, and now the earl drew Arabella over to the large windows and, opening them up, stepped over the sill, lifting her out with him. "Walk wi me in my mother's garden," he said. "The day is fair and yet warm. What else has my mother told ye of me?"

"That you were a proud boy, even as you are a proud man," Arabella said. "That sometimes you are thoughtless, but never with malice, she says, for you have a kind heart. You are hard on your enemies, but you can also be forgiving. You are loyal to your family and to your friends, and good to your people. Lady Margery says you are a fine soldier as well."

"My mother, it seems, has said a great deal about me," he noted.

"Your mother would have us mend our differences, Tavis," and here Arabella chuckled once again. "She is eager for grandchildren."

"I can but imagine our bairns," he said softly, stopping to draw her into the circle of his arms once again. "Hot-tempered little lads, and tiny spitfire wenches wi their mother's pale gold hair. Lassie, I must kiss ye,'' he finished in a rush, and tipping her face up, he met her surprised lips with his.

"Ohhhh," she whispered, tasting the texture of his mouth and deciding she liked it. Arabella's arms slipped up about his neck, clinging to him as the pressure from his lips increased upon hers.

Sweet, sweet! She tasted so sweet, he thought, unexpectedly and sharply aware of the new fullness in her breasts as she pressed herself against him. Then without warning her lips opened beneath his, and he was unable to prevent his tongue from insinuating itself into her mouth to find hers. She shuddered with that first contact, her arms tightening even more about his neck in her budding passion.

Arabella did not really understand what was happening to her, but it all seemed quite natural nonetheless. Hazily she remembered back to the first time he had kissed her, and recalled that she had also found herself bereft of reason then too. Did kissing a man always produce such a delicious, if disconcerting effect? When she opened her mouth in an attempt to breathe, and his tongue caressed hers, the result was riveting, to say the least. Emotions she had never before felt, and certainly did not understand, overwhelmed her, forcing her to cling more tightly to his neck.

It had to stop. In a moment he was going to lay her down upon the slope of the garden and take everything she was so unwittingly and innocently offering him. Not that it would not be pleasant for them both, for he would see it was; but what if she felt regret afterward? Her curiosity and inexperience urged her onward to a fate she didn't even know existed. His experience warned him against accepting her offer. He wanted her totally at peace within her own self that the time was propitious for their union. With a sigh, Tavis Stewart broke off their embrace, aching at the hurt in her eyes. "Lassie, lassie," he murmured, caressing her upturned face with a gentle finger, "I am tempted to ask ye for more, but I willna. Nae yet, though ye would tempt a saint, Arabella *Stewart*."

The way he almost crooned her name sent a little shiver of delight down her spine. "Why not yet, Tavis?" she asked him honestly.

"I want ye to know me better and be content," he replied.

She nodded. "Then, too, there is the matter of Greyfaire, my lord. When will ye regain it for me? It is all I can offer you, though it be just a little keep. Still, the pasture land is good, and we've a fine orchard.''

"Yer new English king will nae be ready quite yet to settle such a dispute, lassie," he told her. "There are still little pockets of resistance to him which he must overcome, and then there is his coronation to be scheduled, the opening of parliament, and his marriage to Princess Elizabeth of York. Greyfaire is important to ye, I know, but 'tis a little affair to Henry Tudor.''

Arabella found herself in a quandary. She did not wish to renew her quarrel with Tavis Stewart, especially just when she was trying to make peace with this big man to whom she was, for better or for worse, married. "I know that Greyfaire is a small matter in the politics of England, my lord, but the longer Sir Jasper Keane holds it, the harder, I think, it will be for us to dislodge him. Sooner or later you will kill him, of course, but should my mother bear him a son, it is possible the new king will favor that child over me by virtue of his male sex. That a stranger should hold lands that have belonged to the Greys for so many years is unthinkable. For now there is peace between England and Scotland, and I am told that several troops of young Scotsmen fought with King Henry against King Richard. Surely this is a good time for you to sue King Henry for the return of my lands.''

"Ye must trust me in this matter, Arabella," Tavis Stewart said. "This winter I shall take ye to court to meet my brother, King James. We will tell him of yer plight and let Jemmie sue King Henry for ye. Such a request coming from one king to another will carry more weight than should either ye or I sue the English king. Ye understand, however, that England may refuse even Jemmie; or they may demand Greyfaire be held for our first daughter, whom they will betroth to a husband of the English king's choice. That child will be sent to England to be fostered by her husband's family at an early age in order that she be more English than Scots, and hae no divided loyalties in the event of war between our countries. Or England may simply pay ye what they feel yer lands are worth and end the matter that way. Ye will nae be allowed to live at Greyfaire again, lovey. Yer the Countess of Dunmor now and related to Scotland's king.''

Never to go home to Greyfaire again? Arabella's eyes welled

with tears. Until this moment she had not realized how very much she had really lost—and none of it through her own doing. She was suddenly angry. Angry that all that was important in her life, that was of consequence or of relevance to her happiness, was being or had been decided for her by someone else, usually a man. It wasn't fair! She wanted to control her own life; a somewhat radical thought, she knew. Her sweet mother would be horrified by such an idea. Father Anselm would tell her that women were bound by tradition and God's law to be subservient to men; but that didn't mean, Arabella decided, that she had to like it.

"What is it, lassie?" the earl asked her. "Ye look like a wee thundercloud."

A sharp reply sprang to her lips, but Arabella bit it back, suddenly realizing that to behave in such a manner was childish. Her entire life was not her husband's fault . . . only these last few months concerned him. She had to take charge of her own fate. No one else had the right, but a direct assault upon Tavis Stewart would earn her nothing. "I am angered," she said honestly, "by the fact my ancestral home is in the hands of a stranger who may be more successful at pressing his claim to it than I."

" 'Tis natural ye would feel that way, Arabella," the earl told her.

"Promise me that you will do *everything* to regain Greyfaire for me, my lord," Arabella said. "I do not want royal gold. I want my border keep."

"I dinna need the gold, though that be a somewhat sacrilegious statement for a good Scotsman to make," he told her with some humor. "But it will nae be easy, Arabella Stewart. I will do my best for ye, I swear it."

"I am satisfied that you will, my lord," she answered him, but in her heart she knew that should he fail, she would not let it rest at that.

He smiled at her, and Arabella suddenly realized that it was the first time she had ever seen Tavis Stewart smile. She had seen him laugh, but never had his mouth stretched wide to show her a top row of square white teeth. "Yer such a solemn little puss, Arabella Stewart," he said. "I like ye, lass."

" 'Tis fortunate you do, my lord," she replied with spirit, "since you are bound to me in marriage."

He chuckled. "Shall I court ye, lovey? Ye can scarce call our acquaintance to date a courtship."

Now it was Arabella's turn to chuckle. "Nay, my lord, you have certainly not courted me the way I ever imagined a maid should be courted. Rather you have waged a rough wooing of my person. I think I should like it if you courted me properly."

"And how long is this courting to last?"

"If you please me, Tavis Stewart, then I shall go home to Dunmor with you after your sister's wedding on December fifth," Arabella told him. There was a long moment of silence, and then she said, "You have not asked me what will happen if you do not please me, my lord."

"I dinna need to know," he said softly, "for I shall please ye well, my little English spitfire." And he tipped her chin up with his fingers and touched her mouth once again with his. "I have never wooed a woman properly, Arabella Stewart, but ye will hae nae cause for complaint, I promise ye."

Would his kiss always send that delicious little ripple down her backbone? Arabella wondered. She hoped so! And when he took her hand in his big paw and led her through his mother's gardens, all rational thoughts seemed to drift away. They did not speak now, and, indeed, there seemed no need to speak. The September day was fair and the air yet warm. Above a bed of Michaelmas daisies several fat bumblebees hovered, their gossamer wings beating the air and, by some miracle, holding up their plump black and yellow bodies.

"When will you go to court?" Arabella finally asked, breaking the silence.

"Not until after Twelfth Night," the earl replied. "I would take ye wi me, lassie. Both Jemmie and his queen are anxious to meet ye. The hunting is too good now for me to leave Dunmor, particularly since my brother doesna need me."

"I have heard it said that your king is not well liked among his nobility," Arabella noted. "Why is that? You seem to hold him in great affection, and I do not think you would feel that way if he were not a good man, Tavis."

The earl sighed. "James is a man of peace in an age that esteems militaristic values and all that goes with it. He despises violence and all martial pastimes; but even so, he might have redeemed himself in the eyes of the nobility if he at least sat a horse well, but alas, he doesna. If the truth be known, my brother is afraid of horses. He is most like his mother, Marie of Gueldres, who was the niece of Burgundy's duke, Philip the Good. She was raised at the Burgundian court, and was a lady of great wit, intellect, and piety. Jemmie even favors her with his olive skin, dark eyes and hair; and though he has always been a handsome man, he has a foreign look to him which has nae endeared him to many.

"He had two younger brothers, Alexander, Duke of Albany, and John, Earl of Mar. Both were Stewarts in face and form, and totally narrow Scots in their thinking. Several years ago they were arrested upon suspicion of treason, and God knows, Albany aspired to the throne. Mar died in prison, but Albany escaped to France, where the French king arranged an aristocratic marriage for him but would nae help him overthrow Jemmie, so Albany crossed the channel to England. Yer King Edward was more than willing to meddle in a business that was nae his own. He publicly recognized Jemmie's brother as King Alexander IV of Scotland and sent his brother, Duke Richard, with an army to invade Scotland."

"That was the summer my father was killed," Arabella said. "I never really understood it. I remember the summons coming from the king and my mother begging him not to go. My father laughed and said 'twas no more than a border skirmish, for all King Edward was involved. He said the Scots king would not allow himself to be so easily unseated by a younger brother; that King Edward supported the usurper merely to annoy Scotland, for relations between our two countries had not been going well."

"Nay, they hadna," the earl replied. "Jemmie marched south to meet the challenge to his throne. Unfortunately he took with him a group of his favorites, none of whom excelled particularly in the warlike arts, some of whom did excel in the arts, and all of whom were most cordially disliked by the nobility. Robert Cochrane, who was the architect of the Great Hall at Stirling Castle, was my brother's chief favorite. He was a pompous, overbearing man, lacking in humor and hated by most who knew him. Jemmie chose Cochrane to be his Master of the Artillery over a number of eminently well-qualified men. It was like putting a light to gunpowder.

"We were camped at Lauder when the Earl of Angus and his group of other nobles seized Cochrane and five others and hung them over Lauder Bridge. The rumors of these creatures of Jemmie's, and the king himself, had so revolted Angus and his party that, unaware of Albany's full treason against James—for Alexander Stewart had secretly sworn his and Scotland's fealty to England—they had decided to replace James wi his younger brother. They forced the king to witness the execution of his friends, and then escorted him back to Edinburgh.''

"Were you with him? Why did you not help him?" Arabella demanded.

"I did," the earl told her. "When my half brother Alexander had gone to England, I sent one of my own Dunmor Stewart clansmen to join up with his party. While Angus was bringing Jemmie back to Edinburgh a prisoner, I rode for the borders and met up wi my clansman, who had stolen a document which clearly detailed Albany's perfidy. We brought it to the capital, and when Albany arrived there at the reception that had originally been planned to welcome him as Scotland's new king, he found a far different reception than he had anticipated.

"Angus, who is a basically decent man, was shocked that, in his passion to rule, Alexander Stewart would betray his country into England's hands. Albany was forced to reconcile his differences with Jemmie, who remained king, and Duke Richard returned to England. Yer King Edward's only gain was the town of Berwick, which Duke Richard had captured wi Albany's assistance before they arrived in Edinburgh," said Tavis Stewart.

"And where my father was killed," Arabella answered quietly. "Where is the Duke of Albany today, my lord?"

"Dead, lass. Jemmie tried to win his brother's loyalty by giving him a wee bit of power as Lieutenant of the Kingdom, but Albany was, the following year, discovered once again in treasonable intrigues. When he fled to England, he learned that his former sponsor, King Edward, was dead, and Duke Richard was now King Richard. Richard had no time for Albany, and so he moved on to France. Last year he invaded Scotland wi another long-exiled rebel, the Earl of Douglas. They were defeated at Lochmaben. Douglas was captured and imprisoned. Albany fled back to France, where he was killed in a tournament this spring.''

"And so your king is no longer threatened by his enemies," Arabella said.

"Kings always hae enemies, lassie," the earl remarked dryly.

"Most kings are faulted for going to war, but my brother is faulted for working so assiduously to keep the peace between Scotland and England. His nobility do nae understand him, for they do nae wish to change, but the world around us is changing."

"You love King James, I can see," Arabella noted. "Are you alike at all? You must be, that you can understand him so well."

Tavis Stewart laughed. "My love for Jemmie began when I was but a wee lad. As I hae told ye, his mother was most kind to my own mother despite the difficulty of their positions. Although my father was killed when I was three, Queen Marie nae forgot that I was his son. Jemmie was nine when our father died, and his mother brought him to Roxburgh, showing him to her late husband's armies and exhorting them to victory that they would do honor to King James II's memory. She had her way, for the Scots successfully stormed Roxburgh and took it. Several days later my brother Jemmie was crowned at Kelso Abbey.

"Jemmie, however, was still a child, and child kings can be dangerous, for many wish to rule through them. Yer King Edward formed an alliance wi the Earl of Douglas and the Lord of the Isles that would hae partitioned Scotland between them. They intended to rule as vassals of England. My brother's government avoided that danger by refuting their Lancastrian interests and signing a truce wi yer king. For a time we hae peace here in Scotland.

"When Jemmie was twelve his mother died. It was a great loss for us all, for the queen's loyalty to her son and to Scotland could not be circumvented. Still, Jemmie had Bishop Kennedy of St. Andrews to advise him, and the bishop, too, was loyal as the queen had been; but he died two years after the queen. I was only eight years old then, but I remember my mother and stepfather speaking of the dangers involved, for Jemmie was only fourteen."

"Were they afraid that you might lose Dunmor?" Arabella asked.

"Nay, I think not, for Dunmor has always been a Stewart stronghold, and Ian Fleming was holding it in my name at the time, and he was loyal beyond question. I think they simply feared a civil war which might hae encouraged England to invade us despite the truce between us. The Boyd family, however, settled everything for us all. They seized the young king at Linlithgow and brought him to Edinburgh. Sir Alexander Boyd was Jemmie's military tutor and the governor of Edinburgh Castle, where Jemmie was now housed. God, how he hates the place, even today!

"Lord Boyd of Kilmarnock, the other conspirator, sent to my stepfather, Lord Fleming, saying that I was to be brought up to Edinburgh to keep my elder sibling company. By that time the Boyds had supreme power and there was nae refusing them. Lord Boyd had married his son to Jemmie's sister, Princess Mary. I stayed wi my brother for several years until the Boyds made a match for him wi Princess Margaret of Denmark. After the wedding, Jemmie sent me home to Dunmor, saying that he now intended to assert his own royal authority over those who had ruled in his name.

"I was very angry wi him when he told me, for I wanted to stay and fight the Boyds wi him, but he would nae let me. 'Ye've kept me company, laddie, these past few years,' he told me, 'and good company ye hae been, for all yer still a child. I couldna live wi such grand memories as we hae if I let anything happen to ye.' So I went home to Dunmor wi my memories of a kindly elder brother who taught me that a man need nae be cruel in order to be a real man. I returned to Dunmor wi an appreciation of music and the arts, for Jemmie loves these things best. I learned that a man may esteem and value beauty wi out losing his manhood."

"And what happened to the Boyds?" Arabella was enjoying her husband's tale.

"Sir Alexander was executed, and Lord Boyd fled Scotland wi his son to live in exile. They were presumptuous to have seized the king in his youth. When they did they took the chance that they would pay such a penalty for their audaciousness, as indeed they did pay."

"So there has been a happily ever after for your brother, my lord, hasn't there?" Arabella said.

"Lassie," the earl said, lifting his wife up to set her upon a low wall, that he might look at her, "until the Royal Stewarts totally control their nobility, no Scots king will ever hae a happy reign. My brother's greatest loves, after his children, are music and architecture. He is well-informed regarding European painting, and even commissioned Master Hugo van der Goes to make an altarpiece for him which contains portraits of himself and Queen Margaret upon several of the panels. He collects classical manuscripts, and has encouraged our poets to their finest works. The beautiful coinage we hae here in Scotland is a result of Jemmie's influence and patronage.'' The earl grinned ruefully. ''He's nae a man easily understood by his earls and clansmen. They find it easier to dislike him because he is different than they are. They will nae take the time to know or understand him, and since Cochrane and his ilk were hung, Jemmie will make no concessions to them or to his public in the matter of favorites. The current favorite is young John Ramsay of Balmain.''

''What does the queen think of all of this?'' Arabella was curious, for she had never heard that King James's marriage was not a happy one.

''Queen Margaret is the kindest, gentlest woman I have ever known,'' Tavis Stewart said feelingly. ''She has loved and supported Jemmie from the first moment she laid eyes upon him; and he, in turn, has loved and respected her as well. Whatever faults or weaknesses my brother may hae, his wife hae stood by him through it all. She is goodness beyond belief, lassie. Jemmie knows this and hae never abused her in any way for it, nor taken advantage of her sweetness.''

''How complex a man your brother sounds,'' Arabella said. ''I have known few people outside of Greyfaire, except for cousin Richard and Sir Jasper Keane, but then neither of them was what they seemed.''

He nodded and was pleased by her words, for it indicated to him that although Arabella might not be very educated—though few women really were—at least she had a good intellect and could learn. He had married her in haste in an effort to gain revenge upon another; and in doing so, he realized now that he had to accept her for what she was. It was a relief to know she was capable of change. Then Tavis Stewart considered the uncomfortable possibility that his young wife most certainly had similar thoughts about him. He wondered what her conclusions were as he lifted her from the garden wall to continue their stroll.

From the windows of her private apartments Lady Margery Fleming watched her eldest son and his wife as they walked and talked amongst her flowers. She smiled, well-pleased, and her husband—who had many times seen that smile—chuckled as, coming to her side, he slipped an arm about her comfortable waist. She looked up at him, her eyes bright with satisfaction. "I'll hae a grandchild from those two by this time next year," she said with certainty.

Ian Fleming laughed. "It took Tavis long enough to come calling, my dear," he noted.

"Aye, he's proud," she answered, the doting fondness in her tone evident. "Still, I knew he'd come eventually, and now that I've had time to cool Arabella's ire at being stolen away, I can see she is more amenable to him. I like the lass, and she'll be a good wife to him. Her mother has raised her well, for all her own loose behavior, which I am pleased she nae showed before her daughter."

"Dinna be hard on Arabella's mam, my dear," Lord Fleming cautioned his spouse. "The lass loves her, and even I have heard of Sir Jasper's reputation wi the ladies. He could be a Stewart for all his charm. That he seduced the poor woman is plain, for never hae I heard Arabella speak of her mother that she did nae speak of her wi love. I dinna think the little lass could love her mam were she a wicked woman."

"Aye," his wife agreed grudgingly. "Yer probably right, Ian. My tongue is ever getting ahead of my good sense."

Lord Fleming gave his wife a little squeeze. "Yer anxious for Arabella to love Tavis, my dear, and jealous of anything that might make the lass long for her home. Dinna fear. She is his wife, and all will be well between them if we but gie them a chance. Turn yer thoughts to our Ailis's wedding now, Margery."

Lady Fleming nodded, but then her eyes strayed back to the garden and she smiled. "Look Ian! He's kissing her again!"

Ian Fleming shook his head with a grin. By now, he thought, he ought to be used to his wife's interest in any and everything. "The lass looks as if she likes it," he observed.

"Aye," Margery Fleming said softly. "If he kisses her like his father used to kiss me . . ." and she sighed gustily, her eyes overflowing with memories of a time past.

Lord Fleming had accepted long ago the fact that the father of his wife's eldest child would always hold a special place in her heart. It was rare she even mentioned King James II. He felt no jealousy, for Margery had not even been his wife then, nor promised to him, and since their marriage she had been faithful and true. "However Tavis kisses, my dear," he replied quietly, "it is obviously pleasing to Arabella, for she seems loath to cease their pleasant sport. I wonder if we should not emulate our children, Margery," and Lord Fleming turned his wife about, giving her a warmly passionate kiss.

"Ohh, Ian!" she cried, blushing rosily with delight. "How naughty ye are!"

"Why should the young hae all the fun?" he demanded.

"I dinna ever say they should," she replied coyly, and taking his hand in hers, Lady Fleming led her husband into her bed-chamber, smiling.

Chapter 7

*R*owena Keane lay writhing with the agony of her birth pangs. She did not remember the process ever taking so long or being so painful. Her travail had begun two days ago, and now on the night of November thirtieth she knew that both her life and her labor were fast coming to an end. Father Anselm, bless him, had remained by her side for all these many hours. She had already made her full confession and received absolution. She had but two regrets. That she would not live to see her daughter again to tell her how much she loved her, and to beg Arabella's forgiveness; and the fact that she would not live to raise this new child, if in fact the child should live.

Arabella. Her beloved daughter. How angry Jasper had been when he learned that the girl was alive, and the wife of the Earl of Dunmor. It was said that the Scotsman had stolen Jasper Keane's bride with the express purpose of replacing his own, who had been murdered by Sir Jasper himself. Rowena was no longer surprised by anything that was said about her husband, and gossip, if nothing else, had a way of finding its way to Greyfaire. She had wanted to communicate with Arabella, but Jasper had forbidden the priest to write to the girl. Scotland was the enemy, he said pompously. The wench had made her bed, and now must lie in it; and if she regretted it, which she certainly must, that was unfortunate. There would be no sympathy or succor for her at Greyfaire or from any of Greyfaire's inhabitants. It astounded Rowena, simple as she was, that Jasper could so easily forget that poor Arabella was in Scotland because of his actions, and through no fault of her own. Still, now as she felt her life's force ebbing away with her effort to birth her child, Rowena knew she could not leave this earth without warning Arabella of the danger involved in treating with Sir Jasper Keane. It was surely too late to ask for her daughter's forgiveness.

"Tell . . . Arabella . . ." she ground out painfully, trying to form her thoughts, but distracted by another contraction. Still she would not be denied, for this was too important. "Tell Arabella . . . not to trust Jasper . . . for he is . . . evil!'' she gasped, triumphant in her small success.

"Lady, there is nothing I shall withhold from Greyfaire's rightful mistress,'' the priest assured her, "and none here with us now will deny you your dying wishes either,'' he concluded sternly, his glance taking in Elsbeth and the village midwife.

Elsbeth burst into tears and knelt by her mistress's bedside, half sobbing. "I'll be faithful, m'lady, I swear it!'' she promised.

The priest nodded, satisfied. The midwife, he knew, would say nothing, for like others who belonged to Greyfaire, she was unhappy with Sir Jasper Keane's tenure but helpless to do anything about it. Her silence was a small blow against this false lord. Elsbeth, however, was a different matter. Three months earlier she had delivered a healthy son whose father would not marry her in order to give the boy a name. Elsbeth had been devastated, for she had firmly believed that Seger would wed with her. Her devastation turned to anger when she learned that her lover had a wife, or so he claimed, in the vicinity of Northby. He also had several other children, Elsbeth consequently learned to her mortification, by several other women. She believed him when he told her these things, for already he had turned his attentions to another of Greyfaire's gullible young girls. Still, there was always the chance, the priest thought, that in order to curry favor with her former lover, Elsbeth might reveal the secrets of the birthing chamber.

"If you betray the Lady Rowena, girl,'' he warned Elsbeth, "I'll deny you the sacraments, and your family as well. Remember what misery and shame your illicit passion has brought you . . . and brought this poor lady as well,'' he finished, lowering his voice at his last thought.

"The child is being born now,'' the midwife said dourly.

A feeble cry sounded, and the priest crossed himself in thanksgiving for the birth.

" 'Tis a wee boy,'' the midwife said, "but he'll not live long, for he already has the look of death about him.''

"Thank . . . God!'' Rowena Keane whispered, and they all understood her meaning.

"Go and fetch Sir Jasper, girl,'' Father Anselm ordered Elsbeth. "Say nothing more than his wife has been delivered of a son.''

Elsbeth nodded and fled the room.

"Give . . . him to . . . me," Rowena said weakly.

The midwife had finished cleaning the baby of the evidence of his hard birth, and now she wrapped the child in swaddling clothes and gave him to his mother.

Rowena weakly cradled her son, her soft blue eyes filling with tears. "Poor baby," she said low.

The door to the bedchamber was flung rudely open and Jasper Keane strode into the room. "Where is my son?" he demanded loudly. "Give me the boy!" He was half drunk, and stumbled as he came across the room.

Rowena nodded to the midwife, who took the baby from her and handed him to his father.

Jasper Keane looked down at his son's wizened features for a long moment and then, staring directly at the priest, he asked, "Will he live?"

"I think not, my lord," Father Anselm replied. "He should be baptized immediately."

Jasper Keane nodded. "Call him Henry," he said, handing the baby to Elsbeth.

"What, my lord?" Rowena struggled into a half-seated stance, and with the last of her strength, mocked her husband. "Not *Richard*, after he who gave you all of this good fortune? Where is your gratitude?"

Sir Jasper walked to his wife's bedside and looked down at her. "Even with death beginning to lurk within your eyes, sweet Row, you are still a beauty," he noted. "Nay, the boy will be called Henry that the king knows my loyalty. As for Richard, aye, I owe him a small debt for Greyfaire, but after I have properly mourned you and our Henry, sweet Row, I shall take another wife, and the Greys of Greyfaire will be but a memory, if indeed they are remembered, even as Duke Richard. I intend founding a dynasty. I shall build a large church here in my village upon the site of the church that now stands. You and our son shall have your part in my dynasty, for I shall see you eventually entombed in the family vault there. The first of many," he finished with a chuckle.

Rowena gave a sharp bark of laughter at these words. "You will end your days . . . alone, Jasper," she said, falling back upon her pillows. "All alone . . . and sooner than later." Her eyes closed and her breathing grew labored for a time.

Fascinated, Jasper Keane watched his wife in her death throes. As death approached her, Rowena seemed to have more courage and strength than he had ever known her to have. She had always been so meek and pliant. She was certainly the loveliest woman he had ever possessed, and an excellent bed partner. He had to admit to himself that he would miss her, despite her inability to give him a healthy son. Then once again her blue eyes opened, and Jasper Keane felt the blood in his veins freeze and the hair upon the nape of his neck prickle with apprehension.

Rowena stared directly at Jasper Keane and in a hollow voice said, "You will never have Greyfaire, Jasper." There was a long pause, and finally she continued, "You . . . are curst!" Then the life fled from her eyes.

He stood rooted to the spot where he was standing until finally the priest moved forward and gently closed Rowena's sightless eyes. Behind him the infant whimpered weakly, and turning, Father Anselm signaled to Elsbeth to follow him with the child to the family chapel. "Will you come, my lord?" he asked the baby's father.

Wordlessly he shook his head in the negative, and pushing past the priest, stamped back down to the hall, where he proceeded to get drunk, finally falling into a stupor in the hour before dawn, even as Henry Keane breathed his last, tortured breath. By the time Jasper Keane awoke in the midday, his head aching, his mouth foul, the grave for his wife and infant son had been dug and stood ready. In Greyfaire's small church Rowena had been laid out in her coffin in her finest gown, her golden hair newly washed and braided into a single thick plait, her arms cradling her dead child.

The good folk of Greyfaire village had spent the morning in solemn procession past the bier, and now waited anxiously for Sir Jasper Keane that they might bury their poor lady. When he finally came, accompanied by his captain, Seger, it was midafternoon and close to sunset, for it was December first. Jasper Keane glanced briefly at the woman who had been his wife for such a short time, and then signaled the priest to begin.

The church was cold. The service brief. Jasper Keane lingered at the gravesite only long enough to shovel a clot of dirt upon his wife and son's coffin. It was FitzWalter who lovingly completed the task of filling in the grave as the last red-orange rays of the sun sank behind the western hills. Rowena had been laid to rest beside her first husband, Henry Grey, even as all who knew her best realized she would want to be. His sad task done, FitzWalter returned to the keep and found Sir Jasper Keane and Seger in the hall with two pretty servant girls, already half drunk, and obviously preparing for a long night of wenching. They did not notice either his arrival or his departure from the hall, for with a scornful look at the pair, the keep's captain had quickly taken his leave. It was unlikely that Sir Jasper would miss him this night.

FitzWalter was a man of unusual height, a height made even more unique by the fact he was also slender to the point of emaciation. His lack of girth was deceiving to those who did not know him, for though he was thin, he was strong and wiry. He had a long head and a sensitive, almost mournful face with intelligent, light-colored eyes and a high forehead. He kept his sandy-colored hair cropped short. His most distinctive feature, however, was his very deep voice.

"I'll be at the cottage," he told the watch, and then crossing over the keep's drawbridge before it was raised for the night, he hurried down the hill to the small stone house Lord Grey had given him and his family years before. There was pale gray smoke rising from his chimney, visible even in the deepening twilight. A light shone warmly through the front window of the cottage. FitzWalter opened the door to his home and, ducking beneath the low lintel, entered within, where his wife Rosamund, his son Rowan, and four of his daughters were seated at the trestle table. His three eldest daughters were already married and gone to live with their husbands' families.

"You're not needed at the keep tonight?" his wife inquired.

"He's got Seger with him," FitzWalter said grimly. "They've Derward the huntsman's daughters to keep them company, and both will be well fuddled by morning. They're loose jades, the pair of them."

"They've no mother to tell them better," Rosamund said quietly.

"Thank God Wanetta, Scirleah, and Nellwyn are wed and away from Greyfaire," FitzWalter said. "Sir Jasper will now have no restraints upon him with Lady Rowena dead. There won't be a lass around who is safe from his roving eye." He fixed his gaze on the youngest of his daughters. "You, Jane, what is your age?"

"Nine, Da," the girl answered.

"And you, Eba?"

"Seven, Da."

"And my wee Annie?"

"Five, Da," the smallest child lisped.

FitzWalter nodded. "They should be safe, but you, Lona, you won't be unless I marry you off. Rad's grandson would be a good match for you, and you know it."

Rosamund saw the mutinous look flash in Lona's eyes and she quickly said, "Lady Arabella promised Lona that she should be her own personal maid, husband. Lona can look higher than Rad's grandson, I think, and besides, Sir Jasper would be apt to take the droit du seigneur of our girl should she be a bride. 'Tis just the sort of thing that would give him pleasure."

FitzWalter nodded in agreement with his wife. "Aye, he would enjoy forcing a hapless virgin. I'd not wish that on our Lona." He was silent a long moment, and then he said to his daughter, "Are you brave enough to ride over the Chevoits to tell Lady Arabella of her mother's death and to ask that she take you into her service, Lona?"

Lona never hesitated. "Aye, Da!" she told him.

"Husband!" Rosamund spoke sharply, and her warning glance took in her younger daughters, who were wide-eyed and fascinated by this table conversation.

"You've heard nothing, my girls," FitzWalter said quietly to Jane, Eba, and Annie. "If you should tell anyone of our words, we could lose our very lives. Do you understand?"

The three nodded solemnly and chorused in unison, "Aye, Da!"

"Then get to your pallets, my girls; say your prayers, remembering poor Lady Rowena's sweet soul, and go to sleep," their father told them.

The three arose from the table and scrambled obediently up the narrow staircase of the cottage to the loft above, where their childish voices were shortly heard droning their prayers.

FitzWalter smiled fondly after them, and then turning, said to his remaining daughter, "You'll go before dawn, Lona, and your brother will accompany you. I'm giving you Lady Arabella's mare to take to her. Rowan, you'll have that black gelding, but you must be back by night. Neither Seger nor Sir Jasper know the number of horses in the stable, so they will not miss the mare. The sky tonight told me that there will be rain by morning, and so it's unlikely either of those two will venture forth from the keep tomorrow. Sir Jasper will want to enjoy his 'inheritance' for a bit, I'm certain. When Lona is missed, we'll simply say she ran off because she didn't want to marry Rad's grandson. Everyone knows her feelings on that matter, don't they, Lona?'' her father finished with a small attempt at humor.

"You mustn't hurt the boy's feelings," Rosamund said soft-heartedly.

"Don't worry, Mother, it won't," Lona said, laughing. "Rad's grandson doesn't like me any better than I like him. Besides, he's got his eye on our Jane, and she really likes him."

"Does she, now?" their mother said, surprised. "Well now, that certainly puts a different light on matters, doesn't it?"

Her family laughed at her, for Rosamund was a matchmaker at heart, and she was, in fact, such a good one that all of the village relied upon her in matters of the heart.

"Where am I to take Lona?" Rowan demanded. He was a practical young man, very much like his father.

" 'Twas the Earl of Dunmor who stole our lady away, and 'tis said he wed her himself to replace the bride that Sir Jasper killed," FitzWalter replied. "Take Lona to Dunmor Castle, for if Lady Arabella isn't there, they will know where she is. Say Lona is her body servant, escaped Greyfaire with the news of Lady Arabella's mother. It should be safe to leave your sister then and return home, but use your judgment, Rowan, in that matter."

"How do we get the horses without being caught, Da?"

FitzWalter smiled. "I've taken horses from Greyfaire many a time, my lad. One wall of the stable is an outer wall of the keep, and there's a small door in it just big enough to slip a horse through. It's well hidden from the outside, and none has ever found it over the years, for if they did, Greyfaire would not be safe. John, the stableman, sleeps sound, and even if he did wake, he'd say nothing. He hopes to marry your aunt Elsbeth and won't want to get in bad with me. I'll take care of it, my bairns." He chuckled at his children's surprised faces. "There's much you don't know," he told them. "Now, Lona, dress warm. As many petticoats as you've got, and stockings as well. 'Twill be a cold, wet ride. Best you both seek your beds, for you'll need all your strength tomorrow."

His children gone, FitzWalter sat by the fire, accepting a wooden goblet of cider from his wife, who then sat by his knee.

"What will happen now, husband?" she asked him.

"I don't know, though I expect Sir Jasper will sue the king for possession of Greyfaire and seek another wife as quickly as possible. That is why I'm sending Lona to Lady Arabella. She is the last of the Greys, and if I know her as I think I do, she will not easily relinquish her lands to Sir Jasper Keane. She will fight him for them."

"But can she regain Greyfaire, husband? She has wed with a Scot," Rosamund said.

"I do not know, wife, for I am not privy to such matters concerning the nobility, but I do not want Sir Jasper Keane as my master, and so I will do whatever I can in my own small way to oust him. If Lady Arabella is content to be only the Earl of Dunmor's wife, then I can do nothing more; but I believe that if she knows her mother is dead in childbirth, Lady Arabella will seek to avenge her, even as her husband seeks to avenge his own honor in the matter of Eufemia Hamilton."

"But what will happen to us, to our family," fretted Rosamund, "if Sir Jasper learns that you seek to betray him?"

"I will do nothing more than I have told you, wife," FitzWalter replied. "I will get word to Lady Arabella, no more. Who will know I have done it? Lona will be gone and Rowan safely back. Besides, does not Lady Arabella have the right to know of her mother's death that she might pray for the poor lady's soul?"

Rosamund nodded slowly. "You are right, husband," she said, and believed the words even as she spoke them. FitzWalter had never done anything to endanger his family, and she knew he would not risk their safety even now.

"Come to bed," FitzWalter told her, and when they were settled comfortably together, he calmed her fears while using her vigorously to their mutual satisfaction. He left her sleeping, a soft smile upon her face, an hour or more before the dawn. Slipping silently through the night, he climbed the hill to the keep, and using the only key to the secret stable door, FitzWalter let himself into the keep.

Once inside he stopped and listened. From the loft above came the lusty snores of John, the stableman, coupled with a more delicate wheeze that indicated to FitzWalter that John had a woman with him. Elsbeth, the captain considered, for the stableman loved her deeply. Hearing the whimper of a small baby, FitzWalter knew he was right, for Elsbeth would not leave her child, being a good mother. He had best hurry, for his nephew was beginning to awaken with hunger, and that meant Elsbeth would awaken also to feed her son. Best she know nothing.

He moved instinctively to the proper stalls, saddling first the gelding and then Lady Arabella's little mare. The horses were alert to him, but still sleepy enough to be silent. Quickly he led them to the rear of the building and through the secret door. Holding the reins of both animals in one hand, he turned and relocked the door behind him. Then he led the horses quietly down the hill to his cottage, the darkness hiding them from the sleepy watch upon the walls.

Inside the house he found Rosamund already awake, ladling oat porridge into trenchers of yesterday's bread for her son and daughter. The siblings ate quickly, washing down their meal with a shared wooden goblet of brown ale. Both understood the need for haste, for they must be away from Greyfaire long before first light, lest anyone see them. When they had finished, Rosamund pressed a small basket into her son's hand. "For the journey," she said, and then turned to Lona. "I don't know if we'll ever meet again, daughter," she began seriously, "but remember all I have taught you, trust in God, and be loyal to Lady Arabella." She then hugged Lona awkwardly, finishing, "Christ and his blessed Mother watch over you, my child. Get word to me whenever you can."

It was in that instant that Lona realized precisely what was happening, and for a brief moment tears threatened to overflow her bright eyes. Then, however, she considered the wonderful adventure she was about to begin, and the fact that if Lady Arabella took her into her service, she would be a servant to a countess. None of her family had ever risen that high! Giving her mother a quick kiss, she said, "And God keep you safe too, Mother. Farewell!"

" 'Twill rain within the hour," FitzWalter warned his son, and Rosamund took her own fine heavy wool shawl and put it over her daughter's head. Then together she and her husband escorted their children outside and watched as they rode away.

"Will they be safe?" she asked her husband.

"Aye, they've nothing to steal but the horses, and Rowan is quick-witted enough if stopped to claim protection of the Earl of Dunmor's wife. Besides, the wild weather we'll soon have will keep most all to their shelters this day."

They stood watching as the darkness swallowed up both horses, and soon they could not even hear the gentle clop of the animals' hooves. FitzWalter smiled, satisfied. Dawn would not break for more than an hour yet, and it would be a dark dawn this day. He felt the first splash of rain upon his grizzled cheek, and taking his wife's hand, led her back into the cottage. He pushed her down upon their bed and loosened his clothing. The small danger of removing the two horses from the keep's stable was beginning to drain from him, and this relaxation of tension always made him as randy as a young billy goat. Rosamund smiled into his face and raised her chemise for him. FitzWalter chuckled, for he knew that they were both thinking the same thing. That there was time for a little more pleasure before the day's duties began. Age, he decided, had its compensations.

Outside the cottage the rain had begun to fall in earnest, and reaching the crest of the first hill beyond Greyfaire, Lona pulled her mother's shawl tightly about her, softly cursing the weather. Just ahead of her Rowan grinned, hearing his sister's words. He hadn't known she was familiar with such colorful phrases. After all, she was a girl. He pulled his own rough wool cape about him and hunched his head into his shoulders. It wasn't going to be an easy day, and he had a long way to go before he'd see his home and a warm bed again.

They rode on, and night became day. The rain fell in silvery sheets out of a gray sky, never lessening in its intensity as the hours crawled by. They rode without speaking, Lona following behind her brother, who prayed silently to himself that his father's directions were accurate. Although there were no signs or other indications, Rowan knew suddenly, as if there had been, exactly when they crossed over into Scotland.

"We're on t'other side, Lona," he told her. "Shouldn't be too much farther," and, indeed, in less than two hours' time the walls of Dunmor Castle rose up before them.

Wearily they trotted over the open drawbridge, the horses sensing the possibility of a dry shelter. They were not stopped until they had passed through the portcullis into the castle courtyard. Rowan slid easily from the gelding to meet the curious gaze of the man-at-arms who came forth to greet him.

"Well, well, what hae we here?" the clansman demanded.

"I'm Rowan, FitzWalter's son, come from Greyfaire with Lady Arabella's body servant and word of my lady's mother."

"The earl and his wife are at Glen Ailean for the wedding of his lordship's sister in three days' time," came the reply.

"Is it far?" Rowan asked. "And can you direct me?"

"Three miles, nae more," the clansman said. "Let me get my captain's permission and I'll take ye myself."

Lona sneezed, and then she sneezed several times again.

"Why, the lassie is soaked clean through," the man-at-arms said, looking closely at the girl. "Would ye nae like to take her inside the castle for some broth before I take ye on?"

"No," Lona said, settling the matter herself, "but I thank you, sir. I must get to my mistress as quickly as possible, for the news I carry is of great importance."

The man hurried off, and Rowan said, concerned, "We could stop for a bit, Lona, if you want."

The girl shook her head. " 'Tis already almost midday, Rowan, and 'tis growing colder. This rain will be snow by nightfall, and it grows dark early, being December. You must return to Grayfaire lest you be discovered missing. 'Twould make Seger suspicious, and then he'd begin poking about. If he does, he'll find me gone, and my lady's mare as well. Da would have a difficult time explaining that to Sir Jasper, and though he professes to be content to allow Da to remain the Captain of Greyfaire Keep, Seger covets his authority and his place. Now that poor Lady Rowena is dead and there are no more Greys at Greyfaire, who knows what will happen. Times are not good, brother, and I don't want our father to lose his place, and our family their home. Sir Jasper has no kindness in his soul."

He considered her words and thought her wise for a girl. He was a bit abashed at himself, for he would have never thought that his father could be in danger. His father had always seemed so all-powerful to Rowan. Yet Lona's words made good sense, so when the clansman returned to say he might escort them to Glen Ailean, Rowan thanked him and they continued immediately upon their way.

Cheviot Court, Lord Fleming's house at Glen Ailean, was in a proper uproar that day, for the bride had discovered a blemish upon her cheek that sent her into a fit of tears, for she was certain it would not be gone by her wedding day. It was into the midst of this confusion that FitzWalter's children arrived. Arabella, coming down the main staircase of the house, saw them standing in the reception room, Lona sneezing once again, and fell upon them with a shriek of joy. The clansman grinned, pleased at having served the new countess, whom few had really seen yet, as she had been living here at Glen Ailean.

"Lona! Rowan! How is it you are here? What of my mother? What of *Greyfaire*? Speak! Speak!"

Lona sneezed again.

"Ohh, dear," Arabella said, "you are soaked, both of you, poor things!" She turned to the clansman. "Will you take Rowan to the kitchens that he may dry out, please? Lona, come with me!"

"Mistress . . . Lady Arabella," Rowan said. "I cannot stay. Da took the horses from the keep by stealth, and I must get the gelding back before 'tis discovered missing. Lona has brought you your own mare, which Da says is to remain."

"You cannot leave until you are dry, Rowan," Arabella said firmly. "Go to the kitchens and I will find other garments for you while you eat. Your horse will need a rest as well. 'Tis a bad day to be out."

" 'Tis good advice, lad," said the earl, entering the reception room, for he had learned of the new arrivals. "Fergus, take the boy to the kitchens, and then stable his horse properly."

"Aye, m'lord!" the clansman answered, and then he smiled half shyly at Lona. "I hope ye've nae caught the ague, mistress," he told her, and then turning abruptly, he escorted Rowan out.

Lona felt a blush suffuse her already hot cheeks. The young clansman was certainly a handsome fellow. She might learn to like this dank, cold gray land after all.

"Arabella, go to my mother and tell her of yer servant's arrival," the earl said. "The lass will need a hot bath and dry clothes herself. Let me gie her a wee dram of whiskey to warm herself, and then I will take her to the kitchens to bid her brother farewell before I send her along to ye."

Arabella flashed her husband a warm smile, pleased at his kindness toward Lona and Rowan. Then she hurried off.

The earl turned to Lona, even as he poured her a small whiskey. "The news, lass?"

"Lady Rowena is dead, my lord. In childbirth. The boy with her." She took the proffered dram and gulped it down, gasping suddenly as it hit her stomach like a fireball and spread heat throughout her veins. "By our lady! 'Tis powerful drink, my lord!"

Tavis Stewart laughed. "Aye, lassie, that it is," he agreed with her. "Finish yer story though, lest my wife return."

Lona nodded. "My father is FitzWalter, the captain of Greyfaire Keep, my lord. He cannot openly oppose Sir Jasper Keane for fear of endangering my mother and our family; but his loyalty is with the Greys of Greyfaire. He wanted Lady Arabella to know of her mother's death. He says Sir Jasper will move quickly to consolidate his position."

"Aye, he will," the earl remarked. "I know I would if I were in his place. And ye, lass? What of ye? Yer father sent ye to Dunmor for safety's sake, I imagine. Yer a pretty wench, and Sir Jasper, as we all know, has a roving eye."

Lona blushed and a small giggle escaped her, but then she caught herself. "My aunt Elsbeth was Lady Rowena's personal servant, my lord, and I was being trained to serve Lady Arabella. My father did, indeed, send me from Greyfaire for safety, but he could just as easily have married me off, for I had offers. I prefer, however, to enter my lady's service, if she will have me."

Tavis Stewart had spent the last three months courting his hot-tempered English bride, who was still his wife in name only after six months of marriage. Though he was just beginning to admit it to himself, he was falling in love with Arabella. He wanted her at Dunmor, and he wanted her in his bed. He knew all about FitzWalter, his wife Rosamund, Rowan, Lona and all their siblings, for Arabella had told him everything of her life. His wife had missed Lona, and pretending that he would "allow" her to remain with Arabella could just possibly win this game of courtship that they had been playing this whole long autumn.

"Aye, she'll hae ye, lassie," he said to Lona. "She's missed ye greatly. I must, however, ask ye a great favor."

"Anything, my lord!" Lona promised. Arabella was so lucky,

she thought. This great lord was even more handsome than Sir Jasper!

"My sister, Ailis, is to be married on the fifth day of this month. If ye tell my wife of her mother's death, 'twill throw a pall over the festivities. 'Tis not as if Arabella could slip quietly away to mourn alone. She is my wife, and I am head of my family. Such news could spoil Ailis's wedding, and I am most doting of her, for she is my youngest sister."

"I am willing, my lord, but my lady will pester me to death for news of Greyfaire, and if I avoid the issue, she will begin to wonder what is wrong. I cannot lie to her," Lona said, distressed.

"Aye, she is as determined as a rat terrier," the earl said with a chuckle, "but if ye will pretend to be ill, Lona, she will nae question ye until ye are well enough again. Can ye do it?"

"Aye, my lord, but can I fool the others in this house?"

A knock sounded upon the door, and the earl called out his permission to enter. Flora bustled into the room. A grin lit Tavis Stewart's handsome features. "Flora will help us, lassie!" he said, and then quickly explained the predicament.

When he had finished, Flora nodded. "I'll take Lona to bid her brother farewell in the kitchens, my lord, and that will gie ye time to find yer lady mother and tell her of our plan. No sooner than the lad is on his way, ye must faint, lass. Can ye do it?"

"Aye," Lona said calmly. "I can."

"Good lass," the earl approved. "Dinna fret about telling yer lady the news of her mother, for I will do that after the wedding."

In the kitchen Lona bid her brother a fond farewell. The heat of the ovens and the fireplaces had quickly dried his wet clothing. He was well warmed by a hot meal, and several mugs of October ale as well. The clansman called Fergus had remained to keep him company, and upon closer inspection Lona decided he was indeed handsome. His hair was poker straight and dark, and his blue eyes twinkled as he easily bantered with the kitchen maids, of whom he was an obvious favorite. Wet and bedraggled, Lona had never before in her life felt so unattractive. For some reason it bothered her, and she turned her irritation on Fergus.

"My brother must be away quickly, you great lout!" she

scolded. "Yet here you sit stuffing your face, and encouraging him to do likewise."

"Give over, Lona," Rowan replied mildly. "I'll be soaked to the skin soon enough as it is. Give us a moment more."

"If Seger catches you gone, it will go the worst for Da and the others," Lona said, and her voice breaking, tears spilled down her cheeks, to her great mortification.

Fergus leapt up. "Dinna greet, mistress," he begged her, his handsome face openly distressed. "We'll go now, and I'll ride wi yer brother to sight of Greyfaire meself. Ye dinna fear for him."

"God go with you, Rowan," Lona managed to say, and then she fled the kitchens, Flora hurrying after her.

Arabella was upset to learn of Lona's illness, but Lady Margery assured her that it wasn't at all surprising, considering the "poor lass" had ridden across the border in a heavy downpour.

"Why, the child was wearing four petticoats, two of them flannel, and they were wet clear through," Lady Margery said. "As for her shawl . . . !"

"When will I be able to see her?" Arabella asked. "I would have the news of Greyfaire, madame."

"It will be several days before yer poor Lona is up and about, my dear," Lady Margery replied. "I'm certain she hae nothing of such import to tell ye that it canna keep. She'll be fine after Ailis's wedding to Robert Hamilton."

Arabella had to be satisfied with her mother-in-law's assessment of the situation, for to have questioned her further would have been extremely rude. In the six months she had lived in Scotland, she had allowed herself to be easily absorbed into this large and loving family. Despite having been raised as an only child in the relative isolation of Greyfaire Keep, Arabella had not found it difficult to become a Stewart. Ailis Fleming's wedding to the young laird of Culcairn was the first really festive occasion Arabella would be partaking in, and if Lady Margery said that Lona would be all right, then she was content to accept her word in the matter and enjoy the wedding.

December fifth dawned cold and, to everyone's surprise, fair. December wasn't a month for sun, as a rule, and everyone considered it an excellent omen for the future happiness of the bride and groom. Ailis Fleming was considered most fair in a gown of white velvet, the bodice of which was rather tight fitting, with a long waist and a low vee neckline exposing her pretty bosom. The bodice of the gown had a wide shawl collar generously trimmed in ermine, as were the tight-fitting sleeves and the hem of the gown, including its long train, lined in gold brocade. She wore no jewelry but her betrothal ring and a jeweled rosary which was attached to a delicate gold chain about her waist. Her hair was loose to signify her purity and maiden state.

In a matching cape trimmed in fur about her shoulders, she was escorted from Cheviot Court to the church by her father; the wedding party, her family, and the assembled guests followed. Once inside the stone church, Arabella looked about her and found the entire scene one of rather barbaric splendor: Clansmen in red, green, and blue plaid of the Murray clan to which the Fleming family belonged; the red and blue tartan of the Hamilton family with its narrow white stripe; and the green, black, dark blue, and red plaid of the Stewarts of Dunmor, crowded the church along with the more colorful and intricate garb of the ladies.

Everyone was curious to see Tavis Stewart's bride, who, if the rumors were true, had yet to grace either his bed or his castle, though frankly, many of the ladies could not understand why. The Earl of Dunmor had the Stewart charm, as many of the women present would attest. And there was that delicious story that she was English, and he had stolen her out of the church on her wedding day to another man. Knowing that the earl and his wife would certainly be at the wedding of Ailis Fleming to Robert Hamilton, few of their friends, relations, and neighbors had turned down the invitation to come to the event.

Arabella did not disappoint them. Her gown was of pale blue velvet and cloth of silver, trimmed in snowy ermine; and she had bound up her beautiful hair in a gold and pearl crespinette. About her neck, extending in fact from one shoulder to the other, the countess wore a wide, flat necklace of pearls and aquamarines set in a filigree of red Irish gold. Upon each of her fingers was a jeweled ring. Her handsome husband in his kilts was most attentive, which but added to the intrigue.

When the religious ceremony was over and the guests had all trooped back to Cheviot Court for the banquet, neither the Earl's nor his countess's behavior gave anyone a clue as to their relationship. They were every bit the happily married couple. Indeed, when separated occasionally during the hours of the festivities, Tavis Stewart was seen to seek out his wife's location and stare longingly at her. It was most confusing.

"Ye are wed wi her, aren't ye?" demanded his half sister, Princess Mary, who was wed to her second husband, Lord James Hamilton, a distant cousin of the bridegroom's. "Truly wed?"

Tavis Stewart laughed and kissed his attractive sibling's cheek. "Colin wed us in June, even as he wed Ailis and Rob today."

"That tells me nothing," his elder sister replied dryly. "They say she has yet to live at Dunmor. Is it true?"

"Aye," he told her honestly.

"Ah-hah!" she pounced. "Then 'tis true!"

"What 'tis true, Mary?"

"Yer wife is still a maid!" the princess said in whispered tones.

"God's foot, Mary! What has that to do wi ye?" the earl demanded irritably. "Our life is nae for public tittle-tattle."

She laughed knowingly. "Why, Tavis," she almost purred with satisfaction, "yer in love, aren't ye? And may the blessed Mother help ye, ye dinna know what to do about it. Ye've spent so much time in service to our brother, the king, that despite yer handsome face and twenty-eight years, ye dinna know how to act wi a wife. The little lass has ye all flummoxed, and I find it most amusing!" She laughed again, and the sound had a decidedly wicked tone to it.

He flushed uncomfortably, and his sister suddenly felt sorry for him.

"Hae ye made any progress wi her, Tavis?"

"Aye, and perhaps tonight she will come home wi me to Dunmor. We made a bargain several months back, and I dinna think she will renege on it."

"What does she want of ye?" Mary Stewart Hamilton said matter-of-factly.

He grimaced. "She wants her home back, Mary. She wants Greyfaire Keep back in her hands, though she understands she canna live there herself, as she is my wife. She wants it for our eldest daughter, whom she is willing to allow the English king to betroth to someone of his own choosing, but she'll nae be happy until Sir Jasper Keane is sent packing and Greyfaire is back in her hands again."

The princess considered a moment, and then she said, "Well, 'tis the lass's dowry, Tavis. I can understand her position. Ye'll simply have to get it back for her, and considering all ye've done for Jemmie over the years, he should help ye. When are ye going to court?''

"After Twelfth Night," he told her.

"Speak to Margaret first," his sister counseled. "She'll help ye. Remember the fuss over her dowry?''

"Jemmie was wise to accept the Shetlands and the Orkneys in lieu of King Christian's gold. The gold would hae been long gone, but those islands will remain forever a part of Scotland,'' the earl noted.

"Aye,'' his sister told him, "land is better, and understanding that, surely ye understand Arabella's point wi regard to Greyfaire.''

"I ne'er said I dinna understand it, Mary, but I dinna know if I can regain Greyfaire. I will try, and I know that Jemmie will help me, but this whole matter rests upon the whim of an English king. I canna predict what he will do.''

"Surely yer wife understands that," Princess Mary said.

"Arabella understands only what pleases her, Mary. She's a fierce spitfire, my wee wife.''

"I nae thought I'd see the day when Tavis Stewart would dance a jig to a little English pipe," his sister said, and giving him a quick kiss on the cheek, she moved away to join her husband.

Why was it, the earl considered, that all women had the sting of the bee in their power? He could actually feel the smart of irritation his sister's words had caused him, although he couldn't quite pinpoint the pain. Then he felt a gentle touch upon his arm, and looking down, saw his wife.

"You look like a thundercloud, my lord," she said.

"My sister Mary can be waspish," he said.

"Your mother introduced us earlier, and I found the princess to be most charming," Arabella said sweetly. "Perhaps she but told you something you did not wish to hear." She took his hand. "Come, my lord, it is time to put the bride and groom to bed.''

"Yer the only bride I wish to put to bed, madame," he said low.

"My lord!" She blushed furiously.

"Ye promised, lass. Ye said ye would come home wi me to Dunmor after Rob and Ailis were wed." His dark eyes held her prisoner, and Arabella, half frightened, turned away as if she would flee him. His hands fell upon her shoulders and he drew her back against him, his lips brushing softly against her hair. "Lassie, I want ye," he crooned.

"What of love?" she whispered. Her heart was hammering and she was finding it difficult to breathe.

"Damn, lass, can ye nae see that I've fallen in love wi ye? I spend more time here than I do at Dunmor just to be wi ye. There are those who would laugh themselves to tears to see Tavis Stewart, the Earl of Dunmor, holding embroidery threads between his two hands that his wife might wind them. Only a man in love is that foolish."

She laughed softly. "You have been most patient about my threads, my lord."

"I hae been most patient about everything, lassie," he answered her, his words heavy with meaning.

"I am afraid," she said quietly.

"Aye, most maidens are," he acknowledged.

"Your mother told Ailis there is pain," Arabella said.

"The first time, when the maidenhead is pierced," he agreed, "but yer a brave lass, I know, and ye can swallow yer fear." His hands slipped down to encircle her waist, and his lips pressed soft kisses along the side of her face. One hand moved up to cup her right breast.

"My lord!" she gasped softly. "The others will see!"

His fingers gently crushed her breast a moment, and he murmured softly in her ear, "What matter, lass? They will simply say that the Earl of Dunmor is mad wi love for his beautiful little wife."

For a brief moment Arabella closed her eyes and allowed the delicious sensations her husband's proximity was giving her to engulf her entire being. "I do not know if I love you," she finally managed to say, her lips and her brain somehow coordinating the words together.

"Do ye hate me, then?"

"Nay!"

"Dislike me?"

"Nay."

"Do ye like me at all?"

"Oh, aye my lord, I do!"

"Can we nae build on that, lassie? Come home wi me to Dunmor this night, and we will begin," he entreated her.

He must love her, she decided. He did not have to beg her to accompany him to Dunmor. He was her husband. Her lord. She was his to do with as it pleased him, and yet he had courted her these past months with charm and sweetness. He could force her, and yet she did not think he would. To deny him his husbandly rights any longer would not be fair, and such childishness on her part could turn his thoughtfulness to enmity. "I will come home with you, my lord," she said softly, "but first we must put the bride and groom to bed. Come now, for we have kept the others waiting long enough." She turned about, gently removing his hands from her person, and taking one of those hands in hers, she led him back to the others. "I must help Ailis," she said, and he nodded.

A toast was called for, and while the gentlemen were engaged in drinking it, the bride and the other ladies made good their prearranged escape from the hall, laughing and running up the staircase of the house to a bedchamber that had been prepared for the bridal couple's wedding night. After a few days' sojourn with his in-laws, the laird of Culcairn would take his bride home to his newly rebuilt house; and on Christmas Eve Day his sister Meg would marry Gavin Fleming from that house.

"No bride needs a marriageable sister-in-law mooning about her house," Meg said firmly, "and ye'll hae yer hands full as it is wi Mary and wee Geordie, and the other bairns to come."

This wedding night, Meg's impending nuptials, and the open secret regarding Arabella and her husband, led to the unusually noisy high jinks on the part of the ladies.

"Is there a knife beneath the mattress?" demanded Princess Mary.

"What on earth for?" Arabella said.

"To cut the pain when he breaks her maidenhead, silly!" came the reply, and the others laughed.

"Ahhh," sighed one lady, "there's nothing finer than a good upstanding cock on a man! 'Twill cover a multitude of sins."

"Ye should know," chortled another woman. "Three husbands ye've had, Annie Home, and how many bairns now?"

"Eight," came the reply. " 'Tis nae my fault I keep wearing out the poor laddies, but my Duncan says he'll nae leave me a widow like the other two."

There was much good-natured laughter over this sally as the ladies helped Ailis to remove her beautiful wedding gown.

"Ye dinna seem fearful, Ailis," Princess Mary remarked.

"Nay, madame," Ailis replied. "Why would I fear the man I love best of any in this world?"

The other women nodded, smiling at Ailis's reply. 'Twas a love match to be sure, and it would be a happy marriage, they were all certain. Little Mary Hamilton came racing into the room.

"The gentlemen are coming!" she cried.

Ailis stood naked within the chamber.

"Quick!" said her mother, giving the girl's long hair a last brush, "Into bed wi ye, daughter, unless ye wish to display yer charms for all the gentlemen to see!"

Ailis was helped into the big bed, the covers drawn up, and a gossamer light white shawl was draped about her shoulders.

"God bless ye and keep ye, my dearie," said her mother, bending to kiss her daughter's cheek, and then standing, she ordered, "Open the door!"

Mary Hamilton yanked open the portal just as the gentlemen arrived, preparing to pound upon it. They tumbled into the room laughing and shouting, pushing the groom before them good-naturedly. Robert Hamilton had been divested of all of his clothing excepting his shirt, which hung halfway between his thigh and his knee. He was flush with wine, excitement, and embarrassment.

"We've given him just enough wine to assure he does well by ye, madame," the earl announced.

The laird blushed a deeper hue of red.

"Will ye not come to bed, sir?" Ailis said calmly, as if the whole thing were an everyday event. She drew back the coverlet on one side of the bed.

The laird of Culcairn was gently led to his place by his in-laws, his shirt whisked from him, causing him to almost dive between the sheets next to Ailis, allowing the wedding guests a most enticing, if brief, view of his flanks. The caudle cup was brought with much ceremony and drunk by all, beginning with the bride and groom, who, trying to ignore the lewd remarks and rowdy behavior of their family and friends, almost sighed with relief as they departed; sharing a first marital joke after little Mary Hamilton, drawing the door shut behind her, called out innocently, "God grant ye both sweet repose, Rob and Ailis."

Ailis Hamilton looked at her young husband and giggled as he murmured piously, eyes cast to the heavens, "God forbid!"

Below in the hall the earl found his mother and said, "Arabella is coming home to Dunmor wi me tonight, Mother. We would like to depart as quietly as possible, and wi out fanfare, since our marital state is an open secret throughout the borders."

Margery Fleming laughed softly. "Then I would suggest ye take yer wife, my Stewart son, and slip away now while the guests are still involved in their drinking and their merrymaking."

He nodded with a happy grin.

"Hae ye told Arabella yet about her mother, Tavis?" his mother inquired.

"Nay, but I will tell her before the morrow. Like most maids, she is shy of her bridegroom, and I hae nae pressed her until now. I dinna want her to hae another excuse to deny me, Mother, and once I hae calmed her fears of the unknown, I shall be in a better position to comfort her in her sorrow," the earl said.

Margery Fleming's eyes were damp with tears as she said, "Ye canna remember yer father very well, Tavis, but ye are like him in many ways. History will remember my James as a hard and fierce man, but there was a kind, a gentle, and a thoughtful side to him as well, that he dared show to only a very few. I hae come to love Arabella, but her temper can be wicked, and often she acts wi out thinking. Ye will need to exercise all yer patience wi her. Ye will need to show her that part of ye that yer father showed me. It may nae be easy, my son."

"Will I ever grow too old for yer advice, my lady?" he teased her gently.

"Of course not," she said pertly. "Every man should listen to his mother no matter his age," and then giving him a kiss upon his smooth cheek, she said, "I will send Flora and Lona to Dunmor tomorrow. Take yer wife and go."

He kissed her hand, and with a smile moved away from her, his eyes seeking out Arabella, whom he spotted across the room in animated conversation with Meg Hamilton. Slipping his arm about his wife, he said quietly, "Bid Margaret good night, lassie. 'Tis time to go, and I would make our exit as discreetly as possible.''

Meg's eyes widened at the implication of his words, and seeing momentary panic rising in her friend's eyes, she curtsied quickly, saying as she did so, "Good night, Arabella. Good night, my lord,'' and she hurried off, looking for someone with whom she might converse. Lady Margery. Mary. Anyone.

"I have already spoken wi my mother, lassie. She says 'tis a good time to slip away. Flora and Lona will return to Dunmor on the morrow.'' His arm still about her tiny waist, he guided her from the hall. "Bring me lady's cloak,'' he instructed a servant in the reception area of the house, "and have our horses brought around immediately.''

"Aye, my lord,'' came the obedient answer.

Arabella was almost numb with a combination of nervousness and fear. "My clothes—'' she began weakly.

"Yer possessions will come wi Flora and Lona tomorrow,'' he said quietly, and drew her into the comforting circle of his arms. "Dinna be afraid, Arabella Stewart. I love ye.''

"Enough to leave me here for but a little while longer, my lord?'' she asked him.

He laughed gently. "Lassie, lassie, yer making a great to-do over little. I'm taking ye home to love ye, not eat ye alive. Ye've been my wife for over six months now, and I've been patient, but the longer we delay our coming together, the more dreadful the initial act will seem to ye. Hae ye heard any shrieks of terror or anguish from the bridal chamber above?''

Arabella shook her head saying, "But surely Rob cannot already have . . .'' Her words died off.

He grinned wickedly at her. "Perhaps, and perhaps not, lassie, but one thing I know for certain, both he and my sister were hot to couple wi each other, even as I am hot to couple wi ye. Love is sweet, my wee English wife.''

"And bitter too, I am told,'' Arabella said.

"Aye, at times bitter too,'' he answered her honestly, "but 'tis more sweet, I promise ye.''

Their conversation was terminated by the returning servant who brought their capes. The earl carefully draped an ermine-lined and -trimmed velvet cloak that matched his wife's gown about her shoulders. With sure fingers he fastened the closings and drew the fur-trimmed hood up over her head. Then he quickly drew his own cape about him, and taking his wife's hand, drew her out of the door of Cheviot Court, where their horses awaited. Lifting Arabella up onto the back of her little dappled gray mare, he mounted his own stallion.

This was the moment of decision, Arabella thought, as panic again threatened to overcome her. What in God's name was she afraid of? But she knew. Her mother's actions had shown her that passion was as strong as any other weapon used by man against woman. She didn't know if she wanted to be bound to this man, any man, by yet another chain. Helpless once more to decide her own destiny. Greyfaire's destiny. Still, if a man could bind a woman to him in this fashion, was it not possible for a woman to bind a man in the same way? She had to take the chance if she was to know, and if it was not so, what else was there for her?

"Madame?" His tone was questioning.

Arabella looked up at her husband and smiled shyly at him. "I am ready to go home now, my lord," she said.

≋ *Chapter 8*

*D*unmor Castle was judiciously quiet as its earl and countess rode across its drawbridge into the castle courtyard.
A stableman ran out to take their horses, bobbing a brief bow
as he gathered up the reins in his callused hand.

"Are ye hungry or thirsty, lovey?" the earl politely inquired
of his wife as they mounted steps to the door leading to the entry
hall.

"Nay, sir," she answered him softly, and then gasped in surprise as he picked her up to carry her across the threshold of his
home into the castle.

"Though we were wed here," he told her, "ye hae never
entered Dunmor as my wife until now. This is yer home, Arabella Stewart, and I welcome ye wi all my heart. There has been
no lady of the castle here since my grandmother's time. Her
portrait is in the picture gallery. I'll show it to ye tomorrow.
Her name was Jean Gordon, and she was the youngest daughter
of a great highland family."

The servant who held the door never even blinked as the earl
moved past him bearing his beautiful wife in his arms; but he
was unable to restrain a quick grin as his master strode purposefully up the main staircase of the house with his countess
still nestled within his embrace. There would soon be bairns at
Dunmor again, praise God!

Arriving at the door to his apartment, the earl reached out
one hand to open it, and walking into his dayroom, kicked the
door closed behind him. Calum, his manservant, was nowhere
in evidence, and the earl smiled to himself. Calum was incredibly discreet. The earl set his wife down, brushing a kiss across
her lips as he did so.

"I'm a proud man, Arabella Stewart, and so I tell ye that in
the veins of our children will run the blood of the kings of
Scotland. Never in his wildest dreams could yer father, may God
assoil his brave soul, for all he was an Englishman, hae imagined such a marriage for ye as we hae made. He would hae nae

appreciated the low and craven coward yer cousin Richard chose to wed ye. A man so lacking in honor he would nae come after his stolen bride, but choose instead to force her helpless mother to the altar that he might rob ye of yer rightful inheritance. I vow to ye now, Arabella Stewart, on this our wedding night, that I will nae rest until Sir Jasper Keane hae met wi justice, and I will do my best to see that yer beloved keep of Greyfaire is restored to ye. Remember, though, that I am but a man. I can only try, lassie.''

She nodded, touched by his words. She knew so little about this man who was her husband. She was beginning to realize that he was a marvelous puzzle, but each little piece of that puzzle she managed to uncover offered an enticing glimpse of a rather complex man. She wondered if she would ever know him completely.

''Ye'll nae suffer as my wife, Arabella,'' he told her softly as he led her into his bedchamber. ''I can be a hard man, but if ye'll but try, lovey, I'll make ye happy, I swear it!'' His lips brushed her brow, and then he undid her cloak and laid it upon a chair. Turning her about, the earl began to undo his wife's intricate gown with extremely skilled fingers.

For good or for evil, Arabella thought, she was his wife. She remembered her parents' happy marriage; how they had loved one another to the exclusion of all others; how gentle and considerate her father had always been with her mother, even though Henry Grey must surely have been disappointed by Rowena's inability to produce other children for him, particularly sons. She had thought to have that same good fortune with Jasper Keane, but in her heart she knew Sir Jasper would have probably made her life a misery. Her parents' marriage had been a miracle, Arabella thought to herself, too practical to expect another miracle, for all Tavis Stewart said he loved her. He had married her, and he wanted her in his bed that he might get heirs on her. It could be no more than that, though she was grateful for his kind words, said, undoubtedly, to soothe her fears.

Arabella felt the last of the fastenings on her bodice release, and he drew the garment off. ''I do not know if we can make each other happy, my lord,'' she said stiffly, turning about to face him, ''but we are wed, and I will not deny you your rights over me. I know my duty. Do what you will, for I will not hinder you.''

For a moment he did not know if he could contain his amusement. She was so serious in her intent, but he could still see that she was nervous, for all she sought to mask her feelings from him. She was a wee, proud lass, he thought, and felt a small surge of gratification, for he admired her fierce spirit which, he had only begun to realize, was so like his own. Her fear, he knew, came from ignorance and innocence. Tavis Stewart loosened the tapes holding his wife's skirts up and released the garment so that it fell to the floor, leaving his wife to stand in her chemise.

"I will leave ye to divest yerself of the rest of yer garments, madame, while I remove mine," he said calmly. He would soon calm her girlish fears, but by the time the new day dawned, he would have taught Arabella that in passion there is no fear, only pleasure. Without another word he stripped his clothing off.

The rest of her garments? He wanted her to remove all of her clothing? Arabella snuck a peek at her husband, who was methodically removing his garments and placing them neatly upon a chair. Was he going to take them *all* off? She had never seen a naked man. Swallowing hard, she bent to roll down her knit stockings even as she stepped from her shoes. Turning her back to him, she undid the ribbons that fastened her chemise, and drawing a deep breath, slipped it off. Without turning about, Arabella climbed into the big bed, pulling the coverlet up to her chin even as she turned over onto her side, her back still to him.

As the bed gave beneath his weight Arabella stiffened, her heart thumping madly. Her first instinct was to leap from the bed and flee to some nebulous hiding place, but she quickly remembered she had given him her word to neither deny nor to hinder him in the consummation of their marriage.

"Ye have not undone yer hair, lovey," he said. "Sit up and I will do it for ye."

Carefully she pulled herself into a seated position, her bare back visible to him, clutching the bedclothes to her chest. Tavis Stewart let his eyes slide down the graceful line of her spine. Then reaching out, he began to draw the pins from her hair, setting them upon the bedside table, his fingers unweaving her thick braids until her pale gold hair obscured the curve of her back and spread across his lap. Its texture was soft, and a faint perfume he sniffed, heather, rose from it. The sight and the touch of it actually aroused him. He had never in his life seen such beautiful hair as Arabella possessed. Gently he turned her about, and not at all prepared for the soft kiss he placed upon her lips, her mouth made a little O of surprise.

"Tell me what ye know of men and women, lassie," he gently asked, "other than the kissing and touching," he amended, swallowing down a chuckle when she blushed bright pink.

What did she know of men and women? Nothing! She knew absolutely nothing, thanks to her sweet but silly mother, who somehow, despite her assurances to the contrary, had never gotten around to explaining that rather important matter to her daughter. Arabella suddenly realized that she was mortified to find herself at such a disadvantage, and it was all her own fault. When Lady Margaret had offered to explain such things to her as she was explaining them to Ailis, Arabella had put her off in prickly fashion, embarrassed to admit her own mother's failure of duty. Furious with everyone, Arabella said sharply, "My lord, what should I know? A respectable woman coming to her marriage bed expects that her husband will educate her in all that she must know."

"A wise mother," he replied, "prepares a lass so she may nae be fearful of the unknown."

"I am not afraid," Arabella lied boldly, staring into the dark curls upon his chest.

"Good!" The earl grinned wickedly into the firelit gloom of the bedchamber. "Let us begin your tutelage, madame." He stretched his length out next to her, reclining upon one hip.

He had the longest legs, she thought, fascinated.

"Gie me yer hand, wife," he demanded of her.

"What for?" she answered suspiciously.

"That ye might meet wi the instrument of yer maidenhead's destruction, lassie," he said, grasping her hand in his. "Ye must learn to touch me, for in touch there is great pleasure."

Arabella snatched her hand away. "I cannot!" she cried.

"Perhaps it is too soon," he agreed with her in a reasonable tone. "In that case I shall touch ye," and before she had the chance to fully comprehend his meaning, his arm was cradling her back, and a hand was fondling her bare breasts.

"Ohhhh," she said softly, as much taken aback by the melting she felt in her bones as by his touch upon her sensitive flesh. Aware that her naked body was fully exposed to him even as his was to her sight, she found she had no time for embarrassment, for everything about this moment was so new and unfamiliar.

Tavis Stewart sighed deeply with pleasure at his first real look at Arabella. "Lovely," he said almost to himself as he cupped a breast in the curve of his palm and found that it fit perfectly. Bending his dark head down, he leaned forward to kiss the nipple, his tongue snaking out to encircle the hard crown of flesh which had been soft and pliant just moments before. Unable to restrain himself, he took the nipple into his mouth and suckled upon it.

"Ohhh," she cried out again, her resolve not to hinder him disappearing as she considered that perhaps her lack of knowledge in these matters would put her at a severe disadvantage with him. Squirming away from his teasing tongue, she fended him off. "My lord! Please, I beg of you, do not do that! If you would couple with me, then do so, but this dallying unsettles my nerves!"

Tavis Stewart burst into laughter, much to his bride's extreme mortification. He was unable to help himself, but seeing her outraged expression, he quickly regained control of himself. "If, lassie, I was of a mind to simply couple wi ye, I would not," he told her. "Yer a virgin, lovey, and I would nae give ye any hurt; but such delicacy of feeling aside, I canna couple wi ye until *I* am ready to do so, and alas, I am not."

"Why not?" she demanded, her tone quite plainly asking why he did not find her irresistible enough to be driven by blind lust.

"Because as lovely as ye are in face and form, Arabella Stewart, I am nae aroused by ye yet," he said bluntly, forcing his face to remain unsmiling, though he was near to another fit of laughter. "That part of me that ye refuse to entertain wi yer soft, wee hand needs to be encouraged. That's what the kissing and the touching are for, lassie." Leaning forward, he nibbled on her earlobe.

"I do not understand any of this," Arabella admitted grumpily, thinking that his attentions to her earlobe were not unpleasant at all.

He could not restrain the grin that simply refused to be stayed, despite his efforts not to offend her; and Arabella, really looking at him for probably the first time, was suddenly aware of what an attractive man her husband was when he was not frowning.

He was not handsome like Sir Jasper Keane, but though that craven was fair to gaze upon, his soul was as black as night. Tavis Stewart was surely not pretty, for his face was too angular, but for all that his features appeared to have been hewn from rock, he was pleasant to gaze upon.

"Now, lovey," the earl said gently to her, "ye must tell me exactly what ye do know of lovemaking, for though yer mam did nae instruct ye as she might have, lasses have an instinct in these matters, I know."

"I have seen the horses in the pasture and the dogs in the hall," Arabella told him honestly. "Once my father even let me watch as the bull was brought to the heifers, though my mother complained; but even I know that people do not mate in such fashion."

"Nay, they do not as a rule," he answered her.

"Must we do this *thing* now, my lord?" she pleaded with him.

"Aye, we must," he said quietly, and tipped her face up so that their eyes met. "Are ye nae the least bit curious, lovey, as to what all this fuss over love is about?"

His eyes were green! A dark, foresty green. She had never before dared to look so deeply into them, and the open look of passion in them almost took her breath away. Arabella shivered, and silently damned her mother for her silly thoughtlessness, for something within her desired to please this man. She wondered if Sir Jasper Keane would have been as patient with her as Tavis Stewart was now being. Nay, he would not have. Jasper would have put his own pleasure above all else, and the realization that admission brought her somehow angered her. What a little fool she had been!

"Dinna be afraid of me, lassie," the earl murmured softly. "I am said to be a skilled lover, and I will treat ye gently."

Still aggravated with herself Arabella snapped, "Is your man-root as big as your pride, my lord?"

"Only sometimes, lovey," he shot back with a chuckle, and kissed her mouth.

With the touch of that firm mouth against hers, Arabella felt her body flooded with a delicious warmth. Thoughts not in her head minutes before were suddenly swirling about in her brain. She was in bed. *Naked.* With a handsome man. *Equally naked.* They were going to make love, a not wholly unpleasant prospect, even if she was more frightened than she chose to admit. Well-schooled in kissing by her husband over the autumn months, Arabella opened her mouth to him, and his tongue plunging between her lips began a leisurely exploration.

She felt scalded as his tongue boldly caressed hers, and as he enfolded her within his embrace, the nipples of her breasts thrust forward suddenly to press against his furred chest. The softness of those dark curls was more irritation, however, than soothing. She found herself squirming nervously, which only increased their proximity to one another, and she sought to pull away.

"Nay, lass," he whispered against her mouth, and then his voice thickened slightly. "Jesu, yer sweet!" His head dipped once again to her breasts, which were now firm, the nipples so engorged that she thought they might burst open.

Her head began to swim as he kissed the sensitive flesh of her bosom. His tongue encircled her nipples again, each in its turn, and he suckled once more upon a sentient little point, groaning with his pleasure. Each time his lips tightened and drew upon her, Arabella could feel a corresponding tug in that secret and forbidden place between her thighs. Was this pleasure she was beginning to feel beneath her nervousness? She suddenly yearned to touch him, and yet she did not know if she should, or even quite how to go about it.

His mouth continued to give her pleasure, transferring itself from one nipple to the other while his other hand began to smooth over the taut flesh of her belly. She almost cringed beneath this new touch; not that she found it unpleasant, for she didn't. It was simply odd to have a man caressing her so intimately. His fingers strayed lower, brushing over her Venus mont as if by accident, and Arabella shifted nervously again. The hand returned to her belly and her breasts, causing her to murmur with soft contentment.

"Open yer eyes, lovey," Tavis Stewart said to his bride, and Arabella's light green eyes flew open to look blushingly into her husband's dark green ones. She had not even realized her eyes were closed. "Yer the bonniest lass I have ever known," he told her tenderly, and then he brushed her lips with his.

"You do not have to tell me that, my lord," she answered him shyly. "I know my duty as your wife, although I will admit to being grateful for your patience with me in this matter."

"If I tell ye that yer bonnie, Arabella, 'tis because I think ye are," the earl replied. "This marriage had come about through matters not of our making, lovey, but I think myself a fortunate man to have found so beautiful a mate."

"And had I not been bonnie, my lord?"

"I would hae still made ye my wife, lassie, but nae gained a hundredth of the pleasure from ye that yer beauty gies me. Dinna be angry wi me, for 'tis man's nature to appreciate beauty."

"You are blunt, my lord, and honesty, I have been taught, is a great virtue," she answered him.

"Will ye gie me yer hand now, lassie?" he said. "I need yer touch. Nay! I crave it." He took her hand in his and drew it, unresisting now, to his burgeoning manhood. "Dinna be afraid, lovey," he encouraged her. "He's a fierce laddie in battle, but easily tamed if ye'll be but kind to him."

Bravely Arabella reached out, her fingers wrapping about the length of hard flesh. To her great surprise it felt warm and alive. Indeed, it pulsed with a vigorous life force that she could feel most distinctly beneath her touch. "Are all men fashioned so, my lord?" she asked him. "It seems overlarge to fit within my sheath," she noted, careful not to look at either the earl or his manhood, for she was yet shy.

Tavis Stewart was astounded to discover that his bride's gentle touch was like being scorched with wildfire. He was hard put to maintain his equilibrium. For the first time in his life he seriously understood the real meaning of lust, and he was not quite certain that he felt just a little ashamed. He wanted this exquisite girl adorning his bed. He wanted her body with every fiber of his being, and he was not sure that a man should feel so strongly about his wife, about any woman. "Some men," he answered her carefully, "are smaller, while others are larger, although we Stewarts are said to be endowed better than most."

"Is my touch pleasurable to you, my lord?" she inquired of him innocently.

"Aye," he said slowly, hoping his voice did not betray the fierce fire within him that he was so desperately trying to bank. He could scarcely fall on his bride like a mad dog. "Does my touch please ye?" he asked her; although he knew the answer, he did want to hear it from her lips.

"Aye," she said, nodding, carefully choosing her words, "but I am not certain, Tavis, that I should feel such pleasure. Is it right and proper? Does the church not teach us that copulation is for the mere purpose of procreation only?''

"I dinna think there should be any shame in a man and his wife enjoying themselves as they go about God's work, lassie,'' he said with a rich chuckle.

"My lord! You come close to blasphemy!'' she scolded him.

The earl had suddenly had enough of talking. Rolling swiftly onto his back, he drew Arabella atop him, kissing her most soundly.

"Ohhhh,'' she gasped, coloring with embarrassment at this new position in which she found herself. It was so *intimate*.

His hands clasped themselves about her slim waist. She could actually feel his fingers marking her tender skin. Slowly he lifted her up and drew her forward until her breasts hung like two small ripe fruits just above his handsome face. Lifting his head up slightly, he began to tease her nipples with his lips, and teeth, and tongue once more.

Instinctively her hands flew out to brace themselves against his shoulders. "Ohhh! You must not do that, my lord! Ohhh! Ohhh!'' She was beginning to tingle all over.

His answer was a noise that sounded like a cross between a growl and a groan. His face pushed itself into the valley between her lovely breasts, and then with an agility that stunned her, he turned them once again so that she lay beneath him now. He was careful not to crush her beneath his weight, pinning her with only half of his great body. His mouth fused against hers, and Arabella's head spun wildly. Even so, she was cognizant of his fingers once again straying to that forbidden zone.

"Don't,'' she pleaded with him.

"I must,'' he whispered against her lips, and she felt the invading digits slipping between her nether lips, touching for the first time a part of her that sent a wave of pleasure into the core of her very being. "Easy, lass,'' he soothed her trembling body as he gently aroused her; caressing the little bud of her sex until she was squirming beneath his hand, until she was unable to suppress a confused whimper, for she had suddenly and quite distinctly felt the pleasure, yet she was still not certain she should admit to it. He leaned forward to feather soft kisses across her brow, her cheeks, her quivering lips. Then his fingers began a far deeper and more intimate exploration of his bride.

Arabella stiffened. She could not help it. Her awareness of

the serious intent this dalliance intimated could not be denied. She was unable to prevent the words that tumbled forth from her mouth.

"My lord!" The words were half sobbed, though she had struggled to keep her voice calm. "I am afraid!"

"Aye, lassie, I know," he answered her, rubbing his cheek against her face, "but dinna be afraid of me, lovey. I would only gie ye sweet pleasure."

"Are you . . . aroused by me now?" she asked him, and trembled at his reply.

"Aye," he told her honestly. "Yer nae just bonnie, Arabella Stewart. Yer damnably desirable, and I desire ye more than I can tell ye, lovey."

His fingers invaded her more deeply, and she cried out softly, more with fear, however, than with any pain he was causing, for indeed he strove desperately not to hurt her. He was discovering that the knowledge that he was the first man to ever touch her was a far more potent aphrodisiac than he could have anticipated. He was burning to possess her completely. He could never remember wanting a woman so badly as he wanted his young bride. Acutely aware of every nuance of her virgin body, he knew that he could no longer deny himself the pleasure of possessing her.

His teasing fingers had more than confirmed her virgin state. Now he moved them gently back and forth within the innocent silken casing of her warm, perfumed flesh, coaxing forth the sweet evidence of her own artless desire. Unable to hide that desire, not even totally aware of it, her ingenuous young body moved in a way that encouraged his fingers. He knew that she was now ready to receive the full measure of his bridegroom's love and homage.

Swinging over Arabella, he fit her slender form between his two powerful thighs, pinioning her firmly so that she could not escape him and do herself harm. Leaning forward, he kissed her mouth, her fluttering eyelids, her forehead. He could see the simple truth of her fright in her madly beating heart which fluttered quite plainly in the shadowed valley between her breasts.

Arabella hated the helplessness she was feeling at this moment. He was so strong, and even though she knew the act of love between a man and his wife could be good and was certainly acceptable in both the church and polite society, she felt a small flame of resentment. A small whisper of fear still nagged at her, and despite her good intentions to allow him his way, her arms flew suddenly up to fend him off. *She would not yield herself to him!*

Tavis Stewart caught her wrists between one of his hands and firmly held them captive above her head. With his other hand he guided his engorged manhood between her resisting thighs and directly to the mark. For a brief moment he debated the course he would take, finally deciding the pain would be no less for her whether he went gently or ended the agony for her by taking her without further ado. The look of terror on her beautiful face settled him on the latter course.

Arabella was pale and trembling. Her obviously overactive virgin's imagination was frightening her beyond all reason. Better to make the unknown the known, he thought, and so deciding, the earl thrust hard into his bride's unyielding body, leaning forward as he did so to absorb her startled cry into his own mouth as he kissed her a most passionate kiss.

Her body ached with his entry. She felt as if someone had driven a red hot poker into her vitals. Although his kisses successfully silenced her sobs, Arabella could hear her own cries within her very brain. She was being stretched and stuffed beyond bearing! The burning pain of his possession almost suffocated her with its intensity; but then as fiercely as it had begun, the agony began to drain away, until suddenly it was simply no more, or at least not enough to complain about. The very walls of her tight sheath seemed to have stretched to accommodate his manhood. Though a light sheen of perspiration dotted her face and her body, at least her initial fear had vanished. As he lifted his lips from her own, Arabella gasped in a mouthful of air.

"Yer a brave lass," Tavis Stewart said approvingly. "The worst is over now, my sweet, wee *wife*. Now will come the pleasure." He began to move on her, slowly, drawing himself almost completely out of her, plunging himself back within her. Each time appearing to drive deeper and yet deeper into the seemingly endless depths of her. He had freed her hands now, but they remained where he had confined them.

The tears she had tried not to shed were now slipping down her face unchecked, and she understood them not. He had not been unkind to her. Indeed, he had done his best to make her passage into womanhood as easy for her as possible. This was the way her life was supposed to be. A woman wed. Rarely was the man of her own choosing. This man appeared to be a good man, and she could consider herself fortunate. Love was a rarity, like a unicorn, a fairy tale. Perhaps it would come later. Perhaps not. Could she love this big, fierce Scot now delving into her with such passion and vigor? She suspected that through some odd quirk of fate she had wed a better man than she perhaps deserved. Her poor mother, who had known only kindness and caring from her father, was undoubtedly finding her life much harder as the wife of Sir Jasper Keane.

"Lass! Lass!" groaned the earl desperately, and then he rolled away from her.

It was the tone of his voice that brought Arabella back to herself, and as the fullness of him drained away she felt, much to her surprise, regret. An almost sad and poignant regret.

"Damn!" her husband swore angrily. "I gave ye nae pleasure, lovey, and for that I do most humbly apologize. Ye made me feel so like a green boy again, I seemed to hae nae control of myself." Raising himself up upon an elbow, he kissed her forehead. "Will ye forgie me, Arabella?"

"I do not understand you, sir," she said softly, feeling shy of their new closeness. "Ye were kind to me, and more than honest. You said there would be pain first, and there was. You said it would fade away, and it did. What more is there? What else do I not know?"

Looking down into her flushed features, he said softly, "Why, much more, lassie. A sweetness that melts the bones and makes the heart ache flows between two lovers." His finger stopped one of her tears, and he brushed it away. "Dinna fret, lovey. I'll make it better for ye the next time. I would hear ye cry wi passion, nae pain."

She blushed again. "You are a bold man, my lord. The boldest I have ever known."

"I'm the only man ye've ever known, Arabella Stewart," he replied huskily. "There is proof of my words upon the very sheets. Yer maidenhead, lost for all to see." He pointed to the linens beneath them and to her bloodied thighs. Then reaching out he cupped her head in his big hand and drew her up to him. Their lips were almost touching as he murmured, "I want more of ye, lovey! More than ye even realize ye hae to gie me," and his mouth crushed down on hers.

For a moment she felt as if she were drowning, but desire is communicative as Arabella was quickly discovering. She could not stop herself from wrapping her arms about his neck to draw him even closer; realizing even as she did that she liked the feel of his hard, masculine body against hers. She was unable to resist meeting him kiss for kiss; her lips becoming more skilled with each passing minute than she had ever thought them to be. Where earlier she had fought against the rising tide of excitement within her own body, she now no longer struggled against the inevitable. Her husband had not lied to her. There was pleasure in passion, and Arabella realized, though it did surprise her a little, she wanted that pleasure.

He sensed this end to the hostilities between them, and it but fueled his own hunger to once again possess her. The firm flesh of her young breasts was like a magnet, drawing him to them, binding themselves to him. He covered them with quick, hot kisses. His mouth closed over the nipples, suckling upon them, scoring them lightly with his teeth, inciting her to dig her fingernails into the nape of his neck even as she murmured her obvious contentment of his actions.

His lips strayed below, crossing her torso, causing her to draw her breath in sharply, particularly when his tongue began to slowly trace an irregular pattern across her tingling, shivering flesh. He rubbed his face into her belly, inhaling her fragrance. Then suddenly he was kissing the curve of her jawline, his lips moving down her neck to bury themselves into the hollow of her throat, where he growled low as her very pulses pounded wildly beneath his mouth, even as she turned her head to nip sharply at his earlobe.

Why, she wondered in a brief moment of clarity, why had she been so fearful of this marvelous wildness? She had not known! She had not known! Arabella almost purred her approval as he probed once more into her yet tender sheath, moving rhythmically upon her with careful, measured strokes which soon set her whimpering with frustration, for the manroot she had feared too large but minutes ago now seemed not large enough.

Watching her from between half-closed eyes, the earl saw the subtle changes in her face even as passion caught her in its thrall. He smiled with satisfaction. "All right, lovey," he murmured softly to her, "I'll take ye home now!"

Arabella felt as if she had been swept up into a fiery maelstrom. She could feel the powerful thighs pressing against her thighs as if he were guiding her. She managed to open her eyes for a moment, and the sight of him above her made her shiver, though whether from fear or passion she was not certain. He appeared so fierce, so savage in this possession of her. Her head was whirling, and she closed her eyes once more. She was suddenly and most acutely aware of a strange feeling that was beginning to permeate her from the soles of her feet to the top of her head.

She felt like a child chasing a bright, yet elusive butterfly. There was something she wanted badly, but she did not know quite what it was. Arabella's body caught the rhythm meted out by her husband. As they moved together in their wild passion, a fullness began to build within her, overwhelming her, almost suffocating her in its intensity. *She wanted it!* She did not understand what it was that she wanted, and surely she was going to die from the unbelievable sweetness flooding her body, her mind, and her very soul—but she cared not! *She wanted it!*

Satisfied that his young bride had at last attained the full perfection of passion, Tavis Stewart took his own release once more. Pleasured, he drew Arabella into the comfort of an embrace, and was amused when she sighed deeply and fell quickly into a quiet sleep. He grinned to himself. The lass was either going to kill him or keep him the happiest man in all of Scotland, he thought. He was not sure that he was ever going to get enough of his adorable wee English wife, but he did know that this marriage, made in haste and anger, would be well-consummated before he and Arabella appeared in the Great Hall of Dunmor Castle tomorrow morning. Knowing innocence made wise, the earl took his rest while he could.

When he awoke it was yet dark, and by the chill permeating the room, he knew the fire to be low, if indeed it had not gone out entirely. Arabella lay next to him, curled like a small cat against his side, the warm puff of her breathing soft against his shoulder. Gingerly the earl moved away from her, sliding his big frame from the bed. He padded across the floor to the fireplace, where the coals still glowed with a deep orange light. Kneeling, he laid a fresh log upon them and then fed the coals small bits of tinder until the fire flamed up once more, the blaze spreading a cheerful golden glow and a friendly warmth throughout the room.

"Tavis?"

He arose at the sound of her voice and returned to their nuptial bed. "The fire was about to go out, my love," he told her, and he cradled her within his arms.

"Will Lona and Flora come home today?" she asked him sleepily.

"Aye," he said.

"I have not yet spoken to Lona about conditions at Greyfaire under Sir Jasper's rule; nor have I had any word of my mother. She must surely be near her time."

He had to tell her, Tavis Stewart realized. *Now.* Before the morning, when Lona would return. There was no time left. His arm tightened about her. "Lona did indeed bring word of yer mother, Arabella," he began, and felt her tense against him. "Ye must nae be angry at Lona," he quickly continued. "I would nae let her tell ye lest it spoil our joy in Ailis's wedding to Rob. Can ye understand that, lassie?"

She nodded, a sinking feeling suddenly welling up in the pit of her stomach. *Mama!* The word echoed in her brain, and she knew even before he said the terrible words. *She knew!*

"Yer mother is dead, Arabella, and the bairn wi her." He let her digest his words, and then when she said nothing, he continued. "Sir Jasper would nae allow her to communicate wi ye, but Father Anselm, and yer good FitzWalter, saw that Lona was sent to ye wi yer own little mare on her death. Yer mother wanted it, and she wanted ye to know that she loved ye, and hoped ye'd forgie her."

It was then that Arabella began to weep. Great, tearing, gulping sobs of raw anguish that almost broke Tavis Stewart's heart. "*Forgive her?* She wanted me to forgive her? Why should she need my forgiveness, Tavis? She saved me from that dreadful man. I do not believe for one moment that she really loved him. She was lonely after my father's death, and she was incapable of managing without a man to tell her what to do."

"Yer nae like her, are ye?" he observed wryly.

She looked up at him, her eyes like rain-washed gems with her sorrow. Then she shook her head slowly and said simply, "Nay."

He hugged her close against him, and she began to vent her sorrow once more while he crooned soft words and phrases of comfort to her. Finally her grief seemed to abate, to his relief, for he was quite soaked with her tears.

"I am alone now," she said.

"Ye hae me, lassie," he answered quietly.

She looked at him again. A solemn, thoughtful look. He was a good man, this great border lord who had stolen her away from Greyfaire, wed her in anger, and then this night initiated her into womanhood with such overwhelming tenderness and care. Lifting her face to him, she said softly, "Kiss me," and as his lips touched hers with gentle passion, she was overcome with sadness once more. Her arms wound about her husband's neck and she wept again. How fortunate she was to have Tavis Stewart! Why should she be so blest when her sweet and simple mother had been so curst.

And as if he could see her very thoughts, the Earl of Dunmor said comfortingly, "Dinna think on it, lassie. Yer gentle mam is safe in Heaven wi yer father now, and I suspect she is far happier there wi him than here wi out him."

"This is all the fault of Sir Jasper Keane," Arabella said, and suddenly her voice was hard.

"Aye," the earl agreed, "and ye may be certain, my wee English wife, that the devil will pay for his misdeeds. I'll see to that, I promise ye."

"You *must* see he does, Tavis Stewart, for there are but two people upon whom I can rely in this world. You, and me."

In the months to come, Tavis Stewart would remember his bride's words with growing foreboding. For the moment, however, he was content to love her sorrow away.

Part II

HER LADYSHIP
OF DUNMOR

▓ *Chapter 9*

*T*avis! Welcome, man! Welcome!'' Scotland's king stepped
across the floor to meet his half brother, enfolding him in
a warm embrace. He was a handsome man, with his French
mother's olive skin, dark hair, and fine, dark eyes. Stepping back
from his younger but taller brother, he said, "And this wee
lassie is yer countess, is she?"

"Aye, Jemmie, she is," the earl said, and drew his wife
proudly forward. "This is Arabella Stewart."

The Countess of Dunmor curtsied to the king, her deep blue
velvet skirts puddling prettily about her as she dipped her knee.

James Stewart took her hand and raised her up, smiling as he
did so. "Welcome to ye, my lady of Dunmor. Yer a far lovelier
lass than my brother deserves."

Arabella blushed prettily. "Thank you, sire," she said, "but
I find I am most content with the marriage I have made."

The king chuckled. "Yer outspoken, lass, just like a good
Scots woman, for all ye were born and raised on the other side
of the border. Come now, for this is nae a formal court, I fear.
Ye will want to meet the queen, of course, and my heir, Jamie."
He led her to the dais where Queen Margaret sat and made the
introductions.

Arabella curtsied again.

"Why, my dear, how fair ye are," the queen said in kindly
tones. "Come and sit by my side that I may know more of ye."

At the queen's command a small upholstered stool was brought
and set beside the queen's chair.

"Sit down, my lady of Dunmor," Margaret of Denmark said,
and when Arabella had settled herself, the queen continued. "I
was sorry to learn of yer recent sorrow. I know how very sad I
was when my mother died. Like you, I was far from home and
did not learn of it for several months. I will remember yer mother
in the mass, of course."

"Thank you, madame," Arabella said. "I am grateful for
your prayers for my mother. When I think of her wed to that

▓ *Chapter 9*

"*T*avis! Welcome, man! Welcome!" Scotland's king stepped
across the floor to meet his half brother, enfolding him in
a warm embrace. He was a handsome man, with his French
mother's olive skin, dark hair, and fine, dark eyes. Stepping back
from his younger but taller brother, he said, "And this wee
lassie is yer countess, is she?"

"Aye, Jemmie, she is," the earl said, and drew his wife
proudly forward. "This is Arabella Stewart."

The Countess of Dunmor curtsied to the king, her deep blue
velvet skirts puddling prettily about her as she dipped her knee.

James Stewart took her hand and raised her up, smiling as he
did so. "Welcome to ye, my lady of Dunmor. Yer a far lovelier
lass than my brother deserves."

Arabella blushed prettily. "Thank you, sire," she said, "but
I find I am most content with the marriage I have made."

The king chuckled. "Yer outspoken, lass, just like a good
Scots woman, for all ye were born and raised on the other side
of the border. Come now, for this is nae a formal court, I fear.
Ye will want to meet the queen, of course, and my heir, Jamie."
He led her to the dais where Queen Margaret sat and made the
introductions.

Arabella curtsied again.

"Why, my dear, how fair ye are," the queen said in kindly
tones. "Come and sit by my side that I may know more of ye."

At the queen's command a small upholstered stool was brought
and set beside the queen's chair.

"Sit down, my lady of Dunmor," Margaret of Denmark said,
and when Arabella had settled herself, the queen continued. "I
was sorry to learn of yer recent sorrow. I know how very sad I
was when my mother died. Like you, I was far from home and
did not learn of it for several months. I will remember yer mother
in the mass, of course."

"Thank you, madame," Arabella said. "I am grateful for
your prayers for my mother. When I think of her wed to that

awful man, however, I think perhaps it is best she is dead and with my father, who loved her above all women. Besides, Sir Jasper but married her in an attempt to steal Greyfaire from me, but I will not let him do it!''

"Greyfaire is yer childhood home?" the queen inquired.

"Aye, madame, but more important, it is my inheritance, for I am the last of the Greys of Greyfaire. It is my dowry as well. Without it I come to my husband worse off than a shepherd's daughter. Sir Jasper Keane was chosen as a husband for me by King Richard, who was wed to my mother's cousin, Anne Neville. King Richard was a good man, but he was not aware of Sir Jasper's wicked reputation, for from the moment of his ascension to England's throne, he had all the difficulties he could manage simply in order to retain his ordained place."

"My husband says he was the best of the Plantagenets," Queen Margaret remarked, "but continue with yer tale, my lady of Dunmor."

"There is little more to it, madame. Unbeknownst to King Richard, to me, and to my mother, Sir Jasper Keane had murdered Eufemia Hamilton, who was my lord's betrothed wife. Tavis desired revenge."

The queen's blue eyes sparkled. "I understood that he kidnapped ye from the church on yer wedding day. Is it true?"

Arabella laughed. "Aye, he did. He arrived just as Father Anselm was beginning the service, and he offered to meet Sir Jasper in single combat. That craven, however, hid behind the priest's skirts and demanded sanctuary of the church. So Tavis stole me away and wed with me himself two days after. I'd heard by then that Sir Jasper had forced Father Anselm to marry him to my mother even as Tavis rode over the border with me."

"She died in childbirth, I understand," the queen said.

"Aye," Arabella answered, not certain just how much of the truth the queen actually knew, but in an effort to protect Rowena's reputation, she said, "My mother was not a good breeder, madame. She lost several children by my father. I am her only surviving offspring." Arabella's eyes filled with tears. "I shall never forgive Jasper Keane! It is not, you realize, that I do not believe that Tavis is the better man, for I do; but had Sir Jasper accepted my husband's challenge, my mother might have been saved from him. If he had beaten Tavis, he would have wed with me. If he had lost, he would have been dead and my mother alive this day!''

The queen, who knew that Rowena Grey had been several months gone with child before her hasty and scandalous marriage, reached out and patted Arabella's shoulder. Her gallant effort to protect her dead parent, even if her reasoning was faulty, was touching. Queen Margaret approved of her ladyship of Dunmor's filial loyalty. ''I do not attempt to understand God's will, my dear,'' she said, ''and oft times I find it difficult to even accept it, but accept it we must as good daughters of Holy Mother Church. Our gracious Lord has given ye a new family, my lady, and with God's blessing ye will bear children of yer own. They will never take yer mother's place in yer heart, but ye can best serve her memory by raising them well as she raised ye.''

''And as ye raised me, little mother!''

''Jamie!''

A tall and extremely handsome boy had joined them. He had a quick and winning smile that reached all the way to his bright blue eyes. His hair, unlike his dark-haired father and his blond mother, was bright auburn red.

''My lady of Dunmor,'' he said, catching Arabella's hand in his and raising it to his lips, which lingered perhaps a trifle longer than they should have. His eyes held hers in thrall for a moment, and Arabella was shocked by the raw sensuality she saw lurking within their depths. Prince James was a boy, a lad no older than herself, yet his boldness bespoke a man, and a man of far more experience than even she, a married woman, had. Arabella disengaged her hand with as little fuss as she could, but though the boy's face was a mask of polite charm, those wicked blue eyes told her that he had read her very thoughts.

The queen, however, did not seem to notice, and her tone was almost doting as she said, ''Jamie, yer a naughty laddie! Will ye not at least wait for me to properly introduce her ladyship, yer new aunt, to you? Arabella, my dear, this is our eldest son and Scotland's heir, James, whom we call Jamie. Make yer bow, ye wicked scamp!'' his mother scolded lovingly, and when he had, she said, ''Jamie, yer uncle Tavis's bride, Lady Arabella.''

Arabella arose from her stool and curtsied to the future king, blushing furiously as he took the opportunity to look boldly down her bodice.

"Madame," the prince said in proper tones, "yer presence at my father's court makes it a far fairer place. Welcome."

"I thank you sir," Arabella said politely.

"I am going to steal Lady Stewart away from ye, Mother, for ye hae been monopolizing her since her arrival. I would take her about and introduce her to all here."

"Of course, Jamie," his mother agreed, " 'tis a fine idea." Then she turned to Arabella and said, "Come back to me if ye grow tired of all this hubbub, my dear."

Arabella could not see any way to escape the prince, and so she curtsied to the queen, saying, "Thank you, madame, for all your kindness."

The prince took Arabella by the hand and led her across the room, but instead of introducing her to anyone, he drew her into an alcove. "Yer the most beautiful woman I hae ever seen," he declared.

"My lord, your compliment is overly extravagant," Arabella said in what she hoped passed for a severe tone.

The prince laughed. "I hae been told ye are a spitfire, my beauty. I like a wee bit of spice in the wooing."

"I would hope you would not even attempt to woo me, my lord, for I am content with my husband." Arabella was shocked by the prince's attitude.

He grinned engagingly at her. "I would make love to ye, my beauty," he said, and leaning forward, kissed her breast just as it swelled from her bodice.

Arabella started as if she had been scalded. "*My lord!* How dare ye!"

"I would dare anything in pursuit of passion, my beauty," came the disconcerting reply.

"*How old are you?*" Arabella demanded, suddenly deciding the only way to treat this saucy boy was to treat him as a child.

"I bedded my first wench when I was ten, my beauty. I'm a Stewart, and we're known for our warm natures."

"Ye'll soon be known for yer warm bottom, my royal nephew," came Tavis Stewart's stern voice, "unless ye behave yerself and dinna attempt to seduce my wee wife."

"Uncle!" The prince turned and grinned up at the earl. "Ye canna expect me to ignore this beautiful creature ye've wed."

"I expect ye to behave yerself in her presence, Jamie."

"I would try, Uncle, but the amorous culuch will nae allow it."

"If ye dinna want to find yer culuch shortened by several inches, laddie, ye'll keep yer wicked ways away from my wife. Now run along and find a more willing playmate."

"Madame." The prince grinned mischievously, and bowing, departed.

"He's really quite harmless," Tavis Stewart told his wife.

"He's a child," Arabella said, "and far too knowing a child. Why, he told me he bedded a woman when he was ten."

The earl laughed. "He probably did," he agreed. "He's a Stewart, lovey, and Stewarts mature quickly, particularly Stewart princes. Besides, the rumor concerning Jamie's father makes him more anxious than he might normally be to prove his own manhood."

"What rumors?"

"Such things need not concern ye, lovey. The rumors are nae true, and they are but the wicked ravings of jealous men. My brother has nae chosen his friends because of their pedigree, though there are those who think he should. The people he likes best are those who are interested in the arts and in the sciences. They are nae usually found amongst the nobility. Consequently, my brother's earls and barons believe themselves slighted by their monarch. They are a contentious lot, particularly the wild highland lords. They seek to gie themselves reasons why Jemmie does nae pay them the due they believe is owed them."

"How easily ye explain it away," came a soft voice.

They turned and Tavis Stewart said, "Nae only did ye bell the cat, Angus, ye creep like one."

The Earl of Angus smiled, but it was a cold smile. "I'm nae afraid to speak my mind, even to the king," he said. "Ye tread a very fine line like a rope dancer, Tavis Stewart, but ye will one day hae to make a choice like the rest of us."

"I'm a Stewart, Angus. My loyalty will always be to the Stewarts," the Earl of Dunmor replied.

"But which Stewart, my lord? The father or the son?"

"I canna believe yer fool enough to dabble in treason, Angus, particularly in light of the fact 'twas ye who hung Cochrane and his ilk."

"Ye liked that arrogant bastard no better than we did," the Earl of Angus replied.

"Nay, I dinna, but I dinna hang him either."

"Introduce me to yer wife," the Earl of Angus said and turned his gray eyes on Arabella. "Jamie was correct when he said she was a rare beauty, for all she's English."

"Many of Scotland's queens have been English, my lord, and I do not think Scotland has suffered for it," Arabella said pertly.

The Earl of Angus laughed. "So the rumor is correct, and she's a spitfire as well," he said. "Is it true ye wed her after tearing the clothes from her fair form, Tavis?"

"My wife, Arabella," the Earl of Dunmor said through gritted teeth. "Arabella, this 'gentleman' is Archibald Douglas, the Earl of Angus, whom we call 'Bell the Cat.' "

"Why do they call you that, my lord?" Arabella demanded.

"The summer we lost Berwick to England, madame, his nobles were, for the most part, in disagreement wi the king. We sat in the kirk at Lauder discussing what we would do," the Earl of Angus began. "The king had—and here I believe even yer husband will agree wi me—put his favorites, all of them incompetent, in command of his armies, bypassing the logical choices. No one dared to confront him wi this until Lord Grey—perhaps a distant relation of yers, madame—said, 'Will no one bell the cat?' meaning speak wi the king. For a long time there was silence, and then I said that I would bell the cat. From that time on I hae been called 'Bell the Cat Angus,' and I am proud of it, madame, for on that day we rid Scotland of several men who took the king from his duties."

"Ye murdered wi out trial or just cause most of poor Jemmie's only friends," Tavis Stewart said. "I agree wi ye, Angus, that my brother was wrong to put these men in charge of the armies, but ye could hae solved the situation wi out murder. Jemmie is a good king who has kept peace for Scotland most of his reign. The arts have flourished under my half brother's benevolent rule. Surely ye dinna want the chaos of constant war like the damn highland lords. Those uncivilized wild men live for strife to the detriment of their people, and ye know it."

"The arts! Pah! Music, architecture, painting, and poetry! What twaddle, Dunmor! These things are best left to the French and Italian courts. Foreigners all! These things hae nothing to di wi the Scots, or wi Scotland!" the Earl of Angus said.

Before Tavis Stewart might speak up again in his brother's defense, Arabella said spiritedly, "Just what does this have to do with Scotland and the Scots, my lord? Have you any idea of how you look to the rest of the world? A land where men run about in skirts, their lower limbs bare to the elements? A gray land where many of the peasants still live in turf houses because they have no strong claim to the land they work and cannot, or will not, build warmer, safer stone houses for fear of being evicted. A land that makes music by blowing through a sheep's innards! Though I wear silks, velvets, and damasks, my lord, and there are figs, almonds, raisins, and dates in my kitchens and fine wines in my cellar, these things, as well as most of our furniture, come from England, France, Spain, and Italy. The Scots export little save animal skins, wool, and fish. Their reputation abroad is for brawling and bold women. King James attempts but to bring some of the beauty of Europe to this northern land. What is wrong with that, my lord? The king's own grandfather, James the First, was a poet of some renown."

"A man who spent eighteen years as a captive in England, and then came home wi an English wife," Angus said sharply. "He was a good king though, madame. A *real* man who rode, and wrestled, and was bloody skilled wi both the bow and the spear. He had great strength, and he loved the machinery of war. He knew how to govern!"

"He was a poet and a musician as well as a soldier, my lord," Arabella told the Earl of Angus.

"Perhaps, but he was a soldier first, madame, and this James who rules us now is nae. Why, the poor bairn can barely sit a horse," Angus said scornfully.

"He does not need to in order to keep the peace between England and Scotland, sir!"

Archibald Douglas looked down from his great height into the blazing green eyes of the Countess of Dunmor, and he began to chuckle. She was a wee bit of a lass, but she was not in the least afraid of him, or even slightly intimidated by him. "Tavis Stewart," he said, "are ye certain this wife of yers is English? She sounds more Scot to me, and she's surely as brave as a Scot."

"I was not aware, my lord, that the Scots had a priority on bravery," Arabella snapped, and turning on her heel, stalked off back toward the queen.

The Earl of Angus broke into guffaws of laughter. "She'll breed ye up a feisty quiverful of bairns, Tavis, but God bless me, she's got the sting of a dozen wasps in that tongue of hers."

"Arrogant, pompous ass!" Arabella muttered to herself as she stamped across the room, not particularly watching where she was going until she bumped into another person. "Ohh, sire," she gasped, mortified, and her eyes focused themselves. "I do beg your pardon!" Blushing, she curtsied quickly.

"Nae fault, lassie," the king said in kindly tones, "but yer pretty face tells me yer angered. What has distressed ye?"

"The Earl of Angus is a damned fool, sire!" The words were out of her mouth before she could stop them.

The king nodded sagely. "There are times, madame, when I would agree wi yer astute judgment. What hae he said that hae distressed ye so?"

"Sire," Arabella said, "I am only a woman, and I have not had the advantages of a great education, but common sense tells me that peace is better than war. War destroys lives and property. Progress cannot be made in times of strife. I know that there are times when men have no other alternatives than to fight, but it seems to me, sire, that the Scots prefer to fight first and find the cause for their war after the fact."

James Stewart chuckled, vastly amused by his petite sister-in-law's clever judgment of his race. "Why, lassie, ye hae lived but a short time amongst us, yet ye know us well," he said.

"Sire, I have had the Scots at my back door my whole life. How could I not know them well?" Arabella said.

"Angus hae always been critical of me, lassie," the king said. "He hae ever been a hothead. He does nae understand that a king must rule wi his head as well as his sword."

"He does not understand the arts, sire," Arabella said earnestly. "While all about us in Europe and England there has been a great flowering of music and poetry and painting, here in Scotland all that is encouraged is to grow cabbages and carrots!"

Now the king laughed openly. He had not enjoyed a conversation so very much in months. His half brother's lovely bride was a delight. "Which of the arts di ye prefer, Arabella Stewart?" he asked her.

"Music, I think, sire. Mind you, I am not a musician myself, but my mother and I loved to sing together in the hall at Greyfaire. My father always said 'twas a waste to give shelter to a roving Irish minstrel, for we two sang the songs better. Mother and I, however, insisted that the minstrels be invited in, for how else could we have learned new songs? Ohh, sire, there is so much to know, and I know so very little!'' the young Countess of Dunmor declared passionately.

He was touched. Learning was not a virtue well appreciated by the Scots at this point in time, although Scotland possessed two fine universities, one at Edinburgh and another at Glasgow. There were no laws requiring education of even the gentry's sons. It was not thought that a good Scotsman needed to learn how to read, or write, or do simple sums so that his bailiff would not cheat him. A good Scotsman needed to know how to fight well, die well, and futter a woman well enough that he might be reasonably certain that his sons were his own. As for Scotswomen, if a man did not need to know how to read or write, certainly a woman didn't.

''What is it ye would learn, lassie?'' the king asked her.

''Everything!'' Arabella replied.

Again James laughed. ''What would ye begin wi?'' he demanded.

She thought a moment and then said, ''History, sire. The history of Scotland. I do not know if I shall ever be considered a Scot by those about me, but my husband is a Scot, and my children will certainly be, but for one, and I would know the history of their native land that I may better understand it.''

The king was pleased by her desire, but he was also intrigued by part of her statement: *but for one*. ''What do ye mean, my dear, that all yer bairns but for one will be Scots?''

Arabella suddenly realized what she had said and clapped her hand to her mouth. ''I have spoken out of turn, sire, for 'tis a matter best discussed with you by Tavis. He would be angry, I fear, should I bring it to your majesty's attention before he did.''

''And yer of a mind to obey him?'' the king teased her gently, still curious. ''Why, lassie, ye must love him to be so biddable, for I suspect ye could hold Dunmor Castle by yerself if called upon to do so, yet in this secret matter yer all meek and mild.''

Arabella blushed, unable to think of a single way in which she might defend herself.

James Stewart patted her shoulder. ''Dinna fret, lassie, I'll nae press the matter, for my brother's hot Stewart temper is every bit as peppery as yer own. Yer well matched, and right glad I am for it!''

Tavis Stewart had managed to disengage himself from the Earl of Angus and moved across the room to join his wife and brother. A beautiful woman unexpectedly blocked his passage.

"Tavis Stewart, it is good to see ye once again. I hae missed ye, my lord," she murmured into his face.

"Lady Morton," he responded coolly.

"What, my lord? I hae never known ye to greet me in such cold fashion," the beauty declared, her amber eyes growing dark with her annoyance. "Ye hae always been a most passionate lover," she said softly.

Tavis Stewart, to his irritation, found himself leaning forward to hear her words. Lady Morton's décolletage left little to the imagination. A whiff of her favorite perfume, heavy with musk, assailed his nostrils. It was a little trick of hers, the earl knew, to lower her voice so that a man found himself leaning forward to hear what she had to say. "Madame, I am a married man now," he told her.

Sorcha Morton laughed, tossing back her bright red hair in another familiar gesture. "I am aware of it, my lord. 'Twas the scandal of the court last summer. Did ye really tear the clothes from the poor wee creature's back before ye wed her?" Lady Morton shivered. "Aye, I'm certain ye did! How absolutely delicious, Tavis. Yer poor little English bride must hae been terrified of such savagery."

Across the king's chamber the Countess of Dunmor saw the beauty in animated conversation with her husband and said to the king, "Who is that woman, sire, who makes so free with my husband?"

The king hid a smile. " 'Tis Lady Sorcha Morton, my dear. She is a widow several years, for old Lord Morton died leaving her little."

"She dresses well for a lady with little," Arabella noted tartly. Lady Morton's dark green velvet gown was lavishly trimmed in rich brown marten. "How is it that she can afford to come to court?"

" 'Tis nothing ye should worry about, my dear," the queen said as she joined them. She had observed her husband in conversation with Arabella and was frankly curious to learn what was making him smile so much, for the king was not a man who smiled easily under any circumstances. She slipped her arm through Arabella's. "Lady Morton, my dear, is a woman who seems to attract wandering gentlemen. She lives, I suspect, off their foolish generosity. She is not the sort of woman ye should know, though she does frequent the court. Since she has broken no laws, I cannot forbid it in good conscience. It is best to ignore her."

"Is my husband one of those 'gentlemen'?" Arabella asked softly.

"Aye, lassie, in the past he was," the king replied, and then said to his wife, "Now, Maggie, dinna look daggers at me. 'Tis best the lassie know. She can hardly believe that Tavis was celibate until he set eyes upon her, and besides, 'twas but a brief fling. Sorcha Morton is too predatory and obvious a female for my brother. Frankly, I think 'twas curiosity on Tavis's part."

"Curiosity?" said the queen. "I have never seen anything interesting about that woman, Jemmie. Have ye?"

The king laughed. "I hae nae found any woman interesting but ye, my Maggie," he answered smoothly.

Now it was the queen who laughed, shaking her head at him. "Ye are too clever by far, sire," she said, and then turning to Arabella, told her, "Go and fetch yer husband, my dear. Tavis looks extremely uncomfortable to me, and 'tis yer duty as a good wife to rescue him from that female dragon."

Arabella curtsied to their majesties and then made her way the rest of the distance separating her from her husband. Reaching him, she took a leaf from the queen's book and slipped her arm through his. "My lord," she pouted at him, "I have missed your company these past few minutes." Her face was tipped up to his, her light green eyes wide with ingenuousness. She pointedly ignored Lady Morton.

The Earl of Dunmor grinned down at his beautiful wife. He could hear the faint edge behind her honeyed tones, and he was extremely amused by her pretense that he was alone. "Well, lovey, then I suspect I shall hae to take ye home and prove my devotion to ye."

Arabella smiled brilliantly. "Ohh, my lord, how wicked you are! Come along now, naughty man! You have made me most eager to depart." Then pulling at his arm in a most playful fashion, the Countess of Dunmor drew her husband away from where he had been standing with Lady Morton.

Sorcha Morton was mortified to find herself both so blatantly ignored and so obviously deserted. Tavis Stewart had made no attempt to even introduce her to his wife, and worse, had not bid her farewell. "Ye'll pay for that slight, my lord!" she murmured softly after them. "And ye also, ye simpering bitch!"

"Madame, madame, dinna look so openly angered. It does nae become ye," the prince said softly as he joined her. He slipped his arm about her waist and dropped a kiss upon her shoulder.

"He hae insulted me, yer highness," she replied in as soft a tone. "I will nae forgie him!"

"Is he a good lover, my uncle?" the prince demanded.

"Aye," she replied, her eyes going smoky with the memory.

"I am better," Jamie said quietly.

Sorcha Morton turned and looked into the prince's eye. "Are ye, my wee princeling? Are ye indeed?"

"Aye," he drawled, "I am. I can easily make ye forget my uncle, madame."

"His passion, perhaps," she said, "but the insult he and his milk-faced wife hae done me, *never*!"

"Where do ye lodge, madame?" Prince James inquired.

"At my cousin Angus's house," she said.

"Yer a Douglas, madame? I was nae aware of it."

"I was born a Douglas, yer highness," Lady Morton replied.

"Albeit an unimportant one," the Earl of Angus said, joining them.

"So ye wish to futter Sorcha, do ye, Jamie? She's a hot piece, I can assure ye, for I broke her in myself many years ago," the earl said.

"Nae *that* many years ago!" the lady snapped at him.

"I dinna say ye were too old for him, Sorcha," Angus replied. "Indeed, I think yer just right, for he's a lusty young fellow. Are ye nae that, Prince Jamie? I've wenched wi the royal laddie myself on several occasions, eh my lord?"

The prince laughed heartily even as his eyes strayed across the room to where his uncle and beautiful new aunt were now bidding his parents a good evening. Arabella Stewart was the loveliest woman he had ever encountered, and he was frank in admitting to himself that he wanted her; but for now he would assuage his passions on Sorcha Morton, who was, if her legend was even half true, a born and extremely skilled whore. Who knew what she could teach him?

The Earl and Countess of Dunmor departed Stirling Castle for their own house outside the town. They were escorted by their own men-at-arms, for no one of any consequence traveled without protection. It was late afternoon, and although Arabella was hungry, for they had not eaten since morning, she was equally curious about her husband's old paramour.

"Lady Morton is very beautiful, my lord. Was she your mistress for very long?" Arabella said in a voice carefully modulated to show him that though she was interested, she was not particularly concerned.

"An extremely brief time, lovey," he answered her calmly, although he was greatly startled by her query. That she was aware of Sorcha Morton's past relationship with him he had no doubt, for her exquisitely timed performance in the king's rooms was perfection.

"Why brief?" she asked, pursuing him, not quite yet satisfied.

"She bored me," Tavis Stewart told his wife. "The worst thing that lovers can do is to bore one another, and Sorcha's behavior lacks both spontaneity and originality."

"You obviously did not bore her, my lord," Arabella said sharply.

He laughed, and she bit her lip, vexed that she should have shown him her irritation so easily. "Men, as a species, never bore Sorcha," the earl replied. " 'Tis another of her faults, lassie. She lacks discrimination."

"You are harsh, my lord, in your judgment."

"Lovey, make up yer pretty little head. Are ye defending Lady Morton, or do ye wish to scratch her eyes out?" He was grinning with absolutely smug delight.

Arabella had a strong urge to lean over and box his ears, but she restrained herself admirably. "I was simply considering the possibility, my lord, that a man might bore a woman every bit as much as she might bore him," Arabella told her husband tartly, and kicking her horse into a canter, she rode off ahead of him down the hill from Stirling Castle.

He pushed his own mount into a faster pace and hurried after her. Catching up with her, he shouted, "Madame, I demand ye nae ride ahead of me like some Gypsy wench. Yer the Countess of Dunmor, and I'll thank ye to remember it! I'll nae be left standing in the road again like some spurned fool!''

"And I will thank you, my lord, not to ever again embarrass me publicly by consorting openly at court with your whore!'' she shouted back at him.

"She is nae my whore! What passed between us was over and done wi months ago! I didna even know ye existed at that point in time,'' he gamely defended himself.

Arabella drove her horse into a headlong gallop as they reached a flat stretch of road below the castle hill. Her temper was rising as each moment passed, and she did not know why, except the thought of Tavis Stewart in the arms of Sorcha Morton, even before her husband knew her, rendered her helpless with rage. Why did she feel so strongly over this past history? It didn't matter. She just wanted to get away from him and from her fury, and only a good gallop would help her ride off her anger. Behind her, her husband and his clansmen thundered on in their attempt to catch up with her.

And if the Countess of Dunmor was angry, her husband was equally so. Tavis Stewart did not immediately understand his wife's irrational behavior. What he did comprehend, however, was that he had been made a fool of by Arabella, and in front of his own men. Furious, he galloped after her, the blood singing in his ears. When he caught up with her he was going to give her the beating that she deserved for all of her appalling behavior. He was going to take her home to Dunmor Castle and fill her belly with his child, and she would stay there while he came to court. She was not fit to be at court. He had been forced to wed her, and he had been a fool to think this marriage could be anything else but one of convenience.

His stallion drew abreast of her mare and the earl reached out to catch at the other horse's bridle. With a shriek Arabella attacked him with her riding crop. She would not be defeated by this bullying lecher. She would not! Startled that she would accost him thusly, the earl changed his tactics. Quickly reaching out, he wrapped his arm tightly about his wife's waist and lifted her from the back of her mare to his own saddle. As her horse galloped on, one of his men rode up to catch the beast.

Surprised to find herself in her husband's arms, Arabella began to pummel him with her fists, and he had some slight difficulty in controlling his stallion. Pulling the animal to a halt,

Tavis Stewart leapt to the ground and placed his wife on her feet. Arabella swung on him with a fist, and he ducked the blow.

"I hate you!" she screamed at him. "I want to kill you!" Her pale features were bright with her fury.

"Why?" Her vehemence took him somewhat off guard. Why the hell should she hate him?

"The thought of you with that . . . that . . . bitch! The thought that you lay with her even as you have lain with me is unbearable!" Arabella said.

Jealous. She was jealous! Suddenly his anger dissolved, and grasping his wife by the shoulders, he looked down into her face. *"Why?"* he demanded.

"Because I love you! I love you, you arrogant bastard! I love you!" Arabella shouted at him, and then she slapped him across his face with every ounce of her strength, even as she burst into tears.

He shook his head at the vagaries of women, even as he rubbed his cheek. "I love ye too, Arabella Stewart," he said softly. "Perhaps we should go home, lassie, so I may prove the depth of my devotion to ye."

Had she actually uttered those fateful words? Why had she said them? Arabella allowed her husband to place her back upon his saddle, even as he mounted up behind her. She felt weak now that her wrath had drained away, and she leaned back, silently wondering just when it had gone and what had possessed her to utter those fateful words. She couldn't possibly love him. Love was pure, and airy, and sweet! Wasn't it? It couldn't be this dreadful feeling that left her bereft at the thought of losing this man to another woman. It couldn't be!

Tavis Stewart drew his horse to a halt before the door to his town house. Dismounting, he lifted his wife down, cradling her in his arms, carrying her inside past the startled servants and up the stairs to their bedchamber. Behind him he could actually feel the delighted amusement of his clansmen, and their approval as well. Arabella's hot temper was but an indication to them that she would give Dunmor strong children.

Entering their bedchamber, he ordered Flora and Lona out with a silent nod of his head. They closed the doors behind them, even as he set Arabella upon her feet and began the process of disrobing her. She stood mutely, even meekly, as he removed her velvet bodice and her long skirts. Her body was too young, too perfect for a corset, and she wore none, so he removed her camisa, leaving her to stand nude in her stockings and her shoes. He quickly removed them, and taking her face between his two hands, he kissed her passionately.

For a moment her lips remained lifeless, but suddenly she was kissing him in return. Kissing him with a fervor that left him breathless with his own rising desire. Her slender fingers pulled his garments from him; his elegant doublet, his silken shirt. Her lips were leaving his and moving across his chest. He kicked his shoes off, standing first on one foot and then the other to draw his stockings off as she unfastened his kilt, which she let fall to the floor.

He slid to his knees before her, his mouth scorching a fiery path across her torso. She whimpered, holding his dark head in tender embrace even as he pressed his lips into the shadowed valley between her breasts. Beneath his lips he could feel the frantic beat of her heart, and he was consumed with passion for his wife as he had never before been consumed with passion for a woman. His manhood was hot and hard with his need for her. Leaning back upon his haunches, he lifted her up and then gently impaled her, sliding into her silken love cave, groaning as she wrapped her legs about him, gluing her lips to his once again.

Instinctively she rode him, arms tangled about his neck, pressing forward just slightly so that her firm young breasts pushed against his chest. He slid his hands beneath the twin halves of her bottom, drawing her closer, reveling in the working of her muscles beneath the soft flesh.

"Tell me!" he gasped, pulling his head away from hers.

"Tell you what?" she whispered back at him, unable to meet his gaze, for he had certainly never taken her like this, in this way, upon the floor.

"Tell me that ye love me, Arabella Stewart, as I love you!"

She shook her head wordlessly.

"Tell me! Ye said it out on the high road, lovey, for all to hear. Say it now but for me, my wee wife!"

"I was mistaken! It cannot be love that I feel, my lord. There is too much pain!" she cried softly.

"Aye! There is pain in love, Arabella Stewart, but there is sweetness too. Ye love me, lassie, and I love ye too. Tell me now," he coaxed her gently, and taking her face in his hands, looked deep into her eyes.

"God help me," she sobbed, "but I do love you, Tavis Stewart! *I do!*" and she began to cry.

"Nay, lassie, dinna greet," he said, and covering her beautiful face with his kisses, he pressed her back upon the floor before the softly glowing fire and pushed deep into her. "I love ye," he murmured into her hair, unfastening it now from its intricate arrangement of braids, letting his fingers comb through the silkiness of it. "I love ye, Arabella Stewart, and tonight we will make a bairn between us. A fine, strong bairn, and I dinna care, lassie, if it be a son or a daughter. It will be a bairn created from the love we hae for each other. The love and the passion!"

She heard him; heard his words even as her own desires began to soar with his expert loving. She wanted his child! Aye, she did, and she remembered that Meg had said wanting a man's child was an indication that you really loved him. A son for Dunmor, or a daughter for Greyfaire? Dunmor was a certainty. Greyfaire was not. Arabella shuddered with her passion, but even as she did, the insidious thought that her destiny was once again being planned for her without her consent crept into her consciousness.

"I cannot be content without Greyfaire!" she cried.

"I will get ye yer damned keep back, madame," he promised her, "but first I will get ye wi my bairn!"

The intensity of his voice excited her. "Fill me full of your seed, Tavis Stewart," she said to him fiercely. "Fill me full! I would have a daughter for Greyfaire!"

"A son for Dunmor!" he countered, and laughed when she sank her teeth into his hard shoulder in her heated desire.

Chapter 10

*T*he Earl of Dunmor's passion for his young wife was a scandal that delighted a court seldom amused by anything. No man but the king might speak with Arabella Stewart, that he was not in danger of being challenged to a duel—even Prince James, who it seemed took great pleasure in teasing his uncle with regard to his wife. Jamie Stewart had all the qualities of a perfect Renaissance prince. He was intelligent, even as his father was, and well-educated; but where the king was solemn and thoughtful in his manner, the prince was charming, spirited, warm-hearted, and gay. The king was standoffish except with those who took his fancy; the prince was far easier to know. If he had one fault, it was his appetite for the ladies, particularly in view of his youth. Women twice his age sought his bed, and the prince disappointed few of them. The Countess of Dunmor, however, continued to elude Jamie Stewart, a fact that made her appear even more desirable in the prince's eyes.

The Scottish nobility, always restless, rarely content with their lot, were openly favorable of the heir over their king, even as they had once favored James III's younger brothers over the king. The resulting chaos that had followed their previous meddling was still fortunately bright within their collective memories, and so the earls, the highland lords, and the bonnet lairds on the borders held their peace for the time being. Besides, Jamie was young despite his vigorous wenching, which was approved of and encouraged by his father's enemies. His brothers were younger yet, and no one wanted another minority king controlled as James III had been controlled in his youth by the Boyds, or as James II in his minority had been controlled by Sir Alexander Livingstone and Sir William Crichton. Scotland wanted a strong king, and James III, despite his deep love for the arts and his ability to keep the peace, simply did not fill the bill.

Arabella liked the king. He was kind and soft-spoken, even if he did find it difficult to make decisions. One decision he did make was to teach his young sister-in-law the history of his land. Each day before the dinner hour the Countess of Dunmor came to her brother-in-law's private rooms in Stirling Castle, beautiful rooms designed by the king's late favorite, Robert Cochrane, where she sat at the king's knee and listened as he spoke of Scotland's history. She was soon familiar with the savage and fierce Malcolm Canmore and his queen, Margaret, who had attained sainthood. It was this gentle Margaret of England, a princess of Alfred's line, who brought Scotland its first taste of civilized living, and in the process, lessened Celtic power and influence. That had been four centuries back.

Two centuries ago William Wallace of Elderslie had leapt into prominence following King Edward I of England's brutal subjugation of Scotland. Wallace, a young man of great height who was renowned for his strength and his courage, led Scotland in its War of Independence against the English. Eventually captured and viciously executed by the English, Wallace's legend of bravery encouraged the Scots to choose another leader, one Robert Bruce. It was Bruce's daughter, Margery, who married Walter, the High Steward of Scotland, and from whom the Royal Stewarts were descended.

Arabella was fascinated by it all, for she had not really known how closely intertwined the two countries really were, or fully understood the reasons for the deep and often painful bitterness engendered between England and Scotland. She now comprehended better the king's desire for peace with his southern neighbor. It was not weakness on James's part. It was survival. The English, united as a nation for centuries, had been able to grow and prosper. The Scots, divided by petty rivalries, had not. They were two hundred years behind their neighbors to both the south and upon the European continent itself.

Prince James frequently joined them in their lessons. His love for his father was evident, even if his respect was not. Jamie did not understand the king's need for friends who were of a humbler rank than he, and yet the prince was no snob. Still, he was uncomfortable in the presence of the king's physician, William Scheves, and William Elphinstone, a wise and kind jurist whom his father had raised from a lowly church office to the important bishopric of Aberdeen. These were men with no power or wealth or rank behind them. Nonetheless, the prince came often, if only to flirt with Arabella Stewart, who, in spite of herself, had begun to succumb to the charming side of his personality, even if she did not approve of his licentiousness.

One afternoon the prince escorted her to the Great Hall of Stirling Castle after her lesson with the king. "Why," he asked her bluntly, "will ye nae lay wi me, Arabella Stewart? Am I nae fair to look upon, and surely ye hae heard that I am an excellent lover."

As startled as she was by his directness, Arabella could not help but reply in kind, despite his rank. "My lord," she said, "I know that the women of this court are loose in their behavior, but I am not. I love my husband, and I honor his name, even as he honors mine. I do not approve of infidelity, though it may flourish about me. I would be your friend, my lord, but if you persist in this foolish and reckless pursuit of my person, I shall be forced to speak to my husband and to your lady mother regarding your behavior."

"Madame, you are hard," Jamie Stewart replied, his hands placed over his heart for effect.

Arabella laughed. "My lord, do not think to weasel me with your charm, for I am determined not to be taken in by you."

The prince stopped, and taking her hand, drew her about to face him. "This is nae coyness, madame? Ye mean what ye say? There is nae hope for me?" he demanded, searching her face for a sign, however small, of some encouragement.

"I am resolved to be faithful to my lord husband, highness," Arabella said quietly.

"He is a fortunate man," the prince replied.

"I am a fortunate woman, my lord," Arabella said softly.

"If I could but find a love like yers, madame . . ." Jamie Stewart said.

"In time, my lord, you will. You are young yet, despite your great height and your wicked ways," she teased, and he chuckled.

"But I may count upon yer friendship, Arabella Stewart?"

"Aye, my lord, you have it," she told him.

They arrived in the Great Hall of Stirling Castle to learn that King Henry VII had finally, on the eighteenth day of January, married Princess Elizabeth of York at Westminster.

"He didna dare wait any longer," the Earl of Angus said. "The commons petitioned him at Christmas to stop dragging his feet and marry the wench. Henry Tudor's claim to his throne is nebulous at best. His wife's claim could be said to be stronger, and if the truth be known, young Edward, the boy earl of Warwick, has the strongest claim of all, being the last surviving, legitimate male Plantagenet. His late father, the Duke of Clarence, was older than King Richard.''

"Henry Tudor,'' the king said, taking up the tale, ''and his wife are both great-great-grandchildren of John of Gaunt and his third wife, Katherine Swynford. They had four bairns, three lads and a lassie, but the bairns were born illegitimate, for after the death of his first wife, Blanche of Lancaster, the Duke of Lancaster was forced by political necessity to wed Constanza of Portugal despite the fact he hae already fallen in love wi Lady Swynford. After his second wife died, John of Gaunt wed wi his true love and legitimized their bairns, who had taken the family name of Beaufort. The Tudor's mam is Lady Margaret Beaufort, the great-granddaughter of the duke and his last wife, descended through the line of their eldest son, John Beaufort, the Duke of Somerset. Elizabeth of York, however, descends through the line of Joan Beaufort, the only daughter of John of Gaunt and Katherine Swynford. She was wed to Ralph Neville, the Earl of Westmorland. She was his first wife. His first had borne him nine children. Joan Beaufort bore him fourteen more. It was the youngest daughter of that match, Cecily, who wed Richard, Duke of York; and together they fathered King Edward IV and King Richard III, among others.''

Here Arabella took up the tale from the king. ''My mother was a Neville,'' she said. ''She was raised by the Earl of Warwick, Richard Neville. I have seen Lady Cecily Neville many times. She was called the 'Rose of Raby' in her youth, for she was very beautiful. She still is, though she be an old lady. But all of this still does not tell me why King Henry lagged in his duty to wed with Princess Elizabeth.''

''I think,'' the king said thoughtfully, ''that Henry Tudor wanted to affirm his own rights to England's throne before taking the York heiress to wife. There are some, I am told, who support him only for the sake of his wife's family. 'Tis hard on a man for his people to feel that way.''

''And there is trouble yet brewing for that Welshman,'' Angus said. ''The boy earl will be a rallying point for the Yorkist rabble, for all King Henry's lodged him in the Tower and made good his promise to marry the York heiress. That bodes well for

Scotland, for the English canna give us difficulties when they hae their own difficulties at home. 'Twould be a good time to regain Berwick back, I think.''

The other lords in the hall hearing his words nodded in agreement, but the king said, "I want peace wi England, Angus, and ye need nae shake yer head at me either. The violence that goes on on the border is horrific. It must be stopped once and for all!''

"Aye, and we'll stop it only when we regain Berwick and teach the English nae to meddle wi the Scots!'' Angus roared. "Yer weak, Jemmie Stewart! Yer father, God assoil him, and yer grandfather, God assoil him, would nae have sued meekly for peace as ye do!''

The king said nothing, but in his dark eyes there was a hopeless look, for he knew men like the Earl of Angus would never understand his policies.

"So you would wage war along the border, would you, my lord?'' Arabella said furiously. "If you lived upon that land as I have lived my entire life, you would not be so eager to cause trouble! How dare you criticize the king for keeping the peace! You sit in the hall of your fine castle, safe from your enemies, planning havoc upon innocents, and you smugly think yourself the better man because you are as quick with your sword as you are undoubtedly to take offense. You never smell the smoke of burning cottages, do you? Or care that the hooves of your horses have destroyed kitchen gardens meant to feed a family through a winter? Do the cries of innocent women being raped by your men even reach you, or does the blood lust ringing in your ears deafen you to them and to the shrieks of their children being murdered? You and your ilk make me ill, my lord, and lest you think I single the Scots out in this matter, be assured that I despise my own kind for the similar crimes that they commit here in Scotland. The madness must stop, and I for one support the king in his efforts. He is the best man of you all!''

For a moment the Earl of Angus was rendered speechless by Arabella's outburst, and then he said scathingly, "Dunmor, can ye nae keep yer woman under control?''

Tavis Stewart saw it coming, but for the life of him he was unable to react swiftly enough. His countess, ever quick with her fists, doubled her small hand and hit Archibald Douglas a mighty blow that staggered him, much to his surprise and his deep embarrassment. The earl, thrown off balance, tottered backward a brief moment and then he grew beet red in his face. "Jesu Christus!" he roared, his hand going to the dagger at his waist, his gaze locking onto the Earl of Dunmor.

"Oh no, my lord!" Arabella shouted at him. " 'Tis not my husband with whom you have a quarrel, 'tis me! Do you think I am afraid of *you*? I am not! Choose your weapon, and I will meet you anywhere to settle this matter, should you feel your 'honor' has been compromised."

Now the Earl of Angus was truly rendered speechless, and all about them the court gaped between them, trying to make sense of the entire matter. The queen found herself close to laughter, and bit her lip sharply to contain her mirth. How many times, she thought, she had wanted to smack the arrogant Archibald Douglas herself, but she had never considered that a woman would do such a thing. Tavis Stewart swallowed back his own mirth, all the while wondering how the hell he was going to extricate both himself and his wee termagant of a wife from this mire she had gotten them into. It was then that the king spoke.

"My honor hae been offended by ye, Archibald Douglas, but in turn I hae been well defended by the Countess of Dunmor. I consider this matter closed now. Do ye both understand me?"

Arabella curtsied prettily. "Aye, my liege," she said, smiling.

"Aye!" the Earl of Angus growled shortly. In truth he was relieved, for the king had actually extricated him from an extremely tricky situation. The damned spitfire had challenged him, laughable as it was, and then he had been totally confused as to how he would answer her. A man certainly couldn't meet a woman in martial combat, yet how could he have walked away without seeming a coward? He looked at the Earl of Dunmor and muttered, "Ye hae best take a stick to yer countess, Tavis, lest ye one day find her wearing yer kilt."

The remark stung, but Tavis Stewart smiled engagingly and said, "She would look fetching in a kilt, Angus, for her legs are prettier than ye could imagine."

His remark had the effect of breaking the tension that had enveloped the room, and there was relieved laughter. The queen nodded to her Irish minstrel, and he began to play a merry tune upon his lute.

"We would beg yer leave to depart, Jemmie," the Earl of Dunmor said to his half brother, and the king nodded, his dark eyes twinkling.

"Dinna be hard on Arabella," he said low to Tavis Stewart. "She hae given me the best entertainment I hae had in many a month. I approve her loyalty, but more important, brother, she is as quick-witted as she is quick-tongued. These are nae bad traits, even in a woman."

Before the earl might answer the king, Arabella quickly said, "If I have offended you, sire, I beg your pardon. I allowed my dislike for the Earl of Angus to overcome my good sense and my good manners." Though her words were soft, the Countess of Dunmor did not look in the least contrite.

"I will admit to liking a quieter evening, madame," the king said, "but ye did gie us a grand amusement."

" 'Twill nae happen again, Jemmie," Tavis Stewart said quietly, and with a bow, escorted his wife from the Great Hall of Stirling Castle.

Outside a coach awaited them, for the weather had turned bitterly cold and the riding was harsh. They entered the coach and it moved off down the hill. Arabella sat silently, waiting for her husband to speak. She had not missed the edge in his voice when he had promised the king that she would not have another outburst. The wind blew through the joints of the coach and she shivered, drawing the fur-lined cloak about her.

"Angus is right," Tavis Stewart said. "I ought to beat ye."

"You would not!" she answered him, shocked.

"Nay, but I should," he replied. "God's bones, madame! Ye speak with fervor against violence upon the border, and then ye most violently assault poor Archibald Douglas wi yer fists!"

"He insulted the king!"

"Jemmie is more than capable of handling Angus and his ilk, lovey. He hae spent his life wi men like that."

"Archibald Douglas is the most arrogant man I have ever met!" Arabella fumed.

"Nay, lovey, he is not," Tavis Stewart replied. "Oh, he is proud. All the Douglases are proud, but he loves Scotland, and he is loyal."

"To whom, I wonder?" Arabella said.

"Dinna ever 'wonder' that aloud in public," her husband

warned her. "Angus wants what is best for Scotland, Arabella. Nothing more."

"And what is best for Scotland, my lord? I am not a fool. I know there are those who would set the prince above his father. If civil war should come, Tavis Stewart, who will you support? Your half brother who is king? Or your nephew who will one day be king? What is actually best for Scotland? Another minority? Who will rule then?"

They were hard questions that his wife put to him, and the Earl of Dunmor did not have the answers. There were other considerations as well. England, always a thorn in the paw of the lion in the north, as Scotland was known, was currently undergoing serious dynastic changes. What it would all mean for Scotland was uncertain. Henry Tudor, despite his astounding victory over Richard III at Bosworth, was not yet entirely secure upon the throne he had usurped, despite his recent marriage to Elizabeth of York. The new queen's brothers were presumed dead, and Henry claimed to have the last Plantagenet heir under lock and key within the Tower.

Still, there had been disquieting rumors from Ireland. It was being said that young Edward Neville, the boy-earl of Warwick, was safely in the custody of the great Earl of Kildare; that the boy in the Tower was an imposter. Gerald Fitzgerald, the eighth Earl of Kildare, was the Lord Deputy of Ireland. A member of the most powerful Anglo-Norman family in Ireland, he controlled more of that land than any other Irishman had controlled since the last great High King, Brian Boru. Would he back the boy in his charge against the new Tudor dynasty? Was that boy in fact the legitimate Earl of Warwick, or an imposter, as some were already claiming? No. England was not yet safe from civil strife.

The Earl of Dunmor could see his elder half brother's point in the argument. England needed no outside troubles, and it was a good time to make a peace with the English. On the other hand, it could also be a good time to strike out at the English, who, busy with their other difficulties, would be helpless to defend themselves . . . or would they? Whatever else the English were, they were good fighters, Tavis Stewart allowed with a small grimace.

They remained at court, and Arabella managed not to engage the Earl of Angus in battle, although it was not easy. Archibald

Douglas, recovered from his initial shock at being challenged by a woman, suddenly saw the humor in the whole situation and took great delight in teasing the Countess of Dunmor. The entire court watched, eagerly waiting for the next explosion.

"He will not leave me be," Arabella said to the king one day. "I have promised Tavis that I will not again display my temper before you, sire, and I am a woman of my word."

"Ye must think of another way to stop him then, lassie," the king told her. "I am certain if ye think on it, ye will find a way."

"And your majesty would not object?" Arabella said. "I know that this earl is a powerful man and important to your majesty's cause."

The king chuckled. "Angus is loyal to Scotland first, lassie, but that doesna mean he is loyal to me."

"But you are Scotland, sire!" Arabella cried.

James III smiled sadly. "I am Scotland's king, lassie, and that doesna always mean the same thing, I fear, though it should." Then he patted her little hand, which in her distress she had placed upon the arm of his robe. "If ye take yer revenge upon Archie, my dear, dinna tell me of it beforehand lest I feel guilty; and above all, be subtle. It is difficult to be angry at a jest well played, even if that jest is upon ye."

Arabella considered for several weeks just how she would get back her own upon Angus, and then she knew. Archibald Douglas had one weakness. He loved fruit. Fruit was a rare commodity in Scotland in the dead of winter, and to make matters worse, it was Lent. Almost every day was a fast day but for Sunday, which, because it had been set aside as the Lord's Day, was considered, even in this season of penance, a feast day. Through Flora, whose elder sister was the housekeeper in the Stirling town house, Arabella managed to obtain a supply of fresh green figs. With Lona at her side, the Countess of Dunmor ventured into the kitchens of the town house and personally prepared the figs in a sweet syrup. Draining the fruit, she stuffed each one with an almond and rolled it in pulverized sugar. Then lining a small Florentine basket of filigreed silver with a bright scrap of silk, she filled it with the figs.

Lona could scarcely contain herself. "He'll get one surprise, he will, m'lady, when he eats them figs," she said, giggling.

"I think after this," Arabella said, "Archibald Douglas will leave me be. I do not know how much longer I can restrain my temper, for he has tried me sorely these last few weeks.''

''I can only hope,'' Flora fretted, ''that yer husband will nae be too angry wi ye, m'lady.''

''I think Tavis will be relieved,'' Arabella laughed. ''No one is more aware than he of my great restraint toward Lord Douglas.''

That Sunday evening at the Great Hall of Stirling Castle, the Earl of Angus once again attempted to bait the Countess of Dunmor into a show of her fiery temper, but Arabella merely laughed.

''My lord,'' she said, ''I do not wish to quarrel with you. Really I do not. To show my good faith, I have made for you, with my own two hands, a small gift. Knowing your love for fruit, I managed to obtain some fine green figs and prepared them as my mother taught me.'' She turned. ''Lona, bring the basket for Lord Douglas.''

''Why, madame,'' the Earl of Angus said, caught completely off guard. ''This is most surprising.'' He looked down at her and thought again, as he had been thinking of late, that she was really a most beautiful girl. Unlike the wonderfully statuesque Scots women to whom he was used, there was something exciting about her petiteness. She was wearing a gown of scarlet velvet tonight which made her fair skin seem even fairer by contrast. Her pale gold hair was unlike anything he had ever seen before, and those light green eyes she possessed were almost mysterious.

''Sir,'' Arabella said sweetly, ''we are not children, and we should both know better than to quarrel before their majesties. Having begun this matter between us so publicly, I feel it is my duty to end it as publicly.''

Archibald Douglas wondered if that pretty rosebud mouth of hers would be sweet to kiss, and in his heart he knew the answer. ''Then ye are capitulating to me, madame?'' he said, unable to restrain himself from just a tiny prick.

''I did not think to exhibit good manners, my lord, was to acknowledge defeat,'' Arabella answered calmly, while those about her were amazed that she had not shown her anger toward Angus. ''Ahh, here is my Lona with the basket, my lord.'' The Countess of Dunmor took the pretty silver piece from her servant and, smiling, handed it to Lord Douglas.

For a moment he hesitated, and then said, "How do I know, madame, that ye dinna seek to poison me?"

Arabella rolled her eyes comically, inferring to all about her that dealing with this earl was like dealing with a silly child. She took two plump fruits from the basket, and popping one into her mouth, offered the other to the queen, who accepted it without hesitation. When she had finished the sweet she smiled up innocently at Lord Douglas and said, "There, my lord! I have eaten the fruit myself and given one to the queen. Certainly you cannot believe I would harm either myself or her majesty? Will you not now accept my gift, that we may make a good end to this affair between us?"

The Earl of Angus smiled down, pleased, upon the Countess of Dunmor. "Very well, madame," he said expansively and popped one of the fruits into his own mouth. His eyes lit up, even as he quickly chewed and swallowed the fig. "By God, madame! These are delicious! I'll nae share a one!" and he began eating the fruits as quickly as he could stuff them into his mouth and swallow them down.

Arabella curtsied to the Earl of Angus and moved off, suddenly finding her husband at her side.

Tavis Stewart took his wife's arm and murmured into her ear, "Ye didna tell me ye intended suing for peace wi Angus, lovey. Why do I wonder what ye hae done?"

"You need not fret, my lord. I have not poisoned him, though it was tempting," she answered him mischievously.

"What hae ye done?"

"I have purged him, my lord."

"*What!*" The Earl of Dunmor stopped in his tracks.

"I have purged him," Arabella repeated, "but do not fret, my lord. The fruit I ate and the one I gave the queen were untreated."

The Earl of Dunmor burst out laughing. He simply could not help it. "Lassie," he managed to wheeze, "I hae best get ye out of here, for Angus will kill ye for certain."

"He will not be in any condition to," Arabella answered her husband. "Besides, I have not yet paid my respects to their majesties this evening, and I would not miss what is to come for anything, Tavis. Surely you will grant me my small victory?"

"I shall probably hae to defend yer small life." He chuckled, escorting her over to the royal couple upon their dais, bowing to his brother as his wife curtsied.

"Those figs are delicious," the queen said. "Will ye not gie me the recipe, my dear?"

"Certainly, your majesty, but those we ate are just the tiniest bit different than those the Earl of Angus is now so greedily cramming into his mouth. I fear he will be slightly ill," Arabella said.

The king chuckled even as a roar was emitted from the Earl of Angus's mouth. The Great Hall of Stirling Castle grew suddenly silent and the crowd of courtiers parted as Archibald Douglas doubled up, stumbling his way across the floor toward the Earl and Countess of Dunmor.

"Ye hae poisoned me!" he howled, clutching at his middle.

"Nay, sir, I have not!" Arabella said with as much outrage as she dared to muster. "Do you see either the queen or myself in your condition?"

The Earl of Angus felt another strong cramp gripping his bowels and groaned piteously. "Ye hae poisoned me," he repeated.

"And again, my lord, I tell you nay," Arabella replied. "I have merely purged you," she finished sweetly.

"Purged me?" In the interval between his belly grips her words penetrated his brain. *"Ye purged me?"* His words rang with indignation.

"Aye, my lord, I purged ye," Arabella said. "My mother, may God assoil her sweet soul, taught me that when a man is filled with an unhealthy choler, it is best to purge him of it. You, my lord, needed purging, and so I have done just that. I would suggest, however, my lord, that you make your excuses to their majesties, for you will shortly need the necessary."

A spasm attesting to the truth of her words passed over the Earl of Angus's handsome face, which was now dappled with beads of sweat. "Madame," he gasped, "I would offer ye my sword but that I do nae wear it in the royal presence. I surrender to ye, Arabella Stewart, for I would rather hae ye as a friend than an enemy." His face grew almost green then, and with a hasty bow to the king and queen, the Earl of Angus fled the room even as it erupted with laughter over his unfortunate plight.

"I dinna think Archie will trouble ye any longer," the king remarked wryly.

"Nor do I, sire," Arabella answered him.

" 'Twas really very naughty of ye, my dear," the queen chided the Countess of Dunmor mildly.

"It shall not happen again, your majesty," Arabella promised Queen Margaret solemnly.

The queen burst into a fit of the giggles.

"Ahh, Uncle, what fun it must be to be married to my aunt," Prince James said, joining them. " 'Twas a splendid trick, madame!"

"I thought you liked the Earl of Angus," Arabella remarked to the prince.

"I do," came the reply, "which is why I know that when he has recovered from the gripes to his bowels, no one will appreciate this jest more than Archibald Douglas himself."

" 'Tis nae the proper behavior for a countess of Dunmor," Tavis Stewart grumbled.

"I did not ask to be your wife, my lord," Arabella said sharply. " 'Twas you, if you will remember, who stole me away from my home and forced me to the altar."

"Thereby saving ye from Sir Jasper Keane," Tavis Stewart said, for lack of anything better to say, for he could not deny her words. "Perhaps I should hae left ye to wed wi him, for my revenge would hae been complete by now. Ye would hae killed the bastard before a year of wedded bliss had run its course."

"Then you had best beware, sir, had you not? We have not been wed a year yet," Arabella mocked him, her eyes narrowing catlike.

He grinned suddenly, feeling the excitement rising between them. "Perhaps I shall kill ye first, lovey," and his voice became almost a whisper, "for I surely know how."

She laughed softly, and it was as if they were completely alone. "Aye, my lord," she agreed with him, "you know well how to bring me a *petite morte*."

The passion between them now was almost visible, and the prince felt a stab of serious envy. Though Arabella had made it quite plain she would not betray her husband's honor, Jamie Stewart's desire for the Countess of Dunmor had not lessened a whit. He would have her one day, he vowed. He did not know how, but he would have her. Queen Margaret, though she remained silent, was more than aware of her son's reputation. She saw the lust in her eldest child's face and was concerned.

"Your majesties," the Earl of Dunmor said, bowing to his half brother and sister-in-law, "may my wife and I have yer permission to withdraw the royal presence?"

The king and queen nodded in unison, and as the earl and his countess departed, Margaret of Denmark said, "He is so very much in love with her, I feel almost sorry for him."

"Why, Mother?" demanded Prince James.

"No man, or woman for that matter," the queen said softly, "should love another person so deeply. When ye love that much, ye are more often than not doomed to disappointment because ye make yer lover someone or something he isn't. Eventually ye realize it, and then ye must come to terms with that disappointment, Jamie."

"It seems a small price to pay, Mother," the prince said wisely, "for the pleasure that love brings."

"I speak of love, my son, but ye speak of something entirely different," the queen told him, and then she ruffled his red hair. " 'Tis not important, laddie mine. Ye'll go yer own way in any case."

"Is that nae how it should be, Mother?" he asked her with a smile.

"Aye," she told him, returning the smile, her eyes straying beyond him to Tavis and Arabella, who were just now departing the Great Hall of Stirling Castle.

"Yer a wicked, wild wench," the earl told his wife as they hurried to gain their coach. "I hope that Angus does indeed think yer jest a good one, for I dinna need a feud upon my hands right now."

They entered their vehicle, and no sooner had the door been shut upon them than Arabella slid into his arms, her face raised to his, her lips soft and inviting. "Let's go back to Dunmor," she murmured against his mouth, setting the hair upon the back of his neck a-prickle. "I sense winter about to strike us a fierce blow, and I would be happiest locked away from the world with you, my lord." She kissed him a long, sweet kiss.

"Madame, 'twas ye who wanted to come to court. I should have been just as happy remaining at Dunmor," he said, one hand sliding into the neckline of her dress to cup a breast, even as he nibbled at her lips.

"Mmmmmm," Arabella sighed, pressing against him. "Can

a lass nae change her mind, my lord?'' she teased him, using the Scots idiom for the first time since he had known her.

"We hae no good excuse to leave court right now, lovey,'' he said with genuine regret in his deep voice. "In the spring, perhaps, we can return home, for traditionally the English come raiding in the spring, and I must be at Dunmor to help defend the border.''

But they did not go home in the spring, for Henry Tudor, unsure upon his throne, was as interested in keeping peace along the borders as was James III. For the time being the English king did not need a war with Scotland; and to the disgust of many of his earls, Scotland's king would not let his people make war upon the English.

"This could be the beginning of total peace between us,'' Jemmie Stewart told his younger brother, Tavis Stewart. "I must bring Scotland into the modern world, but as long as she wastes her few resources and the lives of her sons in useless wars, I hae nae a chance. Why can they nae see it as I see it? Why must they live in the past? I need peace, and I need time to accomplish it all, but if nae me, Tavis, then my Jamie! He's a braw bairn and they like him, but I've taught him well, for though they think he's like them, he is nae. That was my mistake. Letting them see me as I really am. I was too honest, but I've taught Jamie better.''

"Aye,'' the earl agreed. "He's got charm, my nephew, and he's strong as well.''

"He'll be a good king when he's old enough, Tavis, but I must hold on until he is. I know, I know,'' the king told his brother. "There are those who agitate to overthrow me and put my son upon the throne, but Jamie will nae betray me ever.''

"Nay, he will not, Jemmie, for he loves ye even if he doesna understand ye.''

"Do ye understand me, Tavis?''

"Sometimes, in some things, but not always in all things.'' The earl grinned, and then he took a deep swallow from the goblet he was holding. "But I love ye too, Jemmie.''

"Would ye ever betray me?'' the king asked quietly.

Tavis Stewart thought a moment, and finally he said, "I dinna know, Jemmie. Not as ye are now, certainly, but time and circumstances change. I honestly dinna know, but this I can tell ye, Jemmie, I will nae ever betray Scotland.''

The king nodded. It was an honest answer, and more than he would have gotten from any other man. "Yer wife says that I am Scotland," he told his younger brother craftily.

"Arabella is young and driven by passions I am only just beginning to explore," Tavis Stewart told his brother. "I do not, however, admit to understanding them or her in the least."

The king laughed. "What man really understands a woman's mind?" he replied. "There are many, Angus for one, I suspect, who think women dinna hae minds. Only bodies like that pretty drab of a cousin of his, Sorcha Morton. Even my laddie hae plowed in that well-tilled field."

"And paid dearly for the privilege, I can assure ye, brother," the earl said. "Sorcha hae expensive tastes, and like an alley cat who will go to whoever will feed it, nae true loyalty. I had a taste, but found it not to my liking. I dinna imagine Jamie stayed too long in that pasture."

"Nay," the king chuckled. "Then, too, he feared his mother would find out. Angus encourages the lad to carnality, and I canna stop him, for my son seems to hae a natural bent for the ladies."

The earl grinned. "He's a true Stewart."

"Yet yer faithful to yer wife, Tavis, as I am to Margaret."

"Perhaps we are unique amongst our family," the earl replied.

The king smiled to himself. His younger brother, with a Stewart mother and a Stewart king for a father, was the quintessential Stewart. He seemed to possess all of the best qualities inherent in the Stewarts. He was handsome, loyal, intelligent, a good horseman, a good soldier, and if his reputation might be believed, a good lover. He was charming, and kind and politic. *Very politic.* The king knew his own total fidelity to his queen, coupled with the pleasure he gained from the company of artistic men, had given rise to stories that left his reputation less than savory. He would neither deny nor confirm those rumors, for he felt to do so was to give them credence; but he realized now that even Tavis Stewart was not certain of the truth of those rumors. Still, his brother was too loyal to even voice his concern in this one matter, and whatever answer James Stewart might have given to the question, should the earl have asked it, the king knew his brother would still continue to love him. There were precious few, he realized, that he might depend on to that extent.

"Indeed," he agreed with his brother, "I think we are unique, Tavis. It is unfortunate, however, that that quality is nae appreciated by the highland earls and their ilk. They will be the death of me yet, I fear. Though the lowland lords and the bonnet lairds complain, they remain loyal to me nonetheless."

"Yer like a bloody rope dancer, Jemmie," the earl remarked. "Ye must step carefully at all times."

"Pray God I dinna fall, brother," the king said. "At least not until my Jamie is old enough to rule wi out the interference of rash and ambitious men."

Chapter 11

*T*he queen was dead. Suddenly, and without any real warning. She had awakened early on the morning of July fourteenth with a sharp cry, and the lady who had hurried to the
queen's bedside had heard her say even as she fell back upon
her pillows, "God and his mother, Mary, have mercy on me."
Then she was gone, and as word of her unexpected death spread
throughout Stirling Castle, the town below, and the very realm
itself, the reaction was the same. Total astonishment and disbelief.

Margaret of Denmark, daughter of King Christian I of Nor-
way and Denmark, was only twenty-nine years old. She had
come to Scotland as James III's bride at the age of twelve. No
one in Scotland, even her husband's fiercest critics, had a bad
word to say about the young queen. She was universally loved
by all, for her nature was sweet, her heart good, and her piety
legend. She had borne her husband three sons; the eldest two of
whom were named James, because when Jamie the elder had
been a small child, it was thought he was ill unto death, and so
the son his mother had borne shortly after his illness began was
also christened James, ensuring that Scotland's next king would
have the same name as the previous three. The queen's third son
was called John.

The king was in a state of total shock; more so than any of
the others, for whatever might be thought of him, he had loved
his wife. He sat silent and staring at a wall in his beautiful
rooms, deaf to all pleas, unable to even give orders for his wife's
funeral. James Stewart had never been the most decisive of men
where his duties were concerned, but at this particular moment
he was virtually useless. Even his young favorite, John Ramsey
of Balmain, whom he had created Earl of Bothwell, could not
reach him.

The king's family, the Stewarts, with help from the kingdom's
greatest lords, planned the queen's funeral; offering a final and
perfect tribute to a gracious lady who, while she lived, had

spurred her husband on in his efforts to put the affairs of his half-savage realm in order. Now it was wondered what would happen without her, and those more practical and less sentimental than others considered a suitable replacement for the grieving royal widower; amongst the candidates, the dowager queen of England, Elizabeth Woodville.

The day of the queen's funeral dawned gray and bleak. All along the road between St. Michael's Chapel at Stirling to the Abbey of Cambuskenneth where the burial would take place, the way was lined with hundreds of common folk, many of whom wept openly for the queen. The black-draped coffin was drawn by black horses caparisoned in black and gold. Before it went black-clad riders upon black horses bearing the flags of Scotland and Denmark, dipped in respect. Other riders carried banners with the quartered Arms of the Danish Royal House and the Lyon Rampant of Scotland. The clergy, all of Scotland's bishops and abbots walking side by side in pairs, the lesser priests—their vestments, their jeweled mitres, their croziers blazing with precious gemstones, making an almost painful flash of color amid all the black—preceded the coffin.

The coffin itself with the queen's own arms upon it was carried by Scotland's six senior earls, and after it came the king, bareheaded and all in black, followed by his sons, the youngest of whom was carried by his nurse; his two younger sisters, Margaret the spinster and Lady Mary Hamilton, the queen's own ladies, the lords and ladies of the court, the royal servants, and all others who had official reason to be there.

"Why are there so many simple people?" Arabella asked her husband. "Surely they cannot have known the queen, and yet their grief seems genuine." The Countess of Dunmor had never before taken part in such a great occasion, and she was not certain if it was all usual.

"The queen," replied her husband in a low voice as they walked, "was generous wi her time and gave audiences to any who asked. When this was known, the ordinary folk began bringing their complaints to her. She never turned them away, and she never hurried them in their tales. She was also openhanded wi those in need, although she hid both her charity and her willingness to listen well, that she nae be taken advantage of by those who didna really need her. She was truly Jemmie's better half, and God help Scotland now that she is gone."

The high requiem mass and the many prayers for the repose of the queen's good soul took up most of the day, which, despite its gloomy outlook, was also warm with unusual midsummer heat. In the hours that followed, the press of too many people jammed into the abbey's small church caused many to faint or even grow ill with the heat and the stench. The stench came from the court's mourning clothing, which were so elegant and expensive that the garments were passed down from generation to generation. Most of the garments were made of velvet, which was too heavy a fabric for a summer's day, and all of the doublets, robes, and gowns were heavy with embroidery. In the interim between important funerals these clothes were stored in airtight chests and dusted with pungent spices to kill several generations of body odors.

There was no air in the abbey church, and eventually, as the bodies of the mourners grew warm, not even the frankincense and myrrh wafted from the censers could overcome the rank reek of ancient sweat mixed with new. Arabella could feel the roil of her belly, and tried desperately to concentrate upon the mourning rosary of jet beads that the king had given members of his family, which now hung in her hands. Her head had begun to ache, and although food had been the furthest thing from her mind this morning when she had arisen, now, even with her upset stomach, she was beginning to feel quite hungry.

At last, to the grateful thanks of the many mourners, the state formalities were over. The king could not at this time abide the thought of returning to his beloved Stirling Castle, and so the court was to move to the place he disliked above all places, Edinburgh Castle. It was as if James Stewart felt in some way responsible for the death of his dearly loved spouse and was punishing himself.

The Stewarts of Dunmor moved along with the rest of the court to the capital city, where they had another town house, which was located on the High Street. Arabella liked Edinburgh, which she found an exciting and colorful place with its open markets and many merchant shops with their wide variety of goods from all over the known world. She did not, however, enjoy traversing the city streets, which were virtual open sewers, populated not only by respectable citizens and not so respectable citizens, but by dogs, pigs, and rats, as well as other assorted vermin. Arabella, like other ladies of the nobility, blocked the stench of the town by carrying a clove-studded orange called a pomander ball.

"Let's go home to Dunmor," the earl suggested to his wife as they idled away the early hours of the morning in their bed some two weeks after the queen's funeral. It was the beginning of August.

"What of the king?" Arabella asked her husband. "He has virtually shut himself away from everyone in his grief. Is it wise to leave him to the mercy of his opponents now?"

"Jemmie must come to terms wi himself sooner than later, lovey. He will nae even see us now, and the court is in mourning for the next few months. Even the most militant of the earls will nae act against the king for the time being. It is a good time for us to leave, and besides, Arabella Stewart, there is something ye hae nae shared wi me yet that ye should," the earl said, kissing the tip of his wife's nose.

Arabella blushed prettily. "My lord, I am not certain of your meaning," she answered him.

"Are ye nae with child?" His dark green eyes searched her face.

"I am not quite certain," she said. "I must speak with your mother first. How did you know?" Her cheeks were still pink.

"Because everything about ye is important to me, lovey, and I have noted that ye hae nae had yer link wi the moon broken in at least two months now."

"But perhaps 'tis something else, my lord," Arabella said. "I need very much to speak with your mother before I am certain. I have never had a child before, and I was but a wee girl when my mother was last with a child by my father; and I did not know she was quickening with Sir Jasper's child last summer."

"Ye hae other symptoms, lovey," he said with a doting smile. "Yer belly hae become fussy of late, and yer pretty titties are growing plumper and rounder. I hae planted my seed deep wi'in ye, and yer already quickening wi my son." His big hand cupped her head, and he kissed her mouth warmly.

Her blush grew deeper, for even after having been married to this man for over a year, and having cohabited with him for the past eight months, she was still a little shy of him. She was embarrassed that he should know her so intimately that he could be certain of her condition even before she was. It was almost a violation, she thought irritably.

He saw the annoyance springing to life in her eyes, and he quickly said, "I am my mother's eldest son, and familiar wi a woman's habits when she is first wi bairn."

"Could you not have waited at least until I told you myself, my lord? I think it indecent that a man should be so aware of a woman's habits!" She could feel her temper beginning to tug at her. "How like a man, so caught up with the superiority of his overweening pride that he would know such things as you do; and further would assume the babe I carry is a son!"

He wanted to laugh, for she was so like a small and golden-furred spitting kitten in her outrage. "Lovey," he told her, controlling his amusement, "I love ye, and everything about ye is important to me. Why sometimes I awake in the night and listen to ye breathe to be certain that ye are all right."

"I wanted to surprise you," she pouted, not quite ready to forgive him despite his declaration of love.

"There are many ways in which ye surprise me, madame," he said softly, and he kissed her once again.

She slipped her arms about his neck and drew him closer to her, pressing the length of her naked body against him. "Take me home, my lord," she said with double meaning.

"Witch," he growled into the golden tangle of her hair, feeling little hands seeking him. With a half groan he rolled over onto his back, taking her with him.

Laughing, Arabella caressed his manhood until he was aching with his eagerness to possess her. Shy in many ways with him, he had discovered, to his amazement, that she had no such reticence when it came to the act of love. It was almost as if she were a different person. In time, he suspected, he would be able to teach her certain refinements of passion that many women would not tolerate. Mounting him, Arabella began to ride her husband, gently at first, more wildly as her own passion increased; her head thrown back, her lips slightly parted, her green eyes half veiled.

Reaching up, he grasped her breasts, teasing at the berry nipples, caressing and fondling the silken flesh. He half sat, leaning his head forward to take one of her nipples into his mouth so he might suckle upon it. Gently he bit down on the tender tip and was rewarded by a soft moan of unmistakable pleasure from his wife. He pinched the other nipple equally gently, for pain was not his goal, only an enhancement of desire. He was rewarded when her sweetly tight little sheath contracted about his throbbing manhood, and Arabella shivered violently the beginning of her own fulfillment. Releasing her nipples, he took control of the situation, gently turning her over upon her back and finishing magnificently what she had so gallantly started.

They lay together in the afterward, feeling the heat of not only their mutual passion, but of the new day as well. In the garden of the town house a thrush sang, even as from the front of the house the cries of the flower seller in from the country sounded. "Sweet lavender and Mary's gold. Roses half a copper penny! Who'll buy? Flowers! Fresh flowers wi the dew yet upon them! Who'll buy?"

"Jemmie will nae miss us," the earl finally said, breaking the silence between them. "He canna deny me the right to take ye home when yer quickening wi my heir and before it becomes too dangerous for ye to travel. Besides, the city is an unhealthy place for ye, particularly now."

"Aye," Arabella agreed, stretching her limbs with contentment. She no longer felt angry with him, for he was really most considerate of her. Then she said, "I cannot wait to see the look upon the face of that alley cat, Sorcha Morton, when she learns I am with child. I do not like the way she eyes you, my lord. As if you were a particularly delectable bit of sweetmeat."

"There is nothing between Lady Morton and myself, lovey, but if the truth be known, I dinna like the way my nephew looks upon ye."

"Are you jealous?" she teased him.

"Aye!"

She laughed, pleased. "Jamie is a boy," she said. "I have a man!"

He was flattered by her quick reply, but still he said, "He may be a lad, but he's got a man's hard cock already, and he well knows how to use it, Arabella Stewart. Remember that lest ye ever underestimate him."

"I shall be safely at Dunmor, my lord," she said sweetly. "The prince shall be gone from my life, even as Jasper Keane is gone from my life."

The king acceded to their wishes to return home to Dunmor, though he would not see either of them, so deeply did he mourn his Margaret. He remained for most of the time within his own apartments, praying for his late wife's soul and generally ignoring the business of his realm. A treaty for a solid peace with England was being negotiated between the two countries in London, and James III was little needed elsewhere. There was no army to lead against the age-old enemy, and if there was discontent among the Scots nobility, it was, for the time being, set aside out of respect for the late queen.

The Earl and Countess of Dunmor came home to the border country on a bright mid-August day. They had been away eight months. The Flemings of Glen Ailean were there to greet them, both Ailis and Meg plump and close to delivering their first children. Happily, Arabella confided her suspicions to them all. Her mother-in-law, after asking her several pertinent questions and discussing Arabella's habits with Flora and Lona, confirmed her son's verdict. In the early spring of the new year, Dunmor would have an heir.

"Or heiress," Arabella said stubbornly, "and if it is a little girl, I will call her Margaret after the queen, God assoil her sweet soul."

"Ye will nae name her after yer own mother?" Lady Margery inquired.

"Nay," Arabella said shortly.

"Surely ye hae forgiven the poor woman," Margery Fleming said.

"Aye," Arabella answered, "but I cannot forget what she did when she allowed herself to become involved with Sir Jasper. She was not a bad woman, belle mère, but she was a foolish and a silly one, I now realize. She might have refused Sir Jasper. It was her right, but she did not. I should never allow any man to use me so!"

"Pray God ye will never find yerself so vulnerable, my child," Lady Margery told her daughter-in-law.

"A woman is only vulnerable if she allows herself to be," the young countess answered with all the assurance of her youth and inexperience.

"Everyone is vulnerable at some time in their life, Arabella," Lady Margery said quietly. "Everyone. Man or woman. There is nae crime in it, for it is the way of the world, my dear."

Arabella shook her head vehemently. "I have been vulnerable to others in the past, belle mère, but I will never again allow anyone to dictate to me how I will live my life. I must be my own mistress! Why is it a man may chart not only his own course, but a woman's as well?''

"Men are the natural rulers of the earth," Lady Fleming said.

"Why?" Arabella demanded.

For once the usually wise lady was at a loss for words, and her daughter and other daughter-in-law looked totally confused by Arabella's simple question.

"Perhaps because God intended it that way," Father Colin finally said.

"How do we know that?" Arabella said, totally unfazed by the church's opinion.

"Because men are naturally wiser than women," Donald Fleming said, his tone just a trifle belligerent. He was still not over his suspicion of Arabella, and these questions of hers only confirmed his mistrust of her.

"Indeed, Donald? Just why is that so? Because they are bigger than women, or perhaps that temperamental little worm that dangles between your legs leads you to think so? I was not aware that a man's cock added to his intellect."

Lord Fleming burst out laughing. Not only did her words amuse him, but the look on his second son's face was more than comical. Donald, who always had something to say and an opinion on everything, was finally and truly at a loss for words. "Arabella," he said, when he finally managed to gain a hold on his own humor, "I vow yer more a Scot than ye are English. The women of our race are noted for their outspoken ways, and ye certainly dinna attempt to conceal yer thoughts or yer feelings from us, do ye, lassie?"

"I do not mean to be bold, my lord," Arabella answered him, "it is just that I do not see why women cannot rule their own lives as men do. Should I not know better than any what is right for me?"

The earl put an arm about his young wife. "It is tradition, madame, that the earls of Dunmor care for all those in their charge. Their wives, however, rule the family and all that concerns it."

"But it is your word, Tavis, in the end that can supplant mine. It is your will that can overrule mine should you so desire it," Arabella said passionately. "I would rule my own life!"

"I will never impede ye in that desire, madame," the earl

told her, "unless, of course, yer desires endanger me or mine. In return I would expect the same of ye. I think that is a fair bargain I offer ye. Do ye nae?"

"Aye, my lord, I do," she answered him, a smile brightening her beautiful features.

"Bah!" Donald Fleming said irritably. "If she were my wife I'd take a stick to her. Ye spoil the wench, Tavis, and she'll make a fool of ye yet for it!"

"If I were your wife, Donald Fleming, I would have poisoned your ale long since," Arabella replied spiritedly, "and any man foolish enough to raise a weapon of any kind to me will find it quickly broken over his head or buried in his heart!"

"Spoken like a true warrior Countess of Dunmor," said her husband with a grin, and he gave Arabella a hard kiss.

Donald Fleming rolled his eyes with exasperation. His English sister-in-law was the most irritating and strong-willed woman he had ever known. He did not understand why his eldest brother would put up with her. His mother patted his arm comfortingly.

"Dinna fret, laddie," she said softly. "One day ye'll meet a lass, and no matter what she does or says, everything about her will be wonderful. 'Tis love, Donald."

"If love forces a man to be less than a man," grumbled Donald, "then I'd just as soon nae find myself in such a state, Mother."

"Gieing a woman her own way where 'twill do nae harm is nae being less than a full man, Donald, but ye'll find that out for yerself one day," Lady Fleming told him with a knowledgeable smile.

"I don't know who would want to wed with Donald," Arabella told her husband in a low tone. "He's like a great, clumsy, ill-tempered old dog."

"He hae good qualities too, lassie," the earl said.

To Arabella's surprise, one of her brother-in-law's good qualities was soon more than apparent, for Meg and Ailis delivered their babies within a few days of each other in late September, and Donald Fleming found himself rendered helpless with love for the two infants, both of whom were boys. The big man was fascinated by the babies, and his rough features softened as he looked upon them. Arabella would even swear that there were

tears in his eyes as he cradled his sister's son at the boy's christening, where he stood as the lad's godfather.

Lona, too, was intrigued with the new babies, taking every
moment she might steal when they were about to coo at them,
and cuddle them. At first Arabella was surprised, for Lona,
coming from a large family, had never before evinced such an
interest in children. Then, suddenly, it occurred to her that her
childhood friend might be in love. Yet Lona had confided nothing to her, and surely she would have, Arabella thought. Still
. . . the Countess of Dunmor decided to keep a close watch
upon her young servant. Indeed, she felt it her duty, for she
could not allow FitzWalter's daughter to be seduced while in her
care!

Arabella's patience was finally rewarded at Martinsmas when
she saw the young clansman called Fergus helping the blushing
Lona to carry a basket of apples into the hall. *Fergus!* Of course,
she thought with a smile. He was always hanging about them
when he was not at his duties. As they sat in the hall one evening
listening to the piper, Arabella spoke softly to her husband.

"The young man who first brought Lona and her brother to
us; Fergus? What can you tell me of him, my lord?"

The earl thought for a moment, and then as his eyes lit with
remembrance he said, "Fergus MacMichael. A good lad wi a
good future. A man-at-arms, but he'll be a captain one day, I
think."

"Has he a wife?"

The earl considered her query a minute, and then shook his
head. "Nay." Then he looked at his own wife. "Why this curiosity, lassie?"

"I think Lona casts her eyes in his direction, and he seems to
be amenable. I would be certain he does not dishonor her, or
break her tender heart, my lord. Lona is not simply my servant,
but my friend."

"I'll speak wi the lad, madame, and be certain he is free to
court Lona," the earl promised his wife.

On the following morning Fergus MacMichael found himself
called into his lord's presence, and Tavis Stewart wasted no time
in coming to the point.

"Would ye court the lass who serves my wife, laddie?"

The young man flushed, but his gaze never wavered from that
of his lord's. "Aye, my lord, I would."

"Yer free to?"

"Aye, my lord."

"Then ye hae my permission, and that of my lady's; but ye'll nae seduce Lona, or shame her."

"Nay, my lord, never!"

"Then we understand each other," the earl said, dismissing his clansman.

Tavis Stewart reported the conversation to his wife that night as they cuddled with each other in their bed. "I hope he'll make yer Lona as happy as ye've made me, Arabella Stewart," he murmured softly, kissing her brow.

And the very next day Lona came blushingly to her mistress saying, "I have a suitor, 'Bella!" Her eyes were bright with her happiness. "I didn't dare to hope he would ever see me in *that* way, but he has!"

"Would it be that handsome young clansman, Fergus MacMichael?" Arabella teased Lona.

"How did you know?!"

"Oh," Arabella said off-handedly, "I've seen the way he looks at you these past months, Lona, and so I asked my husband to be certain that his intentions towards you were honorable. I am assured they are." She chuckled, and then added mischievously, "But not too honorable!"

Lona giggled, confiding in her mistress and friend, "He's got quick hands, 'Bella, and a sweet kiss, I vow."

"And will you wed him if he asks?"

"Perhaps," Lona smiled, "but first I would be courted a bit by the man. Ohhh, 'Bella, he has the bluest eyes!"

The winter came, and with it a strange calm settled over Scotland. The king still mourned his wife, but the queen was now dead six months, and those who negotiated peace in England also seriously considered Elizabeth Woodville as a possible replacement for Margaret of Denmark. Tidbits of news always reached Dunmor first, for messengers returning from England always stopped at the castle. The king's half brother was known for his loyalty and his hospitality. Archibald Douglas, whose border castle of Hermitage was not too far distant, found to his irritation that he was not considered as generous a host. He was forced to visit Dunmor in order to learn what was happening firsthand, for he found that secondhand gossip was usually unreliable.

"Elizabeth Woodville would destroy yer brother," he told Tavis Stewart one night as he enjoyed the earl's fine wine in the Great Hall of Dunmor Castle. "They say she's a woman of great passions. Not at all to Jemmie's taste, though perhaps Jamie would enjoy her favors."

"I hae nae doubt that Henry Tudor would like to rid himself of his mother-in-law," Tavis said, chuckling. "She is a most troublesome jade, I hear, and I dinna think his own mother, Lady Margaret Beaufort, considers her wi much kindness either. The negotiators play wi each other, Archie, and ye know it even as I do. 'Tis peace that is the main order of business between our countries. I dinna think forcing poor Jemmie to the altar wi that English harpie would lead us to a lasting peace."

"But it might lead yer brother into a good fight wi the English," the Earl of Angus laughed.

"There will be nae match between the king and that particular lady," Tavis Stewart said quietly. "The peace treaty is ready for signing, and Henry Tudor has other troubles to worry about that take precedence over Elizabeth Woodville."

"The lad in Ireland," Archibald Douglas said.

"There's talk of crowning him in Dublin," Tavis Stewart said. "That canna set well wi the Tudor."

"He's got an heir now in Prince Arthur," Angus said.

"Aye, but there are still some diehard Yorkists who would choose a boy prince of York over a Lancastrian king," the Earl of Dunmor answered him.

"But the lad is an imposter, or so Henry Tudor says. Why, only recently I hear he dragged the poor little Plantagenet out from the Tower to display." The Earl of Angus thought a moment and then said, "If, of course, the little laddie is the *real* York prince. Mayhap this boy in Ireland is the real York heir."

"It makes no difference to Scotland," Tavis Stewart said. "Let the English fight amongst themselves and leave us in peace."

"Or to gain back Berwick," Angus said slyly.

"Will ye nae ever cease singing that tune, Archie?"

"My lord!"

The earl looked to see Lona. "Aye, lass, what is it?"

"My mistress bade me come and tell you that the babe will shortly be born," Lona said excitedly.

Tavis Stewart leapt to his feet. "Is she all right, lass? Does she nae need me?" He didn't know which way to turn, to Angus's amusement, for Archibald Douglas had never thought to see the Earl of Dunmor so at loose ends, and all over a bairn to boot.

"I do not think she would mind if you sat by her side, my lord."

"My mother!"

"Her ladyship has already sent for Lady Fleming," Lona replied.

"A priest!" the earl cried.

"God's foot, man, yer wife isna dying, and the bairn will nae need christening until he's born," Angus said good-naturedly. "Go on to yer woman, Tavis. I dinna mind my own company as long as yer fine wine holds out."

Lona had already departed the hall, and the earl hurried after her. When he reached Arabella's apartments he was met by Flora, who said matter-of-factly, "Yer mam will nae get here in time, my lord, for never hae I seen a bairn so eager to be born than this one. Why, one moment yer lady was sitting quietly wi her embroidery hoop, and in the next minute she was laboring to bring forth the bairn."

"Flora!" Arabella's voice sounded stridently.

"I'm here, my lamb," the older woman said soothingly, "and here's the cause of all yer troubles himself."

Arabella was half seated in a birthing chair, her legs spread and raised upon two wooden runners. Her beautiful face was flushed, her brow dappled with beads of perspiration, yet she smiled when she saw her husband. "Ohh, Tavis! The babe is coming! Before the night is out we shall have our child!"

"More before the hour's out," Flora muttered beneath her breath as the earl bent to kiss his wife.

Tavis Stewart heard the serving woman's words and he grinned. " 'Tis the first day of spring, lovey, though the winds are yet cold and from the north. I think it is a good omen that our first son be born upon the first day of spring."

"Spring is a young girl," Arabella said. "The king told me that when we were at court last year." Then as a spasm passed over her face, she groaned deeply.

"That's it, my lamb," Flora encouraged her mistress, and then she glanced up at Lona. "Are the blankets warming, lass?"

"Aye! I'm ready," Lona said brightly.

"Lovey, is there much pain?" the earl fretted, and Flora rolled her eyes back in her head.

"Birthing a bairn is nae easy, my lord," she told him.

"I'm all right, my love," Arabella assured him, and then groaned again with even more feeling than the last time.

The earl paled even as Flora said brightly, "That's it, my lady! Aye, there's the wee one's head now. Look, my lord! Lona! Push now, my lamb. Push!"

Arabella groaned and bore down with all her strength. Now Flora was moving into position between the wooden runners and bending down to help her mistress. "Ohhhh, Flora!" Arabella shrieked. "I feel it coming! I feel it coming!"

"Aye, my lamb, here's its little head and shoulders already born. Push but once more. Aye, here's the bairn," Flora crowed as the baby slipped from its mother's womb and into her capable hands. Quickly Flora wiped the birthing blood from the baby with warm oil as it lay upon a mat upon the floor. Then she neatly clipped and knotted the cord, wrapping the baby tightly in its swaddling clothes as the infant scrunched up its little face and screamed with outrage.

"She's her mother's daughter," said the earl, having astutely noted his child's sex as Flora tended to her.

"You are not disappointed?" Arabella said quietly, another spasm passing over her face as she passed the afterbirth.

"Nay, lovey. Yer safe, wee Maggie is safe, and we'll hae other bairns," he told her, kissing her brow again.

"She's a good breeder," Flora said approvingly. "She nae be like her poor mother."

"Give me my daughter," Arabella demanded of her husband, who was now cradling the infant and making soft cooing noises which had strangely quieted the baby. "Is everyone to see this miracle before I am?"

Flora smiled and Lona giggled as the earl handed his daughter to her mother. "Bid yer mother a good evening, wee Maggie," Tavis Stewart said, bending to place the child in Arabella's arms.

Amazement and awe lit the Countess of Dunmor's beautiful features as she gazed upon her offspring for the first time. The infant's features were perfect, and although she did not have a great deal of hair upon her head, what hair she had was pale gold like her mother's. Her skin was pink and healthy looking. Her eyes blue and alert. This was obviously a baby who would survive. "Ohh, my little love," Arabella said softly with delight as she gazed upon her daughter. Lady Margaret Stewart, however, opened up her rosebud mouth and howled loudly, her dainty miniature features growing scarlet with her indignation.

"What is the matter with her?" Arabella cried, frightened.

"She is her mother's daughter," the earl repeated over the din of his offspring's cries. "A spitfire's temper and a mind of her own. It will take a strong-willed Scotsman to tame her, lovey."

"A strong-willed Englishman," Arabella said.

He looked puzzled.

"This is Greyfaire's heiress, my lord. You promised me. Now that Margaret has been born, you must go to the king and see that our daughter's inheritance is restored to her," Arabella said seriously.

"I will provide for my daughter," the earl said as seriously. "And besides, Jemmie is worse than useless in his mourning. He'll do naught for us, lovey."

"You promised me, my lord!" There was an edge to her voice.

"My lady, gie me the bairn," Flora said. "Lona will look after her tonight, and ye need yer rest."

She was tired. Suddenly and without warning, very tired. Arabella allowed her husband to put her to bed after Flora had sponged her down with perfumed water and placed a fresh chemisette of soft white silk upon her body. He laid her gently upon the fragrant lavender-scented sheets, settling her carefully upon her pillows. Then to everyone's surprise, the earl kicked off his house slippers and climbed into bed with Arabella, drawing her tenderly into his arms protectively. "Leave us," he told the two startled-looking women servants, and when they had gone, he spoke softly but firmly to his wife. "I hae given ye my word, Arabella, that I will try to regain Greyfaire for our eldest daughter, and I *will* keep my word to ye. Can ye nae understand that?"

"When?" Her voice, though weak, was implacable.

He nuzzled the top of her head. "When our wee Maggie is a month old, I will go to Jemmie and ask him to petition King Henry. It is all we can do, lovey. The Tudor may not choose to return yer precious Greyfaire to us. I hae told ye before that all we can do is try, but we will try. Ye must be patient, lassie."

"I am not very good at being patient," she said low.

"Then 'tis a habit ye hae best learn if ye are to deal wi the powerful, lovey. Those in positions of authority are effective precisely because they are in positions of control over the impuissant and defenseless. Their power grows wi the vulnerability of others."

"When I was Greyfaire's heiress," Arabella said slowly, "I possessed the power of my station, but I no longer have that power, and I hate it! At least then I was in a position to take charge of my own life. I no longer am."

"Oh, lovey," the earl replied, "dinna let life chafe ye so, for ye will nae be happy if ye do. I would hae ye happy and content. We hae a beautiful daughter, my love, and I thank ye for her. Now try and sleep, for even an easy birth is an exhausting one." He cuddled her in his embrace and kissed her fair head.

Arabella sighed and closed her eyes, yet she could not stop the thoughts that raced through her mind. She wanted Greyfaire back, but it was not merely whim on her part. The thought of Sir Jasper Keane swaggering with pride of ownership about the keep that had been her family's heritage for several hundred years was galling beyond all. He had no right to Greyfaire. He had stolen it, plain and simple. If he wanted a home, let him go back to his own Northby Hall. Surely, using his false charm and his handsome face as he had done with her and her mother, he could find himself another silly, innocent virgin heiress, or some hapless and equally silly rich widow to wed. Then let him rebuild his own ancestral home in which to live, but she would have Greyfaire back for her daughter!

Her daughter. The words echoed strangely in her head. She had a daughter, and by virtue of that very fact she was now a mother herself. *A mother!* She was a mother. In the months she had carried her child it had not seemed real, until now. How could she deny the reality of the infant murmuring in its sleep in the cradle by her bedside? The Countess of Dunmor felt her first strong surge of maternal concern. Greyfaire now belonged to Lady Margaret Stewart, and no one, Arabella decided, was going to deny her daughter her rightful inheritance!

Margaret must have brothers, she thought fuzzily as sleep began to overcome her. At least six strong brothers who would be just like their father. Someday, Arabella decided, someday when her as yet unborn sons were grown, they would go over the border with their clansmen, and their Fleming and Hamilton cousins, and they would burn Sir Jasper Keane's fine new Northby Hall to the ground as their fathers had once done. Arabella smiled with satisfaction even as sleep reached up to claim her for its own.

Realizing that his wife was now deep in the arms of Morpheus, the earl arose carefully from the bed and drew the coverlet over her. Stopping a moment to gaze down at his new daughter, he smiled and then tiptoed from the room. "She's asleep," he told Lona, who was waiting patiently outside the door. "Ye may go in now. Watch over my wee Maggie carefully, lassie."

"I will, my lord. Ohh, 'tis so exciting! I only wish poor Lady Rowena were here to see her grandchild, but yer babe will have Lady Margery."

"Aye," the earl agreed, "and my mother will spoil my wee Maggie fiercely, I've nae doubt."

Lona giggled and nodded vigorously. Lady Margery Fleming had shown serious signs of doting with regard to her two grandsons. This first granddaughter would undoubtedly be a favorite.

The earl returned to his hall to find his mother had just arrived. A servant was even now taking Lady Fleming's cloak, and both his sister Ailis and his sister-in-law Meg were with her.

"Well?" she demanded, hurrying forward. "How is Arabella? How far along is she? Is she comfortable? Is she haeing a hard time of it? I didna want to say anything before now, but I pray she will nae be like her poor mother."

"We hae a daughter," Tavis Stewart said, laughing. "A fine, healthy bairn, Mother. She hae golden hair like my wee spitfire, and her mam's hot temper to boot."

"*What?* Why was I nae called sooner?" Lady Margery said.

"Ye were nae called sooner because there was nae time. Flora tells me that my wife is a natural breeder. Arabella had little warning of the birth and delivered quickly, wi little fuss that I could see."

"Aye, my lady, 'tis true," Flora said as she joined them. "She popped the wee bairn out like I'd pop a grape from its skin, and wi as little trouble too. Once she's had time to heal, his lordship can get another bairn on her, and the next one will be a boy, I vow!" Flora grinned broadly.

"I want to see my granddaughter immediately," Lady Margery said firmly.

"I'll take ye up, yer ladyship," Flora volunteered. "Lona is wi them, watching."

Lady Margery nodded her approval. "We'll be staying the night, Tavis," she said. "I didna come at a gallop from Glen Ailean to turn myself about to go home as quickly. I'll want to speak wi Arabella in the morning about my granddaughter's care. Come along, Ailis! Meg!" She strode from the hall, every inch the matriarch, the two younger women hurrying behind in her wake.

"So ye've a lass, hae ye?" The Earl of Angus arose from his place by the fire and came over to Tavis Stewart, holding out his big hand that he might congratulate him.

A servant came forward bearing a tray with two small silver dram cups upon it, which he offered to his master and his master's guest.

The two men accepted the drams, and Archibald Douglas raised up his cup saying, "Long life, good health, and good fortune to Lady Margaret Stewart!"

The Earl of Dunmor raised his own cup in return. "God willing!" he answered, and together the two gentlemen drank down the potent whiskey which came from Dunmor's own still.

The smiling servant took the empty dram cups away as the two earls returned to seat themselves by the fire.

"Is she bonnie, Tavis?"

"Aye, Archie, she's very bonnie," came the reply.

"I might take her for one of my boys then, if ye'll consider it," the Earl of Angus said.

"I canna, though I thank ye for the compliment. Margaret is already promised."

"To whom?" Archibald Douglas was astounded. The newborn was not even an hour old yet and she was betrothed?

"I dinna know," Tavis Stewart said with a smile, "but he must be an Englishman." Then the earl went on to explain the situation.

"Ye think ye'll get yer wife's inheritance back?" Angus said.

"Perhaps under the circumstances, aye. At the moment the English are more favorably disposed to the Scots than they hae been in years, Archie."

"But I wonder if they are foolish enough to gie a border keep to the daughter of a Stewart earl?'' Angus answered slowly, considering the situation. "Still, even if the lass is raised in England after her sixth year, in those six years ye can make her a Scot for life. It canna hurt to hae a friendly refuge on the English side of the border, Tavis. Yer a clever bastard, by God! But what if ye canna regain yer wife's Greyfaire?''

"If the matter is aired publicly between the two kings, then King Henry will hae to pay Arabella a forfeit in exchange for Greyfaire, although I know that will make her very angry. She will hae her home back and nothing less.''

"Ye must kill Sir Jasper Keane, of course,'' Archibald Douglas said.

"I hae intended doing that in any event,'' Tavis Stewart replied. "There is still that matter of my honor between us, and although it matters to no one else, it does matter to me. I will hae my revenge upon him.''

"They say he hae gone south to serve King Henry. He must still fear yer wife that he would try so hard to solidify his position wi the Tudor.''

"He needs a new wife too,'' Tavis Stewart noted. "He hae neither gold nor sons to recommend him; yet 'twill take time for that lickspittle to worm his way into King Henry's favor. Particularly now wi all the Tudor's troubles yet wi the Yorkists; but should, by chance, Sir Jasper Keane gain the king's promise of confirmation to Greyfaire, he will nae live long enough to enjoy the fruits of his dishonorable conduct. That I can promise any who ask,'' the Earl of Dunmor said grimly.

❧ *Chapter 12*

Henry Tudor looked curiously upon the man before him. His name was Jasper Keane, and he was a knight from the north. The king had a certain instinct where men were concerned, and that instinct was now warning him to be cautious with Sir Jasper Keane.

"So you see, my liege, with my wife dead in childbed, there are no longer any Greys left at Greyfaire Keep. I have been master there for almost three years, and I would beg your majesty's leave to continue on in my duties with the hope that someday I might be considered worthy to be confirmed in my wife's inheritance." Sir Jasper smiled toothily, bowing obsequiously.

"I am not quite certain of the recent history of Greyfaire, Sir Jasper. You must refresh my memory. Your wife was the heiress of Greyfaire? She was born a Grey?"

Jasper Keane considered lying, but then thought better of it. There were too many alive and even now in the king's favor who could tell Henry Tudor the truth. "Rowena, may God assoil her sweet soul," he began piously, "was married to Henry Grey, the last Grey lord of Greyfaire, sire. When she was widowed, I wed her."

"There were no offspring of her first marriage?" the king queried.

"A daughter," Sir Jasper said shortly.

"She is dead?" the king pressed gently.

"The wench was carried off in a border raid by the Scots," he said.

"She is dead?" the king repeated.

Again Sir Jasper considered lying. When several days after Arabella's abduction the word had come that the Earl of Dunmor had married her, Jasper Keane had been made a laughingstock in the district. There had already been a great deal of nasty talk about his hasty marriage as it was. Yet, here again, he dare not lie. "I understand the girl was married off to some nobly-born bastard, sire, but I could not say for certain. She has not communicated with me, even when her mother died. She is a feckless, spoilt wench who cares for naught but herself, I fear.''

''Still,'' the king considered aloud, ''she is Greyfaire's rightful heiress,'' and seeing the play of emotions cross Sir Jasper's face, Henry Tudor knew he was wise not to promise the man anything concrete. There had been fury in the man's eyes for a brief moment before he had quickly masked his emotions. ''Have you land of your own, Sir Jasper?'' the king asked in pleasant tones, not quite ready to shut the door upon this man.

''My home was destroyed by the Scots,'' Sir Jasper Keane said tightly.

The king nodded. ''So Greyfaire Keep is now your home?''

''Aye, my liege.''

Sir Jasper Keane obviously did not have the wherewithal to rebuild his own house, the king thought. He was hungry for legal possession of Greyfaire Keep. With it he might attract a wife with some substance of her own. He motioned to his secretary, who bent down to hear his master's words. ''This Greyfaire. Is it important? Rich? Large? In other words, is it worth having?'' he demanded in low tones.

''It is a small border keep, majesty, and virtually impregnable. There is no real wealth attached to it. One village and some acreage. Its only real value is in its location. The Scots usually invade from that direction, and it has always served as the first warning outpost for England in the north.''

The king considered, and then said to his secretary, ''You have heard. If you were me, would you give this keep over to Sir Jasper, or would you seek the heiress in Scotland?''

''I think, sire, that I would consider long on it before making *any* decision. It is not that I question this knight's word, but we really know naught of this matter but what he has told us. I think I would investigate it further, for your majesty would not willingly do Greyfaire's heiress an injustice. Let this knight prove his loyalty to you first before you reward him. He was, I have heard, a staunch Yorkist.''

The point was well taken by Henry Tudor. ''I think, Sir Jasper, that I am not in a position to grant you Greyfaire Keep at this time,'' the king began. ''England has, as you well know, been but recently invaded by one Lambert Simnel, masquerading as the boy earl of Warwick, the last of the royal Plantagenets, and an army of diehard Yorkists, Irish rabble, and German mercenaries. It is to be hoped that this is the last challenge made to my throne, but until I defeat this challenge, I cannot possibly consider your request. You were a trustworthy Yorkist yourself, I understand, Sir Jasper. Do you not desire to help those who would usurp my throne?''

Jasper Keane felt panic welling up. Damn Rowena's treasonous connections! Thank God she was dead. If he were clever he just might salvage his hopes. ''It is true, sire, that I supported Richard of Gloucester during his reign, and his brother King Edward before him. It is true that my late wife was Queen Anne Neville's favorite cousin, but I have sworn my oath to uphold your rights, sire, and I will not break that oath. There are none who can say that I ever broke my sacred oath. Let me prove my loyalty to you. I have knowledge of a great and secret nature that might be of importance to your majesty.''

So, his late wife had been Anne Neville's cousin, Henry Tudor thought. He had not known this, but obviously Sir Jasper thought he did. What else was this man not telling him? ''What knowledge?'' the king demanded.

Sir Jasper looked nervously at the king's personal secretary, but when the king made no move to send the man away, he spoke anyway. ''Your queen's young brothers live, sire. They were hidden at Middleham Castle by their uncle Richard for safety's sake.''

''And they are still there?'' Henry Tudor's voice was almost afire in his excitement.

''Nay, they were moved immediately after your majesty's victory at Bosworth Field to the Tower, I am told. One of the two knights assigned to personally guard the princes is my relation. For obvious reasons, the princes were moved in secret with no fanfare. My late wife knew of this, and it was through her I first learned of it. That is how I was able to place my cousin in the prince's train.''

The king's mind was reeling with the serious implications that Sir Jasper's words intimated. Worse, how could his wife's two young brothers be incarcerated in the Tower and he not know about it? One surviving York prince was bad enough, but three could bring the whole kingdom down around his ears. He chose his words carefully. ''This is an interesting tale you tell me, Sir Jasper, but of course it is not possible that my wife's brothers survived their uncle's ill intent. It is equally impossible that Edward and Richard Plantagenet are currently imprisoned within the Tower without my knowledge. Nevertheless, I will investigate what you have told me, for I know you would not fabricate such a tale simply to curry my favor. You have divulged this in order to prove your loyalty to me, and I am pleased by your display of faithfulness. Go now and join with my army as we prepare to meet the invader. If we both survive this assault upon England, we will talk again on this matter regarding Greyfaire Keep."

Sir Jasper Keane bowed ingratiatingly several times as he backed from the room, thinking that all was not lost, even if he was not yet Greyfaire's legal lord.

When the door had closed behind him, the king turned to his secretary. *"Find out!"* was all he said.

"And if it is true?" his secretary asked.

"Is it not your purpose in life to solve such problems for me?" the king said coldly. "You will take care of the matter for me, but I do not ever again want to have it mentioned in my presence."

"Of course, your majesty," the king's secretary said tonelessly.

"It is *my* son, Arthur, who will one day be England's king," Henry Tudor replied. "I will defeat these rebels and bring a lasting peace to England. There have been too many years of strife."

"God is surely on your majesty's side," his secretary answered.

"Aye," the king said with a smile. "I believe he truly is!"

And all of Europe believed, when on the sixteenth day of June in that year of our Lord, 1487, Henry Tudor defeated the diehard Yorkists and the boy they called Edward, Earl of Warwick, but whom the king called Lambert Simnel. The boy, who was ten years of age, was taken into the royal household. Some of the rebels were punished and forfeited their lives. Others were forgiven and paid large fines. A three-year peace treaty was signed between Scotland and England, hopefully guaranteeing the safety of the north. It seemed that God did, indeed, approve of Henry Tudor and the dynasty he was founding.

Scotland, however, did not benefit from God's goodwill in that same year. Plague had broken out throughout the countryside. It appeared that another bad harvest was fated, portending another hungry winter. The highland earls and chieftains fought with one another for lack of a common enemy, and grumbled incessantly about the many weaknesses of James III. The weather was horrendous, and the Countess of Dunmor was feuding publicly with the Earl of Dunmor.

"A month!" Arabella shouted at her husband. "You promised me that when Maggie was a month old you would go to your brother so that he might treat with his fellow king over my daughter's rights to Greyfaire. She is nine and a half months old, Tavis, and you have not done it! You gave me your word and I accepted it, for you are an honorable man."

"Damnit, Arabella," he roared back at her, "hae ye no concept of anything but yer own desires? Ye know the difficulties that Jemmie faces right now."

"They are difficulties of his own making this time, Tavis. You know it as well as I do. Seeking to divert the Earl of Home's revenues from Coldingham Priory into his own pocket is certainly provocative, my lord, and your brother well knows it! The queen's death has changed him, Tavis. He is not the man we once knew. In the first months after Queen Margaret's death he cloistered himself within his own apartments, ignoring the business of his government. Now, suddenly, he has decided he needs another choir, but he does not want to pay for that choir out of his own pocket, so he has reached into Lord Home's pocket in an act of petty revenge, for Lord Home has spoken out against an English match for Scotland's royal house."

"*An English match?* 'Tis nae one wedding Jemmie speaks of, Arabella. 'Tis three! Himself, Jamie and Ormond, the other James. Three English women wi all their servants and personal attendants overrunning the Scots court. One we might accept, but three makes it seem like a conquering invasion of Scotland by England. Can ye nae see that?"

"All of which has nothing to do with our daughter's rights to Greyfaire," snapped Arabella.

" 'Tis nae a good time to reason wi Jemmie, lovey," the earl said stubbornly.

"And when will be a good time, Tavis? All hell is about to break loose here in Scotland over your brother's highhandedness. I know you love him. I do too, but as a king he is not well liked. There are many who would overthrow him given the provocation. His whole life Jemmie Stewart has been indecisive, yet suddenly he has roused himself from his languor and is inviting civil war in the process. Are you aware, my lord, that the king has petitioned Pope Innocent to close Coldingham and divert its revenues to the Chapel Royal at Stirling?''

"He is the king, Arabella. It is his right," her husband replied.

"Lord Home does not think so. God's foot, my lord, those members of the Home family with a bent to religious orders have always taken those orders at Coldingham Priory. They consider it *their* priory. For how many generations has a Home sat in the prior's chair in that religious house? Lord Home himself is the priory's hereditary bailiff.''

"The Homes have always been the one great border family who hae given my brother trouble," Tavis Stewart said. "He and Lord Home are mortal enemies. They always hae been.''

"And so the king has taken it upon himself to come out of his stupor and bait them? 'Tis madness, and again I say it has nothing to do with our daughter's rights over Greyfaire Keep. You must go to Jemmie and ask him to speak with King Henry. Perhaps this matter will divert him from his path of self-destruction.''

"It is nae the proper time, lovey.''

"It is nae the proper time, my lord? There will never be a better time than now for King James to ask King Henry. There is peace between our two countries at this moment. You know as well as I do that if a civil war breaks out, England is apt to break that peace even as Scotland would have broken it had the Yorkists prevailed at Stokefield last June and caused a civil war in England. You cannot be so blind that you do not see that!''

He was amazed by her grasp of the political situation. How his wee English wife had grown in intellect in the almost three years since he had stolen her from Greyfaire church and married her. It was, of course, his brother's tutoring. Jemmie had opened the door to Arabella's mind, and in doing so had lit a fire for learning in her that could not seem to be quenched. She read any and everything she could get her hands on, though God only knew his library was not a large one. While they had been in Edinburgh she had found a stall in the marketplace that sold volumes brought from France and Italy. She was correct in her assessment of the situation, and yet he believed that he was equally correct in his handling of the matter.

"I cannot go to Jemmie now, lovey," he said in a tone he hoped conveyed to her that the matter was closed for the time being.

"If you will not protect our daughter's rights, my lord, then I must, of necessity, do so myself," Arabella told him in equally implacable tones.

The Earl of Dunmor departed his castle to hunt down a wolf who had been terrorizing his villages. He had learned that when his wife was in one of her moods it was best to allow her the space of several days' time to calm her temper. When he returned home four days later with the wolfskin as a gift which she might use to trim a gown and a cloak, he discovered to his shock that his countess had set forth for Edinburgh almost immediately after he had left Dunmor. The message she had left him was curt and to the point.

I have gone to the king.

With a smothered curse the Earl of Dunmor threw the parchment into the fire and glowered at Flora, who had been his wife's messenger. "Did she take the coach?" he demanded.

"She rode," said Flora, "and she would nae hae gone had ye done yer duty by Lady Maggie, my lord."

" 'Tis nae the time to approach Jemmie," he roared at the serving woman, who was not in the least intimidated.

"There is nae a time that is quite right in this matter, my lord. The king is a good man, but ye've spent yer entire life worrying about his delicate sensibilities. If the king is as soft as they say he is, it is because everyone hae treated him so, yet he doesna treat others wi the same care. He hae always been like a great clumsy beastie where men were concerned, an ye know it. He offends those who could help him and favors those who but seek the advantage for themselves. He doesna hae any common sense. Yer lady was right to go to Edinburgh and seek yer child's rights. In the spring the feuding will begin, and there will be nae time for the king to show kindness toward any."

"Indeed, Flora, and how do ye know this?" the earl inquired.

"All the common people know it, my lord. Has it nae always been like this?"

Her words gave Tavis Stewart food for thought, and upon reflection he realized the truth of those words. His nephew was almost grown, and if not fully mature, was certainly old enough to be successfully used against his father, though not old enough to rule alone without strong guidance. The Earl of Dunmor knew from where that guidance would come. It would come from Archibald Douglas, from the Homes, from the Hepburns of Hailes and other border families. It would become necessary to choose sides, Tavis Stewart knew, if an attempt was made to overthrow his half brother. And what would he do? He didn't honestly know at this moment.

He contemplated going after his wife, but then realized chasing after Arabella would make him look foolish, and she had probably considered that very fact when she decided to seek out the king herself. He was angry at her for going, and at the same time he worried about her reception at court. Since his sister-in-law had died, the court had been very much, and quite exclusively, a man's world. Would Arabella, sheltered and so unversed in such a world, be able to cope?

Arabella, however, by her very inexperience, had contended quite well. She had traveled up to the capital city with only Lona and a troop of her husband's clansmen for protection in her train. She had gone immediately to Edinburgh Castle and sought an audience with her brother-in-law, who, for lack of anything else to do, was delighted to see a friendly face.

"Arabella, lass," the king said, beaming at her as she curtsied to him. "Where is my brother? Hae he nae come wi ye?"

"Tavis is hunting wolves, my liege," Arabella said sweetly, "and I have come up to Edinburgh alone to beg a favor of your majesty."

"I am deeply fond of Tavis Stewart," the king replied, "and I would nae do anything that would displease him, lass, even for ye. Yer not at odds wi him in this matter ye would raise wi me, are ye?"

"Nay, sire," Arabella said. "My husband and I are in complete agreement regarding this matter, but Tavis feels that we should not disturb your majesty at this time. I, on the other hand, feel that the matter, though important to us, will be such a slight thing in your majesty's eyes that you cannot possibly be disquieted by it. So I have come to Edinburgh to beg a boon of you, sire."

"Wi out yer husband's knowledge, madame?" the king gently inquired.

"I left him a note, sire," Arabella said innocently.

The king burst into guffaws of genuine amusement. In the months since his wife's death he had not found anything so humorous. "She left him a note," he cackled, poking his favorite, John Ramsey, the Earl of Bothwell, in the ribs. "Why, I'll wager even now my brother is spurring his horse for Edinburgh! Hee! Hee!"

"Indeed, my lord," Ramsey of Balmain replied in a bored tone.

"Well, lassie," the king finally said, regaining control of his emotions, "what is it that ye want of me?"

"You know the story, sire, of how my husband abducted me from my home. If the truth be known, I have not been unhappy with my marriage, despite its unorthodox beginnings, but I was, sire, the heiress of Greyfaire Keep. I am the last of the Greys of Greyfaire, and although Tavis has never complained, I brought him no dowry, for Greyfaire was my dowry. When my lord stole me away, the man I was to have wed married my mother instead. She died in childbed several months later, and now, I am told, this man is petitioning King Henry for possession of Greyfaire Keep. It is neither his right nor his heritage. He is a wicked man.

"I would have my home back, your majesty. Oh, I know I can never again really possess Greyfaire, for I am wed to a Scot and King Henry is no fool to give an English border keep to a Scots earl; but if my daughter Margaret might have Greyfaire, I should rest content. I would allow King Henry to match my child with a bridegroom of his own choosing, and I should send my daughter into that bridegroom's house to be fostered after her sixth birthday. Greyfaire Keep would then remain in the hands of a descendant of the Greys, which is as it should be, your majesty. Will you not intercede with King Henry for your niece, my lord? Surely he will listen to you, for I am of little importance myself." Arabella looked up trustingly into the king's eyes.

"Och, lassie," Jemmie Stewart replied, " 'tis indeed a slight request in the scheme of the world, but I can see how important it is to ye that ye would come through late winter weather to see me and ask my aid. Of course I will gie ye that aid! King Henry will see the advantage to such a match, even as I do. Having the current king of Scotland's niece and the future king of Scotland's first cousin in his power canna be but a pleasant thought to him. I approve of an English marriage. If I can but negotiate a match for myself and my lads, I will regain Berwick back as part of the bargain. What think ye of that, lassie?''

"Ye will surely silence Bell the Cat, my lord, if you do.'' Arabella chuckled. "What will he complain about then, I wonder?''

"I'm certain he will think of something,'' Ramsey of Balmain interjected sharply. He was dressed in garments striped yellow and black, and Arabella thought how very much the slender man resembled a wasp.

"I think not, my lord,'' she replied. "Rather he will be surprised to learn that diplomacy is every bit as successful as war, and far less damaging to both property, not to mention life and limb.'' She turned to the king. "You will write to King Henry, my lord?''

"Aye, lassie, I will, and this very day, I promise ye. Where are ye staying?''

"At the house on the High Street, sire. I will but remain the night, and then I must hurry home, for I have left Maggie with a wet-nurse, and she has never before been without me.''

"Stay wi'in the castle, Arabella, until I hae had my secretary make a copy of the letter I will dictate to him for ye. Then ye may take it back to Dunmor to show my brother that ye didna anger me by yer innocent request. Tell me, lass, is yer bairn named in honor of my own Margaret?''

"Aye, my lord, she is.'' Arabella answered simply.

Jemmie Stewart nodded silently, and then with a slight wave of his hand, indicated that she might leave him.

Arabella curtsied to the king, and dismissed, backed from the room. In the antechamber she found herself face to face with the prince. He had grown even taller in the months since she had last seen him, and although she knew him to be somewhat younger than she was, he had all the appearance of a grown man now.

His eyes raked her boldly. "Madame, it is good to see ye back at court.'' He swept her a bow, catching her small hand up in his and kissing it.

"My lord,'' she said politely, and disengaged her hand from his, to his open amusement.

"How long will ye be staying, my lady of Dunmor? I hae missed seeing yer lovely face."

She ignored the compliment. "I return home tomorrow, my lord."

"So soon?" His look was one of disappointment, and then he said, "My uncle is nae wi ye?"

"My husband hunts the wolves that have been terrorizing our villages. I came to Edinburgh on an errand for him, and as my mission is complete, I will return home tomorrow," Arabella answered the prince.

"Then ye will take supper wi me tonight," Jamie Stewart said.

"Certainly not!"

"Ye canna refuse me, *Aunt*," he said softly. "I am the heir to Scotland's throne. Insult me, and ye do yer family a disservice."

Arabella suddenly found herself in a quandary. Was Jamie telling her the truth, or was he merely attempting to gain his own way in this matter? She honestly did not know, but she also found she did not like the idea that he would bully her with his royal position in an effort to gain his own way.

"I will have my supper in the hall with the rest of the court, my lord," she told the prince. "I cannot refuse you if you wish to sit with me."

"There are no women at court since my mother died, madame," the prince answered. "I would have ye take supper wi me in my private apartments."

"Surely, my lord, you understand that to have supper with you in your apartments, no matter how innocent such a meeting between us would be, should certainly compromise my reputation. I know you would never do that to either me or to your uncle, who is so fond of your highness."

The prince laughed. "Ye may attempt to elude me, Arabella Stewart, but I will nae let ye. 'Tis lonely and dull here at court now that there is no queen or pretty maids. All that I have are my studies and the company of my younger brothers and our tutors."

For a moment he almost sounded like the boy he should have been, but the Countess of Dunmor, wary, saw the mischievous light lurking in the prince's eyes behind the pitiful look of innocence he was attempting to turn on her. She was in a complete quandary as to what to do, when the Earl of Angus joined them. "My lord," she said brightly, "the prince is having a supper party in his apartments this evening, and I am certain he wants you to come! Is that not so, my lord?"

"I shall be delighted to join ye," Archibald Douglas said with a grin before the prince might tell him nay.

"I hae best go and tell my servants to prepare for us then," Jamie Stewart said, realizing that he had been bested in his attempt to seduce the Countess of Dunmor this day. "If I ever go to war, Aunt," he told her, "I can only hope that ye are on my side." Then with a bow he was gone.

The Earl of Angus chuckled. "Madame, ye must, indeed, hae been desperate to call upon me for my aid." He took her arm in his and they began walking. "He's a braw laddie, our wee prince."

"He's a wily young lecher and should have his ears boxed," Arabella said furiously. "He has been most outspoken in his desire to take me to his bed. How dare he, my lord! I have certainly not encouraged him, nor would I ever betray my husband or put the horns of a cuckold upon his head."

The Earl of Angus could see that she was very upset, and so he did not tease her. Instead he said, "The prince is at least a real man, unlike his father. It pleases us to see that that is so, for we must look beyond the day when James III rules in this land."

"The king is far different than any man I have ever known," Arabella admitted, "but I see no reason for you to dislike him so greatly, my lord. Like you, he prefers the company of men. The difference is that the men he likes are not always of the nobility, and are men whose interests and tastes are more refined than yours. You suggest some unnatural relationship between the king and his friends; and yet the king fathered three sons, and Queen Margaret openly adored and respected her husband. I suspect you now dabble with the idea of setting the son above his father. I think you are wrong."

Archibald Douglas, who was not normally respectful of a woman's intelligence, suddenly found himself respecting the young Countess of Dunmor for speaking bluntly, even if she was wrong. She could influence her husband, and Tavis Stewart would certainly be of help to their cause. "Madame," he began slowly, carefully choosing his words, "I dinna dislike the king,

but he is a weak man, and no matter how deep yer friendship
wi him may be, ye must admit the truth of that. England now
has a strong king. The kings before Henry Tudor had other
problems. Richard spent most of his reign fighting to maintain
his tenuous hold upon his throne. His brother before him, Edward, was involved wi not only threats to his kingship, but was
forced to contend wi serious family problems as well. And before him, poor feeble-minded Henry of Lancaster, a pawn to
his lords, a pawn to his wife's ambitions. But now, Arabella
Stewart, now England has Henry Tudor, and the Yorkists hae
nothing left but a boy-earl in the Tower and a pretender in the
king's kitchens.''

"There are King Edward's sons, Edward and Richard," Arabella said faintly.

"Those poor laddies are surely dead, madame, if nae at their
uncle's hand, then certainly at Henry Tudor's. He will hae no
serious threat to his kingship left living. Not for himself, and
nae for his son. King Henry Tudor is England's king for as long
as he shall live. Now Scotland needs a strong king," Archibald
Douglas told her.

"Perhaps you are correct, my lord, but perhaps you are not.
A king is anointed with God's own holy oil at his crowning, and
it is not for us, mere mortals, to question God's judgment. This
king will reign in Scotland until God wills it otherwise. To think
treason is to go against God's own order, my lord.''

"Divine Right," Angus said with a smile. "Aye, a king rules
by *Divine Right*, but sometimes we mere mortals must gie God
a wee bit of a helping hand, madame.''

Arabella was forced to laugh. "My lord," she said, "you are
incorrigible, but what's worse, you are wrong and refuse to acknowledge it. Still, I cannot argue with you, as you have rescued
me from a most difficult position. You may admire the prince's
manly behavior toward women, but I know you would not want
the wife of a friend forced into a compromising situation.''

Now it was Archibald Douglas's turn to laugh. "Madame, ye
made it impossible for me to refuse ye. I dinna think young
Jamie was pleased to have found his cleverly planned rendezvous turning before his own eyes into a supper party for three.''

"Do you mean he would not even have fed me?" Arabella
demanded, outraged.

"Why prepare supper when ye dinna mean to eat it?" Angus

said with a grin. "Jamie is a careful young fellow wi his gold. He can be generous when he chooses, but I've nae known him to be deliberately wasteful."

Arabella suddenly found herself giggling. "Oh, my lord," she gasped, looking up into Archibald Douglas's blue eyes, "I think I see why my husband is fearful of allowing me to roam unprotected and alone. The prince is a sly fox, but I am obviously just a lamb."

Archibald Douglas chuckled. " 'Tis true," he agreed with her, "and yet, madame, I hae seen ye turn into a wee fierce thing when angered. Still, anger is nae defense against a prince of the blood royal."

"Please do not leave me with Prince James," Arabella said, suddenly sobered and serious. "I cannot accede to his implied demands, and yet I cannot openly insult him without incurring his enmity. I know he will one day be king, but that should not give him the right to bully any woman into his bed."

"It is your very refusal that makes ye so tempting, madame," the Earl of Angus said. "Jamie Stewart is nae used to ladies who say nae to him. I will nae leave ye alone wi him, however, I promise ye. I could nae face yer husband if I did, for I know the prince desires ye, and Tavis knows it too. Why on earth did ye come up to Edinburgh wi out him?"

Arabella explained to the Earl of Angus why she had come, and he nodded his understanding.

"Ye were right to take this matter into yer own hands, madame," he told her. "Tavis Stewart is a good man, but he treats his half brother too softly. Besides, if ye raise yer wee Maggie correctly, she'll always be loyal to the Stewarts, even though she lives in England, an Englishman's wife."

"I would have her be loyal to Greyfaire, and its people first, after God," Arabella said quietly. "That is where my daughter's duty will lie, my lord. Politics and war are a man's domain. Nurturing is a woman's."

"Yet sometimes women involve themselves in politics, madame," the Earl of Angus noted.

"How can that be?" she asked him.

"When a woman influences her husband one way or another, she is in her own way involving herself in his affairs, is she nae?"

"Indeed, my lord, she is," Arabella admitted, "although I

have never thought of a woman's good influence in that light. I think it is a woman's Christian duty to guide her husband where she may.''

''A female mind is a treacherous bog, madame,'' the Earl of Angus teased her. ''Woe to the man who loses himself in an attempt to understand it.''

Together the Countess of Dunmor and Archibald Douglas passed the next hour in the castle's Great Hall speaking on various subjects. Arabella began to gain new respect for Angus, and he, in turn, admitted to himself that she was not only a beautiful woman, but a fascinating and clever one as well, particularly considering her youth and inexperience. When finally a page came to tell them the prince was ready to receive them, they followed the boy arm in arm, ignoring the stares of both the curious and the envious.

The prince greeted them warmly and apologized for the plainness of the fare upon his table. ''I did nae hae the time to prepare properly,'' he said.

''You must not invite people to supper so precipitously, my lord,'' Arabella teased him.

''Madame, it is nae supper I hae in mind when I look at ye,'' the prince shot back wickedly.

''Then it should have been Lady Sorcha Morton you asked to your rooms, Jamie Stewart, and not me,'' Arabella said mischievously. With Angus for support, she was feeling braver than she might have had she been alone with the prince.

The two gentlemen burst out laughing, and Angus asked, ''How is my cousin, laddie?''

''I could nae tell ye, Archie, for our acquaintance was but a brief one. Sorcha's repertoire is nae very large or involved, I fear, despite yer early tutelage of the lady. She hae, I am told, set her sights on a wealthy merchant in the city.''

Angus nodded. ''She needs a husband, and she needs a rich one, for her tastes are expensive. The gentlemen of her own class nae hae the funds to waste upon a woman that Sorcha needs for her personal adornment.''

The prince grinned. ''She could nae seem to see the advantage in pleasing a future king,'' he said, and his blue eyes twinkled.

The meal was a simple one, for the castle kitchens had not the guidance of a mistress any longer. There was a roasted capon, venison, a rabbit pie, and a salmon poached in white wine. There was bread, cheese, and a bowl of apples. A rich Burgundy wine accompanied their supper, which was no sooner over than a young page appeared.

"The king would see the Earl of Angus," the lad piped.

"Then I must return to the hall," Arabella said quickly, "for I am certain the king's secretary has my parchment ready for me by now."

"Ye will stay, madame," the prince ordered, catching her hand. He turned to Archibald Douglas. "Ye may go, my lord."

The Earl of Angus cast Arabella a look that told her that although he sympathized with her predicament, he could no longer interfere. The prince's dismissal of him, and his directive to Arabella that she remain, made it impossible for him to intercede on her behalf any further. He stood, and with a bow to both the prince and the Countess of Dunmor, he departed.

As the door closed behind the earl, the prince turned, and raising Arabella's hand to his lips, he turned it and placed a kiss upon the soft, sensitive flesh of her inner wrist. "Now, sweetheart, we are finally alone." His look was a smouldering one.

"If you touch me, Jamie Stewart, I shall scream," Arabella told him bluntly, snatching her hand from his grasp.

"What is it about me, madame, that you find so repugnant?" the prince demanded angrily.

"First answer me this, my lord. What is it you want of me?" she countered.

He had the good grace to flush, and then he said, "I think, madame, ye know precisely what it is I want of ye."

"You wish to take me to your bed and make love to me, do you not?" Arabella said frankly. "Well, my lord, I do not wish you to make love to me. I love my husband, and I consider your pursuit of me offensive. I do not wish to dishonor my lord's good name. You know this, for I have been more than candid with you in this matter. I do not understand why you continue in your pursuit."

"Yer certainly outspoken, madame," the prince noted dryly.

"If you force me to your will, Jamie Stewart, and surely you could, for you are far bigger than I, you will commit an act of rape. When you release me, I shall go directly to my husband and tell him of your behavior toward me. What do you think

Tavis Stewart will do, my lord, when he learns you have coerced his wife into your bed and then compelled her to your will?''

The prince stood up, and walking around the table, stopped behind Arabella. He placed his hands upon her velvet-clad shoulders. "I've nae known a woman like ye, Arabella," he said softly. Bending, he kissed her throat lingeringly and one hand slipped down into her bodice to cup a breast. He fondled her breast, teasing gently at the nipple which hardened beneath his thumb. "Yer so soft, hinny-love, and so sweet," he murmured.

Arabella sat perfectly still beneath his touch.

"How many men hae ye known, sweetheart? Yer husband and nae other, I'll wager. I am young, I know, but already I am acclaimed as the finest lover in all of Scotland. Let me love ye, Arabella Stewart! *Let me love ye!*''

"I will never betray Tavis willingly, Jamie Stewart," she told him coldly. "Now remove your hand from my bodice this instant! I would leave, and if you try to stop me, I shall cry the castle down about your royal ears!" It was as if his invasion of her bodice had suddenly given her the strength to defy him. Arabella decided that the fact Jamie Stewart was heir to Scotland's throne should not give him license over her person.

Reluctantly he complied with her demand, and she arose from the table, shaking her skirts angrily. "One day ye will want something of me, sweetheart," he said softly, kissing her neck once more. "Eventually everyone wants some boon of a king. Before ye ask it of me, Arabella Stewart, remember what the price will be, for nae even a king's favors are free."

"You are not Scotland's king yet, my lord prince, and pray God you will not be until you have learned that you cannot have everything you want simply because you are a Royal Stewart!" the Countess of Dunmor snapped.

"I canna wait to get ye in my bed, Arabella Stewart." The prince chuckled. "I like spice and can nae ever get enough of it. Ye must keep my uncle a verra happy man."

He was the most determined man she had ever met, Arabella thought as she traveled home the following day. She debated whether she should tell her husband of her encounter and decided, in the interest of family unity, she would say only that she and the Earl of Angus had taken supper with the prince. She had met Angus in the hallway outside the prince's apartments.

The page who had come to fetch him, Angus told her, had disappeared the moment he had exited Jamie Stewart's apartments, and Angus had learned quickly enough that the king had not summoned him. It had all been a trick of the prince's to get Arabella alone. Realizing that, Archibald Douglas had returned posthaste to rescue the Countess of Dunmor.

"I should hae known ye didna really need my aid," he said to her as he explained the prince's ruse.

"Oh, my lord, I most certainly did need you," she told him. "I was terrified and had no idea how I was going to extricate myself from the situation until the prince boldly put his hands upon me. I became so angry that he was forced to let me go. I do not think women usually become angry with Jamie Stewart."

"Only when he refuses them," Angus chuckled, and she burst out laughing.

"He is so damned persistent," Arabella grumbled.

"He'll be a good king one day," the earl replied.

Arabella was not unhappy to see the turrets of Dunmor Castle rising up before her. She had been gone from her home for ten days, and she had missed her daughter terribly. First, however, she had to contend with her husband, whom she had no doubt would be very angry with her. The Countess of Dunmor strode boldly into the Great Hall of her castle to find herself face to face with Tavis Stewart.

"Well, madame, did ye get what ye wanted from my brother?" he demanded.

"Aye, I did," she answered him, thrusting a rolled parchment into his hand.

The Earl of Dunmor unrolled the parchment and scanned its contents, nodding. "By God, my wee spitfire, ye did stir Jemmie to action, didn't ye? It doesna mean, however, that ye'll get yer precious Greyfaire back for Maggie. Ye realize that, don't ye?"

"I will get Greyfaire back, Tavis. I swear it!" she told him. "It was my dowry, and 'tis Maggie's now. I'll not let Jasper Keane and his ilk have it! I'll tear the keep down stone by stone myself rather than allow *that* bastard to have it." Then she flung herself into his arms. "Ohhh, 'tis so good to be home, my lord!"

"What a wench ye are, lassie," he murmured against her hair, and then he picked her up in his arms.

"*My lord!*" she squealed. "I have not seen Maggie yet."

"Ye'll see her in the morning," he said, and stamped out of the hall and up the stairs with his wife.

"Did you miss me, my lord?" Arabella said softly, nibbling at his earlobe.

"Vixen!" he grumbled at her.

"Did you catch the wolf?" She bit down sharply on the morsel of flesh.

"Aye, damnit, lovey! Aye, I did," he admitted.

"And you'll admit that you were wrong and I was right about approaching the king?" she pressed.

"Only if ye'll admit yer a disobedient baggage," he teased her, kicking open the door to her apartments and striding through into her bedchamber. "*Out!*" he commanded Flora, who was awaiting her mistress, and then he dumped Arabella upon the bed, flinging himself atop her. "Now, madame, I would hae a welcoming kiss of ye!" and his lips came down upon hers.

Arabella made a distinctively satisfied sound and stretched sensually, her arms coming up around his neck. "Mmmmm," she purred, sighing deeply as his mouth moved to press kisses along the column of her throat. His fingers fumbled expertly with her laces and he pulled her loosened bodice off. Impatiently his hand gripped at the neck of her chemise, and with a quick motion he tore it away, burying his dark head between her breasts. She thrust herself against the warmth of his lips, turning within his grasp so that he might kiss the twin mounds of perfumed flesh.

"*Sweet, sweet,*" he groaned, a hand seeking beneath her skirts, trailing leisurely upon a silken thigh, finding the throbbing core of her.

She twisted beneath him, making soft little whimpering noises in the back of her throat, moving a hand between them, reaching beneath his kilt to find his manhood, stroking it urgently until he was hard and even more eager for her than he had first been.

Their mouths met again, tongues intertwining, and he was pushing her skirts above her thighs that he might mount her. "Look at me, my passionate wee spitfire," he growled fiercely. "*Look at me!*"

Arabella's light green eyes flew open to stare deeply into her husband's dark green ones. Her eyes widened with pleasure, never looking away from his gaze even as he pushed deeply into her. "Ahhhhh," she sighed once more, and then smiled at his answering groan. "Tell me you love me, Tavis Stewart," she said softly.

"I love ye, Arabella Stewart," he answered her, smiling down into her face. "Aye, I love ye, and ye well know it!"

"Aye, I do," she whispered against his mouth, and then her eyes closed slowly as she floated away on a cloud of pleasure that the wonderful union of their two bodies brought her.

"Ahh, spitfire," he moaned, driving them both hard in his own quest for fulfillment, and when his passion broke, he was, as always, careful not to let his weight harm her delicate form. Rolling off her, he pulled her into the comfort of his embrace, covering her beautiful face with kisses.

Arabella sighed with contentment. "Is it always this way between husband and wife?" she asked him.

He thought a moment, and then he said, "Nay, 'tis sad to say, 'tis not, lovey. We, however, are nae just husband and wife. We are lovers, my wee wife, and there the difference lies."

"Then 'tis different with each woman?" she queried.

"Aye."

"How?" she demanded.

"My passion for ye is tempered by my love for ye," he said slowly, choosing each word with care so she might understand. "There are women who may arouse a man's baser nature so that he desires to futter them, but he wants nae more of them than that. The same holds true for certain women. They wish but one thing of a man—that he be a lover. No more. For us 'tis different, for nae only do I love ye wi all my heart, lassie, I desire ye as well, and I seek to gie ye my bairns. Do ye understand that?"

"Yet men give women they do not love children, do they not, my lord?"

"Aye, yet men give women they do not love children."

"You have, my lord."

"I hae been more careful than most," Tavis Stewart answered honestly, "but ye know that I hae three bairns by lasses in my villages. There are two lads, and one little lass."

"Do you ever see them, my lord?"

"When I am in the neighborhood, aye. I hae denied none of them, for having got them on their mothers, they are my responsibility," the earl told his wife.

"You are such a good man," she purred in a deceptively

sweet voice, and then rolling over, she raised herself up, looked down into his face with a smile, and grabbing a handful of his dark hair, yanked it with all her might. "There will be no more lasses in the villages, my lord, lest you incur my undying wrath!" She pulled his hair a second time for emphasis.

"Owww!" Tavis Stewart yelped, for she was not gentle.

"Say it, my lord! *No more lasses!*" Arabella demanded.

"No more lasses," he agreed with a rueful grin, reaching up to caress her bare breasts. "How could I want any other, spitfire, when I hae ye for my wife?" The softness of her skin, the fact that her pretty nipples were puckering with arousal, set his own pulses racing. Wrapping an arm about her waist, he tumbled her onto her back once more and drew her skirt and petticoats off. Naked now but for her stockings with their ribboned garters, his wife was a most fetching sight.

"The fire's gone out," Arabella said softly, "and the chamber is chilled, my lord."

The earl arose from the bed, and going to the fireplace, rebuilt the blaze. Then turning, he removed his shirt, his kilt, and the rest of his garments. "I'll warm ye, lovey," he replied low.

Arabella Stewart held out her hand to her husband. "Come to bed, my lord," she told him. "Ye've scarce begun to welcome me home."

With a smile of delight, the Earl of Dunmor joined his wife.

Chapter 13

*P*ope Innocent granted the petition of King James III of Scotland in the matter of Coldingham Priory. After all, had not King James sought out and then sent abroad to learn their art the finest musicians in Scotland? He had. Did not King James encourage the collegiate churches to form choirs and to craft instruments, all of which were promoted as an inspiring part of the church services to the greater glory of God? He had. The pope, being advised of all of this, as well as the king's own devoutness and the devoutness of his late queen, Margaret, was favorably disposed toward Scotland's king.

The king had also requested of the pope that he have the authority from Rome—Scotland being so far from it, and from the Rota—to choose and select for himself all aspirants for ecclesiastic offices, and to have domain over the funds attached to those church appointments. His earls would no longer have the opportunity to use the church's authority for their own designs. This, too, the pope granted King James III.

Suddenly, like a master games player, the king was exerting his royal authority, and his earls, for the most part, did not like it. For all their complaints, they were more comfortable with an indecisive James Stewart, for it gave them the excuse to run wild in defiance of the king's wishes. The *new* James was not at all to their taste. He threatened their authority in matters that they had always considered to be in their own personal jurisdiction.

The king, however, had the enthusiastic support of his parliament for probably the first time in his entire reign. There were some among the nobility who agreed with his stand, and the clergy were certainly on his side, but it was from the members of the Third Estate within the parliament that the king received his strongest support. These upright representatives of the growing middle class and the poor were greatly encouraged to see the king taking charge and attempting to put his realm in order at last. They had for too long suffered at the hands of the earls.

In an effort to aid the king, the parliament passed an act making it a treasonable offense to challenge James III with respect to his acquisition of Coldingham Priory. The Earl of Home, his brother—the now displaced prior of Coldingham—and their kinsman Patrick Hepburn—Lord Hailes—were suddenly gone from court. James III sent his herald to Home Castle with a harsh message demanding their immediate return. The Homes were in contempt of parliament. The King's herald, to hear him tell it upon his return to Edinburgh, barely escaped with his life. The Homes had torn up the Royal Warrant, boxed his ears, and stripped him of his cloak of office before sending him away.

"There will be war before summer," the Earl of Angus told Tavis Stewart. "Home will nae accept this decision, and Jemmie hae gone too far now to retreat or even compromise. We'll soon hae no choice and will hae to choose sides ourselves. The king hae already sent the prince to Stirling."

"Jamie?" the Earl of Dunmor asked.

"Aye. Ormond and young John are wi their sire, but Jamie hae been sent away. He is nae allowed outside the castle gates, and can only walk upon the ramparts and fly his falcons for exercise, I am told," Archibald Douglas replied.

"Poor lad," Tavis sympathized. "He grows so irritable if too many days go by and he canna ride." Then he pierced the Earl of Angus with a sharp look. "And what will ye do, Archie, when ye must choose sides?"

"Like ye, Tavis, I will wait and see. I dinna find treason a pleasant thought."

Arabella, sitting at the highboard with the two men, was strangely silent, for she usually had an opinion on everything. In her own mind she had examined the situation and found that although the king was lacking in many ways, he was a good man and should not be threatened by his nobility for acting in Scotland's best interests and not theirs. Angus was so certain of some sort of military encounter. The thought of war frightened her. She had lost her father to war. The thought of losing her husband did not please her.

In late January the Earl of Home, along with Lords Lyle and Grey and the Hepburn of Hailes came to Stirling Castle at the head of a large body of men. Lord Home, for all his anger toward the king over Coldingham Priory, was a decent man known for his honesty as well as his boldness. The prince welcomed him, or so it appeared to those who viewed the encounter. Master John Shaw, the governor of the castle, admitted the earl and his party despite the king's express orders that no one, except those coming under royal insignia, be admitted. Master Shaw was not a rebel. He was just so overcome by the Earl of Home's powers of reason and great charm that he forgot he would have to answer to the king for Prince James's departure.

Several hours later the prince, dressed all in scarlet, left Stirling Castle at the head of the great troop of men. Behind him rode the Earl of Home, Lords Hailes, Lyle, and Grey. As they exited the castle ramp, their men, seeing the prince leading the four lords, cheered, as did the castle's guard. A small girl, known for her gift of second sight, daughter of one of the castle guards, called out after the prince in the Celtic tongue, "Blessings on ye, O King!" but young Jamie Stewart did not stop to acknowledge her words, if he even heard them. Those about the child, however, were shaken.

The prince and his adherents went to Linlithgow Palace, where they set up their headquarters and waited, but nothing happened. Scotland's lords were strangely silent as they mulled over this turn of events. Suddenly they were not certain of anything, for though James III did not suit them, the prince was young. Perhaps too young to rule. Jamie Stewart and his supporters sat waiting at Linlithgow for those who never came, while the king went north to Aberdeen to reassure himself of the loyalty of the northern lords, all the while ignoring his eldest son and his heir's precipitous behavior.

February was gray and grim, with periods of snow followed by periods of mild weather that left the countryside a thawed mush. Word came to Dunmor Castle that the prince was ill.

"It hae ever been thus," the Earl of Dunmor told his wife. "Jamie hae the constitution of a bull when he is happy, but let him be unhappy, and he suffers physically from a flux of the bowels, aches and pains in his head, neck, and joints."

"It is his own guilty conscience," Arabella said unsympathetically. "He is in defiance of his own father and consorting with those who would rebel against the king. I wish you could go to him and tell him so, but I know you cannot."

"Nay, I canna," he agreed. "If I were to show myself at Linlithgow, there would be those who would say I was supporting my nephew, and in opposition to my brother."

March brought better weather, and the prince, his health improved, celebrated his birthday. His greatest gift was the arrival of the Earl of Angus to his banner, to be followed shortly thereafter by the Earl of Argyll. The kings of England and France, however, sent messages of reprimand to Prince James for his seeming rebellion against his father. The king, in the company of his northern lords and their armies, came to within five miles of Linlithgow, the royal army camping beside the Firth of Forth while the king took up residence in a nearby castle.

A skirmish was fought, the prince's army being led by the Earl of Angus, while the Earl of Home, to his immense irritation, was forced to remain at Linlithgow protecting the prince. A truce was negotiated in which the king would relinquish his full powers to his eldest son and heir, who would act as regent until he was considered old enough to be crowned king; at which point James III would abdicate in the son's favor. The agreement, attested to by four witnesses for either side, was signed and sealed, but the king, upon his return to Edinburgh, disavowed the agreement and announced that he would fight his son first before he turned over his kingdom to him. The Earl of Dunmor finally sent his nephew a message of support, albeit reluctantly.

"How can you support him against your own brother?" Arabella demanded of her husband.

"Jemmie is nae longer worthy of my support," Tavis Stewart said grimly. "He did nae hae to sign that agreement wi Jamie, but he did. He was, therefore, by all the laws of chivalry, bound to keep his word. For God's sake, Arabella, he is the king! If the king canna keep his word, then what can the world expect of such a king? He hae lost his creditability."

"He is your brother," she said furiously, "and he is God's chosen king of Scotland. When you rebel against your brother, you not only commit the sin of Cain, you defy God's will!"

"I will nae support a man who canna keep his word," Tavis Stewart said.

"And I cannot support your rebellious nephew," she answered him.

"I speak for the Stewarts of Dunmor," the earl told his wife.

"You do not speak for me, my lord," she replied angrily.

"Aye, I will admit to that," he agreed, "for nae one knowing ye, Arabella Stewart, would say ye were wi out a tongue of yer own."

The Countess of Dunmor reached for the nearest object to come to hand, a silver candlestick, and threw it with her unerring aim, directly at her husband, who, after almost three years of marriage to the woman he called his "wee English spitfire," had considerably sharpened reflexes and ducked.

The prince sent word throughout Scotland that he was at odds with an unjust king. He invited all who would support him to join him, and Tavis Stewart left Dunmor with a thousand men following his banner and in his wake. It was not considered a large force, for the great northern earls and their counterparts in the borders could muster easily up to thirty thousand clansmen to follow them; but it was considered psychologically important that the king's beloved half brother was supporting his nephew rather than his elder sibling, who had always been so good to him.

It was openly acknowledged, however, that the Countess of Dunmor supported the king and had quarreled violently and publicly with her husband prior to his going. In this opinion she stood alone, for even her husband's stepfather and half brothers followed Prince James and his forces to victory at Saunchieburn on the eleventh day of June in the year of our Lord, 1488. There was a shadow upon the new king's victory, however. James III, having been convinced by his advisors to leave the battlefield after the battle was well under way and obviously lost, had been found murdered beside the millstream of Bannockburn. There were five stab wounds to his chest and stomach, any one of which could have been the death blow. He was buried quickly, but with honor.

On the twenty-fifth day of the month, King James IV was crowned at Scone. It was a hurried affair, for the Scots feared the English king might try and intervene. The new king's younger brothers—the other James, who was now Duke of Ross, and young John—were brought to join their sibling lest some unhappy faction use them against their eldest brother, which was entirely possible. Scotland's lords were already feuding even as the new king was being crowned.

There had been no parliament yet to appoint the new office holders, and there was, therefore, no new order of precedence. The earls and the other nobles fought for places like jealous children. The Earl of Angus was insulted by the Earl of Home's proprietary manner, for despite the fact that Archibald Douglas had been acting as the new king's regent, Home considered that since he had taken the former prince from Stirling in January, the act that precipitated the events leading up to today, he was the greater of the two. Home had also quarreled with his brother, the Prior of Coldingham at this point, and the Earl of Argyll was no longer on speaking terms with Lord Grey, although no one knew why. At least a third of Scotland's nobility were not in attendance at Scone, and a number of bishops were missing as well. The young king, in an effort to give some semblance of dignity to his coronation, banned all from the chapel of Scone at his anointing, save his two younger brothers. His lords, however, noisily jostled with one another in the doorway, craning their necks in an attempt to see the king as he was anointed, murmuring loudly with their discontent over their banishment.

Afterward, in the Great Hall of Scone, James IV sat calmly accepting the Rite of Fealty from Scotland's lords, both great and small. The king was garbed in all black. Above him the clan banners of all those present swung almost imperceptibly in the air currents caused by the heat of the day rising from the hall and the open windows. The largest banner, however, was the king's own, the Lion Rampant, gold upon bloodred.

When the Earl of Dunmor, coming last, had given his oath to his nephew, the young king raised his uncle from his knees himself, saying, "I thank ye, Tavis Stewart, for yer fealty and for yer support of my cause. I know how verra much ye loved my father."

"Ye loved him too, laddie," the earl said. "None of this was yer doing, but ye would be well advised to exercise yer authority over yon pack of unruly dogs immediately, else ye find yerself in yer father's position one day; but perhaps nae. Jemmie was a hard man to know, but ye hae yer mother's charm and sweetness about ye. Just be strong, laddie."

The prince nodded. "I will take yer advice, Uncle, for 'tis both good and honest advice, lovingly given." Then his blue eyes twinkled. "I hae heard that yer countess did nae agree wi ye in our cause."

The Earl of Dunmor flushed and muttered, "Ye know Arabella hae a mind of her own, yer majesty. I canna seem to curb her."

"Perhaps ye should nae, Uncle. I like yer wife the way she

is, and I suspect ye do too. If ye change her, she will nae be the woman ye love," the king said wisely.

Tavis Stewart chuckled. "Aye, yer right, nephew." He hesitated a moment, and then he said, "Just one more word of advice, Jamie Stewart. Ye intend stripping Ramsey of his earldom, do ye nae?"

The king nodded. "I do," he replied low.

"Then gie the earldom of Bothwell to Patrick Hepburn. Home is a good man, but he hae a tendency to get above himself, and he is riding perhaps a wee bit too high at the moment. The Hepburn of Hailes will balance him off nicely. Since they're related, there should be no bad blood between them over this, and besides, Hepburn hae earned his earldom. He's a true border lord, and a good man in a fight."

The king smiled, and it was a relieved smile. "Ye hae saved me a great deal of trouble, Uncle, for although I intended taking Bothwell from Ramsey of Balmain, I didna know to whom I should gie the title, but yer right. Patrick Hepburn is the perfect man!"

"Yer quick to assess a situation, Jamie," the earl told his nephew. " 'Tis a good trait. Would that yer father had had it. Hae ye been able to learn yet who was responsible for his death?"

A shadow passed over the king's young face. "Nay, Uncle, I hae not. Ye know how poor a horseman my father was. He either fell or was thrown from that large grey he rode outside of Beaton's mill at Bannockburn. He was still conscious and sent the miller's wife for a priest. She brought back a man claiming to be a cleric, who asked to be left alone wi my father to hear his dying confession. After a time she returned to the room where the king's grace had been carried and found my sire stabbed to his death, and the 'priest' gone."

"Could the miller and his wife hae been involved, Jamie?" the earl asked.

"Nay, Uncle. They hae both been questioned thoroughly, and were horrified and frightened by the whole event. The poor goodwife kept repeating over and over again: 'He were nae a strong king, but he were a guid man. I could see it in his eyes.' She kept telling me that I should ne'er forget my father, for a man hae but one father. God's bones, Uncle, I feel so guilty over my father's death!" the young king admitted miserably.

"Ye hae nae found the murderer or the men behind the murder, Jamie?''

The king shook his head.

"So be it then," the Earl of Dunmor said. "Ye must get on wi yer own life, Jamie, and wi this business of ruling Scotland.''

"Do ye nae care?" the king said half bitterly. *"He was yer brother!''*

"Aye, Jamie, I care, but Jemmie is gone and nothing will ever bring him back to us. If we could find those responsible, I would slay them wi my bare hands myself, but if ye canna apportion blame, then 'tis best to let it go and move on, laddie. Yer father is safe for all time wi yer mother at Cambuskenneth, and ye are Scotland's king. 'Tis the fate for which ye were born. *Now rule!''*

His nephew upon his throne, the Earl of Dunmor departed for his home. Despite the turn of events of the past few weeks, he found his countess not one whit more disposed to the new king. As always, her main concern was for the return of Greyfaire.

"Did you not ask Jamie if among his late father's correspondence there was not some reply from King Henry regarding my petition for the return of my home?'' She was looking particularly beautiful on this hot summer's day. Her long hair was braided into a single thick plait, and she wore a simple gown of pale blue silk.

He had missed her, he thought to himself as his eyes feasted greedily on her smooth, creamy skin, which was just faintly damp with the heat of the day. She smelt of heather, her favorite fragrance. Drawing her into his arms, the earl kissed his wife and said with some humor, "Between the battles, the state funeral, and the coronation, lovey, there was nae time to discuss yer Greyfaire.''

"But you will speak to your nephew about it soon?'' she replied.

"I will try, lassie," he told her honestly, "but Jamie hae much to do before he sits solidly upon his throne. He must mend many fences, dole out new offices and honors, and gain creditability wi the kings of both France and England. Yer wee problem is the least of Jamie's trials.''

Arabella opened her mouth and as suddenly shut it. They had been over this ground a thousand times, and they were still at opposite ends of the spectrum. For Tavis everything took precedence over Greyfaire, but for Arabella, Greyfaire was paramount. She had gone to James III to help her solve her problem, and she would probably end up having to go to this new king as well, for her husband had his Dunmor, and Greyfaire mattered little to him. He would have been just as happy if Maggie wed with a Home, or a Douglas, or a Hepburn one day.

"Yer thinking again," he accused, half playfully.

"Aye," she admitted.

"When ye think," he told her, "ye hae a tendency to do dangerous things."

Arabella laughed. "I dinna think so," she teased him.

"Come to bed," he said.

"Why, my lord!" She feigned shock. " 'Tis not even sunset yet."

He peered through the windows. "Another hour, at least," he agreed.

" 'Tis much too warm a day to be cooped up in a bedchamber," Arabella told him. "I have a far better idea."

"Ye do?"

"Aye, my lord," she drawled, and taking him by the hand, led him from the castle out across the drawbridge. "I discovered this place with Maggie, for she is suffering with her teeth, and the heat does not help. Your mother recommended I rub pounded clove on her gums, and it does help, but not entirely. The trick is to distract her from the pain," Arabella explained. "I take her walking, and we only recently found this little stream flowing beside this small grove of trees here in the meadow. The trees shelter our bathing place from sight of the castle."

"Ye swim?" He was surprised.

"Aye," she said. "My father taught me when I was small." Arabella began to unlace her gown as she spoke. "Our daughter loves the water and is as agile as a wee froggie." Undoing her bodice, she laid it carefully upon the grass beneath the trees. "The stream bed is sandy here and not too deep. I never let Maggie out of my hands, however, though she protests mightily. I think if I let her she would swim away." The Countess of Dunmor's long skirt and petticoats dropped to the ground, and stepping out of them, she gathered them up to place them with her bodice. She was wearing no stockings, he discovered when she kicked off her slippers, and was clad only in her chemise now. Looking curiously at him, she said sweetly, "Will you not join me, Tavis, or do you not swim?" Arabella stripped aside her chemise and tossed it onto the pile of clothes. "Ohhh, how I love the feel of warm air upon my body!" she told him ingenuously.

He had thought he was past being surprised by her behavior, but he was not. This was a new Arabella. One he had not seen before. An impudent little woodland sprite with saucy breasts, and saucier buttocks that flashed before him now as she moved to enter the water. He felt himself growing hot with the need to possess her, and he wondered if a wife should be as tempting as his wife was.

Arabella turned her head toward him, the waters of the little stream lapping at her mid-thigh. "Are you coming, my lord?" she said softly, and then she bound up her long braid, the tip of which was already wet. With a laugh she splashed into the water and paddled about.

The earl considered a long moment as he decided whether he could reach the safety of the water before she discovered the state of his desire for her. His manhood was already hard and thrusting beneath his kilts. Casually he bent and, having kicked off his shoes, drew his stockings off. Slowly he undid his shirt, careful to keep his back to her, unaware that she was admiring his long torso and muscled shoulders.

"Why are you so poky?" she teased him.

The Earl of Dunmor dropped his kilts and turned to face his wife.

"Oh!" she said, and then she began to giggle.

"Madame," he said fiercely, "I will nae be mocked!" and he strode purposefully into the cold water toward her.

Mischievously she splashed him, shrieking with feigned terror as he launched himself toward her, evading him skillfully as he moved to within easy grasping distance of her. "Catch me if you can, my randy lord!" she cried as she scampered to the other side of the stream bed.

With a roar he was after her, lumbering about noisily in the water until, with a surprisingly quick lunge, he did indeed catch her, and drawing her wet, squirming body inexorably to him, he covered her mouth in a burning kiss even as she pressed his lips firmly with her own. They kissed for what seemed a very long time, and then he murmured, "Madame, hae ye ever been fucked in the water?'' even as he slowly impaled her upon his throbbing manhood.

Her slender arms wrapped about his neck, her wet body squirming against him in her passion. ''Oh, you are a wicked man, Tavis Stewart, to tease a body so,'' she moaned against his mouth, and she rubbed her breasts provocatively against his broad chest.

His big hand cupped her buttocks, reveling in the springy flesh that pressed into his palms as her legs squeezed his waist. ''Ahh, lovey,'' he groaned, ''I hae missed ye, and 'tis past time our Maggie hae a baby brother. Did ye nae promise me a son for Dunmor, Arabella Stewart?''

''Aye, I did,'' she agreed. ''Ohhh, Tavis! Do not cease your sweet torture! Ohh, I cannot bear it! *I cannot!*'' Her body shuddered with sweet fulfillment as she first threw her head back, the column of her throat straining with her passion, and then with a small, satisfied sigh, dropped her head upon his shoulder.

Slowly he walked from the water, cradling her in his arms, still buried deep within her sweet sheath. With great control he slipped to his knees, laying her upon her back, covering her face with warm kisses which seemed to revive her, and her light green eyes fluttered open.

''I missed you too, my lord,'' she told him with understated simplicity.

''I know,'' he replied, his mouth twitching with amusement. Then he began to pump her with deep strokes, his strong thrusts drawn out and protracted, tarrying within her, bringing her almost to the point of tears as he deliberately stroked her ever-rising desires. It was not easy for him to hold his own hungers in check, but he had discovered soon after the consummation of their marriage that his wife had an enormous capacity for loving. It was not a bad tendency for a wife to have, he thought, particularly as she seemed totally satisfied with him and showed no inclination to other men. He was certain of that, having been more than well aware of his nephew's interest in Arabella and her most firm refusal of Jamie's favors.

Beneath him Arabella thrashed, her ecstasy growing with every passing moment. She clawed wildly at him, raking her small nails sharply down his long back, eliciting a grunt of irritation from him, causing him to drive even deeper into her sweetness. She reeled with the intoxication and the intensity of his fire, as leaning forward he took one of her nipples in his mouth and bit down gently, albeit firmly, upon it. Shrieking softly, she tried to twist away from him, but he held her hips in a tight grasp, suckling hard upon her flesh, feeling her wonderfully tight passage begin to contract about him.

"I die!" she sobbed. "Ohh, I die!" and she shivered violently with the intensity of her ardor.

He could wait no longer, for her own rapture but fueled his. "I also!" he groaned, pouring a libation of his lusty juices into her love grotto.

They lay together upon the sweet green grass amid a tangle of exhausted limbs for what seemed the longest time. They half dozed while about them drowsy honey bees droned in the summer clover. To the west the sun was sinking slowly in a blazing glory of red-gold and purple. Above them in a tree a crow called loudly, warning all within his voice of the hawk who was hunting his evening meal, while near them a family of young rabbits peered curiously at the two naked humans lying upon the warm ground.

Finally Arabella sighed; a sound replete with satisfaction. "You were most pleasurable, my lord," she said with great understatement.

"As were ye, madame," he answered her.

"I suppose we must return to the castle," Arabella noted sadly, reaching out to pick up her chemise and put it on.

He grinned up boyishly, his dark eyes brimming with mischief. "Unless, of course, ye want to run away wi me, madame. Shall we walk out like a simple Jock-upon-the-land and his lass, Arabella Stewart? Living in a wee cottage? I shall hunt and fish for our daily sustenance, and ye will weave garlands wi which to adorn my triumphant brow when I return home wi a brace of conies."

Arabella laughed. "My lord, you are more romantic than a green maid having thoughts about her first lover," she teased him.

"Would ye nae love me, lass, if I were a humble man?" he asked.

"There is not a humble bone in your body, Tavis Stewart," she told him bluntly. "It is not within the nature of the Stewarts to be humble, particularly falsely so. A humble man would not have aspired to my hand. Indeed, he would not have even dared to entertain thoughts of me. I love you, and you, by God's grace, are the Earl of Dunmor. Earls live in fine castles, and that is where we had best hurry lest the drawbridge be raised against us!'' Arabella stood up, and putting her skirt on, fastened its tapes even as she slipped into her slippers.

''Honest to a fault,'' he said. ''Yer nae a woman to dissemble, are ye, lovey?''

''Nay, I am not. A woman who is not honest with her husband is a fool, my lord, as is a husband who is not honest with his wife.'' Bending, she picked up his kilts and handed them to him.

The earl dressed himself quickly, and then taking his wife's hand, they strolled back to the castle; not noticing the men-at-arms guarding Dunmor's entry, who grinned at each other knowingly as they passed. It was a good summer that year. The harvest looked as if it would be fruitful. There was peace upon the border, and Scotland's new king was loved by all of his people.

❊ *Chapter 14*

*T*hey had spent Christmas at Dunmor. The Earl and Countess of Dunmor had hosted their entire family, which seemed
to be growing by leaps and bounds. Both Ailis and Meg had two
children, and Ailis admitted to be ripening with a third already.
Donald Fleming had fallen in love at long last. She was the well-
loved bastard daughter of the new Earl of Bothwell, Patrick
Hepburn, who, upon learning of his child's warm feelings toward her bluff suitor, had offered her a dowry consisting of a
small estate with a fine stone house upon it, and all the coins
she might grasp in her two hands from her father's treasury
chest.

The girl, whose name was Ellen, was a clever creature. She
coated her hands with glue in order that whatever she touched
might stick to them; and rather than being angry with her, Patrick Hepburn was amused that this child of his, so casually
begotten upon one of his clansmen's sisters, should prove so
quick-witted. It reflected well upon him, he decided, to have so
canny a daughter, but then he had always loved her, for she was
a particularly winning girl. The wedding was to be held in the
spring, after Easter.

Margery Fleming sat at her son's highboard looking out over
the hall with particular pleasure. Five grandchildren already, a
sixth upon the way, and the last of her children to be married
shortly, with the hope of more grandchildren to come. She had
never felt more at peace in her entire life, or more content, but
for one small problem. She turned to Arabella and said hopefully, "Can we hope ye'll hae a son for Dunmor in the new year,
my dear?"

Arabella smiled. "We can always hope, belle mère," she
answered, "but, of course, I also hope for the return of Greyfaire in the new year too."

"There hae been no word from the English king, then?" Lady
Margery asked.

Arabella shook her head in the negative. "Tavis and I are

going to court just before Twelfth Night. There may be a message awaiting us that has been overlooked in the transition between King James and his late father, may God assoil Jemmie Stewart's good soul. I hope so, belle mère! Greyfaire is in a sad state right now. Sir Jasper is with King Henry's court and has neglected the keep, the village, the land, and my people. Lona's brother comes over the border every now and then to bring me word, and I send back what encouragement I can and all the coin I can spare. Their harvest was no better than ours last year, and there is hunger at Greyfaire too.''

Lady Margery pondered a moment, but she knew that she must ask. ''What if King Henry VII will not return Greyfaire to ye, Arabella?''

''*He must!* I will go to England if I have to, but I will regain Greyfaire, belle mère, for our Margaret!'' Arabella answered her mother-in-law passionately. ''Jasper Keane will not have it! Not while I have breath in my body!''

Lady Margery could see that her eldest son's wife was determined, and she wondered if Tavis realized how determined Arabella really was. She suspected he did not quite understand the young woman's deep feelings in the matter, and she worried that her son's lack of comprehension could lead to a serious rift between the two. She decided to speak with Tavis about Arabella's strong determination regarding the return of Greyfaire; but before she could find the right moment in which to approach her son, the Earl of Dunmor and his countess were off to court. Disappointed, Lady Margery resolved to broach the subject on their return if nothing was resolved by then.

James IV kept a merry court. For lack of a queen, he had asked his aunt, Margaret Stewart, to come to court and oversee the many noble young ladies who were flocking there in search of husbands. Princess Margaret Stewart was a tall, gaunt woman in her mid-thirties, with the long, straight Stewart nose. She had been convent-bred, but was far too independent of nature to become a nun. Her brother, King James III, had invited her to court when she was just past twenty, in hopes of snaring a husband for her before her small beauty failed entirely; but the princess had no wish to marry. She was a well-educated, highly intelligent woman with a passion for music, mathematics, and astrology. She had little patience for her brother's earls, half of whom could not even speak Scots English, and most of whom

were totally ignorant in learning. Although he adored her, her
brother was finally relieved to accede to her request to remain a
maiden lady, and he installed her in a fine house on Castle Hill
in Edinburgh from which she held her own court of sorts.

Now Princess Margaret, in answer to her kingly nephew's
plea, came to Linlithgow, riding upon her white mare and followed by several ox-drawn carts containing her belongings, as
well as her train of personal servants. If there was anxiety at her
coming amongst the young noblewomen, Margaret Stewart soon
dispelled it, for she was a woman of great wit and originality.
She might expect proper behavior of the women at court, but
she was certainly not a prude. Although she had enjoyed independence and solitude for most of her life, the king's aunt found
she was ready for a change. The young people of the court were
fascinated by her, for Margaret Stewart was unique amongst her
sex. She was a free woman, and she answered to none regarding
her behavior. Still, she was devout and mannerly, for all her
intellect.

Her apartments became a gathering place for young and old
alike; and her rooms were as interesting as the princess herself
was, for they were crammed with all manner of things that she
had collected over the years, and many other things which had
simply taken her fancy. The "Royal Aunt," as she was fondly
called, seemed not to mind that her quarters were as cluttered
and as messy as a magpie's nest with all her possessions. They
were warm, inviting rooms whose very disorder seemed to encourage everyone who entered them to discussion.

Arabella particularly enjoyed being a part of the Royal Aunt's
group, for women were encouraged to speak their minds before
her. One afternoon they were discussing a particular point regarding morality when the young Countess of Dunmor spoke
up, saying to the gentleman who had been expounding his view,
"You infer, sir, that only men need be concerned with honor.
Women, also, have honor."

"I think ye confuse honor wi virtue, madame," came the
reply.

"And I think you, sir, are a pompous ass!" Arabella retorted
as the room erupted into giggles.

"Gie us an example of a woman's honor as opposed to virtue,
my dear," said the Princess Margaret.

"Of course, madame," Arabella said. "My own circumstances are a perfect case in point. I came to Scotland due to an affair of honor between the gentleman King Richard had chosen for me to wed and the Earl of Dunmor. Their quarrel had nothing to do with me, and yet the honor of my family, *my honor*, was compromised when Tavis Stewart stole me away and wed me. Now my home, Greyfaire, which I inherited upon my father's death, is in the hands of my enemy. The honor of the Greys of Greyfaire, of whom I am the last surviving member, will continue to have a stain upon it until my home is restored to me. My husband has promised to do this for me.''

"Hah!" scoffed the gentleman Arabella had mocked. "How can a Scotsman reclaim an English border keep? He canna, madame, and what will ye do when he finally admits to ye that he canna?''

"Why, to satisfy honor," Princess Margaret teased, "the Countess of Dunmor would hae nae choice but to divorce her husband.''

There was more laughter at this solution, and one pretty young woman said pertly, "If ye decide to divorce him, madame, I would be the first to know.''

"Nay," said another woman. "Tell me! Tavis Stewart is the bonniest gentleman I've ever seen.''

"And, I've heard," spoke up a third lady, "a magnificent lover. Is that true, my lady of Dunmor?''

Arabella blushed prettily, but before she could extricate herself from the situation, the princess said with mock severity, "Ladies, ladies! These discussions are meant to be intellectually elevating," and then she adroitly changed the subject, to Arabella's great relief.

The Earl and Countess of Dunmor entered into the frivolity of the court. Arabella possessed her soul of patience regarding Greyfaire until the month of April had begun. Neither Tavis nor the king had said anything to her regarding the matter, and it was now close to four years since she had left her home. Rowan FitzWalter had only recently contacted his sister Lona, and Lona had passed on to Arabella the news that Greyfaire was in a sorry state. Sir Jasper had taken all the able-bodied young men with him to court, impressing boys as young as twelve into his military troop, that he might influence the king. Rowan had only escaped because his father, forewarned, had sent him out hunting that day. Half the trees in the orchards had come down with

a canker, and if not already dead, were dying. The village and
the keep had both suffered from epidemics of white throat, the
spotting sickness, and the sweating sickness. There wasn't a
family that had not lost either a child, an elder, or a parent.

"Rowan says our two youngest sisters, Eba and Annie, have
died," Lona said sadly. " 'Twas the spotting sickness."

"I must do something," Arabella said desperately.

"M'lady, you could do nothing about the spotting sickness,"
Lona said with perfect logic. "That was God's will, and as for
the canker in the orchard, no one can prevent canker in the fruit
trees."

"Without a Grey," Arabella said solemnly, "Greyfaire has
lost its luck. I must get it back!"

"What must ye get back, sweetheart?" the king demanded,
entering Arabella's bedchamber unannounced.

Lona's eyes widened with surprise, but she kept her wits about
her and curtsied prettily to the king. He grinned mischievously,
and taking a small gold ring from his pinkie, dropped it down
Lona's bodice. Lona gave a little shriek of surprise and then
blushed scarlet.

The king chuckled and said, "Yer dismissed, lassie," and
gently shoved her out the door, closing it firmly behind Lona
before Arabella might protest.

The Countess of Dunmor eyed her sovereign warily. "My
lord," she said coolly, nodding her head in greeting.

"Madame," he replied, eyeing her dishabille, for Arabella
was attired in her petticoats and under bodice. Her beautiful
pale gold hair was unbound and spread across the floor by her
feet.

There was a long silence between them as Arabella waited
for the king to state the purpose of his visit, and finally when he
did not, she said, "Why are you here, my lord? You know that
my husband is in the north treating with the Gordons on your
behalf."

"Aye, but I have had news from England in response to the
request my late father made to King Henry for ye," James Stewart said. "Henry Tudor is reluctant to return Greyfaire Keep to
ye in light of yer marriage to my uncle. Sir Jasper Keane has
entreated him for the property, but the English king has not yet
made a decision in that direction either. He writes to us that he
will consider the possibility of assigning Greyfaire Keep over to

Lady Margaret Stewart, daughter of Arabella Grey and Tavis
Stewart, provided that he has the final say in a choice of a husband for your daughter. He then goes on to say that though he
hae made no decision in the matter, the thought of a minority
heiress possessing such a strategic piece of land disturbs him,
and he wonders if Sir Jasper might not be a better choice.''

''No!'' Arabella's voice was strangled. ''Not Jasper Keane!
Never! I will kill him myself before I allow that man to possess
Greyfaire!''

''What choice hae ye in the matter, Arabella?'' the king said.

''I can go to England!'' she cried. *''I must!''* The Countess
of Dunmor began to pace her bedchamber. ''If I could but speak
with King Henry, I could make him understand the situation. I
could tell him of Jasper Keane's perfidy toward me and toward
my poor mother, may God assoil her sweet soul. Surely Henry
Tudor is an honorable man, and if I can but gain an audience
with him, I can explain it all to him far better than anyone can
explain it in a letter.''

''How will ye gain an audience with him?'' James Stewart
asked, fascinated by her determination. Until this minute he
had only seen Arabella in terms of an adorable young woman
whom he wished to possess. He was intrigued by this new side
of her.

''You will write to King Henry, my lord,'' she answered him,
''and I will carry the message to him personally.''

''And what will I say, sweetheart?'' he asked her, amused.

''You will ask your fellow king to give me an audience,''
Arabella said with great simplicity. ''He will hardly refuse me
when the request comes from his fellow monarch, and I am
standing there before him.''

James Stewart burst out laughing. He did not know which
amused him more. Her audaciousness or the indignant expression she was now wearing upon her beautiful face.

''Do not dare to laugh at me!'' Arabella said angrily, stamping
her foot at him. ''There is absolutely nothing funny or foolish
about my plan.''

''Nay, sweetheart,'' the king said, putting his own emotions
firmly under control, ''there is, indeed, nothing funny or foolish
about ye, but what makes ye think I will help ye?''

''But why, my lord, would you refuse me? My daughte. is
your own cousin, sire. Having Margaret the heiress of such a

strategic place on the English side of the border could hardly be detrimental to Scotland.''

James Stewart crossed the room to where Arabella stood and drew her tightly to his side. Her fragrance assailed his nostrils, making him almost dizzy with his rising desire. ''Once, Arabella Stewart, I told ye there would come a day when ye wanted a favor from me. Do ye remember that?''

''A-Aye,'' she said softly.

''And do ye remember also the price for that favor, sweetheart?'' The king's hand crept up her torso to cup a small, perfect breast.

Arabella resisted the urge to pull away from him and slap his face. Instead she stood very still and said, ''I remember, my lord.''

''And are ye willing to pay the price for my aid, 'Bella,'' he murmured, his lips moving down the side of her neck to her shoulder.

''Please, my lord,'' Arabella said. ''You are my husband's nephew, and he is your friend. Surely you would not extract such a price from me.''

''Indeed, madame, I would, for like ye, I am determined to have what I desire, and as ye desire the return of yer home, I desire ye.''

''Is there no other way, my lord?'' she pleaded with him. ''Is there nothing else I might give you that would satisfy such a debt between us? I love Tavis Stewart.''

''But ye love yer Greyfaire more, I think,'' James Stewart said. He turned her so that she was forced to look up at him, and bending, he brushed her mouth lightly with his. ''Yer such a wee bit of a creature, sweetheart.'' His voice was tender, but then it hardened. ''What can ye possibly gie me, Arabella Stewart, that I dinna already hae? I am an anointed king, and though my earls are no less fractious now than they were in my father's time, I am able, for all my youth, or perhaps because of it, to rule them well. I am nae a rich man, but then neither am I a poor one. My country, though it has suffered with several bad harvests, has survived, and we are nae threatened by any of our enemies at this time. Indeed, both France and England seek to court Scotland. *And*, sweetheart, I hae the most beautiful women in the land seeking my bed. I lack for nothing but my heart's desire, and that is ye. So if ye would hae me intercede for ye wi King Henry, ye must yield yerself to my wishes.''

"I do not need your help," Arabella said proudly. "I will go to England without it.''

"I will nae let ye go," he told her calmly.

"You cannot stop me!" she cried, attempting to pull away from him, but he would not release her.

"I can," he said. "Do ye think my uncle, when informed of yer plans, will concur wi them? Ye know he will nae.''

"I do not need his permission," Arabella said, and the king laughed with genuine amusement.

"I dinna know how ye and my uncle hae managed to remain wed wi out killing each other," he said. "Do ye ever agree on anything, 'Bella?''

"Of course!" she said irritably. "Whatever our differences, my lord, we love one another.''

The king grew serious once more. "I will nae let ye leave here wi out yer husband's permission, madame, and if ye defy me in this matter, I will tell him of yer plans. Wi out me, ye will nae go to England, nor will ye succeed wi out my aid.''

"I cannot put the horns of a cuckold on my husband's head," Arabella told the king firmly.

"He need nae know, sweetheart," James said. "I am nae a man who must boast amongst his friends in the hall of his conquests.''

"I cannot," Arabella said.

"Then ye will hae to resign yerself to losing yer beloved Greyfaire, madame. Are ye prepared to do that?''

Tears welled up in the Countess of Dunmor's eyes. For the last several years she had dreamed of regaining her childhood home. She might have been able to let that dream go had it not been for Sir Jasper Keane. The thought of him possessing Greyfaire was more than she was able to bear. "I must think on it," she said low.

Dear God! What was she to do? How could she betray Tavis Stewart when she loved him so very much? And yet . . . and yet had he not promised to regain Greyfaire for her? But he had not, and she sensed that having made the effort, he would accept the English king's judgment in the matter. But she could not! She could not leave Greyfaire to the tender mercies of Sir Jasper

Keane, and she could not betray her husband by giving herself to Jamie Stewart's lust.

Then she heard a voice in her mind, and she remembered the discussion on honor that she had partaken in but a short while ago in the Royal Aunt's chambers. She remembered the gentleman who had asked her what she would do when Tavis finally admitted to her that he could not regain Greyfaire for her. She recalled the princess's quick retort:

"Why, to satisfy honor, the Countess of Dunmor would hae nae choice but to divorce her husband."

For a moment she felt as if her heart had stopped in her chest. Was there no other choice? She wanted Greyfaire, and obviously only she could regain it. The honor of her family demanded it, and if she had to sacrifice her own happiness . . .

He saw the indecision and all the other emotions churning inside her, welling up in her eyes, playing across her beautiful face. He could almost taste his victory, and the taste was sweet.

Finally Arabella spoke, and what she said could not have surprised him more than if she had hurled a thunderbolt at him. "If I agree to your terms," she said slowly, "then you must do one thing for me first. Men, my husband in particular, are most fond of speaking about their honor. 'Twas an affair of honor that brought me to Scotland, as you well know. Were it not for honor, I should be in possession of Greyfaire now, and not here before your majesty. Well, women are possessed of honor too, my lord, and if I must compromise my own honor in order to regain what is rightfully mine, I will not discredit my husband's name in the process. You are Scotland's king, and whatever you desire is done. Obtain for me a divorce from the archbishop of St. Andrew's. When you have done that, I will grace your bed, and afterward you will let me return to England that I may regain what is mine. Our liaison must be a secret one, however, for whatever Tavis may think of me, I would not have him shamed publicly, for I love him. Sadly, I love Greyfaire too. You Stewarts are wrong to attempt to make me choose between you and my home, for I cannot."

"But ye hae," the king said.

"Nay, I have but done what I must do to restore my family's honor," Arabella said quietly. "I have done no more than my husband or any other man would have done in a similar situation. Why should it be different simply because I am a woman?"

"Yer certain ye wish to do this?" the king said, feeling just the faintest twinge of guilt.

"As certain as your majesty is that he desires to bed me," Arabella said quietly. There was an elegant dignity about her that made James Stewart uncomfortable.

The young king flushed, and was irritated that she made him feel so guilty. "Ye dinna hae to divorce my uncle," he said, his tone just short of surly.

"Ye dinna hae to futter me either, my lord," she mocked him in his own Scots-English, "but you desire to possess me more than you love your uncle. I, however, love Tavis Stewart, and I will not allow either of us to bring dishonor to his name or to the Stewarts of Dunmor! If you will help me without extracting this terrible price from me, I will be your majesty's grateful servant forever; but if you will not, then I must do what is right even if you will not."

"Dinna seek to instruct me, madame," the king said angrily. "I am long past lessons."

"Your father, may God assoil his good soul, once told me that no one is past learning. A man who ceases to learn becomes valueless to those about him, for he can offer them nothing new," Arabella retorted sharply.

James Stewart yanked her hard against him and ground his mouth down upon hers in a punishing kiss. Furiously, Arabella pulled her head away from him, but the king took her chin between his thumb and forefinger, holding her fast. "When ye speak to me in future, madame, I want to hear words of love and cries of sweet passion only issuing forth from between your delectable lips. Nothing else!" He kissed her fiercely once again, leaving Arabella somewhat breathless. "Yer husband will nae be back for several weeks, madame, for his mission to the Gordons at Huntley and the Leslie laird at Glenkirk is delicate and will take time. Ye will hae yer divorce before the week is out, 'Bella, and ye will be in my bed not long afterward."

"One night," she said.

"A week," he told her.

"You cannot keep such a secret for a week," she said, tears springing into her light green eyes.

He considered her words and realized that she was correct, though the knowledge annoyed him. It was not a secret that could be long kept. "Three days, then," he said grudgingly, "but nae here at Linlithgow. I've a small hunting lodge in the borders. We'll go there."

"No!" she cried. "You are the king. You cannot simply run off to *hunt* as you did when you were a prince. You will be missed! As king you cannot go alone, and even the loyalest servant will gossip. My identity will become known. Do not pretend you want anything else of me other than my body, my lord, and that being so, are not the nights enough? You must surely know—for the first day we came to Linlithgow, I discovered it—that there is a secret passage from this room leading to another room within the palace."

"Nay," he said, surprised. "I didna know. Show me, madame!"

Arabella moved across the bedchamber to the fireplace wall, and pressing a corner of the paneling, she stepped back as a small door swung open. Taking a candlestick from the table, the king stepped through into the passage and moved forward. Within a moment the flickering candle disappeared from sight. She stood awaiting his return, and for the first time since this encounter with James Stewart had begun, Arabella felt herself overwhelmed by a great sadness.

What in the name of God was she doing? She loved her husband. Loved him with every fiber of her being. They had a child, but of course it was really Margaret for whom she was doing this, she told herself. Greyfaire would be inherited by Lady Margaret Stewart, for she would never marry again, Arabella decided. With FitzWalter's help she would hold the keep for England until the day her daughter married. Then, as Rowena had once planned, she would go to the Dower House to live out her old age. A tear slipped down her face. *What was she doing?* Angrily she brushed it away, wishing at the same time that she could rid herself of her doubts as easily.

The king popped back into her view and exited the passage saying, "It leads to a small library next to my apartments! I can go there to 'read,' asking that I not be disturbed, and no one shall know that I am really wi ye. 'Tis perfect!" He grinned, pleased. "I shall come to ye tonight, sweetheart!"

"Nay, you will not, my lord!" she told him. "Not until the archbishop assures me that I have my divorce. I will not lie with you until I do, lest I compromise *my* honor."

He was disappointed, for the anticipation of possessing this lovely woman for whom he had hungered for so long was great, but he also knew how fragile her state of mind was. She could change that mind at any moment should he press her, and he did not want her to do so. If he felt any guilt at the wrong he was doing to his uncle, James Stewart had not yet begun to contemplate that, for he was driven by but one thing—his need for Arabella. "I understand, madame," he said gravely, and then bowing formally to her, he left her chambers.

When she was certain that he was gone, Arabella put her head in her hands and wept. Again she was assailed by doubts, by the wisdom, or lack of wisdom, of what she was doing. Was Greyfaire really that important to her? It was naught but a little stone keep on the English side of the border. Dunmor Castle was far grander, and she had grown to love it too. Yet Greyfaire was her ancestral home, and she had been a Grey far longer than she had been a Stewart. If it had been anyone other than Jasper Keane, she might have been able to let it go; but she could not relinquish her hold on Greyfaire that *he* might have it. He was not worthy of Greyfaire, that debaucher of women, that murderer of innocents. She had to regain her rights to Greyfaire. She had to regain it for Margaret.

Tavis had sworn to help her, and yet he had not. There was always something that took precedence for him over her problems. It was not that he didn't care, for Arabella was certain her husband did care, but like most men, he put his own concerns above those of his wife's. She had waited four years for him to act in her behalf, and yet he had never been able to find the time to do so. She had gone to King James III herself, and even that had not stirred him to action on her part. She had no other choice. She needed the king's help, and Jamie would not give it to her unless she gave him her body in return.

Arabella sighed deeply. And when she had regained Greyfaire, what then? A life of loneliness lay before her, for Tavis would certainly never forgive her. He would remarry, and some other woman's son would be Dunmor's heir. She could never love another man. Arabella maintained no illusions about the king. James Stewart, as young as he was, had a great appetite for women. If the rumors were true, and she certainly had no reason to doubt them, he was a vigorous and tireless lover. He was, at this moment in time, actively seeking a mistress. She knew should she aspire to the position, it could be hers.

Poor James, Arabella thought. He was not a bad man, but he was certainly a thoughtless one. He had not, she was certain, considered for even the briefest moment Tavis's feelings should he learn that his nephew had seduced her. Yet he would be a good king, for unlike his late father, James IV was a decisive young man. He saw what he wanted and he took it, as she certainly could attest. The court poet, William Dunbar, had recently written an amusing satire regarding one of the king's amorous seductions. Jamie was pictured as a fox, while Master Dunbar had portrayed the lady as a lamb.

> *The fox was neither ragged nor lean*
> *A lustier reynard was never seen:*
> *He was long tailed and large withal.*
> *The silly ewe-lamb was much too small*
> *to answer "nay" when he said "yea."*
> *Good luck to her, whatever befall!*
> *She didn't flee him, strange to say.*

The court had laughed for several weeks over the poem, and even the lady involved was able to see the good-natured humor in her predicament. At least there would be no poetry about the king's seduction of the Countess of Dunmor. With God's good luck, no one would know.

"M'lady?" Lona was standing by her side. "The king said I might come in, m'lady." The girl shifted nervously, suddenly more aware than she had ever before been in her life of the differences between herself and her childhood friend.

"Oh, Lona," Arabella said, looking up, the evidence of tears quite plain upon her face, "do not look so frightened. It's all right."

Lona hesitated, and then bravely she said, slipping back into the familiar address of their childhood, "No, it ain't, 'Bella. You've been crying, and you aren't one for easy tears. We've been friends since the cradle, and I know I'm just your servant, and you're a fine lady and all, but I know you better than any living, and it ain't all right. If you don't want to tell me, then that's another matter, but don't tell me it's all right when I can see it ain't!"

It was probably the longest speech Lona had made in her entire life. It came from her heart, and Arabella knew that she could confide in Lona without fear. "No, it really isn't all right, Lona," she told her servant. "I am going to divorce the earl."

"What?" Lona's face registered her total astonishment. " 'Bella, you can't!"

"I must," Arabella answered, and then she went on to explain the situation to Lona.

"That's just plain daft," Lona said matter-of-factly when her mistress had finished with her explanations. "Listen, m'lady, we'll just sneak out of Linlithgow tonight, and no one, especially the king, will be the wiser. He don't dare to pursue you openly."

"Go to the door, Lona, and open it," Arabella instructed her servant, and when Lona obeyed, flinging the door wide, she found her way firmly blocked by two guardsmen.

"Well!" Lona said, closing the door with a bang. "If that don't beat all! How did you know, 'Bella?"

"I didn't, really, but the king said he would not let me go, and so I suspected I would find myself under guard sooner or later," Arabella told her friend.

"What about the secret passage?" Lona said craftily.

"I imagine we will now find it locked from the other side should we check," Arabella replied, "but go through and see, Lona. Perhaps there is a chance."

Taking the candle the king had so recently set down, Lona popped into the passageway, disappearing quickly, only to return as quickly. "Locked!" she told Arabella.

"Jamie is no fool," the Countess of Dunmor said.

"He has no right to do this to you, m'lady, even if he is a king," Lona said indignantly. "What will the earl say when he finds out? He'll come after you for certain!"

"No, Lona, he will not. With luck, Tavis will never know of my liaison with the king. He will assume I have been my usual willful self, and he will be very angry with me. Angry enough that I believe he will seek elsewhere for another wife. I could not remarry him under the circumstances; knowing that I had lain with his nephew. He would feel dishonored, though I divorce him in order not to dishonor him. He would feel betrayed by Jamie, and I cannot do that to him, for Tavis has always held the Stewarts above all. He is a man who prizes loyalty. Let him think it is I who have been disloyal to him, not the king. Dunmor is not important like Angus, or Argyll, or Huntley, but Tavis is a Royal Stewart, and I will not be responsible for causing a rift within the clan.''

"Give Greyfaire up, 'Bella!" Lona cried. " 'Tis not worth your unhappiness."

"To Sir Jasper Keane? *Never!* Not while there is breath in my body, Lona! What of your family? Already that bastard has drained off our youth, leaving the keep to be defended by old men, women and children. The orchards are dying for lack of care, and half the fields lie fallow for want of young men to work them. Greyfaire's people will go half hungry this winter despite the good growing year, thanks to Sir Jasper Keane, who makes merry at King Henry's court while my people starve! No, Lona! I will not let Greyfaire go."

"What of wee Mistress Maggie?" Lona demanded.

"I intend taking Margaret with us," Arabella said. "I cannot leave my daughter behind."

Lona shook her head. "The earl is going to kill you for certain, m'lady," she told her mistress gravely. "That little lass is the light of his life."

"If he cared so very much about Margaret," Arabella said tartly, "he would have seen to her inheritance instead of avoiding the issue."

Lona clamped her lips shut at that, for she knew there was no arguing with Arabella when she set her mind to something. She wished she could speak with her father, who was the wisest person she had ever personally known. She did not think FitzWalter would approve of Arabella divorcing her husband in order to gain King James's help so that she might recover the rights to Greyfaire for her daughter's dowry. Was Greyfaire really worth all the misery that Arabella was going to cause both herself and the man she loved? Lona somehow did not think it was, but then she had not been the heiress to Greyfaire Keep. She was only one of FitzWalter's girls. The nobility thought differently than just plain folks did.

Lona sighed gustily. Fergus MacMichael had been courting her for some months now. She had held him off, encouraging him one moment, flirting with other men the next, to poor Fergus's distress. Still the young clansman had not given up on her, Lona thought with a small smile. "Get it all out of yerself, lassie," he had told her patiently before she had left Dunmor to come to court with Arabella. "When we wed I'll nae put up wi yer casting eyes on other men."

"Indeed," she had answered him pertly. "You've not asked me to marry you, Fergus MacMichael, and I'm not sure I would if you did!"

He had chuckled, a rich, knowing sound that had sent little shivers up and down her backbone. "The day I first laid eyes on ye, Lona, as bedraggled as a wet sparrow ye were too, I knew ye were mine," he said.

Lona sighed again. He was a man, was Fergus MacMichael! For a minute she closed her eyes and remembered his arms about her, his warm lips upon hers. She wanted to be his wife, and now that she was in danger of losing him, she realized it plainly. Damn 'Bella, and her pigheaded passion for that mouldering heap of stones called Greyfaire! Could she not see that Dunmor was better? She didn't have to do this! She could refuse the king and go home. Why did she persist in her stubbornness? Still, she loved Arabella Grey, and she would remain loyal to her even at the cost of her own happiness, Lona told herself. At least she would see Fergus a final time when they went to Dunmor to fetch wee Maggie.

For the next few days they were kept busy packing, for Arabella had decided she would leave for Dunmor Castle as soon as her divorce from Tavis Stewart was granted and her debt to the king paid. The court need only know that Arabella longed for her child, and as her husband was away, had decided to return home. There would be no gossip about a divorce because no one would know about it until the Earl of Dunmor told them himself. She would leave it to Tavis to say what he pleased about the matter. She would not even mind if he intimated that it was he who instigated the proceedings.

Arabella returned from the Great Hall one evening to be greeted by a grim-faced Lona who handed her a rolled parchment. With suddenly shaking fingers she undid the dark purple ribbon holding the tightly bound parchment closed and spread it open upon the table. The written words formally dissolving her marriage to Tavis Stewart swam before her eyes. Several quick tears splashed down upon the parchment before she could catch them, and she wiped at them with her sleeve, smearing the ink in several places.

"Send it back to the bishop, m'lady," Lona begged her. "Tell

him 'twas all a mistake and that you don't want a divorce from
his lordship!''

"I have the right to use my maiden name again," Arabella
said tonelessly, and then rolling the parchment back up and tying
it, she handed it to Lona. "Put this in a safe place, Lona, and
see to my bath. I expect the king will be visiting me tonight. In
just a few more days we will begin our journey home to Greyfaire. Won't you be glad to see your father, and mother, and
Rowan and your sisters again?''

Lona almost wept with frustration. It was so obvious that
Arabella was miserable. She was ruining her whole life, and
Lona suspected that she knew it. Why was she deliberately and
heedlessly pushing forward with her own destruction when she
could, with just a word, save herself?

"Don't dally, Lona," Arabella scolded her servant, and then
she shivered. "God's bones, I'm cold!''

Lona moved silently about the room. There was nothing that
she could say that would make any difference now. Hurrying to
the door, she called the page who was at their disposal these
days and sent him off to arrange for bathwater. Within a short
period of time, footmen were trekking into the apartments with
buckets of hot water run up from the kitchens for her ladyship,
the Countess of Dunmor. Since the trip was not a short one,
Lona poured several of the buckets into the black iron cauldron
she kept over the fire in the dayroom in order to have boiling
water with which to reheat the tub when necessary.

Arabella wandered aimlessly from room to room as the work
was being done, and when the last footman had departed the
apartments, Lona helped her mistress to disrobe, and pinning
up her long, glorious hair, settled her in the tub, which was
fragrant with the scent of heather.

"All right," said Lona, sounding more like her own mother
than like herself. "What's done is done, 'Bella! If you're determined to go through with this folly, then you had best put a
smile on your face, for no man likes a sour woman.''

The sharp words had a steadying influence on Arabella. Lona
was right. No one had forced her into this position. She had had
the option of giving Greyfaire up. It was she who had decided
not to do so. Nothing, she knew, was free in this life, even for
Arabella Grey. If the king kept his part of the bargain—and

certainly obtaining her a divorce was included in that agreement—then she would keep her part of the bargain.

A knock sounded upon the door, and Lona scurried to answer it. She returned bearing a carved wooden box. "The page wore no badge, or insignia or service, but I think I've seen him with the king's people," Lona said.

"Open the box," Arabella commanded her servant.

The girl complied and then said, "There's another parchment, and . . . ohhh! Oh, 'Bella! 'Tis the most beautiful strand of pearls I've ever seen!" She held up a long rope of luminescent pearls, just faintly tinged with pink, from which hung a carved heart of red-gold studded with smaller pearls.

"Oh my!" Arabella exclaimed, surprised. She had hardly expected such a gift. Then her common sense took over. "Open the parchment," she instructed Lona, "and let me see it."

When Lona held out the parchment, Arabella scanned it carefully. Jamie Stewart had more than kept his bargain. Not only had he written to King Henry regarding her plight and requesting the return of Greyfaire for his young kinswoman, Lady Margaret Stewart, as the copy Lona was holding attested to, he had enclosed a second message to Henry Tudor introducing his fellow monarch to Lady Arabella Grey. There was no way the English king could avoid seeing Arabella without giving offense to his fellow ruler in the north.

"I am now deeply in the king's debt, Lona," Arabella told her serving woman with a gusty sigh. "Put these away, for they are important, and then scrub me well. The king, I am told, is offended by those who do not bathe."

"Perhaps, then," Lona replied with a giggle, "you shouldn't, m'lady." She replaced the parchments in the box and set them aside before taking up a cloth to soap it.

Arabella could not refrain from chuckling, but then she grew serious again. "Oh, Lona! I am so confused, for I know not if what I do is right, and yet I cannot help myself! It is as if the very stones of Greyfaire cry out to me."

" 'Tis done now, 'Bella, and it seems to me you have little choice left. I suppose you could tell the king that you had changed your mind, but I suspect that it would anger him greatly. We both know that you must keep your bargain, and that being your father's daughter, you will. Best to put a good face on it. My father always said that those who show weakness will be devoured by those who don't. You've been strong all along, m'lady. This is not the time to grow weak.''

Arabella nodded. "Aye," she said quietly, and then standing up, she stepped from her tub.

Lona took a towel from the rack by the fire where it had been warming and briskly rubbed her mistress down until her soft skin was dry and glowed with good health. "I'll get ye a clean silk shift," she told her mistress.

"She will nae need it," the king said. He was standing in the secret door which had opened silently. "Ye may go, lassie," he told Lona. "Yer dismissed for the night."

Without a word Lona curtsied to the king and departed the bedchamber, closing the door behind her as she went.

"I do not like being taken unawares, particularly before I have finished my toilette," Arabella said coldly, "and in future, my lord, I will dismiss my own servants."

"Proud," the king said. "Proud and beautiful. Such pride must surely be inborn that the heiress of a tumbled-down stone keep would have it in such measure." His blue eyes swept slowly over her, examining her carefully with a connoisseur's practiced eye. "Damn me, madame, but you are even lovelier than I could have possibly anticipated. Methinks our bargain is a poor one that I must let you go after only three nights of bliss."

Naked! She was standing naked before a man other than her husband, Arabella thought, and yet she was not in the least embarrassed by her situation. It was most puzzling indeed. "A bargain, my lord, is a bargain," she said calmly, "and if I remember correctly, there was no guarantee of bliss. You agreed to intercede with King Henry on my behalf, and I agreed to allow you three nights in my bed; but there was certainly no discussion of bliss."

The king chuckled. "Do ye nae think, madame, that we are capable of gieing each other bliss?" he said, casually removing his silk shirt and his hose, which were the only garments that he had been wearing. He stood before her naked, and seeing that Arabella's gaze was somewhat fixed somewhere past his right shoulder, he chuckled again. "I am said to be a fine figure of a man, sweetheart. Would ye nae look at me? I am certainly enjoying looking at ye."

"I did not think you had come to *look*, my lord," Arabella answered archly, annoyed at having shown such cowardice be-

fore him. She turned her cool gaze upon the king, her green
eyes sweeping boldly over him as if she were quite used to
perusing naked men. He was, as he said, a fine figure of a man;
big and tall, with long limbs that were well fleshed and a long
torso that was lightly covered with auburn hair matching that
upon his bush and upon his head. She willed herself not to blush
as her glance moved over the most intimate part of him. He was
certainly most well-endowed, but then as her husband was always reminding her, the Stewart men were.

She had great strength, James Stewart thought, watching her
face carefully as she looked her fill at him. He would have almost
thought her a woman of vast experience had not the most delicate blush of pink stained her cheeks. He doubted that she herself was even aware of the blush, for it was so faint. Walking
over to Arabella, he pulled the tortoiseshell pins from her hair
slowly, one by one, watching with delight as her pale gold tresses
tumbled to the floor, cloaking her like a silken mantle.

James Stewart reached out and took a handful of her hair
between his fingers, feeling the wonderful texture as he rubbed
those fingers together. He raised a handful of hair to his lips,
kissing it, tasting it, inhaling its wonderful and elusive fragrance. "Magnificent," he said with deep and sincere feeling.
"Never hae I seen such magnificent hair! Its beauty is such that
I want to bathe in it!"

"Bathe in my hair?" she mocked him. "My lord, what nonsense you speak."

"Nay," he said. "Take yer beautiful hair, sweetheart, and
rub it all over my body. I must feel yer hair upon me!"

Tavis had loved her hair, Arabella thought sadly. He, too, had
liked to take her hair and rub it over his skin, but he had never
said that he wanted to bathe in it. It was, however, what he was
doing, she considered, catching up her hair in her hands and
stroking his skin with it. "Like this, my lord?" she murmured
softly.

"Aye," he said, almost purring, his eyes closed for a moment
as he enjoyed the double sensation of her hair and her hands
upon him. Then after a while his blue eyes opened and he looked
down into her face. "Kiss me, Arabella," he commanded her,
his hands tightening about her waist as he lifted her up level with
him.

She had never kissed another man but Tavis, she thought, as

a wave of panic suddenly swept over her. Not like this. Not intimately; but triumphing over her tumultuous emotions, she put her lips upon his. After a moment, however, the king pulled away from her, laughing softly.

"Why sweetheart," he said gently. "yer shy of me. 'Tis most charming. Perhaps I ask too much of ye. 'Tis I who should be instructing ye, for other than my uncle, ye really are an innocent, aren't ye?" Swinging her into his arms, he carried her over to the bed and set her down upon it.

"I have known no other man but Tavis Stewart," she answered the king honestly. "I am no wanton, my lord."

Again James Stewart felt a prick of guilt, but he pushed it away. He was a king, and kings had certain rights over their subjects that other men did not. Arabella's decision to divorce her husband had been her decision. He had certainly not asked it of her, nor had it been necessary to their liaison that she do so. "Nay, Arabella," the king agreed, joining her upon the bed, "yer nae a wanton." He lowered his head so that their faces almost touched. "Open yer mouth to me, sweetheart," he bid her, and when she obeyed him, he put his lips upon hers even as his tongue reconnoitered forward to surprise hers. She stiffened at its touch and sought to draw away from him, but he would not let her. "Nay, sweetheart," he said, raising his head from her that he might speak. "Gie me yer wee pink tongue that mine may love it. Watch them as they entwine and play wi each other."

His words had a strange, almost hypnotic effect upon her. Her eyes followed the erotic ballet that their two tongues were performing. She could not for the life of her look away. His tongue was strong. It seemed to master hers, and she shivered even as she felt a thrill of excitement race through her. It had not occurred to Arabella before this moment that she might actually respond to the king's lovemaking. She had honestly believed that good women respond only to the love of their husbands. Perhaps she was not really a good woman, or perhaps this was simply some sort of temptation that she must resist. Yet if the king was displeased with her, he might take back his aid. She could not be certain that he had actually sent a letter to King Henry. To her decided embarrassment, a small moan escaped her.

"Aye, sweetheart," the king encouraged her, "dinna be fearful of me or of the passion I will raise in ye.'' He began to cover her face with hot kisses, nibbling upon her dark gold eyelashes as he did. Her head fell back, and he kissed her throat. Then his tongue began to lick slowly over the slender column, savoring the silky texture of the faintly perfumed flesh.

Arabella shivered once again, suddenly clearly aware that when the king had made his pact with her he had not, as she believed, meant their three nights to be so quickly over. James Stewart did not want merely to futter her and be gone. He did not intend to use her like a common whore. He wanted all of her, and the thought was terrifying. No man, Arabella instinctively realized, had the right to demand that much of any woman.

He let his lips rest momentarily within the faintly pulsing hollow of her throat. There was something about the life force throbbing beneath his mouth that was incredibly sensual. Though she allowed him free access to her person, he could sense both confusion and resistance within her. He could understand both. The confusion stemmed from her basic innocence. He could sense her rising desire, but he knew that that same desire brought about an instinctive struggle within her against it. James Stewart had not had a great deal of experience with innocent women, but as greatly as he wanted her, he knew he could not enjoy himself fully until he could help her overcome her own resistance to passion. Then, too, there was that intriguing thought: Had she ever known real passion? Surely she had to have known it, for his uncle's reputation was typically Stewart.

Why did he not simply take her and be done with it? Arabella wondered nervously. She had never been tested like this before, and she did not know for how much longer she could maintain a cool detachment. He was so gentle. She had not expected gentleness. His lips began to move on her again, his tongue slipping from between them occasionally to caress her. It was that tongue more than anything else that made her so nervous. He seemed to be tasting her flesh and relishing it.

The king had refrained from touching her with his hands up to this point, but now he could no longer resist. Rolling onto his back, he pushed himself into a sitting position and then pulled Arabella back against him, positioning her between his outspread legs. He cupped both of her breasts within his palms, teasing at the outthrust nipples with his thumbs. ''Ye hae a pair of the prettiest titties I hae ever seen, sweetheart,'' he complimented her. "They are like ripe fruits, plump and sweet." He bent and kissed her shoulder, brushing her long hair aside as he did.

His hands were strong, and yet he took great care with her tender flesh. For the briefest moment Arabella allowed her eyes to close, imagining that it was her husband who was caressing her, and yet the king's touch was a distinctly different one. *Her husband.* She had to stop thinking of Tavis Stewart as her husband. He was not her husband. She had no husband, and there was no reason for her to feel guilt about her situation. James Stewart was a handsome young man and a skilled lover. He was taking every care to ensure her pleasure, and if the truth be known, her predicament was not such a terrible one.

He felt her suddenly relax a little, and he said, "What are ye thinking, sweetheart?"

"I think," she said, carefully choosing her words, "that you are not a bad man. You are canny, my lord, and I believe you will be a good king, for you are not afraid to take what you want."

The king laughed. "Ye are an interesting woman, Arabella," he told her. "Here I am striving to rouse yer passions, and ye are considering my qualifications as king."

She turned her body slightly so she might look at him. "I think it is important to know the person with whom you are dealing, my lord. You think of me as a mere female to be conquered on the altar of love, but I think of myself as a warrior. My goal is the return of my home. I fight for that gain even as a man would fight. Only my weapons are different. My goals, however, are the same."

"Then ye yield yerself only in order to reach yer goal," he said, his tone just slightly aggrieved. "Do ye nae find me attractive then, madame?"

The time had come, Arabella realized, to put away her childish ideals. Even devoid of experience, she knew that a man's ego was far more fragile than a woman's. "Oh, Jamie Stewart," she told him softly, "I have been raised to be a good woman, and I suddenly find it is possible that I might enjoy being a bad one. My conscience pricks me sorely, and aye, you are more than attractive, my lord. You are wickedly handsome. Perhaps that is why I am just a little afraid." Were those honeyed words coming out of her mouth?

"Afraid, sweetheart? Why afraid?" the king asked her, now all solicitous concern. "Ye need nae be afraid of me. I only want to love ye."

" 'Tis that very love of which I am afraid, my lord," Arabella told him. "I cannot love you, Jamie Stewart, for if I did, I should not want to go, and I must go."

James Stewart's sensuous mouth brushed her lips lightly, and his eyes were warm. "Ye know I would hae ye stay, sweetheart," he said, "but I will also understand yer going . . . if ye must." His hands began to fondle her breasts again. "But let us dinna think of yer going, Arabella, when we are just beginning." His voice was thick with his rising passion.

Arabella closed her eyes once again in an effort to will away her guilt. There could be no more talk between them, and the king was far too sensitive to women to be fooled by a sham of amorousness on her part. He would accept reticence and shyness, but that reticence must soon melt away, and her shyness must turn to desire lest she displease the monarch. He turned her, cradling her against an arm, and lowering his bright auburn head, he began to lick at one of her nipples, his skilled tongue slowly encircling the hard little nub of flesh. Her breasts had always been sensitive, and Arabella gasped softly as a small prickle of pleasure raced through her.

The king sensed her vulnerability immediately. Sliding down onto his back, he drew her atop him and pulled her up so that he might have free access to both of her breasts. He kissed and licked at the plump flesh, finally suckling upon each nipple in its turn.

The prickles were fast turning into fiery darts of pleasure, and Arabella heard herself moaning softly as her breasts grew hard and swollen with their desire. Her fingers began to tangle themselves into his hair, kneading at his head aimlessly in an effort to gain surcease even as he laid her on her back and, leaning over her, began to nuzzle her torso. He kissed at the silken flesh of her belly, his head moving inexorably lower and lower even as her heart pounded wildly with the blinding realization that he was not going to stop.

He was hard. Dear God, but he was hard. He felt that if he reached down and touched himself, that his great Stewart cock would snap and break off. He wanted to drive himself into her without any further delay, but he would not . . . not yet. *Not quite yet.* His hand smoothed over her Venus mont, and she shuddered. Quickly spreading her with his fingers, he lowered his head and touched her with his tongue.

Arabella stiffened and cried out softly, for the touch, so warm and so intimate, was totally unexpected.

The king raised his head a moment and said, "Did my uncle never use ye in this fashion, sweetheart?"

"N-nay!" she half sobbed.

"Dinna be afraid, Arabella. 'Twill gie ye pleasure far greater than ye can imagine," and lowering his head again, he began to tongue her, first with slow, broad strokes, and then as she grew hot with her passion, with quick, flickering motions that seemed to drive her wild with unfeigned delight.

It was too much, Arabella thought. There had never before been such incredible sweetness. Why had Tavis denied her this delight? She felt as if a star were bursting within her brain, just behind her eyelids. "Ohhhh," she moaned, and her now fevered body began to thrash. "Ohhhh, yessss! Ohh, yes, my lord!" It was all too delicious. Simply too delicious, and then she shivered hard with her pleasure.

James Stewart was astounded and delighted as well. How could his uncle not have given Arabella this delight? Was Tavis one of those damn fools who believed a man futtered a wife differently than he futtered other women? Surely not! He pulled himself level with her once more. "Did I gie ye pleasure, sweetheart?" he asked her, fully knowing what her response would be, and when she nodded dreamy-eyed at him, he said, "Then the time hae come for ye to gie me equal pleasure. Open yerself to me, Arabella."

She slipped her arms about his neck, and drawing his head down to hers, she kissed him sweetly, her little tongue hurrying into his mouth to play with his. She felt him seeking, and shifted herself to better accommodate him, but he fit only the tip of his organ within her moist sheath. Puzzled, she drew back and looked at him questioningly.

"Let us play a wee game, sweetheart," he said, his blue eyes twinkling. "Let us see which one of us needs the other first." His lips met hers again.

Men, Arabella thought, amused, were such children. Yet this child was a clever devil who fully enjoyed and devoured female flesh with gusto. He would also expect her to break first, she realized, and contemplated if she would. No. 'Twas what he expected. Let him get what he did not expect, Arabella decided, even as she returned his kisses with passion.

He wanted her! Dear heaven how he wanted her, he thought, as he moved teasingly on her, but she would not surrender. The kisses between them became more frantic, and finally James Stewart could no longer bear the tension. Slowly and deliberately he pushed himself into her sheath, groaning with pure relief as he did so. Her soft laughter inflamed him, and he began to move skillfully upon her until it was she who was crying for release. When he had at last acceded to her plea, she shuddered again and again, her golden head finally falling to one side, her breathing so faint that he wondered if perhaps he had killed her.

She had the answer to her question, Arabella realized, as her body lay replete with satisfaction against the equally contented body of the king. A man, other than a husband, could indeed give a woman carnal pleasure, but it was different too. She did not dislike Jamie, but there was no special warmth between them now as there had been between herself and Tavis in the afterward. She and the king had nothing more between them than the shared experience of a coupling, and however pleasurable it had been to her body, the love was lacking, and her heart ached with loneliness. It was a sobering, indeed a terrifying revelation, and she was now committed to live with that knowledge for the rest of her life; but surely Greyfaire was worth it. *Wasn't it?*

Part III

MY LADY OF
GREYFAIRE

*A*rabella Grey came back to Greyfaire almost four years after she had left it. It was April, and her white mare nickered softly as her equine memory was triggered by some familiar sight or scent. They stood on the crest of a hill overlooking the keep, and Arabella suddenly thought that it all looked so forlorn and shabby. Though the day was chilly and the air damp with impending rain, no smoke came from the cottages in the village below. She shivered with a sense of imminent doom.

"You are certain, Rowan, that Sir Jasper is not in residence?" she demanded of FitzWalter's son for what was probably the sixth time that day.

"Nay, m'lady, he ain't there. He hasn't been at Greyfaire in months. If he had come, me dad would have sent word."

"Let us go down then," Arabella said, and turning, called to Lona, astride a brown gelding with little Margaret. "Come on, Lona. We're almost home now."

They began their descent down the hill even as the first spatterings of rain began to hit them.

"Why is there no smoke from the cottages?" Arabella wondered aloud.

"Most of the old women are in the fields and in the orchard, m'lady, while the old men keep watch on the heights. There ain't no one home in the cottages. The young 'uns and their mams are out in the fields too. Sir Jasper sends his man Seger once or twice a year to see if any of the young boys left has growed enough to serve him. We tried to hide our lads at first, but Sir Jasper has a list of all the families he sends with Seger. There ain't no escaping for most."

"Yet you are still here, Rowan," Arabella observed.

"Aye, I am," Rowan said matter-of-factly. "Me dad told Sir Jasper that as I would take his place one day, I should stay and learn all there was to learn about defending Greyfaire. Sir Jasper laughed and replied that he would not argue with my father over one lad, for he valued my father's loyalty and needed him to defend Greyfaire in his absence. So I don't have to hide anymore when Seger comes, m'lady.''

Arabella nodded. ''I wonder how the other mothers feel about you,'' she said quietly.

Rowan had the good grace to flush. ''It ain't easy, m'lady,'' he admitted. ''No girl will walk out with me, for all have brothers forced into Sir Jasper's service; but my father does need me, m'lady, and in the beginning—before Seger came with his damned list—I was able to hide several lads. They live in a small cave near the village, for they cannot go home lest they be caught, for we never know when Seger will come.''

''And if he comes while I am at Greyfaire?'' Arabella wondered aloud.

''We'll kill him so he'll carry no tales,'' Rowan said bluntly.

''How many lads are in hiding, Rowan?''

''A full dozen, m'lady.''

''Good! I will need them to guard me when I go south to King Henry's court.''

''You're going to court, m'lady? Why?'' Rowan asked her.

''Because the king must confirm my rights to Greyfaire, as Sir Jasper seeks my lands for himself,'' Arabella told him.

''But you are Greyfaire's mistress, m'lady!'' the young man cried. ''You are the last of the Greys.''

''That is true, Rowan, but I have been in Scotland these past years while Sir Jasper has had charge of Greyfaire. What can the king know of me but what Sir Jasper has told him? I do not want Greyfaire for myself, but for my daughter. If the king will allow the line of descent to pass to my daughter, then Greyfaire will have a new beginning. I will ask the king to match Margaret with an English husband so there will never be any doubt as to the loyalty of Greyfaire Keep or its people.''

They had come down off the hill as they talked and ridden through the practically deserted village. Now, as they came out again on the road leading to the castle, the Greyfaire folk saw them and came running from the fields, calling out their welcome. Arabella almost wept aloud, for most of the women, all of whom she remembered well, were altered in appearance. Those who had been inclined to plumpness were hollow-cheeked, and those who had been slender were gaunt. The young had become old, and the old frail and birdlike. Still they smiled and cried warm words of welcome to her.

"The mistress is home!"

"God bless you, Lady Arabella!"

" 'Twill be all right now. The rightful lady of the keep is on the land again."

"Welcome home, m'lady!"

"Greyfaire has its Grey back. Now the luck will come again!"

FitzWalter came from the keep to greet her, kissing her hand, his eyes filled with tears. "So you're home," he said with great understatement.

"Aye, I'm home at last, FitzWalter," she said, and then smiled at them all. "Thank you for your welcome, good people of Greyfaire. Tomorrow at noon you will all come to the hall, and I will tell you of my adventures and of my plans for the future. Now go to your homes, for the rain is falling harder as each minute passes." Then turning, she entered the keep.

When night had fallen and Margaret had been settled in a warm, dry bed, Arabella Grey sat in her hall and marveled that she had never before realized how poor a place her home was. It was clean, at least, and she knew that she probably had FitzWalter's wife Rosamund to thank for that. The stone floors were well-swept, and the rushes and sweet herbs were fresh, but other than the highboard and a few chairs, there was nothing of note when one compared it with the Great Hall of Dunmor Castle, or Stirling, or Linlithgow. Arabella's sharp eye noted that there were several panes of precious glass missing from two of the four windows. The gaping holes had been stuffed with fabric.

"What happened to the windows?" she asked FitzWalter, whom she had invited to eat with her.

"Sir Jasper's men, the ones he brought with him on his last visit, are a rough lot," came the dry answer.

"Glass is costly," Arabella grumbled aloud.

"Have you any gold?" FitzWalter queried her.

"I possess very little coin, and what I have I must keep for my trip south," she answered him.

"Jewelry then," FitzWalter persisted.

"I brought nothing with me that belonged to the earl," she said quietly.

"You brought his daughter," FitzWalter said, "and if you think he'll not come after her, you're sadly mistaken."

"Margaret is my child too," Arabella reminded him sharply. "Besides, Tavis is in the north on King James's business. It will be several weeks before he returns south, and I will be long gone with my daughter before then. When he comes to Greyfaire—and I believe he will—you will tell him the truth. That I have gone to King Henry to regain my rights and that of Lady Margaret Stewart."

"You didn't have to divorce him to do any of this," FitzWalter said. "I know the man stole you away, but Lona says you love him. If you love him, then why divorce him?"

Had he been anyone else, she would have dismissed him from her table, not to mention her service; but he was FitzWalter, the man she had known her entire life. Greyfaire's loyal captain. Loyal to the keep. Loyal to the Greys. He had remained steadfast to both despite Sir Jasper Keane. FitzWalter would not settle for any less than the truth, and she would not give him any less.

"In order to obtain King James's aid, it was necessary for me to yield myself to him in the fullest sense," Arabella said. "I divorced Tavis Stewart that I might not shame him with my conduct by placing the horns of a cuckold upon his head."

To her surprise, FitzWalter nodded and said, "Aye, then you did the right thing, m'lady. No Grey would act with dishonor. Your father would be proud of you."

"I hope you will tell the earl that when he comes raging over the hills in a month or two," Arabella said with a small attempt at humor.

"I won't be here," FitzWalter said. "Rowan will tell him, for I am going with you."

"But Greyfaire is your responsibility," Arabella said.

"Aye, it is," FitzWalter agreed, "but Greyfaire is safe in my son's hands, and there is peace between England and Scotland, m'lady. You, however, are the last of the Greys, and you should not travel without the protection of someone in authority. There is no one else with whom I would entrust your safety, and there is no one here at Greyfaire with the experience I have."

Arabella thought carefully for a few long moments, and then she said, "Aye, you will come with me, FitzWalter, for I do need you. It is not my safety alone that must be protected, but my daughter's as well. If the king will reaffirm my right to Grey-faire, then Margaret becomes its heiress.''

"Not *if*, m'lady," FitzWalter said, "but *when*."

She flashed him a bright smile at his words. "Aye," she told him, "you are correct, FitzWalter. *When!*"

"What will you tell the people tomorrow?" he asked her.

"The truth," she answered. "That I must go south in order to regain what is mine. That when I do I will bring their sons home. At least those who wish to come, for there will be some who do not."

He nodded. "Aye. A few will have taken to soldiering and will find life here too dull for them. If they survive their youth, however, they'll come home again one day and be glad of the peace here."

"I will need more than peace to rebuild Greyfaire's prosperity," Arabella said thoughtfully.

"You need a rich husband," FitzWalter said bluntly.

Arabella laughed. "Nay, my old friend, no more husbands for me!"

"Perhaps he'll take you back," FitzWalter ventured.

"I do not want him back," Arabella said fiercely. "He claimed to love me, and yet he could not do this one little thing for me. No time was ever the right time to aid me in recovering *Greyfaire*. My home meant nothing to him, though it meant the world to me. How could he love me and not understand that? I do not need Tavis Stewart. I have Greyfaire, and I have my daughter."

FitzWalter said nothing more. It was no use arguing with her. Arabella had always been stubborn. Until she regained her rights to the keep, it would do no good to tell her that the orchards had to be replanted, and that sheep would make a good cash crop if they could just find the coin with which to accomplish these miracles. Greyfaire had never been the most prosperous place, but never before had they had such hard times, and that was part of the difficulty. The times were changing. This peace with Scotland portended an end to Greyfaire's value as England's first warning beacon. Certainly there would be small outbreaks of hostilities between the two nations in future, but FitzWalter still sensed a change.

Arabella stayed at Greyfaire just long enough to reassure her people that all would be well. She explained to them as best she could the difficulty of her situation, but most could not quite grasp her plight. All they knew was that Arabella was *the* Grey of Greyfaire, and therefore the right *must* be on her side. She was forced to leave it at that. The weather had turned fair, and the fields were suddenly lush and green with the promise of a good harvest this year. The orchards were flowering, and where trees had been taken down due to blight, the earth had been first scorched with fire to cleanse it and then laced with steaming manure to enrich it before the new seedlings had been placed carefully in the ground. They were now being tenderly cared for by several women and two elderly men.

The lady of Greyfaire started south on a bright, late spring day. She was accompanied by fifteen young men-at-arms, including the dozen Rowan had hidden, and three others who had magically appeared from their own self-imposed exile, being somehow overlooked by Seger during one of his early visits. FitzWalter's blue eyes had twinkled with amusement at the arrival of these young men, but he had said little, arranging instead for them to be fitted for leather breastplates; inquiring politely if they had enough arrows for their long bows; seeing that they had new swords from the smithy.

Fergus MacMichael arrived the morning of their departure, increasing their number to sixteen. As Lona had confided in her parents her love for the young clansman, no further explanation was necessary, although the Scotsman justified his arrival by saying, "I've come to keep a watch over the earl's bairn."

FitzWalter had nodded solemnly and agreed. " 'Tis good, and you are welcome amongst us, lad."

As deeply disappointed as Rowan was, not to be going with them, he was filled with pride at being left in charge of Greyfaire Keep. He listened attentively to his father's last-minute instructions, nodding, but then as FitzWalter turned to mount his horse, Rowan said, "What if Sir Jasper comes?"

"Bar the gate and deny him entry," Arabella snapped. "He will not put his foot inside my keep again if I have anything to say about it."

"What if Seger comes, m'lady?"

"Kill him!" Arabella said sharply. "It will take us several weeks to reach the king, traveling as we will be with my child. If Seger came before we reached his majesty, he could get back to Sir Jasper, and I would lose the element of surprise. I cannot afford to be at any more of a disadvantage than I already am.''

"I hope he comes,'' Rowan said.

"Pray he doesn't, lad,'' his father replied. "He won't be alone, and you might have to kill a friend as well.''

"And the Earl of Dunmor?'' Rowan asked, hesitant, but aware it was a sticky predicament which he was being left to handle, and wanting to do it right.

"Give him my compliments,'' Arabella added dryly, "and cooperate with him in every way, Rowan. When I return, I want to find Greyfaire as I have left it. Intact and beginning to thrive again. He will want but one thing of you. My daughter. Tell him she is with me, and allow him access to the keep that he may be certain you tell him the truth. Above all, Rowan, be respectful of Tavis Stewart. He is a good man.''

They headed south, traveling at a brisk pace, but one that would not needlessly tire little Margaret. The child was quickly becoming spoilt by the doting attention of all the men about her. Each wanted his turn carrying the little girl, and Margaret spent her days moving delightedly from one friend to another, being sung to, cosseted, and given small treats. The weather was good, and Margaret slept soundly through each night, worn with the fresh air and her adventures.

FitzWalter had carefully planned their trip so that they might spend most of their nights in the guest houses of the various convents, monasteries, and abbeys along their route. Several nights, however, they were forced to camp in the open. If FitzWalter had ever been south of Middleham Castle, he did not volunteer the information, but Arabella trusted him to get them safely to wherever King Henry and his court were currently in residence.

It was the middle of May when they reached Sheen, where the king had come to hunt and enjoy the fine weather. FitzWalter arranged for Arabella, Lona, and Margaret to stay at a nearby convent, explaining to the Mother Superior that his mistress had traveled almost the entire length of England in order to pledge her fealty to the king and confirm her right to the keep of which she was heiress. She was a widow, FitzWalter told the nun, and had little money, but—and here FitzWalter dug deep into his own doublet, finally withdrawing a silver coin—his mistress wanted the convent to have the little she could spare.

"It is good that your mistress acknowledges God's might and power over us all," the Mother Superior said. "Our blessed Lord, Himself, has told us we should not store up treasures for ourselves here on earth, for it is the soul which must be cared for above all else. Your mistress, her orphaned child, and her servant are welcome in this house."

"You told her I was a widow?" Arabella said, surprised.

"Aye," he answered calmly. "I could hardly tell her the truth, now could I?"

Lona snickered, but was silenced by a look from her mistress.

"Now that I am here," Arabella admitted, "I do not know how to go about getting an audience with the king."

"Ask Mother Mary Bede," FitzWalter said. "I have an idea she will know. She's a tough but knowing old bird."

"You have no connections?" the Mother Superior said, surprised.

"Not with this court," Arabella replied.

The nun raised a questioning eyebrow and fingered her ebony and silver crucifix thoughtfully. She awaited Arabella's account.

"My father was a cousin of Queen Elizabeth Woodville's first husband, and my mother was Queen Anne Neville's cousin and childhood companion. It was King Richard who arranged my marriage," Arabella explained, building upon FitzWalter's lie and mixing it with the actual truth, concluding, "My husband was a Scot, and King James has given me a letter of introduction."

The nun thought a moment and then said, "It is your father's connections that will help us here, Lady Grey. The king does not like his mother-in-law—and with good reason, I think—but the queen holds a certain fondness for her surviving parent. My brother, who is a priest, serves as the queen's confessor. We will apply through him to Queen Elizabeth for an audience. If you are clever, my child—and I think you must be to have undertaken such a journey—then it is the young queen who will aid you. You have much in common, being young mothers. Your royal introduction certainly cannot hurt."

Several days later it was all arranged. Lady Arabella Grey would be received by Queen Elizabeth the following afternoon at Sheen.

"It could not be better," FitzWalter said. "It is unlikely the queen even knows Sir Jasper, or will come in contact with him. You'll be able to plead your case in a sympathetic atmosphere.''

"But will the queen be willing to aid me?'' Arabella fretted. "What if she does not like me? Women who are breeding are given to strange fancies, and it is said the queen is with child again.''

"Just be yourself,'' FitzWalter counseled. "The queen knows what it is like to be stripped of all she holds dear. She will understand your plight better than most, my lady.''

Arabella dressed carefully for her audience with the queen. She had brought but one gown she deemed suitable. It was of a deep blue silk, rather tight fitting, with a long waist and wide shawl collar which was trimmed in a wide band of silver brocade. The low neckline of the gown revealed the shadowy area between her breasts, but was quite modest by most standards. A modest sheer-white lawn veil was held upon her head by a pretty silver circlet. Her hair beneath was braided and looped up at her temples, giving a square effect. About her waist was a girdle of silver links from which fell a small silver crucifix and a pomander ball. She was the picture of a respectable, widowed noblewoman.

"Leave the child with me,'' Mother Mary Bede instructed Arabella. "She may play in the kitchens, where there are new kittens, and Sister Mary Grace is baking honey cakes.''

Although Arabella was worried that Margaret might be frightened without her, the little girl put her hand trustingly into that of the gaunt nun and trotted off.

"Well, that's one less worry,'' said Lona, who was accompanying her mistress to court.

The horses had been combed and curried, and their coats glistened as they rode slowly down the road to Sheen. The king and his family in residence, the road was a busy one this day, with much going to and fro. There were those who provisioned the king and court, carrying or driving their wares. There were merchants hoping to gain favor. There were courtiers, and hangers-on and their servants. There were soldiers. Lona's eyes were wide and curious, her head swiveling every which way at some new sight; but Arabella rode, eyes straight ahead, refusing to be distracted, considering for the hundredth time just how she should approach the queen. To her surprise, it turned out to be far easier than she had anticipated.

Elizabeth of York was a sweet-faced young woman with thick flaxen braids and beautiful light blue eyes. She received her guest in a small private garden, for the afternoon was pleasant and warm. She had with her but one attendant, a discreet lady who busily plied her embroidery needle without even looking at her mistress's visitor. Arabella, kneeling meekly before the queen, was asked to rise and state her case. The priest who had brought Arabella to the queen also remained by her side.

Kissing the queen's hand, Arabella then stood and explained as carefully as possible her difficulties regarding Greyfaire. She finished by saying, "So you see, madame, if I might just lay my case before the king and win his approval, I could return home to reassure my people. They do not understand any of this and are frightened, as you may well imagine. I am, however, a woman of no great importance, your majesty. Had it not been for Mother Mary Bede's brother, Father Paul, I should not have even had a means of redress to you despite the letters I carried. I only want my rights, and those of my daughter Margaret, confirmed so I may return home. I am no woman of the world, merely a simple country woman."

"Why is your husband not with you, Lady Grey?" the queen asked, curious.

"I divorced my husband, madame. He swore a sacred oath that he would aid me in my quest to regain Greyfaire, and yet he did not. He swore an oath to me that he would give our daughter, at age six, into the keeping of an English husband so that King Henry would be assured of Greyfaire's continuing loyalty, and yet suddenly he began to speak of matching Margaret with a Home or a Hepburn."

"You are certainly a woman of strong character, Lady Grey," the queen noted, just a trifle shocked. "Did your husband not oppose this divorce?"

"King James believed my cause was just, madame, and he is my husband's nephew," Arabella replied, not quite answering the queen's question. "The archbishop of St. Andrews also concurred. It is not a decision I made lightly, madame. I love my husband."

"Then your pain is certainly doubled, Lady Grey," Elizabeth of York answered, "yet I understand better than many what it is to lose everything you hold dear. In my case I could do nothing and was at the mercy of others to solve my problems. You are very brave, I think, to attempt to right your own wrongs. I will certainly bring your plight to my husband's attention as quickly as possible, and I will arrange for you to have an audience with the king.''

"For whom will you arrange an audience, Beth?" Henry Tudor had entered the queen's garden and overheard the last part of his wife's sentence. He was a serious-faced man, already slightly stooped with the worries of his office. He had a long, prominent nose, and fathomless eyes that seemed to register little if any emotion, and yet those eyes softened when they gazed upon the queen.

Elizabeth arose and curtsied prettily to her husband. "This is Lady Arabella Grey, my lord, and she needs your majesty's aid greatly.''

"You would have an audience of me, my lady? Then say on, for you have my ear," the king told Arabella, who curtsied deeply at the king's entry and handed him James Stewart's letter of introduction.

Once more Arabella told her story.

When she had finished, the king said, "A border keep such as yours, however small, needs a man." Henry Tudor briefly scanned the parchment she had given him before handing it to his servant. He vaguely remembered a recent communique from the Scots king regarding this matter.

"I have a man, sire," Arabella answered. "FitzWalter, who was my father's captain, has had Greyfaire in his keeping ever since my father was killed seven years ago. His son Rowan stands behind his father, ready to take his place one day when he is needed. We are a small keep, sire, but we have ever been loyal.''

"Sir Jasper Keane is loyal," Henry Tudor said, curious to see what reaction his words would have. He was not disappointed.

"Jasper Keane is loyal to himself first, sire!" Arabella said furiously. "He murdered a noble Scots woman, and then refused to give her betrothed husband the satisfaction of honorable combat. Instead he hid behind an elderly priest to save his cowardly skin, thus endangering all of Greyfaire. His actions have caused the difficulties that I face. His marriage to my mother was an open scandal, and he was responsible for her death as well. Jasper Keane betrayed King Richard in an effort to steal my property. I cannot believe a man of your majesty's nobility and good reputation would retain such a man as a friend, or reward such a craven creature for his shameful perfidies!''

The queen and the few about her were somewhat aghast by Arabella's angry words, but the king's mouth twitched with frosty amusement.

"You speak bluntly, madame, for a humble petitioner."

"Sire, I have given everything I have to regain my home. If you refuse me, what more can I lose?" Arabella asked honestly.

"Tell me how you came to be involved with Sir Jasper," the king said. "Did your father match you?"

"No, sire, King Richard matched us."

"Yet you claim to be a woman of no importance," the king said craftily.

"I am not, sire, but my mother, may God assoil her sweet soul, was Anne Neville's beloved cousin and friend. When my father was killed in England's defense, my mother, who was a gentle creature and helpless without my father's counsel, asked Queen Anne to arrange a match for me for Greyfaire's sake. Sir Jasper Keane was King Richard's choice. Neither my mother nor I had ever laid eyes on him prior to the king's decision; and Sir Jasper, wicked knave he is, had no sooner laid eyes on my mother than he seduced her, poor frail lady she was.''

"Do you seek revenge then, madame?" Henry Tudor asked.

"If I were a man, sire, I should have long ago had satisfaction of Sir Jasper Keane, but alas, I am a weak woman. I must meekly swallow my anger and pray God for my poor mother's soul; but I would do those things on my own land. Jasper Keane has no right to Grey lands. He has his own lands at Northby, though his house was burned by the Scots," she concluded, a small smile touching the corners of her mouth.

"What of another husband for you, madame?" the king inquired.

"I would prefer to not marry again, sire," Arabella said. "Managing Greyfaire so that my child's inheritance is safe and prosperous will take all my time. I would not have the time for another husband, or other children. Life in the north has never been easy, my lord, and Sir Jasper has neglected Greyfaire badly while forcing our young men and boys into his service that he might impress your majesty.''

"How old is your daughter, madame?" the king asked.

"Just two, sire.''

"Would a Percy suit you, madame? A minor one, of course," the king said, gently acknowledging her unimportance. "Sir Henry has a young bastard of whom he is quite fond. The lad is six now and being raised in the Percy nursery. His mother, the daughter of one of Percy's captains, died in childbed with him. The Percys are a difficult family at best. Giving them a small heiress for this child might help to bind them to me."

"The Percys know Greyfaire," Arabella said thoughtfully, "but if you are not quite certain of their loyalty, leave the keep in my hands until after the marriage between my daughter and the Percy bastard is consummated. I would even prefer that there be no marriage ceremony until Margaret is at least fifteen."

"There must be a formal betrothal, however, if the Percys agree," the king replied. "I cannot promise them an heiress whose dowry is to remain in her mother's hands until a consummation without offering some sign of good faith."

"And another thing," Arabella said boldly. "Instead of my daughter going to the Percys, have them send the boy to me when he is ten."

"What, madame?" The king looked astounded.

"Sire," Arabella said in a reasonable tone, "you do not really trust the Percys, you say, but to put them in your debt you would match their favored bastard with my heiress daughter. If the Percys are indeed tempted to disloyalty against your majesty, would it not be better that the boy come to me that I may teach him to be your majesty's faithful servant, rather than that the Percys possibly teach my Scots-born daughter to be treasonous and turn her keep against you?"

"By the rood, madame," the king said admiringly, "you are a clever woman! Aye! The Percy lad will come to you. We will say it is so you may teach him of Greyfaire firsthand. 'Tis most plausible."

They had walked to the far end of the queen's garden that the others might not hear them and gossip about their conversation.

"Then you will reconfirm my right to Greyfaire, my lord, and that of my daughter?" Arabella said hopefully.

"It would seem a prudent course, madame, particularly if what you have told me about Sir Jasper Keane is indeed true," the king answered slowly, "but it is my habit to always sleep upon such a decision. Then, too, I must sound out Sir Harry as to whether such a match between his cub and your child is acceptable to the Percys. You do not lodge at court, do you?''

"Nay, my lord, I have not the means. My child, my servants, and I have been staying at St. Mary's-in-the-Fields, close by Sheen.''

"Your daughter is with you?'' The king seemed surprised.

"Aye, sire, she is. Margaret is far too young to be separated from her mama, and I could not bear to be far from her,'' Arabella admitted.

"But the rigors of travel,'' the king protested.

"Margaret is a strong and healthy lass, praise God, and she seems to thrive on travel,'' Arabella told him.

"Would that my son Arthur be the same,'' the king said softly.

"May the queen bear your majesty a fine, strong son before year's end,'' Arabella said graciously.

"I will send to St. Mary's when I wish to see you again, Lady Grey,'' the king told her in dismissal.

Arabella curtsied low and kissed the king's outstretched hand, but as she arose, her lovely face plainly bespoke her concern.

"I will not keep you waiting more than a day or two, madame,'' Henry Tudor reassured her. "I am certain, given the importance of your visit to court, that you can manage until then.''

"Of course, my lord,'' Arabella said, her face now composed, even as her mind recalled the number of coins left in her purse. Traveling was more expensive than she had anticipated. With another curtsy to her sovereign, Lady Grey hurried back up the garden to bid the queen farewell and to thank her for her kindness. "God bless your grace,'' she said. "I will beseech our Lord for your safe delivery and a healthy son come autumn.''

Elizabeth of York smiled sweetly. "Thank you, Lady Grey. I pray that your audience with my husband, the king, has been a successful one, and that I have truly been of aid to you.''

"I have hope, your grace,'' Arabella said quietly, not wishing to appear smug, although her heart was racing with excitement.

She was almost certain that Henry Tudor would return Greyfaire to her!

"Then I have done my duty toward you as your queen," came the gracious reply. "If I do not see you again, Lady Grey, I bid you Godspeed."

Arabella curtsied a final time, kissing the queen's beringed hand gratefully, and backed slowly from her presence accompanied by Father Paul.

"The king has granted your request, madame?" the priest asked.

"Not yet, Father, but he has promised to render his decision to me within two days' time," Arabella told him.

"Then he will," Father Paul answered, "for Henry Tudor is a meticulous man in all matters. He is not like so many of these great ones who promise yet do not find the time to grant. You will hear. You will hear."

Arabella reached into her purse. God, there were so few coins left, and yet she knew she must reward the priest for his intervention on her behalf. Almost reluctantly she drew a silver coin forth and pressed it into the cleric's hand. "I wish," she apologized, "that it might be more, holy Father, but I have little left, a long journey ahead of me, and my child to consider. Still, I would thank you for all your kindness toward me, and ask that you remember my mother, the Lady Rowena, in the mass."

"Of course, my daughter," Father Paul said in kindly tones, fingering the coin and mentally computing its value without even looking at it. He moved to help her mount her mare when an unpleasantly familiar voice interrupted their conversation.

"Christ's bones! Is it you, Arabella, my pet?"

Her head snapped up and her angry eyes met those of Sir Jasper Keane.

"By God," Sir Jasper drawled admiringly, his gaze boldly assessing her, "you've grown into a rare beauty, my pet! Why, you're fairer than your mam, I'll vow."

"Do not dare to speak of my mother, you foul devil," Arabella said in a tight, angry voice. "She lies dead because of you!"

He laughed nastily. "She lies dead because she could not keep her legs closed to me."

Arabella hit him with all her strength, the Grey signet ring on her finger opening a cut upon his cheekbone just below his right eye. She was speechless with the violence of her anger.

Stunned by the fury he saw in her face, Sir Jasper Keane stepped back a pace, his hand clutching at his wound, which was pouring forth blood all over his fine sky-blue satin doublet. *"Bitch!"* he finally managed to grate out. "You will pay for that, I swear it!"

She felt no fear at his words, only a cold and deep rage that seemed to spread throughout her entire body, numbing it. "Should you ever approach me again, sir, I will kill you where you stand," she said icily, and then turning, mounted her horse.

Shocked by events he could not understand, Father Paul climbed upon his mule, and not knowing what else to do, rode off after her. "My daughter," he said when he finally managed to catch up with her, "what manner of behavior is this that you would strike a gentleman? Men were put upon this earth by our God in order that they might rule their women and the beasts. Your disrespect has, I fear, placed your mortal soul in great jeopardy."

"That man is responsible for my mother's death, Father. He was to wed with me, and when I was carried off by the Scots, he forced my mother to the altar, thereby causing her death from shame, *and* all in order that he might steal my property! He is a dreadful man! A devil out of Hell!"

"But," the priest admonished her gently, "he is a man."

Arabella snorted impatiently. She was grateful to Father Paul for having gotten her an audience with the queen, but the man was an innocent fool. "And is that dangling piece of flesh between a man's legs God's way of conferring superiority, Father? I would think that those of us chosen to conceive and bear life were far superior."

The priest's eyes grew round with his shock, and he mouthed the word *Blasphemy!*

To soothe him, she softened her tone and said, "I will pray for God's forgiveness for my evil temper, Father, and I will pray for my enemy as well that I may learn to forgive him." Blessed Mother, how she dissembled in order to get her way. If she had erred, then that was surely her sin, not her personal belief that

women were as equal as any man, and in some cases superior.
How often Tavis had teased her that though she be English by
birth, she was a Scot in her heart and mind. Perhaps he was
right. Perhaps he had been right about a lot of things. She was
so close to regaining her heart's desire, and yet she was unhappy.
Why?

Sir Jasper Keane stood watching her departure. Now that the
surprise of seeing Arabella Grey here at Sheen was fading, he
was beginning to wonder what had brought her here. Where was
her husband, that border bandit bastard who called himself an
earl? There had been no one with her but a priest, and that in
itself was strange. He would have hardly thought a single priest
a fit escort for the king of Scotland's aunt by marriage. Where
was her retinue? Her servants? Had she indeed even been married, or had it been but a hoax to embarrass him? Most important of all, *why was Arabella Grey here?*

Sir Jasper Keane hurried to his lodgings and sent for his man,
Seger.

"My lord, your face . . ." Seger began, his voice actually
concerned.

"It is not important," his master told him. The wound had
already begun to clot. "I have just seen Lady Arabella Grey,
Seger. She was coming from the queen's garden. I would know
why she was there. Why is she not in Scotland? I would have
answers, man. Quickly!"

"Very good, my lord, I will see what I can find out, but you
really must let me take care of that cut upon your face. It is quite
deep and will surely scar your handsome face if not properly
treated. How badly depends upon how quickly I may treat the
wound," Seger fretted.

"Very well," Sir Jasper replied ungraciously, "play physician if you must, but then find me the answers that I seek,
for I will not rest easy until I learn why she was here." He
suddenly realized that the gash Arabella had opened upon
his cheek was beginning to pain him. "She will pay," he
said almost to himself. "That curst spitfire will pay for all
her insults to me!"

"If we could but find where she is staying, my lord, perhaps
we might take her back to Greyfaire, where you could bring the
bitch to heel until she was like a tamed hound, fawning and
licking at your feet," Seger suggested knowingly.

"She has become a great beauty, Seger," Sir Jasper said almost musingly. "She has far surpassed her mother, and has a look about her that only comes to a woman well-loved. I should not be unhappy to have her in my bed for all her vile temper. If she were in my clutches, I should beat the devil right out of her, I swear it!"

"She is really yours by right, my lord," Seger murmured evilly. "If we could but get her back to Greyfaire . . ."

A look of stunned comprehension suddenly lit Sir Jasper's handsome face. "Greyfaire!" he shouted at Seger. "She has come for Greyfaire! Of course! Why else would she leave her life in Scotland but for that damned wretched keep she so prizes?"

"But Greyfaire is yours, my lord," the captain said.

"No, it is not," his master answered. "King Henry has yet to confirm my rights to Greyfaire, and now that that troublesome bitch has come to claim the keep for herself, my claim has been challenged."

"Surely the king will not award such a strategic keep, even one as small as Greyfaire, to a mere woman, my lord," Seger soothed.

"Nothing is ever certain when dealing with royalty, you fool!" snapped Sir Jasper. "Remember that lest you lose your head one day by making such an error in judgment."

"What will you do then, my lord?"

"What I planned to do in the first place, Seger. You will learn the truth of Lady Arabella Grey's visit to the queen, and then you will tell me. Though I feel it in my bones that the wench has come to usurp my position, it is but idle speculation until proven otherwise. Come and let us bind up my wound. Then you will seek out the answers that I need to my many questions."

"She cannot hope to prevail against you, my lord," Seger said with certainty. "She is but a woman."

"Do not be a bigger fool than you already are, Seger," his master told him. "The church teaches us that even God could not prevail against a woman, for did Eve not disobey him? Women are dangerous creatures, and you must never forget that."

"But God punished Eve, my lord."

"Yet she survived, Seger, and so does her sex. They survive to drive men to madness, but I will not let Arabella Grey best me in this contest of wills. Greyfaire will be mine. There is no way I will let her win."

※ *Chapter 16*

A rabella Grey stood once more before her king. Two days had passed since she had last been at Sheen. She had been brought with much public display through the king's antechamber, where a roomful of petitioners milled about, awaiting a chance to present their cases before the king or to one of his favorites who could gain his ear. There had been no other women in the throng. As she curtsied low, Arabella wondered if the king would notice that she was wearing the same gown she had worn the other day. They were alone, for the king had dismissed all his servants and advisors.

"Sir Jasper Keane has petitioned me once again to assign the keep at Greyfaire over to him," the king began.

Arabella remained silent, instinctively knowing that Henry Tudor was not through. Still, her upper teeth worried her lower lip as she wondered what was to come.

"With the peace between Scotland and England, Greyfaire does not really hold the importance it once did. I have investigated the matter carefully, and I can see no reason to give the ancestral home of the Greys to Sir Jasper Keane. He must return to Northby, and those men now in his service who have been impressed from Greyfaire and wish to return home will be told that they may do so."

Arabella fell to her knees, relief pouring through her. "Thank you, your grace," she half sobbed.

The king pulled her to her feet. "Get up, madame, you have not heard *all* I have to say." He drew her across the room and, after seating himself, indicated that she sit in a chair opposite. "Nothing, madame, is free in this life. Everything has its price, and I will not dissemble by pretending otherwise with you. I will return you your beloved Greyfaire, madame, but only on certain conditions."

Her face was ablaze with joy. "*Anything* sire!" she told him.

"A poor choice of words, madame," the king told her dryly. "You leave yourself nothing with which to bargain."

"But I will do whatever I must to regain Greyfaire," Arabella told him earnestly.

"Will you indeed?" Henry Tudor said, feeling almost sorry for Lady Grey, who was, he had finally decided, really quite innocent of the world for all her time at the Scots court. Still, that innocence could, and would, be useful to him. He fixed Arabella with a piercing look and said, "You are really a most beautiful woman, madame. There is something about you . . . something mysterious, and yet there is an artless ingenuousness that charms me. A freshness, a naiveté, for all your marriage and the fact that you are a mother. You are a most alluring little creature."

Holy Mother, Arabella thought. He wants to lie with me!

Henry Tudor saw the look that quickly crossed her face and was quickly gone. His laughter was brief and harsh. "Put all thoughts of carnality from your mind, madame," he reassured her. "What little passion flows through my veins I reserve for my queen."

Arabella flushed, but wisely held her tongue.

"Charming," the king noted, observing the blush, "and it is just that sort of charm that can be useful. I want you to go to France for me, madame."

"France!" Such a request had been the furthest thing from her mind.

"France," the king said.

"But why?" Arabella asked. She didn't want to go to France. She wanted to go home to Greyfaire!

"Because I need eyes and ears in France, madame. The French would plot against me, and I must know before they even attempt their perfidy what it is that they would do."

"But how can I be of help in such an endeavor, your grace? I am a simple country woman. I have no knowledge of politics or court intrigues. Are the French not your friends, sire? Did they not support your desire to be England's king?"

"The French did indeed support me, madame, but they supported me because it suited their convenience to do so. As long as Duke Richard and Duke Henry fought over that fine, meaty bone called England, the English were well-occupied and could not cause the French difficulties elsewhere. Now, however, I am England's king, *and now* I sit firmly upon my throne. France is once again the enemy, although there is no outright war between us, nor do I expect one. I do, however, need to know if the French will continue to support me, or if they will conspire with my enemies to dethrone me, even as they did your late cousin Richard. I need eyes and ears at the French court. Eyes and ears who will be trusted because it is believed those eyes and ears are my enemy's. This is no matter for diplomats who spend so much time couching their language in fine terms that no one can understand what it is they are saying. I want you to be my eyes and ears, madame.''

Arabella was astounded. ''But I am not your majesty's enemy,'' she said. ''What could I possibly learn in France that would help your grace?''

''Would you be my enemy if I refused to return Greyfaire to you, madame, and instead awarded it to Sir Jasper Keane?'' he demanded.

''But you promised . . .'' she began, her voice a half sob, her heart plummeting.

''Put not your trust in princes or in any child of man,'' the king said. ''My mother taught me that. She had it from a priest, she said. I think it a fine motto, but do not look so stricken, madame. Hear me out and all will make sense, I promise. Greyfaire is yours. I would be less than the king I am if I did not uphold your rights in this matter. The papers will be drawn making Lady Margaret Stewart your heiress to the keep. This, however, will not be made public. Instead it will be believed that I have denied you the return of your keep. You have no husband. No home. No place in either Scotland or England. You are an outcast thanks to Henry Tudor, and so you will flee to France to join other exiles at the French court. Who will suspect that you are my eyes and my ears under those circumstances, madame?''

''I have no monies with which to travel,'' Arabella said, her practical nature reasserting itself.

''You will be provided for, madame, but not on any lavish scale, mind you. Your genteel poverty, along with your beauty, should aid you in attracting suitors. Associate only with those who are powerful and can aid you with their loose talk.''

''My lord, just what is it you are asking me to do?'' Arabella was clearly aware that King Henry was not merely suggesting a simple visit to France.

''Whatever you must, madame, to gain your ends,'' the king

replied bluntly, his eyes meeting hers and never wavering for a moment. They were hard eyes.

"Do you ask me to whore for you?" she demanded softly.

"No, madame, I ask you to whore for England if you must," he answered her.

"You are England," Arabella said quietly.

A slow smile briefly lit the king's stern features. "So I am, madame, and it is good that you recognize it. I hold the power of life and death over all in this land."

"For how long must I play this game, your grace?"

"A year at the most. No longer," he promised her.

"A year!" It sounded more like a hundred years, and she sighed deeply. "My daughter—" she began, but he cut her off.

"Lady Margaret Stewart will remain in England, madame. I will have nothing deterring you in your purpose, and a child would make you vulnerable. She will come to live in the royal nurseries with my son Arthur and the new baby that the queen is to bear in the autumn. She will be quite safe. You cannot send her to Greyfaire, for it will not publicly belong to you any longer. Besides, her father might come galloping over the border seeking her return, madame, and I am certain you do not want that."

"But how will you explain her presence, your grace?" Arabella asked the king.

"Why, I will say that I have taken pity on the Scots king's wee niece whose willful mother ran off to France in a vile temper when I refused to grant the silly woman the rights to her family's keep," Henry Tudor said with a frosty smile.

"There is no other way?" Arabella said.

"Did you yourself not say *anything*, madame?"

"But to take my baby from me," Arabella cried. " 'Tis cruel!"

"Perhaps," the king agreed, "but 'twill guarantee me your good behavior, madame. You are hardly likely to betray me while I hold the life of your daughter in my hands."

"Should I hear anything of note, your grace, how will I communicate it to you?" Pushing her turbulent emotions aside, Arabella was beginning to think of the difficulties and the dangers involved in what the king was demanding of her.

"Lord Anthony Varden will be your contact, madame. Whatever it is that you hear, you will pass on to Lord Varden. He will see that your news reaches England. You can trust him with your life, madame, but God willing, you will not have to do so. Tony Varden is believed to hate me because of a quarrel between his family and my stepfather's family. He has lived in France for many years, and he is one of my loyalest friends, though none know it.''

"He must be to have given up his estates and his country for your grace,'' Arabella said quietly.

"Tony is a second son,'' the king replied. "He was destined for the church, but desired it not. The quarrel between us is entirely fabricated. He was with me in Brittany when we decided to try this ploy against the French. Since it has appeared to work, he has remained in France for several years now. He will be your mentor, madame, telling you whatever it is you will need to know. Trust him.''

"It would seem, sire, that I have no other choice,'' Arabella answered the king.

"You have a choice,'' Henry Tudor told her. "You may refuse me, madame, without any fear of my ill will.''

"But if I do, your grace, you will not return Greyfaire to me, will you?''

"Come, madame,'' the king replied, not truly answering her question, "why so squeamish? You tell me that you can hold your keep in the event of an attack, and I have accepted your word for it. I treat you as I will wager no man has ever treated you . . . as an equal. I have returned your home to you, and in return I ask that you serve the crown as any man would serve it.''

"Would you ask a man to whore for you, sire?'' Arabella demanded tartly.

"If necessary, madame, aye! Men and women fight with different weapons, a fact of which I am certain you are well aware. Tony Varden has proved a most valuable spy for England. I cannot be certain that some of his information was not gained in pillow talk. You need not compromise yourself, Lady Grey, if you do not choose to, but a man is more apt to confide in a woman he is enamored of than simply a mere acquaintance. Remember, you go to France to be of use to me.'' The king reached over and took her chin in his hand. "You really are beautiful, madame. I think there is much a man might dare for you, and though you blush most becomingly at my words, you are nonetheless a woman grown. You have no maidenhead to protect. If the thought of taking a lover is unpleasant to you, madame, and perhaps that is a side of your nature you find distasteful, swallow your qualms and remember what you do you do for England, for Greyfaire, and for your most grateful king.'' He loosed his grip upon her chin and smiled his brief smile.

''A year at the most? You swear it?'' The thought of leaving Margaret behind for a year was unbearable.

''At most,'' he promised her, and sensing her concern, continued, ''Lady Margaret will be cared for with kindliness, I assure you. If it will set your heart at ease, I will confide in the queen that you are not the heartless creature you appear, but in truth a gallant and brave Englishwoman who has gone to France to valiantly serve her country in thanks for our generosity toward her. I will explain that the child had been left behind for her own safety, and indeed, that is the truth.''

''Your majesty is most thoughtful,'' Arabella said with wry understatement. ''How will I contact Lord Varden? Will it not seem odd if I seek him out?''

''Tony will seek you out. One exile aiding a beautiful countrywoman will appear most natural to the French, who brazenly claim to appreciate womankind far more than other races,'' the king told her.

''And how will we begin this charade, sire?'' There was little left to discuss, Arabella realized.

''You will run weeping from my closet, madame, cursing my name as you flee through my crowded antechamber which, at this moment, is filled to overflowing with every petitioner, gossip, and sycophant at court. Sir Jasper Keane is undoubtedly there himself right now. I have sent for him to tell him that he may not have Greyfaire, but that the crown has decided to confiscate it. I will then give your Greyfaire men the choice of staying with Sir Jasper or returning home under royal protection. It will take little time for word to travel, madame, as to the cause of your distress. Though disappointed himself, Sir Jasper, I suspect, will ease his own great dissatisfaction by spreading his version of these events and blackening your good name.''

''My daughter? How will Margaret find her way into the royal nursery?'' Arabella was still concerned.

''I shall have the queen send one of her women to St. Mary'.-

in-the-Fields late this afternoon to fetch the child and smuggle her into Sheen."

"So soon?"

"You leave for France tomorrow, madame. I want you gone quickly before one of the more gallant members of my court, moved by your beautiful face, pities your plight and attempts to petition me on your behalf. I will give Sir Jasper several days to gloat, even while he is publicly complaining that I would not give him Greyfaire. The French have spies in my court, and the story will be in France perhaps even before you are, legitimizing your arrival at King Charles's court. Sir Jasper tells me that you are called the 'Spitfire' because of your quick temper. Your behavior will, therefore, seem quite in character."

There was no escape, Arabella realized, from King Henry's will. If she wanted Greyfaire back, then she must go to France. The king had said it plainly. Without Greyfaire she was homeless. How could she care for Margaret under such circumstances? "I have not lied to your grace when I said I am virtually penniless," she told him. "I have but two silver pieces and half a dozen copper coins left to my name. If I am to depart on the morrow, I will need monies now. You have spoken bluntly to me. Now I would be plain with you. I do not mean to give offense, my lord, but it is said that you are close with a coin. You tell me you cannot be lavish with your support, and yet you expect me to travel to France, join the French court, and attract important men that I may gain information useful to England. How am I to attract them, sire, without funds? I have no monies and no clothing. Frenchwomen are known for their elegance of garment. I will be a drab English sparrow, lost in a court of radiant peacocks. If I am to be a fine jewel to tempt your enemies, your grace, then you must fit me into a proper setting," Arabella concluded, looking directly at the king.

"Hmmmmm," Henry Tudor considered, "I had not thought of that, madame, but do you tell me you have no garments but those you wear?"

"I brought but one dress suitable for your court, sire, when I journeyed from the north. My other gowns are barely suitable for traveling."

"Why is that, madame? Was your husband not generous with you?" The king looked thoughtful. "Scotsmen *are* rumored to be penurious."

''Tavis Stewart was most generous, your grace, but as I divorced him, I did not think it right I take anything but the barest essentials. I left the bulk of my wardrobe and jewels at Dunmor, bringing only this one good gown and the oldest of my garments.''

Henry Tudor was astounded. Women, his wife and mother excepted, were a greedy and rapacious lot, he knew; and yet here was this radiant beauty claiming otherwise. Once again he felt a small twinge of guilt in his treatment of Lady Grey, but he thrust it away, for a man could not be a strong king if he allowed a nagging conscience to overrule his good sense. ''You must not appear wealthy, madame, for then the question will arise from whence your wealth comes,'' the king considered. ''Still, you must have decent clothing, I will admit. As I must confide in the queen regarding your child, I shall have to seek her aid in this matter as well.''

''I shall need clothing for my maid as well, your grace,'' Arabella said, feeling braver now. ''Lona must come with me, for no lady of quality, even a poor one, would travel without her servant. I will take several of my own men-at-arms too. I cannot travel unprotected in a foreign land. My own people will never betray me. I need, however, to confide in them the true purpose of my trip to France if I am to retain their loyalty. They are simple men, and they have borne much for my sake. I cannot strain that trust further and keep their unswerving support. Their lips will stay sealed if I ask it.''

The king nodded his agreement. ''An allowance, clothing, and your own people about you,'' he said. ''That should suffice you, should it not?''

''I must have money to transport my horses as well, your grace,'' Arabella told him. ''Do not forget that my people and I will have to travel from the French coast to Paris. I could, of course, send my beasts home, but would it not seem strange that in my mad flight I took the time to act in a logical manner? Besides, I imagine transporting my own horses is probably less expensive than buying new ones in France.'' Arabella was more than well aware of the king's penchant for economy.

''Indeed, yes,'' Henry Tudor agreed. ''You will have an allowance for the horses as well, madame. *Is there anything else?*''

''There remains but the matter of my funds, sire,'' Arabella said sweetly.

"They will be delivered to you by my wife's waiting woman when she comes to fetch your daughter," the king said.

Arabella shook her head. "Nay, your grace, I would have the monies now. If you do not give me enough, I am unable to argue with you, for I have no further excuse for an audience." She did not trust the king's generosity.

"*What, madame?* Would you haggle with me as with a fish monger?" he demanded, outraged.

"I must be certain that what you give me is sufficient, your grace," Arabella said stubbornly. "I am not only responsible for myself in this matter, but for Lona and my men as well. I cannot ask them to come with me into another country unless I know that I have the means by which I may at least feed and shelter them. Remember that once I get to Paris I must find a place for us all to live. It may be some time before I can attract the *proper* suitor. If his nature is not a munificent one, I may still be forced to pay for my own shelter." She smiled mischievously at the king. "Wealthy and powerful men are not always of an extravagant and philanthropic nature. The Scots do not have a monopoly on that sort of behavior, do they now, your grace?"

Henry Tudor looked sharply at the beautiful young woman standing before him. Was she mocking him? Until this moment he had not believed her capable of such real cleverness, but as it was beneath him to argue with her, he walked across the room to an oak cabinet, and pulling open a drawer, pulled out a velvet pouch of coins. Thoughtfully he weighed the bag in his palm for a moment, and then he handed it to her.

Arabella hefted the pouch and then handed it back to the king. " 'Tis not enough," she said bluntly.

Henry Tudor glowered at her. "Madame, your extravagance will beggar me," he snapped.

"Would you have me starve to death before I am able to be of service to you, sire? A bony woman will offer no attractions to a lusty man, and Frenchmen, I am told, like their women pleasing to the eye," she told him boldly.

He reached again into the open drawer of the oak chest, this time drawing out a larger bag, which jingled appreciably with its weight of coins.

Arabella took the pouch from him, and opening it, spilled the gold coins out upon the table, swiftly counting them. "I will also need a bag of silver, and one of coppers as well,'' she told the king. She scooped the gold back into its velvet container even as the king, past arguing with her, drew forth two other bags and handed them to her.

"Are you *now* satisfied, madame?'' he asked her sharply.

Arabella carefully secreted all three pouches upon her person, and looking up at the king, said with a small grin, "I must be certain not to jingle as I hurry through your antechamber cursing you, your grace.''

"Why do I entertain the notion, madame, that that is the part of our little charade that you will enjoy the best?'' he said.

"How astute of your grace,'' Arabella told him in even tones.

"Our business is concluded, madame,'' the king said.

Arabella curtsied at his dismissal and then inquired, "Shall I begin to weep and howl now, sire?''

Henry Tudor nodded, and then started at the piercing shriek she emitted.

"Ohhhhhh! 'Tis not fair, your grace! Ohhhhhh! Where shall I go? What shall I do? How shall I feed my poor daughter?'' Arabella howled.

"You should have thought of that before you left your husband to come on this fool's errand, madame. If you are wise, you will return to Scotland and beg your husband to take you back. If he will not, at least if you are fortunate he may care for the child you have in common,'' the king said in a loud voice. "You have made your own bed, and now you must lie in it.''

"Never!'' Arabella sobbed. "Never will I return to that Scots barbarian! Have mercy, your grace! Have mercy! Give me back Greyfaire!''

"Give a border keep to a woman?'' the king's voice boomed scathingly through the door into the antechamber. "Madame, surely you jest with me. Ah-hah! Hah! Hah! A woman defending a border keep in England's name? What nonsense! Begone, madame! Begone from me this instant!'' The king strode over to his door and flung it wide, sending the several courtiers who had been listening at it scattering across the room. Henry Tudor was hard put not to laugh, which would have undoubtedly caused even more gossip amongst his court, for he was not a man easily given to mirth. "Go back to Scotland where you belong now, madame, and take your brat with you! Greyfaire Keep is no longer yours! *Begone!''*

Arabella paused long enough in the doorway to allow the roomful of people a good look at the tragic figure she wished to portray. Her pale gold hair glistened in the afternoon light coming through the windows. She looked particularly beautiful, very fragile and painfully vulnerable. Turning once more to look at the king, she shouted willfully, "I will not go back to Scotland! *I won't!* You cannot make me!" Then bursting into fulsome tears, she pushed right through the astounded crowd of gentlemen in the king's antechamber, sobbing piteously and bitterly as she went.

She had to hurry, Arabella thought as she went. She was going to begin laughing if she did not make her exit quickly. Her keen eye had already spotted Sir Jasper Keane across the room, a smug smile of triumph upon his handsome face. She suddenly realized that Jasper Keane was becoming jowly with too-good living. His handsome visage had begun to coarsen, and he would definitely run to fat with age. What had she ever seen in him? What had Rowena ever seen in him?

She was almost to the door on the far side of the room when she remembered, and turning a final time, she half sobbed, half shouted at the king, "Damn you, Henry Tudor! Damn you for the usurping devil you are, and damn you as well, Jasper Keane!" Then she fixed her gaze upon the rest of the chamber and said in clear and poignant tones, "What help is there for any of you here, my lords, when this king whom you have taken to yourselves would rob a helpless woman of her patrimony?" More tears filled her eyes and spilled down her beautiful face, drawing sympathetic signs from several. "What am I to do?" she whispered pathetically. Then turning, she was gone from them.

There! she thought, as she hurried out into the courtyard to find her horse. *That* would certainly set tongues to wagging! Particularly as she knew Sir Jasper Keane would, in an effort to appear even more important than he actually was, add to the story his own version of the events that brought them to today's little drama. What a shame women did not go on the stage. She had been quite convincing, she believed. She had even seen a few looks of pity cast her way.

Arabella mounted her horse and rode away from Sheen at a brisk trot, returning to St. Mary's-in-the-Fields convent, where she gathered her people together. Shepherding them out into the orchards where they would not be overheard, she told them of her interview with the king. FitzWalter was angry.

"King or no, Henry Tudor is wrong to ask such a thing of you, my lady!"

Her men-at-arms murmured their assent, but Arabella held up her hand to still their complaints.

"What other choice have I, FitzWalter? You know there is none if Greyfaire is to be saved from strangers," she told him.

"What could the king do if we merely returned home and held the keep against him?" FitzWalter demanded.

Arabella shook her head. "I am no traitor, old friend, and neither are any of you. To defy the king would be to commit treason. There is no choice but to do the king's will. Lona, FitzWalter, I will want you and six of the men to accompany me to France. The rest of you will go home and reassure our people that I have not truly deserted them. You cannot, however, tell them the truth of the matter lest you compromise my value to the king, and he, in a fit of pique, deny me Greyfaire after all. Rowan FitzWalter will continue to be in charge of the defense of Greyfaire. The king, I imagine, will see to the rest, as he is pretending to confiscate the keep from the Greys. Decide among yourselves who is to go, but I will take none who has a wife, save FitzWalter, for we are likely to be gone a full year."

She moved away, walking through the orchard in an effort to calm her distress over her daughter's imminent departure. Perhaps she had been wrong to bring Margaret with her to England. Perhaps she should have regained her family's rights to Greyfaire first, and then returned to Scotland for Margaret. She had stolen Margaret from her father, from her grandparents, from her native land. Now England's king was taking Margaret's mother from her. She would be placed in a strange nursery, alone, with people she did not know. What if she cried in the night? Would someone hurry to comfort her, or would they leave Margaret to weep alone and frightened in the dark? Arabella suddenly realized that she was crying, the tears slipping hot and fast down her face. "Oh, holy Mother," she whispered, "what have I done?"

" 'Tis a fine time to be asking that, my lady," Lona said, joining her. "Margaret will be all right. She's healthy, and like her parents, adventurous. Mark my words, m'lady, she'll enjoy her time in the royal nursery, and the queen will see there is no unkindness done to her.''

"How do you know it is Margaret I weep for?" Arabella demanded, not a little aggravated to be so transparent.

"Greyfaire is yours again, 'Bella, so you cannot weep for it; and you only weep for the earl in the night when you think I'm asleep and can't hear you," Lona said matter-of-factly. "So 'tis your child you break your heart over, for you are a good mother, even if you were not the best of wives.''

"What do you mean I was not a good wife?" Arabella demanded, outraged by Lona's searing honesty. "How dare you speak to me so!''

" 'Tis true you are the lady of Greyfaire, and I but one of FitzWalter's lasses,'' Lona said quietly, "but the difference in our births has never before lessened our friendship, 'Bella. I have always spoken plainly to you, and I always will. The earl loves you with his whole heart despite your odd beginnings, but you always put Greyfaire ahead of everything else, including your own heart. I think you a fool for it, and I think even you have begun to question the wisdom of your actions. Your arrogant pride will drive you to France, and God only knows what fate awaits us there. If you could but swallow that pride and return to Scotland, the earl would, I know, pardon you and take you back. Forgive me if I offend you, my lady. You may send me home if you so choose, but I cannot keep silent any longer.''

Arabella stood stock-still as Lona's words assaulted her. In one sense Lona was right, and Arabella knew it; but on the other hand she was wrong. Lona could not possibly understand the ties that bound her to Greyfaire Keep. "I will not send you home, Lona," she told her servant and friend quietly. "Though your words wound me, I would not have you mouth lies in an effort to please me. I value your friendship far too much, even if we cannot agree on this matter.''

"Do you love the earl?" Lona said.

"Aye, I think I do, though I try to deny it to myself; but there is no going back, Lona. Disabuse yourself of any such notion. If you think my pride great, the Stewart pride is greater yet. I have dealt Tavis Stewart's dignity a mortal blow, and he will never forgive me." Her light green eyes filled with tears and she turned away from Lona in an effort to hide her sadness.

Lona's own eyes grew moist with sympathy, but before either of them might indulge themselves in a good cry, FitzWalter joined them.

"The matter of the men is settled, my lady, but eight of the lads, including the young Scot, will go with us. I realized your funds are less than generous, but these men need little to survive. The others will leave at first light for Greyfaire."

Arabella nodded and said sadly, "Would that we might go with them."

"We must fetch little Lady Margaret," Lona said. "You must prepare her for this separation. What we will do about her clothing I do not know, for we brought little, and she must remain with the court for many months."

"There is an open market in the nearby village, and today is market day," FitzWalter said to Arabella. "Give Lona some coins, and I will send her with one of the men to see if she can find any clothing for the child."

"Make certain it is clean and free from vermin," Arabella instructed her servant, giving her a silver piece and several coppers.

Lona hurried off, and FitzWalter, after appointing one of his men to accompany her, returned to Arabella's side.

"You're certain that you wish to do this," he asked, and when she nodded, he said, "What of Sir Jasper?"

"The king will refuse his request for Greyfaire, tell him he is confiscating it, and send him packing back to Northby," Arabella told her captain.

"What of our good Greyfaire lads?"

"The king will offer them the choice of returning home or remaining in Sir Jasper's service. It is the same choice we would have offered them."

"Aye," he agreed, " 'tis fair."

"Mama! Mama!" Lady Margaret Stewart came running through the orchard on fat little legs, her short skirts flying.

Arabella's mouth trembled, but FitzWalter admonished her sharply.

"You must be brave for the wee lass's sake, my lady," and Arabella nodded, quickly brushing away an errant tear.

"Ahh, poppet," she said, lifting her daughter up into her arms and kissing the child's neck, "where have you been?"

"Cook gave me an apple," replied Margaret, "and the old lady says I may have a kitten." She then popped her thumb in her mouth, the effort of her vast communication having exhausted her. Her eyes were heavy with a sudden need for sleep.

"Stay here with her beneath the trees," FitzWalter suggested. "There is time enough to tell her, my lady, when the queen's woman arrives. The less time she has to ponder the situation, the better it will be."

Taking his advice, Arabella laid her now half-sleeping daughter upon the sweet grass beneath the apple trees and sat next to her. Margaret was quickly asleep as her mother watched over her, memorizing every little nuance of her sweetly plump baby's face. The child had dark hair like her father, and it curled damply over her head and at the nape of her neck. Soft dark eyelashes spread themselves like small silken fans across her pink cheeks. Margaret's eyes, when revealed, were the lovely blue of Arabella's mother. She was altogether a most pleasing child to look upon, with plump and dimpled limbs and natural grace. The thought that she must leave this small creature behind was breaking her mother's heart, but Arabella knew that the king was actually wise in his judgment that the little girl remain in England. Margaret made her vulnerable, and Arabella knew she could not be vulnerable in this dangerous game she was to play in France for England. Reason told her that Margaret would be safe and well cared for in the royal nurseries. Her mother's heart resisted it all. She dozed, her hand protectively upon her daughter, only to be awakened by Lona's voice calling her.

"My lady. My lady."

Arabella's eyes opened and focused slowly.

"I have found some suitable garments for Lady Margaret," Lona said, "and I have packed everything in anticipation of her departure. The queen's lady is here and awaits your pleasure."

Arabella scrambled to her feet, careful not to awaken her sleeping child. "Give me a few minutes with the lady," she instructed Lona, "and then bring Margaret to us." She hurried away through the orchards and back to the convent guest house, where a cloaked woman awaited her in the dayroom. As the lady threw back the hood to her cape Arabella gasped and curtsied low. "Your grace!" she said, surprised.

The queen laughed softly. "The king explained to me that you have volunteered to go to France and aid our friend Lord Varden in return for his majesty's kindness to you. I think you wonderfully brave, Lady Grey! I should not have the courage for such a venture. When he told me that you feared to take your little girl along, and asked that we look after her, I knew you to be a good and caring mother. He asked that I send one of my women to fetch the child, but I could not allow that, Lady Grey. I knew that you would rest more easily if we spoke together as one mother to another. I give you my word that Lady Margaret Stewart will be cared for even as my own son, Arthur, and this new child I will birth before year's end. I am the eldest of my siblings, and like my mother I involve myself in the daily running of my nursery. I will see Margaret almost every day, and I promise to love and cuddle her even as you would. I will not let her forget her brave mama, I promise you."

"Madame . . ." Arabella was rendered almost speechless, and she burst into tears.

"Oh dear!" the queen said nervously. "I did not mean to distress you, Lady Grey. I only meant to help."

Arabella quickly regained control of her emotions, for she did not wish to offend the young Elizabeth of York. "Madame, I am indeed overwhelmed by your kindness! If I weep, it is because it is so hard to leave my little one."

"Oh, of course," the queen said earnestly, her own lovely blue eyes filling with sympathetic tears. "I hate it when we travel from place to place in the warm seasons and my son must be left behind."

"My lady." Lona was entering the dayroom carrying Margaret, who now rested, was bright-eyed and alert.

"Oh, what a beautiful little girl!" the queen cried. Her hand went to her belly. "Though I know I must give England more sons, I do hope this babe is a daughter."

Lona's eyes grew round with recognition, but she wisely remained silent.

"Margaret," Arabella said, taking her child from her servant,

"I must go away for a little while, and you are to stay with this kind lady. She has a little boy your age, and a new baby to come."

Margaret looked at the queen, who smiled at her. "Pretty lady," Margaret said. "I take my kitten!"

"Oh, Margaret, I do not know," Arabella said.

"Of course she may take her kitten," the queen agreed, smiling again at Margaret.

"We go now," Margaret said. "Lona, get Mittens!"

Arabella nodded, and Lona ran to fetch the little gray cat with the two white front paws that Mother Mary Bede had given to Margaret.

"Get down," Margaret said, squirming impatiently.

"Can I not give you a farewell hug and a kiss?" Arabella laughed, squeezing her daughter lovingly and kissing her pink cheek.

"Down!" Margaret demanded.

The queen chuckled. "She is like her mother, I think."

"And her father too," Arabella admitted. "There is much that is Scot in Margaret, I believe," she said, reluctantly placing her daughter upon the floor even as Lona returned to put Mittens in the little girl's arms.

Margaret slipped a trusting hand into the queen's hand, and looking up at her, said, "We go now!"

"Bid your mother a sweet farewell, Lady Margaret Stewart," the queen said in kindly, but firm tones.

Margaret half turned and curtsied to her mother. "Farewell, Mama," she said brightly. "I go now with pretty lady."

Arabella knelt before her daughter. "You must call the pretty lady, 'your grace,' Margaret."

"Your grace," Margaret parroted.

"Very good," Arabella said, and then she took the little girl's face in her two hands. "I love you, my child. Do not forget that, and do not forget me. I will come back to fetch you, and we will go home to Greyfaire soon. God protect you, my Margaret, and keep you safe until we meet again." Arabella kissed her daughter a final time.

Margaret smiled. "Farewell, Mama," she said again, and then turning, trotted off with the queen without a backward glance.

Arabella remained kneeling, feeling the very heart drain out of her, but Lona said in practical tones, " 'Tis always that way with little ones who know they are loved. They are never afraid to do something new. She'll be safe, 'Bella. Imagine the queen herself coming to fetch our Margaret! She's a great lady, our young queen."

Chapter 17

F<i>rance.</i> Its coastline glowed distinct through the pearlescent haze of dawn. Arabella gazed upon it with a sense of disbelief. Only yesterday she had been in England, but fair skies, a brisk wind, and swift seas had transported her from Dover to Calais in less than a day. Calais, of course, had been in English hands since the Battle of Crécy in 1346. It had been captured by the third King Edward after a siege that had lasted almost a year. It was from here she would set off for Paris, and although they had brought their own horses, Arabella intended purchasing a small carriage and animals to draw it. Even if she must play the poor exile, she would do it with the kind of elegance she knew the French would appreciate. Though she spoke excellent French, and she knew FitzWalter had a knowledge of the language, it would not do for her to bargain for her vehicle and the horses. Better they land at Calais where they could do business with their own kind.

By coincidence the captain of their vessel had a brother-in-law who, he said, could help them, and upon landing they were directed to the inn of the Six Burghers, which was owned by that worthy gentleman. FitzWalter had polished his cuirass until it shown brightly, and he wore a helmet of the same metal upon his head. His men were equally impressive, despite their simple breast plates of leather. Riding up to the inn with their lady, they were immediately recognized for gentry, and several stablemen hurried out to help with the horses.

"Where is your master?" FitzWalter demanded of one of the grooms. "Fetch him at once!"

As the man hurried off, FitzWalter winked at Arabella in conspiratorial fashion.

The innkeeper, a large, tall man with a distinct limp, came forth to greet them. "My lady, welcome, and how may I be of service to you?" he said.

"I wish to purchase a coach and horses," Arabella said. "I

have been told by Master Dennis of the *Mermaid* that you have such equipages for sale.''

''Aye, my lady, I do,'' the innkeeper said politely. ''They are not new vehicles, of course, but serviceable.'' As he spoke he was mentally assessing the worth of this young noblewoman. A rich woman would have traveled with her own carriage and horses. A poor woman would not even be speaking with him. The only question remaining was how much he might squeeze from this lady.

''You will have my mistress and her maid escorted to a private room where they may refresh themselves in peace,'' FitzWalter said sternly, guessing the innkeeper's thoughts. ''You and I will conclude this business between us.''

''Certainly, Captain,'' the innkeeper said, bowing just slightly. ''Marie!'' he shouted at a serving wench. ''Take m'lady and her servant to the Rose Room at once.''

The buxom serving girl hurried over and, with a bow, invited Arabella and Lona to follow her into the busy inn. Several of the men leered invitingly in her direction and were not discouraged, to their delight. The two Englishwomen were taken to a small, pretty room, and upon entering, Arabella was hard pressed to decide why it was called the Rose Room. Then she looked through one of the chamber's windows and saw a rose garden beyond. Marie brought them a basin of scented warm water and linen towels with which to dry themselves, and then scampered out, to return a few moments later with a tureen of rabbit stew, a newly baked cottage loaf, a crock of sweet butter, a wedge of Brie, a bowl of lovely red-black cherries, and a pitcher of sweet white wine.

''Allow me to serve you, m'lady,'' she said. ''You must be ravenous. The sea air can make one hungry when you are not used to it.''

''Sit down, Lona,'' Arabella instructed her servant. ''There is no need for us to stand on ceremony here. Marie, we will serve ourselves. Please see that my captain and my men are fed and the horses watered.''

The serving girl curtsied and skipped off.

They were hungry, but still they ate slowly, savoring the well-prepared meal. The stew was rich with small onions and carrots that swam in a tasty herb-flavored gravy; the bread was crusty on the outside, but soft and chewy in its interior. When they had almost finished, FitzWalter joined them.

"I've concluded the bargain with our innkeeper friend, Master Bartholomew," he said. " 'Tis a small coach that should attract neither robbers nor attention. Just the sort of vehicle a poor but proud young noblewoman would have. The innkeeper was eager to part with it, for 'tis not large enough to suit most people, and he's had it hanging about for some time now, I gather. The interior is surprisingly luxurious, if a trifle worn."

"How many horses did you buy?" Arabella asked.

"Three," FitzWalter said. "Lona's gelding will make the fourth. Since she'll not be riding him if she's riding in the coach, it seemed a pity to waste the coin. Your mare can be tied behind to follow, m'lady."

"Have you eaten?"

"Aye." He nodded.

"Then give us but a few minutes to attend to ourselves, and we shall be on our way," Arabella said.

"I've hired a young man to drive us to Paris," FitzWalter told her.

"Was that wise?"

"Master Bartholomew tells me the roads in France are as safe as any," FitzWalter said dryly, "which means we should get through to Paris without losing our possessions or being murdered, if we are lucky, my lady. I'd rather have all our men free to concentrate upon defense. The lad I've hired knows the roads well and is going up to Paris to see his married sister, who has just had her first child. The innkeeper assures me he can handle the carriage and is trustworthy. If he is not, I have promised Master Bartholomew that I will return to Calais to wreak a wee bit of havoc upon his corpulent person."

Arabella laughed. "I trust he took you seriously," she teased.

"You have five minutes, my lady," FitzWalter told her.

It took them over a week to reach Paris, rising early, traveling the entire day long with brief stops to rest the horses. As it was June, the sun did not set until late, and until the twilight faded, it was still possible to navigate the coach along the bumpy, dusty roads. The inns in which they stayed were barely habitable places, several of which did not even have suitable accommodations for a lady of rank, and so Arabella was forced to sleep in the hayloft of the inn's stables, for FitzWalter would not allow his mistress to associate with common travelers.

When at last they reached Paris, they put up at an inn recommended by their host in Calais, Les Deux Reines, whose owner, Monsieur Reynaud, welcomed them warmly. Upon learning that the English lady would need a house, the French innkeeper happily informed them that, by chance, he owned a charming small stone house on the Seine, just south of the city, that he believed madame would adore.

"I can see," he said, "that madame is not used to living in a city, and frankly, madame, city living is not healthy. One must be born and bred to it in order to properly survive. This petite maison will be just to madame's taste, I assure you. It is well-furnished, and the rent is most reasonable."

"We will talk," FitzWalter growled, but Monsieur Reynaud was not in the least intimidated by the big Englishman.

The two men argued back and forth for over an hour, and finally the bargain was struck. Arabella would take possession of the house on the morrow. FitzWalter refused to pay Monsieur Reynaud his year's rent, however, until they had seen the house.

"I will send my serving wenches to make certain that the house is aired and dusted," Monsieur Reynaud purred charmingly. "Madame will be most happy at Maison Riviere, I promise it."

On the following morning they rode to Maison Riviere and discovered to their surprise that Monsieur Reynaud had not exaggerated in the least the virtues of his property. The small stone house had two stories and an attic, as well as a cellar which was fairly dry despite the house's proximity to the river Seine. Mounting the steps to the house, they entered into a small hallway. The main floor of the building consisted of four rooms. The cellar beneath, which was high, contained the kitchens, a buttery, a scullery, and a room for storing wines. The second floor of the building held the sleeping chambers, and the attics above would house several men-at-arms.

Maison Riviere was well-aired and clean. It was furnished in worn, but nicely polished oak furniture. There was not a great deal of it, but enough to give the impression that Arabella was struggling to keep up appearances. There was even a small, if overgrown, garden facing the riverside, and someone had gone to the trouble of gathering a bunch of flowers which they had placed in an earthenware pitcher with a slightly cracked lip. A scrawny white cat marked with several black patches was in firm possession of the kitchen stoop.

"Feed him," Arabella ordered. "He will keep the mice away."

"Madame is pleased, then?" Monsieur Reynaud inquired solicitously.

" 'Twill do," she answered him shortly.

"Madame will need servants," the innkeeper said.

"Madame has little with which to pay servants, monsieur," Arabella said with a small smile that set the innkeeper's heart to racing.

"A woman to cook, a girl or two to clean from the village nearby, madame. Give them a few coppers a month, a place to sleep, their food, and they will be happy," he told her. "I must assume a lady of madame's rank will go to court. Soon she will find new friends. She will want to entertain," he added slyly.

"He's right," FitzWalter said softly at her shoulder.

"I know," Arabella replied in English, "but I must first count our funds to see what we can afford."

"Tell our new landlord to send the women around this afternoon, my lady. We must have a cook at least."

"You will send me several women from which I may choose my servants this afternoon, Monsieur Reynaud," Arabella instructed him.

The innkeeper bowed and departed.

FitzWalter assigned the eight men-at-arms to their new duties. Two would serve in the house and share a room in the attic. Two others would reside in a single-room cottage at the back of the garden by the river. FitzWalter would make his bed in a small chamber on the second floor of the house with Fergus Mac-Michael; the rest of the men would bed down in the little stable belonging to the house and Lona would sleep on a trundle in her mistress's room.

Monsieur Reynaud had left a basket of food for them so they would not go hungry until the cook was chosen from the candidates he was sending. Shortly after the noon hour, however, a great, gaunt woman, accompanied by two younger versions of herself, arrived at the door of Maison Riviere and announced, "I am Barbe, and these are my daughters, Avice and Lanette, madame. Monsieur Reynaud has sent us to serve you. Whatever wages you would pay us we will accept gladly, for I am widowed, and my daughters and I must support ourselves. Monsieur Reynaud says you would not be unfair.''

Then before Arabella might protest, Barbe, her daughters following in her wake, moved past her and, without another word, found their way to the kitchens. Within minutes they had the fires going and Barbe was directing the two men-at-arms assigned to the house by FitzWalter to fetch her water from the house's well and bring her more firewood. As the big woman spoke no English and the Greyfaire men no French, her methods of communication were somewhat comical, though successful. To Arabella's amazement, the cook also set about to teach them two simple words.

"C'est l'eau!" she told them when they had brought her water, and she plunged her big reddened hand into the bucket, bringing it up and drizzling the liquid through her sausagelike fingers. *"L'eau!"* she said a second time for emphasis, and then cocked her head at them.

The two young men looked at her, puzzled, and then Lona, catching on, said, ''It must be the French word for water. Repeat her words, you two dimwits! She's trying to teach you.'' Lona swished her own hand about in the bucket. *"L'eau,"* she said, and the men echoed her.

Barbe grinned broadly. *"Bon!"* she said, obviously pleased, and pointed to the firewood they had also brought. *"Bois de chauffage,"* she pronounced slowly.

''Firewood!'' Lona said excitedly. *"Bois de chauffage* is firewood!''

"Bon!" came the reply. *"Barbe."* The cook pointed to herself and looked to the others.

''Lona,'' Lona said, her fingers touching her own chest, and then she pointed to her two companions in turn. ''Will. John,'' she told the cook.

''Weel. Jean,'' Barbe said, grinning broadly at the two.

''I am obviously not going to be given a choice in the matter,'' Arabella said laughingly. ''I only hope she can cook as well as she can teach you all the French tongue.''

''She probably can,'' FitzWalter said. ''Our wily landlord has so far been honest with us.''

''What am I to pay her?'' Arabella wondered aloud.

''I'll take care of it,'' FitzWalter said. ''I'll see if they plan on living here, in which case they can sleep in the room off the kitchen. The fireplace backs up to it, and it should be warm in winter.''

Arabella nodded and left everything to FitzWalter, realizing even as she returned to the small salon on the main floor of the house how fortunate she was to have this man in her service. Without him, she would have faltered a hundred times, for FitzWalter obviously knew the world beyond Greyfaire, and she, but for her time in Scotland, did not.

In a day or two she would have to consider how she might go about joining the French court. The French king, Charles VIII, was just nineteen years old and had been king since his father's death six years before. Intellectually, he was considered backward and slow, and so his father had given him a regent in the person of his brilliant eldest sister, Anne of Beaujeu, who was married to Pierre de Bourbon. Charles VIII's first cousin and heir-presumptive, Louis, the Duc d'Orléans, was furious. Wed to another of Charles's elder sisters, Jeanne de Valois, he feared that the Bourbons would usurp his position as lieutenant general of the kingdom. He was also in love with his sister-in-law Anne, an open secret known to everyone in France.

Louis rashly tried to have his marriage to Jeanne de Valois put aside, citing his wife's physical imperfections. Jeanne, a charming and intelligent woman, was a hunchback with a pronounced limp. Foolishly, he spoke publicly of his love for Anne of Beaujeu, and that lady, to whom duty and honor meant more than passion, ordered her bold brother-in-law's arrest. Warned, Louis fled to Brittany, a grave error in French eyes, as Brittany's duke was a thorn in France's side.

A number of noblemen of consequence allied themselves to the Duc d'Orléans, but Anne of Beaujeu would not yield an inch. Indeed, she raised an army of twelve thousand men under the leadership of Louis de la Tremoille and defeated the rebels in July of 1488. Duc Louis was taken prisoner and incarcerated in the château at Lusignan. At first he was kept alive on only bread and water, his captors disregarding his high rank. His wife, the good Jeanne, intervened on his behalf, but although his diet was changed to a more humane one, he remained imprisoned. Anne continued to rule France in her brother's name, for he, it was thought, was not yet ready to rule alone.

Charles VIII was briefly in residence in Paris at his Hotel de

Valois. With the summer upon them he would soon be returning to his favorite home, the château at Amboise. Unversed in the protocol of court life, Arabella silently cursed Henry Tudor. How in the name of heaven was she supposed to join the French court? If she could not decide on some clever scheme to accomplish this feat, she would be useless to the English king and would lose Greyfaire. Her dilemma was solved for her with the arrival of a letter.

Astounded that anyone in Paris should send her a message, Arabella broke the seal and unrolled the parchment. As her eyes flew over the words, she felt relief pouring through her.

> *Madame. It has come to my attention that another victim of Henry Tudor's rapacious greed has found her way to Paris. I would be honored if you would be my guest at a small fete that the king is giving on Midsummer's Eve at the Hotel de Valois. My coach will call for you at four.*

The missive was signed, Anthony Varden.

"Who is it from?" FitzWalter demanded.

"Lord Varden," Arabella replied. No further explanation was necessary, as FitzWalter knew who Anthony Varden was. "He is sending his coach for me on Midsummer's Eve. We are to attend a fete given by the king."

FitzWalter nodded and returned to polishing his sword, but Lona began to fuss.

"That's but three days away, my lady! How am I to alter one of those gowns that the queen brought for you in *that* time?"

"*Lona.*" Arabella spoke a gentle warning.

Lona looked to where Avice was sweeping the salon and shrugged. "She don't know what I'm saying, my lady, when I speak English. Why, my French is far better. I don't think she speaks half a dozen words of English, and *no* surely ain't one of them. The slut has bedded four of the men already, and has her eye on Fergus MacMichael, but if she makes an attempt in that direction, I'll scratch her wicked eyes out!"

Arabella laughed, but FitzWalter cautioned, "Never assume anything, lass. Besides, what if someone were listening at the door who could understand you? They'd wonder why our queen was kind to our lady under the circumstances. In future be more careful, daughter."

"The queen was kind because she felt guilty," Lona said sharply, "and well she should! I'll be more careful in the future though, Da."

On Midsummer's Eve Arabella was ready when Lord Varden's coach called for her. The queen might have been charitable, but she had chosen the gowns she gave Arabella well, with an eye for the most flattering colors. Arabella suspected that the gowns had come from the queen's own wardrobe, for although Elizabeth of York's hair was darker, she was also a blond. She was taller, however, and so the hems of the garments had been raised; and she was slightly stockier than Arabella, though not as ample in the bosom. Clever Lona had recut the bodice using the excess material from the skirts.

Arabella's gown was of sky-blue silk, having a bare shoulder and a low neckline, with tight-fitting sleeves ending at the wrist. The overgown was a brocade shot through with a pale gold metallic thread, almost the same color as Arabella's hair. A gilt leather girdle encircled her hips. From it hung a silver-gilt tussoire that helped to hold up the skirt which had an underskirt of ivory brocade embroidered with gold and small seed pearls. A long train lined in ivory satin added an elegant touch. Her shoes matched her gown, and her jewelry was spare. She wore a simple gilt chain about her neck, from which hung a pear-shaped pearl drop. On her hands she had only her signet ring.

Lona handed her a pair of ivory kidskin gloves embroidered with seed pearls, and a drawstring bag of blue silk containing a pomander even as an elegantly attired gentleman entered the hallway.

"Lady Grey. I am Anthony Varden. Welcome to Paris!" He bowed politely, but the smile he gave her was dazzling.

Arabella was astounded, though she hid her surprise well. That this man should be Henry Tudor's friend stunned her. Unlike the king, who was a somber man, Anthony Varden was obviously a gentleman who enjoyed life to its fullest, a fact that amazed Arabella, considering Lord Varden's physical appearance. Though the nobleman had the face of an angel, he was small of stature—no taller than Arabella herself—and one of his shoulders was just slightly higher than the other. Remembering her manners, she curtsied.

"Merci, my lord. I am indeed grateful for your kindness."

He offered her his arm. "Then, madame, let us depart, for

Midsummer's Eve is upon us and the festivities will soon begin. All of Paris will be celebrating, and it will be hard to get our carriage through the streets as it is.''

Once inside the coach and safely under way, Anthony Varden turned to Arabella, saying, "It is safe to speak here, Lady Grey. My servants are English and loyal beyond all to king and country." He assessed her frankly. "God's bones, I can see why Henry sent you. You are ravishing, madame, and will surely lure several big fish into your nets for us.''

Had it been another man, another time or place, Arabella might have been offended. Instead she laughed weakly. "I think the king mad to have sent me here," she answered Lord Varden. "I have spent most of my life away from cities and courts; and I am no wanton to lure a man.''

Looking even more closely at her, Anthony Varden could see that she was telling the truth. Damn Hal for a fool, he thought, but they would all simply have to make the best of the matter. "I would not want a woman of experience in this matter, Lady Grey," he told her gently. "It is your naiveté that is so alluring. As for the rest, I will guide you. You need fear nothing, for I am your friend and will not desert you.''

"I am not even certain what I am to do, or how I am to act," Arabella admitted nervously. "I am really a country mouse, my lord.''

He smiled. A warm smile that reached all the way to his gray eyes. "Did you not spend some time at the Scots court, my dear?''

"Aye, my lord, I did. My husband was half brother to his majesty, King James III, and is uncle to the current king," she told him, not certain how much he knew of her background. "My former husband," she quickly amended. "We did not, however, spend a great deal of time at court, for Tavis loves his home at Dunmor.''

"The French court," said Lord Varden, "is a sophisticated court, but despite the sophistication, human nature is the same the world over, I have found. Familiarize yourself with its charming, dangerous, and jaded inhabitants. In particular I would have you be aware of Adrian Morlaix, the Duc de Lambour. He is close with both the Beaujeu faction at court and the young king himself. 'Tis a rare feat balancing between those two. He is privy, I suspect, to certain information that would be of use to King Henry.''

"How will I know him, my lord?''

"He will seek you out sooner than later, my dear, for the Duc de Lambour is a great connoisseur of beautiful women. As you are new to court, *and* beautiful, you will be eagerly sought out by the gentlemen. I would suggest you be chaste with them all. Most will eventually fall away, but Adrian Morlaix will not. The challenge your virtue presents will prove totally irresistible to him.''

"And shall I eventually succumb to him, my lord?'' Arabella said softly. For some reason she felt close to tears.

Anthony Varden could see the moisture shining in her eyes, and he again silently damned his Tudor friend. "That must be your choice, and yours alone, Arabella Grey. It very well may be that you can play the game and win it without surrendering your chastity. But highborn women who take lovers are never ostracized here, so if it must come to that, you need not distress yourself unnecessarily. Besides, a woman as beautiful as yourself surely cannot live without love. To entrap the Duc de Lambour in Cupid's snare would make you a *succès fou*, my dear, I assure you.''

"Does he not like women, then? Is he married?'' Arabella inquired curiously.

Anthony Varden laughed. "Oh, Adrian Morlaix likes women very much, I assure you; and aye, he has a wife. A mousey little thing of a surprisingly robust nature, who dutifully presents him with a child every other year. He keeps her away from the court, although I did see her once several years ago, when they first wed. She and their children live in a large château in Normandy which the duc visits, but only often enough to get another child on her. Adrian stays with the court most of the time, acquiring and discarding mistresses with shameful rapidity.''

"He sounds a most dreadful man,'' Arabella said.

"But he is not,'' Lord Varden assured her. "He is charming, witty, and surprisingly kind, but he does bore easily.''

"And yet you expect me to intrigue him so that he will bare his innermost thoughts to me? My lord, I fear we are all doomed to disappointment, for if the elegant and sophisticated beauties of the French court cannot hold the Duc de Lambour's interest, how on earth do you think I can?''

"My dear madame," her companion said, "have you no serious idea as to your beauty, and how that beauty can be used to ensorcel a man?" He chuckled. "If you are truly innocent of the wiles you may employ, I shall advise you. Simply, but sweetly, refuse all offers of a licentious nature until he sincerely begs. Be exactly what you are, and you will, I promise you, succeed beyond our wildest dreams."

The carriage was drawing to a stop.

"You will not leave me?" Arabella felt a trifle panicky.

"I will be at your side the entire evening, my dear, although I imagine my behavior will disappoint the many who will see and covet you. I shall make it clear, however, from the start that we are not lovers, although I regret the fact. I am simply a sympathetic countryman."

The coach came to a full stop and a footman leapt down to open the door and hand them both out. About them were other carriages and a swirl of elegantly-garbed people within the courtyard of the Hotel de Valois, which was built about a quadrangle, one end of which opened onto the street, and the other end of which opened into a garden. Lord Varden offered Arabella his arm, and they began to thread their way through the crowd. He nodded and bowed as they went to many of their fellow guests, whose eyes widened with speculation at the beautiful woman on his arm.

"There is the regent, the Duchesse de Bourbon," he murmured low to Arabella, tilting his head just slightly to his left. "Be brave, my dear, for I am about to introduce you." He stopped before the duchesse and swept her a bow as Arabella curtsied low. "Bonjour to you, madame la duchesse," Lord Varden said. "May I present my fellow countrywoman and fellow exile, Lady Arabella Grey?"

"You have left England of your own free will, madame?" the regent inquired.

"I have left England because that miser who calls himself our king has robbed me of my small property, madame la duchesse, and all because I am a woman. He said a mere female could not hold a small keep, and so he stole it from me," Arabella said, her voice bitter.

"And he did not give you another property of the same value in return, madame? Why is this?" Anne of Beaujeu demanded.

"Non, madame la duchesse," Arabella said, "he gave me

nothing in return, for my family, all of whom are dead but for me, were related to our late King Richard.''

"Ahhhhh," the Duchesse de Bourbon replied understandingly. " 'Tis the way of kings, I fear, *ma chère madame*, to wreak their vengeance upon the families of their rivals, but this English king of yours shows a lack of chivalry to disenfranchise a helpless woman with no man to defend her. I wish you better fortune here in France.'' The regent turned away from them to greet others, and dismissed, they strolled about the gardens.

"She is no beauty," Arabella remarked of Anne of Beaujeu, "but she is most elegant.''

"She favors her mother more than her father," Lord Varden said, "but she does have the Valois nose and thick neck. Fortunately, she possesses her mother's sense of style. Charlotte of Savoy was a great lover of luxury and had an excellent eye for fashion.''

"What is King Charles like?" Arabella looked about her for someone who might be France's king.

Lord Varden chuckled. "Charles? Look, my dear, over there. The lad with the flaming red head. *That* is the king.''

"That puny, ill-made boy!" Arabella was astounded, for there was nothing royal about France's king at all. He was short, and yet his legs were too long and spindly-shanked for his torso. His head was far too large for his body, and the globular eyes that stared out at the world were just a trifle nearsighted, giving him the vague appearance of someone who was not particularly bright. He had a large and long hooked nose which came near to touching his upper lip, lips that were thick and wide. His round chin was pierced by a deep cleft. "God's bones, sir, tell me that this king has something to recommend him, for he is surely the ugliest man I have ever seen!" Arabella whispered.

"He has little to recommend him," Anthony Varden said, restraining the laughter, which threatened to well up and burst forth. Lady Grey was most outspoken. "The king is of a nervous temperament. He is hasty and headstrong as well; yet he is a strangely affable young man for it all, my dear, but look! There is the Duc de Lambour just entering the garden. We must contrive to reach the king's presence at almost the same time, that he may get his first look at you," Lord Varden said, suddenly serious.

Arabella turned and her heart beat just a little faster with her nervousness. The gentleman coming through the stone archway from the courtyard was tall and extremely well-favored. He was garbed entirely in crimson, a color that well suited his fair skin and dark hair. He was the height of elegance with his doublet embroidered richly in gold threads, small pearls, and black jets. One leg of his hose was solid red, but the other was striped in black and gold. There were large pearl buttons decorating his sleeves. His girdle was of delicate gold links, and from it hung a pouch called an *escarcelle*, which Arabella knew would contain a knife and a spoon. About his neck he wore a heavier gold chain with a circular pendant upon which was engraved a coat-of-arms; and upon each of his fingers the Duc de Lambour wore a ring. His hair was cut short and close in front of the ears. He was clean-shaven.

Arabella was not even aware as she stared at the duc that Lord Varden was propelling her inexorably toward the king. She almost started visibly when she heard him say, "Your majesty, I would present a fellow exile, my countrywoman, Lady Arabella Grey."

Fortunately, she had the presence of mind to curtsy low, even as the king said in a beautiful voice that was totally at odds with his undistinguished person, "We welcome you to France, madame." A large hand reached out to tip her face up to his. "Why, Anthony, she is as fair as I am ugly," the king noted with a wry laugh. He turned to the Duc de Lambour. "Is she not exquisite, Adrian? Even you who collect beautiful women like butterflies must admit that she is outstandingly beautiful."

Arabella blushed prettily, to the king's delight.

"And modest as well, this petite rose d'Anglaise. How charming to find a woman who can yet blush at a compliment here in my court. Well, Adrian, what do you think of her?"

He had azure-blue eyes, Arabella realized, as the Duc de Lambour looked directly at her. Beautiful light blue eyes the color of a summer's sky. She blushed again at his frank scrutiny.

"A rare beauty indeed, my liege," Adrian Morlaix said quietly.

"You must beware of this rogue, madame," the king playfully warned her. "He is a seducer of beautiful women."

"*Only* beautiful ones, my liege?" Arabella said, and the king laughed heartily.

"She has thorns, this petite rose d'Anglaise!" He almost sounded as if he approved.

"Do not all women have thorns, my liege?" the duc drawled lazily, but he was unable to conceal the flicker of interest in his eyes as he gazed anew upon Arabella. "You are married, madame?"

"I was, once, monseigneur," she answered him, not feeling it necessary to explain further. He would assume, of course, that she was not a virgin, and therefore, fair game.

"Be warned, my lord duc," Anthony Varden said, but half in jest. "Lady Grey is not only my countrywoman, but my distant kinswoman, which is why she came to me for succor. You will have to seek elsewhere for this evening's seduction."

"Dearest Tony," Arabella returned, her hand upon Lord Varden's arm in familiar fashion, "do not fret yourself. I have, in my time, protected my virtue on any number of occasions from 'gentlemen' such as my lord duc. I did not waste my time at King James's court like so many of those Scotswomen who are far too loose with their morals to please me. I am sure that my lord duc recognizes a virtuous woman when he sees one."

"Are you without passion then, madame?" the duc asked her.

Once again Arabella flushed. "My lord!" she said, sounding shocked by his unspoken suggestions.

The Duc de Lambour laughed, however. "No," he said, "you are not without passion, madame. I can see that."

"Adrian," the king smiled at his friend, "you are incorrigible. My confessor says that your company imperils my soul."

"My liege, I should remove myself from your presence altogether if I ever believed that I was truly a danger to you," the duc said. "Besides, your majesty's example of fidelity to your affianced, the lady Margaret of Austria, is an example to us all."

"Not to you, mon ami!" the king chuckled, and then he turned again to Arabella and Lord Varden. "May you be happy in France, madame," he said by way of dismissal, and they moved off back into the crowd of guests. When they were out of hearing, the king said, "The way your eyes follow her, Adrian, I can see Madame Grey is of interest to you."

"Do you think she is really virtuous, my liege, or is it a pose?" the duc wondered aloud. "Either way, aye, I am intrigued. However long it takes, I will make the beauteous petite rose d'Anglaise, as you call her, mine. Certainly such a lovely widow will be in need of comforting sooner or later."

"She is not a widow," the king said softly.

"What!"

"Adrian, you of all people know there is little I do not know about what goes on in my kingdom. They called my father the 'Spider King,' and I am first and foremost the Spider's son, although I would hope I had more charm and a kinder heart than Louis XI. It pleases me to allow my sister and her husband to rule for me at this moment, for they do what I would do, and soon enough I must take up the responsibilities that are mine. For now, however, I am content, but I am also well-informed. Madame Grey divorced her husband, a Scots earl, in an effort to regain her English properties for their child. When the Tudor king refused to return those properties, the lady fled to France, leaving her child behind in the king's care as she could no longer support the child herself. Her husband, I am told, will not have her back now, and as the infant in question is a daughter, it does not matter to him. Fortunately, King Henry's queen is of a charitable nature and accepted the little girl into the royal nurseries.

"Madame Grey has taken a small house on the river just outside the city. She has little if any means, I understand. Eventually she will need either a husband or a noble protector, *mon chère* Adrian. Other than her beauty, she has nothing to recommend her on the marriage market, and marriage, as you well know, is not a matter of beauty. It is a matter of monies, lands, and advantageous alliances for people of our class. La petite rose d'Anglaise will not find a husband amongst the French nobility. Her beauty, however, might be used to entrap some wealthy merchant with a desire for a young and noble wife, but *c'est domage*! To waste such loveliness on some fat burgher."

"One might believe that you were encouraging me in my seductions, my liege," the Duc de Lambour said mischievously.

"Hah!" the king's laughter sounded sharply. "You need no encouragement from me, mon ami. Hein?"

"What kind of a man lets a woman like *that* get away?" the duc said. "I wonder if he misses her."

The king shrugged his shoulders. "It does not matter, mon ami. His loss may be your good fortune *if* the lady can be wooed."

In the weeks that followed, however, it appeared that Arabella could not be enticed from the path of virtue. With Lord Varden, who at first was believed to be her lover, a myth quickly disavowed by the Englishman himself, Arabella traveled to the Loire region, for the king had moved the court to Amboise, his favorite residence, for the summer months. It was Anthony Varden who arranged their shared accommodation, although it was Arabella who, in exchange, brought her servants to oversee the running of the household.

Her association with the late Scots king, James III, and her short time at his court, had strangely, and to her very great surprise, been enough of an exposure to society to assure her success at the French court, where she quickly honed her social skills. She had a good intellect which, coupled with a sharp tongue and a keen eye for observation, soon brought her a reputation as a woman with a quick wit. This engendered her favor with the elders of the court and the women. It was her beauty, nonetheless, that lured the men. Madame Grey was a challenge that no French man could resist. Madame Grey was a virtuous woman.

Wagers began to be placed as to when la petite rose d'Anglaise would succumb to passion, and who would be the fortunate man to overcome her charming, if silly, scruples. The Duc de Lambour was, of course, a heavy favorite, despite Madame Grey's vehement refusals of his overtures d'amour. Adrian Morlaix had never been known before to fail in his objective, although even he could not yet claim having stolen a kiss from the lady in question. To date, no man had.

The entire court watched with delight the whole summer long and into the warm days of early autumn. It was far more interesting than wondering what the English or those who ruled the duchy of Brittany would do next. Would Madame Grey be defeated in this guerre d'amour? Would the

Duc de Lambour grow as tired of the chase as the lady's many other suitors who had now fallen away? What was a poor harvest in several of the northern provinces compared to this? It was all so fascinating!

Chapter 18

What do ye mean she is *gone*?" The Earl of Dunmor's eyes were steely. "Where is Arabella?"

Margery Fleming felt tears beginning to well within her eyes. "She hae left ye, Tavis," she said once again. "She hae divorced ye and returned to England."

"Divorced me?" His jaw dropped.

"Wench was always more trouble than she was worth," Donald Fleming said darkly.

Tavis Stewart rounded on his brother and hit him a blow that sent him flying. *"Shut up, Donald!"* he snarled dangerously. "I want to know the entire truth of this matter." He turned back to Lady Margery. "Mother?"

" 'Tis yer own fault," she began.

"My fault?" The earl looked aggrieved.

"Aye, yer fault!" Angry now, Lady Margery began to shout at her eldest son. "Ye would nae aid her in her attempts to regain her home, Tavis. How would ye feel if Dunmor had been taken from ye?"

"The king wrote to the English," he said defensively.

"Aye, but only after Arabella herself went to Edinburgh to beg him for his help. She felt that ye dinna care, and I truly wonder if ye did. Everything else took precedence in yer life over helping Arabella win back Greyfaire."

"But why divorce me?" he asked, puzzled.

"Without yer aid, or that of yer nephew, what other choice did she hae, ye damned fool? With Jemmie dead, and Jamie king, and ye not in the whit interested, she felt alone. How could she go to King Henry as yer wife, wi out yer support, and ask him to return her property? She hae to be totally free of ye. She hae nae other choice. Yer inaction forced her to it! Do ye think the English would return Greyfaire to an English woman with a Scots husband wi out royal intercession? She needed ye, and she needed yer help, but ye would not gie it to her."

"Yer nephew, however, helped her obtain the divorce," Donald interjected slyly. "I never knew Jamie to be of a charitable nature, Tavis. Do ye nae wonder what she gave him in return for his 'kindness'?" He snickered loudly.

Tavis Stewart went white about the lips. "I'll kill him," he said slowly. "I'll wring his bloody neck!"

"Tavis!" His mother spoke sharply. " 'Tis treason ye mouth. He is yer blood relation, yer brother's son."

"When did that ere stop one Stewart from murdering another?" the earl demanded fiercely.

" 'Twill solve nothing, my lad," Lady Margery said quietly. "Arabella is gone and taken Margaret wi her. That Jamie aided her is of nae importance, and I do not for one minute, Tavis, believe Donald's inferences. Yer brother hae always been of a jealous nature. The question here is, what do ye want to do about it? Do ye want yer wife and child back?"

"She hae made her choice, mother. She hae chosen Greyfaire over me. I wish her happiness of it, but I will go over the border tomorrow and bring my daughter back. *Margaret is mine!*" Tavis Stewart said bitterly.

His mother hit him a blow that staggered him. "Yer a great fool, Tavis Stewart! A great, prideful fool! Arabella rode out from Dunmor wi tears in her eyes. She loves ye!"

"Not enough!"

"Why do ye insist she choose, my son? Why can she nae hae both ye and Greyfaire? She but wanted it as a dowry for Margaret, and such a dowry would hae made the bairn a proper heiress."

"For an English husband," he said.

"The border English are nae different than we border Scots," his mother reminded him, and then her voice softened. "Ye love her, Tavis Stewart. Dinna allow yer pride to overrule yer heart, lest ye regret it in the years to come. Remember, ye need a son."

"There are other women who would be happy to be my wife, mother," he said coldly. "Loyal women."

"Arabella was nae disloyal," Lady Margery said, her voice rising again, and she smashed her fist into his shoulder once more. "This is yer own making, Tavis Stewart, and ye are too stubborn to admit to it. If ye hae one grain of sense in that head of yers, ye'll go over the border tomorrow and fetch Arabella back. Then ye'll remarry her and gie her yer undivided attention to helping her get Greyfaire back. 'Tis nae so great a matter, and I dinna see why ye would allow this terrible thing to happen over something so small.'' She punctuated her speech with a third blow to his arm.

The earl began to laugh as he rubbed his shoulder, for his mother had not been gentle.

''And what,'' she demanded furiously, ''is so damned funny, ye great oaf?''

''I just now realized,'' the earl said, ''how very alike ye and Arabella are, Mother. She hae never been loath to use her fists, my wee spitfire.''

''Then ye'll go and fetch her home?'' his mother said.

''I dinna know, Mother. I must think on it. The lass hae hurt me greatly. Do ye think because I am a man I canna feel heart-sore? She and the bairn are safe at Greyfaire for now, and I must consider well whether I want this hotheaded English lassie back in my life,'' the earl said.

''And who would ye replace her wi?'' Lady Margery said scornfully. ''There's been nae who could please ye until Arabella Grey, but perhaps in yer highland travels for the king ye met some puling wench wi watered milk in her veins instead of a hot blood who would serve to get yer sons on. All cats, I am told, are gray in the dark. Well, did ye?''

''Nay.''

''I thought as much! Go and fetch yer wife, Tavis, lest ye live to regret yer folly. What of Sir Jasper Keane? What if he is at Greyfaire?''

''God help him if he is,'' the earl said with a small smile. ''The man's very life would be in mortal danger if Arabella catches him in her keep, Mother. The lass would disembowel him herself and relish every moment of it.''

''Aye, she would,'' Donald agreed, still rubbing his sore jaw.

''What if Arabella goes south to see King Henry, Tavis? Hae ye considered that?'' his mother goaded him.

''To London?'' the earl said.

''Wherever the court is, and 'tis south, as ye know,'' Lady Margery said. ''Her English king could order her marriage to another in return for Greyfaire. Then where will our Margaret be?''

''How long hae she been gone?'' the earl asked his mother.

''Almost three weeks now,'' came the answer.

"Why did no one inform me?"

"We didna know where ye were, Tavis."

"And as I think on it, Mother, how is it that ye know where my wife went and are privy to her very thoughts?" he wanted to know.

"I probably should nae hae known at all, Tavis, but for chance. I came to Dunmor the day before Arabella's departure to fetch an old cradle that lay in the attics. It was my mother's, and I wanted it for Ailis's new baby. I could see how nervous Arabella was to see me, and then Flora told me that she was planning to leave for England on the morrow, taking wee Margaret wi her. I went to Arabella's apartments and begged her to confide in me, which she finally did. She didna really wish to go, but she did nae know what else to do."

"She might hae waited for me to come home," the earl said.

"Aye!" Donald agreed.

"Shut up, Donald!" his mother snapped, and then turned her full attention again to her eldest offspring. "And what would ye hae done when ye came home, Tavis? Ye dinna need to tell me, for I know and so did Arabella. Ye would hae put her off once again, wheedling and cajoling her and trying to get a son on her in an effort to make her forget Greyfaire."

"But why can she nae forget it?" the earl cried. "From the moment we met, that damned pile of English stones hae come between us! Another man I could contend wi, but Greyfaire is worse than any lover! She is bewitched by it!"

"Why should she forget *Greyfaire*?" Lady Margery demanded. "Could ye forget Dunmor were it taken from ye, Tavis? Should Arabella have numbered her days only from your meeting and put aside her life before then?"

"But I am a man," he said. "I am the Earl of Dunmor and lord of the castle."

"Why should it be any different for Arabella, my son? She was Greyfaire's heiress and lady of the keep. It is a part of her very soul. If ye canna understand that, then ye will never understand her and ye dinna deserve her. Besides, as the last of the Greys, she takes her obligations most seriously. The Greys have been at Greyfaire for several centuries, even as the Stewarts hae been here at Dunmor. Ye could nae expect her to simply desert Greyfaire and leave her people to the tender mercies of Sir Jasper Keane, could ye? A woman who would do such a thing would nae be worthy to be Dunmor's countess." Lady Margery put her hand upon her son's arm. "Go and fetch her home, Tavis," she finished.

"And if she is nae at *Greyfaire*?" he asked.

"Then go south and find her," his mother counseled wisely.

"I must go back to Edinburgh, Mother. Jamie only let me come home to oversee my estates before I return north again," the earl told her.

"If yer going after that wench, then do it, damnit!" Donald said irritably. "Ye dinna owe Jamie Stewart for anything, Tavis. He didna bother to tell ye that yer wife hae divorced ye wi his complicity and returned to England, did he? He can send someone else north. The highland chiefs will gie him difficulties no matter what he does. 'Tis their nature to quarrel wi one another and wi anyone else who crosses their path. They hae always been more trouble to the Stewarts than they were worth, in my opinion. Find yer wife and bring her back, though why ye want the troublesome wench I dinna know. Ye'll nae be content or happy unless ye do. Even I can see it, though it pains me to admit it."

Lady Margery nodded her agreement. "Donald is right," she said, and her eyes twinkled as she continued, "though it surprises me to hear myself say such a thing, for when do we ever agree, Donald, my son, except perhaps in yer choice of a wife? I do approve the Hepburn lass, for she is a good lass and loves ye. I canna understand why, for yer a prickly bear of a man, a surly sort, and that's the truth, but perhaps she sees a different side of ye than the rest of us."

"I'll send a messenger to Jamie on the morrow before I head south," the earl told them. "I'll be long gone before Jamie can tell me nay. He'll nae dare, however, to come between Arabella and me again. Yer right, Mother, when ye complain that I hae nae considered Arabella's feelings in this matter. I see now that if I am to defeat this wee stone keep that my wife loves above all else, then I must help her to regain it. Only then, when it is safe and once more in her firm possession, will it cease to be a rival to me. Only then may we get on wi our lives."

And in the morning, as the Earl of Dunmor's clansman rode north to Edinburgh to seek the king, the earl himself and an armed party of men turned south toward England. At Greyfaire they found Rowan FitzWalter, who, after ascertaining their identity, opened the keep to them, welcoming the Earl of Dunmor with courtesy. Meat and drink were set out in the little hall for them.

"Her ladyship has gone south to seek King Henry," Rowan FitzWalter told the earl before he might even ask. "Wee Maggie is, of course, with her mother. My father and fifteen of our best lads escorted them, and my sister Lona has gone to serve my lady."

The earl had already noted the shabby condition of the keep and of its lands. "What hae happened here, laddie?" he asked Rowan.

"Sir Jasper Keane," Rowan replied bitterly. "The harvests have been poor the last few years, my lord, but Sir Jasper took what little we had without a care for Greyfaire's people. There has been starvation, and several families, on the land for many generations, departed it to seek a better life elsewhere. Sir Jasper stole our strongest and finest men and boys to make up a troop of soldiers that he might impress King Henry. Then blight struck the orchards, killing off most of the older fruit-bearing trees. He did not care. He took what he could, while leaving us to sicken and starve.

"When our lady returned home she filled us with hope, and she set us to repairing the damage Sir Jasper Keane had inflicted upon Greyfaire. She showed us how to cleanse the earth in the orchards of the canker that had killed the trees, and she had us replant seedlings that in several years will bear fruit again. There is no luck for us without a Grey on the land, my lord. The old women said it in the first months that Lady Arabella was gone, and though many scoffed at first, we came to realize that it was true," Rowan finished.

Tavis Stewart nodded at the conclusion of Rowan's tale and felt a bit guilty. Had he not ignored Arabella's pleas, perhaps none of this would have happened. Oh, the orchards would still have gotten canker, for such was a whim of nature, but as for the rest of it . . . together, he and his wife could have prevented much suffering. It was unlikely that Greyfaire would ever recover, but that thought he kept to himself.

God only knew he had been wrong enough times in his life, but looking about him, Tavis Stewart realized that Greyfaire had never been either a rich or a prosperous place. At best they had survived, perhaps more comfortably than other places, but no more than that. What had held it all together was a series of good masters that the Grey lords had been, but the Greys were no more, excepting his wee spitfire. She was going to need his help whether she realized it or not. Arabella was fighting a losing battle with Greyfaire even if she was not quite ready to face the truth, but when she did face it, he wanted to be the one to comfort her. Whatever had happened between them, he loved her. He knew now that his mother had been right when she had told him that he would not want any woman less than Arabella Grey to bear his name or his sons.

The earl chose two of his men to accompany him south, and then instructing his captain to render the keep any help necessary, he told his clansmen to return to Dunmor as soon as possible. Tavis Stewart departed Greyfaire wiser, yet sadder. It pained him to realize now how his wife had suffered the knowledge of Sir Jasper Keane's neglect of Greyfaire; of how she had so desperately tried to help these people she considered her responsibility; and all without his assistance, because he had been too busy going about his own affairs to take but a moment to hear her concerns and to render her his aid. Then he smiled to himself. She was a strong woman for all her small size.

He found the king at his favorite residence of Sheen, and although Henry Tudor was surprised, he granted the Earl of Dunmor an audience. "Do you come on your nephew's business, then, my lord?" he asked even before the earl had straightened himself up from his bow.

"Nay, yer majesty. I seek my wife, whom I am told came south seeking yer aid."

So, Henry Tudor considered, he loves her despite everything. "Lady Grey informed me, my lord, that she had been granted a divorce from you," the king said.

"Aye," the earl admitted, "but I intend remarrying her as soon as I find her. 'Tis a foolish misunderstanding between us that I will correct."

"Lady Grey is in France, my lord, on *my* business," the king told the earl. "That knowledge, of course, I must beg you to keep secret. I but tell you that you do not attempt to commit some foolish act based upon your passion for her."

"And Greyfaire?" the earl asked, knowing that somehow it was involved in this affair, else Arabella would have never left England.

"Do I have your word as a gentleman, my lord, that our conversation today will go no further than this room?" the king demanded.

The earl nodded reluctantly, for he needed to know Arabella's fate.

"The lady agreed to render England service in France in exchange for her keep's return," the king said coldly. "She must serve me a year, and then, *only then*, will I restore her rights to Greyfaire Keep. She is believed to be an exile, and it is thought that I have confiscated her property for myself because of her connection with my late predecessor."

"In other words," Tavis Stewart said evenly, keeping his rising anger under strong control, "ye hae asked my wife to spy for ye?"

Henry Tudor's cold eyes met those of the earl's. "Aye," he said shortly.

"Is my daughter wi her mother?"

"Your daughter is safe in my nurseries, my lord, where she will remain, a bond for her mother's good behavior and usefulness to the crown. When my lady Grey returns home to England," the king replied, "I will release Lady Margaret Stewart into her custody."

The earl nodded slowly. The English king had thought of everything. "Yer a ruthless bastard," he said frankly to Henry Tudor.

"No more than your own king, my lord, but then we are both Celts, are we not? I am a Welshman, for all I wear England's crown. Your king oversaw the patricide of his own father in order to rule, and I—well, there is much I have done to gain my throne that I should as lief forget."

"Jamie did nae kill his father!" Tavis Stewart defended his nephew. "His sorrow over Jemmie's death was so great that he hae a belt of iron links made to wear about his waist that he nae ere forget the incident."

Henry Tudor laughed sharply. "My lord," he said, "it makes no difference whether your king intended his father's death or not. The man was murdered as a direct result of his son's rebellion, *and* King James knows it. His is the responsibility, and that is why he wears a belt of iron about his middle. He has accepted that responsibility as a good king would. Now, you must emulate your own lord and accept the path Lady Grey has taken.''

"It would seem, your majesty, that I hae no choice in the matter, but I would hae my bairn to carry home.''

"You are correct, my lord. You have no choice in the matter at all. As for your child, as I have told you, she is safe and well cared for in my own nurseries. My son Arthur tags after her like a small puppy. He would be devastated to lose her company at this time. Your little one has her mother's charm.'' He smiled a brief, cold smile.

"Ye hae nae right to keep Margaret,'' the earl said, desperately attempting to keep a rein on his temper.

"I have every right, my lord. If I allowed you to take her back to Scotland with you, you would then, I suspect, hurry off to France to fetch your wife back. Not that she would come, for she is most determined to regain her properties. You would, however, distress her needlessly and distract her from her goals. So, my lord, I shall keep your child safe. Lady Grey will remain in France, content in the knowledge that a good performance upon her part will bring her Greyfaire Keep and a reunion with her child in a year's time. You are not a stupid man, and so I am content that you fully understand me and will argue no further with me on this matter,'' the king concluded.

Never had Tavis Stewart felt so close to violence in his entire life. His jaw ached with gritting his teeth, but with superb control he bowed to Henry Tudor, accepting the dismissal with as good a grace as he could. "I thank ye, yer majesty, for yer courtesy in seeing me,'' he said.

The king inclined his head slightly in acknowledgment. "Do not go quite yet, my lord. I have several questions I would ask of you. You have, I assume, been to Greyfaire recently. In what condition did you find the keep? Is it in good repair?''

"The keep itself, aye. The people, however, hae been much abused by Sir Jasper Keane. He took the able-bodied men, leaving the women, the children, and the aged folk to care for the land. The orchards suffered wi blight, and they dinna know what to do until my wife returned. There hae been starvation, and some families hae left. They are more heartened, nonetheless, wi my wife's visit.''

"Who defends the keep?''

"Rowen FitzWalter, the captain's son, for FitzWalter himself is wi Arabella," the earl said.

"Would you advise that I send someone to oversee Greyfaire?" the king said. Then he chuckled. "But asking you that, my lord, is like asking the wolf to shepherd the lambs, isn't it?"

"The English and the Scots are nae at war, yer majesty, and 'tis my nephew's most earnest wish that ye nae be. Ye hae asked me a fair question, sire, and 'twould go against my honor were I to gie ye a less than honest answer," Tavis Stewart said. "Rowen FitzWalter is as capable as any to defend Greyfaire Keep. He was born and raised there. He takes his responsibilities most seriously, for it is hoped that one day when his father is too old to carry out his duties, Rowan will succeed him. If ye would help, though, the people of Greyfaire could use a donation of grain for both themselves and their livestock to get them safely through the winter months. My wife hae given them her permission to take small game, and in the autumn, one deer per family."

"She is a good chatelaine," the king said, his voice brimming with approval. "By addressing what problems she could immediately, she raised their spirits, thereby encouraging them to even greater efforts on her behalf. Greyfaire Keep will soon again be prosperous under her guidance. 'Tis good."

"I do not think that Greyfaire hae ever been really prosperous, yer majesty," the earl told the king. " 'Tis a small estate wi a bleak outlook."

"Then why does she desire it so greatly?" the king wondered aloud.

" 'Tis her home, sire," the earl said simply. "Her heart seems to be there."

"Women are foolish, if necessary, creatures," Henry Tudor said, "but it is fortunate for us that they are, eh, my lord?" He smiled his brief, wintery smile. "You can do me a small service, Tavis Stewart. I would send a clerk north to Greyfaire Keep to evaluate its condition and its needs. I should appreciate it if you would escort him for me. I shall not keep you. You may leave this afternoon."

"As yer majesty wishes," the earl replied. He could hardly refuse England's king so small a favor, particularly as this same king held Lady Margaret Stewart in his keeping. It was also quite obvious that Henry Tudor did not want Tavis Stewart remaining at his court or in England any longer than necessary. By sending this clerk with the Scots, he guaranteed their swift departure.

"We will not keep you any longer," the king said, reverting to a more formal tone.

"Sire." The earl bowed politely a final time and backed from the audience chamber.

He waited in the courtyard at Sheen for less than an hour before a young, tonsured priest joined him, saying that he was the clerk sent by the king.

"I ride well, my lord, and I will not keep you," the priest said.

Resigned to the fact that he would not even be allowed a small glimpse of his daughter, the Earl of Dunmor mounted his stallion, and signaling to his small party, rode from the English court. He had spoken to no one but the king and the king's secretary. He had seen no one, for Henry Tudor had given him an early audience, and few if any courtiers were about. Had they been, they would not have recognized him, although they might have been curious. Now, however, it was as if he had not existed at all for the English court.

If Henry Tudor was foolish enough to believe that he would be satisfied to simply sit back and wait for Arabella to return to England from France, the earl reflected, then he would find he was sadly mistaken. He would not ever endanger their daughter, but Scotland and France were old and strong allies. England and France were not. He had to respect Arabella's duty to Henry Tudor. She had done what any man would have done, he was surprised to realize, to regain her property. She was playing at the game of politics and power, but he wondered if perhaps she was not out of her depth. What could she possibly learn for Henry Tudor that would be of value to him?

More importantly, he suddenly perceived, was *how* she would go about gathering that information. She had neither wealth nor a powerful family or friends helping her. She had but two assets in her favor. Her intelligence, *and her beauty*. It was the latter that concerned him. Did the English king actually expect Arabella to barter herself in her effort to gain information? The dawning realization that that was exactly what Henry Tudor expected sickened him. Arabella was no wanton, but he knew she would do whatever she had to do to regain her property.

God, what a fool he had been! Tavis Stewart thought helplessly. If he had only supported his wife's efforts to regain her
birthright, instead of treating her needs as those of a willful
child. That had been his problem from the start. He had seen
Arabella as a stubborn child, and she was not. She was a strong
woman who would not be gainsaid in a matter in which she
believed herself to be in the right; and who was to say she was
not?

The French were a hot-blooded race. Arabella would be
but helpless prey to some lustful monseigneur. She was
alone and unfamiliar with the ways of the world. No matter
Henry Tudor! He must go to France to protect his wife. *His
wife.* She was no longer his wife in the eyes of the church.
She was a free woman. Free to do as she pleased. Free to
remarry, if some gentleman should take her fancy. *Remarry.*
She could not! Yet what if it suited the English king's plans
that she marry some French monseigneur? Tavis Stewart
bared his teeth in a grimace. He'd kill any man who would
attempt to marry Arabella!

Tavis Stewart arrived home at Dunmor to find his nephew's
personal messenger awaiting him. He was to join the king at
Falklands Palace immediately upon his return. The messenger
had been at Dunmor for over two weeks. With a sigh of resignation, the earl spent one night in his own bed before heading
north. He could not ignore his own king's direct summons.

"Ye took yer damned time," Jamie said in aggrieved tones
when they finally met.

"I only arrived back at Dunmor four days ago, sire," the
earl said.

"Ye were in England. " The king's tone was accusatory.

"Aye. I saw King Henry himself," Tavis Stewart replied.

"Did ye now? And who else did ye see? Were any of those
Scots traitors who fled my justice there fawning over the Tudor
and plotting my demise?"

"I saw no one but the king and his secretary," the earl replied. "I went for one reason, and one alone. *Arabella.* I want
my wife back."

"Yer wife divorced ye, Uncle. Accept it and leave it be. 'Tis
time ye choose another wife."

"Jamie," the earl said quietly, "if ye were nae my king, I
should thrash ye wi'in an inch of yer young life. Why did ye

allow Arabella to divorce me? Nay, ye dinna answer, for I already know."

"Ye do?" James Stewart shifted his feet nervously.

"Aye, I do. The little wench felt wi out yer aid or mine she could nae go to King Henry as a Scots earl's wife requesting the return of her property. So she convinced ye to help her gain a divorce that she might return to England a free woman wi no divided loyalties. Yer a romantic young fool, Jamie, to hae let her cajole ye into such an action, but I forgie ye, nephew. At least ye understood Arabella's distress better than I. I could only see that she was being stubborn."

James Stewart felt a trickle of sweat roll icily down his back in his relief. When his uncle had said "he knew," the king expected that possibly he might end up like several of his kingly ancestors, dead before his time at the hand of a family member. Obviously Tavis knew nothing of his brief idyll with Arabella. The king felt uncomfortably guilty over the incident. His uncle had always been loyal, and more than that, he had worked unceasingly to help quiet the highland lords that Scotland's wounds might be healed, that their country emerge from the medieval mindset that held it back from the progress being made in other lands.

He was king, James Stewart thought ruefully, and yet he had used his power childishly; wielding it to compromise a virtuous woman who needed his help. He felt not just guilty. James Stewart felt ashamed that he had permitted his lust to overrule his kingly honor. He was a man who loved women, but in loving Arabella he had hurt her. He had allowed her to destroy her marriage to his uncle, a man she loved so deeply that she would leave him rather than bring discredit to his name. Would that his moral principles had been as high.

"I want to go to France," his uncle was saying. "Arabella is there."

"What is she doing in France?" the king demanded, astounded.

"Henry Tudor confiscated her property because of her family's relationship with King Richard," the Earl of Dunmor said carefully, remembering his promise to the English king, but regretting that he must dissemble with his own liege. "Having no place in England, and feeling she could not return to Scotland, Arabella fled to France. She is living at the French court, I am told, on what little she has. It cannot be easy for her.''

James Stewart nodded. "Perhaps," he said, "I could see that she was sent a small income, Uncle, until you can get to France.''

" 'Tis kind of ye, Jamie, but wi yer permission I intend leaving almost immediately. There's always a vessel at Leeds sailing for France," the earl said.

"I canna gie ye my permission, Uncle. Not right now. I need ye to go into the highlands once again. I need ye to go to Glenkirk Castle. I have decided to send out ambassadors to several European nations, even as the English are doing. The lord of Glenkirk is the man I want as Scotland's ambassador to a small duchy on the Mediterranean called San Lorenzo. If Scotland is to prosper, we must expand its trade with other lands. I am determined that we will. We will need a haven of safety in the Mediterranean where our ships can replenish their supplies and their water on long voyages. Though the French be our allies, I do not want to be entirely dependent on them. We will also be in competition with them, for I intend that our trade be more than just furs, hides, and salted fish. These we will sell in exchange for luxury goods to be either resold in European markets or here at home.

"Patrick Leslie is a man of great culture, for all he is a highland lord. He is widowed and shows no signs of remarrying at this time. Other than his two children, he has no obligations but to his lands. I shall arrange for his cousin to manage them while he serves me," the king said.

"Is he aware that he is to 'serve' you, nephew?" the earl asked dryly, already knowing the answer, but wanting to hear it from Jamie.

" 'Twill be yer job, Uncle, to convince him that he should," the king told Tavis Stewart. "Did ye know he was one of the few highland chiefs to support me against my late father? I know not why, but I shall certainly ask him when we meet. I require that ye bring Patrick Leslie to me, and 'twill nae be easy, I know. He will take some convincing, for he will be loath to leave his lands. I dinna want to *order* him to me, but I will if I hae nae other choice.

"Go to Glenkirk and try and convince Patrick Leslie to come to me willingly. Take whatever time ye need, wi'in reason, of course. When ye hae been successful, I will send ye to France on royal business that ye may attempt to woo yer wife back. In the meantime, I will see that Arabella does nae lack for anything."

"She'll nae take so much as a groat from us, Jamie, for she is a proud creature, as ye well know," the earl replied.

The king chuckled. "She will game, Uncle, as they all do at the French court. When she does, she will win, I promise ye. Yer lady is also of a practical nature. If she needs funds and wins, she will nae lose her gold in further gaming, but she will put it aside for a rainy day. Ye need hae no fear that Arabella will starve."

"I am nae worried about Arabella starving, Jamie," Tavis Stewart said. "I fear that loneliness may drive her into another man's arms. *That* is my greatest fear, nephew."

"Then put that fear aside, Uncle," the king told him. "Arabella Grey loves ye above all men. Of that I am more certain than any."

"I pray ye be right, Jamie."

So the Earl of Dunmor rode into the highlands to Glenkirk on king's business. He was warmly welcomed by Patrick Leslie, the lord of the castle. For the long weeks of late summer and into the fall, Tavis Stewart remained at Glenkirk; stalking deer in the hills surrounding the castle, fishing for trout and salmon in the icy streams that abounded on the estate, lingering over generous drams of Patrick Leslie's peat-smoked whiskey from the Glenkirk stills during long autumn evenings in the castle's Great Hall, where the Leslies' personal piper played movingly, seeming to know every tune ever composed for the pipes. It was very much a comfortable, bachelorlike existence despite the lord of Glenkirk's two children; a red-haired little girl of ten, named Janet, and a sturdy six-year-old boy who was called Adam.

Broaching the king's business was a tricky matter, but finally one day as they played at golf on Patrick Leslie's small course, Tavis Stewart felt he could wait no longer. The days were growing visibly shorter as winter approached. "Patrick," he began, "my nephew, the king, tells me that ye supported him against his father."

"Aye," Patrick Leslie said shortly. "I felt Jamie hae the right on his side in the matter."

"The king wishes to reward ye for yer loyalty and hae asked me to bring ye to him," the earl told him.

Patrick Leslie shook his dark auburn head. His green-gold eyes were serious when he finally spoke. "I'm nae a man for the court, Tavis, as ye are. I'm a simple highland chief, as my father was before me, and my grandfather before him, and on back into the mists of time. I did what I believed right in the matter between the king and his father. I do not believe I should be rewarded for merely doing my duty."

"Nonetheless, Jamie would hae ye come," the earl told him, thinking that his nephew could use more honest men like this about him. "I am instructed to stay at Glenkirk until ye will agree. As I hae some rather pressing business in France, I hope ye'll quickly change yer mind, my lord."

Patrick Leslie swung his golf club, hitting the ball down the misty greensward. He peered after it, and then apparently satisfied with his shot, said, "I am flattered that the king would do me honor, Tavis, but I'll nae leave Glenkirk. I am nae unacquainted wi kings and their whims. If I go to court, the next thing ye know I'll nae be able to get home, for the king will want some wee favor or other of me even as he does of ye. Surely ye miss Dunmor, man, but can ye get back? Nay, for yer here doing yer nephew a wee favor, and then yer off to France, ye tell me—on royal business, I'm quite certain, though ye hae not said it. Thank ye, but I hae no desire to leave Glenkirk."

"Then I must remain here until I can convince ye otherwise, Patrick," the earl said pleasantly. "Is yer little lass betrothed?"

"Nay, for I'm not of a mind to lose her yet," the lord of Glenkirk answered.

"The king could make a better match for the lass than ye could, I'll wager," Tavis Stewart told him. "Ye could bring her and that braw laddie of yers to court wi ye. They would enjoy it, I've nae a doubt."

"We hae a fine Christmas here at Glenkirk," its lord replied calmly. "If yer determined to remain here, ye should know that. Perhaps ye would like to ask yer wife to join ye."

Tavis Stewart felt despair to the depths of his soul. Patrick

Leslie was going to prove more than merely difficult in this matter, but the earl knew his nephew would not allow him to leave Glenkirk yet. He would have to remain a longer period of time before Jamie could be reasonably convinced that he must issue a royal summons to this highland chief. Patrick Leslie would not be able to avoid a royal summons.

Christmas came and went, as did Twelfth Night. The Earl of Dunmor was finally ready to admit defeat. He had been at Glenkirk for six months and had been unable to move its lord one whit in his resolve to stay exactly where he was. He sent a message to the king, who finally responded with a royal summons for the lord of Glenkirk. There could be no refusal now. Patrick Leslie must attend his king as quickly as possible, *and* he was to bring his two children. This last, Tavis Stewart knew, was so that Patrick would have no excuse for hurrying home before Jamie was quite finished with him.

"After all my hospitality to ye," Patrick Leslie said mournfully, "ye would do this to me?"

"Jamie will hae his way, my friend," the Earl of Dunmor said, "and ye hae best remember that. If ye'd gone when I first invited ye, there would nae hae been this need for a royal summons."

"But the bairns too?"

"They'll hae a good time, man, and 'twill be good for them to see a bit of the world outside of Glenkirk. They'll appreciate it far more when they return than if they knew nothing else."

"May I have a sword, Father?" little Adam Leslie asked his sire. "I would pledge my loyalty and my arms to the king!"

"Silly puppy!" his sister Janet teased. "The king hae no need of a runny-nosed bairn, does he, Father? I, however, am almost of marriageable age. Perhaps Father will find a husband for me at court." She tossed her red-gold curls.

"Hah!" her younger brother mocked. "What man would look at a wench wi no titties, and ye, Mistress High and Mighty, are as flat as the drawbridge!"

"Ohhhhh!" Janet Leslie looked outraged. She charged across the distance that separated her from her brother, a dangerous look in her eye. Adam Leslie, however, was practiced in the art of escaping his sister's wrath, and scampered off, howling with mirth, turning about every few steps to make faces and stick his tongue out at Janet.

The men chuckled at the antics of the two children, who in reality adored one another.

"Well," the earl said, "now that this matter between ye and the king is settled, I'll hae a chance to see my own little lass soon enough."

"Aye," the lord of Glenkirk said sadly, "but it will take us a week or so to prepare for the journey. Then we'll be on our way. Ye'll accompany us, my lord?"

"Aye, 'tis my nephew's wish. I think he fears ye'll nae come, royal summons or nay, if I dinna personally escort ye. So I will. I must get to Leeds anyway if I am to embark to France."

" 'Tis dangerous to cross the waters in the winter," Patrick Leslie noted.

"Aye, but I must go," the earl told him. "I should hae gone months ago, but that ye are a hard man to convince. Still, a few days more or less at this point canna matter, can it?"

But the day before their departure, a fierce winter storm struck Scotland, howling through the highlands with determined and icy ferocity. The snowdrifts were blown high in its wake. It was several weeks before the inhabitants of Glenkirk Castle could possibly leave, for the tracks that passed for roads were blocked with several feet of snow. Only when the first mild winds of March came with their accompanying rains could they finally depart.

Patrick Leslie gazed back at his castle with a look of proprietary pride, but his daughter wept sudden tears. The Earl of Dunmor, seeing her sorrow, said, "What is it, lassie? Dinna be sad, for ye'll enjoy the court, and soon ye'll be safely home again."

Janet Leslie wiped her eyes vigorously with her sleeve and then said low, "I suddenly had the strangest feeling, my lord, that 'twould be a very long time before I see Glenkirk again. But surely that is nonsense!"

"Indeed, lass, it must be. Dinna look back. I never do, for there is nae point in it, ye know. Always look forward, Janet Leslie, for I promise ye the world is a wonderful adventure just awaiting ye!"

❧ Chapter 19

"The Duc de Lambour said something quite interesting today, Tony." Arabella Grey sipped her sweet pale wine from a slender silver goblet. She and Lord Varden had just finished the fine supper that Barbe had prepared; a game pie in a flaky crust, with large pieces of nutty truffles and delicate oniony shallots in a rich wine-flavored gravy.

"What?" Lord Varden, manners aside, dipped a crusty chunk of bread into the remaining gravy, and sopping it up, popped it into his mouth.

"He has been importuning me again to become his mistress," Arabella replied, "and so I reminded him of his poor wife in Normandy. I said he should accept the example of the king's fidelity to the lady Margaret of Austria. The duc laughed and told me that betrothals are made to be broken. When I asked him what he meant by such a thing, he changed the subject. Do you think that important?"

"It could be," Lord Varden said slowly, suddenly interested. "You see, Arabella, part of Lady Margaret's dowry from her father, Maximilian of Hapsburg, are the provinces of Franche Comté and Artois, which the French very much want back. There is only one thing that could tempt Charles from this match. *Brittany.* You will have to find out for us, Arabella, if the king's betrothal is about to be broken. King Henry would very much like that information. It is extremely valuable. Princess Anne of Brittany is to wed with Maximilian himself, now that he is widowed. Should that match be broken for France, then France would have a strong hand in European politics, which should not suit England at all."

Arabella sighed. "There is only one way I am going to pry such information from the duc," she said, and from the resigned tone in her voice, Lord Varden knew what would come next. "I must finally succumb to his advances. There seems to be no other choice in the matter."

He took her hand. "We are friends, Arabella, are we not?"

376

and she nodded. "You are young and beautiful, and I believe of a passionate nature. What you must do, you do for England, and you must not feel guilt over it."

She laughed, for his kindness was touching. "Tony," she replied honestly, "what I do, I do in order that I may regain my lands. What kind of a woman does it make me, I wonder, that I would barter my *virtue* for land? Still, if I had it to do again, I should make my bargain with the devil himself if in the end I could get Greyfaire back for my daughter. Do men not often make such difficult decisions and bargains to obtain whatever it is they would have? You fight with swords, and knives, and artillery. A woman's weapon is her intellect, though many would not credit such a thing. When intellect fails, however, a woman has her soft white body with which to fight, and if men have but one universal weakness, it is their lust."

He stared at her, astounded. Until this moment he had thought of Arabella Grey as an innocent young woman, caught in a web of power and unable to free herself. He suddenly knew better. "You frighten me, Arabella," he said.

She laughed again. "It is my curse that I am petite and delicate of form and coloring. Men think me helpless, Tony, but in this instance, isn't that what we want? *I am a virtuous woman*, and it pains me that I must give up that virtue to gain my goals, but as God is my witness, I will! I have held the duc off as long as I dared, but he will shortly lose his interest if I do not yield myself to his passion. If this tiny scrap of information that I have provided you with can possibly lead to something that will help King Henry, and thus expedite my debt to him, then I will become the duc's mistress."

Lord Varden found himself admiring her determination. Her analysis of the situation was absolutely correct, though why he was surprised, he could not determine, for Arabella had never made any effort to hide her intelligence. "You will surrender gracefully, of course, my dear," he said wryly.

"I shall acquiesce with such delicacy of feeling and innocent distress that he will believe himself to have won a mighty victory. I can only hope he finds me worth all the wooing," Arabella teased her friend mischievously.

Now it was Lord Varden who laughed. "Never doubt yourself, my dear." He chuckled. "You must consider too that the

duc must also prove himself in the lists of love if you are to enjoy
yourself as well.''

"I am not certain, Tony, that I should enjoy myself," Arabella told him, but her green eyes were twinkling. "Somehow
it does not seem right that having gone against all I was taught
to believe, I enjoy myself.''

"If you cannot," he told her, "you could displease the duc.
Remember, my dear, that once you have committed yourself to
an action, you must fully follow through. Have no regrets. Regrets are such a waste of time. To err is human, but to regret
erring is to regret being human. It is a warm, flesh and blood
woman the duc desires.

"Since you must compromise yourself, at least enjoy it. You
do not intend making such behavior a habit, Arabella, and besides, I will wager that you have never known any man but your
former husband. Men have more advantage over women in passion, for they are allowed to digress from the straight and chaste
path without fear of condemnation, unless, of course, they make
a spectacle of themselves. It is your duty to be naughty, my
dear. Take advantage of it!''

"My lord, you are totally incorrigible!" Arabella told him,
laughing. "I will admit to being curious, however, about other
men.'' She felt no guilt in not discussing her adventure with
James Stewart. That was an entirely different thing, and it was
not Lord Varden's business.

"Then this, my dear, will offer you an opportunity to indulge
your curiosity,'' he answered her. "I have but one question.
When?''

"The duc has asked me to celebrate Twelfth Night with him,''
Arabella told Anthony Varden. "He is having a small fete, and
has invited me to be his guest. The opportunity is perfect, for
he will undoubtedly attempt to seduce me once again that evening.''

"Aye,'' her companion agreed. "I suspect he will.'' Anthony
Varden did not tell Arabella that until she had spoken of it, he
was totally unaware that the Duc de Lambour was giving a
Twelfth Night fete. He would wager that no one else at court
knew either. The duc was obviously making a last attempt to
cajole Arabella to his bed. He considered whether he should tell
her, and decided he must. He did not want her suddenly deciding to change her mind.

"I think, my dear, that you may be the duc's only guest on Twelfth Night," he said. "I have not been invited, and the duc always includes me when he invites you."

"Indeed?" Arabella noted, her delicate eyebrows arching in surprise.

"This may be your last opportunity with him," Lord Varden warned her.

"It would appear so, Tony. I thank you for your warning. I am indeed committed to my course now, aren't I?"

He nodded, and then he said gallantly, "I envy the duc his 'conquest,' Arabella."

She colored, and then she asked him the question that she had wanted to ask him since they had met. "Why are you not married, Tony?"

"I was," he said. "She was a Breton lady. We met at the Duke of Brittany's court when I was with King Henry in his youth. We were wed but a few months when she sickened and died of a fever. Few remember her, or that I was ever wed. Since then there has been no one. As I serve the king in this rather odd manner, I dare not take a wife, for it would make me vulnerable. In a service such as this, Arabella, one cannot be vulnerable, as you well know. A wife would complicate my life, for living in France as I do, she would probably be French. How could I keep the life she could not share with me secret from her? It would be nearly impossible. I am safer without a wife and children to fret me.

"As a younger son, I have nothing in England. No lands, no monies. The king has promised me, however, that when my effectiveness here in France comes to an end, he will see that I have an estate on which to retire. Only then will I remarry and have children."

She understood. Had not Henry Tudor used her little Margaret against her? "I pray I can gain valuable information from the duc, Tony. I so long to go home again! My wee Margaret will have grown greatly these past months. I miss her so much!"

"What if you fall in love with the duc, my dear?" he asked her. "It is possible that it could happen, you know. I believe that even now you like him, although perhaps you have not considered it. When passion becomes an added ingredient to your relationship, who knows what will happen?"

"I do not believe that love will ever enter into my association

with Adrian Morlaix," Arabella told Tony. "He simply desires
me—my body, really. I, in turn, desire information from him
that he might not otherwise divulge except in pillow talk."

"But he does not know that, my dear," Lord Varden said.

"I, however, do," Arabella responded wisely. "I dare not
allow myself to love again, Tony. Love, I have found, makes
one heartsore."

"Aye," he agreed, "it does, but to be without love, my dear,
gives far greater pain, I believe. When my Jeanne-Marie was
alive, I ached in the hours that we were apart. My life, it seemed,
was only full and perfect when we were together. Her love en-
cased me with a warmth of feeling the like of which I have not
known since. When she first died, I felt as if I had died, and
when I realized I had not, I cursed the fates that had left me to
walk this earth without her. To be forced to live when Jeanne-
Marie was not here to share my life gave me more anguish than
the pain of a few hours separation, for in those few hours there
was always the knowledge that I would see her again. I no longer
have that certainty, and, naturally, the pain has dulled over the
years. It has never left me, mind you, and, of course, I have my
many happy memories. Ahh, Arabella, I would be in love again,
but alas I dare not at this time either! If your heart responds to
Adrian Morlaix's heart, do not deny yourself that joy! Is not life,
my dear, for living to the fullest?"

Joy? Love, a joy? Love had always been more sorrow than
joy, Arabella thought to herself. Her mother had loved Jasper
Keane, and having suffered bitterly for it, was finally forced to
give her life up in a final tribute to love. She herself had loved
Tavis Stewart, and though he claimed to love her, he had treated
her like a child rather than as a wife. A toy to be cuddled and
kissed, but certainly not taken seriously. The only good thing
to have come of such a love was her wee Margaret, from whom
she was now separated. No, she was never going to allow herself
to be taken in by love again!

She would think on her rendezvous at Twelfth Night with
Adrian Morlaix. What would she wear? Her costume must be a
mixture of demureness and seduction, and she would wear nothing beneath it but a sheer, silk camisia. *Ivory velvet!* Her gown
would be of ivory velvet to compliment her pale gold hair, to
hint at virtue; a virtue he would enjoy despoiling, and which
she would allow him to despoil before the night was out. Ara-

bella shook her head at her thoughts. How hard and calculating she had become, she considered; but were she not, she realized, this could all destroy her.

Ivory velvet. Trimmed in gold threads and seed pearls. An underskirt of gold brocade. And her hair. She would not wear it as she usually did, in a crown of braids atop her head which gave her added height. Her hair on Twelfth Night would be dressed with silk ribbons and seed pearls which would be intertwined into one long and large fat braid. He would, like all men, seek to undo her hair, and she should make it as easy for him as possible. And she would wear no jewelry. That would give a further impression of simplicity, as would her plain burgundy-colored velvet cloak with its hood trimmed in rich marten.

She bathed carefully on Twelfth Night, instructing Lona to perfume the warm water with her favorite white heather fragrance. Her long hair had earlier been washed.

" 'Tis a wonder you don't catch your death of cold with all the bathing you do," grumbled Lona. "So much water can't be healthy, my lady, but then I suppose I should be used to your little crochets by now, shouldn't I?"

"And I used to your constant chattering," teased her mistress.

"Chattering?" Lona's tone was suddenly aggrieved. "Just because I worry aloud over your eccentric ways is no cause to say I chatter, my lady!"

Arabella laughed and soothed her servant and friend. "Dearest Lona, I but tease you because I love you," she said.

"Well now," said Lona, "that puts a different complexion on things, don't it?" She helped her mistress from the tub, and having dried and perfumed her, wrapped her snugly in a warmed towel. Fetching the silk camisia, she noted, "You ought to wear something warmer than this tonight, my lady. 'Tis bitter out, and that's certain."

" 'Twill spoil the line of my gown," Arabella said casually, but Lona raised her eyebrows questioningly, causing her lady to continue warningly, "I will hear no more about it, Lona."

Lona nodded, not in the least offended. She had learned what she needed to know in just those few words. Fetching the ivory velvet bodice and the two skirts, she helped Arabella to dress. Next Lona sat Arabella down, carefully arranging her skirts that they might not wrinkle, and braided Arabella's thick, pale gold hair, carefully weaving in the strands of delicate pearls and silk ribbons as she did so. "There," she said when she had finally finished, " 'tis as good a job as any, my lady, if I do say so. You look beautiful."

Arabella was wearing dainty slippers upon her feet, but because of the snowy ground, Lona fitted her mistress with heavy clogs for outdoors over the little velvet sollerets. Helping her lady into the coach, Lona wrapped a heavy fur rug about her knees and placed flannel-wrapped hot bricks about her feet. Though the journey to the duc's Hotel de Lambour was a short one, the January night was bitterly cold, and few if any Parisians were out and about.

"Put the horses in the duc's stables and then find shelter for yourselves in his kitchens," Arabella instructed the six men who had accompanied her when they had reached their destination. "I will call for you when I am ready to return home."

Allowing the duc's servants to remove the bricks from about her feet and help her from the carriage, Arabella hurried into the mansion.

"Ma Belle! Welcome," Adrian Morlaix said, coming forward to greet her. He kissed her hand lingeringly as a servant took her cape.

She lifted her eyebrows questioningly. "Have I mistaken your invitation, my lord? Have I come on perhaps the wrong night?" The house was quite silent, and his garb—a fur-trimmed velvet brocade gown in his favorite scarlet—quite casual. "Did you not invite me to a Twelfth Night Fete, monseigneur?"

"I did," he said, "and I hope you will forgive me my little deception, ma Belle, but you are to be my only guest," he told her.

"Monseigneur!" Arabella pretended shocked surprise. "You are very wicked! I fear that you will ruin my reputation. Please send for my coach. I really should not stay under the circumstances."

"Will you not stay just a little while, ma Belle? I would give you your gift. Would you not like it? A few minutes cannot damage your spotless reputation, chérie," he said softly, and Arabella allowed herself to be cajoled even as he led her up the hotel's flight of marble stairs to a small salon where a bright fire burned merrily.

"I love presents!" Arabella told him, adding wistfully, "It has been so long since I have received one."

"I would fill a room full of presents for you," he said extravagantly, "if you would but let me!"

The blush that rose to Arabella's cheeks was an honest one, for there was sincerity in the duc's compliment. "I have a small gift for you," she told him, and handed him a little package wrapped in a piece of cloth of gold and tied with a red silk ribbon. "You must open it at once!"

With a smile the duc undid the ribbon and unwrapped the parcel. Inside he found a fine pair of Florentine leather gloves, dyed a clear bright scarlet color and embroidered with black jets and gold beads. "Ma Belle!" He was genuinely touched, for he knew the gloves to be of the best quality, and her income meager at best. "These are beautiful, and I thank you!"

"I won at cards before Christmas," she told him airily in answer to his unspoken question.

He laughed. "For a woman of such unimpeachable virtue, you are becoming quite adept at survival," he teased. Then he handed her a delicately carved pearwood box. "For you, ma Belle."

What did the beautiful little box contain? Arabella wondered. Would the gift be an indication of the esteem in which he held her? With strangely clumsy fingers she lifted the carved gold latch that held the box fastened, and raising the lid, gazed, stunned, at the exquisite square-cut ruby with its dainty filigreed gold chain nestling in the white velvet. *"Ohhhhhh,"* she half gasped, half whispered, unable to move, unable to say anything else.

With a smile of satisfaction Adrian Morlaix lifted the jewel from the box and fastened it about Arabella's neck. The ruby lay glowing just above the shadowed valley between her breasts, shimmering against her fair skin.

Arabella turned her head just slightly and looked up at the duc. "Oh, monseigneur," she murmured, " 'tis the most beautiful thing I have ever possessed in my whole life!" Their eyes met suddenly, and she saw the desperate passion in his, but barely masked. "Ohhh," she said again, even as his mouth came down on hers for the very first time, setting her own pulses to racing furiously. It had been so long since she had tasted a man's lips on hers, and how could she have forgotten the lesson that Jamie Stewart had unwittingly taught her; *that passion without love could exist between a man and a woman.* Oh, holy Mother, Arabella prayed silently, let me be strong in my resolve!

"Oh, Belle! Ma Belle! Ma petite et précieuse Belle! I must have you! Do not say nay to me ever again, ma Belle! I worship at the shrine of your beauty! I adore you!" the duc declared passionately, an arm now firmly about her waist, one hand plunging into her bodice to cup a plump breast. "Ahh, ma Belle! I am wild with love for you!" The hand fondled her breast expertly, its fingers pinching teasingly on her nipple.

"Oh, monseigneur," she cried softly, but she did not struggle or attempt to remove the marauding hand. *"We must not!* What of your spouse?" Did she sound too coy? Pray God she did not sound coy! Arabella could barely suppress the soft moan that escaped from between her lips. His touch felt marvelous!

"Anne-Claude is in Normandy, ma Belle. I do not love her. *I love you!* 'Twas but a marriage of convenience. Give me your lips again, chérie," he pleaded, and Arabella found she was unable to refuse him, no matter her firm intentions.

His kisses were intoxicatingly sweet. Deep, hungry kisses that seemed to warm her to the soles of her feet. She was quite aware that he was carefully undoing her bodice even as he kissed her, and finally she felt it incumbent upon herself to once again protest, lest on reflection he grow suspicious of her sudden acquiescence. Tearing her head away from him, she caught his big hands in her little ones, pleading softly. "This is wrong, monseigneur. Surely it is wrong!"

"Tell me that you do not feel passion for me as I feel it for you!" he demanded of her fiercely, his blue eyes blazing with his determination to have his will.

"I . . . I . . . I do not know!" she cried, knowing that even as she spoke, she did know, and he knew too. She did indeed feel passion.

"You lie," he told her, and the bright blue eyes shone with his triumph. Ripping the neck of her camisia away, he cupped her now naked breasts in his two hands, murmuring as he bent to cover the creamy flesh with hot kisses, "You are mine, ma petite Belle! *Mine alone!"*

Arabella's heart hammered wildly at his masterful tone. She would have never expected it of the elegant and civilized Duc de Lambour.

Releasing her breasts, he held her against him while the fingers of one hand skillfully undid the tapes holding her skirts up. They fell away from her, puddling to the floor with just the barest noise. The duc tore the remainder of her silk undergarment away and carelessly threw it from him. Her only adornment now was the ruby she wore about her neck. As he slowly undid her braid, she thought her legs would give way, but they did not. Spreading her hair over her shoulders, he stepped back a moment and smiled. Then picking her up, he walked across the room and laid her upon a large, dark fur rug spread before the warm fire. His impassioned gaze as he looked down upon her sent a flush of sudden pink embarrassment to her face.

"Mon Dieu!" he said feelingly, "you are perfection, ma Belle! In my wildest dreams I could not have imagined such exquisite perfection!" He turned away from her momentarily as he disrobed himself.

There was some humor in the situation, Arabella considered as she watched him, faintly amused to see that Adrian Morlaix's knees were just a trifle knobby, though his other parts were certainly well-made and upstanding. It was fortunate that she had decided to yield herself to the duc, because he had obviously decided he would have her whatever the cost. She had not really considered how desperately he desired her, for she had never thought of herself as the kind of woman who drove men to passion; but then there had been Jamie Stewart. What was it about her that made men such damned fools?

The duc now knelt and lay beside her on his side, letting his fingers wander provocatively over her flesh, placing little kisses upon her face and again smiling warmly at her. "I will not hurt you, ma Belle," he said sincerely. "These past months I have come to treasure your chasteness, even though it meant I must be denied your loveliness. I cannot, however, deny myself any longer. I love you, and I would have you love me."

"Oh, Adrian," she murmured, using his name for the first time, "whatever we may feel for one another, surely this is wrong of us." *Careful*, Arabella thought, amazed that she could think at all; she could not continue to protest when she was, in fact, yielding herself to him. Still, just a trifle more demurral before she allowed him the final victory. She sighed deeply.

"Ma Belle," he said quietly, "life is so very short that to waste one precious moment of it is surely a crime against God.

We have wasted so many moments these past months, but no more! I am mad for you! I suspect were your adorable little conscience not so strict with you, that you would admit to some feeling for me. Hein?''

"Ohh, monseigneur," Arabella whispered, hiding her face in her hands.

"Admit it, ma Belle! You love me too!" he said, pulling her hands aside.

"What if I should disappoint you?" she fretted, neatly side-stepping his question, although he did not notice it, so intent was he on his pursuit of her. "I have known but a husband's loving. I am no courtesan, skilled in the arts of Eros, Adrian. You have pursued me for months. What if the reality we find in each other's arms is not as wonderful as the anticipation? I will have compromised myself for naught!"

"You are charming, ma Belle," he answered, smiling down on her indulgently. "Your lips are like the first strawberries of summer, my love. When I kissed you I could feel you thrill with my very touch. Your breasts are like sweet ripe peaches, royal fruits worthy of a king. I shall never be able to get enough of them. I shall touch and taste and explore every inch of you, ma Belle, and there is no way under heaven in which you shall disappoint me, I swear it!"

"But what if you should disappoint me?" she asked him gravely. He should not futter her as he futtered other women, Arabella thought to herself. To retain his interest, she must be clever. To simply surrender herself to him would be most fool-ish. Let him not be totally satisfied with their relationship until he was certain in his own mind that he was the best lover she, or any other woman, could possibly have. Until she obtained the information she needed from him, this entanglement could not end. It would not be easy, she suddenly realized, but she would succeed, and in the wake of her success would come the return of Greyfaire Keep and a journey home to reclaim her child.

"Disappoint you?" His tone was startled. Such an impossible thing had obviously never occurred to him.

"My husband was a fine lover," Arabella said candidly. "He gave me much pleasure. I have heard it said, however, that not all men are equal when it comes to love. Have I been misin-formed? Is this not so?" she finished ingenuously.

"Aye," he said slowly, "I have heard it said that such a thing 'tis so; but no woman I have ever loved, ma Belle, has had cause for complaint. I swear it!"

Arabella smiled seductively up at him now. The firelight cast a molten glow over her body, making it warm with color, deepening the gold of her hair, reflecting itself in the ruby that nestled just above her plump breasts and in the pale green shade of her eyes. "If that is so, Adrian, then you must kiss me again, for I found the taste of your kisses as sweet as the finest wine, and even now, monseigneur, I thirst!"

The Duc de Lambour felt his heart leap in his chest at her words. She was the most fascinating woman he had ever met. A mixture of innocence and sensuality that he found wildly exciting. He kissed her again, and to his delight felt her lips part beneath his, her tongue tentatively seeking his own. He groaned with his pleasure and shifted his body so that he lay half over her.

Arabella allowed herself to be swept up in the passion of the moment. With an answering moan of pleasure, she put her arms about his neck, pressing her breasts into his chest, feeling the wiry hair of that chest tickling her flesh. The hard length of his manhood pressed insistently against the side of her thigh as Arabella's fingers softly rubbed the sensitive flesh on the nape of his neck, causing the hairs there to raise.

The duc freed himself reluctantly from her lips and began to press warm kisses upon her closed eyelids and at that sensitive junction of her jaw just beneath her ear. *"Ma Belle,"* he murmured throatily, "you intoxicate me!" His lips moved down the side of her neck to her shoulder, which he bit sharply, causing her to cry out. Instantly his tongue snaked out to soothe the pain away, and having done so, moved on to lick at her nipples. His lips parted to take each nipple in its turn within the warmth of his mouth, where he suckled hard upon it.

"Oh! Oh!" she whimpered. She had forgotten how good a man's mouth felt upon a woman's breasts, and she squirmed with pleasure beneath his touch. Her hand stroked his dark head, encouraging him in his efforts. "Oh, yes!" she said. *"Oh, yes!"*

He cradled her within the curve of an arm and fondled her, saying, "So, ma Belle, the sweet fruits of your breasts are sensitive to the pleasures of my touch. Perhaps I may please you after all."

"Perhaps," she agreed, and then gasped as his fingers found a most sentient and susceptible portion of her anatomy. *"A-dri-annn,"* she cried, amazed at how quickly he had actually begun to arouse her. It had been a very long time, she realized, since she had felt *this* particular sensation.

Reluctant she might have been, Adrian Morlaix considered, but she was nonetheless a hot little piece of female flesh. Already her love juices were flowing, bedewing his fingers even as they thrust themselves into her sweet flesh. He had to taste her! He could not remember having ever been so quickly aroused by a woman. He could feel the very lust to possess her boiling in his veins with such intensity he almost feared for his life, his heart was beating so violently. Twisting his body about, he positioned himself between her outstretched legs and found her with an extremely facile tongue, teasing the little jewel of her sex until it was standing stiff.

Had she been struck with lightning, Arabella would have reacted no differently. Her body arced wildly but briefly as his fingers dug into her soft flesh to hold her to his will. *"Oh!"* she sobbed sharply. "Oh! Oh! Oh!" as the first small waves of pleasure began to sweep over her.

Satisfied, he laughed and raised his head from her. "Do I please you yet, ma Belle?" he teased.

Arabella panted uncontrollably for a moment, and then she gasped, "You come near, monseigneur, but not quite yet!"

"Vixen!" he said, laughing again, and then pulling himself up, pushed himself slowly into her love grotto. "I shall make you cry with a greater passion than you have ever known, ma Belle," he promised her fiercely.

Having regained a small measure of control over her emotions despite his invasion of her person, Arabella taunted him, "We shall see, monseigneur."

He began to pump her, moving smoothly and rhythmically, as if to some unheard and primitive cadence, but Arabella knew enough about men to know that a man as madly aroused as was Adrian Morlaix was usually lacking in self-restraint. If she could but bring him to his own crisis, even if it meant sacrificing hers, he would be intrigued beyond all and eager to retain her company, if for no other reason than he desired a victory over her. His vows of love, she thought, were but a charming ruse to gain his way. She did not believe the Duc de Lambour loved anyone but himself.

She thrust herself up to meet him, but her very thoughts had cooled her own ardor enough, and he was finally unable to hold back his own passion. With a great cry he took his release, falling at last exhausted upon her and almost crushing her with his weight. Tenderly Arabella caressed him, even as she murmured sweetly, "Has it been so long then, monseigneur, since you have had a woman? Ah well, perhaps next time."

With a groan he rolled away from her, and looking up at her with sorrow in his blue eyes, he said, "You have defeated me, ma Belle, and I, to my shame, have disappointed you. Give me but a few minutes to regain my strength and we shall try again. It has never happened before, and I vow it shall not happen again."

"My lord," she told him, "if I did not achieve perfection, I did at least enjoy myself very much. There is no shame in that, is there? You are a most tender and vigorous lover. I can only hope that I did not disappoint you."

"*Never!* You are perfection, ma Belle! Pure perfection! I shall never let you go from me! You must be mine for always and ever!" he told her passionately.

Arabella arose from the fur rug, and walking to a nearby table containing a carafe of wine and some goblets, poured the duc the sweet, refreshing beverage. She was a little amazed, and perhaps just a bit frightened, by her ability to detach herself from her feelings. It made her uncomfortable to realize she could be so calculatingly cold. Still in all, it must be done for Greyfaire's sake.

"You must have some wine as well," the duc said as she handed him his goblet.

"Wine makes me sleepy," she said. "Unless, of course, you would prefer that I sleep, Adrian."

"You will not sleep this night, ma Belle," he said with total sincerity.

"I cannot possibly stay the night," she protested. "What has passed between us, Adrian, should be a private thing between us alone."

"I want you for my mistress, Arabella," he said seriously. "I want you with me at all times, not scuttling back and forth between my hotel and that wretched little house you rent in that backwater village outside of the city.''

"It is all I can afford,'' she said quietly and with dignity.

"I want you here,'' he told her.

"I cannot live in your house, Adrian,'' Arabella said, shocked. "What would people say? What would your wife say? And what of my own people who have followed me into exile? I will not desert them, for they did not desert me!''

"Then let me buy you a small house in a good neighborhood here in Paris at least,'' he begged her. "A place where we may both meet and be private.''

"I do not know . . .'' Arabella hesitated. She needed to talk with Tony about this. She did not know how far she might go before she would be considered déclassé by the French court. She could not afford that, and so she put Adrian Morlaix off. "You must give me time to think, Adrian,'' she replied. "I had hoped one day to remarry and to have other children. Oh, I am not such a fool to believe that a member of the court would marry me. After all, I have nothing, but perhaps some well-to-do merchant would be pleased to have me, despite my lack of a dowry, simply for my fine connections, which have a certain value. If I should give this all up to become a public scandal, what will happen to me when you grow tired of me, monseigneur? No, no! I must have time to carefully consider all of this.''

"I will never repudiate you, ma Belle,'' he told her. "Have I not said that I love you?''

"Oh, Adrian,'' she answered him, "you do not really love me. How could you? You do not know me. I am flattered nonetheless that you would say it, and perhaps you even believe it, but I do not think it possible. Still, I might wish it so, and yet I dare not! Oh, kiss me once again, my darling! Let us forget such things as conventions and making decisions this night! I will stay as long as I can and take what sweetness from you that I dare, but as for the morrow, who can say, monseigneur?'' Her lips brushed his provocatively. "Who amongst us can say?''

He had not exaggerated when he had told her that she would not sleep that night. After their first encounter, he was eager to prove to her his superiority as a lover. Arabella, however, would not allow him a complete victory, and consequently he remained fascinated by this woman he could not seem to conquer. Never before had he met a woman he could not send into spasms of passion, but he seemed unable to lead the beautiful English-woman down the same path he had led so many others.

Another man might have been angered by such developments, but Adrian Morlaix was not. Indeed, he was intrigued, for Arabella was certainly not a cold woman. She was vibrant and warm and now welcomed his advances enthusiastically. She had an aptitude for lovemaking few women he had ever known had. He simply could not bring her to a final surrender. He began to wonder if she were one of those rare women who enjoyed love-making but were unable to fully participate because they could not completely trust themselves to a lover's care. He had never encountered such a woman before, and only time would tell.

In the early hours of the cold January dawn, Arabella's coach returned to her little house on the river Seine. Both FitzWalter and Anthony Varden were waiting for her.

"Are you all right?" her captain-at-arms demanded bluntly.

"Aye," she answered calmly.

"Then I'll get some sleep," he said, and departed.

"Pour me some wine, Tony," Arabella said, moving across the room to the little salon's fireplace. She was chilled to the bone from her short journey, and held out her hands to the flames to warm them.

"I must assume the lateness of your return means that you have yielded your person to our friend, the duc," Lord Varden said, handing her a goblet of wine. "How may I put this delicately?" he mused a moment.

"You needn't." She chuckled and took a deep draught of the wine as she turned to face him. "No, I learned nothing tonight that would be of any possible use to England; and aye, I believe he is yet interested in me. He wanted me to remain with him, but I refused him, of course. He next suggested that he purchase a house for me in a good neighborhood of Paris where we might be alone. I told him that I must think on his second suggestion. What am I to do, Tony? You must tell me how far I dare go, for I do not know."

Lord Varden considered the matter, and after some minutes he said, "You must tell him no, my dear. You would destroy your good reputation and your usefulness to us if you did otherwise. There is no scandal in your visiting the duc's hotel here in Paris, even for a few days' time; or joining him at his château in the Loire for a bit, as long as you possess your own home. A home that is totally unconnected with the Duc de Lambour. No one will think badly of you when the word gets about that you are the duc's 'chère amie.' It was expected that eventually Adrian Morlaix's charm would prevail over your virtue. You cannot, however, flaunt your relationship. To live permanently with the duc, or even accept the gift of a house on such a short acquaintanceship, would also be totally unacceptable. The proprieties must be preserved, my dear Arabella.''

"I thought as much," Arabella told him, "though a house in the city would have been nice. It is so dank here by the river." She sighed, mocking herself slightly. "It is acceptable for the poor but virtuous petite rose d'Anglaise to accept the duc's love, but nothing more, except mayhap some bejewel baubles, eh Tony?''

He chuckled. "Aye," he said. "A king may keep a mistress in style, but with discretion, though most kings have no understanding of the word. A duc may simply have a chère amie, and a duc's affair must be even more discreet lest the church involve itself and make an example of the noble sinner, which they dare not do with a king.''

"I shall keep myself from the duc for the next several days," Arabella told him. "I would have his lust rebuild itself, and I know that he is most taken with me.''

"What a clever little wench you are," Lord Varden said. "You are indeed learning to play the game. I can almost feel sorry for the duc. You will end by breaking his heart, I fear.''

"Better than he breaking mine," Arabella said stonily, suddenly weary and unaccountably distressed. "You will forgive me, Tony, but I am tired. I would seek my bed.'' She put down her goblet and, curtsying, left him.

Lona lay snoring on the settle by the fire in her mistress's bedchamber. Arabella crept past her, leaving her servant to her dreams. She did not choose to explain to Lona the missing silk camisia. With chilled fingers she undid her clothes, leaving them where they fell, and quietly lifting the lid of the storage chest, took out a fresh camisia to sleep in. She needed a bath, but that would have to wait for the morning, when she awoke. Arabella crawled into her cold bed. The sheets were icy, and she shivered for some minutes.

As she began to grow warmer she could smell the scent of their lovemaking on her body, and she shuddered distastefully.

If she had learned one thing this night, it was that though there could be passion without love between a man and a woman, that passion was rendered totally meaningless without the love. Arabella felt the tears slipping down her cheeks. She hated what she was doing. She despised herself, and she despised Henry Tudor for having brought her to this. Still, the choice had been hers. She could have told him no, yet she had not. She must share equal blame in this matter, whatever happened.

Men! Holy Mother, how she hated men! The only men she had ever known who had not hurt her in some way were her own father—God assoil his good soul—and dear Father Anselm. As for the others! King Richard had, in attempting to do her a kindness, betrothed her to Sir Jasper Keane. Jasper Keane had betrayed her with her own mother while trying to steal her property, and then allowed her to be carried off by the Scots. *By Tavis Stewart.* Tavis, in the main, had not been a bad man, but he had refused to keep faith with her, thereby leaving her at the mercy of Jamie Stewart, who had seduced her in return for his help; and Henry Tudor, who had made her a whore in return for his aid. *Men!* They knew nothing but how to make war and their women unhappy!

Well, Arabella thought, rubbing her cheeks with a clenched fist, she would use them even as they had used her. She would regain Greyfaire, whatever the cost, and when she did, she would take Margaret and go home. She would never again be beholden to anyone, particularly a man. When she returned to England, she would run her own life as she saw fit, answering to no one. As for the Percy family, should King Henry betroth Margaret into it, she would make the king send the boy to her that she might raise him properly to respect Margaret. She would not allow to happen to her daughter what had happened to her. She would protect Margaret from any who would do her hurt. She would no longer be victimized as her own mother had been victimized, nor would she allow her daughter to be taken advantage of by *any* man. Margaret Stewart would learn to stand on her own two feet.

Arabella shifted herself, trying to find a more comfortable position in her bed. It had been many months since she had known a man's loving, and she was sore with the duc's attentions. He was a most vigorous lover, and he had been determined to bring her to total fulfillment. Arabella smiled to herself, past her tearful stage now. She was not so foolish that she did not realize she might take her pleasure while still maintaining her own independence, but not yet. Let him work for his victory. *Let him really fall in love with her.* Let him be as helpless before her as women usually were before men. It was a strangely comforting thought.

She must finally come to terms with what she was doing, Arabella considered. She was not at ease with any of it, but there could be no guilt or shame on her part. She was a warrior doing battle for Greyfaire. She was in the service of her country and her king. She must win her battle, and she would. Whatever it took to attain her goal, she would be a lady victorious when this was finally over. She could return to England content in her own mind. Nay, she would not be helpless. *Not ever again.* It gave her aching heart solace to know that. She slept.

✖ *Chapter 20*

I promised ye that ye could go to France, Uncle, when ye won Glenkirk for me, and ye have done it," Jamie Stewart said, his eyes dancing merrily.

"Ye did nae say I was to wet-nurse some damned bride ye were sending for some damned French duke," his uncle grumbled.

The king stretched out his long legs and toasted his stockinged feet before the fire. "The regent, Anne de Beaujeu, hae requested that in the name of the Old Alliance between France and Scotland, I send her a suitable bride for Jean-Claude Billancourt, the Duc de St. Astier. The duc, the last of his unfortunate line, is twenty-seven and comes from an ancient house. Unfortunately, over the last two hundred or so years male members of the Billancourt family are born suffering from a peculiar nervous disorder which leads them to believe that they are hounds. Not constantly, mind ye, but enough that when the disorder does appear in a particular generation, it is difficult to find a wife for the gentleman in question. As a consequence the family hae become most ingrown, for the bridal market amongst the French nobility is narrow for them.

"The duc suffers with more frequency than hae past members of his family. 'Tis an interesting disorder, Uncle, for it does nae, mind ye, inflict the women of the family, just the men. Nor hae the madness been passed by brides of this family onto their own bairns when they wed outside their immediate family. The Billancourt family hae been weakened, however, over the years, for who would want to send the best of their lasses to such a family? The regent did nae gie me this information, for she, of course, would hae me believe that France was honoring Scotland wi this request."

"But ye hae yer sources at the French court, don't ye, Jamie," his uncle said, amused.

"Aye, I do," came the bland reply as the king wiggled his toes.

"And knowing the kind of man this duc is, ye would send one of our fine lasses to him for the sake of the Old Alliance? I canna believe it of ye, Jamie," Tavis Stewart said sternly.

"Dinna fret yerself, Uncle, dinna fret; but hear me out. I hae, as ye are undoubtedly aware, been lately taken by Mistress Meg Drummond, and I would pursue her wi vigor, but for one thing. There is a lady, known to me in the past, who would force herself back into my life. She will nae accept that we are quit, and indeed, Uncle, we hae been quit for several years now, but my kingly rank seems to encourage the lady onward.

"She is of good family, mind ye, but a thorn in my side. The French regent requests a wife for her half-mad duke. I need a far-distant husband for this troublesome jade. The solution is obvious, Uncle. My lady subject dare nae refuse my wishes. 'Tis providential, is it nae?"

The Earl of Dunmor arose from his own chair by the fire, and going to the sideboard, poured them both drams of the king's own whiskey. Returning to his place, he handed his nephew one of the goblets. "And just who is the 'lady' ye would unburden yerself of, Jamie?" he demanded, and then swallowed his whiskey.

"*Sorcha Morton,*" the king said, bursting into laughter as his uncle choked on the potent liquid that had but slid halfway down his throat.

The earl's face grew red with his effort to force the whiskey back down, and when he had finally succeeded, he said, gasping, his eyes watering with his efforts, "*Sorcha Morton!* God's bones, Jamie! Ye'll nae make her go, and even if ye did, she'd nae be anything but trouble. She'll destroy the Old Alliance in a month! Are ye a madman?"

James Stewart restrained his laughter, for he could see that his uncle was truly concerned. "Dinna fret, Uncle," he repeated. " 'Tis all right. Lady Morton is eager to go. The thought of a rich French duke has proven irresistible to her. Her prospects here in Scotland are dismal. Sorcha, ye see, hae no funds, nor any hope of funds. Angus is quit of her, for she is too difficult for him to stomach any longer. She hae slept her way through my court, and there are none who would retain her services, for she is an unpleasant woman at best. She canna bring herself to enter the marriage market of the merchant class because she is too proud of her lineage. What is left for her?

That is why she attempted to insinuate herself back into my favor, but I certainly dinna want her either. I was contemplating what in the name of God I could do wi her when I received the regent's message.

"I immediately wrote Madame Anne that I had the perfect candidate; a beautiful widow of the Douglas family; childless, for her husband was elderly, but of fertile stock. The regent expressed her approval as well as her delight. They were formally betrothed over a month ago. I am supplying Sorcha wi a small trousseau and an honor guard which ye will be in charge of, Tavis. Ye sail from Leeds in two days' time. Yer to escort Lady Morton to her bridegroom, and ye will witness the marriage before ye are free to pursue yer own interests. I want to be certain she is firmly wed."

"And does the blushing bride know of her bridegroom's wee infirmity, Jamie?" the earl asked his nephew.

"Aye," came the surprising reply, "she does. As much as I would hae liked to send Sorcha away to face that little surprise alone, I feared her reaction. So I told her, but it doesna matter to her. She says if she can get wi child, the bairn is likely to be sound as this difficulty dinna strike consecutive generations. 'Tis really all she cares about now. Having a home and a family. She'll rule her poor duc wi an iron hand."

"That she would sell herself for such a thing shames me as a Scot," the earl said coldly.

"Dinna be so harsh in yer judgments, Uncle," the king counseled him. "Sorcha Morton does what she must to survive. So do we all."

" 'Tis different for us," the earl said.

"Nay," the king told him, " 'tis no different, Uncle."

Tavis Stewart stared gloomily into the fireplace. Whatever his nephew said, Lady Morton had sold herself to the highest bidder. *And what of Arabella?* a voice inside his head asked. What has she had to do in order to survive? In order to regain Greyfaire? And 'tis all yer fault, whatever it might be, the voice in his head concluded.

"This is the last thing I'll do for ye, Jamie," the earl said grimly. "I've gotten Glenkirk for ye, and helped ye to calm yer wild highland lords, but after I escort this noble bawd to France, we are quit! I would win my wife back, and a fine impression I will make arriving in France wi Sorcha Morton in tow. Knowing

that wench, she will spend the entire journey attempting to compromise me!''

The king laughed, but then grew sober as his uncle said,
''What does yer source at the French court say of Arabella,
Jamie, and dinna tell me ye dinna know because I'll call ye a
liar if ye do. Ye asked. Of that I'm certain.''

James Stewart wrestled with his conscience. He didn't want
to hurt his uncle, but Tavis was going to learn the truth sooner
or later. Perhaps it would be best if he knew and could spend
his journey growing used to the idea, possibly even deciding
upon a suitable course of action to follow, if indeed there was
one. ''The rumor, Uncle, is that Arabella is the Duc de Lambour's mistress,'' he finally said. ''It is a recent thing, I am
informed, although the duc has pursued her most relentlessly.''

The earl nodded stonily but said nothing.

''I thought to see that she win at cards whenever she played,
in order that she hae enough monies, Uncle,'' the king said in
a clumsy effort to soften the blow, ''but she rarely plays, for she
canna afford it. She is careful wi her funds, and obviously has
none to waste. She lives, I am told, in a wee house that she rents
in a little village outside of Paris. She hae her maidservant and
some men-at-arms wi her from her home. She lives simply.
Though it is said the duc would buy her a hotel of her own, she
will nae accept it. She insists upon her independence. A novel
idea, is it nae?''

Tavis Stewart was forced to smile. ''Aye, 'tis novel,'' he
agreed, ''but nae for Arabella.''

''I know ye love her, Uncle, but she's a strong woman,''
the king said. ''Ye think because she is small of stature that she
canna survive wi out ye, but yer wrong.''

''I know she can survive wi out me, Jamie,'' the earl told his
nephew. ''She is a strong, independent woman, and has already
proved her capability, but I dinna want her to hae to survive wi
out me, Jamie. Can ye understand that? I dinna think so, laddie,
for ye've never loved a woman. Oh, ye've made love to them,
but hae ye really loved one?''

''Had ye asked me that question a month ago, Uncle, I should
hae had to tell ye nay, but now that I know my sweet Meg, 'tis
different than before,'' the king admitted. ''The thought of being wi out her is nae to be borne. I canna imagine how I could
hae been happy before I met her.''

The earl nodded. "Then perhaps ye do know how I feel about my wee spitfire, Jamie." Tavis Stewart grinned wryly at the king. "Very well, laddie, I will escort the 'blushing bride' to France for ye," he said, "but warn Lady Morton that I'll nae be irritated by her bad behavior. She's to conduct herself properly, or the French duc over the water will be a widower before he's a bridegroom, I swear it!"

The king laughed, saying, "I will tell Sorcha that she must be good, but I can nae guarantee she will, Uncle."

Strangely, however, Lady Sorcha Morton was a model of propriety during the whole of the journey. She was more subdued than at any time since Tavis had known her. Frankly curious, he joined her in her coach just before they reached Paris. Lady Morton rode alone, for she preferred it that way. Her female servants had their own vehicle.

"Jamie must hae lectured you sternly," he teased her, and Sorcha Morton smiled.

"He did nae hae to, Tavis. I dare nae jeopardize this marriage. It is, I think, the last chance I shall ever have, and who knows, I may even be happy."

"Hae ye fallen so low then, Sorcha, that ye would wed a man who sometimes thinks he's a hound?" he asked her, regretting the unkind words even as he spoke them, remembering his conversation with the king, and Arabella's own difficult position.

" 'Tis an honorable offer," Sorcha Morton replied with dignity, "and I need a husband, my lord. The late Lord Morton left me quite penniless, as ye well know, and my fine Douglas relations hae given nothing but their scorn. I whored to earn my daily bread, Tavis, but I no longer hae the freshness of my first bloom, and I wish to settle down now that I hae had my fill of adventuring. I am twenty-four years old. Who could I wed wi at home? This French husband I am to hae will know nothing of me but that I am a suitable match, and I hae been sent by the king of Scotland to be his bride. My naughty past will be my own business, and I assure ye that I shall be a model wife to the duc.

"I am told that his delicate health keeps him at his château in the Loire Valley most of the year. 'Twill suit me fine. I will hae my bairns, and after I hae given the duc a houseful of heirs, perhaps I will come to court. I will be a respectable matron then, and whatever may hae happened in my past will be long forgotten by any in France who might know of my reputation. Ye mock me because I would wed a man who suffers from fits, but tell me, Tavis Stewart, what man, if any, is perfect? Ye surely are nae. Did yer own wife nae divorce ye?"

"Touché, madame," he admitted. "Forgive me, Sorcha, that I spoke roughly to ye, but I fear for ye so far from home and wed to a madman."

"Not so much that ye would make me an offer yerself, Tavis Stewart," she mocked him.

"I hae a wife," he said.

"Who left ye, my lord," she reminded him again, and then she laughed. "Besides, yer nae good enough for me now! I'll hae the duc for all his madness, and my bairns will walk wi kings." She drew a miniature from her satin drawstring bag and showed it to him. "This is my duc," she said. "He dinna look as if he is dangerous."

The earl took the little painting and gazed at it. The Duc de St. Astier had a narrow, esthetic face with a long nose and a full sensuous mouth. His eyes were a watery blue, and his hair a dull brown, into which the artist had attempted to instill some life by painting in golden highlights. If his look was vacant and without expression, at least he did not look cruel, Tavis Stewart thought. Perhaps Sorcha Morton had not made such a bad bargain after all. "He looks a gentle laddie, Sorcha," the earl told her. "Be kind to him."

"He is rich, Tavis," she replied, her amber eyes glittering in anticipation, and in that moment he saw a glimpse of the old Sorcha Morton. "I shall hae any and everything I ever wanted," she told him excitedly.

Because the wedding had been arranged between the regent, Madame Anne, and King James, it would be celebrated at Notre Dame, the great cathedral on the Ile de la Cité near the royal palace. King Charles rarely stayed in the royal palace, preferring his Hotel de Valois on the occasions when he was forced to come up to Paris from his beloved Amboise. Immediately after the nuptials the entire court would leave for the Loire Valley. It was already late spring, and with the warm weather, there was always the threat of plague.

As the representative of the king of Scotland, it was Tavis Stewart's duty to escort Sorcha Morton to the altar where her bridegroom awaited her. She was magnificently gowned in rich cream-colored satin, heavily embroidered in pearls, which quite suited her red hair, caught up in a gold caul. Her long train was of cloth of gold and fell from bejeweled bands on her shoulders. It was embroidered with both the Douglas and the St. Astier coats of arms.

The Earl of Dunmor almost stumbled over his own feet when his eyes found Arabella Grey, and if he was startled when he saw her, her look was one of far greater surprise. She seemed to be escorted by two gentlemen; a small fellow with a merry smile, who was dressed in green and gold satin; and a tall, handsome man garbed in deep rose silks who seemed almost proprietary of Arabella's person. She was fetchingly gowned in pale pink silk and cloth of silver.

"She's his whore, I'm told," Sorcha murmured softly, also noting Arabella. Within minutes of becoming the Duchesse de St. Astier, Lady Morton was quickly recovering her previously lost spirit, as well as her vitriolic tongue.

Arabella was finding it hard to breathe. The press of un-washed bodies in the cathedral had been bad enough, but to suddenly see Tavis was, she was certain, more than she was quite up to this day. She had been glad when Adrian had told her that they had finally found a bride for poor Jean-Claude Billancourt. He was a kind man for all his infirmity. An infusion of fresh blood, Adrian had said, that would hopefully eradicate the madness in the next several generations of the ducs de St. Astier. Learning the bride's identity, Arabella had wisely held her tongue. She was hardly in a position to criticize. Sorcha Morton might have the morals of an alley cat, but if James Stewart had sent her to France, there was a good reason for it. Tavis Stewart, however, was a different matter.

"What is it?" Lord Varden murmured softly to her, seeing her look of consternation.

"The gentleman escorting the bride is my . . . is Tavis Stewart," Arabella said low.

Tony nodded understandingly.

Arabella heard neither the choir nor the droning sermon of the bishop of Paris, who was performing the ceremony. She had thought that she had come to terms with herself regarding her position as Adrian Morlaix's mistress. It was hardly a secret, but both she and Adrian were well-liked. It had been expected from the moment he had seen her and evinced his desire to have her that she would eventually be his. Their behavior was discreet and their relationship accepted. When she returned home to England, it was unlikely anyone would learn of her French involvement, as she had come to think of it. Now, here was Tavis Stewart come amongst them, and she already felt the censure in the stiff set of his neck.

Sorcha Morton was once again a married woman. Here in France she would not be known by her Celtic name, Muire Sorcha. Her name would be Frenchified, and she would be Marie-Claire, Duchesse de St. Astier. It quite suited the woman who now swept proudly down from the altar on the arm of her bridegroom. At the great doors to the cathedral the newly-married couple greeted their guests. The duchesse's amber eyes narrowed as Arabella was presented to her, and she might have made some scathing comment, but Arabella curtsied prettily and, wishing the bride and groom good fortune, passed quickly by. Behind her, however, Adrian was caught by poor Jean-Claude Billancourt, who was pitifully eager to show off his beautiful wife. The crowds closed about Arabella, cutting her off from her escorts.

"So, madame," a familiar voice hissed in her ear, "I come to France to find ye playing the whore. Is there nothing ye will nae do in order to regain possession of that wretched scrap of borderland known as Greyfaire?" He could have bitten off his tongue even as the words spilled angrily from his mouth. This was not what he wanted to say to her. This was not the way he had meant to begin, but when he had seen her with the Duc de Lambour, he had known that all Jamie had told him was true.

"How dare you accost me?" she hissed back, shaking off his hand on her elbow.

His fingers closed cruelly about her arm, halting her flight. "Ye owe me an explanation, madame!"

Arabella looked angrily up at him. "I owe you nothing, my lord," she said fiercely. "You forfeited your rights over me when you failed to honor your promise to me to retrieve my property. It was not even for me, Tavis. It was for our child."

"And where is our daughter?" he demanded.

"Safe, and where you will not find her!" Arabella snapped.

"In Henry Tudor's nurseries, ye mean," he said.

Suddenly Arabella's face crumbled and she looked eagerly to

him. "You've seen our Margaret? Is she well? Is she happy? Did she remember you?"

In that moment all his anger dissolved. "Nay," he said. "Yer English king would nae let me see her. It was last autumn. Ye'd already left for France."

"My dear." Anthony Varden was by her side. "Before the duc sees you and wonders with whom you are speaking so heatedly, we had best go."

Arabella nodded, but Tavis Stewart said fiercely, "I've come to take my wife home, sir, and who the hell are ye in the first place?"

"I am Anthony Varden, my lord earl, and your behavior, however well-meaning, is placing Arabella in a most difficult position. You would not want her sacrifice of these past months to be in vain, now would you? Find your way to Adrian, my dear, while I give Lord Stewart your excuses," Lord Varden said quietly, placing his small frame directly in the path of the Earl of Dunmor.

"Arabella!" His voice cut into her heart like a knife, but she did not falter as she moved away from him.

"My lord, come with me and we will talk," Lord Varden said, escorting his companion out of Notre Dame and into the great square in front of the cathedral. "I have been expecting you for some months now, my lord," Anthony Varden said bluntly. "The king wrote me that you had been to Sheen."

"I understood that you were an exile, Lord Varden," the earl said. "An enemy of King Henry."

"So it is said," Anthony Varden replied with a gentle smile. Then his voice became urgent. "My lord, you must not interfere with Arabella. Soon she will have what she has come to France for, and King Henry will return Greyfaire to her. You took Greyfaire from her once, my lord. Do not do it again, for she will certainly then never forgive you."

"What do you know of me and of Arabella?" the earl asked angrily. He was beginning to realize that he was in the middle of a situation he could not control.

"Everything, my lord, for Arabella and I have become good friends," Lord Varden said gently, seeing the earl's rising frustration and feeling sympathetic toward him. "Exiles often do, you know. My home was near York."

"You are a spy," the earl said softly, suddenly comprehending, "and you and Henry Tudor have made my wife a spy as well."

"Your wife has fought for her property as hard as any man. That her methods and weapons have not been what you would use does not matter, my lord earl," Lord Varden told him.

"Are ye nae afraid that I will betray ye, sir?" Tavis Stewart said.

Lord Varden grinned up at the big Scotsman. "Now why would you do that, my lord? Do you not love Arabella Grey? Are Scotland and England not at peace? Has not King Henry offered his infant daughter, the princess Margaret, born last November, to your own king as a wife? Why, my lord, we are practically family."

Tavis Stewart could not help laughing at his last remark. "My nephew will nae accept an English wife, man, but yer right. Our countries are at peace. Still, I dinna like the idea that Arabella is in any danger."

"You love her greatly, I can see," Lord Varden said. "It's written all over your face, my lord, but under the circumstances, I would prefer you masked your cow eyes toward Lady Grey. When she has returned to England, my lord, then you two may settle your differences and reacquaint yourselves. France is not the place to do this, and now is certainly not the time. Go home, my lord earl. Arabella is in no danger except through you. The Duc de Lambour is a very jealous man."

"She is my wife," Tavis Stewart said stubbornly.

"She *was* your wife," Lord Varden answered him.

"I dinna recognize the divorce," the earl replied.

"You do not have the luxury of that choice, my lord," Lord Varden told him. "You say you love her and you fear for her safety, yet you persist in endangering her. I do not understand you."

Tavis Stewart groaned with despair as the reality of the situation hit him. He had stumbled into something that had absolutely nothing to do with him, and what was worse was that Lord Varden was correct when he said that if he, Tavis, could not mask his passions for Arabella, he would endanger her safety. He had to go. Besides, he could not bear to stay and watch the Duc de Lambour being so possessive of her without soon giving in to jealousy and rage. "I will leave tonight," he said to Lord Varden.

"She'll be home soon, my lord, and once she is at Greyfaire, perhaps you will come raiding again," he finished with a smile.

"She told you how we met?" the earl said.

"Aye," Lord Varden told the earl. " 'Twas a bold thing you did when you carried her off."

"And she has never forgiven me for it," the earl said sadly.

"But she will once she has regained Greyfaire," said Lord Varden wisely, "for she loves you too, my lord. She has never denied it."

The wedding guests adjourned to the palace, just a short stroll from the cathedral, where a small banquet was served to celebrate the Duc de St. Astier's nuptials. Afterward, and with almost indecent haste, the king and his friends departed for the Loire. The king feared that the cherries in his orchards at Amboise would ripen and spoil before he got there. They were his favorite fruit.

"We shall have a fete, Adrian," he said loudly to the Duc de Lambour, "and you, ma petite rose d'Anglaise, will rule over my fete as its queen of beauty and love. Will you like that?"

Arabella smiled winsomely at King Charles and curtsied most prettily. "I shall be honored, sire," she said.

"You look exactly like a cherry blossom in that gown of yours, madame," the king continued. " 'Tis a most fetching pink, is it not, Adrian?"

"I adore ma Belle in any of her gowns," the duc replied gallantly.

"Or without them," the king said wryly, and led the ensuing laughter.

The new Duchesse de St. Astier looked hard at Arabella, and turning to her husband, asked softly, "Why does the king make such a fuss over the Duc de Lambour's whore?"

Jean-Claude Billancourt blanched. "Marie-Claire," he said in quiet but disapproving tones, "the Duc de Lambour is the king's close and dear friend. As for Madame Grey, perhaps she is indeed the duc's chère amie, but there is no harm in it. She is a most charming and delightful woman who is well-liked by all here. She has many friends and is quite respectable. Perhaps you are not used to such things, coming from an uncivilized and backward land like Scotland, but here certain relationships are tolerated as long as they are discreet. You will have to learn to hold your tongue, chérie, else I dare not let you associate with polite society." He patted her hand. "I'm certain that you will learn quickly, Marie-Claire, ma belle femme, *n'est-ce pas*?"

Sorcha lowered her head as if with remorse and bit back the sharp reply that rose to her lips. There would be time, she decided, once she had established herself in her husband's affections, to wreak her revenge upon Arabella Grey for the slights that had been inflicted upon her several years ago, when Arabella was the Countess of Dunmor. How the mighty had fallen, Sorcha thought with satisfaction. She looked up at her husband. "Of course, mon mari," she said in sweetly lisping tones, "and you will teach me all I need to know, will you not?"

The besotted bridegroom kissed his wife's smooth, perfumed hand eagerly, his eyes straying to her half-naked bosom. "We shall stay the night in Paris at my hotel," he said meaningfully. "Tomorrow is time enough to be on the road, chérie."

The court adjourned to the Loire Valley, where Lady Grey and Lord Varden were the guests of the Duc de Lambour at his charming and intimate château, Rossignol. The château, a Gothic structure with whimsical pepper-pot turrets, sat on a hillock overlooking the river. It was surrounded by a forest on three sides, but on the fourth a vineyard rolled down to the Loire. Rossignol was positioned in such a way that it appeared to be the only habitable structure for miles, although it was not. It was actually just several miles distance from the king's home at Amboise.

"Does your wife never come here?" Arabella asked her lover. She had been comfortably settled in an apartment immediately next door to that of the duc's rooms, which were obviously meant to be those of the duchesse.

"No, my wife has never been here," Adrian answered her. "She rarely leaves Normandy. I prefer that she stays with the children, for they are her primary duty." He dropped a kiss on her silk-clad shoulder. "I have never brought any woman here to reside in these apartments since I became duc. The rooms were especially refurbished for you," he told her. "Do you like the crimson velvet? My vineyards grow a grape that makes wine that color. You shall have it tonight, ma Belle!"

"We cannot," she told him. "We have been invited to Amboise, for the king is giving a party for the Duc and Duchesse de St. Astier."

"He seems most taken with the bride and groom," Adrian Morlaix remarked.

"Perhaps he is considering his own marriage to Margaret of Austria," Arabella said.

"Charles will never marry the Hapsburg wench," the duc told her.

"They are betrothed," Arabella said, sounding logical and most female.

"Betrothals can be broken," he said.

"So you have told me before, but for whom would the king do such a thing, Adrian?" She turned about and kissed him lightly on the mouth. "If we were betrothed, would you cast me off?"

"Vixen," he laughed, and then he grew serious. "You must not repeat this, of course, ma chérie, but Louis of Orléans has been secretly proposing for some time now that the king marry Princess Anne, the heiress of the duchy of Brittany. It is most important that Brittany be made a part of France. Franche Comté and Artois are not even adjoining territories. Brittany is much more important to us."

"But the king imprisoned Louis in Lusignan over two years ago," Arabella said, "and to my knowledge he is still there."

"But his wife, Jeanne de Valois, the king's sister, is constantly intervening on behalf of her imprisoned husband," the duc said. "Although the king still smarts over the Guerre Folle, he is near to forgiving his cousin Louis. Until Charles has children of his own, which means finally taking a wife, Louis remains his heir. The king has always been most fond of him, which accounts for the harshness of his sentence on Louis. He felt most betrayed by Louis's conduct."

"But Anne of Brittany is to marry Maximilian of Hapsburg, Margaret's father, now that his wife, Mary of Burgundy, has died," Arabella said in a tone that implied that Adrian Morlaix must simply have his facts incorrect, or that perhaps she wasn't intelligent enough to understand all of this.

"Would you like to place a small wager on the chances of that ever happening, ma Belle?" he teased her. "France will not let Maximilian have Brittany, I promise you." He tumbled her onto the bed and tickled her unmercifully.

Arabella squealed and hit at him with her fists. "Men! You

are all mad!'' she said. "Stop, Adrian! *Stop!* We shall be late if you do not cease this instant!''

Reluctantly he arose from her bed. "Very well, madame,'' he said, "but prepare yourself to accept my vengeance for this slight tonight when we return.'' Then, with a grin he left her, whistling.

When she was certain that he had gone, Arabella called to Lona. "Go to Lord Varden and tell him I must speak with him privately as soon as possible. Go carefully, for I do not want it looking like I sent for Tony. Do you understand?''

"Then it would be better if you waited until tonight and spoke with him at the king's fete,'' Lona counseled wisely. "Oh, I know you are anxious, 'Bella, to get us home again to Greyfaire, but you must be careful. To misstep now would be a great tragedy.''

Arabella nodded. "Aye,'' she agreed. " 'Tis true that I'm impatient. Dear heaven, Lona! We've been gone over a year now, and Margaret has probably already forgotten me!''

"Just a little bit longer, my lady. You've been most brave. Even me da says he's proud of you. You're a true Grey right enough!''

A true Grey. Arabella almost laughed aloud at Lona's kindly though innocent words. What would her parents, God assoil their good souls, and her illustrious ancestors think of this last descendant of theirs, who, using her body, sold herself in order to retain what they had so bravely earned with their loyalty and their swords? Well, she had done the best she could, and now that she had the information she had sought for all these months, she could actually think of going home to Greyfaire at last.

It was indeed valuable knowledge she possessed. Charles VIII's father, the old Spider King himself, had made the betrothal between Margaret of Hapsburg and his son. To not only break off the engagement between the young French king and that lady, but to steal Anne of Brittany from beneath the nose of Maximilian of Hapsburg was no mean feat, if it could be done. Maximilian was not going to take kindly to such a monstrous and double insult. Wars had been fought over less, Arabella knew. She also realized the danger of France possessing Brittany, which until now had been England's loyal ally. Aye, 'twas important information, and certainly more than paid for the return of Greyfaire. Her heart soared with joy.

She was unable, however, to hide her happiness that night, and the duc remarked, "I can see that already the salubrious air here in the Loire is doing you some good, ma Belle. You have really been too pale all this winter."

"Perhaps it is something more," the king said slyly. "Is it, madame?"

"I do not know, sire," Arabella replied in honeyed tones, "but I can indeed say I have never been happier."

The king had arranged for a troupe of entertainers, and as the rope dancer began her turn, Arabella heard Tony Varden murmur in her ear, "Meet me in the rose garden, my dear. Your Lona has told my Will that you have information for me." Lord Varden moved on, craning his neck as if most interested in the performance that was so entrancing everyone else.

Certain that no one was looking at her, Arabella moved discreetly to the back of the crowd of nobles and walked unhurriedly toward the rose garden. Once there, she strolled casually amid the fragrant bushes, fanning herself with a peacock's feather fan with a carved ivory handle set with silver, which the duc had given her. To any who bothered to look, she was simply bored with the entertainment, or perhaps too warm in the early evening heat.

"Good evening, my dear." Lord Varden joined her, kissing her hand. "What is it that you would tell me?"

"The French intend breaking off the king's betrothal to Margaret of Austria in favor of Anne of Brittany," Arabella said low, and then proceeded to tell him everything that the duc had told her.

"God's blood!" Lord Varden said, whistling softly. "That is a piece of news, my dear! King Henry will be most pleased with you."

"I want to go home now," Arabella said. "The king said no more than a year, Tony, and a year has passed. I have gotten the information that we sought, and I want to go home. I need to see my daughter, who has undoubtedly forgotten she has a mother by now. I long to be at Greyfaire, which will surely be mine once again. I have more than earned it and expiated my debt to the king."

"I must send this news to England first, Arabella," Lord Varden said.

"Let me be your messenger," Arabella pleaded softly.

Lord Varden shook his head. "I cannot allow you to return to England without the king's permission," he told her.

"I cannot continue to be Adrian Morlaix's whore, Tony," she replied. "No matter how hard I try and convince myself that what I have been doing is right, it is wrong! I have done what I must in order to save my home. I shall have to live with the memory of that for the rest of my life. I can continue no longer, however. Let me go home!"

"You shall go nowhere, Arabella Grey, but to the Bastille!" a familiar and venomous voice hissed. Sorcha Morton, now Duchesse de St. Astier, appeared from behind a tall rosebush. "And you also, my lord! Neither of you will go anywhere but to the executioner."

Lord Varden paled momentarily. Arabella, however, but a moment ago near tears, suddenly became a tigress. *"Indeed, Madame la Duchesse?"* she snarled back. "And why do you think I should go to the Bastille?"

"You are a spy," the duchesse said low. "I shall inform on you, and not only endear myself to my husband, but to my new king as well. This is my revenge on you for all your insults at King James's court. You will end your days unloved! A toothless old hag far from your beloved Greyfaire!"

"Beware, Madame la Duchesse," Arabella warned her. "You are far from home and think your past a secret thing, but if you dare to expose me, I shall expose you! How do you think the most noble and proud Duc de St. Astier will appreciate grafting on his ancient family tree a brand new bride who whored her way through the Scots court with shameless abandon? I know some rare tales of you, Sorcha Morton, including the incestuous relationship you had with not one, but several of your cousins. Say one word to anyone about what you have just overheard here this night, and you will find your marriage quickly annulled. As for you, my dear Sorcha, you will be sent home in disgrace to face an embarrassed king. There is nothing for you in Scotland now, and I doubt that Jamie Stewart would be happy to see you back under any circumstances. He has fallen in love, I hear, and indiscreet, cast-off old amours are certainly not welcome in his life. Betray me and you will end your days in the gutter from whence you surely sprang! I have not come so close to victory to have you snatch it from me. I will kill you first!" Arabella

declared, her green eyes blazing dangerously, her hands clench-
ing and unclenching themselves into fists.

"*Bitch!*" replied Sorcha, now near tears herself. "I hate you
so much that I shall be unable to hold my tongue. I fear you will
ruin me!"

"Hold it but three days, madame," Lord Varden said coax-
ingly in gentle tones, "and we will be gone from France. With
the temptation removed, Madame la Duchesse, you may, in
good conscience, remain silent forever." Taking her hand, he
smiled winningly into her eyes.

"Why can I not expose you *after* you are gone?" the duchesse
demanded petulantly.

"It will look as if you were in collusion with us, my dear,"
Lord Varden warned, still holding her hand and gazing into her
amber eyes.

"Can you not be content knowing that you have driven us
from France before we have fully completed our mission?" Arabella lied, her tone sounding most aggrieved.

The duchesse brightened. "I have stopped you, haven't I?"
she said, and she smiled happily.

"Indeed you have, my dear," Lord Varden told her, smiling back at her warmly. "Be content in having done that, *and*
in your incredible good fortune at marrying your duc. The
little knowledge we have been able to glean in these many
months of trying is certainly not of any vital importance to
France's safety. No wars will be caused over it." He raised
her hand to his lips and kissed it lingeringly. "If you can
keep our little secret, my dear duchesse, I shall send you a
pretty bauble from Calais."

"A wedding gift, my lord?" Sorcha said coyly, moving
against him provocatively.

Anthony Varden smiled slowly down into her face. "Something for you alone, *my dear*," he said softly, and then, "What
an adorable mouth you have, duchesse. I do not believe I kissed
the bride, did I?"

To Arabella's intense amusement, Sorcha giggled girlishly
and presented her lips to Lord Varden for a kiss. He obliged the
lady with a deliberately unhurried embrace that left her frankly
breathless.

The new duchesse, however, recovered quickly. "I am sorry
you must leave France, my lord," she said boldly.

"I, as well, my dear duchesse," Lord Varden told her sincerely.

"We are going to be missed," Arabella said practically.

"I am afraid Lady Grey is correct," Lord Varden said with a great show of reluctance. Releasing the duchesse's hand, he then tucked it through his arm. "You will allow me to escort you back to the entertainment, of course, my dear." Ignoring Arabella, he began to lead Sorcha Morton back up the gravel path from the rose garden.

Alone, Arabella strolled once more through the fragrant bushes. It was unfortunate that the new Duchesse de St. Astier had overheard her conversation with Anthony Varden. Arabella was not comfortable with the idea that Sorcha Morton would keep their secret willingly. Hopefully, the threats of exposure regarding her past conduct, and Tony's sensual charm, would keep the bitch in line; but Arabella did not want to trust either of their lives to chance. One good thing had come from all of this, however. She was going to get to go home immediately. When and how they would travel would, of course, be up to Lord Varden.

"Here you are, ma Belle." Adrian Morlaix was by her side. "Did the entertainment bore you, chérie?"

"Aye," she responded languidly. "And I am warm in this gown as well. I thought perhaps to cool myself amid the roses, but there is no breeze," Arabella complained, fanning herself rapidly to punctuate the point.

"Mayhap you will be cooler out of your gown," he murmured, and kissed her mouth lightly. "I have a surprise for you, ma Belle."

"What is it?" she demanded. "Oh, Adrian, you are so generous! The jewelry and gowns you have lavished upon me are outrageous."

" 'Tis neither jewelry nor gowns, chérie," he told her. " 'Tis something I believe you will like even better."

"You are not going to tell me, are you?" she pouted, and he felt his passion rising. He could never get enough of her, and his greatest sorrow was that although she enjoyed his lovemaking, never had he been able to rouse her to the fullest.

"We will take our leave of the king as soon as we dare," he promised, and kissed her again.

It was two hours, however, before they were able to ride back across the countryside to Rossignol. The summer night was warm and still, the air sweet with newly mown hay. A large moon, pale and creamy in color, cast a bright golden light over them as they rode. When they neared the château they could hear the song of the nightingales for which the estate was named, singing in the trees. For a brief moment Arabella could not help but consider how perfect it all was.

As they descended from their mounts, the duc said to her, "When may I come to you, ma Belle?"

"I must bathe," she told him. "I shall not be cool until I do, monseigneur. Lona will knock upon your door when I am ready to receive you."

"Then I will bathe too," he told her, leaving her at the door to her apartments.

Arabella attended to herself in a leisurely manner. This might be the last night that she was forced to yield herself to Adrian Morlaix. In a strange way, she felt sad, for the duc was not an unkind man, and had always treated her gently and with respect. He did not know that she had become his mistress merely in an effort to gain information for England. He accepted her for what he thought she was. An impoverished English noblewoman, driven from her country by an unjust king. Lest she feel too sorry for him, however, Arabella forced herself to remember that he had made her his mistress for precisely that reason. Because she was helpless and undefended. He had used her unfortunate circumstances to lure her from the path of virtue; except that a woman who used her body in the way she had could hardly be considered virtuous, Arabella concluded. Well, it was almost over and done with. In time she hoped the memory would be not be so painful. She would, however, never forget this time in her life.

"Well, you're washed again, though I can't see that you was dirty to begin with," Lona said. Then lowering her voice she continued, "Did you speak with Lord Varden?"

Arabella nodded. "I will tell you when there is less danger of being overheard," she whispered back.

Lona undid her mistress's long hair from atop her head, where it had been pinned, and brushed it free of tangles. Arabella's hair fell in waves almost to the floor. "Will you want a camisia?" Lona asked.

"Nay," Arabella told her. "It is too warm. Open the win-

dows that I may get whatever breeze comes in the night.'' She
walked across the bedchamber to the great carved-oak bedstead
which was draped in rich crimson velvet brocade hangings heavily embroidered with gold thread bumblebees, hummingbirds,
and wildflowers. The bed's mattress was topped with a feath-
erbed and covered in rose-scented linen sheets and a down coverlet which had been drawn down. Arabella reclined seductively
upon one elbow atop the bed. ''I believe I am ready to receive
my lord now,'' she said drolly.

Lona grinned wryly at her mistress and bustled about the
chamber tidying it up. When she had finished, she snuffed all
the candles but the ones on the bedside table and the mantel,
checked the wine carafe to make certain that it was full, and
curtsying to her mistress, said, ''I bid you a good night, my
lady.''

''Knock on the duc's door to let him know I am ready for him
now, Lona,'' Arabella said.

Lona curtsied again and rapped sharply on the door connecting the duc's bedchamber with that of her mistress. Then she
hurried out.

The door had barely closed behind her when the other door
opened and the duc stepped across the room. Like Arabella,
he was nude. Walking to the bed, he bent and kissed her.
Something was wrong! Arabella started nervously and drew
back, wondering what the problem was. Then she heard a
familiar laugh and gasped in shock as a second Adrian Morlaix, equally au naturelle, came through the connecting
door.

''You could not fool her, Alain,'' he said in pleased tones.
''You may be my mirror image, but you do not kiss women as
I do.''

''I have never had any complaints about my kisses, Adrian,''
the first man said in slightly annoyed tones.

Was she going mad? Arabella's head swiveled between the
two men. ''Adrian?'' she finally managed to gasp to neither man
in particular, for she could honestly not tell them apart. ''Who
is this man, and why have you allowed him to enter my bedchamber?'' Instinctively she reached for the coverlet to shield
her body from the bold stare of the man who appeared to be the
duc's identical twin.

''Get into bed, Alain,'' the duc commanded his companion

as he himself lay on one side of his mistress. He kissed her quickly and continued, "Do not be angry, ma Belle. This is the surprise I have promised you. This gentleman is my half brother, Alain de Morlaix."

"Your half brother!" Why on earth was she repeating his words?

"Allow me to explain, chérie."

"Please do, monseigneur. In fact, I believe that you most certainly do owe me an explanation for introducing a stranger into my bed!" She glowered at Alain de Morlaix.

He smiled engagingly at her, and she realized that although he looked exactly like the duc, his eyes, in fact, were dark brown, unlike Adrian's, which were blue. "Do not be angry, petite," he said softly. "Let Adrian defend his conduct before you condemn it."

Arabella found herself sitting, large goose-feather pillows at her back, between the two men. "Well, Adrian?" she demanded.

"Alain's mother and my mother were half sisters," the duc began. "Louisa, Alain's mama, the elder by a year, was my grandfather's bastard. The girls, however, were raised together and were inseparable. So much so that when my mother married my father, Louisa came with her rather than be left behind. My father was a man of great appetites, and with my mother's permission, took Louisa as his mistress. Alain and I were conceived at approximately the same time. We were born in the same hour, on the same day, although I am the elder by several minutes. It was important to my mother that I be born first, and the effort of birthing killed her. My father then married Louisa, although the marriage was considered morganatic. We have two younger sisters, Marie-Phillipa, which was my mother's name, and Marie-Louise. They and I are legitimate. Alain is not."

"I do not," Arabella said sternly, "see what this has to do with our situation."

"Alain is my dearest friend," Adrian Morlaix said. "I share all my thoughts with him, even the ones that distress me. You, ma Belle, have given me great pain, although I realize that you never meant to do it, chérie. It hurts me that I am unable to bring you into the full flower of passion when we make love.

Never before has this happened to me. I realize, of course, that the fault is not mine. The fault lies in you, ma Belle, but I would nonetheless bring you that special happiness, for I do quite adore you.

"It occurred to me that perhaps two men could accomplish what one has been unable to do. Under normal circumstances I should never share my mistress with anyone, but since I have decided to do this for you, mon amour, I could only share you with one man in this whole world, my brother Alain. Like me, he is skilled in the arts of Eros and Venus. Together we shall bring you to the heights of ecstasy, ma Belle!"

Arabella didn't know whether to laugh or to cry. All these months she had been holding Adrian Morlaix in thrall with her cool and elegant demeanor while in the throes of passion. It had never occurred to her that her seeming inability to attain *la petite morte* with him would give him such distress that he would propose such a solution! She had even intended that tonight she would yield herself fully so that his memories of her would be happy ones once she was gone. Her sudden disappearance would, of course, be confusing to him. What in the name of heaven was she to do? "My lord," she began, but he stopped her mouth with his hand.

"This frightens you, ma Belle. I can see it in your eyes, but you must not be afraid. Alain and I will be the most gentle and the most considerate of lovers, chérie. You will know pleasure this night as you have never before known it, I promise you." He touched her cheek. "Look how she blushes, Alain. Is it not charming? I believe that ma Belle is shy at the thought of sharing herself with us both."

Alain de Morlaix turned her face to his and smiled at her. It was an incredibly sweet smile. "You must not be shy of us, ma petite," he told her. "We mean you no harm." He put his arm about her. "Why, she is trembling, Adrian! We must reassure her this instant!"

"Give me your lips, ma Belle," the duc ordered quietly. She turned to face him, shrugging off Alain's arm. He kissed her ardently, his tongue pushing past her teeth into her mouth.

Arabella wasn't certain that she shouldn't be afraid of these two men. Their voices were gentle, and they claimed that their intent was as well. She obviously had no chance at escape from them, and yet, how did one woman make love to two men at the same time? Was such a thing even possible? Had it been done before? What kind of men did such a thing? *What kind of woman did such a thing?* If she protested more volubly, would they cease? Somehow she didn't think so. Perhaps if she was quiet and cooperative, if she allowed herself release and convinced the duc his brother was no longer a necessity in their bed, just perhaps Alain de Morlaix would be quickly sent away. Nonetheless the duc could hardly be surprised if she left him after this. The situation, though frightening, was also providential.

The duc held her face between his two hands. He pressed her mouth fiercely even as she felt two other hands sliding around and cupping her full, round breasts in an embrace. The effect was most startling. Arabella shrieked, but Alain de Morlaix murmured softly in her ear.

"Non, non, chérie. Do not be afraid of me. How lovely your breasts are. They are like the first firm apples of the autumn." He fondled her flesh enthusiastically. "Perfection! They are pure perfection!"

She did not know if it was his touch, or his words, or simply the piquancy of the situation, but Arabella felt her breasts, suddenly tender, swelling and growing fuller within the palms that fondled them. Gently he pinched her nipples, pulling them out to their fullest length between his two fingers, and then tweaking them quickly with his thumbs until she thought she would scream with the sharpness of the sensation.

Alain de Morlaix nipped at the lobe of her ear. Slowly and deliberately his tongue licked at the inner shell of that same ear as he murmured low into it, "Already my manroot grows eager to sheath itself within your delectable little body, ma petite. I am wild with my desire for you, chérie." He kissed her ear and then said, "Adrian, give me her lips now. Surely you have sated yourself of them by now."

The duc released her mouth reluctantly from his embraces, saying to his brother as he did so, "I shall never grow tired of ma Belle's kisses, Alain, for they are as sweet as the nectar of the gods. Still, I will relinquish them to you for a time, mon frère, but you must promise to give them back."

The duc then leaned forward and, bending his dark head,

began to suckle upon her sensitive breasts even as his brother turned Arabella's head toward him and kissed her lips with hot kisses.

She was assailed by a plethora of sensations racing over her whole body. Neither man seemed to care at this moment whether she participated in their lovemaking at all. Their sole aim, and both were quite determined in it, was to arouse her to the fullest heights of desire. Arabella knew that they were going to succeed quite easily in this intent. She did not believe that a marble statue could have resisted the gentle lust of these two handsome men.

There was, of course, a certain humor in the situation. Adrian Morlaix would never know how hard she had struggled over these past months, how terribly difficult it had actually been to restrain herself from showing her true emotions. He was a wonderfully passionate man, and several times she had come perilously close to revealing herself. That it had all been but a sham to retain his attentions until she learned what she had come to learn no longer seemed important. That she had succeeded in deceiving him so well was a certain comfort and a humorous thought in this unexpected and difficult situation in which she now found herself. Still, her conscience troubled her even as her passions were slipping out of her control.

Hands. She was no longer quite certain whose hands began to stroke every inch of her body lovingly. Her shoulders. Her bosom. Her belly. Her thighs. Her buttocks. There was not a part of her that they did not touch. She was like a child's doll, helpless to their will, being turned this way and that way as the two eagerly explored and loved her. Her mind was reeling with their kisses and their touches. She burned fiercely one moment, shivered wildly the next. Arabella began to moan softly, unable any longer to deny or even delay the pleasure that the duc and his younger brother were giving her. She began to strain her body toward their delicious caresses.

"Ahhh, ma Belle," the duc purred, pleased to see her reaction. "You are beginning to feel the passion, aren't you?"

"Ohhhh, yesss!" Arabella gasped. "Oh! Oh! Ohhh, yesss!"

Smiling, Adrian Morlaix sat back against the goose-feather pillows propped against the bed's carved linen-fold headboard. He drew Arabella into a half-reclining position against his hard chest. Alain de Morlaix then began to kiss her torso, his lips moving lower and lower across her taut, perfumed flesh. His tongue flicked out against her skin, causing her to start nervously even as he drew her legs open to him, and the duc crushed her breasts in his hands, kneading the flesh almost painfully as Alain finally reached the sensitive jewel of her womanhood. Arabella cried out sharply as, opening the soft and vulnerable folds of flesh that hid her little pearl from his immediate sight, his tongue began to love her quite expertly; stroking her with long, slow touches, suckling on her until she was wild with needs she had denied for months; until her own desires were as uncontrollable as the cries that she could not sustain.

"Mon Dieu! Mon Dieu!" Alain cried excitedly. "She is like honey, Adrian! I cannot get enough of her! I cannot!" He lowered his head again, his tongue worrying at Arabella's flesh hotly as the first wave of tempestuous fulfillment began to wash over her.

"Take her, mon frère! Take her!" Arabella heard the duc say savagely. "Take your pleasure now, but leave the culmination for me, I beg you, for my own desires long to be sated!"

By some miracle his words managed to penetrate Arabella's consciousness. They shook her to her core, but what in God's name had she actually expected to come from such a ménage a trois? Still, her conscience fought a final battle to prevent this sensual madness. "Non! Non!" she cried. "Non, Adrian, non!"

The duc gently caught her little hands in his, restraining her. Cradling her in a tender embrace, he looked down into her face, and placing his lips against hers, said softly in soothing tones, "Non, ma Belle. Do not struggle against our pleasure."

Arabella was half fainting, but even so she could feel Alain de Morlaix now firmly astride her, his hard thighs pressing against her, his manhood penetrating her with a slow but sure thrust. He groaned with unfeigned delight as he began to move upon her, his body almost shaking in his excitement.

"Chérie! Chérie! What bliss! Mon Dieu, what bliss!" he cried aloud, and then, "Sacre bleu, Adrian! She has unmanned me

like some untried boy!'' Alain collapsed atop her, half sobbing
with his frustration.

''The night is young yet, mon frère.'' The duc laughed,
not in the least disturbed by his brother's brief performance.
''Ma petite rose d'Anglais has much to give, and we shall
take it all, n'est-ce pas?'' He gave his sibling a moment to
recover himself, but then, attuned to Arabella's delicate
state, he at last said, ''Alain, dismount and let me finish
what you have but started. I believe that ma Belle is near to
total and complete fulfillment thanks to our mutual efforts
on her behalf!''

Arabella struggled to open her eyes, for although her senses
were aroused, she still felt shame and had not quite been able
to face the sight of both men using her. She felt Alain de Morlaix
moving off her, and finally able to focus, saw Adrian mount her.
He smiled down into her face.

''Do not fight it, ma Belle,'' he murmured. ''Let the passion
take you and sweep you away!''

She felt him thrust hard, and then he was filling her full of
himself, and in that terrible instant she knew she was lost. There
was no way she would prevent him from gaining his victory this
time, and the truth was that his victory would be hers as well.
Her arms wrapped themselves about him, drawing him down
against her even as she pushed herself up to meet his downward
movement. Her legs wound about his torso as she clawed at his
back, her nails digging hard into him.

Adrian Morlaix threw back his head and laughed aloud. ''You
cannot resist this time, ma Belle!'' he cried. ''At last you are
completely mine!''

Never before had Arabella felt as she felt at this moment. Her
heart was pounding wildly within the cavity of her chest, yet all
of her concentration seemed to be focused on the violent storm
rising from deep within her. She knew that she was totally out
of control, but the fear building inside her stemmed from the
realization that she was unable to govern or contain her passion
any longer, rather than from the passion itself. It threatened to
overcome her entirely. Suddenly, in a burst of pure clarity, she
understood that only by surrendering to this overwhelming passion could she survive it. Slowly, for her fear was almost as
great as her desire, she let go of her grip on reality and was
swept wildly up into the maelstrom. *Up. Up. Up.* Until suddenly

she was falling, falling, falling into a warm and endless darkness. She could hear the sounds of a woman screaming, and the cries of a man well-satisfied; but certainly it had nothing to do with her. Like a small frog in the deep depths of its pond, she pushed herself away from it. Away into the swirling darkness where only the safety of nothingness awaited her.

■ *Chapter 21*

"M y, God!" Lord Varden said anxiously. "You look like the very devil himself, Arabella. What has happened?"

"I am not certain that I want to discuss it, Tony," she told him. "You have come, I presume, to tell me when we can leave. Please, let it be soon!"

"The king plans a day-long hunt tomorrow in his forest," Lord Varden said. "It is the perfect time for us to leave, although there will be some questions, I'm certain, about our disappearance," he told her, and then he took her hand. "Arabella, you really don't look well at all. Are you certain that you are all right?"

"Tony," she asked him, "have you ever shared a woman with another man?"

Lord Varden looked startled by her question, and then he blushed as he said, "Well, on one or two occasions, my dear, I—" He stopped suddenly, and blanching, said, "God's bones! Are you telling me that the Duc de Lambour . . . that Adrian Morlaix . . . God's bones, Arabella! Such a thing is not to be borne! You are a decent woman, not some common trull!"

"Oh, I bore it, Tony, for I had no other choice," she told him. "Did you know that Adrian has a half brother who might be his twin? Only their eye color is different. His name is Alain de Morlaix."

"But why would Adrian do such a thing?" Lord Varden wondered aloud. "It is obvious that he adores you. In fact, he is in love with you, much to the court's amusement."

"And it was for just that very reason that he did what he did to me last night," Arabella said. "I played the game too well, Tony. I was so cool in passion in order to retain his interest, that he felt he must give me complete fulfillment, as he so delicately put it." She laughed ruefully. "Since he himself was unable to accomplish that feat alone," Arabella continued, "he shared me with the one man he could share me with without being

422

jealous. His half brother Alain.'' She shuddered, and Lord Varden put a comforting arm about her.

"Are you strong enough to make this trip, Arabella?" he inquired of her, concerned.

"I *must* make this trip, Tony, for I cannot bear the thought of another night like last night. They planned to spend the entire night with me, and had their delicate attentions not rendered me unconscious for over an hour after their first assault, they might have. When I finally came to my senses at last, Adrian had, in a fright, sent Alain away. I began to weep and could not stop for some time, though my poor duc begged me to cease. Finally I fell asleep after he swore to me that he would not allow Alain back in my bedchamber that night.

"Let me rest today. Adrian has not visited me this morning. He was called to Amboise quite early, I am told. When he returns I shall be very angry with him. He will not spend the evening in my bed, and I shall cry sick tomorrow for the hunt. We will be long gone by the time he returns, for you may rest assured that the king will have them all back to his château for a feast afterward.''

"With luck," Lord Varden told her, "we may well be gone a full day before the duc even notices that we are gone. I shall go off on the hunt myself, however, but I will slip away during the first chase and meet you at the inn at Villeroyale. We will continue on to Calais from there.''

"We must travel round-the-clock, Tony, but for brief stops. I do not want Adrian catching up with us, and we cannot rely on the Duchesse de St. Astier to keep our secret. Sorcha is not reliable, and she hates me, though she has no real cause. We cannot trust our safety to her goodwill, for she has none.''

"I fear you are right, Arabella," Lord Varden said. "She persisted in keeping me by her side last night when we returned to the entertainment, and all her questions were of you. She is fearfully jealous, and you are correct when you say you believe her to be harboring a grudge. She is.''

"I was newly married to Tavis Stewart when we went up to court for my first visit," Arabella explained. "Sorcha—she was Lady Morton then—attempted to rekindle her old friendship with my husband. I do not think I was too harsh in my objections.'' She smiled a small smile, and Lord Varden was relieved to see it, for her pallor was greatly unnerving him. "Beware that she does not take advantage of you, Tony," Arabella teased him.

He chuckled. "She will not have the chance."

"Only because we are leaving," she said.

"That too," Lord Varden admitted, "but in actuality, our duchesse will not have the time. Poor Jean-Claude Billancourt had one of his attacks last night and insisted that his wife sleep in the kennels with him. No one dared to interfere, and so the lady is much the worse for wear this morning, for I am told the St. Astier hounds do not like her very much. So when she was not servicing her lord and master as a good bitch does, she was kept busy fending off the other dogs, several of whom—and I have this on the very best authority, my dear—nipped at her. She finally struck her husband on the head, rendering him temporarily unconscious, and then called for the servants to release them from the kennels, which they did immediately, fearing for the duc's life."

"Poor Jean-Claude," Arabella sympathized. "How is he?"

"Quite recovered from his fit, so I have heard, but he does have a most dreadful headache," Lord Varden replied.

Arabella could not help but giggle at this.

There was a knock upon the door and Lona bustled in. "The duc is back," she said, "and heading this way, I've not a doubt."

Lord Varden stood up. "I will return to my own rooms," he said and hurried out.

"Quickly," Lona told her mistress, for she knew everything that had transpired the night before, "into your bed, my lady!" and she took Arabella's robe de chambre from her, laying it across a chair. "Will you see him?"

"If I do not," Arabella said, "there is the danger that someone will tell him that Lord Varden was here, and he will wonder why I would see Tony but not him."

"Lord Varden didn't abuse you!" Lona said sharply.

"Still," Arabella told her, "it is best I face him now. Then perhaps he will leave me be for the rest of the day."

The knock upon the door sent Lona scurrying to answer it. She opened the door, and curtsying to the duc, admitted him before departing.

"Ma Belle!" Adrian Morlaix said as he sat down upon the bed and took her hand in his.

Arabella snatched her hand away as if it had been scalded. "*I detest you!''* she hissed at him. "How do you dare to face me after what you did to me last night?! I never want to see you again!''

"Don't be angry, ma Belle," he pleaded with her. "What I did, I did for you. I could not bear seeing you so close to passion yet unable to attain it. I love you!''

"Liar! You do not love me at all! If you loved me, you should not have treated me like a whore! Like some common trull, passing me about like a sweetmeat to be shared! Go away! I hate you!''

"Non, ma Belle, you do not hate me. You are angry, and I understand your anger, but it will pass," the duc answered her, and leaning over, he kissed her cheek.

"I will never forgive you,'' Arabella said honestly.

"Of course you will, ma petite rose d'Anglaise. Of course you will," he told her with perfect confidence. "Our adventures d'amour of last night were a shock to you, I understand that, but you will admit that you reached out for passion as you have never before reached out for it. You attained *la grande petite morte*, ma Belle! You were magnificent, and I adore you for it!''

Arabella glowered at him stonily.

The duc chuckled, convinced that she was just having a tantrum; a tantrum that she would soon get over. He caught up her hand again and kissed it. "If I promise you never to introduce another into our bed again, ma Belle, will you forgive me?''

"Leave me!'' she commanded him icily, ignoring his query.

Rising from the bed, the duc departed her bedchamber, certain that in time his beautiful English mistress would forgive him, although he really did not understand her anger. There had been no real harm done. He and Alain had, indeed, been most tender and gentlemanly.

Arabella kept to her apartments all day, refusing even to join the duc and his guests for dinner. When he entered her bedchamber late that evening, he found Lona sitting by her mistress's bedside. The servant stood and curtsied.

"My lady is not well, my lord, and has taken a sleeping draught," she told him. "She begs that you make her excuses to the king tomorrow, but she says she will not be able to join the hunt.''

"Is she truly ill?" he asked Lona. "Or is she simply being petulant?''

"My lord!" Lona looked indignant at the suggestion that her mistress might be shamming.

"That is no answer," the duc persisted.

"Last night was too much for her, my lord," Lona said bluntly. "My lady is suffering from nerves, the headache, exhaustion, and the effects of too much weeping. She is a gentle soul and has been badly used, though I know you will not like to hear it."

The duc looked uncomfortable beneath Lona's direct gaze. Finally he said, "When she awakens, Lona, tell her that I love her. Reassure her that the events of last night will never be repeated again, as I earlier promised her. I shall make her excuses to the king, and I shall make my own as well, for I will not leave her side in her illness."

"My lady will be pleased to know that you've repented of your wickedness, my lord; but she'll have a fit if you don't join the hunt," Lona told him frankly. "She likes King Charles very much, and she wouldn't want him worried needlessly. If you don't go on the hunt tomorrow, the king will, indeed, fret that her ladyship was so poor that you stayed home as well. Someone like that new duchesse—who hates my lady, and would grasp any opportunity to do her a bad turn—is certain to start a rumor of plague then. The next thing you know, we'll all be forced to pick up and settle somewheres else for the summer. Why, the king might even decide to go to Normandy for the waters, and my mistress could scarce be your guest in Normandy, my lord, could she?"

"You're a clever girl, Lona," the duc noted with a chuckle, having fully understood the servant's not-so-veiled hints. "You can assure me, however, that your mistress is not seriously ill?"

"Aye, my lord, I can."

"Then I shall spend the day hunting tomorrow with the king and his guests. Tell your mistress when she awakens that I will undoubtedly return home late from Amboise. I shall not see her until the day after tomorrow, at which time I shall expect her to have made a full recovery. Do you understand me, Lona?"

"Aye, my lord," Lona told him with a knowing grin and another pert curtsy.

"Good night, then," the duc said, and returned through the connecting door to his own rooms.

When the door had clicked firmly shut and Lona could no

longer hear the duc's footsteps, she said softly, "He is gone, my lady."

Arabella rolled over and sat up. " 'Twas nicely done, Lona," she said, "and 'twas quick thinking on your part when he said he would stay home with me. Thank you."

"I'm as anxious to go home to England as you are, my lady, and so are the others too," Lona told her.

"The trip will not be easy," Arabella said. "We will travel without ceasing, stopping only to change the horses and to eat."

"I'll not be unhappy to see the back of France," Lona said. "This life is too rich for me, my lady. I long for the simplicity of the borders. Besides, 'tis past time Fergus and I were wed. What shall I pack for you?"

"Only a few changes of clothing, Lona, for I'll not need all these beautiful clothes at Greyfaire. You may pack the jewelry that the duc has given me, however, for God knows, I have earned it! I shall not wear any of it ever again, but it can be placed with a goldsmith in York and drawn upon for funds to help me keep the estate in the bad years."

In the early hours of the dawn, Arabella watched from the high windows of her rooms as the duc and Lord Varden rode out from Rossignol to join the royal hunt at Amboise. The château's servants, a small staff, for the duc preferred it that way, were far too busy with their own tasks to notice the departure of their master's leman. Besides, it was not their business to question Arabella. The coach had been quietly and carefully loaded in the dark hours before the dawn, when the château's grooms-men had slept unawares in their loft above the stables. The mare that Arabella had brought from England was at her house outside of Paris, for the duc had given Arabella a new mare after their first night together, and she felt it unnecessary to bring both horses to Rossignol. They would retrieve Arabella's English mare on their journey to Calais and leave behind the other beast. FitzWalter and the Greyfaire men escorted their mistress, drawing no attention at all, for such was their usual habit.

Several hours later they reached the inn at Villeroyale where they stopped to await Lord Varden. He arrived shortly before noon. After eating, they set out once again, and for the next several days they traveled round-the-clock, stopping only to change the coach horses, relieve themselves, and eat. From their third day onward until they arrived at Calais, there was the increased danger of pursuit. Arabella had left the duc a brief note saying that she could not forgive him for his conduct toward her and that she hoped he would accept her decision in this matter and not follow her. She had not wanted to do this, but Lord Varden had insisted that she could not simply disappear without causing an uproar. It was always possible that the duc would accept her judgment, but if he did not, perhaps his ego would allow him to believe she would return of her own accord in a few days after she had worked her temper off. These few days could give them the time they needed to reach Calais. Lord Varden had sent one of his own men ahead to arrange for their immediate passage across the channel to England. They must escape France without delay lest the Duchesse de St. Astier betray them.

They reached the safety of Calais in five-and-a-half days' time, even with a brief stop at Arabella's small house outside of Paris to collect her mare. They had arrived at Maison Riviere in the middle of the night. Fergus MacMichael crept into the stable to retrieve the beast while the stableboy hired to care for it slept quite soundly during his foray. He left a silver piece by the lad's head, knowing that when the boy discovered the coin and the missing horse, he himself would depart lest he be blamed for being negligent in his duties. The silver would give him a new start in life. They fled on through Paris, leaving the city well behind them even before the dawn.

Arriving in Calais, however, they met with a serious delay. A severe summer storm was rolling in from the channel, and no ships, their own included, would put out to sea before it had run its course. Lord Varden's agent had arranged for their accommodations in a neat little inn near the harbor called The Wild Rose. Since there were but three guest rooms available at the inn, there would be no others but themselves. The Wild Rose was too small a place to encourage neighborhood traffic, and an extra coin to the landlord ensured their complete privacy. Although Calais was technically an English possession, Arabella knew that she would not be entirely comfortable until they were safely on English soil once more.

After two days the storm had dissipated and the captain of their vessel, *The Maid of Dover*, told them that they would be departing on the next tide early the following morning. With luck they would be in England by the late afternoon. It was at the very moment that the vessel's captain left them that Adrian Morlaix chose to make his entrance. Anthony Varden drew a sharp breath even as Arabella paled visibly. Both FitzWalter's and Fergus MacMichael's hands moved to their swords, but awaiting Lord Varden's command.

"So, ma Belle, I have caught up with you at last," he said quietly, and he kissed her hand.

"To what purpose, my lord?" Arabella responded coldly, snatching the hand back. "Did I not make myself quite clear in the message that I left behind for you?"

"I would speak with you alone, ma Belle," he told her softly, meaningfully.

"There is nothing you have to say to me, my lord, that Lord Varden cannot hear," she answered firmly.

"Must our passion be a public thing, then?" he asked her.

" 'Twas you who made it so, my lord, not I," came the cutting reply.

The Duc de Lambour smiled ruefully. "Touché, ma Belle," he said.

"You have wasted your time, my lord, in following after me," Arabella said.

"Nay, ma Belle, I have not. I would have caught up with you earlier, but that a messenger arrived at Amboise from Normandy for me. My wife has died. She choked upon a fishbone," the duc said simply and without emotion.

"May God and his blessed Mother Mary assoil her soul, my lord," Arabella said piously. "I am truly sorry, Adrian."

"I want you to marry me, Arabella," was his startling reply.

She was stunned. Never before had he used her Christian name. He had always called her his *Belle. Never Arabella! Belle.*

"We can be married secretly, here in Calais, with Tony as our witness. I cannot let you go from me, but I must formally mourn Claude-Marie for a full year. It is her due, as she was the mother of my children," the duc continued in a matter-of-fact tone.

He had asked her to marry him! For a moment Arabella thought that she would weep. Had she misjudged Adrian Morlaix? "I cannot marry you, Adrian," she said finally.

"Then it is true," was his answer.

"What is true?" she demanded, but in her heart she knew to what he would refer.

"The Duchesse de St. Astier told me in deepest confidence that you and Tony are spies in the pay of England," Adrian Morlaix said sorrowfully.

Lord Varden laughed heartily. "What a tale," he said mockingly. "What on earth could that Scots whore possibly think to gain by such a tale? Poor Billancourt! Did you know, Adrian, that our new duchesse is rumored to have serviced every man in King James's court? A most amazing feat if it is true, and it does appear to be. When she became too troublesome, the king sent her to France. So much for the *Old Alliance*! Let us hope that the St. Astiers' heirs are indeed of their blood."

The duc ignored Lord Varden; his blue eyes looked directly at Arabella. *"Are you?"* he said quietly.

Arabella hesitated a moment, and then she said in as quiet a tone, "Aye." No more. Whatever Adrian Morlaix had done to her, she felt his proposal of marriage entitled him to the truth.

"Why?"

"For Greyfaire," she said simply.

"For Greyfaire? You betrayed me for a piece of land?" he demanded.

"Oh, Adrian," Arabella said gently, and she was unable to restrain a small laugh, "I did not betray you. King Henry simply placed me in the French court to watch and to listen. He fears that your King Charles will betray him as the French, indeed, betrayed King Richard several years ago. Did you know that that poor king was of my family? Henry Tudor merely seeks to solidify his place upon his throne. I have not betrayed you."

"You will tell your king what I told you regarding King Charles's possible marriage plans, however, won't you?" The Duc de Lambour looked somewhat aggrieved.

"Aye, 'tis a very sensitive piece of information," Arabella replied reasonably. "You could hardly expect me to withhold such a trump card from my king? 'Tis the only really interesting bit of knowledge I have obtained during my stay in France. It will, nonetheless, regain me my home and the custody of my child, who has languished this past year in the royal nurseries. I would do anything that I had to do for my wee Margaret, *and for Greyfaire*. Indeed, my lord, I have, haven't I?" Arabella's light green eyes never left his gaze as she spoke.

"I love you," he said.

"No," she replied, "you do not, though I think you believe

that you do. Had you really loved me, you could never have shared me with your half brother. You claim you wanted me to feel perfect passion, but had you loved me, Adrian, you would have sought yourself to find a means by which I might have shared that passion with you. You would not have treated me like a whore, but then I cannot really blame you entirely for that, can I, my lord? By becoming your mistress, I played the whore, and obviously I played it quite well. 'Tis a rather startling side to my character I think I should rather have not known about; but 'tis over now.

"I intend returning to England, to my home in the north, and neither you or anyone else will stop me! I shall never again venture far from Greyfaire, I assure you. I shall live a quiet, indeed, a most circumspect life; raising my child to be the new mistress of Greyfaire, and raising her little betrothed husband to both respect and husband not only my daughter, but her estate as well."

The Duc de Lambour looked grieved. "Will you not be lonely, ma Belle?" he asked her sadly. "You speak of your child and of your Greyfaire, but you say nothing of love."

Arabella laughed bitterly *"Love?"* she said scornfully. "By love, my lord, I assume you mean that illusion that is alleged to exist between men and women. There is no such thing except in children's tales, and in the overly romantic songs that are sung by minstrels who wish to please their masters, and the gullible women whom those masters desire to seduce. I have been the recipient of men's love in the past, my lord duc, and I far prefer the solitary life to such a life."

"Let me prove you wrong, Arabella," he begged her. "I know that my conduct several days ago was inexcusable, but if you can find it in your heart to forgive me, ma Belle, I will devote the rest of my life to expiating my sins against you. I love you as I have never before loved any woman!"

"Did you tell your poor Claude-Marie that, Adrian, before you incarcerated her at your château in Normandy? That you loved her as no other? Before you cut her off from your life, using her only as a brood mare to sire your heirs upon? Good manners bids me thank you for your proposal of marriage, and indeed I do, for I know you mean that proposal to be an honorable one. Common sense and hard experience tells me that my answer to you now is as it was before. *No!* Do not waste your time appealing to my heart, Adrian. I do not have one.''

"Mon Dieu!" he groaned. "You are cruel, chérie!"

"And you are kind, monseigneur?" she asked him. "When I bid you adieu in my letter several days ago, Adrian, I was kind. As kind as I dare be, for men are never really kind to the women they profess to care for, I have found.''

"Then there is no hope for us at all, ma Belle?"

"None," she answered him firmly.

"Come, Adrian, mon ami," Lord Varden said kindly. He wished to draw the duc's attention away from Arabella before the duc's disappointment turned to anger and thoughts of revenge. Adrian Morlaix was a most proud man. "Come and share a carafe of wine with me. You have ridden hard and far, I know. You will need strong evidence to refute the Duchesse de St. Astier's charges against us, should she speak publicly and indiscreetly. You certainly want to retain your friendship with the king.''

"I will not be guilty of treason," the duc said stubbornly, but he allowed Lord Varden to lead him to a table in the inn's taproom in whose entry they had been standing.

"There is no treason involved, mon ami," Anthony Varden said soothingly. "A bit of pillow talk that may or may not come to anything; and no one knows that it was said. Certainly you may easily silence the viperous tongue of Madame Marie-Claire by an intimate knowledge of her past, which I am certain Arabella will be pleased to pass on to you. As for Lady Grey's and my disappearance, you can simply say we returned to Paris. That you were able to trace us that far, but after that you lost our trail; that Barbe, Lady Grey's cook, told you we might be going to Hainault or Cleves, she wasn't certain. Say that Arabella fought over what you considered a trifle, and then she left you in a pique. Say I accompanied her because I am her friend and was bored. That because she amused you better than any other mistress you have ever had, you sought to bring her back, but alas, you could not find her. Ho hum, mes amis! Soon, another delectable creature will come along to keep you happy, and in the meantime you must go into mourning for Claude-Marie. In a year you will seek a new wife, *n'est-ce pas?*"

"You make it sound all so inconsequential, Tony," the duc

grumbled as he downed his first goblet of wine and then held out the goblet for more.

"It is all inconsequential, Adrian," Lord Varden replied, "and by your casual attitude you will make this seem nothing more than a trifle, an amusement. Remember, you have your children to think about, Adrian, particularly your two sons. You do want them to have the king's favor, do you not? Think of them first and foremost. Not of yourself and your personal disappointment." He refilled the duc's goblet and beckoned Arabella, who seated herself at their table. "Why don't you tell the duc the Duchesse de St. Astier's history, Arabella?" Lord Varden suggested. "Before he is too drunk to absorb it all, for we are both going to get quite drunk tonight, Adrian, aren't we? For old time's sake, eh?"

A small smile touched the duc's lips. "Oui, mon ami, we are going to get very drunk," he agreed, and Arabella began her tale of Sorcha Morton.

When she had finished, the duc was already beginning to be in his cups, and at a little nod from Lord Varden, she arose and slipped from the room. In the night she heard them singing bawdy songs in the room below her chamber, and she giggled to herself in the darkness. Tony was going to have a terrible head in the morning, bless him.

Lona woke her before dawn. "His lordship says we're to hurry, my lady. The tide turns in less than an hour."

Arabella rose and began to quickly dress. "How is Lord Varden?" she inquired anxiously.

"Perky as a courting wren," Lona replied.

"But how could he spend the night drinking with the duc and not be ill?" Arabella wondered aloud.

Lona chuckled. "I asked him the same thing, my lady, for I heard them singing too. Do you know what he told me? That after the first gobletful of wine, he kept refilling his cup with well-watered wine. He drank one goblet to the duc's three. By the way, he and me da put the duc to bed in Lord Varden's room. The innkeeper has instructions to treat the poor man with tender loving care when he awakens, for he'll have a sore head to be sure. Lord Varden has paid the bill for all, including the duc's men who are lodged in the stables with our own fellows."

Arabella could not help but smile at Lona's explanation. Tony really was a wonder, considering the circumstances. "Get me some bread and cheese,'' she said to Lona, ''and some fruit as well; and we'll need some for the voyage too! I'm starving! It must be the sea air.''

They sailed from Calais before the sun had risen, and with the sun came a brisk breeze from the southeast that sent their ship scudding across the English Channel to land them at Dover before the sunset. Arabella wept unashamedly to be back in England, and even Lord Varden's eyes were suspiciously moist with emotion, for he had not been in England in almost ten years.

''We'll overnight in Dover,'' Tony told her and sent his men to find a respectable inn for Arabella.

''And tomorrow?'' she asked him.

''We'll depart for Sheen, for the king will certainly be there and no other place at this time of year. He always spends Midsummer's Eve at Sheen. At least he has in the years since he has been king.''

''Can we start early?'' Arabella asked him.

''Before dawn, if you wish, my dear,'' Lord Varden told her, and they did. He had already dispatched a rider ahead, that King Henry know of their coming and be prepared to see them. He could see that Arabella had but two thoughts in her head. To be reunited with her little daughter, and to return north to Greyfaire as quickly as possible. Anthony Varden could not blame her for wanting to put the past year behind her. He would have told her of the deep admiration he felt for her had he not been afraid of her scorn. She was, he believed, a very brave woman. Her bitterness was but a defense behind which she hid the heart she claimed to be missing.

They arrived at Sheen, putting up at a nearby inn and finding that one of the king's servants was already awaiting them.

''His majesty will see you at ten o'clock tomorrow morning,'' they were told. ''His majesty wishes Lady Grey to know that her daughter is in excellent health and spirits, and most anxious to be reunited with her mother.'' The king's servant bowed, and without another word, departed.

''Where will you go, Tony, now that your service to Henry Tudor in France is over?'' Arabella asked her friend. They sat together in a private dining room eating a wonderful meal of good English beef, English cheddar, and October ale. Upon the sideboard was a basket of strawberries and a bowl of clotted Devon cream.

"Hal always promised me my own estate, my dear. Hopefully it will be somewhere near York, where my family comes from originally," Lord Varden told her.

"Have you any family left?"

"My elder brother, Simon, who will undoubtedly be relieved to learn that I am not the rebel he was at first so pleased to believe I was. Simon is slow of wit, you see. He was delighted to see me discredited before our father, whose favorite I was. Only when it dawned upon him that my ill fortune might reflect on him did he fret. It will also be a relief to him to learn I have my own properties." Lord Varden chuckled. "I shall also ask the king for a wife, that I may forestall any matchmaking on my brother's and his wife's part. They are singularly sour people and would undoubtedly choose for me a pious female with neither beauty, intellect, nor humor about her. I do not know if I can ever love another woman as I did my first wife, but I would hope to enjoy her company at least. Particularly as she will be the mother of my children."

Arabella nodded. "It seems as good a basis as any to make a marriage on, Tony."

"And you, my dear? What of you?"

"It is as I told Adrian yesterday, Tony. I have given up everything for Greyfaire and for my wee Margaret. I have accepted that and will build my life around those two."

"What of the Earl of Dunmor, my dear? Do you not think he could find it in his heart to forgive you? Could you not make a new beginning with him?" Lord Varden said hopefully.

"Nay, Tavis does not want me back, and why should he, Tony? 'Twas I who divorced him, after all. When he came to France, we fought almost immediately, and then he did not even bid me farewell when he departed for Scotland. Nay, he considers himself well rid of me and who knows, perhaps he is right. My own Lona once accused me of being a bad wife to Tavis Stewart. It was a courageous judgment for a maidservant to make against her mistress, but she was correct, I fear, and though she not be my equal in rank, we are friends. I cannot fault her. Besides," and here Arabella smiled almost mischievously, "I do not think I have done anything Tavis Stewart need forgive me for, Tony."

It was a pointedly honest assessment of the situation, and Anthony Varden was once more impressed with Arabella Grey's grasp of the state of her circumstances. He did not know another woman who would have been so direct, so honest; and he wasn't certain that he was comfortable with her bluntness. Women, he believed, should be a bit softer, a bit more dependent upon a man than Arabella Grey was. Still, he liked her.

Early the following morning Anthony Varden and Arabella Grey appeared before King Henry at Sheen. The sun was barely up, and the king had come directly from mass. Henry Tudor wanted as little fuss as possible regarding the restoration to his good graces of Lord Varden and Lady Grey. A careful man, he wanted no probing questions asked concerning his decision to return these two to his favor. His advantage over France was in keeping secret his knowledge regarding King Charles's marriage plans. How he would use the information obtained by Arabella Grey he did not know yet; but use it he eventually would. He chuckled aloud to himself. The little French king was more dangerous than he had thought, for like most, he assumed the young man a dullard, but Charles was not a dullard at all. He was the Spider's son, and blood would always tell. Maximilian of Hapsburg was a damned fool to believe he might snatch Brittany away from French domination. Aye, this information that Arabella Grey had brought to him was most valuable indeed.

"Tony!" The king clasped his old friend in a royal embrace, and stepping back, smiled, his little blue eyes bright with friendliness. It was the first real smile Arabella could ever remember seeing Henry Tudor smile. "It is good to have you back with me again, my old friend," the king said warmly.

"Sire," Lord Varden said, his voice thick with emotion and near tears at the gracious welcome.

"What, Tony? Not Hal? Whatever we may be to each other in public, we are still Hal and Tony in private," the king reassured his old friend.

"Thank you, my lord," Lord Varden told the king. "It is good to be in England after so long a time away. Riding up from Dover, I realized that I had almost forgotten how fair a place England is."

"You have been a great help to us, Tony, and we are grateful," the king said with sincerity. He put a friendly arm about Lord Varden. "You will remember I once promised you that when you returned home, I would see you suitably rewarded for your valiant service to the crown.'' The king lifted a sheaf of papers from his desk. Arabella could see the royal seal upon them. He held them out to Lord Varden. "These papers grant you a barony and make you the owner of Whitebridge, an estate north and west of York. It consists of some several hundred acres of land, both pasture, fields, and woods, as well as a fine little castle. By royal decree it will descend through your family in perpetuity. Take it with our grateful thanks, Tony.''

Lord Varden accepted the packet, bowing low to the king as he did so, and then he said, "I would have one additional boon of you, Hal. 'Tis bold of me to ask it after your great generosity, but frankly, I need a wife. Do you think the queen might know of a lady whom she would like to favor and who would make me a good wife? I have been away from England so long that I know of no young ladies I might consider. I must throw myself at your mercy, Hal.''

The king nodded thoughtfully. "You would want a young woman, one who could have children, of course, Tony. The queen has a young maid of honor, an orphan, Lady Anne Millerton, for whom I know she would like a husband. Mind you, the girl's dowry is modest, which has, of course, made it difficult to find a suitable match; but she is a pretty and obedient wench and has, I am told, a most merry disposition. I cannot, however, give her to you without the queen's permission, for my Beth does dote on the girl. She is just fifteen and reminds the queen of her younger sister. Still, as I do not wish a great deal of emphasis put upon your return . . .'' Henry Tudor considered a moment and then called loudly, "Peter, my lad, to me!''

Almost immediately an apple-cheeked young boy ran into the king's chamber and bowed. "My lord?''

"Go to the queen and tell her that I would have her and Lady Anne Millerton wait upon me immediately.''

The lad, who was the king's personal page, bowed again and ran from the room.

Henry Tudor now turned his glance upon Arabella. "Welcome home, Lady Grey. Tony tells me that this vital piece of information regarding King Charles's marriage plans is due to your cleverness, madame. Is this so?''

"Aye, my liege, it is so,'' Arabella replied simply.

"Then you have certainly earned your right to Greyfaire, madame, though I am as yet concerned with the thought of a woman holding that particular keep. Still, there is no war between Scotland and ourselves, and there will be none in the future, God willing. It is a poor place, your Greyfaire, so I am told by the clerk who visited there. Are you certain that you would not accept from us a more prosperous estate for yourself and your child? I would not be mean with a woman who has given so much of herself for England.''

"No, my liege, but I thank you for the offer," Arabella said. " 'Twas Greyfaire for which I fought, and 'tis Greyfaire only that I want and will accept from you.''

"The Percys will not have your lass for their bastard slip, madame," the king said quietly. "They think your lands valueless and not worth having. Lord Percy would seek higher for his brat." He looked at her to see what effect his words would have.

"Lord Percy is a pompous, hotheaded fool, my liege. I would not trust him if I were you," Arabella replied. "Margaret is too young for me to worry that I have not yet found a husband for her. There will be someone in time, sire, and you will approve of him, I know."

The king nodded. "Very well, then, Lady Grey." He handed her a sheaf of papers similar to those he had handed Lord Varden. "These are yours, madame. Greyfaire belongs to you once more, and it may descend through either the male or the female line of your family in perpetuity."

"Thank you, my liege," Arabella said gratefully, and she curtsied low to the king.

At that moment the queen hurried through the door into the king's chamber, a young girl in her wake. Both Lord Varden and Lady Grey made their obeisance.

"My dear lord," the queen said anxiously, "what is it that you would send for me so precipitously?" Her pretty face was livid with distress.

"Calm yourself, Beth. This is Lord Anthony Varden, my old and dear friend of whom you have heard me speak. He has been in France these many years, and he has rendered us many a valuable service," the king told his wife meaningfully. "He has returned now with Lady Grey. You do remember Lady Grey, madame? She will be leaving today for her home at Greyfaire, and has come for her daughter. Tony will also be going north to his estate, Whitebridge. He has asked me if I would make a suitable match for him so that he might take a wife with him.''

The light of understanding dawned instantly in the queen's eyes, and she looked to young Lady Millerton, who, not being a dense girl, also understood where this was leading. Glancing quickly in Anthony Varden's direction, Lady Millerton blushed. She was a pretty girl with brown-gold hair and soft gray-blue eyes. Lord Varden suddenly looked shy and stared down at his feet.

The queen's eyes twinkled at this silent exchange. She liked Anthony Varden's appearance, and he had the look of a good man. "Am I to understand, my dear lord, that you would like to marry my little Anne to Lord Varden?"

"If the lady has no strong objections, madame," the king replied.

The queen turned to her maid of honor. "Anne, what say you? It is an honorable offer, and Whitebridge is a pretty estate. I know it well, for it once belonged to my uncle George, and later to my uncle Richard. I know that my dear lord, the king, would not offer you to just any man, for he is well aware of how I dote upon you, and of the fact that you will always have my friendship.''

Anne Millerton stood perhaps two inches taller than Anthony Varden. She walked across the room to where he stood, and looking into his face, said in a gentle voice, "What say you, my lord? Do you find me pleasing despite my great height? I have heard from his majesty, the king, and I have heard from my lady, the queen, but I have heard nothing from you. I know 'tis most bold of me, and I am not bold by nature, I assure you, but what say you to this match, my lord?''

He was entranced by her, and it was written all over Anthony Varden's face. She was nothing in face or form like his dead wife, but there was a sweetness about Anne Millerton that caught at his heart.

"I say, Mistress Anne," he told her, "that I had forgotten how pretty English girls were, and that if you would consent to be my wife, you would make me the happiest of men. I am a good man, I promise you, and go to mass regularly." He stopped, not knowing what else to say.

"Why then, sir, if you will so generously have me to wife, I

will be right glad to have you as my husband,'' Lady Anne
Millerton said, curtsying to him.

"Good," the king said brusquely. "Then that is settled! Send
for my confessor, Peter, my boy, and we will celebrate this
marriage at once."

"My lord!" The queen was shocked. "There are the banns
to be read, and Anne's trousseau must be made ready, and I
would fete her even as her own dear parents would were they
yet living. This will be no hole-in-the-wall affair if I have anything to say about it!"

"Lord Varden must go north as quickly as possible," the king
said firmly.

"I do not mind a quick wedding," Lady Anne interjected.
"The king has been so generous in choosing me a good husband, madame, that if I must give up the frivolity that usually
surrounds a marriage celebration, I will gladly do so and make
no complaint afterward."

"You see, Tony? You are a fortunate man, indeed. She is a
most sensible girl!" the king said, pleased. "Fetch the priest,
Peter. We will meet him in my private chapel."

"May I go and fetch my daughter now, my liege?" Arabella
asked.

"No!" the king replied. "You will witness Lord Varden's
marriage to Lady Millerton, for Tony would not have it any other
way, would you, my friend?"

"But a few minutes more, Arabella," Lord Varden begged
her. "I have not a doubt that Hal will send us all packing before
the morning is out."

"Indeed I will," the king said. "In time, Tony, you may
return to court, but for now you must go home to Whitebridge."

The king's confessor came and protested volubly at the king's
wishes, but Henry Tudor overcame the cleric's objections so that
he waived the reading of the banns and performed the marriage
ceremony without further delay, uniting Lord Anthony Varden
to Lady Anne Millerton in holy wedlock. The queen, and the
king, and the king's page, Peter, and Lady Arabella Grey wit-
nessed the sacrament; and afterward toasted the somewhat dazed
couple with a goblet of wine.

"We must pack Anne's belongings, my lord," the queen finally said, "and, of course, Lady Grey would like to regain the
custody of her daughter. You and Lord Varden must certainly

have a great deal of catching up to do. As the hour is yet early, perhaps you will take this time to be with your friend before your day begins in earnest. The ladies will meet you in the courtyard within the hour, my lord. Lady Grey is, I assume, traveling north with you, Lord Varden?''

"She is," he admitted.

The queen shepherded the new Lady Varden and Arabella from the king's chamber, Arabella having thanked the king before she departed. "You will find that your daughter has grown taller in the year she has been with us, madame," the queen told Lady Grey. "She is a delightful little girl, if perhaps a trifle willful. Prince Arthur adores her. More so than his own baby sister, but perhaps that is because he can play with your daughter and not with his own sister yet."

Arabella let the queen chatter on, for she was delighted to learn everything she could about Margaret's year. When at last they reached the nursery, having sent Lady Varden to pack her possessions, the nursemaids hurried forward to greet the queen, carrying her son, who, at almost four, was still frail, although quite capable of walking; and a pretty, rosy infant of almost eight months who crowed and clapped her hands happily at the sight of her mother.

"Where is Lady Margaret Stewart?" the queen demanded. "Her mother has come to fetch her."

The eldest of the nursemaids turned and called out in a wheedling voice, "Come, my lambkin, yer mam has arrived to take you away now. Be a good little lass and come to old Sarah, my little sweetheart."

'No!'' The word was issued from a dark distant corner of the nursery.

"Lady Margaret," the queen said sternly, "come forth at once!"

"No! Will not!"

Arabella swallowed back her laughter, and following the sound of the voice, moved slowly across the room. There, in a dim alcove, stood her child, and the queen was correct. Margaret had indeed grown. She was now three years old. Arabella knelt down. "Do you remember me, Maggie?" The child shook her head in the negative. "I am your mother," Arabella continued, "and I have come to take you home with me to Greyfaire."

"I want to stay with Arthur," the little girl said stubbornly, reaching out to finger the gold chain about her mother's neck.

"I am certain that you do," Arabella replied, removing the chain from her own neck and slipping it about her daughter's. "He is a grand playmate, I'm sure, but you have only been visiting with Arthur. Now we must go home again. Would you like to ride with me upon my horse?"

Margaret's eyes grew interested. "Arthur has a pony," she said, and then added slyly, "Can I have a pony too?"

"When we get to Greyfaire," answered her mother cleverly.

"A pony of my very own?" Margaret persisted.

"Aye! And no one else shall be allowed to ride it but you, my wee Maggie," Arabella promised her.

Margaret Stewart moved out of the corner and into her waiting mother's arms for a hug. "Let's go home and get my pony," she said. "Then I will bring him back to show Arthur. May I bring it back to show Arthur, Mama?"

"Someday," Arabella said, picking Margaret up. "Someday, my Maggie!"

Chapter 22

*A*rabella Grey looked at what had once been a prosperous and fruitful orchard. The land was waist high in weeds, and there was not a sign of the young trees she had so carefully overseen the planting of some fourteen months ago. Her eyes turned to the village that had once clustered snug and cheery at the foot of Greyfaire Keep. It was gone. Nothing remained of the neat street of cottages where generations of Greyfaire's people had been born, had lived, and had died; nothing but a few piles of blackened stones, now wet with the summer rain. As Arabella and her party continued up the road to the keep, she noted a few scrawny sheep grazing in the overgrown meadows. Wordlessly she looked to FitzWalter.

"We'll know soon enough," he said grimly.

The drawbridge to the keep was raised in a defensive position, but as they neared it, it began to lower. The wooden drawbridge had been scorched with fire recently and bore the open marks of axes, pikes, and other sharp weapons.

FitzWalter halted their little party. "We don't know who's inside, my lady," he told her. "Let them come to us. We'll not be lambs walking into the lion's maw."

A single rider came forth from the keep, and Arabella said excitedly, " 'Tis Rowan! Rowan! Rowan!" She waved at him, and hearing her voice, he spurred forward to greet them.

"Lady! Thank God and his blessed Mother, 'tis you! Quickly! Into the keep! We never know when they will strike anymore."

"Who, lad?" FitzWalter said, putting his hand upon his son's bridle to stay him. "Have the Scots done this to Greyfaire?"

"*The Scots?* Nay, Da, 'twas not the Scots who destroyed Greyfaire. 'Twas Sir Jasper Keane. Please come now! We must get the drawbridge raised back up again. Even with your few men we have not the force to defeat them should they get the advantage over us."

They followed Rowan into the keep, and the drawbridge was raised, creaking behind them. Within the small courtyard Ara-

bella was shocked to see a number of small wooden huts that
had been constructed against the outer walls. She did not need
to ask. The stench of human waste and from an overpopulation
of farm animals sheltering within the courtyard was overwhelming.

Lona's eyes were wide with amazement. "God help us all!"
she said and clasped little Margaret against her bosom.

"Is the keep habitable?" Arabella demanded.

"Barely," came the reply.

Arabella dismounted her horse and hurried up the steps into
her castle. Within she found a variety of damage. All the windows in the Great Hall were broken, as was most of the furniture. The floors were badly scarred. There was dust and general
filth everywhere. Whatever had happened, she thought angrily,
there was no excuse for this!

"Why has your mother not seen to the castle?" she said to
Rowan.

"She ain't here, my lady. When the troubles got bad, and
most of Greyfaire's folk went south to seek safety and a new
life, I sent my mother and little sister to my eldest sister, Wanetta, in York. She didn't want to go, but I knew Da would have
done the same thing, given the chance. All that's left here, lady,
are the old and the stubborn," Rowan finished gloomily.

"Are there any women capable of working among the stubborn?" Arabella said dryly, and when he nodded, she continued. "Send them to me at once. We must talk, Rowan
FitzWalter, but until this hall is habitable, I will not listen to
anything you have to say." Arabella turned to Lona. "Take
Margaret to my rooms and make them livable if they are not,
Lona. Go with her, Fergus MacMichael, and help her."

"Aye, my lady," Lona answered her, glaring at her brother
furiously. Rowan certainly did not have a great deal of practi-
cality in his nature, Lona decided as she carried her charge
upstairs.

Several women, ageless and openly dispirited, came into the
hall bearing brooms and buckets of water. Arabella directed
them herself, wielding a broom with which she helped to sweep
the hall.

"If you cannot find men to repair this furniture," she raged
at Rowan, "then find me some furniture that isn't broken,

damnit! I do not care how hard the times have been here. You should have kept the hall in readiness for my return.''

He scuttled off, chastened. FitzWalter himself had gone back out into the courtyard to check the stables to see to his men and to get what information he could. Among the remaining women he found several who were capable, and he sent them to the kitchens with instructions to get the ovens going and to prepare food. He was furious at his only son, but he also understood that the boy had done his very best under the circumstances. He had assumed he was leaving Rowan with an easy task. Too many years of soft living, FitzWalter considered, had left him unprepared for the unexpected. An older, wiser man would have pursued Sir Jasper Keane and his men after their first attack, wreaking as many casualties as he could. An older, wiser man would have made certain that Sir Jasper did not come back after that first raid.

By nightfall they had managed to restore some semblance of order to Greyfaire. The windows in the Great Hall were shuttered closed, and a good fire burned in the fireplaces, removing the dank and musty chill from the room. Outside it had begun to rain heavily. The large oak trestle had been returned to the highboard, and several chairs as well. The sideboard was clean and shining with beeswax. On the table were the remains of two capons and a trout. There had been a bowl of peas, but it was now empty. A newly baked loaf had been almost totally consumed, and there was but a shred of cheese left. Arabella did not stand on ceremony this night. FitzWalter, Lona, Fergus MacMichael, and Rowan had all joined her. Wee Maggie was sleeping safely above, watched over by an elderly woman named Nora, who, upon seeing the little lass, had immediately claimed her as her own charge.

Arabella sat back at last, draining her cup empty and looking to Lona to refill it. She finally fixed her gaze on Rowan Fitz-Walter, saying, "Begin at the beginning, Rowan, and leave nothing out. You have done your best, I know, and I am not angry with you."

FitzWalter sent her a grateful look, and even Lona's eyes misted as she poured wine into her mistress's pewter goblet.

"Two months after you left," Rowan began, "Sir Jasper Keane came back to Greyfaire, my lady. The king's clerk was here, cataloging everything he could find. He had told us that the king now owned Greyfaire and that you had been sent into exile in France. The lads who came back, however, reassured the people that you and the king were but playing a game. They said that you would come home soon. At first our folk believed it, but then Sir Jasper came.

"At first he pretended to us that Greyfaire was now his by right of past possession, but the king's priestly clerk told him no and bid him begone. It was then that Sir Jasper and his men went on a rampage and wrecked the inside of the keep. They stripped the king's clerk, and several of Sir Jasper's men—led by that devil, Seger—used him most foully before they whipped him like a dog from the castle. I can still hear his howls. The poor fellow's buttocks were raw and he could not sit without pain for several weeks. We hid him in the caves until he healed well enough to travel. Then we sent him on his way, my lady.

"Sir Jasper, however, left after his men had finished with the poor clerk. We thought ourselves safe, but he was soon back, and he kept coming back. Each time he came, he destroyed a little more of Greyfaire. We never knew when he would strike. He came at all hours of the day and the night. He waited until the harvest was in last autumn, and then he stole it from us. This year he fired the fields each time the crop grew high enough to show promise. We finally stopped planting, my lady. What was the use of it? Sir Jasper destroyed the orchards last spring, just as they were coming into first flower. He drove off the sheep, but for the few you saw that remain. There wasn't enough food to see our people through the winter, and so many families left after Martinsmas, before the hungry times came. I sent Mother and my little sister to York after Christmas.

"In early summer Sir Jasper and his men came and destroyed the village, or what was left of it. No one was hurt, for those remaining had taken to living in the keep by that time. Since then he has been attempting to break into the keep itself. He has stated that if he cannot have Greyfaire, then he will tear it down stone by stone until nothing remains. We have managed to hold him off so far, my lady, and that is the end of my tale."

"Did King Henry know of this?" Arabella wondered aloud.

"I think not, my lady, else the king would surely have sent his troops to rout Sir Jasper," Rowan said innocently.

"I've spoken to everyone," FitzWalter said quietly. "Sir Jasper Keane has become an outlaw, my lady. Although his blackest venom is saved for Greyfaire, he has taken to raiding the helpless throughout the entire Middle Marches; and there seems to be no one strong enough to stop him at the present. Certainly someone in the king's household knows of this, yet no aid has been sent. Therefore, no help will be sent, for though this matter be important to us, it is of no account to the king, who has greater problems. Sir Jasper, after all, poses no threat to Henry Tudor, my lady.''

Arabella thought for several long minutes. She seemed to be wrestling with herself over something, and then she said, "We must send to Dunmor, FitzWalter. The earl has a long-standing grudge to settle with Sir Jasper Keane. I have no doubt that he would welcome the opportunity to do so."

"And you, my lady, are the bait to trap Sir Jasper," Fitz-Walter said with a chuckle. " 'Tis clever! Aye, 'tis clever, and it just could work."

"It must work, FitzWalter, or we shall never again know any peace. I cannot rebuild Greyfaire for Margaret if we are under the constant threat of attack from Sir Jasper Keane." She turned to Rowan. "You will carry a message to the earl for me, and you will leave as soon as I have written it. Sir Jasper Keane, even if he is aware of my return, has not had time to assemble his men. It is unlikely he will attack us in such foul weather. He thinks he has the leisure of time on his side, for he believes us to be helpless. You must ride quickly, for as soon as the weather turns fair, Sir Jasper will seek to strike out at us as quickly as he can." Arabella turned to Fergus MacMichael. "I would send you, Fergus, but that I need your good sword arm, and Fitz-Walter, your experience in battle. Will you stay with us?"

"I will, m'lady," the young clansman replied, and then he boldly said, "but I would have a boon of ye."

"I think I know what you would have," she told him. " 'Tis my Lona to wife, is it not?"

"Aye."

"You have my permission, but 'tis FitzWalter who must have the final say, as Lona is his daughter."

"I've no objection," FitzWalter spoke up, "but let's free ourselves of Sir Jasper Keane first."

Lona brought her mistress parchment and pen before she might even ask, and stood by her shoulder reading the words as

Arabella wrote them, for she had learned to read with her mistress when they were children.

> I have returned to Greyfaire.
> Sir Jasper is even now planning to attack the keep.
> Margaret is with me.
> Arabella Grey of Greyfaire

"You have not asked him for his help at all, my lady," Lona said, puzzled.

"I do not have to," Arabella told her, "and, therefore, Tavis Stewart will never be able to say that I did. He will come because of his daughter, who is in danger."

Lona's eyes grew round, and then she said bluntly, " 'Tis wicked, you are, my lady! Plain wicked!"

Arabella laughed as she rolled the parchment tightly, and sealing it with wax, pressed her signet ring into it hard. "No, Lona, I am not wicked, but I am proud. If there was any way in which I could remove the sting from Sir Jasper's tail myself, I should do it; but I cannot do it alone. I need the Earl of Dunmor's help, and in exchange I give him Sir Jasper Keane, with whom he has had such a long-standing feud. 'Tis more than fair."

"Da?" Lona turned to her father for support, but FitzWalter was grinning broadly.

" 'Tis clever whether you like it or not, Lona lass. 'Tis damned clever, and no one will appreciate that better than the earl himself," FitzWalter said.

Arabella handed the rolled parchment to Rowan. "Go," she said, "and remember, Rowan FitzWalter, that the fate of Greyfaire and all who remain here is in your keeping, my lad."

"I won't fail you, my lady," Rowan promised, and hurried from the hall.

"How long do we have?" Arabella asked FitzWalter.

"Not tomorrow," he told her. "We did not arrive until late today. It is unlikely Sir Jasper has a watch posted in the rain to spy upon the keep, for he had no idea that you would return, and the king's lack of interest in Greyfaire has given him confidence to do anything he wants at any time he desires to do it. Possibly the day after, if the word gets out—and these things do, though God knows how. With luck the earl will be here before

Sir Jasper, and if he is not, we will certainly be able to hold out. You are certain that he will come?''

"He will come,'' Arabella said, assured. ''Not for my sake, but for his daughter's sake.''

''Perhaps Lona is right.'' FitzWalter chuckled again. ''Mayhap you are wicked, my lady.''

And Arabella Grey laughed aloud, feeling truly amused for the first time in many months. ''Aye,'' she admitted to him, ''perhaps I am wicked, FitzWalter.''

The men upon the walls watched carefully all the following day, but the countryside about them was wet and peaceful. More peaceful, it seemed to the frightened residents of Greyfaire, than it had been in many months. The day, however, was gray and rainy. 'Twas not a day a man who believed himself to have all the time in the world would choose to attack his enemies. The night fell and the rain continued, heavier now.

When night had barely fallen, there came a rapping on the postern gate, and looking out the grille, the man on watch saw Rowan FitzWalter, the Earl of Dunmor, and behind them a large group of riders.

"Lower the drawbridge, Wat,'' Rowan FitzWalter said, and the man-at-arms at the postern gate gave the order to do so.

The earl and his clansmen poured into the already crowded castle courtyard, their horses jostling against people and cattle as they came. FitzWalter was immediately there, directing the men and horses to the stable area where they might shelter the wet beasts. A stableboy ran up to take the earl's great stallion, and the earl smiled at him.

"Rub him down good, laddie,'' he said with a smile, and then turned to FitzWalter. ''How bad is it?''

''We only just got back from France ourselves, my lord,'' the captain told him, ''but Sir Jasper, from what I can see, has done a right fine job of destroying Greyfaire. There's nothing left, and most of Greyfaire's folk have gone but for—as my son Rowan puts it—the sick and the stubborn.''

''And when I've finally killed Sir Jasper Keane, FitzWalter, will Greyfaire thrive again?'' the earl asked quietly.

A terrible sadness sprang into FitzWalter's eyes; a knowledge that he obviously found hard to face. Finally he looked directly at the Earl of Dunmor and answered honestly, ''Nay, I think not, my lord, though it pains me to say it. The land will come back in time with hard work and care, and my lady has good credit with the goldsmiths in York; but we have lost our people, my lord. No estate can survive without its people, and there are many who would question my mistress's ability to hold Greyfaire. If her ladyship is Greyfaire's heart—and she is—then Greyfaire's folk are the blood in its veins. There is not enough blood left in Greyfaire's body for it to continue on, to live again.''

"But yer mistress will continue to try, will she nae, FitzWalter?''

"Aye, my lord, she will,'' the keep's captain said fatalistically.

"Then,'' said the earl, ''I must continue to wait for her to come to her senses, though my family harangues me constantly to remarry and hae more bairns.''

"Lady Margaret!" FitzWalter said. "You will want to see our little lady! Oh, she is a right piece of goods, my lord. As willful as her mother, I vow!''

Tavis Stewart burst out laughing. "God help me then, FitzWalter,'' he said. ''One of them is more than I can handle, and I am nae ashamed to admit it either.''

FitzWalter chuckled in agreement.

They came into the Great Hall, and the earl saw Arabella standing by a fireplace warming her hands. A small, dark-haired girl was by her side. Hearing them, Arabella turned, and seeing him, she bent, whispering something to the child, who suddenly sped across the room toward the earl calling, "Papa! Papa!'' Tavis Stewart swept his daughter up into his arms and kissed her soundly, even as he silently marveled at the beautiful sky-blue of her eyes. As he looked past Margaret, snuggled happily in his arms, to meet Arabella's gaze, she saw that his eyes were wet. Turning away, she brushed the tears from her own eyes lest he see them.

Swinging back to face him, she spoke in formal, even tones. "You are most welcome to Greyfaire, my lord. I thank you for coming. You must be thirsty after your long ride. Will you have some ale? I regret I cannot offer you wine, but I returned only two days ago to find my cellars virtually empty, but for a cask or two. We will save what is left to celebrate your defeat of our mutual enemy. Nora, take Lady Margaret. It is past her bedtime. Margaret, bid your father good night. He will be here in the morning to see you, I promise,'' she told her daughter, who looked as if she would rebel, but reassured by her mother's words, she did not.

"Ale will be quite refreshing, madame. My thanks," he said, accepting the pewter goblet as the child was removed from his embrace. What a vixen she was, he thought, and he almost laughed aloud. She was behaving as if his visit were totally unexpected; as if finding himself in the neighborhood, he had simply stopped to visit. He was tempted to say that he had merely come to conduct his daughter to a place of safety, since he had learned Greyfaire would shortly be under siege. He wondered if he told her that whether she would then ask for his help. He doubted it. Arabella would fight Sir Jasper Keane in hand-to-hand combat before she would ask formally for Tavis Stewart's aid. Her pride would be the death of her.

"Your men may bed themselves down in the hall, my lord," she told him in a stiff tone. "A chamber has been prepared in the family apartments for you."

"Thank ye, madame," he said. "Do ye then consider me yet a part of the 'family'?" It had simply been too good to resist, Tavis Stewart considered, his dark green eyes twinkling at her.

She suddenly realized that they were alone. The hall was empty but for herself and the Earl of Dunmor. "This is a small keep, my lord, as you surely realize. Honored guests must, of necessity, be housed in the family apartments," she replied primly.

"Of course, madame," he answered gravely.

"You will be hungry after your journey," Arabella continued coolly. "I regret I can but offer you simple fare, but 'tis hot, well-seasoned, and filling, I promise."

The Earl of Dunmor found himself most tempted to grab the lady of Greyfaire and kiss her quite soundly. She was the most stubborn, most aggravating, most irritating woman he had ever known in his life, but she had totally spoiled him for any other woman. He had not seen her since his visit to France, but somehow the beautiful woman in her plain country garb fascinated him a great deal more than the elegant creature he had encountered in Paris. Whatever had happened between them, Tavis Stewart knew that he loved Arabella Grey; had always loved her; and would never love another woman but her. He wanted her back as his wife, his countess, the mother of his children. This time, however, he would not take her from Greyfaire. This time he would wait until she was ready to leave it of her own free will; until she was ready to come to him. He didn't care how long it took, he would have none but her.

His men were beginning to enter the hall, and the keep's few servants were hurrying in with the food. The men sat themselves down below the highboard, where their hostess, Father Anselm, the earl, and FitzWalter were already seated. Donald Fleming stamped up to the dais and plunked himself into the chair next to his elder brother. Arabella nodded her head in greeting, and he grunted something undistinguishable back at her.

"It is comforting to know that our estrangement has not altered my relationship with your brother, my lord," Arabella said with some small attempt at levity.

"Donald does nae change," Tavis Stewart said, amused. "However, he is a married man now, ye know."

"Donald?"

"Aye, me!" Donald Fleming said belligerently. "Do ye find that strange, madame?"

"Nay, sir, I do not, for does not the church teach that there is a woman for every man? She must be a most special lass, Donald Fleming, to put up with you."

"Aye, she's special," came the retort, "and a biddable lass too, unlike some I'm too polite to mention."

"More ale, Donald Fleming?" Arabella said sweetly, and when he nodded, she poured the contents of the pitcher into his lap. With a particularly violent oath that set the elderly priest to gasping, he leapt up roaring. Arabella cried out in seemingly distressed tones, "Ohh, sir, you must forgive me my clumsiness. I am so nervous with the thought of the battle to come."

Donald Fleming rushed from the table, followed by a manservant whom Arabella had signaled to care for her somewhat wet guest. FitzWalter swallowed his laughter lest he offend Donald Fleming, but it was not easy.

"Ye hae nae changed, spitfire," the earl chuckled, then sobered when he said to her:

"How wise you are to understand that, my lord."

Tavis Stewart nodded. "Aye, lassie," he told her softly, "I do understand. More, perhaps, than even ye may realize."

"Tell me how you will overcome Sir Jasper," Arabella asked him, changing the subject deftly.

"By means of an old ruse," the earl answered. "Before first

light Donald will leave Greyfaire with half of my force. They will be concealed just over yon hills. When our old nemesis attacks, we will catch him in a pincers movement. Donald will fall upon him from the rear, while my half of our clansmen and I will take the offensive and charge forth over yer drawbridge. Sir Jasper will be expecting neither of us because he does nae know we are here. He thinks ye helpless, and will be filled with thoughts of a final victory over Greyfaire. He will be dead before nightfall, madame, I swear it!''

'' 'Tis a good plan, my lord,'' she told him. ''More rabbit stew?''

''Aye,'' he said, and she filled his plate once more, adding a chunk of crusty, fresh bread and a wedge of a hard, sharp cheese.

''I have no sweet,'' she apologized. ''The orchards are gone, and I have not yet had the time to bring supplies in from York.''

''Yer company, Arabella Grey, is sweet enough,'' he replied.

She looked astounded by the compliment. Was it possible that he still cared for her, even after knowing that she had been the Duc de Lambour's mistress while in France? His face betrayed nothing, and Arabella decided that he was simply being polite to her. He had always been quick to turn a pretty phrase. She smiled. ''You are gracious, my lord, but the truth is, I am a poor hostess tonight. I will remedy my circumstances once we have disposed of our enemy. When you come to Greyfaire again, and you must for Margaret's sake, I shall entertain you in far fairer fashion, I promise.''

When the Scots were well filled with stew, and trout, small game birds, bread and cheese, one of them brought out his pipes and began to play. The ale cask was drained, and Arabella saw that another was set in its place before she excused herself from the hall.

''FitzWalter will show you to your room, my lord,'' she told the earl, and curtsying, went to her own rooms, where Lona awaited her mistress.

'' 'Tis to be hoped that Sir Jasper has had himself shriven recently,'' the servant said pertly. ''They say he'll be lying in his grave by this time tomorrow night if the earl has anything to say about it, *and he will!*''

''Pray God and his blessed Mother,'' Arabella said, and she undressed, wondering briefly—before she forced the unsettling thought from her—what it would be like to lie in the Earl of Dunmor's arms again. She shivered, knowing the answer.

"When shall I awaken you, my lady?"

"By first light, Lona. I want to watch the battle from the battlements. I want to see my lord . . . I want to see the earl deliver that wretch, Jasper Keane, his death blow. I hope the bastard sees me looking down on him in his death throes. All that has happened, Lona . . . all that has happened to me these past seven years has been because of Sir Jasper Keane. My mother's death, Jamie Stewart, Greyfaire's destruction, my stay in France! All of that misery due to one man. *I want him dead!*"

"There was good things too, my lady," Lona said quietly. "Your marriage to the earl, and little Margaret."

Arabella said nothing further, instead climbing into her bed. She crossed herself devoutly and turned her back to the maid-servant; but Lona knew that the barb had hit its mark from the flush on her mistress's cheeks.

Arabella should not have slept that night, and yet she did. More soundly than she had slept in months, and when she finally awoke, she heard Tavis Stewart's voice raised in ferocious anger coming from the hall. "Lona? Lona, where are you?" Arabella called, and the girl hurried in, talking even as she came, wide-eyed with the importance of her news.

"The earl is fearful angry, my lady! Sir Jasper Keane is dead! The earl and his brother are having a row the likes of which I have never seen! They're like to kill each other!"

"Give me my robe de chambre!" Arabella said, scrambling from her bed. Quickly she put it on and raced barefoot from her room and downstairs into the hall.

"Ye hae no right!" the earl was shouting at his younger brother, and he hit him a blow that knocked the younger man across the room.

"What the hell hae *right* got to do wi it, damnit?" Donald Fleming shouted back, stumbling to his feet and across the hall to deliver a blow to the earl's jaw.

"I should hae been the one to kill him, not ye!" the earl cried angrily, striking Donald a second time with all of his might and sending him reeling.

"What difference does it make?" Donald roared, staggering to his feet again. "The bastard is dead, and that's all that matters!'' He smashed a fist into Tavis Stewart's midsection, doubling him over.

"Stop it! Stop it this instant! *What is going on?*'' Arabella demanded of the two men. "Lona says that Sir Jasper Keane is dead.''

"Aye,'' the earl said, gasping and straightening himself up. "My brother usurped my rights when he killed him, didn't ye, Donald?'' He stepped threateningly toward the other man.

"Donald, I beg you to explain to me,'' Arabella said, putting herself between the two men.

"Our mam was afraid that Tavis would get himself killed, and there's no heir to Dunmor. Only an heiress, and her being raised *English*,'' Donald began.

Arabella grit her teeth, silently praying she would not lose her temper until this great fool had entirely explained himself.

"I promised Mam that I would see Tavis didna do anything foolish. Sir Jasper Keane is his weak spot, and she feared Tavis's rashness would make him less than careful. So this morning, just before the dawn, we crept from yer keep, and instead of waiting just over the hills to catch Sir Jasper in a pincers movement, I sent several of the lads to seek our Sir Jasper's position. Imagine our surprise to find that the bastard and his men were camped two miles from Greyfaire. The devil probably had thoughts of surprising ye at sunrise.

"We fell upon them in the false dawn,'' Donald continued with a wolfish grin. " 'Twas a glorious battle, even if it was too short. The lads butchered the English neatly, and quickly. All, but Sir Jasper, for I saved him for myself. I knew ye'd nae want him to hae too quick or easy a death, Tavis. 'Twas a pleasure to kill him for ye though he was nae much of a swordsman. More bluster than skill,'' he said, remembering the scene which still played vividly in his mind.

His men had made a circle about them, clearing the bodies of the slain away that the combatants might not stumble and be at a disadvantage.

"Pick up yer sword, my lord,'' Donald Fleming told his antagonist, "and say yer prayers, for ye'll be dead before the sun rises or I'm a disgrace to my father's name.''

Jasper Keane could barely get a grasp upon his blade's hilt, for his hands were wet with fear. His men had been killed before they had even been fully awake. The smell of blood was heavy in the air, and already the carrion birds were circling above them. He was going to die. Instinctively he knew it, and he peed his breeches with his terror.

The Scots encircling him snickered, and his pride pricked, Sir Jasper said, " 'Tis unfair. When I kill you, your men will kill me. I'll not fight you, you damned Scot! You'll have to kill me dishonorably.'' He smiled smugly at Donald Fleming.

"If ye can kill me, and I doubt ye can, my lord, then my men will let ye be on yer way,'' Donald said.

"How do I know I can trust the word of a Scots bandit?'' Sir Jasper replied insultingly.

"Ye can trust my word far more than I would trust yers, Sir Jasper Keane, murderer, ravisher of helpless women, *thief*," Donald said softly. *"Are ye a coward as well, man?''*

With a howl of outrage Sir Jasper leapt forward, taking Donald Fleming off guard and pricking his shoulder so that it bled slightly.

With a pleased grin Donald recovered and went on the attack. For several minutes the two men battled back and forth, but it was quickly obvious that the Scot was the superior swordsman. Slowly, methodically, he drove his English opponent from side to side of the circle in which they fought, amusing himself as Sir Jasper's terror grew. And then finally, seeing the horizon beginning to glow red with the impending arrival of a new day, he ceased toying with the man and, thrusting cleanly and swiftly, put an end to their battle.

"I told ye, man, that ye'd nae see the sunrise,'' Donald Fleming said matter-of-factly.

"Why?'' Sir Jasper Keane managed to gasp.

"Why?'' Donald repeated as his opponent began to sink slowly to the ground, his hands clutched at the bloody blade that pierced him. "Why, for my brother's honor, and, though I should never hae thought I would say such a thing, *for Arabella Grey*.''

A look of total surprise appeared in Sir Jasper's eyes even as the life fled from them and he collapsed to the ground. Donald Fleming pulled his sword from the man's chest, and wiping his blade carefully on the Englishman's doublet, replaced it in his scabbard. His hand went again to the scabbard as he remembered, and then looking at Arabella, he said dourly, "I've brought the body back for ye to see, lady, to ask ye what ye would hae us do wi it.''

"Where is it?" Arabella demanded harshly. Like Tavis, she was somewhat angered not to have been in on the kill, and yet she felt relief that Jasper Keane was dead and Tavis Stewart unharmed.

"In the courtyard," came the brusque reply.

Arabella Grey moved quickly through her hall and out into a surprisingly bright and sunny morning. Above her the sky was a flawless blue and there was not a cloud to be seen, the storm having blown itself away at long last. She descended the steps from the hall but halfway when she saw him. In fact, she almost tripped over him, for Donald had laid Sir Jasper Keane's body out upon those same stone steps. His sightless brown eyes stared up at her, a look of total surprise and yet terrible fear upon his face.

Arabella stared down on Jasper Keane's body. What had even made her think that he was handsome, she wondered? Did death always render a body so insignificant, or had Jasper Keane always been insignificant? Her father had looked as noble in death as he had in life. Perhaps even more so.

"What do ye want done wi the body, lady?" Donald Fleming asked her.

"Show it through the border, both sides, sir, that all may know this cowardly outlaw and his band are dead," Arabella said. "They will never again prey upon the helpless." Turning, she went back into the hall. Just before she reentered the building, however, she swung about and said quite distinctly, "Thank you, Donald Fleming. You have done me a good turn, and I am now in your debt. Should you ever need a favor of me, you have it without question."

Donald Fleming stared after her open-mouthed as she disappeared from his view. "Well, I'll be damned," he said, and then he grinned broadly.

"Ye surely will be damned for this day's work, little brother," the earl said grimly, looking as if he'd like to hit his sibling again.

"Gie over, Tavis. Our mam is right. Ye hae nae the freedom to get yerself killed until ye sire a legitimate male heir on a wife. I've done more this day for Dunmor than ye've ever done."

"Go home, Donald," the earl said wearily.

"Are ye nae coming, man? The fighting is over, though God knows 'twas no real fight at all. Just a wee bit of butchering."

He peered closely at his elder brother. "Yer going to hae a black eye, Tavis," he said.

"So are ye," the earl noted dryly, and then he grinned at Donald. "Are all yer teeth still there, laddie?"

Donald Fleming gingerly felt about his jawline. He spit once or twice, and then he replied, "Ye've loosened two or three of them, man, but I think they'll hold. Why aren't ye coming home now? Not that damned English spitfire still?"

The earl's grin faded and he glared darkly at his younger sibling. "I want to see my daughter," he told him, daring him to refute his explanation.

"Hummmph," Donald said. "Will ye be wanting me to take all the men wi me?"

"Aye, take them all. I'll be home in a few days' time, and there's none fool enough to attack Tavis Stewart, though he rides alone."

Donald Fleming departed with his brother's clansmen, leaving the Earl of Dunmor to his own pursuits; although Donald didn't believe for a minute that Tavis's chief reason for remaining behind at Greyfaire was the little dark-haired lassie who was his niece. The earl remained behind because of that pale-haired English vixen with a temper bigger than she herself was. His brother hadn't been able to bring Arabella Grey to his bridle before. Donald wondered what had changed that Tavis thought he could bring the wench to heel now.

The earl watched his forces leaving, and then he turned back into the hall.

"Father Anselm would say a mass of thanksgiving before we break our fast," Arabella told him, and he followed her to the little family chapel which was off the Great Hall. There was no church now, for the little Greyfaire church had been one of the first things Sir Jasper Keane had destroyed when he had turned outlaw. The chapel was crowded with all the remaining Greyfaire folk. Many were elderly, but there were some young men, and a few women with children. Despite the happiness of the occasion, it was, the earl thought, a pitiful gathering. FitzWalter was right, though Arabella had not yet faced it. Greyfaire was dead.

Afterward in the hall they sat together at the highboard and he was served a hearty breakfast of oat porridge, fresh-baked bread with sweet butter, a honeycomb, and a good brown ale.

"You have sent your men away," she said to him.

"Their job is done, madame, and besides, I realize that ye dinna hae the means at the moment to feed such a great troop," he answered her.

"That was kind, Tavis," she replied, using his name for the first time since he had arrived at Greyfaire. "In another year or two I shall have Greyfaire back to its old self, and my hospitality will not be so niggardly."

"Will ye be able to restore your estate, lovey?" he asked her, slipping without even realizing it into his old form of address.

"Aye! Of course I will!" she insisted.

"How will ye go about it?" he persisted.

"There is no hope of a harvest this year," she began seriously. "It is simply too late in the summer to plant another crop, but we can clear the fields back again so they will be ready for plowing in the spring. I will replant the orchards then too."

"How will ye live through the winter? Yer people will need to be fed," he said.

"I'll buy grain and flour in York," she told him. "We'll dry the grasses we weed from the fields to feed the livestock we have, and then in the spring I'll buy another flock of sheep to replace those that were stolen. There's deer and rabbit in the hills that are mine to hunt. We'll manage, Tavis."

He wanted to tell her that it was all madness. That she should never again be able to rebuild Greyfaire, for she looked at her lands through sentimental eyes. In the best of times it had never been a rich estate, and the times were not particularly good now; but he did not tell her. She would not have accepted his word in the matter, and it would have driven a wedge between them just when he believed there was a chance of his winning her back. Arabella might be proud and stubborn, but she was no fool. Eventually she had to come to her senses. So he listened, and he nodded, and he held his peace, mindful of FitzWalter's approving eyes upon him, and somehow the captain's silent compliance in the matter was comforting.

He remained at Greyfaire for several days, avoiding any serious confrontations with Arabella, remaking his daughter's acquaintance and pretending to himself that they were once again a family. He stood as witness with Arabella at the wedding of his clansman, Fergus MacMichael, and Lona, assuring the young couple that there would be a place for them at Dunmor whenever they decided to return. Finally, however, he could no longer deny that Dunmor and his own obligations as its earl existed. He departed Greyfaire, promising to return as soon as he could.

He came as often as he dared during the autumn months, always arriving with some gift to help her. Several stags, dressed and ready for hanging. A few casks of wine. Bushels of apples and pears, enough to last until the spring. He knew that she shared her bounty with all of her people, and they did not starve, although their rations were certainly not generous. In February the storms came and he could not go to Greyfaire at all. Penned within his own castle, he lashed out in his frustration at anyone who dared to approach him, for he feared for Arabella's safety, as well as that of their daughter.

"Will it nae stop snowing?" he demanded of no one in particular one winter's evening.

His mother, who had been caught at Dunmor by this most recent storm, replied calmly, "It will cease snowing when God wills it, Tavis, and nae a moment before. Do sit down. Yer behaving like a spoilt lad."

"There was barely enough firewood the last time I was there, Mam," he told her. "What if they could nae get it cut in time? They'll freeze to death!"

"Then they will, Tavis, and yer fretting about it will nae change a thing, laddie," came the calm reply. Lady Margery had finally given up any hope of marrying her eldest son off to some good Scots lass. He would rewed Arabella Grey, and no one else, she realized.

When the weather broke, he rode pell-mell across the border to find that they had, indeed, survived the serious weather quite comfortably.

In the early spring sickness struck Greyfaire. Several children and half a dozen elderly souls died of the White Throat. Arabella lived in terror that Margaret would catch the disease, but she did not. The Spotting Sickness followed, however, and here Lady Margaret Stewart did not escape. She fell seriously ill, to the great fright of her mother, who, though she nursed her daughter lovingly and with all of her skill, could not seem to make the child well. In terror Arabella Grey sent for the Earl of Dunmor, who arrived posthaste, looking haggard, and closely followed several hours later by Lady Margery Fleming, bringing her own remedies for her granddaughter, convinced that her greater experience in these matters would prove successful.

Margaret's little body was covered in a great red rash. She burned with fever and complained that her eyes hurt her. They cut her dark curls so that her hair would not sap her waning strength, but it was all to no avail. Lady Margaret Stewart died in her weeping mother's arms just two weeks after her fourth birthday.

In her immediate grief Arabella tried to throw herself from Greyfaire's battlements, but was prevented from doing so by Tavis Stewart. She then fell into a stupor from which she could not be roused for several days, by which time her child was buried next to her maternal grandmother in Greyfaire's churchyard.

The earl mourned, although to a slightly lesser degree, the death of his only legitimate child. It was not that he had not loved wee Maggie, for he had, but in truth he had hardly known her as Arabella had taken her away from Dunmor before her second birthday. He would always remember the dark-haired and winning little girl he had come to know these past few months; but he and Arabella would have other children. Other sons and daughters. In the meantime his chief fears were for the woman he loved.

"We must take her back to Dunmor," Lady Margery insisted. "This wee keep of hers is a damned pesthole, Tavis. Why, I wouldn't be surprised at all to see the plague breaking out here before long. I can nurse her better at Dunmor."

"Nay," the earl replied. "She will never forgive me if I take her from Greyfaire now. She must want to come wi me of her own free will, Mam."

"She's grief-stricken, Tavis," Lady Margery replied impatiently. "She dinna know what she wants, poor lassie. Ye canna know the pain a woman feels when she loses her bairn."

"Ye must trust me in this matter, Mam," he told his mother. "I hae nae known Arabella all these years nae to understand her. I want her back, but I'll nae get her back if I take her away from Greyfaire against her will again. She must gie up this dream of hers; nae because she hae failed, or because a woman canna make such a dream come true; but because she can honestly face the fact that Greyfaire is gone. It hae nae been an easy burden she hae been shouldering—being the last of the Greys—

and she has nae to be ashamed of, Mam. No man could have done better. If I am patient, she will come to accept of her own free will that the battle is lost. And when she can face that loss, she will come home. I dinna care how long it takes. I will be here for Arabella because I love her. Together we will mourn our daughter's loss, and together we will rebuild our lives.''

"Yer a damned romantic fool," his mother said tenderly. "A foolish, romantic Stewart! I only hope that Arabella Grey, when she comes to this great understanding, will also appreciate what a good man she hae in ye." Lady Margery gave her son a hard hug and a motherly kiss. "I'm going home, Tavis. There is nothing more here that I can do for either ye or for poor wee Arabella. God bless ye both, and for heaven's sakes, man, remember Dunmor! Ye canna linger here forever!"

When he had seen her safely off, he returned to Arabella's chamber to find her awake at long last. She was very pale and there were huge, dark circles beneath her light green eyes. Sitting upon the edge of her bed, he took her little hand in his, kissed it and said, "How do ye feel, lovey?"

"Is Margaret really dead, Tavis? Or was it simply a bad dream?" she asked him anxiously, and she shivered, though the day was warm.

"Our wee bairn is dead, lovey," he told her as gently as he might, and worried to himself that her hand was so icy cold. "There was nae help for it, ye know. Mam said we did everything that we could. Many bairns survive the Spotting Sickness wi little discomfort, and others, like Maggie, are struck down so badly that there is simply nothing that can be done for them."

She nodded sadly and a single tear rolled down her cheek. "She was such a little girl," Arabella said helplessly. "Did you see how much she looked like you, Tavis? But for her eyes. Maggie had my mother's lovely blue eyes."

"We buried her next to yer mother, lovey. I thought ye would like it," he told her gently, and climbing into bed next to her, he took her into the warm comfort of his arms.

Arabella closed her eyes wearily and tears streamed from beneath her lashes down her face. "I missed a whole year of her life, Tavis," she whispered tragically. "*A whole year!* King Henry would not let me have her with me in France."

"He was right, lovey," the earl told the grieving mother. " 'Twas too dangerous."

"I did it all for her, Tavis. So she might have Greyfaire. So she might be an heiress in her own right and beholden to none."

"I know," he said.

"Now there is nothing left," Arabella said sadly. "Greyfaire is gone and our daughter is gone." She laughed suddenly. A harsh and terrible sound. "It was *all* for nothing, Tavis. I destroyed our life together, and I sold my body that I might regain Greyfaire for Margaret. Now I have neither. It is surely God's judgment upon me for my overweening pride and my many other sins." She sighed deeply. "Perhaps Father Anselm was right when he told me so long ago that women should be meek and humble, and trust themselves to their men."

Tavis Stewart burst out laughing at this last. He simply couldn't help it. "Arabella Grey," he said finally. "Yer tired, and yer badly worn wi yer grief; but I dinna believe for one moment that ye think ye should be either meek or humble. God's teeth, lassie! Ye dinna know the meaning of either word, but I would nae be displeased if ye would entrust yerself to me again."

"*What?*" She shook off his arms and, turning her head, looked directly at him. She was not sure that she shouldn't be very angry at him for laughing at her, and she was certainly not sure that she fully understood him. "What do you mean," she demanded suspiciously, " 'Entrust myself to you'?"

"Arabella Grey," he said tenderly, "will ye be my wife again? I love ye, and I always hae loved ye. I think that ye hae always loved me too."

"Aye," she said simply. The time for dissemblance between them was long past. She did love him, and whatever anger she may have felt toward him was long gone. That he would want to renew their life together was most tempting.

"Then will ye marry me, lassie? Will ye be my wee English wife once more?"

"I was the Duc de Lambour's mistress," she told him honestly. There must be no secrets between them. Nothing that might ever separate them again.

"I know," he said quietly.

"And it matters not at all to you, Tavis?" she probed skillfully.

"The Duc de Lambour's English mistress was nae my wife," he replied. "Nor was the bold English wench who spent three days wi my nephew, Jamie," the earl told her calmly.

She was thunderstruck. *"You . . . you knew?"* she gasped, and her pale skin grew pink with her blush.

"Aye, I knew," he said. "Nae at first, mind ye, but Donald, in a nasty mood, suggested it, and though I denied it, it set me to thinking. Why did Jamie help ye? Oh, he's a good lad, but nae known for his charity. Ye made some damned unholy bargain wi the laddie. It was then that I understood, lovey. I understood why ye hae divorced me. That ye nae bring shame upon my name. Was that nae the reason, Arabella? And I knew then that ye truly loved me, lassie. Loved me even as I love ye."

"I could not have told you, Tavis," she admitted frankly. "Not that I feared what you might say, for I did not; but I could not drive a wedge between you and your king. Poor Jamie has few souls he can really trust, and you, my darling, have ever been loyal. 'Tis one of the things I love you for, Tavis Stewart. Your sense of honor."

He smiled at her. "I understood that as well, lovey. Are ye nae fortunate to hae so perceptive a man who loves ye?" he teased her.

"Aye, Tavis Stewart, I am," she said with complete sincerity. Then her brow furrowed. "My lord! I cannot leave the few souls who have remained here at Greyfaire to fend for themselves. What can I do? They have been loyal to the Greys to the bitter end. I cannot desert them!"

"Nay," he agreed with her. "Ye canna, but I think I know what ye might do, lovey, to help them. The border is safe for now, wi Sir Jasper Keane having taken up his residence in Hell. Though I expect there'll be plenty of border clashes between England and Scotland in times to come, for 'tis our nature, I fear, to go roving, it will nae ever again be like it was. Let us divide your lands in several portions. We will set upon these lands good tenants to farm them. We will have built stout stone cottages to house them, and the revenues from their rents and kind will be set aside for our next daughter as her dowry. When she marries, the income from the estate will be passed on to her."

"Aye," she agreed, " 'tis a good plan; and the stones for the cottages, Tavis, will come from the keep itself," she told him.

"You would destroy Greyfaire Keep, lovey?" He was astounded.

"The keep was built by the Greys, my lord. Only Greys have

resided here all these centuries, but for Sir Jasper's unfortunate
and brief tenure. I am the last of the Greys. It is only fitting that
I determine the keep's fate. It has outlived its strategic usefulness
now, I fear. If I leave it standing, it will become a haven for
every outlaw roaming the border. What an ignominious end to
a house whose honor has always been paramount. That must
not be, Tavis. Is it not better that I dismantle the keep in order
to put it to better use? Besides, it is half destroyed as it is, thanks
to Sir Jasper.''

Arabella Grey did not leave her lands until the keep had begun
to be dismantled. She had, as the earl suggested, divided her
estate into portions. She awarded those portions to the few young
men who had so loyally remained by her side, giving them the
first year rent-free. FitzWalter had been awarded the largest portion rent free for his lifetime, to be passed on to his male de-
scendants thereafter at a nominal rental.

The first stones removed from the keep were used to rebuild
Greyfaire church, much to the delight of old Father Anselm.
And while the clansmen called from Dunmor worked to tear the
small castle down, the new tenant farmers and their families
tilled their fields, planted their orchards, and cared for the sheep
and cattle, as well as the geese and the laying hens that their
lady had so generously supplied.

One condition of tenancy, however, had been that all the men
take wives. Those without them had chosen to marry the widows
amongst them, thus providing homes for the women, their children, and the few remaining elders. When the keep was finally
dismantled, the clansmen would remain on to help the Greyfaire
folk build their houses before the winter returned. There might
have been some who thought the alliance between the Greyfaire
folk and the clansmen from Dunmor odd, but the two groups
quickly found that they had much in common.

Content that her people were now safe, Arabella Grey, the
heiress of Greyfaire, remarried Tavis Stewart, the Earl of Dunmor, on the tenth of June, in the year of our Lord, 1491.

''Would you not prefer that we be wed at Dunmor?'' she
asked him when she had decided that she might at last leave
Greyfaire.

''Nay,'' he shook his head. ''I married ye at Dunmor the last
time, lovey, and we hae nothing but trouble. This time I will
wed ye where I should hae wed the heiress of Greyfaire in the

first place. We will wed here at Greyfaire. Yer own Father Anselm shall conduct the ceremony, and yer people will be about ye, lassie.''

"And this time, my lord, I shall even wear a wedding gown,'' Arabella teased him mischievously.

"I'll hae ye wi one or wi out one, lovey,'' he told her with a grin. "And afterward—''

"And afterward,'' she interrupted him, "we'll go home, Tavis Stewart!'' She stood upon her toes and kissed his mouth.

"Home?" he said. His arms slipped about her, pulling her close, his dark green eyes smouldering with promises of passion to come.

"Aye, my lord,'' Arabella Grey said, her own eyes bright with unshed tears, and filled to overflowing with her love for him. "Home. *Home to Dunmor!*''

≋ *Author's Note*

*T*he border country between England and Scotland was always a volatile place. On the eighth day of August 1503, Henry VII's eldest daughter, thirteen-and-a-half-year-old Princess Margaret, married the thirty-one-year-old king of the Scots, James IV. It was hoped that this marriage would bring about a final peace between the two nations. Ten years later, however, on September 9, 1513, the young queen of Scotland was widowed. James IV, and practically every adult member of the Scots nobility foolish enough to follow him, was slaughtered in a battle with the English at Flodden Field.

James V, just seventeen months old, was coronated in the Chapel Royal of Stirling Castle on the twenty-first day of September of that same year; his mother's bracelet, newly consecrated, being used to crown his little head. Once grown, James V took first one French queen, and being quickly widowed, took a second. He died following a battle with the English at Solway Moss on December 14, 1542. On his deathbed James V uttered the famous prophecy regarding the crown of Scotland, which had come to the Stewarts through a woman:

> *"It cam wi a lass, and 'twill go wi a lass."*

The morbid portent proved untrue, and his infant daughter Mary inherited the throne of Scotland.

Her history, a novel in itself, has been written many times. Sent to France by her mother to keep her from the English, Mary was first married to and then widowed by young King François II. She returned in her late teens to Scotland, a stranger in her own land, to find herself embroiled not only with her own nobility, but with a fanatical Protestant clergy, neither of whom approved of a woman monarch, and certainly not a Catholic woman monarch. Despite this bigotry, Mary, Queen of Scots, offered religious freedom to all.

The young queen was married a second time in an effort to please her detractors. Her choice, her cousin, Lord Darnley, proved an unfortunate misalliance which produced but one son before Darnley was murdered under mysterious circumstances. Mary took a third husband, James Hepburn, the Earl of Bothwell, and this time she married for love. It was a fatal misstep for a ruling monarch to follow her heart rather than her head, and it would ultimately lead to Mary's downfall. Neither her nobles, the clergy, nor the people would accept her choice. Mary was forced to flee to England, where she was eventually executed; while James Hepburn fled to Denmark, where he died, unjustly imprisoned by the Danish authorities, who to this day refuse to allow his bones returned home to Scotland, which once again found itself burdened with an infant king.

Thus it was that when he was grown, James VI, the son of Mary, Queen of Scots, and the great-grandson of James IV, inherited the English throne from the last member of the Tudor dynasty—Henry VII's fabulous granddaughter, Elizabeth I. One hundred years had passed since little Margaret Tudor had traveled north as a bride, hopeful that this union of the Thistle and the Rose would bring peace. Now, as James VI of Scotland became James I of England, peace—if there can ever be real peace between the English and the Scots—was achieved.

If you have enjoyed *The Spitfire*, I hope you will take the time to write to me and tell me. Since it is my readers for whom I write, it is always a great pleasure to hear from you. And before I close, I want to thank my wonderful secretary, and dearest friend of four and a half years, Donna Tumolo, for her incredible efforts in helping me to get this novel to the publisher on time. Donna is moving to North Carolina, and I will miss her greatly. For now, however, I wish you all Good Reading!

Bertrice Small
P.O. Box 765
Southold, N.Y. 11971

June 12, 1989

ABOUT THE AUTHOR

Bertrice Small is the author of *Adora, Unconquered, Beloved,* and *The Spitfire,* including the Skye O'Malley books: *Skye O'Malley, All The Sweet Tomorrows, A Love for All Time, This Heart of Mine,* and *Lost Love Found.* Ms. Small and her husband live in Southold, New York.

Want to know a secret?
It's sexy, informative, fun, and FREE!!!

❧ PILLOW TALK ❧

Join Pillow Talk and get advance information and sneak peeks at the best in romance coming from Ballantine. All you have to do is fill out the information below!

♥ My top five favorite authors are: _____

_____

_____

_____

_____

♥ Number of books I buy per month: ❏ 0-2 ❏ 3-5 ❏ 6 or more

♥ Preference: ❏ Regency Romance ❏ Historical Romance
         ❏ Contemporary Romance ❏ Other

♥ I read books by new authors: ❏ frequently ❏ sometimes ❏ rarely

Please print clearly:
Name _____

Address _____

City/State/Zip _____

Don't forget to visit us at
www.randomhouse.com/BB/loveletters

**PLEASE SEND TO: PILLOW TALK/
BALLANTINE BOOKS, CN/9-2
201 EAST 50TH STREET
NEW YORK, NY 10022
OR FAX TO PILLOW TALK, 212/940-7539**